AYALA'S ANGEL.

BY

ANTHONY TROLLOPE,

AUTHOR OF "DOCTOR THORNE," "THE PRIME MINISTER," "ORLEY FARM,"
&c., &c.

WARD, LOCK AND CO.,
LONDON: WARWICK HOUSE, SALISBURY SQUARE, E C.
NEW YORK: BOND STREET.

CONTENTS.

CHAPTER I.

iv

CONTENTS.

CONTENTS.

CONTENTS.

CONTENTS.

AYALA'S ANGEL.

CHAPTER I.

THE TWO SISTERS.

When Egbert Dormer died he left his two daughters utterly penniless upon the world, and it must be said of Egbert Dormer that nothing else could have been expected of him. The two girls were both pretty, but Lucy who was twenty-one was supposed to be simple and comparatively unattractive, whereas Ayala was credited,—as her somewhat romantic name might show,—with poetic charm and a taste for romance. Ayala when her father died was nineteen.

We must begin yet a little earlier and say that there had been,—and had died many years before the death of Egbert Dormer,—a clerk in the Admiralty, by name Reginald Dosett, who, and whose wife, had been conspicuous for personal beauty. Their charms were gone, but the records of them had been left in various grandchildren. There had been a son born to Mr. Dosett, who was also a Reginald and a clerk in the Admiralty, and who also, in his turn, had been a handsome man. With him, in his decadence, the reader will become acquainted. There were also two daughters, whose reputation for perfect feminine beauty had never been contested. The elder had married a city man of wealth, —of wealth when he married her, but who had become enormously wealthy by the time of our story. He had when he married been simply Mister, but was now Sir Thomas Tringle, Baronet, and was senior partner in the great firm of Travers and Treason. Of Traverses and Treasons there were none left in these days, and Mr. Tringle was supposed to manipulate all the millions with which the great firm in Lombard Street was concerned. He had married old Mr. Dosett's eldest daughter, Emmeline, who was now Lady Tringle, with a house at the top of Queen's Gate, rented at £1,500 a year, with a palatial moor in Scotland, with a seat in Sussex, and as many carriages and horses as would suit an archduchess. Lady Tringle had everything in the world a son, two daughters, and an open-handed stout husband, who was said to have told her that money was a matter of no consideration.

The second Miss Dosett, Adelaide Dosett, who had been considerably younger than her sister, had insisted upon giving herself to Egbert Dormer, the artist, whose death we commemorated in our first line. But she had died before her husband. They who remembered the two Miss Dosetts as girls were wont to declare that, though Lady Tringle might, perhaps, have had the advantage in perfection of feature and in unequalled symmetry, Adelaide had been the more attractive from expression and brilliancy. To her Lord Sizes had offered his hand and coronet, promising to abandon for her sake all the haunts of his matured life. To her Mr. Tringle had knelt before he had taken the elder sister. For her Mr. Progrum, the popular preacher of the day, for a time so totally lost himself that he was nearly minded to go over to Rome. She was said to have had offers from a widowed Lord Chancellor and from a Russian prince. Her triumphs would have quite obliterated that of her sister had she not insisted on marrying Egbert Dormer.

Then there had been, and still was, Reginald Dosett, the son of old Dosett, and the eldest of the family. He too had married, and was now living with his wife; but to them had no children been born, luckily, as he was a poor man. Alas, to a beautiful son it is not often that beauty can be a fortune as to a daughter. Young Reginald Dosett,—he is anything now but young,—had done but little for himself with his beauty, having simply married the estimable daughter of a brother clerk. Now at the age of fifty, he had his £900 a year from his office, and might have lived in fair comfort had he not allowed a small millstone of debt to hang round his neck from his earlier years. But still he lived creditably in a small but very genteel house at Notting Hill, and would have undergone any want rather than have declared himself to be a poor man to his rich relations the Tringles.

Such were now the remaining two children of old Mr. Dosett,—Lady Tringle, namely, and Reginald Dosett, the clerk in the Admiralty. Adelaide, the beauty in chief of the family, was gone; and now also her husband, the improvident artist, had followed his wife. Dormer had been by no means a failing artist. He had achieved great honour,—had at an early age been accepted into the Royal Academy,—had sold pictures to illustrious princes and more illustrious dealers,—had been engraved, and had lived to see his own works resold at five times their original prices. Egbert Dormer might also have been a rich man. But he had a taste for other beautiful things besides a wife. The sweetest little phaeton that was to cost nothing, the most perfect bijou of a little house at South Kensington,—he had boasted that it might have been packed without trouble in his brother-in-law Tringle's dining-

room,—the simplest little gem for his wife, just a blue set of china
for his dinner table, just a painted cornice for his studio, just satin
hangings for his drawing-room,—and a few simple ornaments for his
little girls; these with a few rings for himself, and velvet suits of
clothing in which to do his painting; these, with a few little dinner
parties to show off his blue china, were the first and last of his extrava-
gances. But when he went, and when his pretty things were sold,
there was not enough to cover his debts. There was, however, a sweet
savour about his name. When he died it was said of him that his
wife's death had killed him. He had dropped his pallette, refused to
finish the ordered portrait of a princess, and had simply turned himself
round and died.

Then there were the two daughters, Lucy and Ayala. It should be
explained that though a proper family intercourse had always been maintained between the three families, the Tringles, the Dormers, and the
Dosetts, there had never been cordiality between the first and the two
latter. The wealth of the Tringles had seemed to convey with it a fetid
odóur. Egbert Dormer, with every luxury around him which money
could purchase, had affected to despise the heavy magnificence of the
Tringles. It may be that he affected a fashion higher than that which
the Tringles really attained. Reginald Dosett, who was neither brilliant nor fashionable, was in truth independent, and, perhaps, a little
thin-skinned. He would submit to no touch of arrogance from Sir
Thomas; and Sir Thomas seemed to carry arrogance in his brow and
in his paunch. It was there rather, perhaps, than in his heart; but
there are men to whom a knack of fumbling their money in their pockets and of looking out from under penthouse brows over an expanse of
waistcoat, gives an air of overweening pride which their true idiosyn-
cracies may not justify. To Dosett had, perhaps, been spoken a word
or two which on some occasion he had inwardly resented, and from
thenceforward he had ever been ready to league with Dormer against
the "bullionaire," as they agreed to call Sir Thomas. Lady Tringle
had even said a word to her sister, Mrs. Dormer, as to expenses, and
that had never been forgiven by the artist. So things were when Mrs.
Dormer died first; and so they remained when her husband followed
her.

Then there arose a sudden necessity for action, which, for a while,
brought Reginald Dosett into connexion with Sir Thomas and Lady
Tringle. Something must be done for the poor girls. That the something should come out of the pocket of Sir Thomas would have seemed
to be natural. Money with him was no object,—not at all. Another
girl or two would be nothing to him,—as regarded simple expenditure.
But the care of a human being is an important matter, and so Sir

Thomas knew. Dosett had not a child at all, and would be the better
for such a windfall. Dosett he supposed to be,—in his, Dosett's way,—
fairly well off. So he made this proposition. He would take one girl
and let Dosett take the other. To this Lady Tringle added her pro-
viso, that she should have the choice. To her nerves affairs of taste
were of such paramount importance! To this Dosett yielded. The
matter was decided in Lady Tringle's back drawing-room. Mrs.
Dosett was not even consulted in that matter of choice, having already
acknowledged the duty of mothering a motherless child. Dosett had
thought that the bullionaire should have said a word as to some future
provision for the penniless girl, for whom he would be able to do so
little. But Sir Thomas had said no such word, and Dosett, himself,
lacked both the courage and the coarseness to allude to the matter.
Then Lady Tringle declared that she must have Ayala, and so the
matter was settled. Ayala the romantic; Ayala the poetic! It was a
matter of course that Ayala should be chosen. Ayala had already been
made intimate with the magnificent saloons of the Tringles, and had
been felt, by Lady Tringle, to be an attraction. Her long dark black
locks, which had never hitherto been tucked up, which were never
curled, which were never so long as to be awkward, were already
known as being the loveliest locks in London. She sang as though
Nature had intended her to be a singing-bird,—requiring no education,
no labour. She had been once for three months in Paris, and French
had come naturally to her. Her father had taught her something of
his art, and flatterers had already begun to say that she was born to
be the one great female artist of the world. Her hands, her feet,
her figure were perfect. Though she was as yet but nineteen, London
had already begun to talk about Ayala Dormer. Of course Lady
Tringle chose Ayala, not remembering at the moment that her own
daughters might probably be superseded by their cousin.

And, therefore, as Lady Tringle said herself to Lucy with her
sweetest smile—Mrs. Dosett had chosen Lucy. The two girls were old
enough to know something of the meaning of such a choice. Ayala,
the younger, was to be adopted into immense wealth, and Lucy was to
be given up to comparative poverty. She knew nothing of her uncle
Dosett's circumstances, but the genteel house at Notting Hill,—No. 3,
Kingsbury Crescent—was known to her, and was but a poor affair as
compared even with the bijou in which she had hitherto lived. Her
aunt Dosett never rose to any vehicle beyond a four-wheeler, and was
careful even in thinking of that accommodation. Ayala would be
whirled about the park by a wire-wig and a pair of brown horses
which they had heard it said were not to be matched in London.
Ayala would be carried with her aunt and her cousin to the show-room

of Madame Tonsonville, the great French milliner of Bond Street, whereas she, Lucy, might too probably be called on to make her own gowns. All the fashion of Queen's Gate, something, perhaps, of the fashion of Eaton Square, would be open to Ayala. Lucy understood enough to know that Ayala's own charms might probably cause still more august gates to be opened to her, whereas Aunt Dosett entered no gates. It was quite natural that Ayala should be chosen. Lucy acknowledged as much to herself. But they were sisters, and had been so near! By what a chasm would they be dissevered, now so far asunder!

Lucy herself was a lovely girl, and knew her own loveliness. She was fairer than Ayala, somewhat taller, and much more quiet in her demeanour. She was also clever, but her cleverness did not show itself so quickly. She was a musician, whereas her sister could only sing. She could really draw, whereas her sister would rush away into effects in which the drawing was not always very excellent. Lucy was doing the best she could for herself, knowing something of French and German, though as yet not very fluent with her tongue. The two girls were, in truth, both greatly gifted; but Ayala had the gift of showing her talent without thought of showing it. Lucy saw it all, and knew that she was outshone; but how great had been the price of the outshining!

The artist's house had been badly ordered, and the two girls were of better disposition and better conduct than might have been expected from such fitful training. Ayala had been the father's pet, and Lucy the mother's. Parents do ill in making pets, and here they had done ill. Ayala had been taught to think herself the favourite, because the artist, himself, had been more prominent before the world than his wife. But the evil had not been lasting enough to have made ba feeling between the sisters. Lucy knew that her sister had been preferred to her, but she had been self-denying enough to be aware that some such preference was due to Ayala. She, too, admired Ayala, and loved her with her whole heart. And Ayala was always good to her,—had tried to divide everything,—had assumed no preference as a right. The two were true sisters. But when it was decided that Lucy was to go to Kingsbury Crescent the difference was very great. The two girls, on their father's death, had been taken to the great red brick house in Queen's Gate, and from thence, three or four days after the funeral, Lucy was to be transferred to her Aunt Dosett. Hitherto there had been little between them but weeping for their father. Now had come the hour of parting.

The tidings had been communicated to Lucy, and to Lucy alone, by Aunt Tringle—"As you are the eldest, dear, we think that you will be best able to be a comfort to your aunt," said Lady Tringle.

"I will do the best I can, Aunt Emmeline," said Lucy, declaring to herself that, in giving such a reason, her aunt was lying basely.

"I am sure you will. Poor dear Ayala is younger than her cousins, and will be more subject to them." So in truth was Lucy younger than her cousins, but of that she said nothing. "I am sure you will agree with me that it is best that we should have the youngest."

"Perhaps it is, Aunt Emmeline."

"Sir Thomas would not have had it any other way," said Lady Tringle, with a little severity, feeling that Lucy's accord had hardly been as generous as it should be. But she recovered herself quickly, remembering how much it was that Ayala was to get, how much that Lucy was to lose. "But, my dear, we shall see you very often, you know. It is not so far across the park ; and when we do have a few parties again——"

"Oh, aunt, I am not thinking of that."

"Of course not. We can none of us think of it just now. But when the time does come of course we shall always have you, just as if you were one of us." Then her aunt gave her a roll of bank-notes, a little present of twenty-five pounds, to begin the world with, and told her that the carriage should take her to Kingsbury Crescent on the following morning. On the whole Lucy behaved well and left a pleasant impression on her aunt's mind. The difference between Queen's Gate and Kingsbury Crescent,—between Queen's Gate and Kingsbury Crescent for life,—was indeed great !

"I wish it were you, with all my heart," said Ayala, clinging to her sister.

"It could not have been me."

"Why not ?"

"Because you are so pretty and you are so clever."

"No !"

"Yes ! If we were to be separated of course it would be so. Do not suppose, dear, that I am disappointed."

"I am."

"If I can only like Aunt Margaret,"—Aunt Margaret was Mrs. Dosett, with whom neither of the girls had hitherto become intimate, and who was known to be quiet, domestic, and economical, but who had also been spoken of as having a will of her own,—"I shall do better with her than you would, Ayala."

"I don't see why."

"Because I can remain quiet longer than you. It will be very quiet. I wonder how we shall see each other ! I cannot walk across the park alone."

"Uncle Reg will bring you."

" Not often, I fear. Uncle Reg has enough to do with his office."

" You can come in a cab."

" Cabs cost money, Ayey dear."

" But Uncle Thomas——"

" We had better understand one or two things, Ayala. Uncle Thomas will pay everything for you, and as he is very rich things will come as they are wanted. There will be cabs, and if not cabs, carriages. Uncle Reg must pay for me, and he is very very kind to do so. But, as he is not rich, there will be no carriages, and not a great many cabs. It is best to understand it all.'

" But they will send for you."

" That's as they please. I don't think they will very often. I would not for the world put you against Uncle Thomas, but I have a feeling that I shall never get on with him. But you will never separate yourself from me, Ayala !"

" Separate myself !"

" You will not—not be my sister because you will be one of these rich ones ?"

" Oh, I wish, -I wish that I were to be the poor one. I'm sure I should like it best. I never cared about being rich. Oh, Lucy, can't we make them change ?"

" No, Ayey, my own, we can't make them change. And if we could, we wouldn't. It is altogether best that you should be a rich Tringle and that I should be a poor Dosett."

" I will always be a Dormer," said Ayala, proudly.

" And I will always be so too, my pet. But you should be a bright Dormer among the Tringles, and I will be a dull Dormer among the Dosetts. I shall begrudge nothing, if only we can see each other."

So the two girls were parted, the elder being taken away to Kingsbury Crescent and the latter remaining with her rich relations at Queen's Gate. Ayala had not probably realized the great difference of their future positions. To her the attractions of wealth and the privations of comparative poverty had not made themselves as yet palpably plain. They do not become so manifest to those to whom the wealth falls,—at any rate, not in early life,—as to the opposite party. If the other lot had fallen to Ayala she might have felt it more keenly.

Lucy felt it keenly enough. Without any longing after the magnificence of the Tringle mansion she knew how great was the fall from her father's well-assorted luxuries and prettinesses down to the plain walls, tables, and chairs of her Uncle Dosett's house. Her aunt did not subscribe to Mudie's. The old piano had not been tuned for the last ten years. The parlour-maid was a cross old woman. Her aunt always sat in the dining-room through the greater part of the day, and of all rooms the dining-room in Kingsbury Crescent was the dingiest. Lucy understood very well to what she was going. Her father and mother were gone. Her sister was divided from her. Her life offered for the future nothing to her. But with it all she carried a good courage. There was present to her an idea of great misfortune; but present to her at the same time an idea also that she would do her duty.

CHAPTER II.

LUCY WITH HER AUNT DOSETT.

FOR some days Lucy found herself to be absolutely crushed,—in the first place, by a strong resolution to do some disagreeable duty, and then by a feeling that there was no duty the doing of which was within her reach. It seemed to her that her whole life was a blank. Her father's house had been a small affair and considered to be poor when compared with the Tringle mansion, but she now became aware that everything there had in truth abounded. In one little room there had been two or three hundred beautifully bound books. That Mudie's unnumbered volumes should come into the house as they were wanted had almost been as much a provision of nature as water, gas, and hot rolls for breakfast. A piano of the best kind, and always in order, had been a first necessary of life, and, like other necessaries, of course, forthcoming. There had been the little room in which the girls painted, joining their father's studio and sharing its light, surrounded by every pretty female appliance. Then there had always been visitors. The artists from Kensington had been wont to gather there, and the artists' daughters, and perhaps the artists' sons. Every day had had its round of delights,—its round of occupations, as the girls would call them. There had been some reading, some painting, some music,—perhaps a little needlework and a great deal of talking.

How little do we know how other people live in the houses close to us! We see the houses looking like our own, and we see the people come out of them looking like ourselves. But a Chinaman is not more different from the English John Bull than is No. 10 from No. 11. Here there are books, paintings, music, wine, a little dilettanti getting-up of subjects of the day, a little dilettanti thinking on great affairs, perhaps a little dilettanti religion; few domestic laws, and those easily broken; few domestic duties, and those easily evaded; breakfast when you will, with dinner almost as little binding, with much company and acknowledged aptitude for idle luxury. That is life at No. 10. At No. 11 everything is cased in iron. There shall be equal plenty, but at No. 11 even plenty is a bondage. Duty rules everything, and it has come to be acknowledged that duty is to be hard. So many hours of needle-work, so many hours of books, so many hours of prayer! That all the household shall shiver before daylight, is a law, the breach of which by any member either augurs sickness or requires condign punishment. To be comfortable is a sin; to laugh is almost equal to bad language. Such and so various is life at No. 10 and at No. 11.

From one extremity, as far removed, to another poor Lucy had been conveyed; though all the laws were not exactly carried out in Kings-bury Crescent as they have been described at No. 11. The enforced prayers were not there, nor the early hours. It was simply necessary that Lucy should be down to breakfast at nine, and had she not appeared nothing violent would have been said. But it was required of her that she should endure a life which was altogether without adornment. Uncle Dosett himself, as a clerk in the Admiralty, had a certain position in the world which was sufficiently maintained by decent apparel, a well-kept, slight, grey whisker, and an umbrella which seemed never to have been violated by use. Dosett was popular at his office, and was regarded by his brother clerks as a friend. But no one was acquainted with his house and home. They did not dine with him, nor he with them. There are such men in all public offices, —not the less respected because of the quiescence of their lives. It was known of him that he had burdens, though it was not known what his burdens were. His friends, therefore, were intimate with him as far as the entrance into Somerset House,—where his duties lay,—and not beyond it. Lucy was destined to know the other side of his affairs, the domestic side, which was as quiet as the official side. The link between them, which consisted of a journey by the Underground Railway to the Temple Station, and a walk home along the Embank-ment and across the parks and Kensington Gardens, was the pleasantest part of Dosett's life.

Mr. Dosett's salary has been said to be £900 per annum. What a fund of comfort there is in the word! When the youth of nineteen enters an office how far beyond want would he think himself should he ever reach the pecuniary paradise of £900 a-year! How he would see all his friends and in return be seen of them! But when the income has been achieved its capabilities are found to be by no means endless. And Dosett in the earlier spheres of his married life had unfortunately anticipated something of such comforts. For a year or two he had spent a little money imprudently. Something which he had expected had not come to him; and, as a result, he had been forced to borrow, and to insure his life for the amount borrowed. Then, too, when that misfortune as to the money came,—came from the non-realization of certain claims which his wife had been supposed to possess,—provision had also to be made for her. In this way an assurance office eat up a large fraction of his income, and left him with means which in truth were very straitened. Dosett at once gave up all glories of social life, settled himself in Kingsbury Crescent, and resolved to satisfy himself with his walk across the park and his frugal dinner afterwards. He never complained to any one, nor did his wife. He was a man small enough to be contented with a thin existence, but far too great to ask any one to help him to widen it. Sir Thomas Tringle never heard of that £175 paid annually to the assurance office, nor had Lady Tringle, Dosett's sister, even heard of it. When it was suggested to him that he should take one of the Dormer girls, he consented to take her and said nothing of the assurance office.

Mrs. Dosett had had her great blow in life, and had suffered more perhaps than her husband. This money had been expected. There had been no doubt of the money,—at any rate on her part. It did not depend on an old gentleman with or without good intentions, but simply on his death. There was to be ever so much of it,—four or five hundred a year, which would last for ever. When the old gentleman died, which took place some ten years after Dosett's marriage, it was found that the money, tied tight as it had been by half-a-dozen lawyers, had in some fashion vanished. Whither it had gone is little to our purpose, but it had gone. Then there came a great crash upon the Dosetts, which she for a while had been hardly able to endure.

But when she had collected herself together after the crash, and had made up her mind, as had Dosett also, to the nature of the life which they must in future lead, she became more stringent in it even than he. He could bear and say nothing; but she, in bearing, found herself compelled to say much. It had been her fault,—the fault of people on her side, and she would fain have fed her husband with the full flowery potato while she ate only the rind. She told him, unnecessarily, over and over again, that she had ruined him by her marriage. No such idea was ever in his head. The thing had come and so it must be. There was food to eat, potatoes enough for both, and a genteel house in which to live. He could still be happy if she would not groan. A certain amount of groaning she did postpone while in his presence. The sewing of seams, and the darning of household linen, which in his eyes amounted to groaning, was done in his absence. After their genteel dinner he would sleep a little, and she would knit. He would have his glass of wine, but would make his bottle of port last almost for a week. This was the house to which Lucy Dormer was brought when Mr. Dosett had consented to share with Sir Thomas the burden left by the death of the improvident artist.

When a month passed by Lucy began to think that time itself would almost drive her mad. Her father had died early in September. The Tringles had then, of course, been out of town, but Sir Thomas and his wife had found themselves compelled to come up on such an occasion. Something they knew must be done about the girls, and they had not chosen that that something should be done in their absence. Mr. Dosett was also enjoying his official leave of absence for the year, but was enjoying it within the economical precincts of Kingsbury Crescent. There was but seldom now an excursion for him or his wife to the joys of the country. Once, some years ago, they had paid a visit to the palatial luxuries of Glenbogie, but the delights of the place had not paid for the expense of the long journey. They, therefore, had been at hand to undertake their duties. Dosett and Tringle, with a score of artists, had followed poor Dormer to his grave in Kensal Green, and then Dosett and Tringle had parted again, probably not to see each other for another term of years.

"My dear, what do you like to do with your time?" Mrs. Dosett said to her niece, after the first week. At this time Lucy's wardrobe was not yet of a nature to need much work over its ravages. The Dormer girls had hardly known where their frocks had come from when they wanted frocks,—hardly with more precision than the Tringle girls. Frocks had come—dark, gloomy frocks, lately, alas! And these, too, had now come a second time. Let creditors be ever so unsatisfied, new raiment will always be found for mourning families. Everything about Lucy was nearly new. The need of repairing would come upon her by degrees, but it had not come as yet. Therefore there had seemed, to the anxious aunt, to be a necessity for some such question as the above.

"I'll do anything you like, aunt," said Lucy.

"It is not for me, my dear. I get through a deal of work, and am obliged to do so." She was, at this time, sitting with a sheet in her lap, which she was turning. Lucy had, indeed, once offered to assist, but her assistance had been rejected. This had been two days since, and she had not renewed the proposal as she should have done. This had been mainly from bashfulness. Though the work would certainly be distasteful to her, she would do it. But she had not liked to seem to interfere, not having as yet fallen into ways of intimacy with her aunt. "I don't want to burden you with my task-work," continued Mrs. Dosett, "but I am afraid you seem to be listless."

"I was reading till just before you spoke," said Lucy, again turning her eyes to the little volume of poetry, which was one of the few treasures which she had brought away with her from her old home.

"Reading is very well, but I do not like it as an excuse, Lucy.

Lucy's anger boiled within her when she was told of an excuse, and she declared to herself that she could never like her aunt. "I am quite sure that for young girls, as well as for old women, there must be a great deal of waste time unless there be needle and thread always about. And I know, too, unless ladies are well off, they cannot afford to waste time any more than gentlemen."

In the whole course of her life nothing so much like scolding as this had ever been addressed to her. So at least thought Lucy at that moment. Mrs. Dosett had intended the remarks all in good part, thinking them to be simply fitting from an aunt to a niece. It was her duty to give advice, and for the giving of such advice some day must be taken as the beginning. She had purposely allowed a week to run by, and now she had spoken her word,—as she thought in good season.

To Lucy it was a new and most bitter experience. Though she was reading the "Idylls of the King," or pretending to read them, she was, in truth, thinking of all that had gone from her. Her mind had, at that moment, been intent upon her mother, who, in all respects, had been so different from this careful, sheet-darning housewife of a woman. And in thinking of her mother there had no doubt been regrets for many things of which she would not have ventured to speak as sharing her thoughts with the memory of her mother, but which were nevertheless there to add darkness to the retrospective. Everything behind had been so bright, and everything behind had gone away from her! Everything before was so gloomy, and everything before must last for so long! After her aunt's lecture about wasted time Lucy sat silent for a few minutes, and then burst into uncontrolled tears.

"I did not mean to vex you," said her aunt.

"I was thinking of my—darling, darling mamma," sobbed Lucy.

"Of course, Lucy, you will think of her. How should you not? And of your father. Those are sorrows which must be borne. But sorrows such as those are much lighter to the busy than to the idle. I sometimes think that the labourers grieve less for those they love than we do just because they have not time to grieve."

"I wish I were a labourer then," said Lucy, through her tears.

"You may be if you will. The sooner you begin to be a labourer the better for yourself and for those about you."

That Aunt Dosett's voice was harsh was not her fault,—nor that in the obduracy of her daily life she had lost much of her original softness. She had simply meant to be useful, and to do her duty; but in telling Lucy that it would be better that the labouring should be commenced at once for the sake of "those about you,"—who could only be Aunt Dosett herself,—she had seemed to the girl to be harsh, selfish,

and almost unnatural. The volume of poetry fell from her hand, and
she jumped up from the chair quickly. "Give it me at once," she
said, taking hold of the sheet,—which was not itself a pleasant object ;
Lucy had never seen such a thing at the bijou. "Give it me at once,"
she said, and clawed the long folds of linen nearly out of her aunt's
lap.

"I did not mean anything of the kind," said Aunt Dosett. "You
should not take me up in that way. I am speaking only for your good,
because I know that you should not dawdle away your existence.
Leave the sheet."

Lucy did leave the sheet, and then, sobbing violently, ran out of the
room up to her own chamber. Mrs. Dosett determined that she would
not follow her. She partly forgave the girl because of her sorrows,
partly reminded herself that she was not soft and facile as had been
her sister-in-law, Lucy's mother ; and then, as she continued her work,
she assured herself that it would be best to let her niece have her cry
out upstairs. Lucy's violence had astonished her for a moment, but
she had taught herself to think it best to allow such little ebullitions
to pass off by themselves.

Lucy, when she was alone, flung herself upon her bed in absolute
agony. She thought that she had misbehaved, and yet how cruel,—
how harsh had been her aunt's words ! If she, the quiet one, had misbehaved, what would Ayala have done ? And how was she to find
strength with which to look forward to the future ? She struggled
hard with herself for a resolution. Should she determine that she
would henceforward darn sheets morning, noon, and night till she
worked her fingers to the bone ? Perhaps there had been something of
truth in that assertion of her aunt's that the labourers have no time to
grieve. As everything else was shut out from her it might be well for
her to darn sheets. Should she rush down penitent and beg her aunt
to allow her to commence at once ?

She would have done it as far as the sheets were concerned, but she
could not do it as regarded her aunt. She could put herself into unison
with the crumpled soiled linen, but not with the hard woman.

Oh, how terrible was the change ! Her father and her mother who
had been so gentle to her ! All the sweet prettinesses of her life ! All
her occupations, all her friends, all her delights ! Even Ayala was
gone from her ! How was she to bear it ? She begrudged Ayala
nothing,—no, nothing. But yet it was hard ! Ayala was to have
everything. Aunt Emmeline,—though they had not hitherto been very
fond of Aunt Emmeline,—was sweetness itself as compared with this
woman. "The sooner you begin to labour the better for yourself and
those about you." Would it not have been fitter that she should have

been sent at once to some actual poor-house in which there would have been no mistake as to her position?

That it should all have been decided for her, for her and Ayala, not by any will of their own, not by any concert between themselves, but simply by the fantasy of another! Why should she thus be made a slave to the fantasy of anyone? Let Ayala have her uncle's wealth and her aunt's palaces at her command, and she would walk out simply a pauper into the world,—into some workhouse, so that at least she need not be obedient to the harsh voice and the odious common sense of her Aunt Dosett! But how should she take herself to some workhouse? In what way could she prove her right to be admitted even then? It seemed to her that the same decree which had admitted Ayala into the golden halls of the fairies had doomed her not only to poverty, but to slavery. There was no escape for her from her aunt and her aunt's sermons. "Oh, Ayala, my darling,—my own one; oh, Ayala, if you did but know!" she said to herself. What would Ayala think, how would Ayala bear it, could she but guess by what a gulf was her heaven divided from her sister's hell! "I will never tell her," she said to herself. "I will die, and she shall never know."

As she lay there sobbing all the gilded things of the world were beautiful in her eyes. Alas, yes, it was true! The magnificence of the mansion at Queen's Gate, the glories of Glenbogie, the closely-studied comforts of Merle Park, as the place in Sussex was called all the carriages and horses, Madame Tonsonville and all the draperies, the seats at the Albert Hall into which she had been accustomed to go with as much ease as into her bed-room, the box at the opera, the pretty furniture, the frequent gems, even the raiment which would make her pleasing to the eyes of men whom she would like to please—all these things grew in her eyes and became beautiful. No. 3, Kingsbury Crescent, was surely, of all places on the earth's surface, the most ugly. And yet,—yet she had endeavoured to do her duty. "If it had been the workhouse I could have borne it," she said to herself; "but not to be the slave of my Aunt Dosett!" Again she appealed to her sister, "Oh, Ayala, if you did but know it!" Then she remembered herself, declaring that it might have been worse to Ayala than even to her. "If one had to bear it, it was better for me," she said, as she struggled to prepare herself for her uncle's dinner.

CHAPTER III.

Lucy's TROUBLES.

THE evening after the affair with the sheet went off quietly, as did many days and many evenings. Mrs. Dosett was wise enough to forget the little violence and to forget also the feeling which had been displayed. When Lucy first asked for some household needlework, which she did with a faltering voice and shame-faced remembrance of her fault, her aunt took it all in good part and gave her a task somewhat lighter as a beginning than the handling of a sheet. Lucy sat at it and suffered. She went on sitting and suffering. She told herself that she was a martyr at every stitch she made. As she occupied the seat opposite to her aunt's accustomed chair she would hardly speak at all, but would keep her mind always intent on Ayala and the joys of Ayala's life. That they who had been born together, sisters, with equal fortunes, who had so closely lived together, should be sundered so utterly one from the other; that the one should be so exalted and the other so debased! And why? What justice had there been? Could it be from heaven or even from earth that the law had gone forth for such a division of the things of the world between them?

"You have got very little to say to a person?" said Aunt Dosett, one morning. This, too, was a reproach. This, too, was scolding. And yet Aunt Dosett had intended to be as pleasant as she knew how.

"I have very little to say," replied Lucy, with repressed anger.

"But why?"

"Because I am stupid," said Lucy. "Stupid people can't talk. You should have had Ayala."

"I hope you do not envy Ayala her fortune, Lucy?" A woman with any tact would not have asked such a question at such a time. She should have felt that a touch of such irony might be natural, and that unless it were expressed loudly, or shown actively, it might be left to be suppressed by affection and time. But she, as she had grown old, had taught herself to bear disappointment, and thought it wise to teach Lucy to do the same.

"Envy!" said Lucy, not passionately, but after a little pause for thought. "I sometimes think it is very hard to know what envy is."

"Envy, hatred, and malice," said Mrs. Dosett, hardly knowing what she meant by the use of the well-worn words.

"I do know what hatred and malice are," said Lucy. "Do you think I hate Ayala?"

"I am sure you do not."

"Or that I bear her malice?"

" Certainly not."

" If I had the power to take anything from her, would I do it ? I love Ayala with my whole heart. Whatever be my misery I would rather bear it than let Ayala have even a share of it. Whatever good things she may have I would not rob her even of a part of them. If there be joy and sorrow to be divided between us I would wish to have the sorrow so that she might have the joy. That is not hatred and malice." Mrs. Dosett looked at her over her spectacles. This was the girl who had declared that she could not speak because she was too stupid ! " But, when you ask me whether I envy her, I hardly know," continued Lucy. " I think one does covet one's neighbour's house, in spite of the tenth commandment, even though one does not want to steal it."

Mrs. Dosett repented herself that she had given rise to any conversation at all. Silence, absolute silence, the old silence which she had known for a dozen years before Lucy had come to her, would have been better than this. She was very angry, more angry than she had ever yet been with Lucy ; and yet she was afraid to show her anger. Was this the girl's gratitude for all that her uncle was doing for her, —for shelter, food, comfort, for all that she had in the world ? Mrs. Dosett knew, though Lucy did not, of the little increased pinchings which had been made necessary by the advent of another inmate in the house ; so many pounds of the meat in the week, and so much bread, and so much tea and sugar ! It had all been calculated. In genteel houses such calculation must often been made. And when by degrees,—degrees very quick,—the garments should become worn which Lucy had brought with her, there must be something taken from the tight-fitting income for that need. Arrangements had already been made of which Lucy knew nothing, and already the two glasses of port wine a day had been knocked off from poor Mr. Dosett's comforts. His wife had sobbed in despair when he had said that it should be so. He had declared gin and water to be as supporting as port wine, and the thing had been done. Lucy inwardly had been disgusted by the gin and water, knowing nothing of its history. Her father, who had not always been punctual in paying his wine-merchant's bills, would not have touched gin and water, would not have allowed it to contaminate his table ! Everthing in Mr. Dosett's house was paid for weekly.

And now Lucy, who had been made welcome to all that the genteel house could afford, who had been taken in as a child, had spoken of her lot as one which was all sorrowful. Bad as it is,—this living in Kingsbury Crescent,—I would rather bear it myself than subject Ayala to such misery ! It was thus that she had, in fact, spoken of her new home when she had found it necessary to defend her feelings towards her sister. It was impossible that her aunt should be altogether silent under such treatment. "We have done the best for you that is in our power, Lucy," she said, with a whole load of reproach in her tone.

"Have I complained, aunt ?"

"I thought you did."

"Oh, no ! You asked me whether I envied Ayala. What was I to say ? Perhaps I should have said nothing, but the idea of envying Ayala was painful to me. Of course she——"

"Well ?"

"I had better say nothing more, aunt. If I were to pretend to be cheerful I should be false. It is as yet only a few weeks since papa died." Then the work went on in silence between them for the next hour.

And the work went on in solemn silence between them through the winter. It came to pass that the sole excitement of Lucy's life came from Ayala's letters,—the sole excitement except a meeting which took place between the sisters one day. When Lucy was taken to Kingsbury Crescent Ayala was at once carried down to Glenbogie, and from thence there came letters twice a week for six weeks. Ayala's letters, too, were full of sorrow. She too, had lost her mother, her father, and her sister. Moreover, in her foolish petulance she said things of her Aunt Emmeline, and of the girls, and of Sir Thomas, which ought not to have been written of those who were kind to her. Her cousin Tom, too, she ridiculed—Tom Tringle, the son-and-heir,—saying that he was a lout who endeavoured to make eyes at her. Oh, how distasteful, how vulgar they were after all that she had known. Perhaps the eldest girl, Augusta, was the worst. She did not think that she could put up with the assumed authority of Augusta. Gertrude was better, but a simpleton. Ayala declared herself to be sad at heart. But then the sweet scenery of Glenbogie, and the colour of the moors, and the glorious heights of Ben Alchan, made some amends. Even in her sorrow she would rave about the beauties of Glenbogie. Lucy, as she read the letters, told herself that Ayala's grief was a grief to be borne, a grief almost to be enjoyed. To sit and be sad with a stream purling by you, how different from the sadness of that dining-room in the Crescent. To look out upon the glories of a mountain, while a tear would now and again force itself into the eye, how much less bitter than the falling of salt drops over a tattered towel.

Lucy, in her answers, endeavoured to repress the groans of her spirit. In the first place she did acknowledge that it did not become her to speak ill of those who were, in truth, her benefactors ; and then she was anxious not to declare to Ayala her feeling of the injustice by which their two lots had been defined to them. Though she had failed to control herself once or twice in speaking to her aunt she did control herself in writing her letters. She would never, never, write a word which should make Ayala unnecessarily unhappy. On that she was determined. She would say nothing to explain to Ayala the unutterable tedium of that downstairs parlour in which they passed their lives, lest Ayala should feel herself to be wounded by the luxurious comforts around her.

It was thus she wrote. Then there came a time in which they were to meet,—just at the beginning of November. The Tringles were going to Rome. They generally did go somewhere. Glenbogie, Merle Park, and the house in Queen's Gate, were not enough for the year. Sir Thomas was to take them to Rome, and then return to London for the manipulation of the millions in Lombard Street. He generally did remain nine months out of the twelve in town, because of the millions, making his visits at Merle Park very short ; but Lady Tringle found that change of air was good for the girls. It was her intention now to remain at Rome for two or three months.

The party from Scotland reached Queen's Gate late one Saturday evening, and intended to start early on the Monday. To Ayala, who had made it quite a matter of course that she should see her sister, Lady Tringle had said that in that case a carriage must be sent across. It was awkward, because there were no carriages in London. She had thought that they had all intended to pass through London just as though they were not stopping. Sunday, she had thought, was not to be regarded as being a day at all. Then Ayala flashed up. She had flashed up some times before. Was it supposed that she was not going to see Lucy? Carriage ! She would walk across Kensington Gardens, and find the house out all by herself. She would spend the whole day with Lucy, and come back alone in a cab. She was strong enough, at any rate, to have her way so far, that a carriage, wherever it came from, was sent for Lucy about three in the afternoon, and did take her back to Kingsbury Crescent after dinner.

Then at last the sisters were together in Ayala's bed-room. "And now tell me about everything," said Ayala.

But Lucy was resolved that she would not tell anything. "I am so wretched !" That would have been all ; but she would not tell her wretchedness. "We are so quiet in Kingsbury Crescent," she said ; "you have so much more to talk of."

"Oh, Lucy, I do not like it."

"Not your aunt ?"

"She is not the worst, though she sometimes is hard to bear. I can't tell you what it is, but they all seem to think so much of themselves. In the first place they never will say a word about papa."

"Perhaps that is from feeling, Ayey."

"No, it is not. One would know that. But they look down upon papa, who had more in his little finger than they have with all their money."

"Then I should hold my tongue."

"So I do,—about him; but it is very hard. And then Augusta has a way with me, as though she had a right to order me. I certainly will not be ordered by Augusta. You never ordered me."

"Dear Ayey!"

"Augusta is older than you,—of course, ever so much. They make her out twenty-three at her last birthday, but she is twenty-four. But that is not difference enough for ordering,—certainly between cousins. I do hate Augusta."

"I would not hate her."

"How is one to help one's-self? She has a way of whispering to Gertrude, and to her mother, when I am there, which almost kills me. 'If you'll only give me notice I'll go out of the room at once,' I said the other day, and they were all so angry."

"I would not make them angry if I were you, Ayey."

"Why not?"

"Not Sir Thomas, or Aunt Emmeline."

"I don't care a bit for Sir Thomas. I am not sure but he is the most good-natured though he is so podgy. Of course, when Aunt Emmeline tells me anything I do it."

"It is so important that you should be on good terms with them."

"I don't see it all," said Ayala, flashing round.

"Aunt Emmeline can do so much for you. We have nothing of our own,—you and I."

"Am I to sell myself because they have got money! No, indeed! No one despises money so much as I do. I will never be other to them than if I had the money, and they were the poor relations."

"That will not do, Ayey."

"I will make it do. They may turn me out if they like. Of course, I know that I should obey my aunt, and so I will. If Sir Thomas told me anything I should do it. But not Augusta." Then, while Lucy was thinking how she might best put into soft words advice which was so clearly needed, Ayala declared another trouble. "But there is worse still."

"What is that?"

"Tom!"

"What does Tom do?"

"You know Tom, Lucy?"

"I have seen him."

"Of all the horrors he is the horridest."

" Does he order you about ?"

" No; but he——"

" What is it, Ayey ?"

" Oh ! Lucy, he is so dreadful. He——"

" You don't mean that he makes love to you ?"

" He does. What am I to do, Lucy ?"

" Do they know it ?"

" Augusta does, I'm sure ; and pretends to think that it is my fault. I am sure that there will be a terrible quarrel some day. I told him the day before we left Glenbogie that I should tell his mother. I did indeed. Then he grinned. He is such a fool. And when I laughed he took it all as kindness. I couldn't have helped laughing if I had died for it."

" But he has been left behind."

" Yes, for the present. But he is to come over to us some time after Christmas, when Uncle Tringle has gone back."

" A girl need not be bothered by a lover unless she chooses, Ayey."

" But it will be such a bother to have to talk about it. He looks at me, and is such an idiot. Then Augusta frowns. When I see Augusta frowning I am so angry that I feel like boxing her ears. Do you know, Lucy, that I often think that it will not do, and that I shall have to be sent away. I wish it had been you that they had chosen."

Such was the conversation between the girls. Of what was said everything appertained to Ayala. Of the very nature of Lucy's life not a word was spoken. As Ayala was talking Lucy was constantly thinking of all that might be lost by her sister's imprudence. Even though Augusta might be disagreeable, even though Tom might be a bore, it should all be borne,—borne at any rate for a while,—seeing how terrible would be the alternative. The alternative to Lucy seemed to be Kingsbury Crescent and Aunt Dosett. It did not occur to her to think whether in any possible case Ayala would indeed be added to the Crescent family, or what in that case would become of herself, and whether they two might live with Aunt Dosett, and whether in that case life would not be infinitely improved. Ayala had all that money could do for her, and would have such a look-out into the world from a wealthy house as might be sure at last to bring her some such husband as would be desirable. Ayala, in fact, had everything before her, and Lucy had nothing. Wherefore it became Lucy's duty to warn Ayala so that she should bear with much, and throw away nothing. If Ayala could only know what life might be, what life was at Kingsbury Crescent, then she would be patient, then she would softly make a confidence with her aunt as to Tom's folly, then she would propitiate Augusta. Not care for money ! Ayala had not yet lived in an ugly room and darned sheets all the morning. Ayala had never sat for two hours between the slumbers of Uncle Dosett and the knitting of Aunt Dosett. Ayala had not been brought into contact with gin and water.

"Oh, Ayala!" she said, as they were going down to dinner together, "do struggle; do bear it. Tell Aunt Emmeline. She will like you to tell her. If Augusta wants you to go anywhere, do go. What does it signify? Papa and mamma are gone, and we are alone." All this she said without a word of allusion to her own sufferings. Ayala made a half promise. She did not think she would go anywhere for Augusta's telling; but she would do her best to satisfy Aunt Emmeline. Then they went to dinner, and after dinner Lucy was taken home without further words between them.

Ayala wrote long letters on her journey, full of what she saw, and full of her companions. From Paris she wrote, and then from Turin, and then again on their immediate arrival at Rome. Her letters were most imprudent as written from the close vicinity of her aunt and cousin. It was such a comfort that that oaf Tom had been left behind. Uncle Tringle was angry because he did not get what he liked to eat. Aunt Emmeline gave that courier such a terrible life, sending for him every quarter of an hour. Augusta would talk first French and then Italian, of which no one could understand a word. Gertrude was so sick with travelling that she was as pale as a sheet. Nobody seemed to care for anything. She could not get her aunt to look at the Campanile at Florence, or her cousins to know one picture from another. "As for pictures, I am quite sure that Mangle's angels would do as well as Raffael's." Mangle was a brother academician whom their father had taught them to despise. There was contempt, most foolish contempt, for all the Tringles; but, luckily, there had been no quarrelling. Then it seemed that both in Paris and in Florence Ayala had bought pretty things, from which it was to be argued that her uncle had provided her liberally with money. One pretty thing had been sent from Paris to Lucy, which could not have been bought for less than many francs. It would not be fair that Ayala should take so much without giving something in return.

Lucy knew that she too should give something in return. Though Kingsbury Crescent was not attractive, though Aunt Dosett was not to her a pleasant companion, she had begun to realise the fact that it behoved her to be grateful, if only for the food she ate, and for the bed on which she slept. As she thought of all that Ayala owed she remembered also her own debts. As the winter went on she struggled to pay them. But Aunt Dosett was a lady not much given to vacillation. She had become aware at first that Lucy had been rough to her, and she did not easily open herself to Lucy's endearments. Lucy's life at Kingsbury Crescent had begun badly, and Lucy, though she understood much about it, found it hard to turn a bad beginning to a good result.

CHAPTER IV.

ISADORE HAMEL.

IT was suggested to Lucy before she had been long in Kingsbury Crescent that she should take some exercise. For the first week she had hardly been out of the house ; but this was attributed to her sorrow. Then she had accompanied her aunt for a few days during the half-hour's marketing which took place every morning, but in this there had been no sympathy. Lucy would not interest herself in the shoulder of mutton which must be of just such a weight as to last conveniently for two days,—twelve pounds,—of which, it was explained to her, more than one-half was intended for the two servants, because there was always a more lavish consumption in the kitchen than in the parlour. Lucy would not appreciate the fact that eggs at a penny a piece, whatever they might be, must be used for puddings, as eggs with even a reputation of freshness cost twopence. Aunt Dosett, beyond this, never left the house on week-days except for a few calls which were made perhaps once a m nth, on which occasion the Sunday gloves and the Sunday silk dress were used. On Sunday they all went to church. But this was not enough for exercise, and as Lucy was becoming pale she was recommended to take to walking in Kensington Gardens.

It is generally understood that there are raging lions about the metropolis, who would certainly eat up young ladies whole if young ladies were to walk about the streets or even about the parks by themselves. There is, however, beginning to be some vacillation as to the received belief on this subject as regards London. In large continental towns, such as Paris and Vienna, young ladies would be devoured certainly. Such, at least, is the creed. In New York and Washington there are supposed to be no lions, so that young ladies go about free as air. In London there is a rising doubt, under which before long, probably, the lions will succumb altogether. Mrs. Dosett did believe somewhat in lions, but she believed also in exercise. And she was aware that the lions eat up chiefly rich people. Young ladies who must go about without mothers, brothers, uncles, carriages, or attendants of any sort, are not often eaten or even roared at. It is the dainty darlings for whom the roarings have to be feared. Mrs. Dosett, aware that daintiness was no longer within the reach of her and hers, did assent to these walkings in Kensington Gardens. At some hour in the afternoon Lucy would walk from the house by herself, and within a quarter of an hour would find herself on the broad gravel path which leads down to the Round Pond. From thence she would go by the back of the Albert Memorial, and then across by the Serpentine and return to the same gate, never leaving Kensington Gardens. Aunt Dosett had expressed some old-fashioned idea that lions were more likely to roar in Hyde Park than within the comparatively retired purlieus of Kensington.

Now the reader must be taken back for a few moments to the bijou, as the bijou was before either the artist or his wife had died. In those days there had been a frequent concourse of people in the artist's house. Society there had not consisted chiefly of eating and drinking. Men and women would come in and out as though really for a purpose of talking. There would be three or four constantly with Dormer in his studio, helping him but little perhaps in the real furtherance of his work, though discussing art subjects in a manner calculated to keep alive art-feeling among them. A novelist or two of a morning might perhaps aid me in my general pursuit, but would, I think, interfere with the actual tally of pages. Egbert Dormer did not turn out from his hand so much work as some men that I know, but he was overflowing with art up to his ears ;—and with tobacco, so that, upon the whole, the bijou was a pleasant rendezvous.

There had come there of late, quite of late, a young sculptor, named Isadore Hamel. Hamel was an Englishman, who, however, had been carried very early to Rome and had been bred there. Of his mother question never was made, but his father had been well known as an English sculptor resident at Rome. The elder Hamel had been a man of mark, who had a fine suite of rooms in the city and a villa on one of the lakes, but who never came to England. English connections were, he said, to him abominable, by which he perhaps meant that the restrictions of decent life were not to his taste. But his busts came, and his groups in marble, and now and again some great work for some public decoration ; so that money was plentiful with him, and he was a man of note. It must be acknowledged of him that he spared nothing in bringing up his son, giving him such education as might best suit his future career as an artist, and that money was always forthcoming for the lad's wants and fantasies.

Then young Hamel also became a sculptor of much promise ; but early in life differed from his father on certain subjects of importance. The father was wedded to Rome and to Italy. Isadore gradually expressed an opinion that the nearer a man was to his market the better for him, that all that art could do for a man in Rome was as nothing to the position which a great artist might make for himself in London that, in fact, an Englishman had better be an Englishman. At twenty-six he succeeded in his attempt, and became known as a young sculptor with a workshop at Brompton. He became known to many both by his work and his acquirements ; but it may not be surprising that after a year he was still unable to live, as he had been taught to live, without drawing upon his father. Then his father threw his failure in his teeth, not refusing him money indeed, but making the receipt of it unpleasant to him.

At no house had Isadore Hamel been made so welcome as at Dormer's. There was a sympathy between them both on that great question of art, whether to an artist his art should be a matter to him of more importance than all the world besides. So said Dormer,—who simply died because his wife died, who could not have touched his brush if one of his girls had been suffering, who, with all his genius, was but a faineant workman. His art more than all the world to him ! No, not to him. Perhaps here and again to some enthusiast, and him hardly removed from madness ! Where is the painter who shall paint a picture after his soul's longing though he shall get not a penny for it, —though he shall starve as he put his last touch to it, when he knows that by drawing some duchess of the day he shall in a fortnight earn a ducal price ? Shall a wife and child be less dear to him than to a lawyer,—or to a shoemaker ; or the very craving of his hunger less obdurate ? A man's self, and what he has within him and his belongings, with his outlook for this and other worlds—let that be the first, and the work, noble or otherwise, be the second. To be honest is greater than to have painted the San Sisto or to have chiselled the Apollo ; to have assisted in making others honest—infinitely greater. All of which were discussed at great length at the bijou, and the bijouites always sided with the master of the house. To an artist, said Dormer, let his art be everything,—above wife and children, above money, above health, above even character. Then he would put out his hand with his jewelled finger, and stretch forth his velvet-clad arm, and soon after lead his friend away to the little dinner at which no luxury had been spared. But young Hamel agreed with the sermons, and not the less because Lucy Dormer had sat by and listened to them with rapt attention.

Not a word of love had been spoken to her by the sculptor when her mother died, but there had been glances and little feelings of which each was half conscious. It is so hard for a young man to speak of love, if there be real love,—so impossible that a girl should do so ! Not a word had been spoken, but each had thought that the other must have known. To Lucy a word had been spoken by her mother,— " Do not think too much of him till you know," the mother had said.—

not quite prudently. "Oh, no ! I will think of him not at all," Lucy had replied. And she had thought of him day and night. " I wonder why Mr. Hamel is so different with you ?" Ayala had said to her sister. "I am sure he is not different with me," Lucy had replied. Then Ayala had shaken her full locks and smiled.

Things came quickly after that. Mrs. Dormer had sickened and died. There was no time then for thinking of that handsome brow, of that short jet black hair, of those eyes so full of fire and thoughtfulness, of that perfect mouth, and the deep but yet soft voice. Still even in her sorrow this new god of her idolatry was not altogether forgotten. It was told to her that he had been summoned off to Rome by his father, and she wondered whether he was to find his home at Rome for ever. Then her father was ill, and in his illness Hamel came to say one word of farewell before he started.

"You find me crushed to the ground," the painter said. Something the young man whispered as to the consolation which time would bring. "Not to me," said Dormer. " It is as though one had lost his eyes. One cannot see without his eyes." It was true of him. His light had been put out.

Then, on the landing at the top of the stairs, there had been one word between Lucy and the sculptor. " I ought not to have intruded on you perhaps," he said ; " but after so much kindness I could hardly go without a word."

"I am sure he will be glad that you have come."

" And you ?"

" I am glad too,—so that I may say good-bye." Then she put out her hand, and he held it for a moment as he looked into her eyes. There was not a word more, but it seemed to Lucy as though there had been so many words.

Things went on quickly. Egbert Dormer died, and Lucy was taken away to Kingsbury Crescent. When once Ayala had spoken about Mr. Hamel, Lucy had silenced her. Any allusion to the idea of love wounded her, as though it was too impossible for dreams, too holy for words. How should there be words about a lover when father and mother were both dead ? He had gone to his old and natural home. He had gone, and of course he would not return. To Ayala, when she came up to London early in November, to Ayala, who was going to Rome, where Isadore Hamel now was, Isadore Hamel's name was not mentioned. But through the long mornings of her life, through the long evenings, through the long nights, she still thought of him,—she could not keep herself from thinking. To a girl whose life is full of delights her lover need not be so very much,—need not, at least, be everything. Though he be a lover to be loved at all points, her friends

will be something, her dancing, her horse, her theatre-going, her
brothers and sisters, even her father and mother. But Lucy had
nothing. The vision of Isadore Hamel had passed across her life, and
had left with her the only possession that she had. It need hardly be
said that she never alluded to that possession at Kingsbury Crescent.
It was not a possession from which any enjoyment could come except
that of thinking of it. He had passed away from her, and there was
no point of life at which he could come across her again. There was
no longer that half-joint studio. If it had been her lot to be as was
Ayala, she then would have been taken to Rome. Then again he
would have looked into her eyes and taken her hand in his. Then
perhaps——. But now, even though he were to come back to London,
he would know nothing of her haunts. Even in that case nothing
would bring them together. As the idea was crossing her mind,—as
it did cross it so frequently,—she saw him turning from the path on
which she was walking, making his way towards the steps of the
Memorial.

Though she saw no more than his back she was sure that it was
Isadore Hamel. For a moment there was an impulse on her to run
after him and to call his name. It was then early in January, and she
was taking her daily walk through Kensington Gardens. She had
walked there daily now for the last two months and had never spoken
a word, or been addressed,—had never seen a face that she had recognised. It had seemed to her that she had not an acquaintance in the
world except Uncle Reg and Aunt Dosett. And now, almost within
reach of her hand, was the one being in all the world whom she most
longed to see. She did stand, and the word was formed within her
lips; but she could not speak it. Then came the thought that she
would run after him, but the thought was expelled quickly. Though
she might lose him again and for ever she could not do that. She
stood almost gasping till he was out of sight, and then she passed on
upon her usual round.

She never omitted her walks after that, and always paused a moment as the path turned away to the Memorial. It was not that she
thought that she might meet him there,—there rather than elsewhere,—
but there is present to us often an idea that when some object has
passed from us that we have desired then it may be seen again. Day
after day, and week after week, she did not see him. During this
time there came letters from Ayala, saying that their return to England
was postponed till the first week in February,—that she would certainly
see Lucy in February,—that she was not going to be hurried through
London in half-an-hour because her aunt wished it; and that she
would do as she pleased as to visiting her sister. Then there was a

word or two about Tom—"Oh, Tom—that idiot Tom !" And another word or two about Augusta. "Augusta is worse than ever. We have not spoken to each other for the last day or two." This came but a day or two before the intended return of the Tringles.

No actual day had been fixed. But on the day before that on which Lucy thought it probable that the Tringles might return to town she was again walking in the Gardens. Having put two and two together, as people do, she felt sure that the travellers could not be away more than a day or two longer. Her mind was much intent upon Ayala, feeling that the imprudent girl was subjecting herself to great danger, knowing that it was wrong that she and Augusta should be together in the house without speaking,—thinking of her sister's perils,—when, of a sudden, Hamel was close before her ! There was no question of calling to him now,—no question of an attempt to see him face to face. She had been wandering along the path with eyes fixed upon the ground, when her name was sharply called, and they two were close to each other. Hamel had a friend with him, and it seemed to Lucy, at once, that she could only bow to him, only mutter something, and then pass on. How can a girl stand and speak to a gentleman in public, especially when that gentleman has a friend with him ? She tried to look pleasant, bowed, smiled, muttered something, and was passing on. But he was not minded to lose her thus immediately. "Miss Dormer," he said, "I have seen your sister at Rome. May I not say a word about her?"

Why should he not say a word about Ayala? In a minute he had left his friend, and was walking back along the path with Lucy. There was not much that he had to say about Ayala. He had seen Ayala and the Tringles, and did manage to let it escape him that Lady Tringle had not been very gracious to himself when once, in public, he had claimed acquaintance with Ayala. But at that he simply smiled. Then he had asked of Lucy where she lived. "With my uncle, Mr. Dosett," said Lucy, "at Kingsbury Crescent." Then, when he asked whether he might call, Lucy, with many blushes, had said that her aunt did not receive many visitors,—that her uncle's house was different from what her father's had been.

"Shall I not see you at all, then?" he asked.

She did not like to ask him after his own purposes of life, whether he was now a resident in London, or whether he intended to return to Rome. She was covered with bashfulness, and dreaded to seem even to be interested in his affairs. "Oh, yes," she said ; "perhaps we may meet some day."

"Here ?" he asked.

"Oh, no ; not here ! It was only an accident." As she said this she determined that she must walk no more in Kensington Gardens. It would be dreadful, indeed, were he to imagine that she would consent to make an appointment with him. It immediately occurred to her that the lions were about, and that she must shut herself up.

"I have thought of you every day since I have been back," he said, "and I did not know where to hear of you. Now that we have met am I to lose you again!" Lose her! What did he mean by losing her? She, too, had found a friend,—she who had been so friendless! Would it not be dreadful to her, also, to lose him? "Is there no place where I may ask of you?"

"When Ayala is back, and they are in town, perhaps I shall sometimes be at Lady Tringle's," said Lucy, resolved that she would not tell him of her immediate abode. This was, at any rate, a certain address from where he might commence further inquiries, should he wish to make inquiry; and as such he accepted it. "I think I had better go now," said Lucy, trembling at the apparent impropriety of her present conversation.

He knew that it was intended that he should leave her, and he went. "I hope I have not offended you in coming so far."

"Oh, no." Then again she gave him her hand, and again there was the same look as he took his leave.

When she got home, which was before the dusk, having resolved that she must, at any rate, tell her aunt that she had met a friend, she found that her uncle had returned from his office. This was a most unusual occurrence. Her uncle, she knew, left Somerset House exactly at half-past four, and always took an hour and a quarter for his walk. She had never seen him in Kingsbury Crescent till a quarter before six. "I have got letters from Rome," he said, in a solemn voice.

"From Ayala?"

"One from Ayala, for you. It is here. And I have had one from my sister, also; and one, in the course of the day, from your uncle in Lombard Street. You had better read them!" There was something terribly tragic in Uncle Dosett's voice as he spoke.

And so must the reader read the letters; but they must be delayed for a few chapters.

CHAPTER V.

AT GLENBOGIE.

WE must go back to Ayala's life during the autumn and winter. She was rapidly whirled away to Glenbogie amidst the affectionate welcomings of her aunt and cousins. All manner of good things were done for her, as to presents and comforts. Young as she was she had money given to her, which was not without attraction; and though she was, of course, in the depth of her mourning, she was made to understand that even mourning might be made becoming if no expense were spared. No expense among the Tringles ever was spared, and at first Ayala liked the bounty of profusion. But before the end of the first fortnight there grew upon her a feeling that even bank notes become tawdry if you are taught to use them as curl-papers. It may be said that nothing in the world is charming unless it be achieved at some trouble. If it rained " '64 Leoville,"—which I regard as the most divine of nectars,—I feel sure that I should never raise it to my lips. Ayala did not argue the matter out in her mind, but in very early days she began to entertain a dislike to Tringle magnificence. There had been a good deal of luxury at the bijou, but always with a feeling that it ought not to be there,—that more money was being spent than prudence authorised,—which had certainly added a savour to the luxuries. A lovely bonnet, is it not more lovely because the destined wearer knows that there is some wickedness in achieving it? All the bonnets, all the claret, all the horses, seemed to come at Queen's Gate and at Glenbogie without any wickedness. There was no more question about them than as to one's ordinary bread and butter at breakfast. Sir Thomas had a way—a merit shall we call it or a fault?—of pouring out his wealth upon the family as though it were water running in perpetuity from a mountain tarn. Ayala the romantic, Ayala the poetic, found very soon that she did not like it.

Perhaps the only pleasure left to the very rich is that of thinking of the deprivations of the poor. The bonnets, and the claret, and the horses have lost their charm; but the Gladstone, and the old hats, and the four-wheeled cabs of their neighbours, still have a little flavour for them. From this source it seemed to Ayala that the Tringles drew much of the recreation of their lives. Sir Thomas had his way of enjoying this amusement, but it was a way that did not specially come beneath Ayala's notice. When she heard that Break-at-last, the Huddersfield manufacturer, had to sell his pictures, and that all Shoddy and Stuffgoods' grand doings for the last two years had only been a flash in the pan, she did not understand enough about it to feel wounded; but when she heard her aunt say that people like the Poodles had better not have a place in Scotland then have to let it, and when Augusta hinted that Lady Sophia Smallware had pawned her diamonds, then she felt that her nearest and dearest relatives smelt abominably of money.

Of all the family Sir Thomas was most persistently the kindest to her, though he was a man who did not look to be kind. She was pretty, and though he was ugly himself he liked to look at things pretty. He was, too, perhaps, a little tired of his own wife and daughters,—who were indeed what he had made them, but still were not quite to his taste. In a general way he gave instructions that Ayala should be treated exactly as a daughter, and he informed his wife that he intended to add a codicil to his will on her behalf. "Is that necessary?" asked Lady Tringle, who began to feel something like natural jealousy. "I suppose I ought to do something for a girl if I take her by the hand," said Sir Thomas, roughly. "If she gets a husband I will give her something, and that will do as well." Nothing more was said about it, but when Sir Thomas went up to town the codicil was added to his will.

Ayala was foolish rather than ungrateful, not understanding the nature of the family to which she was relegated. Before she had been taken away she had promised Lucy that she would be "obedient" to her aunt. There had hardly been such a word as obedience known at the bijou. If any were obedient, it was the mother and the father to the daughters. Lucy, and Ayala as well, had understood something of this; and therefore Ayala had promised to be obedient to her aunt. "And to Uncle Thomas," Lucy had demanded, with an imploring embrace. "Oh, yes," said Ayala, dreading her uncle at that time. She soon learned that no obedience whatsoever was exacted from Sir Thomas. She had to kiss him morning and evening, and then to take whatever presents he made her. An easy uncle he was to deal with, and she almost learned to love him. Nor was Aunt Emmeline very exigeant, though she was fantastic and sometimes disagreeable. But Augusta was the great difficulty. Lucy had not told her to obey Augusta, and Augusta she would not obey. Now Augusta demanded obedience.

"You never ordered me," Ayala had said to Lucy when they met in London as the Tringles were passing through. At the bijou there had been a republic, in which all the inhabitants and all the visitors had been free and equal. Such republicanism had been the very mainspring of life at the bijou. Ayala loved equality, and she specially felt that it should exist among sisters. Do anything for Lucy? Oh, yes, indeed, anything; abandon anything; but for Lucy as a sister among sisters, not for an elder as from a younger! And if she were not bound to serve Lucy then certainly not Augusta. But Augusta liked to be served. On one occasion she sent Ayala upstairs, and on another she sent Ayala down-stairs. Ayala went, but determined to be equal with her cousin. On the morning following, in the presence of Aunt Emmeline and of Gertrude, in the presence also of two other ladies who

were visiting at the house, she asked Augusta if she would mind running up-stairs and fetching her scrap-book! She had been thinking
about it all the night and all the morning, plucking up her courage.
But she had been determined. She found a great difficulty in saying
the words, but she said them. The thing was so preposterous that all
the ladies in the room looked aghast at the proposition. "I really
think that Augusta has got something else to do," said Aunt Emmeline.
"Oh, very well," said Ayala, and then they were all silent. Augusta,
who was employed on a silk purse, sat still and did not say a word.

Had a great secret, or rather a great piece of news which pervaded
the family, been previously communicated to Ayala, she would not probably have made so insane a suggestion. Augusta was engaged to be
married to the Honourable Septimus Traffick, the member for Port
Glasgow. A young lady who is already half a bride is not supposed to
run up and down stairs as readily as a mere girl. For running up and
down stairs at the bijou Ayala had been proverbial. They were a
family who ran up and down with the greatest alacrity. "Oh, papa,
my basket is out on the seat"—for there had been a seat in the two-
foot garden behind the house. Papa would go down in two jumps and
come up with three skips, and there was the basket, only because his
girl liked him to do something for her. But for him Ayala would run
about as though she were a tricksy Ariel. Had the important matrimonial news been conveyed to Ariel, with a true girl's spirit she would
have felt that during the present period Augusta was entitled to special
exemption from all ordering. Had she herself been engaged she would
have run more and quicker than ever,—would have been excited thereto
by the peculiar vitality of her new prospects; but to even Augusta she
would be subservient, because of her appreciation of bridal importance.
She, however, had not been told till that afternoon.

"You should not have asked Augusta to go up stairs," said Aunt
Emmeline, in a tone of mitigated reproach.

"Oh! I didn't know," said Ayala.

"You had meant to say that because she had sent you you were to
send her. There is a difference, you know."

"I didn't know," said Ayala, beginning to think that she would fight
her battle if told of such differences as she believed to exist.

"I had meant to tell you before, but I may as well tell you now,
Augusta is engaged to be married to the Honourable Mr. Septimus
Traffick. He is second son of Lord Boardotrade, and is in the
House."

"Dear me!" said Ayala, acknowledging at once within her heart
that the difference alleged was one against which she need not rouse
herself to the fight. Aunt Emmeline had, in truth, intended to

insist on that difference—and another ; but her courage had failed
her.

"Yes, indeed. He is a man very much thought of just now in public
life, and Augusta's mind is naturally much occupied. He writes all
those letters in The Times about supply and demand."

"Does he, aunt?" Ayala did feel that if Augusta's mind was
entirely occupied with supply and demand she ought not to be made to
go upstairs to fetch a scrap-book. But she had her doubts about
Augusta's mind. Nevertheless, if the forthcoming husband were true,
that might be a reason. "If anybody had told me before I wouldn't
have asked her," she said.

Then Lady Tringle explained that it had been thought better not to
say anything heretofore as to the coming matrimonial hilarities because
of the sadness which had fallen upon the Dormer family. Ayala
accepted this as an excuse, and nothing further was said as to the
iniquity of her request to her cousin. But there was a general feeling
among the women that Ayala, in lieu of gratitude, had exhibited an
intention of rebelling.

On the next day Mr. Traffick arrived, whose coming had probably
made it necessary that the news should be told. Ayala was never so
surprised in her life as when she saw him. She had never yet had a
lover of her own, had never dreamed of a lover, but she had her own
idea as to what a lover ought to be. She had thought that Isadore
Hamel would be a very nice lover—for her sister. Hamel was young,
handsome, with a great deal to say on such a general subject as art,
but too bashful to talk easily to the girl he admired. Ayala had thought
that all that was just as it should be. She was altogether resolved that
Hamel and her sister should be lovers, and was determined to be devoted to her future brother-in-law. But the Honourable Septimus
Traffick ! It was a question to her whether her Uncle Tringle would
not have been better as a lover.

And yet there was nothing amiss about Mr. Traffick. He was very
much like an ordinary hard-working member of the House of Commons, over perhaps rather than under forty years of age. He was
somewhat bald, somewhat grey, somewhat fat, and had lost that look
of rosy plumpness which is seldom, I fear, compatible with hard work
and late hours. He was not particularly ugly, nor was he absurd in
appearance. But he looked to be a disciple of business, not of pleasure,
nor of art. "To sit out on the bank of a stream and have him beside
one would not be particularly nice," thought Ayala to herself. Mr.
Traffick no doubt would have enjoyed it very well if he could have
spared the time ; but to Ayala it seemed that such a man as that could
have cared nothing for love. As soon as she saw him, and realised in

her mind the fact that Augusta was to become his wife, she felt at once the absurdity of sending Augusta on a message.

Augusta that evening was somewhat more than ordinarily kind to her cousin. Now that the great secret was told, her cousin no doubt would recognise her importance. "I suppose you had not heard of him before?" she said to Ayala.

"I never did."

"That's because you have not attended to the debates."

"I never have. What are debates?"

"Mr. Traffick is very much thought of in the House of Commons on all subjects affecting commerce."

"Oh!"

"It is the most glorious study which the world affords."

"The House of Commons. I don't think it can be equal to art."

Then Augusta turned up her nose with a double turn,—first as against painters, Mr. Dormer having been no more, and then at Ayala's ignorance in supposing that the House of Commons could have been spoken of as a study. "Mr. Traffick will probably be in the government some day," she said.

"Has not he been yet?" asked Ayala.

"Not yet."

"Then won't he be very old before he gets there?" This was a terrible question. Young ladies of five-and-twenty, when they marry gentlemen of four-and-fifty, make up their minds for well-understood and well-recognised old age. They see that they had best declare their purpose, and they do declare it. "Of course, Mr. Walker is old enough to be my father, but I have made up my mind that I like that better than anything else." Then the wall has been jumped, and the thing can go smooth. But at forty-five there is supposed to be so much of youth left that the difference of age may possibly be tided over and not made to appear abnormal. Augusta Tringle had determined to tide it over in this way. The forty-five had been gradually reduced to "less than forty,"—though all the Peerages were there to give the lie to the assertion. She talked of her lover as Septimus, and was quite prepared to sit with him beside a stream if only half-an-hour for the amusement could be found. When, therefore, Ayala suggested that if her lover wanted to get into office he had better do so quickly, lest he should be too old, Augusta was not well pleased.

"Lord Boardotrade was much older when he began," said Augusta. "His friends, indeed, tell Septimus that he should not push himse forward too quickly. But I don't think that I ever came across anyone who was so ignorant of such things as you are, Ayala."

"Perhaps he is not so old as he looks," said Ayala. After this may be imagined that there was not close friendship between the cousins. Augusta's mind was filled with a strong conception as to Ayala's ingratitude. The houseless, penniless orphan had been taken in, and had done nothing but make herself disagreeable. Young! No doubt she was young. But had she been as old as Methuselah she could not have been more insolent. It did not, however, matter to her, Augusta. She was going away; but it would be terrible to her mamma and to Gertrude! Thus it was that Augusta spoke of her cousin to her mother.

And then there came another trouble, which was more troublesome to Ayala even than the other. Tom Tringle, who was in the house in Lombard Street, who was the only son, and heir to the title and no doubt to much of the wealth, had chosen to take Ayala's part and to enlist himself as her special friend. Ayala had, at first, accepted him as a cousin, and had consented to fraternise with him. Then, on some unfortunate day, there had been some word or look which she had failed not to understand, and immediately she had become afraid of Tom. Tom was not like Isadore Hamel,—was very far, indeed, from that idea of a perfect lover which Ayala's mind had conceived; but he was by no means a lout, or an oaf, or an idiot, as Ayala in her letters to her sister had described him. He had been first at Eton and then at Oxford, and having spent a great deal of money recklessly, and done but little towards his education, had been withdrawn and put into the office. His father declared of him now that he would do fairly well in the world. He had a taste for dress, and kept four or five hunters which he got but little credit by riding. He made a fuss about his shooting, but did not shoot much. He was stout and awkward looking,—very like his father, but without that settled air which age gives to heavy men. In appearance he was not the sort of lover to satisfy the preconceptions of such a girl as Ayala. But he was good-natured and true. At last he became to her terribly true. His love, such as it seemed at first, was absurd to her. "If you make yourself such a fool, Tom, I'll never speak to you again," she had said, once. Even after that she had not understood that it was more than a stupid joke. But the joke, while it was considered as such, was very distasteful to her; and afterwards, when a certain earnestness in it was driven in upon her, it became worse than distasteful.

She repudiated his love with such power as she had, but she could not silence him. She could not at all understand that a young man, who seemed to her to be an oaf, should really be in love,—honestly in love with her. But such was the case. Then she became afraid lest others should see it,—afraid, though she often told herself that she would appeal to her aunt for protection. "I tell you I don't care a bit about you, and you oughtn't to go on," she said. But he did go on, and though her aunt did not see it Augusta did.

Then Augusta spoke a word to her in scorn. " Ayala," she said, " you should not encourage Tom."

Encourage him ! What a word from one girl to another ! What a world of wrong there was in the idea which had created the word ! What an absence of the sort of feeling which, according to Ayala's theory of life, there should be on such a matter between two sisters, two cousins, or two friends ! Encourage him ! When Augusta ought to have been the first to assist her in her trouble ! " Oh, Augusta," she said, turning sharply round, " what a spiteful creature you are."

" I suppose you think so, because I do not choose to approve."

" Approve of what ! Tom is thoroughly disagreeable. Sometimes he makes my life such a burden to me that I think I shall have to go to my aunt. But you are worse. Oh !" exclaimed Ayala, shuddering as she thought of the unwomanly treachery of which her cousin was guilty towards her.

Nothing more came of it at Glenbogie. Tom was required in Lombard Street, and the matter was not suspected by Aunt Emmeline,—as far, at least, as Ayala was aware. When he was gone it was to her as though there would be a world of time before she would see him again. They were to go to Rome, and he would not be at Rome till January. Before that he might have forgotten his folly. But Ayala was quite determined that she would never forget the ill offices of Augusta. She did hate Augusta, as she had told her sister. Then, in this frame of mind, the family was taken to Rome.

CHAPTER VI.

AT ROME.

During her journeying and during her sojourn at Rome Ayala did enjoy much ; but even these joys did not come to her without causing some trouble of spirit. At Glenbogie everybody had known that she was a dependent niece, and that as such she was in truth nobody. On that morning when she had ordered Augusta to go upstairs the two visitors had stared with amazement,—who would not have stared at all had they heard Ayala ordered in the same way. But it came about that in Rome Ayala was almost of more importance than the Tringles. It was absolutely true that Lady Tringle and Augusta and Gertrude were asked here and there because of Ayala ; and the worst of it was that the fact was at last suspected by the Tringles themselves. Some times they would not always be asked. One of the Tringle girls would only be named. But Ayala was never forgotten. Once or twice an effort was made by some grand lady, whose taste was perhaps more conspicuous than her good-nature, to get Ayala without burdening herself with any of the Tringles. When this became clear to the mind of Augusta,—of Augusta, engaged as she was to the Honourable Septimus Traffick, member of Parliament,—Augusta's feelings were—such as may better be understood than described! "Don't let her go, mamma," she said to Lady Tringle one morning.

"But the Marchesa has made such a point of it."

"Bother the Marchesa! Who is the Marchesa? I believe it is all Ayala's doing because she expects to meet that Mr. Hamel. It is dreadful to see the way she goes on."

"Mr. Hamel was a very intimate friend of her father's."

"I don't believe a bit of it."

"He certainly used to be at his house. I remember seeing him."

"I daresay; but that doesn't justify Ayala in running after him as she does. I believe that all this about the Marchesa is because of Mr. Hamel." This was better than believing that Ayala was to be asked to sing, and that Ayala was to be fêted and admired and danced with, simply because Ayala was Ayala, and that they, the Tringles, in spite of Glenbogie, Merle Park, and Queen's Gate, were not wanted at all. But when Aunt Emmeline signified to Ayala that on that particular morning she had better not go to the Marchesa's picnic, Ayala simply said that she had promised;—and Ayala went.

At this time no gentleman of the family was with them. Sir Thomas had gone, and Tom Tringle had not come. Then, just at Christmas, the Honourable Septimus Traffick came for a short visit,—a very short visit, no more than four or five days, because Supply and Demand were requiring all his services in preparation for the coming Session of Parliament. But for five halcyon days he was prepared to devote himself to the glories of Rome under the guidance of Augusta. He did not of course sleep at the Palazzo Ruperti, where it delighted Lady Tringle to inform her friends in Rome that she had a suite of apartments " au première," but he ate there and drank there and almost lived there ; so that it became absolutely necessary to inform the world of Rome that it was Augusta's destiny to become in course of time the Honourable Mrs. Traffick, otherwise the close intimacy would hardly have been discreet,—unless it had been thought, as the ill-natured Marchesa had hinted, that Mr. Traffick was Lady Tringle's elder brother. Augusta, however, was by no means ashamed of her lover. Perhaps she felt that when it was known that she was about to be the bride of so great a man then doors would be open for her at any rate as wide as for her cousin. At this moment she was very important to herself. She was about to convey no less a sum than £120,000 to Mr. Traffick, who, in truth, as younger son of Lord Boardotrade, was himself not well endowed. Considering her own position and her future husband's rank and standing, she did not know how a young woman could well be more important. She was very important at any rate to Mr. Traffick. She was sure of that. When, therefore, she learned that Ayala had been asked to a grand ball at the Marchesa's, that Mr. Traffick was also to be among the guests, and that none of the Tringles had been invited, —then her anger became hot.

She must have been very stupid when she took it into her head to be jealous of Mr. Traffick's attention to her cousin; stupid, at any rate, when she thought that her cousin was laying out feminine lures for Mr. Traffick. Poor Ayala! We shall see much of her in these pages, and it may be well to declare of her at once that her ideas at this moment about men, —or rather about a possible man,—were confined altogether to the abstract. She had floating in her young mind some fancies as to the beauty of love. That there should be a hero must of course be necessary. But in her day-dreams this hero was almost celestial,—or, at least, æthereal. It was a concentration of poetic perfection to which there was not as yet any appanage of apparel, of features, or of wealth. It was a something out of heaven which should think it well to spend his whole time in adoring her and making her more blessed than had ever yet been a woman upon the earth. Then her first approach to a mundane feeling had been her acknowledgment to herself that Isadore Hamel would do as a lover for Lucy. Isadore Hamel was certainly very handsome,—was possessed of infinite good gifts; but even he would by means have come up to her requirements for her own hero. That hero must have wings tinged with azure, whereas Hamel had a not much more ætherealised than ordinary coat and waistcoat. She knew that heroes with azure wings were not existent save in the imagination, and, as she desired a real lover for Lucy, Hamel would do. But for herself her imagination was too valuable then to allow her to put her foot upon earth. Such as she was, must not Augusta have been very stupid to have thought that Ayala should become fond of her Mr. Traffick!

Her cousin Tom had come to her, and had been to her as a New-foundland dog is when he jumps all over you just when he has come out of a horsepond. She would have liked Tom had he kept his dog-like gambols at a proper distance. But when he would cover her with muddy water he was abominable. But this Augusta had not understood. With Mr. Traffick there would be no dog-like gambols; and, as he was not harsh to her, Ayala liked him. She had liked her

uncle. Such men were, to her thinking, more like dogs than lovers.
She sang when Mr. Traffick asked her, and made a picture for him,
and went with him to the Coliseum, and laughed at him about Supply
and Demand. She was very pretty, and perhaps Mr. Traffick did like
to look at her.

"I really think you were too free with Mr. Traffick last night,"
Augusta said to her one morning.

"Free! How free?"

"You were—laughing at him."

"Oh, he likes that," said Ayala. "All that time we were up at the
top at St. Peter's I was quizzing him about his speeches. He lets me
say just what I please."

This was wormwood. In the first place there had been a word or two
between the lovers about that going up of St. Peter's, and Augusta had
refused to join them. She had wished Septimus to remain down with
her,—which would have been tantamount to prevent any of the party
from going up; but Septimus had persisted on ascending. Then
Augusta had been left for a long hour alone with her mother. Gertrude had no doubt gone up, but Gertrude had lagged during the ascent.
Ayala had skipped up the interminable stairs and Mr. Traffick had
trotted after her with admiring breathless industry. This itself, with
the thoughts of the good time which Septimus might be having at the
top, was very bad. But now to be told that she, Ayala, should laugh at
him; and that he, Septimus, should like it! "I suppose he takes you
to be a child," said Augusta; "but if you are a child you ought to
conduct yourself."

"I suppose he does perceive the difference," said Ayala.

She had not in the least known what the words might convey,—had
probably meant nothing. But to Augusta it was apparent that Ayala
had declared that her lover, her Septimus, had preferred her extreme
youth to the more mature charms of his own true love,—or had, perhaps, preferred Ayala's raillery to Augusta's serious demeanour. "You
are the most impertinent person I ever knew in my life," said Augusta,
rising from her chair and walking slowly out of the room. Ayala stared
after her, not above half comprehending the cause of the anger.

Then came the very serious affair of the ball. The Marchesa had
asked that her dear little friend Ayala Dormer might be allowed to
come over to a little dance which her own girls were going to have.
Her own girls were so fond of Ayala! There would be no trouble.
There was a carriage which would be going somewhere else, and she
would be fetched and taken home. Ayala at once declared that she
intended to go, and her Aunt Emmeline did not refuse her sanction.
Augusta was shocked, declaring that the little dance was to be one of

the great balls of the season, and pronouncing the whole to be a falsehood ; but the affair was arranged before she could stop it.

But Mr. Traffick's affair in the matter came more within her range. "Septimus," she said, "I would rather you would not go to that woman's party." Septimus had been asked only on the day before the party,—as soon, indeed, as his arrival had become known to the Marchesa.

" Why, my own one ?"

" She has not treated mamma well,—nor yet me."

" Ayala is going." He had no right to call her Ayala. So Augusta thought.

" My cousin is behaving badly in the matter and mamma ought not to allow her to go. Who knows anything about the Marchesa Baldoni ?"

" Both he and she are of the very best families in Rome," said Mr. Traffick, who knew everything about it.

" At any rate they are behaving very badly to us, and I will take it as a favour that you do not go. Asking Ayala, and then asking you, as good as from the same house, is too marked. You ought not to go."

Perhaps Mr. Traffick had on some former occasion felt some little interference with his freedom of action. Perhaps he liked the acquaintance of the Marchesa. Perhaps he liked Ayala Dormer. Be that as it might he would not yield. " Dear Augusta, it is right that I should go there if it be only for half-an-hour." This he said in a tone of voice with which Augusta was already acquainted, which she did not love, and which, when she heard it, would make her think of her £120,000. When he had spoken he left her, and she began to think of her £120,000.

They both went, Ayala and Mr. Traffick,—and Mr. Traffick, instead of staying half-an-hour, brought Ayala back at three o'clock in the morning. Though Mr. Traffick was nearly as old as Uncle Tringle yet he could dance. Ayala had been astonished to find how well he could dance, and thought that she might please her cousin Augusta by praising the juvenility of her lover at luncheon the next day. She had not appeared at breakfast but had been full of the ball at lunch. " Oh, dear, yes, I dare say there were two hundred people there."

" That is what she calls a little dance," said Augusta, with scorn.

" I suppose that is the Italian way of talking about it," said Ayala.

" Italian way ! I hate Italian ways."

" Mr. Traffick liked it very much. I'm sure he'll tell you so. I had no idea he would care to dance."

Augusta only shook herself and turned up her nose. Lady Tringle thought it necessary to say something in defence of her daughter's

choice. "Why should not Mr. Traffick dance like any other gentleman?"

"Oh, I don't know. I thought that a man who makes so many
speeches in Parliament would think of something else. I was very
glad he did for he danced three times with me. He can waltz as
lightly as——." As though he were young she was going to say, but
then she stopped herself.

"He is the best dancer I ever danced with," said Augusta.

"But you almost never do dance," said Ayala.

"I suppose I may know about it as well as another," said Augusta,
angrily.

The next day was the last of Mr. Traffick's sojourn in Rome, and on
that day he and Augusta so quarrelled that, for a certain number of
hours, it was almost supposed in the family that the match would be
broken off. On the afternoon of the day after the dance Mr. Traffick
was walking with Ayala on the Pincian, while Augusta was absolutely
remaining behind with her mother. For a quarter-of-an-hour,—the
whole day, as it seemed to Augusta,—there was a full two hundred
yards between them. It was not that the engaged girl could not bear
the severance, but that she could not endure the attention paid to
Ayala. On the next morning "she had it out," as some people say,
with her lover. "If I am to be treated in this way you had better
tell me so at once," she said.

"I know no better way of treating you," said Mr. Traffick.

"Dancing with that chit all night, turning her head, and then
walking with her all the next day! I will not put up with such conduct."

Mr. Traffick valued £120,000 very highly, as do most men, and
would have done much to keep it; but he believed that the best way
of making sure of it would be by showing himself to be the master.
"My own one," he said, "you are really making an ass of yourself."

"Very well! Then I will write to papa, and let him know that it
must be all over."

For three hours there was terrible trouble in the apartments in the
Palazzo Ruperti, during which Mr. Traffick was enjoying himself by
walking up and down the Forum, and calculating how many Romans
could have congregated themselves in the space which is supposed to
have seen so much of the world's doings. During this time Augusta
was very frequently in hysterics; but, whether in hysterics or out of
them, she would not allow Ayala to come near her. She gave it to be
understood that Ayala had interfered fatally, foully, damnably, with
all her happiness. She demanded, from fit to fit, that telegrams
should be sent over to bring her father to Italy for her protection.

She would rave about Septimus, and then swear that, under no consideration whatever, would she ever see him again. At the end of three hours she was told that Septimus was in the drawing-room. Lady Tringle had sent half-a-dozen messengers after him, and at last he was found looking up at the Arch of Titus. "Bid him go," said Augusta. "I never want to behold him again." But within two minutes she was in his arms, and before dinner she was able to take a stroll with him on the Pincian.

He left, like a thriving lover, high in the good graces of his beloved; but the anger which had fallen on Ayala had not been removed. Then came a rumour that the Marchesa, who was half English, had called Ayala Cinderella, and the name had added fuel to the fire of Augusta's wrath. There was much said about it between Lady Tringle and her daughter, the aunt really feeling that more blame was being attributed to Ayala than she deserved. "Perhaps she gives herself airs," said Lady Tringle, "but really it is no more."

"She is a viper," said Augusta.

Gertrude rather took Ayala's part, telling her mother, in private, that the accusation about Mr. Traffick was absurd. "The truth is," said Gertrude, "that Ayala thinks herself very clever and very beautiful, and Augusta will not stand it." Gertrude acknowledged that Ayala was upsetting and ungrateful. Poor Lady Tringle, in her husband's absence, did not know what to do about her niece.

Altogether, they were uncomfortable after Mr. Traffick went and before Tom Tringle had come. On no consideration whatsoever would Augusta speak to her cousin. She declared that Ayala was a viper, and would give no other reason. In all such quarrelings the matter most distressing is that the evil cannot be hidden. Everybody at Rome who knew the Tringles, or who knew Ayala, was aware that Augusta Tringle would not speak to her cousin. When Ayala was asked she would shake her locks, and open her eyes, and declare that she knew nothing about it. In truth she knew very little about it. She remembered that passage-at-arms about the going upstairs at Glenbogie, but she could hardly understand that for so small an affront, and one so distant, Augusta would now refuse to speak to her. That Augusta had always been angry with her, and since Mr. Traffick's arrival more angry than ever, she had felt; but that Augusta was jealous in respect to her lover had never yet at all come home to Ayala. That she should have wanted to captivate Mr. Traffick,—she with her high ideas of some transcendental, more than human, hero!

But she had to put up with it, and to think of it. She had sense enough to know that she was no more than a stranger in her aunt's family, and that she must go if she made herself unpleasant to them.

She was aware that hitherto she had not succeeded with her residence among them. Perhaps she might have to go. Some things she would bear, and in them she would endeavour to amend her conduct. In other matters she would hold her own, and go, if necessary. Though her young imagination was still full of her unsubstantial hero,—though she still had her castles in the air altogether incapable of terrestrial foundation,—still there was a common sense about her which told her that she must give and take. She would endeavour to submit herself to her aunt. She would be kind,—as she had always been kind,—to Gertrude. She would in all matters obey her uncle. Her misfortune with the Newfoundland dog had almost dwindled out of her mind. To Augusta she could not submit herself. But then Augusta, as soon as the next session of Parliament should be over, would be married out of the way. And, on her own part, she did think that her aunt was inclined to take her part in the quarrel with Augusta.

Thus matters were going on in Rome when there came up another and a worse cause for trouble.

CHAPTER VII.

TOM TRINGLE IN EARNEST.

Tom Tringle, though he had first appeared to his cousin Ayala as a Newfoundland dog which might perhaps be pleasantly playful, and then, as the same dog, very unpleasant because dripping with muddy water, was nevertheless a young man with so much manly truth about him as to be very much in love. He did not look like it; but then perhaps the young men who do fall most absolutely into love do not look like it. To Ayala her cousin Tom was as unloveable as Mr. Septimus Traffick. She could like them both well enough while they would be kind to her. But as to regarding cousin Tom as a lover,—the idea was so preposterous to her that she could not imagine that anyone else should look upon it as real. But with Tom the idea had been real, and was, moreover, permanent. The black locks which would be shaken here and there, the bright glancing eyes which could be so joyous and could be so indignant, the colour of her face which had nothing in it of pink, which was brown rather, but over which the tell-tale blood would rush with a quickness which was marvellous to him, the lithe quick figure which had in it nothing of the weight of earth, the little foot which in itself was a perfect joy, the step with all the elasticity of a fawn,—these charms together had mastered him. Tom was not romantic or poetic, but the romance and poetry of Ayala had been divine to him. It is not always like to like in love. Titania loved the weaver Bottom with the ass's head. Bluebeard, though a bad husband, is supposed to have been fond of his last wife. The Beauty has always been beloved by the Beast. To Ayala the thing was monstrous ;—but it was natural. Tom Tringle was determined to have his way, and when he started for Rome was more intent upon his love-making than all the glories of the Capitol and the Vatican.

When he first made his appearance before Ayala's eyes he was bedecked in a manner that was awful to her. Down at Glenbogie he had affected a rough attire, as is the custom with young men of ample means when fishing, shooting, or the like, is supposed to be the employ-ment then in hand. The roughness had been a little overdone, but it had added nothing to his own uncouthness. In London he was apt to run a little towards ornamental gilding, but in London his tastes had been tempered by the ill-natured criticism of the world at large. He had hardly dared at Queen's Gate to wear his biggest pins ; but he had taken upon himself to think that at Rome an Englishman might expose himself with all his jewelry. "Oh, Tom, I never saw anything so stunning," his sister Gertrude said to him. He had simply frowned upon her, and had turned himself to Ayala, as though Ayala, being an artist, would be able to appreciate something beautiful in art. Ayala had looked at him and had marvelled, and had ventured to hope that, with his Glenbogie dress, his Glenbogie manners and Glenbogie propen-sities would be changed.

At this time the family at Rome was very uncomfortable. Augusta would not speak to her cousin, and had declared to her mother and sister her determination never to speak to Ayala again. For a time Aunt Emmeline had almost taken her niece's part, feeling that she might best bring things back to a condition of peace in this manner. Ayala, she had thought, might thus be decoyed into a state of submis-sion. Ayala, so instigated, had made her attempt. "What is the matter, Augusta," she had said, "that you are determined to quarrel with me ?" Then had followed a little offer that bygones should be bygones.

"I have quarrelled with you," said Augusta, "because you do not know how to behave yourself." Then Ayala had flashed forth, and the little attempt led to a worse condition than ever, and words were spoken which even Aunt Emmeline had felt to be irrevocable, irremedi-able.

"Only that you are going away I would not consent to live here," said Ayala. Then Aunt Emmeline had asked her where she would go to live should it please her to remove herself. Ayala had thought of this for a moment, and then had burst into tears. "

could not live I could die. Anything would be better than to be treated as she treats me." So the matters were when Tom came to Rome with all his jewelry.

Lady Tringle had already told herself that, in choosing Ayala, she had chosen wrong. Lucy, though not so attractive as Ayala, was pretty, quiet, and ladylike. So she thought now. And as to Ayala's attractions, they were not at all of a nature to be serviceable to such a family as hers. To have her own girls outshone, to be made to feel that the poor orphan was the one person most worthy of note among them, to be subjected to the caprices of a pretty, proud, ill-conditioned minx;—thus it was that Aunt Emmeline was taught to regard her own charity and good-nature towards her niece. There was, she said, no gratitude in Ayala. Had she said that there was no humility she would have been more nearly right. She was entitled, she thought, to expect both gratitude and humility, and she was sorry that she had opened the Paradise of her opulent home to one so little grateful and so little humble as Ayala. She saw now her want of judgment in that she had not taken Lucy.

Tom, who was not a fool, in spite of his trinkets, saw the state of the case, and took Ayala's part at once. "I think you are quite right," he said to her, on the first occasion on which he had contrived to find himself alone with her after his arrival.

"Right about what?"

"In not giving up to Augusta. She was always like that when she was a child, and now her head is turned about Traffick."

"I shouldn't grudge her her lover if she would only let me alone."

"I don't suppose she hurts you much?"

"She sets my aunt against me, and that makes me unhappy. Of course I am wretched."

"Oh, Ayala, don't be wretched."

"How is one to help it? I never said an ill-natured word to her, and now I am so lonely among them!" In saying this,—in seeking to get one word of sympathy from her cousin, she forgot for a moment his disagreeable pretensions. But, no sooner had she spoken of her loneliness, than she saw that ogle in his eye of which she had spoken with so much ludicrous awe in her letters from Glenbogie to her sister.

"I shall always take your part," said he.

"I don't want any taking of parts."

"But I shall. I am not going to see you put upon. You are more to me, Ayala, than any of them." Then he looked at her, whereupon she got up and ran away.

But she could not always run away, nor could she always refuse when he asked her to go with him about the show-places of the city. To avoid starting alone with him was within her power; but she found herself compelled to join herself to Gertrude and her brother in some of those little excursions which were taken for her benefit. At this time there had come to be a direct quarrel between Lady Tringle and the Marchesa, which, however, had arisen altogether on the part of Augusta. Augusta had forced her mother to declare that she was insulted, and then there was no more visiting between them. This had been sad enough for Ayala, who had struck up an intimacy with the Marchesa's daughters. But the Marchesa had explained to her that there was no help for it. " It won't do for you to separate yourself from your aunt," she had said. " Of course we shall be friends, and at some future time you shall come and see us." So there had been a division, and Ayala would have been quite alone had she declined the proffered companionship of Gertrude.

Within the walls and arches and upraised terraces of the Coliseum they were joined one day by young Hamel, the sculptor, who had not, as yet, gone back to London,—and had not, as yet, met Lucy in the gardens at Kensington; and with him there had been one Frank Houston, who had made acquaintance with Lady Tringle, and with the Tringles generally, since they had been at Rome. Frank Houston was a young man of family, with a taste for art, very good-looking, but not specially well off in regard to income. He had heard of the good fortune of Septimus Traffick in having prepared for himself a connection with so wealthy a family as the Tringles, and had thought it possible that a settlement in life might be comfortable for himself, What few soft words he had hitherto been able to say to Gertrude had been taken in good part, and when, therefore, they met among the walls of the Coliseum, she had naturally straggled away to see some special wonder which he had a special aptitude for showing. Hamel remained with Ayala and Tom, talking of the old days at the bijou, till he found himself obliged to leave them. Then Tom had his opportunity.

" Ayala," he said, " all this must be altered."

" What must be altered?"

" If you only knew, Ayala, how much you are to me."

" I wish you wouldn't, Tom. I don't want to be anything to anybody in particular."

" What I mean is, that I won't have them sit upon you. They treat you as—as,—well, as though you had only half a right to be one of them."

" No more I have. I have no right at all."

" But that's not the way I want it to be. If you were my wife——"

" Tom, pray don't."

" Why not ? I'm in earnest. Why ain't I to speak as I think ?
Oh, Ayala, if you knew how much I think of you."

" But you shouldn't. You haven't got a right."

" I have got a right."

" But I don't want it, Tom, and I won't have it." He had carried
her away now to the end of the terrace, or ruined tier of seats, on
which they were walking, and had got her so hemmed into a corner
that she could not get away from him. She was afraid of him, lest he
should put out his hand to take hold of her,—lest something even more
might be attempted. And yet his manner was manly and sincere, and
had it not been for his pins and his chains she could not but have
acknowledged his goodness to her, much as she might have disliked
his person. " I want to get out," she said. " I won't stay here any
more." Mr. Traffick, on the top of St. Peter's, had been a much
pleasanter companion.

" Don't you believe me when I tell you that I love you better than
anybody ?" pleaded Tom.

" No."

" Not believe me ? Oh, Ayala !"

" I don't want to believe anything. I want to get out. If you go
on, I'll tell my aunt."

Tell her aunt ! There was a want of personal consideration to himself in this way of receiving his addresses which almost angered him.
Tom Tringle was not in the least afraid of his mother,—was not even
afraid of his father as long as he was fairly regular at the office in
Lombard Street. He was quite determined to please himself in marriage, and was disposed to think that his father and mother would like
him to be settled. Money was no object. There was, to his thinking,
no good reason why he should not marry his cousin. For her the
match was so excellent that he hardly expected she would reject
him when she could be made to understand that he was really in
earnest. " You may tell all the world," he said proudly. " All I
want is that you should love me."

" But I don't. There are Gertrude and Mr. Houston, and I want
to go to them."

" Say one nice word to me, Ayala."

"I don't know how to say a nice word. Can't you be made to
understand that I don't like it ?"

" Ayala."

" Why don't you let me go away ?"

" Ayala,—give me—one—kiss." Then Ayala did go away, escaping
by some kid-like manœuvre among the ruins, and running quickly,
while he followed her, joined herself to the other pair of lovers, who

probably were less in want of her society than she of theirs. " Ayala, I am quite in earnest," said Tom, as they were walking home, " and I mean to go on with it."

Ayala thought that there was nothing for it but to tell her aunt. That there would be some absurdity in such a proceeding she did feel, —that she would be acting as though her cousin were a naughty boy who was merely teasing her. But she felt also the peculiar danger of her own position. Her aunt must be made to understand that she, Ayala, was innocent in the matter. It would be terrible to her to be suspected even for a moment of a desire to inveigle the heir. That Augusta would bring such an accusation against her she thought probable. Augusta had said as much even at Glenbogie. She must therefore be on the alert, and let it be understood at once that she was not leagued with her cousin Tom. There would be an absurdity;—but that would be better than suspicion.

She thought about it all that afternoon, and in the evening she came to a resolution. She would write a letter to her cousin and persuade him if possible to desist. If he should again annoy her after that she would appeal to her aunt. Then she wrote and sent her letter, which was as follows :

" DEAR TOM,

" You don't know how unhappy you made me at the Coliseum to-day. I don't think you ought to turn against me when you know what I have to bear. It is turning against me to talk as you did. Of course it means nothing ; but you shouldn't do it. It *never never* could mean anything. I hope you will be good-natured and kind to me, and then I shall be so much obliged to you. If you won't say anything more like that I will forget it altogether.

" Your affectionate cousin,

" AYALA."

The letter ought to have convinced him. Those two underscored nevers should have eradicated from his mind the feeling which had been previously produced by the assertion that he had " meant nothing." But he was so assured in his own meanings that he paid no attention whatever to the nevers. The letter was a delight to him because it gave him the opportunity of a rejoinder,—and he wrote his rejoinder on a scented sheet of note-paper and copied it twice ;—

" DEAREST AYALA,

" Why do you say that it means nothing ? It means everything. No man was ever more in earnest in speaking to a lady than I am with you. Why should I not be in earnest when I am so deeply in love! From the first moment in which I saw you down at Glenbogie I knew how it was going to be with me.

"As for my mother I don't think she would say a word. Why should she? But I am not the sort of man to be talked out of my intentions in such a matter as this. I have set my heart upon having you and nothing will ever turn me off.

"Dearest Ayala, let me have one look to say that you will love me, and I shall be the happiest man in England. I think you so beautiful! I do, indeed. The governor has always said that if I would settle down and marry there should be lots of money. What could I do better with it than make my darling look as grand as the best of them.

"Yours, always meaning it,
"Most affectionately,
"T. TRINGLE."

It almost touched her,—not in the way of love but of gratitude. He was still to her like Bottom with the ass's head, or the Newfoundland dog gambolling out of the water. There was the heavy face, and there were the big chains and the odious rings, and the great hands and the clumsy feet,—making together a creature whom it was impossible even to think of with love. She shuddered as she remembered the proposition which had been made to her in the Coliseum.

And now by writing to him she had brought down upon herself this absolute love-letter. She had thought that by appealing to him as "Dear Tom," and by signing herself his affectionate cousin, she might have prevailed. If he could only be made to understand that it could never mean nothing! But now, on the other hand, she had begun to understand that it did *mean* a great deal. He had sent to her a regular offer of marriage! The magnitude of the thing struck her at last. The heir of all the wealth of her mighty uncle wanted to make her his wife!

But it was to her exactly as though the heir had come to her wearing an ass's head on his shoulders. Love him! Marry him!—or even touch him? Oh, no. They might ill-use her; they might scold her; they might turn her out of the house; but no consideration would induce her to think of Tom Tringle as a lover.

And yet he was in earnest, and honest, and good. And some answer,—some further communication must be made to him. She did recognise some nobility in him, though personally he was so distasteful to her. Now his appeal to her had taken the guise of an absolute offer of marriage he was entitled to a discreet and civil answer. Romantic, dreamy, poetic, childish as she was, she knew as much as that. "Go away, Tom, you fool you," would no longer do for the occasion. As she thought of it all that night it was borne in upon her more strongly than ever that her only protection would be in telling her aunt, and in getting her aunt to make Tom understand that there must be no more of it. Early on the following morning she found herself in her aunt's bedroom.

CHAPTER VIII.

THE LOUT.

" Aunt Emmeline, I want you to read this letter." So it was that Ayala commenced the interview. At this moment Ayala was not on much better terms with her aunt than she was with her cousin Augusta. Ayala was a trouble to her,—Lady Tringle,—who was altogether perplexed with the feeling that she had burdened herself with an inmate in her house who was distasteful to her and of whom she could not rid herself. Ayala had turned out on her hands something altogether different from the girl she had intended to cherish and patronise. Ayala was independent ; superior rather than inferior to her own girls ; more thought of by others ; apparently without any touch of that subservience which should have been produced in her by her position. Ayala seemed to demand as much as though she were a daughter of the house, and at the same time to carry herself as though she were more gifted than the daughters of the house. She was less obedient even than a daughter. All this Aunt Emmeline could not endure with a placid bosom. She was herself kind of heart. She acknowledged her duty to her dead sister. She wished to protect and foster the orphan. She did not even yet wish to punish Ayala by utter desertion. She would protect her in opposition to Augusta's more declared malignity ; but she did wish to be rid of Ayala, if she only knew how.

She took her son's letter and read it, and as a matter of course misunderstood the position. At Glenbogie something had been whispered to her about Tom and Ayala, but she had not believed much in it. Ayala was a child, and Tom was to her not much more than a boy. But now here was a genuine love-letter,—a letter in which her son had made a distinct proposition to marry the orphan. She did not stop to consider why Ayala had brought the letter to her, but entertained at once an idea that the two young people were going to vex her very soul by a lamentable love affair. How imprudent she had been to let the two young people be together in Rome, seeing that the matter had been whispered to her at Glenbogie! "How long has this been going on?" she asked, severely.

"He used to tease me at Glenbogie, and now he is doing it again," said Ayala.

"There must certainly be put an end to it. You must go away."

Ayala knew at once that her aunt was angry with her, and was indignant at the injustice. "Of course there must be put an end to it, Aunt Emmeline. He has no right to annoy me when I tell him not."

"I suppose you have encouraged him."

This was too cruel to be borne! Encouraged him! Ayala's anger was caused not so much by a feeling that her aunt had misappreciated the cause of her coming as that it should have been thought possible that she should have "encouraged" such a lover. It was the outrage to her taste rather than to her conduct which afflicted her. "He is a lout," she said; "a stupid lout!" thus casting her scorn upon the mother as well as on the son, and, indeed, upon the whole family. "I have not encouraged him. It is untrue."

"Ayala, you are very impertinent."

"And you are very unjust. Because I want to put a stop to it I come to you, and you tell me that I encourage him. You are worse than Augusta."

This was too much for the good nature even of Aunt Emmeline. Whatever may have been the truth as to the love affair, however innocent Ayala may have been in that matter, or however guilty Tom, such words from a niece to her aunt,—from a dependent to her superior,—were unpardonable. The extreme youthfulness of the girl, a peculiar look of childhood which she still had with her, made the feeling so much the stronger. "You are worse than Augusta!"

And this was said to her who was specially conscious of her endeavours to mitigate Augusta's just anger. She bridled up, and tried to look big and knit her brows. At that moment she could not think what must be the end of it, but she felt that Ayala must be crushed. "How dare you speak to me like that, 'Miss,'" she said.

"So you are. It is very cruel. Tom will go on saying all this nonsense to me, and when I come to you you say I encourage him! I never encouraged him. I despise him too much. I did not think my own aunt could have told me that I encouraged any man. No, I didn't. You drive me to it, so that I have got to be impertinent."

"You had better go to your room," said the aunt. Then Ayala, lifting her head as high as she knew how, walked towards the door. "You had better leave that letter with me." Ayala considered the matter for a moment, and then handed the letter a second time to her aunt. It could be nothing to her who saw the letter. She did not want it. Having thus given it up she stalked off in silent disdain and went to her chamber.

Aunt Emmeline, when she was left alone, felt herself to be enveloped in a cloud of doubt. The desirableness of Tom as a husband first forced itself upon her attention, and the undesirableness of Ayala as a wife for Tom. She was perplexed at her own folly in not having seen that danger of this kind would arise when she first proposed to take Ayala into the house. Aunts and uncles do not like the marriage of cousins, and the parents of rich children do not, as a rule, approve of marriages with those which are poor. Although Ayala had been so violent, Lady Tringle could not rid herself of the idea that her darling boy was going to throw himself away. Then her cheeks became red with anger as she remembered that her Tom had been called a lout,— a stupid lout. There was an ingratitude in the use of such language which was not alleviated even by the remembrance that it tended against that matrimonial danger of which she was so much afraid. Ayala was behaving very badly. She ought not to have coaxed Tom to be her lover, and she certainly ought not to have called Tom a lout. And then Ayala had told her aunt that she was unjust and worse than Augusta! It was out of the question that such a state of things should be endured. Ayala must be made to go away.

Before the day was over Lady Tringle spoke to her son, and was astonished to find that the "lout" was quite in earnest,—so much in earnest that he declared his purpose of marrying his cousin in opposition to his father and mother, in opposition even to Ayala herself. He was so much in earnest that he would not be roused to wrath even when he was told that Ayala had called him a lout. And then grew upon the mother a feeling that the young man had never been so little loutish before. For there had been, even in her maternal bosom, a feeling that Tom was open to the criticism expressed on him. Tom had been a hobble-de-hoy, one of those overgrown lads who come late to their manhood, and who are regarded by young ladies as louts. Though he had spent his money only too freely when away, his sisters had sometimes said that he could not say "bo to a goose" at home. But now,—now Tom was quite an altered young man. When his own letter was shown to him he simply said that he meant to stick to it. When it was represented to him that his cousin would be quite an unfit wife for him he assured his mother that his own opinion on that matter was very different. When his father's anger was threatened he declared that his father would have no right to be angry with him if he married a lady. At the word "lout" he simply smiled. "She'll come to think different from that before she's done with me," he said.

with a smile. Even the mother could not but perceive that the young
man had been much improved by his love.

But what was she to do? Two or three days went on, during which
there was no reconciliation between her and Ayala. Between Augusta
and Ayala no word was spoken. Messages were taken to her by
Gertrude, the object of which was to induce her to ask her aunt's
pardon. But Ayala was of opinion that her aunt ought to ask her
pardon, and could not be beaten from it. " Why did she say that I
encouraged him?" she demanded indignantly of Gertrude. "I don't
think she did encourage him," said Gertrude to her mother. This
might possibly be true, but not the less had she misbehaved. And
though she might not yet have encouraged her lover it was only too
probable that she might do so when she found that her lover was quite
in earnest.

Lady Tringle was much harassed. And then there came an additional trouble. Gertrude informed her mother that she had engaged
herself to Mr. Francis Houston, and that Mr. Houston was going to
write to her father with the object of proposing himself as a son-in-law.
Mr. Houston came also to herself, and told her, in the most natural
tone in the world, that he intended to marry her daughter. She had
not known what to say. It was Sir Thomas who managed all matters
of money. She had an idea that Mr. Houston was very poor. But
then so also had been Mr. Traffick, who had been received into the
family with open arms. But then Mr. Traffick had a career, whereas
Mr. Houston was lamentably idle. She could only refer Mr. Houston
to Sir Thomas, and beg him not to come among them any more till
Sir Thomas had decided. Upon this Gertrude also got angry, and
shut herself up in her room. The apartments Ruperti were, therefore,
upon the whole, an uncomfortable home to them.

Letters upon letters were written to Sir Thomas, and letters upon
letters came. The first letter had been about Ayala. He had been
much more tender towards Ayala than her aunt had been. He talked of
calf-love, and said that Tom was a fool ; but he had not at once thought
it necessary to give imperative orders for Tom's return. As to Ayala's
impudence, he evidently regarded it as nothing. It was not till Aunt
Emmeline had spoken out in her third letter that he seemed to recognise the possibility of getting rid of Ayala altogether. And this he
did in answer to a suggestion which had been made to him. "If she
likes to change with her sister Lucy, and you like it, I shall not object,"
said Sir Thomas. Then there came an order to Tom that he should
return to Lombard Street at once ; but this order had been rendered
abortive by the sudden return of the whole family. Sir Thomas, in
his first letter as to Gertrude, had declared that the Houston marriage

would not do at all. Then, when he was told that Gertrude and Mr. Houston had certainly met each other more than once since an order had been given for their separation, he desired the whole family to come back at once to Merle Park.

The proposition as to Lucy had arisen in this wise. Tom being in the same house with Ayala, of course had her very much at advantage, and would carry on his suit in spite of any abuse which she might lavish upon him. It was quite in vain that she called him lout. "You'll think very different from that some of these days, Ayala," he said, more seriously.

"No I shan't; I shall think always the same."

"When you know how much I love you, you'll change."

"I don't want you to love me," she said; "and if you were anything that is good you wouldn't go on after I have told you so often. It is not manly of you. You have brought me to all manner of trouble. It is your fault, but they make me suffer."

After that Ayala again went to her aunt, and on this occasion the family misfortune was discussed in more seemly language. Ayala was still indignant, but she said nothing insolent. Aunt Emmeline was still averse to her niece, but she abstained from crimination. They knew each as enemies, but recognised the wisdom of keeping the peace. "As for that, Aunt Emmeline," Ayala said, "you may be quite sure that I shall never encourage him. I shall never like him well enough."

"Very well. Then we need say no more about that, my dear. Of course, it must be unpleasant to us all, being in the same house together."

"It is very unpleasant to me, when he will go on bothering me like that. It makes me wish that I were anywhere else."

Then Aunt Emmeline began to think about it very seriously. It was very unpleasant. Ayala had made herself disagreeable to all the ladies of the family, and only too agreeable to the young gentleman. Nor did the manifest favour of Sir Thomas do much towards raising Ayala in Lady Tringle's estimation. Sir Thomas had only laughed when Augusta had been requested to go upstairs for the scrap-book. Sir Thomas had been profuse with his presents even when Ayala had been most persistent in her misbehaviour. And then all that affair of the Marchesa, and even Mr. Traffick's infatuation! If Ayala wished that she were somewhere else would it not be well to indulge her wish? Aunt Emmeline certainly wished it. "If you think so, perhaps some arrangement can be made," said Aunt Emmeline very slowly.

"What arrangement?"

"You must not suppose that I wish to turn you out."

"But what arrangement?"

"You see, Ayala, that unfortunately we have not all of us hit it off nicely ; have we ?"

"Not at all, Aunt Emmeline. Augusta is always angry with me. And you,—you think that I have encouraged Tom."

"I am saying nothing about that, Ayala."

"But what arrangement is it, Aunt Emmeline ?" The matter was one of fearful import to Ayala. She was prudent enough to understand that well. The arrangement must be one by which she would be banished from all the wealth of the Tringles. Her coming among them had not been a success. She had already made them tired of her by her petulance and independence. Young as she was she could see that, and comprehend the material injury she had done herself by her folly. She had been very wrong in telling Augusta to go upstairs. She had been wrong in the triumph of her exclusive visits to the Marchesa. She had been wrong in walking away with Mr. Traffick on the Pincian. She could see that. She had not been wrong in regard to Tom,—except in calling him a lout ; but whether wrong or right she had been most unfortunate. But the thing had been done, and she must go.

At this moment the wealth of the Tringles seemed to be more to her than it had ever been before,—and her own poverty and destitution seemed to be more absolute. When the word "arrangement" was whispered to her there came upon her a clear idea of all that which she was to lose. She was to be banished from Merle Park, from Queen's Gate, and from Glenbogie. For her there were to be no more carriages, and horses, and pretty trinkets ;—none of that abandon of the luxury of money among which the Tringles lived. But she had done it for herself, and she would not say a word in opposition to the fate which was before her. "What arrangement, aunt ?" she said again, in a voice which was intended to welcome any arrangement that might be made.

Then her aunt spoke very softly. "Of course, dear Ayala, we do not wish to do less than we at first intended. But as you are not happy here——." Then she paused, almost ashamed of herself.

"I am not happy here," said Ayala, boldly.

"How would it be if you were to change—with Lucy ?"

The idea which had been present to Lady Tringle for some weeks past had never struck Ayala. The moment she heard it she felt that she was more than ever bound to assent. If the home from which she was to be banished was good, then would that good fall upon Lucy. Lucy would have the carriages and the horses and the trinkets,—Lucy, who certainly was not happy at Kingsbury Crescent. "I should be very glad, indeed," said Ayala.

Her voice was so brave and decided that, in itself, it gave fresh offence to her aunt. Was there to be no regret after so much generosity? But she misunderstood the girl altogether. As the words were coming from her lips,—"I should be very glad, indeed,"—Ayala's heart was sinking with tenderness as she remembered how much after all had been done for her. But as they wished her to go there should be not a word, not a sign of unwillingness on her part.

"Then perhaps it can be arranged," said Lady Tringle.

"I don't know what Uncle Dosett may say. Perhaps they are very fond of Lucy now."

"They wouldn't wish to stand in her way, I should think."

"At any rate, I won't. If you, and my uncles, and Aunt Margaret, will consent, I will go whenever you choose. Of course I must do just as I'm told."

Aunt Emmeline made a faint demur to this; but still the matter was held to be arranged. Letters were written to Sir Thomas, and letters came, and at last even Sir Thomas had assented. He suggested, in the first place, that all the facts which would follow the exchange should be explained to Ayala; but he was obliged after a while to acknowledge that this would be inexpedient. The girl was willing; and knew no doubt that she was to give up the great wealth of her present home. But she had proved herself to be an unfit participator, and it was better that she should go.

Then the departure of them all from Rome was hurried on by the indiscretion of Gertrude. Gertrude declared that she had a right to her lover. As to his having no income, what matter for that. Everyone knew that Septimus Traffick had no income. Papa had income enough for them all. Mr. Houston was a gentleman. Till this moment no one had known of how strong a will of her own Gertrude was possessed. When Gertrude declared that she would not consent to be separated from Mr. Houston then they were all hurried home.

CHAPTER IX.

THE EXCHANGE.

Such was the state of things when Mr. Dosett brought the three letters home with him to Kingsbury Crescent, having been so much disturbed by the contents of the two which were addressed to himself as to have found himself compelled to leave his office two hours before the proper time. The three letters were handed together by her uncle to Lucy, and she, seeing the importance of the occasion, read the two

open ones before she broke the envelope of her own. That from Sir
Thomas came first, and was as follows ;—

"Lombard Street, January, 187—.
"MY DEAR DOSETT,

"I have had a correspondence with the ladies at Rome which has been
painful in its nature, but which I had better perhaps communicate to
you at once. Ayala has not got on as well with Lady Tringle and
the girls as might have been wished, and they all think it will be
better that she and Lucy should change places. I chiefly write to give
my assent. Your sister will no doubt write to you. I may as well
mention to you, should you consent to take charge of Ayala, that I
have made some provision for her in my will, and that I shall not
change it. I have to add on my own account that I have no complaint
of my own to make against Ayala.

"Yours sincerely,
"T. TRINGLE."

Lucy, when she had read this, proceeded at once to the letter from
her aunt. The matter to her was one of terrible importance, but the
importance was quite as great to Ayala. She had been allowed to go
up alone into her own room. The letters were of such a nature that
she could hardly have read them calmly in the presence of her Aunt
Dosett. It was thus that her Aunt Emmeline had written ;—

"Palazzo Ruperti, Rome, Thursday.
"MY DEAR REGINALD,

"I am sure you will be sorry to hear that we are in great trouble
here. This has become so bad that we are obliged to apply to you to
help us. Now you must understand that I do not mean to say a word
against dear Ayala ;—only she does not suit. It will occur sometimes
that people who are most attached to each other do not suit. So it
has been with dear Ayala. She is not happy with us. She has not
perhaps accommodated herself to her cousins quite as carefully as she
might have done. She is fully as sensible of this as I am, and is,
herself, persuaded that there had better be a change.

"Now, my dear Reginald, I am quite aware that when poor Egbert
died it was I who chose Ayala, and that you took Lucy partly in compliance with my wishes. Now I write to suggest that there should be a
change. I am sure you will give me credit for a desire to do the best
I can for both the poor dear girls. I did think that this might be best
done by letting Ayala come to us. I now think that Lucy would do
better with her cousins, and that Ayala would be more attractive
without the young people around her

"When I see you I will tell you everything. There has been no great fault. She has spoken a word or two to me which had been better unsaid, but I am well convinced that it has come from hot temper and not from a bad heart. Perhaps I had better tell you the truth. Tom has admired her. She has behaved very well; but she could not bear to be spoken to, and so there have been unpleasantnesses. And the girls certainly have not got on well together. Sir Thomas quite agrees with me that if you will consent there had better be a change.

"I will not write to dear Lucy herself because you and Margaret can explain it all so much better,—if you will consent to our plan. Ayala also will write to her sister. But pray tell her from me that I will love her very dearly if she will come to me. And indeed I have loved Ayala almost as though she were my own, only we have not been quite able to hit it off together.

"Of course neither has Sir Thomas or have I any idea of escaping from a responsibility. I should be quite unhappy if I did not have one of poor dear Egbert's girls with me. Only I do think that Lucy would be the best for us; and Ayala thinks so too. I should be quite unhappy if I were doing this in opposition to Ayala.

"We shall be in England almost as soon as this letter, and I should be so glad if this could be decided at once. If a thing like this is to be done it is so much better for all parties that it should be done quickly. Pray give my best love to Margaret, and tell her that Ayala shall bring everything with her that she wants.

"Your most affectionate sister,

"EMMELINE TRINGLE."

The letter, though it was much longer than her uncle's, going into details, such as that of Tom's unfortunate passion for his cousin, had less effect upon Lucy, as it did not speak with so much authority as that from Sir Thomas. What Sir Thomas said would surely be done; whereas Aunt Emmeline was only a woman, and her letter, unsupported, might not have carried conviction. But, if Sir Thomas wished it, surely it must be done. Then, at last, came Ayala's letter;—

"Rome, Thursday.

"DEAREST, DEAREST LUCY,

"Oh, I have such things to write to you! Aunt Emmeline has told it all to Uncle Reginald. You are to come and be the princess, and I am to go and be the milkmaid at home. I am quite content that it should be so because I know that it will be the best. You ought to be a princess and I ought to be a milkmaid.

"It has been coming almost ever since the first day that I came among them,—since I told Augusta to go upstairs for the scrap-book. I felt from the very moment in which the words were uttered that I had gone and done for myself. But I am not a bit sorry, as you will come in my place. Augusta will very soon be gone now, and Aunt Emmeline is not bad at all if you will only not contradict her. I always contradicted her, and I know that I have been a fool. But I am not a bit sorry as you are to come instead of me.

"But it is not only about Augusta and Aunt Emmeline. There has been that oaf Tom. Poor Tom! I do believe that he is the most good-natured fellow alive. And if he had not so many chains I should not dislike him so very much. But he will go on saying horrible things to me. And then he wrote me a letter! Oh dear! I took the letter to Aunt Emmeline, and that made the quarrel. She said that I had—encouraged him! Oh, Lucy, if you will think of that! I was so angry that I said ever so much to her,—till she sent me out of the room. She had no business to say that I encouraged him. It was shameful! But she has never forgiven me, because I scolded her. So they have decided among them that I am to be sent away, and that you are to come in my place.

"My own darling Lucy, it will be ever so much better. I know that you are not happy in Kingsbury Crescent, and that I shall bear it very much better. I can sit still and mend sheets." Poor Ayala, how little she knew herself! "And you will make a beautiful grand lady, quiescent and dignified as a grand lady ought to be. At any rate it would be impossible that I should remain here. Tom is bad enough, but to be told that I encourage him is more than I can bear.

"I shall see you very soon, but I cannot help writing and telling it to you all. Give my love to Aunt Dosett. If she will consent to receive me I will endeavour to be good to her. In the meantime, good-bye.

Your most affectionate sister,

"AYALA."

When Lucy had completed the reading of the letters she sat for a considerable time wrapped in thought. There was, in truth, very much that required thinking. It was proposed that the whole tenour of her life should be changed, and changed in a direction which would certainly suit her taste. She had acknowledged to herself that she had hated the comparative poverty of her Uncle Dosett's life, hating herself in that she was compelled to make such acknowledgment. But there had been more than the poverty which had been distasteful to her,—a something which she had been able to tell herself that she might be justified in hating without shame. There had been to her an absence of intellectual charm in the habits and manners of Kingsbury Crescent which she had regarded as unfortunate and depressing. There had been no thought of art delights. No one read poetry. No one heard music. No one looked at pictures. A sheet to be darned was the one thing of greatest importance. The due development of a leg of mutton, the stretching of a pound of butter, the best way of repressing the washerwoman's bills,—these had been the matters of interest. And they had not been made the less irritating to her by her aunt's extreme goodness in the matter. The leg of mutton was to be developed in the absence of her uncle,—if possible without his knowledge. He was to have his run of clean linen. Lucy did not grudge him anything, but was sickened by that partnership in economy which was established between her and her aunt. Undoubtedly from time to time she had thought of the luxuries which had been thrown in Ayala's way. There had been a regret,—not that Ayala should have them but that she should have missed them. Money she declared that she despised ;—but the easy luxury of the bijou was sweet to her memory.

Now it was suggested to her suddenly that she was to exchange the poverty for the luxury, and to return to a mode of life in which her mind might be devoted to things of beauty. The very scenery of Glenbogie,—what a charm it would have for her ! Judging from her uncle's manner, as well as she could during that moment in which he handed to her the letter, she imagined that he intended to make no great objection. Her aunt disliked her. She was sure that her aunt disliked her in spite of the partnership. Only that there was one other view of the case—how happy might the transfer be. Her uncle was always gentle to her, but there could hardly as yet have grown up any strong affection for her. To him she was grateful, but she could not tell herself that to part from him would be a pang. There was, however, another view of the case.

Ayala ! How would it be with Ayala ? Would Ayala like the partnership and the economies ? Would Ayala be cheerful as she sat opposite to her aunt for four hours at a time ? Ayala had said that she could sit still and mend sheets, but was it not manifest enough that Ayala knew nothing of the life of which she was speaking. And would she, Lucy, be able to enjoy the glories of Glenbogie while she thought that Ayala was eating out her heart in the sad companionship of Kingsbury Crescent ? For above an hour she sat and thought ; but of one aspect which the affair bore she did not think. She did not reflect that she and Ayala were in the hands of Fate, and that they must both do as their elders should require of them.

At last there came a knock at the door and her aunt entered. She would sooner that it should have been her uncle ; but there was no choice but that the matter should be now discussed with the woman whom she did not love,—this matter that was so dreadful to herself in all its bearings, and so dreadful to one for whom she would willingly sacrifice herself if it were possible ! She did not know what she could say to create sympathy with Aunt Dosett. "Lucy," said Aunt Dosett, "this is a very serious proposal."

"Very serious," said Lucy, sternly.

"I have not read the letters, but your uncle has told me about it." Then Lucy handed her the two letters, keeping that from Ayala to herself, and she sat perfectly still while her aunt read them both slowly. "Your Aunt Emmeline is certainly in earnest," said Mrs. Dosett.

"Aunt Emmeline is very good-natured, and perhaps she will change her mind if we tell her that we wish it."

"But Sir Thomas has agreed to it."

"I am sure my uncle will give way if Aunt Emmeline will ask him. He says he has no complaint to make against Ayala. I think it is Augusta, and Augusta will be married and will go away very soon."

Then there came a change, a visible change, over the countenance of Aunt Dosett, and a softening of the voice,—so that she looked and spoke as Lucy had not seen or heard her before. There are people apparently so hard, so ungenial, so unsympathetic, that they who only half know them expect no trait of tenderness, think that features so little alluring cannot be compatible with softness. Lucy had acknowledged her Aunt Dosett to be good, but believed her to be incapable of being touched. But a word or two had now conquered her. The girl did not want to leave her,—did not seize the first opportunity of running from her poverty to the splendour of the Tringles ! "But, Lucy," she said, and came and placed herself nearer to Lucy on the bed.

"Ayala——," said Lucy, sobbing.

"I will be kind to her,—perhaps kinder than I have been to you.'

"You have been kind, and I have been ungrateful. I know it. But I will do better now, Aunt Dosett. I will stay, if you will have me."

"They are rich and powerful, and you will have to do as they direct."

"No ! Who are they that I should be made to come and go at their bidding ? They cannot make me leave you."

"But they can rid themselves of Ayala. You see what your uncle says about money for Ayala."

"I hate money."

"Money is a thing which none of us can afford to hate. Do you think it will not be much to your Uncle Reginald to know that you are both provided for ? Already he is wretched because there will be nothing to come to you. If you go to your Aunt Emmeline, Sir Thomas will do for you as he has done for Ayala. Dear Lucy, it is not that I want to send you away." Then for the first time Lucy put her arm round her aunt's neck. "But it had better be as is proposed, if your aunt still wishes it, when she comes home. I and your Uncle Reginald would not do right were we to allow you to throw away the prospects that are offered you. It is natural that Lady Tringle should be anxious about her son."

"She need not, in the least," said Lucy, indignantly.

"But you see what they say."

"It is his fault, not hers. Why should she be punished?"

"Because he is Fortune's favourite, and she is not. It is no good kicking against the pricks, my dear. He is his father's son and heir, and everything must give way to him."

"But Ayala does not want him. Ayala despises him. It is too hard that she is to lose everything because a young man like that will go on making himself disagreeable. They have no right to do it after having accustomed Ayala to such a home. Don't you feel that, Aunt Dosett?"

"I do feel it."

"However it might have been arranged at first, it ought to remain now. Even though Ayala and I are only girls, we ought not to be changed about as though we were horses. If she had done anything wrong,—but Uncle Tom says that she has done nothing wrong."

"I suppose she has spoken to her aunt disrespectfully."

"Because her aunt told her that she had encouraged this man. What would you have a girl say when she is falsely accused like that? Would you say it to me merely because some horrid man would come and speak to me?" Then there came a slight pang of conscience as she remembered Isadore Hamel in Kensington Gardens. If the men were not thought to be horrid, then perhaps the speaking might be a sin worthy of most severe accusation.

There was nothing more said about it that night, nor till the following afternoon, when Mr. Dosett returned home at the usual hour from his office. Then Lucy was closeted with him for a quarter-of-an-hour in the drawing-room. He had been into the City and seen Sir Thomas. Sir Thomas had been of opinion that it would be much better that Lady Tringle's wishes should be obeyed. It was quite true that he himself had no complaint to make against Ayala, but he did think that Ayala had been pert; and, though it might be quite true that Ayala had not encouraged Tom, there was no knowing what might grow out of such a propensity on Tom's part. And then it could not be pleasant to Lady Tringle or to himself that their son should be banished out of their house. When something was hinted as to the injustice of this, Sir Thomas endeavoured to put all that right by declaring that, if Lady Tringle's wishes could be attended to in this matter, provision would be made for the two girls. He certainly would not strike Ayala's name out of his will, and as certainly would not take Lucy under his wing as his own child without making some provision for her. Looking at the matter in this light he did not think that Mr. Dosett would be justified in robbing Lucy of the advantages which were offered to her. With this view Mr. Dosett found himself compelled to agree, and with these arguments he declared to Lucy that it was her duty to submit herself to the proposed exchange.

Early in February all the Tringle family were in Queen's Gate, and Lucy on her first visit to the house found that everyone, including Ayala, looked upon the thing as settled. Ayala, who under these circumstances was living on affectionate terms with all the Tringles, except Tom, was quite radiant. " I suppose I had better go to-morrow, aunt?" she said, as though it were a matter of most trivial consequence.

" In a day or two, Ayala, it will be better."

" It shall be Monday, then. You must come over here in a cab, Lucy."

" The carriage shall be sent, my dear."

" But then it must go back with me, Aunt Emmeline."

" It shall, my dear."

" And the horses must be put up, because Lucy and I must change all our things in the drawers." Lucy at the time was sitting in the drawing-room, and Augusta, with most affectionate confidence, was singing to her all the praises of Mr. Traffick. In this way it was settled that the change, so greatly affecting the fortunes of our two sisters, was arranged.

CHAPTER X.

AYALA AND HER AUNT MARGARET.

TILL the last moment for going Ayala seemed to be childish, triumphant, and indifferent. But, till that last moment, she was never alone with Lucy. It was the presence of her aunt and cousins which sustained her in her hardihood. Tom was never there,—or so rarely as not to affect her greatly. In London he had his own lodgings, and was not encouraged to appear frequently till Ayala should have gone. But Aunt Emmeline and Gertrude were perseveringly gracious, and even Augusta had somewhat relaxed from her wrath. With them Ayala was always good-humoured, but always brave. She affected to rejoice at the change which was to be made. She spoke of Lucy's coming and of her own going as an unmixed blessing. This she did so effectually as to make Aunt Emmeline declare to Sir Thomas, with tears in her eyes, that the girl was heartless. But when, at the moment of parting, the two girls were together, then Ayala broke down.

They were in the room, together, which one had occupied and the other was to occupy, and their boxes were still upon the floor. Though less than six months had passed since Ayala had come among the rich things and Lucy had been among the poor, Ayala's belongings had become much more important than her sister's. Though the Tringles had been unpleasant they had been generous. Lucy was sitting upon the bed, while Ayala was now moving about the room restlessly, now clinging to her sister, and now sobbing almost in despair. "Of course I know," she said. "What is the use of telling stories about it any longer?"

"It is not too late yet, Ayala. If we both go to Uncle Tom he will let us change it."

"Why should it be changed? If I could change it by lifting up my little finger I could not do it. Why should it not be you as well as me? They have tried me, and,—as Aunt Emmeline says,—I have not suited."

"Aunt Dosett is not ill-natured, my darling."

"No, I dare say not. It is I that am bad. It is bad to like pretty things and money, and to hate poor things. Or, rather, I do not believe it is bad at all, because it is so natural. I believe it is all a lie as to its being wicked to love riches. I love them, whether it is wicked or not."

"Oh, Ayala!"

"Do not you? Don't let us be hypocritical, Lucy, now at the last moment. Did you like the way in which they lived in Kingsbury Crescent?"

Lucy paused before she answered. "I like it better than I did," she said. "At any rate, I would willingly go back to Kingsbury Crescent."

"Yes,—for my sake."

"Indeed I would, my pet."

"And for your sake I would rather die than stay. But what is the good of talking about it, Lucy. You and I have no voice in it, though it is all about ourselves. As you say, we are like two tame birds, who have to be moved from one cage into another just as the owner pleases. We belong either to Uncle Tom or Uncle Dosett, just as they like to settle it. Oh, Lucy, I do so wish that I were dead."

"Ayala, that is wicked."

" How can I help it, if I am wicked ? What am I to do when I get
there ? What am I to say to them ? How am I to live ? Lucy, we
shall never see each other."

" I will come across to you, constantly."

" I meant to do so, but I didn't. They are two worlds, miles
asunder. Lucy, will they let Isadore Hamel come here ?" Lucy
blushed and hesitated. " I am sure he will come."

Lucy remembered that she had given her friend her address at
Queen's Gate, and felt that she would seem to have done it as though
she had known that she was about to be transferred to the other
uncle's house. " It will make no difference if he does," she said.

" Oh, I have such a dream,—such a castle-in-the-air ! If I could
think it might ever be so, then I should not want to die."

" What do you dream ?" But Lucy, though she asked the question,
knew the dream.

" If you had a little house of your own, oh, ever so tiny ; and if you
and he—— ?"

" There is no he."

" There might be. And if you and he would let me have any
corner for myself, then I should be happy. Then I would not want
to die. You would, wouldn't you ?"

" How can I talk about it, Ayala. There isn't such a thing. But
yet,—but yet ;—oh, Ayala, do you not know that to have you with me
would be better than anything ?"

" No ;—not better than anything ;—second best. He would be
best. I do so hope that he may be ' he.' Come in." There was a
knock at the door, and Aunt Emmeline, herself, entered the room.

" Now, my dears, the horses are standing there, and the men are
coming up for the luggage. Ayala, I hope we shall see you very often.
And remember that, as regards anything that is unpleasant, bygones
shall be bygones." Then there was a crowd of farewell kisses, and in a
few minutes Ayala was alone in the carriage on her road up to Kingsbury Crescent.

The thing had been done so quickly that hitherto there had hardly
been time for tears. To Ayala herself the most remarkable matter in
the whole affair had been Tom's persistence. He had, at last, been
allowed to bring them home from Rome, there having been no other
gentleman whose services were available for the occasion. He had
been watched on the journey very closely, and had had no slant in his
favour, as the young lady to whom he was devoted was quite as
anxious to keep out of his way as had been the others of the party to
separate them. But he had made occasion, more than once, sufficient
to express his intention. " I don't mean to give you up, you know,"

he had said to her. " When I say a thing I mean it. I am not going to be put off by my mother. And as for the governor he would not say a word against it if he thought we were both in earnest."

"But I ain't in earnest," said Ayala ; " or rather, I am very much in earnest."

"So am I. That's all I've got to say just at present." From this there grew up within her mind a certain respect for the "lout," which, however, made him more disagreeable to her than he might have been had he been less persistent.

It was late in the afternoon, not much before dinner, when Ayala reached the house in Kingsbury Crescent. Hitherto she had known almost nothing of her Aunt Dosett, and had never been intimate even with her uncle. They, of course, had heard much of her, and had been led to suppose that she was much less tractable than the simple Lucy. This feeling had been so strong that Mr. Dosett himself would hardly have been led to sanction the change had it not been for that promise from Sir Thomas that he would not withdraw the provision he had made for Ayala, and would do as much for Lucy if Lucy should become an inmate of his family. Mrs. Dosett had certainly been glad to welcome any change, when a change was proposed to her. There had grown up something of affection at the last moment, but up to that time she had certainly disliked her niece. Lucy had appeared to her to be at first idle and then sullen. The girl had seemed to affect a higher nature than her own, and had been wilfully indifferent to the little things which had given to her life whatever interest it possessed. Lucy's silence had been a reproach to her, though she herself had been able to do so little to abolish the silence. Perhaps Ayala might be better.

But they were both afraid of Ayala,—as they had not been afraid of Lucy before her arrival. They made more of preparation for her in their own minds, and, as to their own conduct, Mr. Dosett was there himself to receive her, and was conscious in doing so that there had been something of failure in their intercourse with Lucy. Lucy had been allowed to come in without preparation, with an expectation that she would fall easily into her place, and there had been failure. There had been no regular consultation as to this new coming, but both Mr. and Mrs. Dosett were conscious of an intended effort.

Lady Tringle and Mr. Dosett had always been Aunt Emmeline and Uncle Reginald, by reason of the nearness of their relationship. Circumstances of closer intercourse had caused Sir Thomas to be Uncle Tom. But Mrs. Dosett had never become more than Aunt Dosett to either of the girls. This in itself had been matter almost of soreness to her, and she had intended to ask Lucy to adopt the more endearing

form of her Christian name; but there had been so little endearment
between them that the moment for doing so had never come. She was
thinking of all this up in her own room, preparatory to the reception
of this other girl, while Mr. Dosett was bidding her welcome to Kings·
bury Crescent in the drawing-room below.

Ayala had been dissolved in tears during the drive round by Kensington to Bayswater, and was hardly able to repress her sobs as she
entered the house. "My dear," said the uncle, "we will do all that
we can to make you happy here."

"I am sure you will; but—but—it is so sad coming away from
Lucy."

"Lucy I am sure will be happy with her cousins." If Lucy's happiness were made to depend on her cousins, thought Ayala, it would not
be well assured. "And my sister Emmeline is always good-natured."

"Aunt Emmeline is very good, only——"

"Only what?"

"I don't know. But it is such a sudden change, Uncle Reginald."

"Yes, it is a very great change, my dear. They are very rich and
we are poor enough. I should hardly have consented to this, for your
sake, but that there are reasons which will make it better for you
both."

"As to that," said Ayala, stoutly, "I had to come away. I didn't
suit."

"You shall suit us, my dear."

"I hope so. I will try. I know more now than I did then. I
thought I was to be Augusta's equal."

"We shall all be equal here."

"People ought to be equal, I think,—except old people and young
people. I will do whatever you and my aunt tell me. There are no
young people here, so there won't be any trouble of that kind."

"There will be no other young person, certainly. You shall go upstairs now and see your aunt."

Then there was the interview upstairs, which consisted chiefly in
promises and kisses, and Ayala was left alone to unpack her boxes and
prepare for dinner. Before she began her operations she sat still for a
few moments, and with an effort collected her energies and made her
resolution. She had said to Lucy in her passion that she would that
she were dead. That that should have been wicked was not matter of
much concern to her. But she acknowledged to herself that it had been
weak and foolish. There was her life before her, and she would still
endeavour to be happy though there had been so much to distress her.
She had flung away wealth. She was determined to fling it away still
when it should present itself to her in the shape of her cousin Tom.

But she had her dreams,—her day-dreams,—those castles in the air which it had been the delight of her life to construct, and in the building of which her hours had never run heavy with her. Isadore Hamel would, of course, come again, and would, of course, marry Lucy, and then there would be a home for her after her own heart. With Isadore as her brother, and her own own Lucy close to her, she would not feel the want of riches and of luxury. If there were only some intellectual charm in her life, some touch of art, some devotion to things beautiful, then she could do without gold and silver and costly raiment. Of course, Isadore would come ; and then—then—in the far distance, something else would come, something of which in her castle-building she had not yet developed the form, of which she did not yet know the bearing, or the manner of its beauty, or the music of its voice ; but as to which she was very sure that its form would be beautiful and its voice full of music. It can hardly be said that this something was the centre of her dreams or the foundation of her castles. It was the extreme point of perfection at which she would arrive at last, when her thoughts had become sublimated by the intensity of her thinking. It was the tower of the castle from which she could look down upon the inferior world below,—the last point of the dream in arranging which she would all but escape from earth to heaven,—when in the moment of her escape the cruel waking back into the world would come upon her. But this she knew,—that this something, whatever might be its form or whatever its voice, would be exactly the opposite of Tom Tringle.

She had fallen away from her resolution to her dreams for a time, when suddenly she jumped up and began her work with immense energy. Open went one box after another, and in five minutes the room was strewed with her possessions. The modest set of drawers which was to supply all her wants was filled with immediate haste. Things were deposited in whatever nooks might be found, and every corner was utilized. Her character for tidiness had never stood high. At the bijou Lucy, or her mother, or the favourite maid, had always been at hand to make good her deficiencies with a reproach which had never gone beyond a smile or a kiss. At Glenbogie and even on the journey there had been attendant lady's maids. But here she was all alone.

Everything was still in confusion when she was called to dinner. As she went down she recalled to herself her second resolution. She would be good ;—whereby she intimated to herself that she would endeavour to do what might be pleasing to her Aunt Dosett. She had little doubt as to her uncle. But she was aware that there had been differences between her aunt and Lucy. If Lucy had found it difficult to be good how great would be the struggle required from her !

She sat herself down at table a little nearer to her aunt than her uncle, because it was specially her aunt whom she wished to win, and after a few minutes she put out her little soft hand and touched that of Mrs. Dosset. "My dear," said that lady, "I hope you will be happy."

"I am determined to be happy," said Ayala, "if you will let me love you."

Mrs. Dosett was not beautiful, nor was she romantic. In appearance she was the very reverse of Ayala. The cares of the world, the looking after shillings and their results, had given her that look of common-place insignificance which is so frequent and so unattractive among middle-aged women upon whom the world leans heavily. But there was a tender corner in her heart, which was still green, and from which a little rill of sweet water could be made to flow when it was touched aright. On this occasion a tear came to her eye as she pressed her niece's hand; but she said nothing. She was sure, however, that she would love Ayala much better than she had been able to love Lucy.

"What would you like me to do?" asked Ayala, when her aunt accompanied her that night to her bed-room.

"To do, my dear? What do you generally do?"

"Nothing. I read a little and draw a little, but I do nothing useful. I mean it to be different now."

"You shall do as you please, Ayala."

"Oh, but I mean it. And you must tell me. Of course things have to be different."

"We are not rich like your uncle and aunt Tringle."

"Perhaps it is better not to be rich, so that one may have something to do. But I want you to tell me, as though you really cared for me."

"I will care for you," said Aunt Dosett sobbing.

"Then first begin by telling me what to do. I will try and do it. Of course I have thought about it, coming away from all manner of rich things ; and I have determined that it shall not make me unhappy. I will rise above it. I will begin to-morrow and do anything if you will tell me." Then Aunt Dosett took her in her arms and kissed her, and declared that on the morrow they would begin their work together in perfect confidence and love with each other.

"I think she will do better than Lucy," said Mrs. Dosett to her husband that night.

"Lucy was a dear girl too," said Uncle Reginald.

"Oh, yes—quite so. I don't mean to say a word against Lucy ;

but I think that I can do better with Ayala. She will be more diligent." Uncle Reginald said nothing to this, but he could not but think that of the two Lucy would be the one most likely to devote herself to hard work.

On the next morning Ayala went out with her aunt on the round to the shopkeepers, and listened with profound attention to the domestic instructions which were given to her on the occasion. When she came home she knew much of which she had known nothing before. What was the price of mutton, and how much mutton she was expected as one of the family to eat per week; what were the necessities of the house in bread and butter, how far a pint of milk might be stretched, —with a proper understanding that her Uncle Reginald as head of the family was to be subjected to no limits. And before their return from that walk,—on the first morning of Ayala's sojourn,—Ayala had undertaken always to call Mrs. Dosett Aunt Margaret for the future.

CHAPTER XI.

TOM TRINGLE COMES TO THE CRESCENT.

DURING the next three months, up to the end of the winter and through the early spring, things went on without any change either in Queen's Gate or Kingsbury Crescent. The sisters saw each other occasionally, but not as frequently as either of them had intended. Lucy was not encouraged in the use of cabs, nor was the carriage lent to her often for the purpose of going to the Crescent. The reader may remember that she had been in the habit of walking alone in Kensington Gardens, and a walk across Kensington Gardens would carry her the greater part of the distance to Kingsbury Crescent. But Lucy, in her new circumstances, was not advised,—perhaps, I may say, was not allowed,—to walk alone. Lady Tringle, being a lady of rank and wealth, was afraid, or pretended to be afraid, of the lions. Poor Ayala was really afraid of the lions. Thus it came to pass that the intercourse was not frequent. In her daily life Lucy was quiet and obedient. She did not run counter to Augusta, whose approaching nuptials gave her that predominance in the house which is always accorded to young ladies in her recognised position. Gertrude was at this time a subject of trouble at Queen's Gate. Sir Thomas had not been got to approve of Mr. Frank Houston, and Gertrude had positively refused to give him up. Sir Thomas was, indeed, considerably troubled by his children. There had been a period of disagreeable obstinacy even with Augusta before Mr. Traffick had been taken to the bosom of the family. Now Gertrude had her own ideas, and so also had Tom. Tom had become quite a trouble. Sir Thomas and Lady Tringle, together, had determined that Tom must be weaned; by which they meant that he must be cured of his love. But Tom had altogether refused to be weaned. Mr. Dosett had been requested to deny him admittance to the house in Kingsbury Crescent, and as this request had been fully endorsed by Ayala herself orders had been given to the effect to the parlour-maid. Tom had called more than once, and had been unable to obtain access to his beloved. But yet he resolutely refused to be weaned. He told his father to his face that he intended to marry Ayala, and abused his mother roundly when she attempted to interfere. The whole family was astounded by his perseverance, so that there had already sprung up an idea in the minds of some among the Tringles that he would be successful at last. Augusta was very firm, declaring that Ayala was a viper. But Sir Thomas, himself, began to inquire, within his own bosom, whether Tom should not be allowed to settle down in the manner desired by himself. In no consultation held at Queen's Gate on the subject was there the slightest expression of an opinion that Tom might be denied the opportunity of settling down as he wished through any unwillingness on the part of Ayala.

When things were in this position, Tom sought an interview one morning with his father in Lombard Street. They rarely saw each other at the office, each having his own peculiar branch of business. Sir Thomas manipulated his millions in a little back room of his own, while Tom, dealing probably with limited thousands, made himself useful in an outer room. They never went to, or left, the office together, but Sir Thomas always took care to know that his son was or was not on the premises. "I want to say a word or two, Sir, about—about the little affair of mine," said Tom.

"What affair?" said Sir Thomas, looking up from his millions.

"I think I should like to—marry."

"The best thing you can do, my boy; only it depends upon whom the young lady may be."

"My mind is made up about that, Sir; I mean to marry my cousin. I don't see why a young man isn't to choose for himself." Then Sir Thomas preached his sermon, but preached it in the manner which men are wont to use when they know that they are preaching in vain. There is a tone of refusal, which, though the words used may be manifestly enough words of denial, is in itself indicative of assent. Sir Thomas ended the conference by taking a week to think over the matter, and when the week was over gave way. He was still inclined to think that marriages with cousins had better be avoided; but he gave way, and at last promised that if Tom and Ayala were of one mind an income should be forthcoming.

For the carrying out of this purpose it was necessary that the door of Uncle Dosett's house should be unlocked, and with the object of turning the key Sir Thomas himself called at the Admiralty. "I find my boy is quite in earnest about this," he said to the Admiralty clerk.

"Oh ; indeed."

"I can't say I quite like it myself." Mr. Dosett could only shake his head. "Cousins had better be cousins, and nothing more."

"And then you would probably expect him to get money ?"

"Not at all," said Sir Thomas, proudly. "I have got money enough for them both. It isn't an affair of money. To make a long story short, I have given my consent ; and, therefore, if you do not mind, I shall be glad if you will allow Tom to call at the Crescent. Of course, you may have your own views ; but I don't suppose you can hope to do better for the girl. Cousins do marry, you know, very often." Mr. Dosett could only say that he could not expect to do anything for the girl nearly so good, and that, as far as he was concerned, his nephew Tom should be made quite welcome at Kingsbury Crescent. It was not, he added, in his power to answer for Ayala. As to this, Sir Thomas did not seem to have any doubts. The good things of the world, which it was in his power to offer, were so good, that it was hardly probable that a young lady in Ayala's position should refuse them.

"My dear," said Aunt Margaret, the next morning, speaking in her most suasive tone, "your Cousin Tom is to be allowed to call here."

"Tom Tringle ?"

"Yes, my dear. Sir Thomas has consented."

"Then he had better not," said Ayala, bristling up in hot anger. "Uncle Tom has got nothing to do with it, either in refusing or con senting. I won't see him."

"I think you must see him, if he calls."

"But I don't want. Oh, Aunt Margaret, pray make him not come. I don't like him a bit. We are doing so very well. Are we not, Aunt Margaret ?"

"Certainly, my dear, we are doing very well ;—at least, I hope so. But you are old enough now to understand that this is a very serious matter."

"Of course it is serious," said Ayala, who certainly was not guilty of the fault of making light of her future life. Those dreams of hers, in which were contained all her hopes and all her aspirations, were very serious to her. This was so much the case that she had by the means thought of her Cousin Tom in a light spirit, as though he were a matter of no moment to her. He was to her just what the Beast must have been to the Beauty, when the Beast first began to be in love. But her safety had consisted in the fact that no one had approved of the Beast being in love with her. Now she could understand that all the horrors of oppression might fall upon her. Of course it was serious; but not the less was she resolved that nothing should induce her to marry the Beast.

"I think you ought to see him when he comes, and to remember how different it will be when he comes with the approval of his father. It is, of course, saying that they are ready to welcome you as their daughter."

"I don't want to be anybody's daughter."

"But, Ayala, there are so many things to be thought of. Here is a young man who is able to give you not only every comfort but great opulence."

"I don't want to be opulent."

"And he will be a baronet."

"I don't care about baronets, Aunt Margaret."

"And you will have a house of your own in which you may be of service to your sister."

"I had rather she should have a house."

"But Tom is not in love with Lucy."

"He is such a lout! Aunt Margaret, I won't have anything to say to him. I would a great deal sooner die. Uncle Tom has no right to send him here. They have got rid of me, and I am very glad of it; but it isn't fair that he should come after me now that I'm gone away. Couldn't Uncle Reginald tell him to stay away?"

A great deal more was said, but nothing that was said had the slightest effect on Ayala. When she was told of her dependent position, and of the splendour of the prospects offered, she declared that she would rather go into the poor-house than marry her cousin. When she was told that Tom was good-natured, honest, and true, she declared that good-nature, honesty, and truth had nothing to do with it. When she was asked what it was that she looked forward to in the world she could merely sob and say that there was nothing. She could not tell even her sister Lucy of those dreams and castles. How, then, could she explain them to her Aunt Margaret? How could she make her aunt understand that there could be no place in her heart for Tom Tringle seeing that it was to be kept in reserve for some angel of light who would surely make his appearance in due season,—but who must still be there, present to her as her angel of light, even should he never show himself in the flesh. How vain it was to talk of Tom Tringle to her, when she had so visible before her eyes that angel of light with whom she was compelled to compare him!

But, though she could not be brought to say that she would listen patiently to his story, she was nevertheless made to understand that she must see him when he came to her. Aunt Margaret was very full on that subject. A young man who was approved of by the young lady's friends, and who had means at command, was, in Mrs. Dosett's opinion, entitled to a hearing. How otherwise were properly authorised marriages to be made up and arranged? When this was going on there was in some slight degree a diminished sympathy between Ayala and her aunt. Ayala still continued her household duties,— over which, in the privacy of her own room, she groaned sadly; but she continued them in silence. Her aunt, upon whom she had counted, was, she thought, turning against her. Mrs. Dosett, on the other hand, declared to herself that the girl was romantic and silly. Husbands with every immediate comfort, and a prospect of almost unlimited wealth, are not to be found under every hedge. What right could a girl so dependent as Ayala have to refuse an eligible match? She therefore in this way became an advocate on behalf of Tom,—as did also Uncle Reginald, more mildly. Uncle Reginald merely remarked that Tom was attending to his business, which was a great thing in a young man. It was not much, but it showed Ayala that in this matter her uncle was her enemy. In this, her terrible crisis, she had not a friend, unless it might be Lucy.

Then a day was fixed on which Tom was to come, which made the matter more terrible by anticipation. "What can be the good?" Ayala said to her aunt when the hour named for the interview was told her, "as I can tell him everything just as well without his coming at all." But all that had been settled. Aunt Margaret had repeated over and over again that such an excellent young man as Tom, with such admirable intentions, was entitled to a hearing from any young lady. In reply to this Ayala simply made a grimace, which was intended to signify the utter contempt in which she held her cousin Tom with all his wealth.

Tom Tringle, in spite of his rings and a certain dash of vulgarity, which was, perhaps, not altogether his own fault, was not a bad fellow. Having taken it into his heart that he was very much in love he was very much in love. He pictured to himself a happiness of a wholesome cleanly kind. To have the girl as his own, to caress her and foster her, and expend himself in making her happy; to exalt her, so as to have it acknowledged that she was, at any rate, as important as Augusta; to learn something from her, so that he, too, might become romantic, and in some degree poetical;—all this had come home to him in a not ignoble manner. But it had not come home to him that Ayala might probably refuse him. Hitherto Ayala had been very persistent in her refusals; but then hitherto there had existed the opposition of all the family. Now he had overcome that, and he felt therefore that he was entitled to ask and to receive.

On the day fixed, and at the hour fixed, he came in the plenitude of all his rings. Poor Tom! It was a pity that he should have had no one to advise him as to his apparel. Ayala hated his jewelry. She was not quite distinct in her mind as to the raiment which would be worn by the angel of light when he should come, but she was sure that he would not be chiefly conspicuous for heavy gilding; and Tom, moreover, had a waistcoat which would of itself have been suicidal. Such as he was, however, he was shown up into the drawing-room, where he found Ayala alone. It was certainly a misfortune to him that no preliminary conversation was possible. Ayala had been instructed to be there with the express object of listening to an offer of marriage. The work had to be done,—and should be done; but it would not admit of other ordinary courtesies. She was very angry with him, and she looked her anger. Why should she be subjected to this terrible annoyance? He had sense enough to perceive that there was no place for preliminary courtesy, and therefore rushed away at once to the matter in hand. "Ayala!" he exclaimed, coming and standing before her as she sat upon the sofa.

"Tom!" she said, looking boldly up into his face.

"Ayala, I love you better than anything else in the world."

"But what's the good of it?"

"Of course it was different when I told you so before. I meant to stick to it, and I was determined that the governor should give way. But you couldn't know that. Mother and the girls were all against us."

"They weren't against me," said Ayala.

"They were against our being married, and so they squeezed you out as it were. That is why you have been sent to this place. But they understand me now, and know what I am about. They have all given their consent, and the governor has promised to be liberal. When he says a thing he'll do it. There will be lots of money."

"I don't care a bit about money," said Ayala, fiercely.

"No more do I,—except only that it is comfortable. It wouldn't do to marry without money,—would it?"

"It would do very well if anybody cared for anybody." The angel of light generally appeared "in formâ pauperis," though there was always about him a tinge of bright azure which was hardly compatible with the draggle-tailed hue of everyday poverty.

"But an income is a good thing, and the governor will come down like a brick."

"The governor has nothing to do it. I told you before that it is all nonsense. If you will only go away and say nothing about it I shall always think you very good-natured."

"But I won't go away," said Tom, speaking out boldly. "I mean to stick to it. Ayala, I don't believe you understand that I am thoroughly in earnest."

"Why shouldn't I be in earnest, too?"

"But I love you, Ayala. I have set my heart upon it You don't know how well I love you. I have quite made up my mind about it."

"And I have made up my mind."

"But Ayala——" Now the tenor of his face changed, and something of the look of a despairing lover took the place of that offensive triumph which had at first sat upon his brow. "I don't suppose you care for any other fellow yet."

There was the angel of light. But even though she might be most anxious to explain to him that his suit was altogether impracticable she could say nothing to him about the angel. Though she was sure that the angel would come, she was not certain that she would ever give herself altogether even to the angel. The celestial castle which was ever being built in her imagination was as yet very much complicated. But had it been ever so clear it would have been quite impossible to explain anything of this to her cousin Tom. "That has nothing to do with it," she said.

"If you knew how I love you!" This came from him with a sob, and as he sobbed he went down before her on his knees.

"Don't be a fool, Tom,—pray don't. If you won't get up I shall go away. I must go away. I have heard all that there is to hear. I told them that there is no use in your coming."

"Ayala!" with this there were veritable sobs.

"Then why don't you give it up and let us be good friends."

"I can't give it up. I won't give it up. When a fellow means it as I do he never gives it up. Nothing on earth shall make me give it up. Ayala, you've got to do it, and so I tell you."

"Nobody can make me," said Ayala, nodding her head, but somewhat tamed by the unexpected passion of the young man.

"Then you won't say one kind word to me?"

"I can't say anything kinder."

"Very well. Then I shall go away and come again constantly till you do. I mean to have you. When you come to know how very much I love you I do think you will give way at last." With that he picked himself up from the ground and hurried out of the house without saying another word.

CHAPTER XII.

" WOULD YOU ?"

THE scene described in the last chapter took place in March. For three days afterwards there was quiescence in Kingsbury Crescent. Then there came a letter from Tom to Ayala, very pressing, full of love and resolution, offering to wait any time,—even a month,—if she wished it, but still persisting in his declared intention of marrying her sooner or later ;—not by any means a bad letter had there not been about it a little touch of bombast which made it odious to Ayala's sensitive appreciation. To this Ayala wrote a reply in the following words :

" When I tell you that I won't, you oughtn't to go on. It isn't manly.   " AYALA."

" Pray do not write again for I shall never answer another."

Of this she said nothing to Mrs. Dosett, though the arrival of Tom's letter must have been known to that lady. And she posted her own epistle without a word as to what she was doing.

She wrote again and again to Lucy imploring her sister to come to her, urging that as circumstances now were she could not show herself at the house in Queen's Gate. To these Lucy always replied ; but she did not reply by coming, and hardly made it intelligible why she did not come. Aunt Emmeline hoped, she said, that Ayala would very soon be able to be at Queen's Gate. Then there was a difficulty about the carriage. No one would walk across with her except Tom ; and walking by herself was forbidden. Aunt Emmeline did not like cabs. Then there came a third or fourth letter, in which Lucy was more explanatory, but yet not sufficiently so. During the Easter recess, which would take place in the middle of April, Augusta and Mr. Traffick would be married. The happy couple were to be blessed with a divided honeymoon. The interval between Easter and Whitsuntide would require Mr. Traffick's presence in the House, and the bride with her bridegroom were to return to Queen's Gate. Then they would depart again for the second holidays, and when they were so gone Aunt Emmeline hoped that Ayala would come to them for a visit. " They quite understand," said Lucy, " that it will not do to have you and Augusta together."

This was not at all what Ayala wanted. " It won't at all do to have me and him together," said Ayala to herself, alluding of course to Tom Tringle. But why did not Lucy come over to her ? Lucy, who knew so well that her sister did not want to see any one of the Tringles, who must have been sure that any visit to Queen's Gate must have been impossible, ought to have come to her.   To whom else could she say a word in her trouble ?   It was thus that Ayala argued with herself, declaring to herself that she must soon die in her misery,—unless indeed that angel of light might come to her assistance very quickly.

But Lucy had troubles of her own in reference to the family at Queen's Gate, which did, in fact, make it almost impossible to visit her sister for some weeks.   Sir Thomas had given an unwilling but a frank consent to his son's marriage,—and then expected simply to be told that it would take place at such and such a time, when money would be required.   Lady Tringle had given her consent,—but not quite frankly.   She still would fain have forbidden the banns, had any power of forbidding remained in her hands.   Augusta was still hot against the marriage, and still resolute to prevent it.   That proposed journey upstairs after the scrap-book at Glenbogie, that real journey up to the top of St. Peter's, still rankled in her heart.   That Tom should make Ayala a future baronet's wife ; that Tom should endow Ayala with the greatest share of the Tringle wealth ; that Ayala should become powerful in Queen's Gate and dominant probably at Merle Park and Glenbogie,—was wormwood to her.   She was conscious that Ayala was pretty and witty though she could affect to despise the wit and the prettiness. By instigating her mother, and by inducing Mr. Traffick to interfere when Mr. Traffick should be a member of the family, she thought that she might prevail.   With her mother she did in part prevail.   Her future husband was at present too much engaged with Supply and Demand to be able to give his thoughts to Tom's affairs.   But there would soon be a time when he naturally would be compelled to divide his thoughts.   Then there was Gertrude.   Gertrude's own affairs had not as yet been smiled upon, and the want of smiles she attributed very much to Augusta.   Why should Augusta have her way and not she, Gertrude, nor her brother Tom ?   She therefore leagued herself with Tom, and declared herself quite prepared to receive Ayala into the house. In this way the family was very much divided.

When Lucy first made her petition for the carriage, expressing her desire to see Ayala, both her uncle and her aunt were in the room. Objection was made,—some frivolous objection,—by Lady Tringle, who did not in truth care to maintain much connection between Queen's Gate and the Crescent.   Then Sir Thomas, in his burly authoritative way, had said that Ayala had better come to them.   That same evening he had settled or intended to settle it with his wife.   Let Ayala come as soon as the Traffics,—as they then would be,—should have gone. To this Lady Tringle had assented, knowing more than her husband as to Ayala's feelings, and thinking that in this way a breach might be made between them. Ayala had been a great trouble to her, and she was beginning to be almost sick of the Dormer connection altogether. It was thus that Lucy was hindered from seeing her sister for six weeks after that first formal declaration of his love made by Tom to Ayala. Tom had still persevered and had forced his way more than once into Ayala's presence, but Ayala's answers had been always the same. "It's a great shame, and you have no right to treat me in this way."

Then came the Traffick marriage with great éclat. There were no less than four Traffick bridesmaids, all of them no doubt noble, but none of them very young, and Gertrude and Lucy were bridesmaids,— and two of Augusta's friends. Ayala, of course, was not of the party. Tom was gorgeous in his apparel, not in the least depressed by his numerous repulses, quite confident of ultimate success, and proud of his position as a lover with so beautiful a girl. He talked of his affairs to all his friends, and seemed to think that even on this wedding-day his part was as conspicuous as that of his sister, because of his affair with his beautiful cousin. "Augusta doesn't hit it off with her," he said to one of his friends who asked why Ayala was not at the wedding,—"Augusta is the biggest fool out, you know. She's proud of her husband because he's the son of a lord. I wouldn't change Ayala for the daughter of any duchess in Europe ;"—thus showing that he regarded Ayala as being almost his own already. Lord Boardotrade was there, making a semi-jocose speech, quite in the approved way for a cognate paterfamilias. Perhaps there was something of a thorn in this to Sir Thomas, as it had become apparent at last that Mr. Traffick himself did not purpose to add anything from his own resources to the income on which he intended to live with his wife. Lord Boardotrade had been obliged to do so much for his eldest son that there appeared to be nothing left for the member for Port Glasgow. Sir Thomas was prepared with his £120,000, and did not perhaps mind this very much. But a man, when he pays his money, likes to have some return for it, and he did not quite like the tone with which the old nobleman, not possessed of very old standing in the peerage, seemed to imply that he, like a noble old Providence, had enveloped the whole Tringle family in the mantle of his noble blood. He combined the jocose and the paternal in the manner appropriate to such occasions; but there did run through Sir Thomas's mind as he heard him an idea that £120,000 was a sufficient sum to pay, and that it might be necessary to make Mr. Traffick understand that out of the income thenceforth coming he must provide a house for himself and his wife. It had been already arranged that he was to return to Queen's Gate with his wife for the period between Easter and Whitsuntide. It had lately,—quite lately,—been hinted to Sir Thomas that the married pair would run up again after the second holidays. Mr. Septimus Traffick had once spoken of Glenbogie as almost all his own, and Augusta had, in her father's hearing, said a word intended to be very affectionate about "dear Merle Park." Sir Thomas was a father all over, with all a father's feelings; but even a father does not like to be done. Mr. Traffick, no doubt, was a Member of Parliament and son of a peer;—but there might be a question whether even Mr. Traffick had not been purchased at quite his full value.

Nevertheless the marriage was pronounced to have been a success. Immediately after it,—early, indeed, on the following morning,—Sir Thomas inquired when Ayala was coming to Queen's Gate. "Is it necessary that she should come quite at present?" asked Lady Tringle.

"I thought it was all settled," said Sir Thomas, angrily. This had been said in the privacy of his own dressing-room, but downstairs at the breakfast-table, in the presence of Gertrude and Lucy, he returned to the subject. Tom, who did not live in the house, was not there. "I suppose we might as well have Ayala now," he said, addressing himself chiefly to Lucy. "Do you go and manage it with her." There was not a word more said. Sir Thomas did not always have his own way in his family. What man was ever happy enough to do that? But he was seldom directly contradicted. Lady Tringle when the order was given pursed up her lips, and he, had he been observant, might have known that she did not intend to have Ayala if she could help it. But he was not observant,—except as to millions.

When Sir Thomas was gone, Lady Tringle discussed the matter with Lucy. "Of course, my dear," she said, "if we could make dear Ayala happy——"

"I don't think she will come, Aunt Emmeline."

"Not come!" This was not said at all in a voice of anger, but simply as eliciting some further expression of opinion.

"She's afraid of—Tom." Lucy had never hitherto expressed a positive opinion on that matter at Queen's Gate. When Augusta had spoken of Ayala as having run after Tom, Lucy had been indignant, and had declared that the running had been all on the other side. In a side way she had hinted that Ayala, at any rate at present, was far from favourable to Tom's suit. But she had never yet spoken out her mind at Queen's Gate as Ayala had spoken it to her.

"Afraid of him?" said Aunt Emmeline.

"I mean that she is not a bit in love with him, and when a girl is like that I suppose she is—is afraid of a man, if everybody else wants her to marry him."

" Why should everybody want her to marry Tom ?" asked Lady
Tringle, indignantly. " I am sure I don't want her."

" I suppose it is Uncle Tom, and Aunt Dosett, and Uncle Reginald,"
said poor Lucy, finding that she had made a mistake.

" I don't see why anybody should want her to marry Tom. Tom
is carried away by her baby face, and makes a fool of himself. As to
everybody wanting her, I hope she does not flatter herself that there
is anything of the kind."

" I only meant that I think she would rather not be brought here,
where she would have to see him daily."

After this the loan of the carriage was at last made, and Lucy was
allowed to visit her sister at the Crescent. " Has he been there ?"
was almost the first question that Ayala asked.

" What he do you mean ?"

" Isadore Hamel."

" No ; I have not seen him since I met him in the Park. But I do
not want to talk about Mr. Hamel, Ayala. Mr. Hamel is nothing."

" Oh, Lucy."

" He is nothing. Had he been anything, he has gone, and there
would be an end to it. But he is nothing."

" If a man is true he may go, but he will come back." Ayala
had her ideas about the angel of light very clearly impressed upon
her mind in regard to the conduct of the man, though they were
terribly vague as to his personal appearance, his condition of life, his
appropriateness for marriage, and many other details of his circumstances. It had also often occurred to her that this angel of light,
when he should come, might not be in love with herself,—and that
she might have to die simply because she had seen him and loved him
in vain. But he would be a man sure to come back if there were fitting
reasons that he should do so. Isadore Hamel was not quite an angel
of light, but he was nearly angelic,—at any rate very good, and surely
would come back.

" Never mind about Mr. Hamel, Ayala. It is not nice to talk
about a man who has never spoken a word."

" Never spoken a word ! Oh, Lucy ?"

" Mr. Hamel has never spoken a word, and I will not talk about
him. There ! All my heart is open to you, Ayala. You know that.
But I will not talk about Mr. Hamel. Aunt Emmeline wants you to
come to Queen's Gate."

" I will not."

" Or rather it is Sir Thomas who wants you to come. I do like
Uncle Tom. I do, indeed."

" So do I."

" You ought to come when he asks you."

" Why ought I? That lout would be there,—of course."

" I don't know about his being a lout, Ayala."

" He comes here, and I have to be perfectly brutal to him. You can't guess the sort of things I say to him, and he doesn't mind it a bit. He thinks that he has to go on long enough, and that I must give way at last. If I were to go to Queen's Gate it would be just as much as to say that I had given way."

" Why not?"

" Lucy!"

" Why not? He is not bad. He is honest, and true, and kind-hearted. I know you can't be happy here."

" No."

" Aunt Dosett, with all her affairs, must be trouble to you. I could not bear them patiently. How can you?"

" Because they are better than Tom Tringle. I read somewhere about there being seven houses of the Devil, each one being lower and worse than the other. Tom would be the lowest,—the lowest,—the lowest."

" Ayala, my darling."

" Do not tell me that I ought to marry Tom," said Ayala, almost standing off in anger from the proffered kiss. " Do you think that I could love him?"

" I think you could if you tried, because he is loveable. It is so much to be good, and then he loves you truly. After all, it is something to have everything nice around you. You have not been made to be poor and uncomfortable. I fear that it must be bad with you here."

" It is bad."

" I wish I could have stayed, Ayala. I am more tranquil than you, and could have borne it better."

" It is bad. It is one of the houses,—but not the lowest. I can eat my heart out here, peaceably, and die with a great needle in my hand and a towel in my lap. But if I were to marry him I should kill myself the first hour after I had gone away with him. Things! What would things be with such a monster as that leaning over one? Would you marry him?" In answer to this, Lucy made no immediate reply. " Why don't you say? You want me to marry him. Would you?"

" No."

" Then why should I?"

" I could not try to love him."

" Try! How can a girl try to love any man? It should come

because she can't help it, let her try ever so. **Trying to love Tom
Tringle !** Why can't you try ?"

" He doesn't want me."

" But if he did ? I don't suppose it would make the least difference
to him which it was. Would you try if he asked ?"

" No."

" Then why should I ? Am I so much a poorer creature than
you ?"

" You are a finer creature. You know that I think so."

" I don't want to be finer. I want to be the sáme."

" You are free to do as you please. I am not—quite."

" That means Isadore Hamel."

' I try to tell you all the truth, Ayala ; but pray do not talk about
him even to me. As for you, you are free ; and if you could——"

" I can't. I don't know that I am free, as you call it." Then Lucy
started, as though about to ask the question which would naturally
follow. " You needn't look like that, Lucy. There isn't any one to
be named."

" A man not to be named !"

' There isn't a man at all. There isn't anybody. But I may have
my own ideas if I please. If I had an Isadore Hamel of my own I
could compare Tom or Mr. Traffick, or any other lout to him, and
could say how infinitely higher in the order of things was my Isadore
than any of them. Though I haven't an Isadore can't I have an image ?
And can't I make my image brighter, even higher, than Isadore ? You
won't believe that, of course, and I don't want you to believe it yourself. But you should believe it for me. My image can make Tom
Tringle just as horrible to me as Isadore Hamel can make him to you."
Thus it was that Ayala endeavoured to explain to her sister something of the castle which she had built in the air, and of the angel of
light who inhabited the castle.

Then it was decided between them that Lucy should explain to
Aunt Emmeline that Ayala could not make a prolonged stay at Queen's
Gate. " But how shall I say it ?" asked Lucy.

" Tell her the truth, openly. 'Tom wants to marry Ayala, and
Ayala won't have him. Therefore, of course, she can't come, because
it would look as though she were going to change her mind,--which
she isn't.' Aunt Emmeline will understand that, and will not be a bit
sorry. She doesn't want to have me for a daughter-in-law. She had
quite enough of me at Rome."

All this time the carriage was waiting, and Lucy was obliged to
return before half of all that was necessary had been said. What was
to be Ayala's life for the future ? How were the sisters to see each

other ! What was to be done when, at the end of the coming summer, Lucy should be taken first to Glenbogie and then to Merle Park ? There is a support in any excitement, though it be in the excitement of sorrow only. At the present moment Ayala was kept alive by the necessity of her battle with Tom Tringle, but how would it be with her when Tom should have given up the fight? Lucy knew, by sad experience, how great might be the tedium of life in Kingsbury Crescent, and knew, also, how unfitted Ayala was to endure it. There seemed to be no prospect of escape in future. "She knows nothing of what I am suffering," said Ayala, "when she gives me the things to do, and tells me of more things, and more, and more ! How can there be so many things to be done in such a house as this !" But as Lucy was endeavouring to explain how different were the arrangements in Kingsbury Crescent from those which had prevailed at the bijou the offended coachman sent up word to say that he didn't think Sir Thomas would like it if the horses were kept out in the rain any longer. Then Lucy hurried down, not having spoken of half the things which were down in her mind on the list for discussion.

<hr />

CHAPTER XIII.

HOW THE TRINGLES FELL INTO TROUBLE.

AFTER the Easter holidays the Trafficks came back to Queen's Gate, making a combination of honeymoon and business which did very well for a time. It was understood that it was to be so. During honeymoon times the fashionable married couple is always lodged and generally boarded for nothing. That opening wide of generous hands, which exhibits itself in the joyous enthusiasm of a coming marriage, taking the shape of a houseful of presents, of a gorgeous and ponderous trousseau, of a splendid marriage feast, and not unfrequently of subsidiary presents from the opulent papa,—presents which are subsidiary to the grand substratum of settled dowry,—generously extends itself to luxurious provision for a month or two. That Mr. and Mrs. Traffick should come back to Queen's Gate for the six weeks intervening between Easter and Whitsuntide had been arranged, and arranged also that the use of Merle Park, for the Whitsun holidays, should be allowed to them. This last boon Augusta, with her sweetest kiss, had obtained from her father only two days before the wedding. But when it was suggested, just before the departure to Merle Park, that Mr. Traffick's unnecessary boots might be left at Queen's Gate, because he would come back there, then Sir Thomas, who had thought over the matter, said a word.

It was in this way. "Mamma," said Augusta, "I suppose I can leave a lot of things in the big wardrobe. Jemima says I cannot take them to Merle Park without ever so many extra trunks."

"Certainly, my dear. When anybody occupies the room, they won't want all the wardrobe. I don't know that anyone will come this summer."

This was only the thin end of the wedge, and, as Augusta felt, was not introduced successfully. The words spoken seemed to have admitted that a return to Queen's Gate had not been intended. The conversation went no further at the moment, but was recommenced the same evening. "Mamma, I suppose Septimus can leave his things here?"

"Of course, my dear; he can leave anything,—to be taken care of."

"It will be so convenient if we can come back,—just for a few days."

Now, there certainly had been a lack of confidence between the married daughter and her mother as to a new residence. A word had been spoken, and Augusta had said that she supposed they would go to Lord Boardotrade when they left Queen's Gate, just to finish the season. Now, it was known that his lordship, with his four unmarried daughters, lived in a small house in a small street in Mayfair. The locality is no doubt fashionable, but the house was inconvenient. Mr. Traffick, himself, had occupied lodgings near the House of Commons, but these had been given up. "I think you must ask your papa," said Lady Tringle.

"Couldn't you ask him?" said the Honourable Mrs. Traffick. Lady Tringle was driven at last to consent, and then put the question to Sir Thomas,—beginning with the suggestion as to the unnecessary boots.

"I suppose Septimus can leave his things here?"

"Where do they mean to live when they come back to town?" asked Sir Thomas, sharply.

"I suppose it would be convenient if they could come here for a little time," said Lady Tringle.

"And stay till the end of the season,—and then go down to Glenbogie, and then to Merle Park! Where do they mean to live?"

"I think there was a promise about Glenbogie," said Lady Tringle.

"I never made a promise. I heard Traffick say that he would like to have some shooting,—though, as far as I know, he ca'nt hit a haystack. They may come to Glenbogie for two or three weeks, if they like, but they shan't stay here during the entire summer."

"You won't turn your own daughter out, Tom."

"I'll turn Traffick out, and I suppose he'll take his wife with him," said Sir Thomas, thus closing the conversation in wrath.

The Trafficks went and came back, and were admitted into the bed-room with the big wardrobe, and to the dressing-room where the boots were kept. On the very first day of his arrival Mr. Traffick was in the House at four, and remained there till four the next morning,—certain Irish Members having been very eloquent. He was not down when Sir Thomas left the next morning at nine, and was again at the House when Sir Thomas came home to dinner. "How long is it to be?" said Sir Thomas, that night, to his wife. There was a certain tone in his voice which made Lady Tringle feel herself to be ill all over. It must be said, in justice to Sir Thomas, that he did not often use this voice in his domestic circle, though it was well known in Lombard Street. But he used it now, and his wife felt herself to be unwell. "I am not going to put up with it, and he needn't think it."

"Don't destroy poor Augusta's happiness so soon."

"That be d——d," said the father, energetically. "Who's going to destroy her happiness. Her happiness ought to consist in living in her husband's house. What have I given her all that money for?" Then Lady Tringle did not dare to say another word.

It was not till the third day that Sir Thomas and his son-in-law met each other. By that time Sir Thomas had got it into his head that his son-in-law was avoiding him. But on the Saturday there was no House. It was then just the middle of June,—Saturday, June 15, —and Sir Thomas had considered, at the most, that there would be yet nearly two months before Parliament would cease to sit and the time for Glenbogie would come. He had fed his anger warm, and was determined that he would not be done. "Well, Traffick, how are you?" he said, encountering his son-in-law in the hall, and leading him into the dining-room. "I haven't seen you since you've been back."

"I've been in the House morning, noon, and night, pretty near."

"I dare say. I hope you found yourself comfortable at Merle Park."

"A charming house,—quite charming. I don't know whether I shouldn't build the stables a little further from——"

"Very likely. Nothing is so easy as knocking other people's houses about. I hope you'll soon have one to knock about of your own."

"All in good time," said Mr. Traffick, smiling.

Sir Thomas was one of those men who during the course of a successful life have contrived to repress their original roughnesses, and who make a not ineffectual attempt to live after the fashion of those with whom their wealth and successes have thrown them. But among such will occasionally be found one whose roughness does not altogether desert him, and who can on an occasion use it with a purpose. Such

a one will occasionally surprise his latter-day associates by the sudden
ferocity of his brow, by the hardness of his voice, and by an apparently
unaccustomed use of violent words. The man feels that he must fight,
and, not having learned the practice of finer weapons, fights in this
way. Unskilled with foils or rapier he falls back upon the bludgeon
with which his hand has not lost all its old familiarity. Such a one
was Sir Thomas Tringle, and a time for such exercise had seemed to him
to have come now. There are other men who by the possession of im-
perturbable serenity seem to be armed equally against rapier and bludgeon, whom there is no wounding with any weapon. Such a one was
Mr. Traffick. When he was told of knocking about a house of his own,
he quite took the meaning of Sir Thomas's words, and was immediately
prepared for the sort of conversation which would follow. "I wish I
might ;—a Merle Park of my own for instance. If I had gone into the
city instead of to Westminster it might have come in my way."

"It seems to me that a good deal has come in your way without
very much trouble on your part."

"A seat in the House is a nice thing,—but I work harder I take it
than you do, Sir Thomas."

"I never have had a shilling but what I earned. When you leave
this where are you and Augusta going to live?"

This was a home question, which would have disconcerted most gentlemen in Mr. Traffick's position, were it not that gentlemen easily disconcerted would hardly find themselves there.

"Where shall we go when we leave this? You were so kind as to
say something about Glenbogie when Parliament is up."

"No, I didn't."

"I thought I understood it."

"You said something and I didn't refuse."

"Put it any way you like, Sir Thomas."

"But what do you mean to do before Parliament is up? The long and
the short of it is, we didn't expect you to come back after the holidays.
I like to be plain. This might go on for ever if I didn't speak out."

"And a very comfortable way of going on it would be." Sir
Thomas raised his eyebrows in unaffected surprise, and then again
assumed his frown. "Of course I'm thinking of Augusta chiefly."

"Augusta made up her mind no doubt to leave her father's house
when she married."

"She shows her affection for her parents by wishing to remain in it.
The fact, I suppose, is, you want the rooms."

"But even if we didn't? You're not going to live here for ever, I
suppose."

"That, Sir, is too good to be thought of. I fear. The truth is we had an idea of staying at my father's. He spoke of going down to the country and lending us the house. My sisters have made him change his mind and so here we are. Of course we can go into lodgings."

" Or to an hotel."

" Too dear ! You see you've made me pay such a sum for insuring my life. I'll tell you what I'll do. If you'll let us make it out here till the 10th of July we'll go into an hotel then." Sir Thomas, surprised at his own compliance, did at last give way. " And then we can have a month at Glenbogie from the 12th."

" Three weeks," said Sir Thomas, shouting at the top of his voice.

" Very well ; three weeks. If you could have made it the month it would have been convenient ; but I hate to be disagreeable." Thus the matter was settled, and Mr. Traffick was altogether well pleased with the arrangement.

" What are we to do ? " said Augusta, with a very long face. " What are we to do when we are made to go away ? "

" I hope I shall be able to make some of the girls go down by that time, and then we must squeeze in at my father's."

This and other matters made Sir Thomas in those days irritable and disagreeable to the family. " Tom," he said to his wife, " is the biggest fool that ever lived."

" What is the matter with him now ? " asked Lady Tringle, who did not like to have her only son abused.

" He's away half his time, and when he does come he'd better be away. If he wants to marry that girl why doesn't he marry her and have done with it ? "

 Now this was a matter upon which Lady Tringle had ideas of her own which were becoming every day stronger. " I'm sure I should be very sorry to see it," she said.

" Why should you be sorry ? Isn't it the best thing a young man can do ? If he's set his heart that way all the world won't talk him off. I thought all that was settled."

" You can't make the girl marry him ? "

" Is that it ? " asked Sir Thomas, with a whistle. " You used to say she was setting her cap at him."

" She is one of those girls you don't know what she would be at. She's full of romance and nonsense, and isn't half as fond of telling the truth as she ought to be. She made my life a burden to me while she was with us, and I don't think she would be any better for Tom."

" But he's still determined."

" What's the use of that ? " said Lady Tringle.

" Then he shall have her. I made him a promise and I'm not going to give it up. I told him that if he was in earnest he should have her."

" You can't make a girl marry a young man."

" You have her here, and then we'll take her to Glenbogie.   Now
when I say it I mean it.   You go and fetch her, and if you don't ⁻
will.   I'm not going to have her turned out into the cold in that
way."

" She won't come, Tom."   Then he turned round and frowned at
her.

The immediate result of this was that Lady Tringle herself did drive
across to Kingsbury Crescent accompanied by Gertrude and Lucy, and
did make her request in form.   " My dear, your uncle particularly
wants you to come to us for the next month."   Mrs. Dosett was sitting
by.   " I hope Ayala may be allowed to come to us for a month."

" Ayala must answer for herself," said Mrs. Dosett firmly.   There
had never been any warm friendship between Mrs. Dosett and her husband's elder sister."

" I can't," said Ayala, shaking her head.

" Why not, my dear ? " said Lady Tringle.

" I can't," said Ayala.

Lady Tringle was not in the least offended or annoyed at the refusal.
She did not at all desire that Ayala should come to Glenbogie.   Ayala
at Glenbogie would make her life miserable to her.   It would, of course,
lead to Tom's marriage, and then there would be internecine fighting
between Ayala and Augusta.   But it was necessary that she should take
back to her husband some reply ;—and this reply, if in the form of
refusal, must come from Ayala herself.   " Your uncle has sent me,"
said Lady Tringle, " and I must give him some reason.   As for expense,
you know,"—then she turned to Mrs. Dosett with a smile,—" that of
course would be our affair."

" If you ask me," said Mrs. Dosett, " I think that as Ayala has come
to us she had better remain with us.   Of course things are very different, and she would be only discontented."   At this Lady Tringle
smiled her sweetest smile,—as though acknowledging that things certainly were different,—and then turned to Ayala for a further reply.

" Aunt Emmeline, I can't," said Ayala.

" But why, my dear ?   Can't isn't a courteous answer to a request
that is meant to be kind."

" Speak out, Ayala," said Mrs. Dosett.   " There is nobody here but
your aunts."

" Because of Tom."

" Tom wouldn't eat you," said Lady Tringle, again smiling.

" It's worse than eating me," said Ayala.   " He will go on when I
tell him not.   If I were down there he'd be doing it always.   And then
you'd tell me that I—encouraged him !"

Lady Tringle felt this to be unkind and undeserved. Those passages in Rome had been very disagreeable to every one concerned. The girl certainly, as she thought, had been arrogant and impertinent. She had been accepted from charity and had then domineered in the family. She had given herself airs and had gone out into company almost without authority, into company which had rejected her,—Lady Tringle. It had become absolutely necessary to get rid of an inmate so troublesome, so unbearable. The girl had been sent away,—almost ignominiously. Now she, Lady Tringle, the offended aunt, the aunt who had so much cause for offence, had been good enough, gracious enough, to pardon all this, and was again offering the fruition of a portion of her good things to the sinner. No doubt she was not anxious that the offer should be accepted, but not the less was it made graciously,—as she felt herself. In answer to this she had thrown back upon her the only hard word she had ever spoken to the girl ! " You wouldn't be told anything of the kind, but you needn't come if you don't like it."

" Then I don't," said Ayala, nodding her head.

" But I did think that after all that has passed, and when I am trying to be kind to you, you would have made yourself more pleasant to me. I can only tell your uncle that you say you won't."

" Give my love to my uncle, and tell him that I am much obliged to him and that I know how good he is ; but I can't—because of Tom."

" Tom is too good for you," exclaimed Aunt Emmeline, who could not bear to have her son depreciated even by the girl whom she did not wish to marry him.

" I didn't say he wasn't," said Ayala, bursting into tears. " The Archbishop of Canterbury would be too good for me, but I don't want to marry him." Then she got up and ran out of the room in order that she might weep over her troubles in the privacy of her own chamber. She was thoroughly convinced that she was being ill-used. No one had a right to tell her that any man was too good for her unless she herself should make pretensions to the man. It was an insult to her even to connect her name with that of any man unless she had done something to connect it. In her own estimation her cousin Tom was infinitely beneath her,—worlds beneath her,—a denizen of an altogether inferior race, such as the Beast was to the Beauty ! Not that Ayala had ever boasted to herself of her own face or form. It was not in that respect that she likened herself to the Beauty when she thought of Tom as the Beast. Her assumed superiority existed in certain intellectual or rather artistic and æsthetic gifts,—certain celestial gifts. But as she had boasted of them to no one, as she had never said that she and her cousin were poles asunder in their tastes, poles asunder in their feelings, poles asunder in their intelligence, was it not very, very cruel that she should be told, first that she encouraged him, and then that she was not good enough for him ? Cinderella did not ask to have the Prince for her husband. When she had her own image of which no one could rob her, and was content with that, why should they treat her in this cruel way?

" I am afraid you are having a great deal of trouble with her," said Lady Tringle to Mrs. Dosett.

" No, indeed. Of course she is romantic, which is very objection-able."

" Quite detestable !" said Lady Tringle.

" But she has been brought up like that, so that it is not her fault. Now she endeavours to do her best."

" She is so upsetting."

" She is angry because her cousin persecutes her."

" Persecutes her, indeed ! Tom is in a position to ask any girl to be his wife. He can give her a home of her own, and a good income. She ought to be proud of the offer instead of speaking like that. But nobody wants her to have him."

" He wants it, I suppose."

" Just taken by her baby face ;—that's all. It won't last, and she needn't think so. However, I've done my best to be kind, Mrs. Dosett, and there's an end of it. If you please I'll ring the bell for the carriage. Good-bye." After that she swam out of the room and had herself carried back to Queen's Gate.

CHAPTER XIV.

FRANK HOUSTON.

THREE or four days afterwards Sir Thomas asked whether Ayala was to come to Glenbogie. " She positively refused," said his wife, " and was so rude and impertinent that I could not possibly have her now." Then Sir Thomas frowned and turned himself away, and said not a word further on that occasion.

There were many candidates for Glenbogie on this occasion. Among others there was Mr. Frank Houston, whose candidature was not pressed by himself,—as could not well have been done,—but was enforced by Gertrude on his behalf. It was now July. Gertrude and Mr. Houston had seen something of each other in Rome, as may be remembered, and since then had seen a good deal of each other in town. Gertrude was perfectly well aware that Mr. Houston was impecunious ; but Augusta had been allowed to have an impecunious lover, and Tom to throw himself at the feet of an impecunious love,

Gertrude felt herself to be entitled to her £120,000 ;—did not for a moment doubt but that she would get it. Why shouldn't she give it to any young man she liked as long as he belonged to decent people? Mr. Houston wasn't a Member of Parliament,—but then he was young and good-looking. Mr. Houston wasn't son to a lord, but he was brother to a county squire, and came of a family much older than that of those stupid Boardotrade and Traffick people. And then Frank Houston was very presentable, was not at all bald, and was just the man for a girl to like as a husband. It was dinned into her ears that Houston had no income at all,—just a few hundreds a year on which he never could keep himself out of debt. But he was a generous man, who would be more than contented with the income coming from £120,000. He would not spunge upon the house at Queen's Gate. He would not make use of Merle Park and Glenbogie. He would have a house of his own for his old boots. Four per cent. would give them nearly £5,000 a year. Gertrude knew all about it already. They could have a nice house near Queen's Gate ;—say somewhere about Onslow Gardens. There would be quite enough for a carriage, for three months upon a mountain in Switzerland, and three more among the art treasures of Italy. It was astonishing how completely Gertrude had it all at her finger's ends when she discussed the matter with her mother. Mr. Houston was a man of no expensive tastes. He didn't want to hunt. He did shoot, no doubt, and perhaps a little shooting at Glenbogie might be nice before they went to Switzerland. In that case two months on the top of the mountain would suffice. But if he was not asked he would never condescend to demand an entry at Glenbogie as a part of his wife's dower. Lady Tringle was thus talked over, though she did think that at least one of her daughter's husbands ought to have an income of his own. There was another point which Gertrude put forward very frankly, and which no doubt had weight with her mother. "Mamma, I mean to have him," she said, when Lady Tringle expressed a doubt.

"But papa?"

"I mean to have him. Papa can scold, of course, if he pleases."

"But where would the income come from if papa did not give it?"

"Of course he'll give it. I've a right to it as much as Augusta." There was something in Gertrude's face as she said this which made her mother think that she would have her way.

But Sir Thomas had hitherto declined. When Frank Houston, after the manner of would-be-sons-in-law, had applied to Sir Thomas, Sir Thomas, who already knew all about it, asked after his income, his prospects, and his occupation. Fifty years ago young men used to encounter the misery of such questions, and to live afterwards often in

the enjoyment of the stern questioner's money and daughters. But
there used in those days to be a bad quarter of an hour while the
questions were being asked, and not unfrequently a bad six months
afterwards, while the stern questioner was gradually undergoing a
softening process under the hands of the females of the family. But
the young man of to-day has no bad quarter of an hour. "You are a
mercantile old brick, with money and a daughter. I am a jeunesse
dorée,—gilded by blood and fashion, though so utterly impecunious !
Let us know your terms. How much is it to be, and then I can say
whether we can afford to live upon it." The old brick surrenders himself more readily and speedily to the latter than to the former manner;
—but he hardly surrenders himself quite at once. Frank Houston,
when inquired into, declared at once, without blushing, that he had
no income at all to speak of in reference to matrimonial life. As to
family prospects he had none. His elder brother had four blooming
boys, and was likely to have more. As for occupation, he was very
fond of painting, very fond of art all round, could shoot a little, and
was never in want of anything to do as long as he had a book. But for
the earning of money he had no turn whatever. He was quite sure of
himself that he could never earn a shilling. But then on the other
hand he was not extravagant,—which was almost as good as earning.
It was almost incredible ; but with his means, limited as they were to
a few hundreds, he did not owe above a thousand pounds ;—a fact
which he thought would weigh much with Sir Thomas in regard to his
daughter's future happiness.

Sir Thomas gave him a flat refusal. "I think that I may boast that
your daughter's happiness is in my charge," said Frank Houston.

"Then she must be unhappy," said Sir Thomas. Houston shrugged
his shoulders. "A fool like that has no right to be happy."

"There isn't another man in the world by whom I would allow her
to be spoken of like that," said Houston.

"Bother !"

"I regard her as all that is perfect in woman, and you must forgive
me if I say that I shall not abandon my suit. I may be allowed, at
any rate, to call at the house ?"

"Certainly not."

"That is a kind of thing that is never done nowadays ;—never,
said Houston, shaking his head.

"I suppose my own house is my own."

"Yours and Lady Tringle's, and your daughters , no doubt. At any
rate, Sir Thomas, you will think of this again. I am sure you will
think of it again. If you find that your daughter's happiness depends
upon it——"

"I shall find nothing of the kind. Good morning."

"Good morning, Sir Thomas." Then Mr. Houston, bowing graciously, left the little back room in Lombard Street, and, jumping into a cab, had himself taken straight away to Queen's Gate.

"Papa is always like that," said Gertrude. On that day Mrs. Traffick, with all the boots, had taken herself away to the small house in Mayfair, and Gertrude, with her mother, had the house to herself. At the present moment Lady Tringle was elsewhere, so that the young lady was alone with her lover.

"But he comes round, I suppose."

"If he doesn't have too much to eat,—which disagrees with him,—he does. He's always better down at Glenbogie because he's out of doors a good deal, and then he can digest things."

"Then take him down to Glenbogie and let him digest it at once."

"Of course we can't go till the 12th. Perhaps we shall start on the 10th, because the 11th is Sunday. What will you do, Frank?" There had been a whisper of Frank's going to the Tyrol in August, there to join the Mudbury Docimers, who were his far-away cousins. Imogene Docimer was a young lady of marvellous beauty,—not possessed indeed of £120,000,—of whom Gertrude had heard, and was already anxious that her Frank should not go to the Tyrol this year. She was already aware that her Frank had—just an artist's eye for feminine beauty in its various shapes, and thought that in the present condition of things he would be better at Glenbogie than in the Tyrol.

"I am thinking of wandering away somewhere ;—perhaps to the Tyrol. The Mudbury Docimers are there. He's a pal of mine, besides being a cousin. Mrs. Docimer is a very nice woman."

"And her sister?"

"A lovely creature. Such a turn of the neck! I've promised to make a study of her back head."

"Come down to Glenbogie," said Gertrude, sternly.

"How can I do that when your governor won't let me enter his house-door even in London."

"But you're here."

"Well,—yes ;—I am here. But he told me not. I don't see how I'm to drive in at the gate at Glenbogie with all my traps, and ask to be shown my room. I have cheek enough for a good deal, my pet."

"I believe you have, Sir ;—cheek enough for anything. But mamma must manage it,—mamma and me, between us. Only keep yourself disengaged. You won't go to the Tyrol,—eh?" Then Frank Houston promised that he would not go to the Tyrol as long as there was a chance open that he might be invited to Glenbogie.

"I won't hear of it," said Sir Thomas to his wife. On that occasion his digestion had perhaps failed him a little. "He only wants to get my money."

"But Gertrude has set her heart on it, and nothing will turn her away."

"Why can't she set her heart on some one who has got a decent income. That man hasn't a shilling."

"Nor yet has Mr. Traffick."

"Mr. Traffick has, at any rate, got an occupation. Were it to do again, Mr. Traffick would never see a shilling of my money. By ——, those fellows, who haven't got a pound belonging to them, think that they're to live on the fat of the land out of the sweat of the brow of such men as me."

"What is your money for, Tom, but for the children?"

"I know what it's for. I'd sooner build a hospital then give it to an idle fellow like that Houston. When I asked him what he did, he said he was fond of 'picters!'" Sir Thomas would fall back from his usual modes of expression when he was a little excited.

"Of course he hasn't been brought up to work. But he is a gentleman, and I do think he would make our girl happy."

"My money would make him happy,—till he had spent it."

"Tie it up."

"You don't know what you're talking about. How are you to prevent a man from spending his wife's income?"

"At any rate, if you have him down at Glenbogie you can see what sort of a man he is. You don't know him now."

"As much as I wish to."

"That isn't fair to the poor girl. You needn't give your consent to a marriage because he comes to Glenbogie. You have only to say that you won't give the money and then it must be off. They can't take the money from you." His digestion could not have been very bad, for he allowed himself to be persuaded that Houston should be asked to Glenbogie for ten days. This was the letter of invitation;—

"MY DEAR MR. HOUSTON,

"We shall start for Glenbogie on the 10th of next month. Sir Thomas wishes you to join us on the 20th if you can, and stay till the end of the month. We shall be a little crowded at first, and therefore cannot name an earlier day.

"I am particularly to warn you that this means nothing more than a simple invitation. I know what passed between you and Sir Thomas, and he hasn't at all changed his mind. I think it right to tell you this. If you like to speak to him again when you are at Glenbogie of course you can. "Very sincerely yours. "EMMELINE TRINGLE."

At the same time, or within a post of it, he got another letter, which was as follows ;—

"DEAREST F,

"Papa, you see, hasn't cut up so very rough after all. You are to be allowed to come and help to slaughter grouse, which will be better than going to that stupid Tyrol. If you want to draw somebody's back head you can do it there. Isn't it a joke papa's giving way like that all in a moment? He gets so fierce sometimes that we think he's going to eat everybody. Then he has to come down, and he gets eaten worse than anybody else.

"Of course, as you're asked to Glenbogie, you can come here as often as you like. I shall ride on Thursday and Friday. I shall expect you exactly at six, just under the Memorial. You can't come home to dinner, you know, because he might flare up ; but you can turn in at lunch every day you please except Saturday and Sunday. I intend to be so jolly down at Glenbogie. You mustn't be shooting always. "Ever your own, "G."

Frank Houston as he read this threw himself back on the sofa and gave way to a soft sigh. He knew he was doing his duty,—just as another man does who goes forth from his pleasant home to earn his bread and win his fortune in some dry, comfortless climate, far from the delights to which he has been always accustomed. He must do his duty. He could not live always adding a hundred or two of debt to the burden already round his neck. He must do his duty. As he thought of this he praised himself mightily. How beautiful was his far-away cousin, Imogene Docimer, as she would twist her head round so as to show the turn of her neck ! How delightful it would be to talk love to Imogene. As to marrying Imogene, who hadn't quite so many hundreds as himself, that he knew to be impossible. As for marriage, he wasn't quite sure that he wanted to marry any one. Marriage, to his thinking, was "a sort of grind," at the best. A man would have to get up and go to bed with some regularity. His wife might want him to come down in a frock coat to breakfast. His wife would certainly object to his drawing the back heads of other young women. Then he thought of the provocation he had received to draw Gertrude's back head. Gertrude hadn't got any turn of a neck to speak of. Gertrude was a stout, healthy girl ; and, having £120,000, was entitled to such a husband as himself. If he waited longer he might be driven to worse before he found the money which was so essentially necessary. He was grateful to Gertrude for not being worse, and was determined to treat her well. But as for love, romance, poetry, art,—all that must for the

future be out of the question. Of course, there would now be no difficulty with Sir Thomas, and therefore he must at once make up his
mind. He decided that morning, with many soft regrets, that he
would go to Glenbogie, and let those dreams of wanderings in the
mountains of the Tyrol pass away from him. "Dear, dearest Imogene!"
He could have loved Imogene dearly had fates been more propitious.
Then he got up and shook himself, made his resolution like a man, ate
a large allowance of curried salmon for his breakfast,—and then wrote
the following letter. "Duty first!" he said to himself as he sat down
to the table like a hero.

Letter No. 1.

"DEAR LADY TRINGLE,

"So many thanks! Nothing could suit my book so well as a few
days at Glenbogie just at the end of August. I will be there, like a
book, on the 20th. Of course I understand all that you say. Fathers
can't be expected to yield all at once, especially when suitors haven't
got very much of their own. I shouldn't have dared to ask hadn't I
known myself to be a most moderate man. Of course, I shall ask
again. If you will help me, no doubt I shall succeed. I really do
think that I am the man to make Gertrude happy.—Yours, dear Lady
Tringle, ever so much,   F. HOUSTON."

Letter No. 2.

"MY OWN ONE,

"Your governor is a brick. Of course, Glenbogie will be better than
the Tyrol, as you are to be there. Not but what the Tyrol is a very
jolly place, and we'll go and see it together some day. Ask Tom to let
me know whether one can wear heavy boots in the Glenbogie mountains. They are much the best for the heather; but I have shot generally in Yorkshire, and there they are too hot. What number does he
shoot with generally? I fancy the birds are wilder with you than
with us.

"As for riding, I don't dare to sit upon a horse this weather. Nobody but a woman can stand it. Indeed, now I think of it, I sold my
horse last week to pay the fellow I buy paints from. I've got the saddle
and bridle, and if I stick them up upon a rail, under the trees, it would
be better than any horse while the thermometer is near 80. All the
ladies could come round and talk to one so nicely.

"I hate lunch, because it makes me red in the face, and nobody will
give me my breakfast before eleven at the earliest. But I'll come in
about three as often as you like to have me. I think I perhaps shall
run over to the Tyrol after Glenbogie. A man must go somewhere

when he has been turned out in that fashion There are so many babies at Buncombe Hall!"—Buncombe Hall is the family seat of the Houstons,—"and I don't like to see my own fate typified before the time.

"Can I do anything for you except riding or eating lunch,—which are simply feminine exercises? Always your own FRANK."

Letter No. 3.

"DEAR COUSIN IM,

"How pleasant it is that a little strain of thin blood should make the use of that pretty name allowable! What a stupid world it is when the people who like each other best cannot get together because of proprieties, and marriages, and such balderdash as we call love. I do not in the least want to be in love with you,—but I do want to sit near you, and listen to you, and look at you, and to know that the whole air around is impregnated by the mysterious odour of your presence. When one is thoroughly satisfied with a woman there comes a scent as of sweet flowers, which does not reach the senses of those whose feelings are not so awakened.

"And now for my news! I suppose that G. T. will in a tremendously short period become Mistress F. H. 'A long day, my Lord.' But, if you are to be hung, better be hung at once. Père Tringle has not consented,—has done just the reverse,—has turned me out of his house, morally. That is, out of his London house. He asked of my 'house and my home,' as they did of Allan-a-Dale.

"Queen's Gate and Glenbogie stand fair on the hill.
"My home,' quoth bold Houston, 'shows gallanter still.
"'Tis the garret up three pair——

"Then he told me roughly to get me gone; but 'I had laughed on the lass with my bonny black eye.' So the next day I got an invite to Glenbogie, and at the appropriate time in August,

"She'll go to the mountains to hear a love tale,
"And the youth——

It will be told by is to be your poor unfortunate coz, Frank Houston. Who's going to whimper? Haven't I known all along what was to come? It has not been my lot in life to see a flower and pick it because I love it. But a good head of cabbage when you're hungry is wholesome food.—Your loving cousin, but not loving as he oughtn't to love,

"FRANK HOUSTON."

"I shall still make a dash for the Tyrol when this episode at Glenbogie is over.

CHAPTER XV.

AYALA WITH HER FRIENDS.

SOME few days after Lady Tringle had been at Kingsbury Crescent, two visitors, who knew little or nothing of each other, came to see Ayala. One was a lady and the other a gentleman, and the lady came first. The gentleman, however, arrived before the lady had gone. Mrs. Dosett was present while the lady remained ; but when the gentleman came she was invited to leave him alone with her niece,—as shall be told.

The lady was the Marchesa Baldoni. Can the reader go so far back as to remember the Marchesa Baldoni ? It was she who rather instigated Ayala to be naughty to the Tringles in Rome, and would have Ayala at her parties when she did not want the Tringles. The Marchesa was herself an Englishwoman, though she had lived at Rome all her life, and had married an Italian nobleman. She was now in London for a few weeks, and still bore in mind her friendship for Ayala, and a certain promise she had once made her. In Rome Lady Tringle, actuated by Augusta, who at the moment was very angry with everybody including her own lover, had quarrelled with the Marchesa. The Marchesa had then told Ayala that she, Ayala, must stay with her aunt,—must, in fact, cease for the time to come to the Marchesa's apartments, because of the quarrel ; but that a time would come in which they might again be friends. Soon afterwards the Marchesa had heard that the Tringle family had discarded poor Ayala,—that her own quarrel had, in fact, extended itself to Ayala, and that Ayala had been shunted off to a poor relation, far away from all the wealth and luxuries which she had been allowed to enjoy for so short a time. Therefore, soon after her arrival in London, the Marchesa had made herself acquainted with the address of the Dosetts, and now was in Kingsbury Crescent in fulfilment of her promise made at Rome.

" So now you have got our friend Ayala," said the Marchesa with a smile to Mrs. Dosett.

" Yes ; we have her now. There has been a change. Her sister, Lucy, has gone to my husband's sister, Lady Tringle."

The Marchesa made a pleasant little bow at each word. She seemed to Mrs. Dosett to be very gorgeously dressed. She was thoroughly well dressed, and looked like a Marchesa ;—or perhaps, even, like a Marchioness. She was a tall, handsome woman, with a smile perhaps a little too continuously sweet, but with a look conscious of her own position behind it. She had seen in a moment of what nature was Ayala, how charming, how attractive, how pretty, how clever,—how completely the very opposite of the Tringles ! Ayala learned Italian so readily that she could talk it almost at once. She could sing, and play, and draw. The Marchesa had been quite willing that her own daughter Nina should find a friend in Ayala. Then had come the quarrel. Now she was quite willing to renew the friendship, though Ayala's position was so sadly altered. Mrs. Dosett was almost frightened as the grand lady sat holding Ayala's hand, and patting it. "We used to know her so well in Rome ;—did we not, Ayala ?"

"You were very kind to me."

"Nina couldn't come, because her father would make her go with him to the pictures. But now, my dear, you must come to us just for a little time. We have a furnished house in Brook Street, near the park, till the end of the season, and we have one small spare room which will just do for you. I hope you will let her come to us, for we really are old friends," said the Marchesa, turning to Mrs. Dosett.

Mrs. Dosett looked black. There are people who always look black when such applications are made to them,—who look black at any allusions to pleasures. And then there came across her mind serious thoughts as to flowers and ribbons,—and then more serious thoughts as to boots, dresses, and hats. Ayala, no doubt, had come there less than six months since with good store of everything ; but Mrs. Dosett knew that such a house as would be that of this lady would require a girl to show herself with the newest sheen on everything. And Ayala knew it too. The Marchesa turned from the blackness of Mrs. Dosett's face with her sweetest smile to Ayala. " Can't we manage it ?" said the Marchesa.

"I don't think we can," said Ayala, with a deep sigh.

"And why not ?"

Ayala looked furtively round to her aunt. "I suppose I may tell, Aunt Margaret," she said.

"You may tell everything, my dear," said Mrs. Dosett.

"Because we are poor," said Ayala.

"What does that matter?" said the Marchesa, brightening up. "We want you because you are rich in good gifts and pretty ways."

"But I can't get new frocks now as I used to do in Rome. Aunt Emmeline was cruel to me, and said things which I could not bear. But they let me have everything. Uncle Reginald gives me all that he has, and I am much happier here. But we cannot go out and buy things,—can we, Aunt Margaret?"

"No, my dear ; we cannot."

"It does not signify," said the Marchesa. " We are quite quiet, and what you have got will do very well. Frocks ! The frocks you had in Rome are good enough for London. I won't have a word of all that. Nina has set her heart upon it, and so has my husband, and so have I.

Mrs. Dosett, when we are at home we are the most homely people in the world. We think nothing of dressing. Not to come and see your old friends because of your frocks! We shall send for you the day after to-morrow. Don't you know, Mrs. Dosett, it will do her good to be with her young friend for a few days." Mrs. Dosett had not succeeded in her remonstrances when Sir Thomas Tringle was shown into the room, and then the Marchesa took her leave. For Sir Thomas Tringle was the other visitor who came on that morning to see Ayala.

"If you wouldn't mind, Mrs. Dosett," said Sir Thomas before he sat down, "I should like to see Ayala alone." Mrs. Dosett had not a word to say against such a request, and at once took her leave.

"My dear," he began, coming and sitting opposite to Ayala, with his knees almost touching her, " I have got something very particular to say to you." Ayala was at once much frightened. Her uncle had never before spoken to her in this way,—had never in truth said a word to her seriously. He had always been kind to her, making her presents, and allowing himself to be kissed graciously morning and evening. He had never scolded her, and, better than all, had never said a word to her, one way or the other, about Tom. She had always liked her uncle, because he had never caused her trouble when all the others in his house had been troublesome to her. But now she was afraid of him. He did not frown, but he looked very seriously at her, as he might look, perhaps, when he was counting out all his millions in Lombard Street. "I hope you think that I have always wished to be kind to you, Ayala."

"I am sure you have, Uncle Tom."

"When you had come to us I always wished you to stay. I don't like changes of this sort. I suppose you didn't hit it off with Augusta. But she's gone, now."

"Aunt Emmeline said something." That accusation, as to "encouragement," so rankled in her heart, that when she looked back at her grievances among the Tringles that always loomed the largest.

"I don't want to hear anything about it," said Sir Thomas. "Let bygones be bygones. Your aunt, I am sure, never meant unkindly by you. Now, I want you to listen to me."

"I will, Uncle Tom."

"Listen to me to the end, like a good girl."

"I will."

"Your Cousin Tom——." Ayala gave a visible shudder, and uttered an audible groan, but as yet she did not say a word. Sir Thomas, having seen the shudder, and heard the groan, did frown as he began again. "Your Cousin Tom is most truly attached to you."

"Why won't he leave me alone, then?"

" Ayala, you promised to listen to me without speaking."

" I will, Uncle Tom. Only——"

" Listen to me, and then I will hear anything you have to say."

" I will," said Ayala, screwing up her lips, so that no words should come out of them, let the provocation be what it might.

Sir Thomas began again. " Your Cousin Tom is most truly attached to you. For some time I and his mother disapproved of this. We thought you were both too young, and there were other reasons which I need not now mention. But when I came to see how thoroughly he was in earnest, how he put his heart into it, how the very fact that he loved you had made a man of him; then how the fact that you would not return his love, unmanned him,—when I saw all that, I gave my permission." Here he paused, almost as though expecting a word ; but Ayala gave an additional turn to the screw on her lips, and remained quite silent. " Yes ; we gave our permission,—I and your aunt. Of course, our son's happiness is all in all to us ; and I do believe that you are so good that you would make him a good wife."

" But——"

" Listen till I have done, Ayala." Then there was another squeeze. " I suppose you are what they call romantic. Romance, my dear, won't buy bread and butter. Tom is a very good young man, and he loves you most dearly. If you will consent to be his I will make a rich man of him. He will then be a respectable man of business, and will become a partner in the house. You and he can choose a place to live in almost where you please. You can have your own establishment and your carriage, and will be able to do a deal of good. You will make him happy, and you will be my dear child. I have come here to tell you that I will make you welcome into the family, and to promise that I will do everything I can to make you happy. Now you may say what you like ; but, Ayala, think a little before you speak."

Ayala thought a little ;—not as to what she should say, but as to the words in which she might say it. She was conscious that a great compliment was paid to her. And there was a certain pride in her heart as she thought that this invitation into the family had come to her after that ignominious accusation of encouragement had been made. Augusta had snubbed her about Tom, and her aunt ; but now she was asked to come among them, and be one of them, with full observances. She was aware of all this, and aware, also, that such treatment required from her a gracious return. But not on that account could she give herself to the Beast. Not on that account could she be untrue to her image. Not on that account could she rob her bosom of that idea of love which was seated there. Not on that account could she look upon the marriage proposed to her with aught but a shuddering abhorrence. She sat silent for a minute or two, while her heavy eyes were fixed upon his. Then, falling on her knees before him, she put up her little hands to pray to him. " Uncle Tom, I can't," she said. And then the tears came running down her cheeks.

" Why can't you, Ayala ? Why cannot you be sensible, as other girls are ?" said Sir Thomas, lifting her up, and putting her on his knee.

" I can't," she said. " I don't know how to tell you."

" Do you love some other man ?"

" No ; no ; no !" To Uncle Tom, at any rate, she need say nothing of the image.

" Then why is it ?"

" Because I can't. I don't know what I say, but I can't. I know how very, very, very good you are."

" I would love you as my daughter."

" But I can't, Uncle Tom. Pray tell him, and make him get somebody else. He would be quite happy if he could get somebody else."

" It is you that he loves."

" But what's the use of it, when I can't ? Dear, dear Uncle Tom, do have it all settled for me. Nothing on earth could ever make me do it. I should die if I were to try."

" That's nonsense."

" I do so want not to make you angry, Uncle Tom. And I do so wish he would be happy with someone else. Nobody ought to be made to marry unless they like it ;—ought they ?"

" There is no talk of making," said Sir Thomas, frowning.

" At any rate I can't," said Ayala, releasing herself from her uncle's embrace.

It was in vain that even after this he continued his request, begging her to come down to Glenbogie, so that she might make herself used to Tom and his ways. If she could only once more, he thought, be introduced to the luxuries of a rich house, then she would give way. Bu she would not go to Glenbogie ; she would not go to Merle Park ; she would not consent to see Tom anywhere. Her uncle told her that she was romantic and foolish, endeavouring to explain to her over and over again that the good things of the world were too good to be thrown away for a dream. At last there was a touch of dignity in the final repetition of her refusal. " I am sorry to make you angry, but I can't, Uncle Tom." Then he frowned with all his power of frowning, and, taking his hat, left the room and the house almost without a word.

At the time fixed the Marchesa's carriage came, and Ayala with her boxes was taken away to Brook Street. Uncle Reginald had offered

to do something for her in the way of buying a frock, but this she
refused, declaring that she would not allow herself to become an
expense merely because her friends in Rome had been kind to her. So
she had packed up the best of what she had and started, with her heart
in her mouth, fearing the grandeur of the Marchesa's house. On her
arrival she was received by Nina, who at once threw herself into all
her old intimacy. "Oh, Ayala," she said, "this is so nice to have you
again. I have been looking forward to this ever since we left Rome."

"Yes," said Ayala, "it is nice."

"But why did you tell mamma you would not come? What non
sense to talk to her about frocks. Why not come and tell me? You
used to have everything at Rome, much more than I had."

Then Ayala began to explain the great difference between Uncle
Tom and Uncle Reginald,—how Uncle Tom had so many thousands
that nobody could count them, how Uncle Reginald was so shorn in his
hundreds that there was hardly enough to supply the necessaries of life.
"You see," she said, "when papa died Lucy and I were divided. I
got the rich uncle, and Lucy got the poor one; but I made myself disagreeable, and didn't suit, and so we have been changed."

"But why did you make yourself disagreeable?" said Nina, opening
her eyes. "I remember when we were at Rome your cousin Augusta
was always quarreling with you. I never quite knew what it was all
about."

"It wasn't only that," said Ayala, whispering.

"Did you do anything very bad?"

Then it occurred to Ayala that she might tell the whole story to her
friend, and she told it. She explained the nature of that great persecution as to Tom. "And that was the real reason why we were
changed," said Ayala, as she completed her story.

"I remember seeing the young man," said Nina.

"He is such a lout."

"But was he very much in love?" asked Nina.

"Well, I don't know. I suppose he was after his way. I don't
think louts like that can be very much in love to signify. Young men
when they look like that would do with one girl as well as another."

"I don't see that at all," said Nina.

"I am sure he would if he'd only try. At any rate what's the good
of his going on? They can't make a girl marry unless she chooses."

"Won't he be rich?"

"Awfully rich," said Ayala.

"Then I should think about it again," said the young lady from
Rome.

"Never." said Ayala, with an impressive whisper. "I will neve think about it again. If he were made of diamonds I would not think about it again."

"And is that why you were changed?" said Nina.

"Well, yes. No; it is very hard to explain. Aunt Emmeline told me that—that I encouraged him. I thought I should have rushed out of the house when she said that. Then I had to be changed. I don't know whether they could forgive me, but I could not forgive her."

"And how is it now?"

"It is different now," said Ayala, softly. "Only that it can't make any real difference."

"How different?"

"They'd let me come if I would, I suppose; but I shall never, never go to them any more."

"I suppose you won't tell me everything?" said Nina, after a pause.

"What everything!"

"You won't be angry if I ask?"

"No, I will not be angry."

"I suppose there is someone else you really care for?"

"There is no one," said Ayala, escaping a little from her friend's embrace.

"Then why should you be so determined against that poor young man?"

"Because he is a lout and a beast," said Ayala, jumping up. "I wonder you should ask me;—as if that had anything to do with it. Would you fall in love with a lout because you had no one else? I would rather live for ever all alone, even in Kingsbury Crescent, than have to think of becoming the wife of my cousin Tom." At this Nina shrugged her shoulders, showing that her education in Italy had been less romantic than that accorded to Ayala in London.

CHAPTER XVI.

JONATHAN STUBBS.

But, though Nina differed somewhat from Ayala as to their ideas as to life in general, they were close friends, and everything was done both by the Marchesa and by her daughter to make Ayala happy. There was not very much of going into grand society, and that difficulty about the dresses solved itself, as do other difficulties. There came a few presents, with entreaties from Ayala that presents of that kind might not be made. But the presents were of course accepted, and our girl was as prettily arrayed, if not as richly, as the best around her. At first here was an evening at the opera, and then a theatre,—diversions which are easy. Ayala, after her six dull months in Kingsbury Crescent, found herself well pleased to be taken to easy amusements. The carriage in the park was delightful to her, and delightful a visit which was made to her by Lucy. For the Tringle carriage could be spared for a visit in Brook Street, even though there was still a remembrance in the bosom of Aunt Emmeline of the evil things which had been done by the Marchesa in Rome. Then there came a dance,— which was not so easy. The Marchesa and Nina were going to a dance at Lady Putney's, and arrangements were made that Ayala should be taken. Ayala begged that there might be no arrangements, declared that she would be quite happy to see Nina go forth in her finery. But the Marchesa was a woman who always had her way, and Ayala was taken to Lady Putney's dance without a suspicion on the part of any who saw her that her ball-room apparatus was not all that it ought to be.

Ayala when she entered the room was certainly a little bashful. When in Rome, even in the old days at the bijou, when she did not consider herself to be quite out, she had not been at all bashful. She had been able to enjoy herself entirely, being very fond of dancing, conscious that she could dance well, and always having plenty to say for herself. But now there had settled upon her something of the tedium, something of the silence, of Kingsbury Crescent, and she almost felt that she would not know how to behave herself if she were asked to stand up and dance before all Lady Putney's world. In her first attempt she certainly was not successful. An elderly gentleman was brought up to her,—a gentleman whom she afterwards declared to be a hundred, and who was, in truth, over forty, and with him she manœuvred gently through a quadrille. He asked her two or three questions to which she was able to answer only in monosyllables. Then he ceased his questions, and the manœuvres were carried on in perfect silence. Poor Ayala did not attribute any blame to the man. It was all because she had been six months in Kingsbury Crescent. Of course this aged gentleman, if he wanted to dance, would have a partner chosen for him out of Kingsbury Crescent. Conversation was not to be expected from a gentleman who was made to stand up with Kingsbury Crescent. Any powers of talking that had ever belonged to herself had of course evaporated amidst the gloom of Kingsbury Crescent. After this she was returned speedily to the wings of the Marchesa, and during the next dance sat in undisturbed peace. Then suddenly, when the Marchesa had for a moment left her, and when Nina had just been taken away to join a set, she saw the man of silence coming to her from a distance, with an evident intention of asking her to stand up again. It was in his eye, in his toe, as he came bowing forward. He had

evidently learned to suppose that they two outcasts might lessen their
miseries by joining them together. She was to dance with him because
no one else would ask her! She had plucked up her spirit and
resolved that, desolate as she might be, she would not descend so far as
that, when, in a moment, another gentleman sprang in, as it were,
between her and her enemy, and addressed her with free and easy
speech as though he had known her all her life. "You are Ayala Dormer I am sure," said he. She looked up into his face and nodded her
head at him in her own peculiar way. She was quite sure that she had
never set her eyes on him before. He was so ugly that she could not
have forgotten him. So at least she told herself. He was very, very
ugly, but his voice was very pleasant. "I knew you were, and I am
Jonathan Stubbs. So now we are introduced, and you are to come and
dance with me."

She had heard the name of Jonathan Stubbs. She was sure of that,
although she could not at the moment join any facts with the name.
"But I don't know you," she said, hesitating. Though he was so ugly
he could not but be better than that ancient dancer whom she saw
standing at a distance, looking like a dog that has been deprived of his
bone.

"Yes, you do," said Jonathan Stubbs, "and if you'll come and
dance I'll tell you about it. The Marchesa told me to take you."

"Did she?" said Ayala, getting up, and putting her little hand upon
his arm.

"I'll go and fetch her if you like; only she's a long way off, and we
shall lose our place. She's my aunt."

"Oh," said Ayala, quite satisfied,—remembering now that she had
heard her friend Nina boast of a Colonel cousin, who was supposed to
be the youngest Colonel in the British army, who had done some wonderful thing,—taken a new province in India, or marched across Africa,
or defended the Turks,—or perhaps conquered them. She knew that
he was very brave,—but why was he so very ugly? His hair was ruby
red, and very short; and he had a thick red beard, not silky, but
bristly, with each bristle almost a dagger,—and his mouth was enormous. His eyes were very bright, and there was a smile about him,
partly of fun, partly of good humour. But his mouth! And then
that bristling beard! Ayala was half inclined to like him, because he
was so completely master of himself, so unlike the unhappy ancient
gentleman who was still hovering at a distance. But why was he so
ugly? And why was he called Jonathan Stubbs?

"There now," he said, "we can't get in at any of the sets. That's
your fault."

"No it isn't" said Ayala

" Yes, it is. You wouldn't stand up till you had heard all about me."

" I don't know anything about you now."

" Then come and walk about and I'll tell you. Then we shall be ready for a waltz. Do you waltz well ?"

" Do you ?"

" I'll back myself against any Englishman, Frenchman, German, or Italian, for a large sum of money. I can't come quite up to the Poles. The fact is, the honester the man is the worse he always dances. Yes ; I see what you mean. I must be a rogue. Perhaps I am ;—perhaps I'm only an exception. I knew your father."

" Papa !"

" Yes, I did. He was down at Stalham with the Alburys once. That was five years ago, and he told me he had a daughter named Ayala. I didn't quite believe him."

" Why not ?"

" It's such an out-of-the-way name."

" It's as good as Jonathan, at any rate." And Ayala again nodded her head.

" There's a prejudice about Jonathan, as there is about Jacob and Jonah. I never could quite tell why. I was going to marry a girl once with a hundred thousand pounds, and she wouldn't have me at last because she couldn't bring her lips to say Jonathan. Do you think she was right ?"

" Did she love you ?" said Ayala, looking up into his face.

" Awfully ! But she couldn't bear the name ; so within three months she gave herself and all her money to Mr. Montgomery Talbot de Montpellier. He got drunk, and threw her out of the window before a month was over. That's what comes of going in for sweet names."

" I don't believe a word of it," said Ayala.

" Very well. Didn't Septimus Traffick marry your cousin ?"

" Of course he did, about a month ago."

" He is another friend of mine. Why didn't you go to your cousin's marriage ?"

" There were reasons," said Ayala.

" I know all about it," said the Colonel. " You quarreled with Augusta down in Scotland, and you don't like poor Traffick because he has got a bald head."

" I believe you're a conjuror," said Ayala.

" And then your cousin was jealous because you went to the top of St. Peter's, and because you would walk with Mr. Traffick on the Pincian. I was in Rome, and saw all about it."

" I won't have anything more to do with you," said Ayala.

"And then you quarreled with one set of uncles and aunts, and now you live with another."

"Your aunt told you that."

"And I know your cousin, Tom Tringle."

"You know Tom?" asked Ayala.

"Yes ; he was ever so good to me in Rome about a horse ! I like Tom Tringle in spite of his chains. Don't you think, upon the whole, if that young lady had put up with Jonathan she would have done better than marry Montpellier? But, now they're going to waltz, come along."

Thereupon Ayala got up and danced with him for the next ten minutes. Again and again before the evening was over she danced with him ; and although, in the course of the night, many other partners had offered themselves, and many had been accepted, she felt that Colonel Jonathan Stubbs had certainly been the partner of the evening. Why should he be so hideously ugly? said Ayala to herself, as she wished him good night before she left the room with the Marchesa and Nina.

"What do you think of my nephew ?" said the Marchesa, when they were in the carriage together.

"Do tell us what you think of Jonathan ?" asked Nina.

"I thought he was very good-natured."

"And very handsome ?"

"Nina, don't be foolish. Jonathan is one of the most rising officers in the British service, and luckily he can be that without being beautiful to look at."

"I declare," said Nina, "sometimes, when he is talking, I think him perfectly lovely. The fire comes out of his eyes, and he rubs his old red hairs about till they sparkle. Then he shines all over like a carbuncle, and every word he says makes me die of laughter."

"I laughed too," said Ayala.

"But you didn't think him beautiful," said Nina.

"No, I did not," said Ayala. "I liked him very much, but I thought him very ugly. Was it true about the young lady who married Mr. Montgomery de Montpellier and was thrown out of window a week afterwards ?"

"There is one other thing I must tell you about Jonathan," said Nina. "You must not believe a word that he says."

"That I deny," said the Marchesa ; "but here we are. And now, girls, get out of the carriage and go up to bed at once."

Ayala, before she went to sleep, and again when she woke in the morning, thought a great deal about her new friend. As to shining like a carbuncle,—perhaps he did, but that was not her idea of manly beauty. And hair ought not to sparkle. She was sure that Colonel

Stubbs was very, very ugly. She was almost disposed to think that he was the ugliest man she had ever seen. He certainly was a great deal worse than her cousin Tom, who, after all, was not particularly ugly. But, nevertheless, she would very much rather dance with Colonel Stubbs. She was sure of that, even without reference to Tom's objectionable love-making. Upon the whole she liked dancing with Colonel Stubbs, ugly as he was. Indeed, she liked him very much. She had spent a very pleasant evening because he had been there. "It all depends upon whether anyone has anything to say." That was the determination to which she came when she endeavoured to explain to herself how it had come to pass that she had liked dancing with anybody so very hideous. The Angel of Light would of course have plenty to say for himself, and would be something altogether different in appearance. He would be handsome,—or rather, intensely interesting, and his talk would be of other things. He would not say of himself that he danced as well as though he were a rogue, or declare that a lady had been thrown out of a window the week after she was married. Nothing could be more unlike an Angel of Light than Colonel Stubbs, —unless, perhaps, it were Tom Tringle. Colonel Stubbs, however, was completely unangelic,—so much so that the marvel was that he should yet be so pleasant. She had no horror of Colonel Stubbs at all. She would go anywhere with Colonel Stubbs, and feel herself to be quite safe. She hoped she might meet him again very often. He was, as it were, the Genius of Comedy, without a touch of which life would be very dull. But the Angel of Light must have something tragic in his composition,—must verge, at any rate, on tragedy. Ayala did not know that beautiful description of a " Sallow, sublime, sort of Werther-faced man," but I fear that in creating her Angel of Light she drew a picture in her imagination of a man of that kind.

Days went on, till the last day of Ayala's visit had come, and it was necessary that she should go back to Kingsbury Crescent. It was now August, and everybody was leaving town. The Marchesa and Nina were going to their relations, the Alburys, at Stalham, and could not, of course, take Ayala with them. The Dosetts would remain in town for another month, with a distant hope of being able to run down to Pegwell Bay for a fortnight in September. But even that had not yet been promised. Colonel Stubbs had been more than once at the house in Brook Street, and Ayala had come to know him almost as she might some great tame dog. It was now the afternoon of the last day, and she was sorry because she would not be able to see him again. She was to be taken to the theatre that night,—and then to Kingsbury Crescent and the realms of Lethe early on the following morning.

It was very hot, and they were sitting with the shutters nearly closed, having resolved not to go out, in order that they might be ready for the theatre—when the door was opened and Tom Tringle was announced. Tom Tringle had come to call on his cousin.

"Lady Baldoni," he said, "I hope you won't think me intrusive, but I thought I'd come and see my cousin once while she is staying here." The Marchesa bowed, and assured him that he was very welcome. "It's tremendously hot," said Tom.

"Very hot, indeed," said the Marchesa.

"I don't think it's ever so hot as this in Rome," said Nina, fanning herself.

"I find it quite impossible to walk a yard," said Tom, "and therefore I've hired a Hansom cab all to myself. The man goes home and changes his horse regularly when I go to dinner ; then he comes for me at ten, and sticks to me till I go to bed. I call that a very good plan." Nina asked him why he didn't drive the cab himself. "That would be a grind," said he, "because it would be so hot all day, and there might be rain at night. Have you read what my brother-in-law, Traffick, said in the House last night, my Lady?"

"I'm afraid I passed it over," said the Marchesa. "Indeed, I am not very good at the debates."

"They are dull," said Tom, "but when it's one's brother-in-law, one does like to look at it. I thought he made that very clear about the malt tax." The Marchesa smiled and bowed.

"What is—malt tax?" asked Nina.

"Well, it means beer," said Tom. "The question is whether the poor man pays it who drinks the beer, or the farmer who grows the malt. It is very interesting when you come to think of it."

"But I fear I never have come to think of it," said the Marchesa.

During all this time Ayala never said a word, but sat looking at her cousin, and remembering how much better Colonel Jonathan Stubbs would have talked if he had been there. Then, after a pause, Tom got up, and took his leave, having to content himself with simply squeezing his cousin's hand as he left the room.

"He is a lout," said Ayala, as soon as she knew that the door was closed behind him.

"I don't see anything loutish at all," said the Marchesa.

"He's just like most other young men," said Nina.

"He's not at all like Colonel Stubbs," said Ayala.

Then the Marchesa preached a little sermon. "Colonel Stubbs, my dear," she said, "happens to have been thrown a good deal about the world, and has thus been able to pick up that easy mode of talking which young ladies like, perhaps because it means nothing. Your cousin is a man of business, and will probably have amassed a large fortune when my poor nephew will be a do-nothing old general on half-pay. His chatter will not then have availed him quite so much as your cousin's habits of business."

"Mamma," said Nina, "Jonathan will have money of his own."

"Never mind, my dear. I do not like to hear a young man called a lout because he's more like a man of business than a man of pleasure." Ayala felt herself to be snubbed, but was not a whit the less sure that Tom was a lout, and the Colonel an agreeable partner to dance with. But at the same time she remembered that neither the one nor the other was to be spoken of in the same breath, or thought of in the same spirit, as the Angel of Light.

When they were dressed, and just going to dinner, the ugly man with the red head was announced, and declared his purpose of going with them to the theatre. "I've been to the office," said he, "and got a stall next to yours, and have managed it all. It now only remains that you should give me some dinner and a seat in the carriage." Of course he was told that there was no dinner sufficient for a man to eat; but he put up with a feminine repast, and spent the whole of the evening sitting next to his aunt, on a back tier, while the two girls were placed in front. In this way, leaning forward, with his ugly head between them, he acted as a running chorus to the play during the whole performance. Ayala thoroughly enjoyed herself, and thought that in all her experience no play she'd seen had ever been so delightful. On their return home the two girls were both told to go to bed in the Marchesa's good-natured authoritative tone; but, nevertheless, Ayala did manage to say a word before she finally adjusted herself on her pillow. "It is all very well, Nina, for your mamma to say that a young man of business is the best; but I do know a lout when I see him; and I am quite sure that my cousin Tom is a lout, and that Colonel Jonathan is not."

"I believe you are falling in love with Colonel Jonathan," said Nina.

"I should as soon think of falling in love with a wild bear;—but he's not a lout, and therefore I like him."

CHAPTER XVII.

LUCY IS VERY FIRM.

It was just before the Tringles had returned from Rome, during the winter, that Lucy Dormer had met Mr. Hamel in Kensington Gardens for the second time, had walked there with him perhaps for half an hour, and had then returned home with a conviction that she had done a wicked thing. But she had other convictions also, which were perhaps stronger. "Now that we have met, am I to lose you again?" he had said. What could he mean by losing, except that she was the one thing which he desired to find? But she had not seen him since, or heard a word of his whereabouts, although, as she so well remembered, she had given him an address at her Aunt Emmeline's,—not knowing then that it would be her fate to become a resident in her Aunt Emmeline's house. She had told him that Ayala would live there, and that perhaps she might sometimes be found visiting Ayala. Now, she was herself filling Ayala's place, and might so easily have been found. But she knew nothing of the man who had once asked whether he was "to lose her again."

Her own feelings about Isadore Hamel were clear enough to herself now. Ayala in her hot humour had asked her whether she could give her hand and her heart to such a one as their cousin Tom, and she had found herself constrained to say that she could not do so, because she was not free,—not quite free,—to do as she pleased with her hand and her heart. She had striven hard not to acknowledge anything, even to Ayala,—even to herself. But the words had been forced from her, and now she was conscious, terribly conscious, that the words were true. There could be no one else now, whether Tom or another,—whether such as Tom or such as any other. It was just that little word that had won her. "Am I to lose you again?" A girl loves most often because she is loved,—not from choice on her part. She is won by the flattery of the man's desire. "Am I to lose you again?" He had seemed to throw all his soul into his voice and into his eyes as he had asked the question. A sudden thrill had filled her, and, for his sake, —for his sake,—she had hoped that she might not be lost to him. Now she began to fear that he was lost to her.

Something has been told of the relations between Isadore Hamel and his father. They were both sculptors, the father having become a successful artist. The father was liberal, but he was essentially autocratic, If he supplied to his son the means of living,—and he was willing to supply the means of very comfortable life,—he expected that his son should live to some extent in accordance with his fancies. The father wished his son to live in Rome, and to live after the manner of Romans. Isadore would prefer to live in London, and after the manner of Londoners. For a time he had been allowed to do so, and had achieved a moderate success. But a young artist may achieve a moderate success with a pecuniary result that shall be almost less than moderate. After a while the sculptor in Rome had told his son that if he intended to remain in London he ought to do so on the independent proceeds of his own profession. Isadore, if he would return to Rome, would be made welcome to join his affairs to those of his father. In other words, he was to be turned adrift if he remained in London, and petted with every luxury if he would consent to follow his art in Italy. But in Rome the father lived after a fashion which was distasteful to the son. Old Mr. Hamel had repudiated all conventions. Conventions are apt to go very quickly, one after another, when the first has been thrown aside. The man who ceases to dress for dinner soon finds it to be a trouble to wash his hands. A house is a bore. Calling is a bore. Church is a great bore. A family is a bore. A wife is an unendurable bore. All laws are bores, except those by which inferiors can be constrained to do their work. Mr. Hamel had got rid of a great many bores, and had a strong opinion that bores prevailed more mightily in London than in Rome. Isadore was not a bore to him. He was always willing to have Isadore near to him. But if Isadore chose to enter the conventional mode of life he must do it at his own expense. It may be said at once that Isadore's present view of life was very much influenced by Lucy Dormer, and by a feeling that she certainly was conventional. A small house, very prettily furnished, somewhat near the Fulham Road, or perhaps verging a little towards South Kensington, with two maids, and perhaps an additional one as nurse in the process of some months, with a pleasant English breakfast and a pleasant English teapot in the evening, afforded certainly a very conventional aspect of life. But, at the present moment, it was his aspect, and therefore he could not go upon all fours with his father. In this state of things there had, during the last twelvemonth, been more than one journey made to Rome and back. Ayala had seen him at Rome, and Lady Tringle, remembering that the man had been intimate with her brother, was afraid of him. They had made inquiry about him, and had fully resolved that he should not be allowed into the house if he came after Ayala. He had no mother,—to speak of ; and he had little brothers and sisters, who also had no mother,—to speak of. Mr. Hamel, the father, entertained friends on Sunday, with the express object of playing cards. That a Papist should do so was to be borne ;—but Mr. Hamel was not a Papist, and, therefore, would certainly be ——. All this and much more had been learned at Rome, and therefore Lucy, though she herself never mentioned Mr. Hamel's name in Queen's Gate, heard evil things said of the man who was so dear to her.

It was the custom of her life to be driven out every day with her aunt and Gertrude. Not to be taken two or three times round the park would be to Lady Tringle to rob her of the best appreciated of all those gifts of fortune which had come to her by reason of the banker's wealth. It was a stern law ;—and as stern a law that Lucy should accompany

I

her. Gertrude, as being an absolute daughter of the house, and as having an almost acknowledged lover of her own, was allowed some choice.
But for Lucy there was no alternative. Why should she not go and be
driven? Two days before they left town she was being driven, while
her aunt was sitting almost in a slumber beside her, when suddenly a
young man, leaning over the railings, took off his hat so close to Lucy
that she could almost have put out her hand to him. He was standing
there all alone, and seemed simply to be watching the carriages as they
passed. She felt that she blushed as she bowed to him, and saw also
that the colour had risen to his face. Then she turned gently round
to her aunt, whom she hoped to find still sleeping; but Aunt Emmeline
could slumber with one eye open. "Who was that young man, my
dear?" said Aunt Emmeline.

"It was Mr. Hamel."

"Mr. Isadore Hamel!" said Aunt Emmeline, horrified. "Is that
the young man at Rome who has got the horrible father?"

"I do not know his father," said Lucy; "but he does live at Rome."

"Of course, it's the Mr. Hamel I mean. He scraped some acquaintance with Ayala, but I would not have it for a moment. He is not at
all the sort of person any young girl ought to know. His father is a
horrible man. I hope he is no friend of yours, Lucy!"

"He is a friend of mine." Lucy said this in a tone of voice which
was very seldom heard from her, but which, when heard, was evidence
that beneath the softness of her general manner there lay a will of her
own.

"Then, my dear, I hope that such friendship may be discontinued
as long as you remain with us."

"He was a friend of papa's," said Lucy.

"That's all very well. I suppose artists must know artists, even
though they are disreputable."

"Mr. Hamel is not disreputable."

Aunt Emmeline, as she heard this, could almost fancy that she was
renewing one of her difficulties with Ayala. "My dear," she said,—
and she intended to be very impressive as she spoke,—"in a matter
such as this I must beg you to be guided by me. You must acknowledge that I know the world better than you do. Mr. Hamel is not a
fit person to be acquainted with a young lady who occupies the place
of my daughter. I am sure that will be sufficient." Then she leant
back in the carriage, and seemed again to slumber; but she still had
one eye open, so that if Mr. Hamel should appear again at any corner
and venture to raise his hand she might be aware of the impropriety.
But on that day Mr. Hamel did not appear again.

Lucy did not speak another word during the drive, and on reaching the house went at once to her bed-room. While she had been out with her aunt close to her, and while it had been possible that the man she loved should appear again, she had been unable to collect her thoughts or to make up her mind what she would do or say. One thing simply was certain to her, that if Mr. Hamel should present himself again to her she would not desert him. All that her aunt had said to her as to improprieties and the like had no effect at all upon her. The man had been welcomed at her father's house, had been allowed there to be intimate with her, and was now, as she was well aware, much dearer to her than any other human being. Not for all the Aunt Emmelines in the world would she regard him otherwise than as her dearest friend.

When she was alone she discussed the matter with herself. It was repugnant to her that there should be any secret on the subject between herself and her aunt after what had been said,—much more that there should be any deceit. "Mr. Hamel is not fit to be acquainted with a lady who occupies the position of my daughter." It was thus that her aunt had spoken. To this the proper answer seemed to be,—seemed at least to Lucy,—"In that case, my dear aunt, I cannot for a moment longer occupy the position of your daughter, as I certainly am acquainted and shall remain acquainted with Mr. Hamel." But to such speech as this on her own part there were two impediments. In the first place it would imply that Mr. Hamel was her lover,—for implying which Mr. Hamel had given her no authority; and then what should she immediately do when she had thus obstinately declared herself to be unfit for that daughter's position which she was supposed now to occupy? With all her firmness of determination she could not bring herself to tell her aunt that Mr. Hamel was her lover. Not because it was not as yet true. She would have been quite willing that her aunt should know the exact truth, if the exact truth could be explained. But how could she convey to such a one as Aunt Emmeline the meaning of those words,—"Am I to lose you again?" How could she make her aunt understand that she held herself to be absolutely bound, as by a marriage vow, by such words as those,—words in which there was no promise, even had they come from some fitting suitor, but which would be regarded by Aunt Emmeline as being simply impertinent coming as they did from such a one as Isadore Hamel. It was quite out of the question to tell all that to Aunt Emmeline, but yet it was necessary that something should be told. She had been ordered to drop her acquaintance with Isadore, and it was essential that she should declare that she would do nothing of the kind. She would not recognise such obedience as a duty on her part. The friendship had been created by her father, to whom her

earlier obedience had been due.   It might be that, refusing to render
such obedience, her aunt and her uncle might tell her that there could
be no longer shelter for her in that house.   They could not cherish and
foster a disobedient child.   If it must be so, it must.   Though there
should be no home left to her in all the wide world she would not
accept an order which should separate her from the man she loved.
She must simply tell her aunt that she could not drop Mr. Hamel's
acquaintance,—because Mr. Hamel was a friend.

Early on the next morning she did so.   "Are you aware," said
Aunt Emmeline, with a severe face, "that he is—illegitimate."   Lucy
blushed, but made no answer.   "Is he—is he—engaged to you?"

"No," said Lucy, sharply.

"Has he asked you to marry him?"

"No," said Lucy.

"Then what is it?" asked Lady Tringle, in a tone which was
intended to signify that as nothing of that kind had taken place such a
friendship could be a matter of no consequence.

"He was papa's friend."

"My dear, what can that matter?   Your poor papa has gone, and
you are in my charge and your uncle's.   Surely you cannot object to
choose your friends as we should wish.   Mr. Hamel is a gentleman of
whom we do not approve.   You cannot have seen very much of him,
and it would be very easy for you, should he bow to you again in the
park, to let him see that you do not like it."

"But I do like it," said Lucy, with energy.

"Lucy!"

"I do like to see Mr. Hamel, and I feel almost sure that he will
come and call here now that he has seen me.   Last winter he asked
me my address, and I gave him this house."

"When you were living with your Aunt Dosett?"

"Yes, I did, Aunt Emmeline.   I thought Aunt Margaret would not
like him to come to Kingsbury Crescent, and, as Ayala was to be here,
I told him he might call at Queen's Gate."

Then Lady Tringle was really angry.   It was not only that her
house should have been selected for so improper a use but that Lucy
should have shown a fear and a respect for Mrs. Dosett which had not
been accorded to herself.   It was shocking to her pride that that
should have appeared to be easy of achievement at Queen's Gate which
was too wicked to be attempted at Kingsbury Crescent.   And then the
thing which had been done seemed in itself to her to be so horrible!
This girl, when living under the care of her aunt, had made an appointment with an improper young man at the house of another aunt!   Any
appointment made by a young lady with a young man must, as she

thought, be wrong. She began to be aghast at the very nature of the girl who could do such a thing, and on reflecting that that girl was at present under her charge as an adopted daughter. "Lucy," she said, very impressively, "there must be an end of this."

"There cannot be an end of it," said Lucy.

"Do you mean to say that he is to come here to this house whether I and your uncle like it or not?"

"He will come," said Lucy; "I am sure he will come. Now he has seen me he will come at once."

"Why should he do that if he is not your lover?"

"Because," said Lucy,—and then she paused; "because——. It is very hard to tell you, Aunt Emmeline."

"Why should he come so quickly?" demanded Aunt Emmeline, again.

"Because——. Though he has said nothing to me such as that you mean," stammered out Lucy, determined to tell the whole truth, "I believe that he will."

"And you?"

"If he did I should accept him."

"Has he any means?"

"I do not know."

"Have you any?"

"Certainly not."

"And you would consent to be his wife after what I've told you?"

"Yes," said Lucy, "I should."

"Then it must not be in this house. That is all. I will not have him here on any pretence whatsoever."

"I thought not, Aunt Emmeline, and therefore I have told you."

"Do you mean that you will make an appointment with him elsewhere?"

"Certainly not. I have not in fact ever made an appointment with him. I do not know his address. Till yesterday I thought that he was in Rome. I never had a line from him in my life, and of course have never written to him." Upon hearing all this Lady Tringle sat in silence, not quite knowing how to carry on the conversation. The condition of Lucy's mind was so strange to her, that she felt herself to be incompetent to dictate. She could only resolve that under no circumstances should the objectionable man be allowed into her house. "Now, Aunt Emmeline," said Lucy, "I have told you everything. Of course you have a right to order, but I also have some right. You told me I was to drop Mr. Hamel, but I cannot drop him. If he comes in my way I certainly shall not drop him. If he comes here I shall see him if I can. If you and Uncle Tom choose to turn me out of course you can do so."

"I shall tell your uncle all about it," said Aunt Emmeline, angrily, "and then you will hear what he says." And so the conversation was ended.

At that moment Sir Thomas was, of course, in the City managing his millions, and as Lucy herself had suggested that Mr. Hamel might not improbably call on that very day, and as she was quite determined that Mr. Hamel should not enter the doors of the house in Queen's Gate, it was necessary that steps should be taken at once. Some hours afterwards Mr. Hamel did call and asked for Miss Dormer. The door was opened by a well-appointed footman, who, with lugubrious face,— with a face which spoke much more eloquently than his words,—declared that Miss Dormer was not at home. In answer to further inquiries he went on to express an opinion that Miss Dormer never would be at home ;—from all which it may be seen that Aunt Emmeline had taken strong measures to carry out her purpose. Hamel, when he heard his fate thus plainly spoken from the man's mouth, turned away, not doubting its meaning. He had seen Lucy's face in the park, and had seen also Lady Tringle's gesture after his greeting. That Lady Tringle should not be disposed to receive him at her house was not matter of surprise to him.

When Lucy went to bed that night she did not doubt that Mr. Hamel had called, and that he had been turned away from the door.

CHAPTER XVIII.

DOWN IN SCOTLAND.

WHEN the time came, all the Tringles, together with the Honourable Mrs. Traffick, started for Glenbogie. Aunt Emmeline had told Sir Thomas all Lucy's sins, but Sir Thomas had not made so much of them as his wife had expected. " It wouldn't be a bad thing to have a husband for Lucy," said Sir Thomas.

" But the man hasn't got a sixpence."

" He has a profession."

" I don't know that he makes anything. And then think of his father ! He is—illegitimate !" Sir Thomas seemed rather to sneer at this. "And if you knew the way the old man lives in Rome ! He plays cards all Sunday !" Again Sir Thomas sneered. Sir Thomas was fairly submissive to the conventionalities himself, but did not think that they ought to stand in the way of a provision for a young lady, who had no provision of her own. "You wouldn't wish to have him at Queen's Gate?" asked Lady Tringle.

"Certainly not, if he makes nothing by his profession. A good deal, I think, depends upon that." Then nothing further was said, but Lucy was not told her uncle's opinion on the matter, as had been promised. When she went down to Glenbogie she only knew that Mr. Hamel was considered to be by far too black a sheep to be admitted into her aunt's presence, and that she must regard herself as separated from the man as far as any separation could be effected by her present protectors. But if he would be true to her, as to a girl whom he had a short time since so keenly rejoiced in "finding again," she was quite sure that she could be true to him.

On the day fixed, the 20th of August, Mr. Houston arrived at Glenbogie, with boots and stockings and ammunition, such as Tom had recommended when interrogated on those matters by his sister, Gertrude. "I travelled down with a man I think you know," he said to Lucy ;—"at any rate your sister does, because I saw him with her at Rome." The man turned out to be Isadore Hamel. "I didn't like to ask him whether he was coming here," said Frank Houston.

"No ; he is not coming here," said Aunt Emmeline.

"Certainly not," said Gertrude, who was quite prepared to take up the cudgels on her mother's behalf against Mr. Hamel.

"He said something about another man he used to know at Rome, before you came. He was a nephew of that Marchesa Baldoni."

"She was a lady we didn't like a bit too well," said Gertrude.

"A very stuck-up sort of person, who did all she could to spoil Ayala," said Aunt Emmeline.

"Ayala has just been staying with her," said Lucy. "She has been very kind to Ayala."

"We have nothing to do with that now," said Aunt Emmeline. "Ayala can stay with whom she and her aunt pleases. Is this Mr. Hamel, whom you saw, a friend of the Marchesa's?"

"He seemed to be a friend of the Marchesa's nephew," continued Houston ;—"one Colonel Stubbs. We used to see him at Rome, and a most curious man he is. His name is Jonathan, and I don't suppose that any man was ever seen so red before. He is shooting somewhere, and Hamel seems to be going to join him. I thought he might have been coming here afterwards, as you all were in Rome together."

"Certainly he is not coming here," said Aunt Emmeline. "And as for Colonel Stubbs, I never heard of him before."

A week of the time allotted to Frank Houston had gone before he had repeated a word of his suit to Sir Thomas. But with Gertrude every opportunity had been allowed him, and by the rest of the family they had been regarded as though they were engaged. Mr. Traffick, who was now at Glenbogie, in accordance with the compact made with him, did not at first approve of Frank Houston. He had insinuated to Lady Tringle, and had said very plainly to Augusta, that he regarded a young man, without any employment and without any income, as being quite unfit to marry. "If he had a seat in the House it would be quite a different thing," he had said to Augusta. But his wife had snubbed him; telling him, almost in so many words, that if Gertrude was determined to have her way in opposition to her father she certainly would not be deterred by her brother-in-law. "It's nothing to me," Mr. Traffick had then said; "the money won't come out of my pocket; but when a man has nothing else to do he is sure to spend all that he can lay his hands upon." After that, however, he withdrew his opposition, and allowed it to be supposed that he was ready to receive Frank Houston as his brother-in-law, should it be so decided.

The time was running by both with Houston, the expectant son-in-law, and with Mr. Traffick, who had achieved his position, and both were aware that no grace would be allowed to them beyond that which had been promised. Frank had fully considered the matter, and was quite resolved that it would be unmanly in him to run after his cousin Imogene, in the Tyrol, before he had performed his business. One day, therefore, after having returned from the daily allowance of slaughter, he contrived to find Sir Thomas in the solitude of his own room, and again began to act the part of Allan-a-Dale. "I thought, Mr. Houston," said Sir Thomas, "that we had settled that matter before."

"Not quite," said Houston.

"I don't know why you should say so. I intended to be understood as expressing my mind."

"But you have been good enough to ask me down here."

"I may ask a man to my house, I suppose, without intending to give him my daughter's hand." Then he again asked the important question, to which Allan-a-Dale's answer was so unreasonable and so successful. "Have you an income on which to maintain my daughter?"

"I cannot just say that I have, Sir Thomas," said Houston, apologetically.

"Then you mean to ask me to furnish you with an income."

"You can do as you please about that, Sir Thomas."

"You can hardly marry her without it."

"Well: no; not altogether. No doubt it is true that I should not have proposed myself had I not thought that the young lady would have something of her own."

" But she has nothing of her own," said Sir Thomas. And then that interview was over.

" You won't throw us over, Lady Tringle?" Houston said to Gertrude's mother that evening.

" Sir Thomas likes to have his own way," said Lady Tringle.

" Somebody got round him about Septimus Traffick."

" That was different," said Lady Tringle. " Mr. Traffick is in Parliament, and that gives him an employment. He is a son of Lord Boardotrade, and some of these days he will be in office."

" Of course, you know that if Gertrude sticks to it she will have her own way. When a girl sticks to it her father has to give way. What does it matter to him whether I have any business or not. The money would be the same in one case as the other, only it does seem such an unnecessary trouble to have it put off."

All this Lady Tringle seemed to take in good part, and half acknowledged that if Frank Houston were constant in the matter he would succeed at last. Gertrude, when the time for his departure had come, expressed herself as thoroughly disgusted by her father's sternness. "It's all bosh," she said to her lover. "Who is Lord Boardotrade that that should make a difference? I have as much right to please myself as Augusta." But there was the stern fact that the money had not been promised, and even Frank had not proposed to marry the girl of his heart without the concomitant thousands.

Before he left Glenbogie, on the evening of his departure, he wrote a second letter to Miss Docimer, as follows ;—

" DEAR COUSIN IM,

" Here I am at Glenbogie, and here I have been for a week, without doing a stroke of work. The father still asks ' of his house and his home,' and does not seem to be at all affected by my reference to the romantic grandeur of my own peculiar residence. Perhaps I may boast so far as to say that I have laughed on the lass as successfully as did Allan-a-Dale. But what's the good of laughing on a lass when one has got nothing to eat. Allan-a-Dale could pick a pocket or cut a purse, accomplishments in which I am altogether deficient. I suppose I shall succeed sooner or later, but when I put my neck into the collar I had no idea that there would be so much up-hill work before me. It is all very well joking, but it is not nice to be asked ' of your house and your home ' by a gentleman who knows very well you've got none, and is conscious of inhabiting three or four palaces himself. Such treatment must be described as being decidedly vulgar. And then he must, know that it can be of no possible permanent use. The ladies are all on my side, but I am told by Tringle mère that I am less acceptable than old Traffick, who married the other girl, because I'm not the son of Lord Boardotrade! Nothing astonishes me so much as the bad taste of some people. Now, it must all be put off till Christmas, and the cruel part is, that one doesn't see how I'm to go on living.

"In the meantime I have a little time in which to amuse myself, and I shall turn up in about three weeks at Merle Park. I wish chiefly to beg that you will not dissuade me from what I see clearly to be a duty. I know exactly your line of argument. Following a girl for her money is, you will say, mercenary. So, as far as I can see, is every transaction in the world by which men live. The judges, the bishops, the poets, the Royal academicians, and the Prime Ministers, are all mercenary ;—as is also the man who breaks stones for 2s. 6d. a-day. How shall a man live without being mercenary unless he be born to fortune? Are not girls always mercenary? Will she marry me knowing that I have nothing? Will you not marry some one whom you will probably like much less, simply because he will have something for you to eat and drink? Of course I am mercenary, and I don't even pretend to old Tringle that I am not so. I feel a little tired of this special effort ; —but if I were to abandon it I should simply have to begin again elsewhere. I have sighted my stag, and I must go on following him, trying to get on the right side of the wind till I bring him down. It is not nice, but it is to me manifestly my duty,—and I shall do it. Therefore, do not let there be any blowing up. I hate to be scolded.

"Yours always affectionately,

"F. H."

Gertrude, when he was gone, did not take the matter quite so quietly as he did, feeling that, as she had made up her mind, and as all her world would know that she had made up her mind, it behoved her to carry her purpose to its desired end. A girl who is known to be engaged, but whose engagement is not allowed, is always in a disagreeable plight.

"Mamma," she said, "I think that papa is not treating me well."

"My dear, your papa has always had his own way."

"That is all very well ;—but why am I to be worse used than Augusta? It turns out now that Mr. Traffick has not got a shilling of his own."

"Your papa likes his being in Parliament."

"All the girls can't marry Members of Parliament."

"And he likes his being the son of Lord Boardotrade."

"Lord Boardotrade! I call that very mean. Mr. Houston is a gentleman, and the Buncombe property has been for ever so many hundreds of years in the family. I think more of Frank as to birth and all that, than I do of Lord Boardotrade and his mushroom peerage. Can't you tell papa that I mean to marry Mr. Houston at last, and that he is making very little of me to let me be talked about as I shall be ?'

" I don't think I can, Gertrude."

"Then I shall. What would he say if I were to run away with Frank ?"

" I don't think Frank Houston would do that."

" He would if I told him,—in a moment." There Miss Tringle was probably in error. " And unless papa consents I shall tell him. I am not going to be made miserable for ever."

This was at Glenbogie, in Inverness-shire, on the south-eastern side of Loch Ness, where Sir Thomas Tringle possessed a beautiful mansion, with a deer-forest, and a waterfall of his own, and any amount of moors which the minds of sportsmen could conceive. Nothing in Scotland could be more excellent, unless there might be some truth in the remarks of those who said that the grouse were scarce and that the deer were almost non-existent. On the other side of the lake, four miles up from the gates, on the edge of a ravine, down which rushed a little stream called the Caller, was an inconvenient ricketty cottage, built piecemeal at two or three different times, called Drumcaller. From one room you went into another, and from that into a third. To get from the sitting-room, which was called the parlour, into another which was called the den, you had to pass through the kitchen, or else to make communication by a covered passage out of doors which seemed to hang over the margin of the ravine. Pine-trees enveloped the place. Looking at the house from the outside anyone would declare it to be wet through. It certainly could not with truth be described as a comfortable family residence. But you might, perhaps, travel through all Scotland without finding a more beautifully romantic spot in which to reside. From that passage, which seemed to totter suspended over the rocks, whence the tumbling rushing waters could always be heard like music close at hand, the view down over the little twisting river was such as filled the mind with a conviction of realised poetry. Behind the house across the little garden there was a high rock where a little path had been formed, from which could be seen the whole valley of the Caller and the broad shining expanse of the lake beyond. Those who knew the cottage of Drumcaller were apt to say that no man in Scotland had a more picturesque abode or one more inconvenient. Even bread had to be carried up from Callerfoot, as was called the little village down on the lake side, and other provisions, such even as meat, had to be fetched twenty miles, from the town of Inverness.

A few days after the departure of Houston from Glenbogie two men were seated with pipes in their mouths on the landing outside the room called the den to which the passage from the parlour ran. Here a square platform had been constructed capable of containing two arm-chairs, and here the owner of the cottage was accustomed to sit, when he was disposed, as he called it, to loaf away his time at Drumcaller. This man was Colonel Jonathan Stubbs, and his companion at the present moment was Isadore Hamel.

"I never knew them in Rome," said the Colonel. "I never even saw Ayala there, though she was so much at my aunt's house. I was in Sicily part of the time, and did not get back till they had all quarrelled. I did know the nephew, who was a good-natured but a vulgar young man. They are vulgar people, I should say."

"You could hardly have found Ayala vulgar?" asked Hamel.

"Indeed, no. But uncles and aunts and nephews and nieces are not at all bound to run together. Ayala is the daintiest little darling I ever saw."

"I knew their father and mother, and certainly no one would have called them vulgar."

"Sisters when they marry of course go off according to their husbands, and the children follow. In this case one sister became Tringlish after Sir Tringle, and the other Dormerish, after that most improvident of human beings, your late friend the artist. I don't suppose any amount of experience will teach Ayala how many shillings there are in a pound. No doubt the Honourable Mrs. Traffick knows all about it."

"I don't think a girl is much improved by knowing how many shillings there are in a pound," said Hamel.

"It is useful sometimes."

"So it might be to kill a sheep and skin it, or to milk a cow and make cheese; but here, as in other things, one acquirement will drive out others. A woman if she cannot be beautiful should at any rate be graceful, and if she cannot soar to poetry should at least be soft and unworldly."

"That's all very well in its way, but I go in for roasting, baking, and boiling.

I can bake and I can brew ;
I can make an Irish stew ;
Wash a shirt and iron it too.

That's the sort of girl I mean to go in for if ever I marry; and when you've got six children and a small income it's apt to turn out better than grace and poetry."

"A little of both perhaps," said Hamel.

" Well, yes ; I don't mind a little Byron now and again, so there is no nonsense. As to Glenbogie, it's right over there across the lake. You can get a boat at Callerfoot, and a fellow to take you across and wait for you won't cost you more than three half-crowns. I suppose Glenbogie is as far from the lake on that side as my cottage is on this. How you'll get up except by walking I cannot say, unless you will write a note to Sir Thomas and ask him to send a horse down for you."

" Sir Thomas would not accommodate me."

" You think he will frown if you come after his niece ?"

" I simply want to call on Miss Dormer," said Hamel, blushing, " because her father was always kind to me."

" I don't mean to ask any questions," said the Colonel.

" It is just so as I say. I do not like being in the neighbourhood without calling on Miss Dormer."

" I daresay not."

" But I doubt whether Sir Thomas or Lady Tringle would be at all inclined to make me welcome. As to the distance, I can walk that easily enough, and if the door is slammed in my face I can walk back again."

Thus it was resolved that early on the following morning after breakfast Isadore Hamel should go across the lake and make his way up to Glenbogie.

CHAPTER XIX.

ISADORE HAMEL IS ASKED TO LUNCH.

ON the following morning, the morning of Monday, 2nd September, Isadore Hamel started on his journey. He had thought much about the journey before he made it. No doubt the door had been slammed in his face in London. He felt quite conscious of that, and conscious also that a man should not renew his attempt to enter a door when it has been once slammed in his face. But he understood the circumstances nearly as they had happened,—except that he was not aware how far the door had been slammed by Lady Tringle without any concurrence on the part of Sir Thomas. But the door had, at any rate, not been slammed by Lucy. The only person he had really wished to see within that house had been Lucy Dormer ; and he had hitherto no reason for supposing that she would be unwilling to receive him. Her face had been sweet and gracious when she saw him in the Park. Was he to deny himself all hope of any future intercourse with her because Lady Tringle had chosen to despise him? He must make some attempt. It was more than probable, no doubt, that this attempt would be futile. The servant at Glenbogie would probably be as well instructed as the servant in Queen's Gate. But still a man has to go on and do something, if he means to do anything. There could be no good in sitting up at Drumcaller, at one side of the lake, and thinking of Lucy Dormer far away, at the other side. He had not at all made up his mind that he would ask Lucy to be his wife. His professional income was still poor, and she, as he was aware, had nothing. But he felt it to be incumbent upon him to get nearer to her if it were possible, and to say something to her if the privilege of speech should be accorded to him.

He walked down to Callerfoot, refusing the loan of the Colonel's pony carriage, and thence had himself carried across the lake in a hired boat to a place called Sandy's Quay. That, he was assured, was the spot on the other side from whence the nearest road would be found to Glenbogie. But nobody on the Callerfoot side could tell him what would be the distance. At Sandy's Quay he was assured that it was twelve miles to Glenbogie House ; but he soon found that the man who told him had a pony for hire. "Ye'll nae get there under twelve mile,—or maybe saxteen, if ye attempt to walk up the glin !" So said the owner of the pony. But milder information came to him speedily. A little boy would show him the way up the glen for sixpence, and engage to bring him to the house in an hour and a half. So he started with the little boy, and after a hot scramble for about two hours he found himself within the demesne. Poking their way up through thick bushes from a ravine, they showed their two heads,—first the boy and then the sculptor,—close by the side of the private road,— just as Sir Thomas was passing, mounted on his cob. "It's his ain sell," said the boy, dropping his head again amongst the bushes.

Hamel, when he had made good his footing, had first to turn round so that the lad might not lose his wages. A dirty little hand came up for the sixpence, but the head never appeared again. It was well known in the neighbourhood,—especially at Sandy's Quay, where boats were used to land,—that Sir Thomas was not partial to visitors who made their way into Glenbogie by any but the authorised road. While Hamel was paying his debt, he stood still on his steed waiting to see who might be the trespasser. "That's not a high road," said Sir Thomas, as the young man approached him. As the last quarter of an hour from the bottom of the ravine had been occupied in very stiff climbing among the rocks the information conveyed appeared to Hamel to have been almost unnecessary. "Your way up to the house, if you are going there, would have been through the lodge down there."

"Perhaps you are Sir Thomas Tringle," said Hamel.

"That is my name."

"Then I have to ask your pardon for my mode of ingress. I am going up to the house ; but having crossed the lake from Callerfoot I did not know my way on this side, and so I have clambered up the ravine." Sir Thomas bowed, and then waited for further tidings. "I believe Miss Dormer is at the house?"

"My niece is there."

"My name is Hamel,—Isadore Hamel. I am a sculptor, and used to be acquainted with her father. I have had great kindness from the whole family, and so I was going to call upon her. If you do not object, I will go on to the house."

Sir Thomas sat upon his horse speechless for a minute. He had to consider whether he did not object or not. He was well aware that his wife objected,—aware also that he had declined to coincide with his wife's objection when it had been pressed upon him. Why should not his niece have the advantage of a lover, if a proper sort of a lover came in her way? As to the father's morals or the son's birth, those matters to Sir Thomas were nothing. The young man, he was told, was good at making busts. Would anyone buy the busts when they were made? That was the question. His wife would certainly be prejudiced,—would think it necessary to reject for Lucy any suitor she would reject for her own girls. And then, as Sir Thomas felt, she had not shown great judgment in selecting suitors for her own girls. "Oh, Mr. Hamel, are you?" he said at last.

"Isadore Hamel?"

"You called at Queen's Gate once, not long ago?"

"I did," said Hamel ; "but saw no one."

"No, you didn't ; I heard that. Well, you can go on to the house if you like, but you had better ask for Lady Tringle. After coming over from Callerfoot you'll want some lunch. Stop a moment. I don't mind if I ride back with you." And so the two started towards the house, and Hamel listened whilst Sir Thomas expatiated on the beauties of Glenbogie.

They had passed through one gate and were approaching another, when, away among the trees, there was a young lady seen walking alone. "There is Miss Dormer," said Hamel ; "I suppose I may join her?" Sir Thomas could not quite make up his mind whether the meeting was to be allowed or not, but he could not bring himself at the spur of the moment to refuse his sanction. So Hamel made his way across to Lucy, while Sir Thomas rode on alone to the house.

Lucy had seen her uncle on the cob, and, being accustomed to see him on the cob, knew of course who he was. She had also seen another man with him, but not in the least expecting that Hamel was in those parts, had never dreamt that he was her uncle's companion. It was not till Hamel was near to her that she understood that the man was coming to join herself; and then, when she did recognise the man, she was lost in amazement. "You hardly expected to see me here?" said he.

"Indeed; no."

"Nor did I expect that I should find you in this way."

"My uncle knows it is you?" asked Lucy.

"Oh, yes. I met him as I came up from the ravine, and he has asked me to go on to the house to lunch." Then there was silence for a few moments as they walked on together. "I hope you do not think that I am persecuting you in making my way over here."

"Oh, no; not persecuting!" Lucy, when she heard the sound of what she herself had said, was angry with herself, feeling that she had almost declared him guilty of some wrong in having come thither. "Of course I am glad to see you," she added, "for papa's sake, but I'm afraid——"

"Afraid of what, Miss Dormer?"

She looked him full in the face as she answered him, collecting her courage to make the declaration which seemed to be necessary. "My Aunt Emmeline does not want you to come."

"Why should she not want me?"

"That I cannot tell. Perhaps if I did know I should not tell. But it is so. You called at Queen's Gate, and I know that you were not admitted, though I was at home. Of course, Aunt Emmeline has a right to choose who shall come. It is not as though I had a house of my own."

"But Sir Thomas asked me in."

"Then you had better go in. After what Aunt Emmeline said, I do not think that you ought to remain with me."

"Your uncle knows I am with you," said Hamel. Then they walked on towards the house together in silence for a while. "Do you mean to say," he continued, "that because your aunt objects you are never to see me again?"

"I hope I shall see you again. You were papa's friend, and I should be so very sorry not to see you again."

"I suppose," he said, slowly, "I can never be more than your papa's friend."

"You are mine also."

"I would be more than that." Then he paused as if waiting for a reply, but she of course had none to make. "I would be so much more than that, Lucy." Still she had no answer to give him. But there comes a time when no answer is as excellent eloquence as any words that can be spoken. Hamel, who had probably not thought much of this, was nevertheless at once informed by his instincts that it was so. "Oh, Lucy," he said, "if you can love me say so."

"Mr. Hamel," she whispered.

"Lucy."

"Mr. Hamel, I told you about Aunt Emmeline. She will not allow it. I ought not to have let you speak to me like this, while I am staying here."

"But your uncle knows I am with you."

"My aunt does not know. We must go to the house. She expressly desired that I would not speak to you."

"And you will obey her—always?"

"No; not always. I did not say that I should obey her always. Some day, perhaps, I shall do as I think fit myself."

"And then you will speak to me?"

"Then I will speak to you," she said.

"And love me?"

"And love you," she answered, again looking him full in the face. "But now pray, pray let us go on." For he had stopped her awhile amidst the trees, and had put out his hand as though to take hers, and had opened his arms as though he would embrace her. But she passed on quickly, and hardly answered his further questions till they found themselves together in the hall of the house.

Then they met Lady Tringle, who was just passing into the room where the lunch was laid, and following her were Augusta, Gertrude, and the Honourable Septimus Traffick. For, though Frank Houston had found himself compelled to go at the day named, the Honourable Septimus had contrived to squeeze out another week. Augusta was indeed still not without hope that the paternal hospitality of Glenbogie might be prolonged till dear Merle Park should once again open her portals. Sir Thomas had already passed into the dining-room, having in gruff voice informed his wife that he had invited Mr. Hamel to come in to lunch. "Mr. Hamel!" she had exclaimed. "Yes, Mr. Hamel. I could not see the man starving when he had come all this way. I don't know anything against him." Then he had turned away, and had gone into the dining-room, and was now standing with his back to the empty fire-place, determined to take Mr. Hamel's part if any want of courtesy were shown to him.

It certainly was hard upon Lady Tringle. She frowned and was going to walk on without any acknowledgment, when Lucy timidly went through a form of introduction. "Aunt Emmeline, this is Mr. Hamel. Uncle Tom met him somewhere in the grounds and has asked him to come to luncheon." Then Lady Tringle curtseyed and made a bow. The curtsey and the bow together were sufficient to have crushed the heart of any young man who had not been comforted and exalted by such words as Isadore had heard from Lucy's lips not five minutes since. "And love you," she had said. After that Lady Tringle might curtsey and bow as she would, and he could still live uncrushed. After the curtsey and the bow Lady Tringle passed on. Lucy fell into the rank behind Gertrude; and then Hamel afterwards took his place behind the Honourable Septimus. "If you will sit there, Mr. Hamel," said Lady Tringle, pointing to a chair, across the table, obliquely, at the greatest possible distance from that occupied by Lucy. There he was stationed between Mr. Traffick and Sir Thomas. But now, in his present frame of mind, his position at the table made very little difference to him.

The lunch was eaten in grim silence. Sir Thomas was not a man profuse with conversation at his meals, and at this moment was ill-inclined for any words except what he might use in scolding his wife for being uncivil to his guest. Lady Tringle sat with her head erect, hardly opening her mouth sufficiently to allow the food to enter it. It was her purpose to show her displeasure at Mr. Hamel, and she showed it. Augusta took her mother's part, thoroughly despising the two Dormer girls and any lover that they might have. Poor Gertrude had on that morning been violently persecuted by a lecture as to Frank Houston's impecuniosity. Lucy of course would not speak. The Honourable Septimus was anxious chiefly about his lunch,—somewhat anxious also to offend neither the master nor the mistress of Merle Park. Hamel made one or two little efforts to extract answers from Sir Thomas, but soon found that Sir Thomas would prefer to be left in silence. What did it signify to him? He had done all that he wanted, and much more than he had expected.

The rising and getting away from luncheon is always a difficulty,— so great a difficulty when there are guests that lunch should never be much a company festival. There is no provision for leaving the table as there is at dinner. But on this occasion Lady Tringle extemporised provision the first moment in which they had all ceased to eat. "Mr. Hamel," she said very loudly, "would you like some cheese?" Mr. Hamel, with a little start, declared that he wanted no cheese. "Then, my dears, I think we will go into my room. Lucy, will you come with me?" Upon this the four ladies all went out in procession, but her ladyship was careful that Lucy should go first so that there might be no possibility of escape. Augusta and Gertrude followed her. The minds of all the four were somewhat perturbed; but among the four Lucy's heart was by far the lightest.

"Are you staying over with Stubbs at that cottage?" asked the Honourable Septimus. "A very queer fellow is Stubbs."

"A very good fellow," said Hamel.

"I dare say. He hasn't got any shooting?"

"I think not."

"Not a head. Glentower wouldn't let an acre of shooting over there for any money." This was the Earl of Glentower, to whom belonged an enormous tract of country on the other side of the lake. "What on earth does he do with himself stuck up on the top of those rocks?"

"He does shoot sometimes, I believe, when Lord Glentower is there."

"That's a poor kind of fun, waiting to be asked for a day," said the Honourable Septimus, who rarely waited for anything till he was asked. "Does he get any fishing?"

"He catches a few trout sometimes in the tarns above. But I fancy that Stubbs isn't much devoted to shooting and fishing."

"Then what the d—— does he do with himself in such a country as this?" Hamel shrugged his shoulders, not caring to say that what with walking, what with reading and writing, his friend could be as happy as the day was long in such a place as Drumcaller.

"Is he a Liberal?"

"A what?" asked Hamel. "Oh, a Liberal? Upon my word I don't know what he is. He is chiefly given to poetry, tobacco, and military matters." Then the Honourable Septimus turned up his nose in disgust, and ceased his cross-examination as to the character and pursuits of Colonel Jonathan Stubbs.

"Sir Thomas, I am very much obliged to you for your kindness," said Hamel, getting up suddenly. "As it is a long way over to Drumcaller I think I will make a start. I know my way down the Glen and should be sure to miss it by any other route. Perhaps you'll let me go back as I came." Sir Thomas offered him the loan of a horse, but this was refused, and Hamel started on his return journey across the lake.

When he had gone a few steps from the portal he turned to look at the house which contained one whom he now regarded as belonging exclusively to himself; perhaps he thought that he might catch some final view of Lucy; or, not quite thinking it, fancied that some such chance might at least be possible; but he saw nothing but the uninteresting façade of the grand mansion. Lucy was employed quite otherwise. She was listening to a lecture in which her aunt was describing to her how very badly Mr. Hamel had behaved in obtruding himself on the shades of Glenbogie. The lecture was somewhat long as Aunt Emmeline found it necessary to repeat all the arguments which she had before used as to the miscreant's birth, as to his want of adequate means, and as to the general iniquities of the miscreant's father. All this she repeated more than once with an energy that was quite unusual to her. The flood of her eloquence was so great that Lucy found no moment for an interposing word till all these evils had been denunciated twice and thrice. But then she spoke. "Aunt Emmeline," she said, "I am engaged to Mr. Hamel now."

"What!"

"He has asked me to be his wife and I have promised."

"And that after all that I had said to you!"

"Aunt Emmeline, I told you that I should not drop him. I did not bid him come here. Uncle Tom brought him. When I saw him I would have avoided him if I could. I told him he ought not to be here because you did not wish it; and then he answered that my uncle knew that he was with me. Of course when he told me that he— loved me, I could not make him any other answer." Then Aunt Emmeline expressed the magnitude of her indignation simply by silence, and Lucy was left to think of her lover in solitude.

* * * * * *

"And how have you fared on your day's journey?" said the Colonel, when Hamel found him still seated on the platform with a book in his hand.

"Much better than I thought. Sir Thomas gave me luncheon."

"And the young lady?"

"The young lady was gracious also; but I am afraid that I cannot carry my praises of the family at Glenbogie any further. The three Tringle ladies looked at me as I was sitting at table as though I certainly had no business in their august society."

CHAPTER XX.

STUBBS UPON MATRIMONY.

BEFORE that evening was over,—or in the course of the night it might be better said, as the two men sat up late with their pipes,— Hamel told his friend the Colonel exactly what had taken place that morning over at Glenbogie. "You went for the purpose, of course?" asked the Colonel.

"For an off chance?"

"I know that, well enough. I never heard of a man's walking twelve miles to call upon a young lady merely because he knew her father; and when there was to be a second call within a few weeks, the first having not been taken in very good part by the young lady's friends, my inquiring mind told me that there was something more than old family friendship."

" Your inquiring mind saw into the truth."

" And now looks forward to further events. Can she bake and can she brew ?"

" I do not doubt that she could if she tried."

" And can she wash a shirt for a man ? Don't suppose, my dear fellow, that I intend to say that your wife will have to wash yours. Washing a shirt, as read in the poem from which I am quoting, is presumed to be simply emblematic of household duties in general."

" I take all you say in good part,—as coming from a friend."

" I regard matrimony," said the Colonel, " as being altogether the happiest state of life for a man,—unless to be engaged to some lovely creature, in whom one can have perfect confidence, may be a thought happier. One can enjoy all the ecstatic mental reflection, all the delights of conceit which come from being loved, that feeling of superiority to all the world around which illumines the bosom of the favoured lover, without having to put one's hand into one's pocket, or having one's pipe put out either morally or physically. The next to this is matrimony itself, which is the only remedy for that consciousness of disreputable debauchery, a savour of which always clings, more or less strongly, to unmarried men in our rank of life. The chimes must be heard at midnight, let a young man be ever so well given to the proprieties, and he must have just a touch of the swinge-buckler about him, or he will seem to himself to be deficient in virility. There is no getting out of it until a man marry. But then——"

" Well ; then ?"

" Do you know the man whose long-preserved hat is always brushed carefully, whose coat is the pattern of neatness, but still a little thread-bare when you look at it,—in the colour of whose cheek there is still some touch of juvenility, but whose step is ever heavy and whose brow is always sad ? The seriousness of life has pressed the smiles out of him. He has learned hardly to want anything for himself but outward decency and the common necessaries of life. Such little personal indulgences as are common to you and to me are as strange to him as ortolans or diamonds."

" I do not think I do know him."

" I do ;—well. I have seen him in the regiment, I have met him on the steps of a public office, I have watched him as he entered his parsonage house. You shall find him coming out of a lawyer's office, where he has sat for the last nine hours, having supported nature with two penny biscuits. He has always those few thin hairs over his forehead, he has always that well-brushed hat, he has always that load of care on his brow. He is generally thinking whether he shall endeavour to extend his credit with the butcher, or resolve that the supply of meat may be again curtailed without injury to the health of his five daughters."

" That is an ugly picture."

" But is it true ?"

" In some cases, of course, it is."

" And yet not ugly all round," said the meditative Colonel, who had just replenished his pipe. "There are, on the other side, the five daughters, and the partner of this load of cares. He knows it is well to have the five daughters, rather than to live with plenty of beef and mutton,—even with the ortolans if you will,—and with no one to care whether his body may be racked in this world or his spirit in the next. I do not say whether the balance of good or evil be on one side or the other ; but when a man is going to do a thing he should know what it is he is going to do."

" The reading of all this," said Hamel, " is, that if I succeed in marrying Miss Dormer I must have thin locks, and a bad hat, and a butcher's bill."

" Other men do."

" Some, instead, have balances at their bankers, and die worth thirty, forty, or fifty thousand pounds, to the great consolation of the five daughters."

" Or a hundred thousand pounds! There is, of course, no end to the amount of thousands which a successful professional man may accumulate. You may be the man ; but the question is, whether you should not have reasonable ground to suppose yourself the man, before you encumber yourself with the five daughters."

" It seems to me," said Hamel, " that the need of such assurance is cowardly."

" That is just the question which I am always debating with myself. I also want to rid myself of that swinge-buckler flavour. I feel that for me, like Adam, it is not good that I should be alone. I would fain ask the first girl, that I could love well enough to wish to make myself one with her, to be my wife, regardless of hats, butchers, and daughters. It is a plucky and a fine thing for a man to feel that he can make his back broad enough for all burdens. But yet what is the good of thinking that you can carry a sack of wheat when you are sure that you have not, in truth, strength to raise it from the ground ?"

" Strength will come," said Hamel.

" Yes, and the bad hat. And, worse than the bad hat, the soiled gown ; and perhaps with the soiled gown the altered heart ;—and perhaps with the altered heart an absence of all that tenderness which it is a woman's special right to expect from a man."

" I should have thought you would have been the last to be so self-diffident."

" To be so thoughtful, you mean," said the Colonel. " I am unattached now, and having had no special duty for the last three months I have given myself over to thinking in a nasty morbid manner. It comes, I daresay, partly from tobacco. But there is comfort in this,—that no such reflections falling out of one man's mouth ever had the slightest effect in influencing another man's conduct."

Hamel had told his friend with great triumph of his engagement with Lucy Dormer, but the friend did not return the confidence by informing the sculptor that during the whole of this conversation, and for many days previous to it, his mind had been concerned with the image of Lucy's sister. He was aware that Ayala had been, as it were, turned out from her rich uncle's house, and given over to the comparative poverty of Kingsbury Crescent. He himself, at the present moment, was possessed of what might be considered a comfortable income for a bachelor. He had been accustomed to live almost more than comfortably ; but, having so lived, was aware of himself that he had not adapted himself for straitened circumstances. In spite of that advice of his as to the brewing, baking, and washing capabilities of a female candidate for marriage, he knew himself well enough to be aware that a wife red with a face from a kitchen fire would be distasteful to him. He had often told himself that to look for a woman with money would be still more distasteful. Therefore he had thought that for the present, at least, it would be well for him to remain as he was. But now he had come across Ayala, and though in the pursuance of his philosophy he had assured himself that Ayala should be nothing to him, still he found himself so often reverting to this resolution that Ayala, instead of being nothing, was very much indeed to him.

Three days after this Hamel was preparing himself for his departure immediately after breakfast. " What a beast you are to go," said the colonel, " when there can be no possible reason for your going."

" The five daughters and the bad hat make it necessary that a fellow should do a little work sometimes."

" Why can't you make your images down here ? "

" With you for a model, and mud out of the Caller for clay."

" I shouldn't have the slightest objection. In your art you cannot perpetuate the atrocity of my colour, as the fellow did who painted my portrait last winter. If you will go, go, and make busts at unheard-of prices so that the five daughters may live for ever on the fat of the land. Can I do any good for you by going over to Glenbogie ?"

"If you could snub that Mr. Traffick, who is of all men the most atrocious."

"The power doesn't exist," said the Colonel, "which could snub the Honourable Septimus. That man is possessed of a strength which I thoroughly envy,—which is perhaps more enviable than any other gift the gods can give. Words cannot penetrate that skin of his. Satire flows off him like water from a duck. Ridicule does not touch him. The fellest abuse does not succeed in inflicting the slightest wound. He has learnt the great secret that a man cannot be cut who will not be cut. As it is worth no man's while to protract an enmity with such a one as he, he suffers from no prolonged enmities. He walks unassailable by any darts, and is, I should say, the happiest man in London."

"Then I fear you can do nothing for me at Glenbogie. To mollify Aunt Emmeline would, I fear, be beyond your power. Sir Thomas, as far as I can see, does not require much mollifying."

"Sir Thomas might give the young woman a thousand or two."

"That is not the way in which I desire to keep a good hat on my head," said Hamel, as he seated himself in the little carriage which was to take him down to Callerfoot.

The Colonel remained at Drumcaller till the end of September, when his presence was required at Aldershot,—during which time he shot a good deal, in obedience to the good-natured behests of Lord Glentower and in spite of the up-turned nose of Mr. Traffick. He read much, and smoked much,—so that as to the passing of his time there was not need to pity him, and he consumed a portion of his spare hours in a correspondence with his aunt the Marchesa and with his cousin Nina. One of his letters from each shall be given,—and also one of the letters written to each in reply.

NINA TO HER COUSIN THE COLONEL.

"MY DEAR JONATHAN,

"Lady Albury says that you ought to be here, and so you ought. It is ever so nice. There is a Mr. Ponsonby here, and he and I can beat any other couple at lawn tennis. There is an awning over the ground, which is such a lounge. Playing lawn tennis with a parasol as those Melcombe girls did is stupid. They were here, but have gone. One I am quite sure was over head and ears in love with Mr. Ponsonby. These sort of things are always all on one side, you know. He isn't very much of a man, but he does play lawn tennis divinely. Take it altogether, I don't think there is anything out to beat lawn tennis. I don't know about hunting,—and I don't suppose I ever shall.

"We tried to have Ayala here, but I fear it will not come off. Lady Albury was good-natured, but at last she did not quite like writing to Mrs. Dosett. So mamma wrote, but the lady's answer was very stiff. She thought it better for Ayala to remain among her own friends. Poor Ayala! It is clear that a knight will be wanted to go in armour, and get her out of prison. I will leave it to you to say who must be the knight.

"I hope you will come for a day or two before you go to Aldershot. We stay till the 1st of October. You will be a beast if you don't. Lady Albury says she never means to ask you again. 'Oh, Stubbs!' said Sir Harry; 'Stubbs is one of those fellows who never come if they're asked.' Of course we all sat upon him. Then he declared that you were the dearest friend he had in the world, but that he never dared to dream that you would ever come to Stalham again. Perhaps if we can hit it off at last with Ayala, then you would come. Mamma means to try again.—Your affectionate cousin,   NINA."

THE MARCHESA BALDONI TO HER NEPHEW, COLONEL STUBBS.

"MY DEAR JONATHAN,

"I did my best for my protégé, but I am afraid it will not succeed. Her aunt Mrs. Dosett seems to think that, as Ayala is fated to live with her, Ayala had better take her fate as she finds it. The meaning of that is, that if a girl is doomed to have a dull life she had better not begin it with a little pleasure. There is a good deal to be said for the argument, but if I were the girl I should like to begin with the pleasure and take my chance for the reaction. I should perhaps be vain enough to think that during the preliminary course I might solve all the difficulty by my beaux yeux. I saw Mrs. Dosett once, and now I have had a letter from her. Upon the whole, I am inclined to pity poor Ayala.

"We are very happy here. The Marchese has gone to Como to look after some property he has there. Do not be ill-natured enough to say that the two things go together;—but in truth he is never comfortable out of Italy. He had a slice of red meat put before him the other day, and that decided him to start at once.

"On the first of October we go back to London, and shall remain till the end of November. They have asked Nina to come again in November in order that she may see a hunt. I know that means that she will try to jump over something, and have her leg broken. You must be here and not allow it.. If she does come here I shall perhaps go down to Brighton for a fortnight.

"Yes;—I do think Ayala Dormer is a very pretty girl, and I do think, also, that she is clever. I quite agree that she is ladylike. But I do not therefore think that she is just such a girl as such a man as Colonel Jonathan Stubbs ought to marry. She is one of those human beings who seem to have been removed out of this world and brought up in another. Though she knows ever so much that nobody else knows, she is ignorant of ever so much that everybody ought to know. Wandering through a grove, or seated by a brook, or shivering with you on the top of a mountain, she would be charming. I doubt whether she would be equally good at the top of your table, or looking after your children, or keeping the week's accounts. She would tease you with poetry, and not even pretend to be instructed when you told her how an army ought to be moved. I say nothing as to the fact that she hasn't got a penny, though you are just in that position which makes it necessary for a man to get some money with his wife. I therefore am altogether indisposed to any matrimonial outlook in that direction.—Your affectionate aunt,

"BEATRICE BALDONI."

COLONEL STUBBS TO HIS COUSIN NINA.

"DEAR NINA,

"Lady Albury is wrong; I ought not to be at Stalham. What should I do at Stalham at this time of year, who never shoot partridges, and what would be the use of attempting lawn tennis when I know I should be cut out by Mr. Ponsonby? If that day in November is to come off then I'll come and coach you across the country. You tell Sir Harry that I say so, and that I will bring three horses for one week. I think it very hard about poor Ayala Dormer, but what can any knight do in such a case? When a young lady is handed over to the custody of an uncle or an aunt, she becomes that uncle's and aunt's individual property. Mrs. Dosett may be the most noxious dragon that ever was created for the mortification and general misery of an imprisoned damsel, but still she is omnipotent. The only knight who can be of any service is one who will go with a ring in his hand, and absolutely carry the prisoner away by force of the marriage service. Your unfortunate cousin is so exclusively devoted to the duty of fighting his country's battles that he has not even time to think of a step so momentous as that.

"Poor Ayala! Do not be stupid enough to accuse me of pitying her because I cannot be the knight to release her; but I cannot but think how happy she would be at Stalham, struggling to beat you and Mr. Ponsonby at lawn tennis, and then risking a cropper when the happy days of November should come round.—Your loving cousin,

"J. S."

' My dear Aunt,

"Your letter is worthy of the Queen of Sheba, if, as was no doubt the case, she corresponded with King Solomon. As for Ayala's fate, if it be her fate to live with Mrs. Dosett, she can only submit to it. You cannot carry her over to Italy, nor would the Marchese allow her to divide his Italian good things with Nina. Poor little bird! She had her chance of living amidst diamonds and bank-notes, with the Tringle millionaires, but threw it away after some fashion that I do not understand. No doubt she was a fool, but I cannot but like her the better for it. I hardly think that a fortnight at Stalham, with all Sir Harry's luxuries around her, would do her much service.

"As for myself and the top of my table, and the future companion who is to be doomed to listen to my military lucubrations, I am altogether inclined to agree with you, seeing that you write in a pure spirit of worldly good sense. No doubt the Queen of Sheba gave advice of the same sort to King Solomon. I never knew a woman to speak confidentially of matrimony otherwise than as a matter of pounds, shillings, and pence. In counsels so given, no word of love has ever been known to creep in. Why should it, seeing that love cannot put a leg of mutton into the pot? Don't imagine that I say this in a spirit either of censure or satire. Your ideas are my own, and should I ever marry I shall do so in strict accordance with your tenets, thinking altogether of the weekly accounts, and determined to eschew any sitting by the sides of brooks.

"I have told Nina about my plans. I will be at Stalham in November to see that she does not break her neck.—Yours always, J. S."

CHAPTER XXI.

AYALA'S INDIGNATION.

Perhaps Mrs. Dosett had some just cause for refusing her sanction for the proposed visit to Albany. If Fate did require that Ayala should live permanently in Kingsbury Crescent, the gaiety of a very gay house, and the wealth of a very wealthy house, would hardly be good preparation for such a life. Up to the time of her going to the Marchesa in Brook Street, Ayala had certainly done her best to suit herself to her aunt's manners,—though she had done it with pain and suffering. She had hemmed the towels and mended the sheets, and had made the rounds to the shops. She had endeavoured to attend to the pounds of meat and to sympathise with her aunt in the interest taken in the relics of

the joints as they escaped from the hungry treatment of the two maidens
in the kitchen. Ayala had been clever enough to understand that her
aunt had been wounded by Lucy's indifference, not so much because
she had desired to avail herself of Lucy's labours as from a feeling
that that indifference had seemed to declare that her own pursuits were
mean and vulgar. Understanding this she had struggled to make
those pursuits her own,—and had in part succeeded. Her aunt could
talk to her about the butter and the washing, matters as to which her
lips had been closed in any conversation with Lucy. That Ayala was
struggling Mrs. Dosett had been aware;—but she had thought that
such struggles were good and had not been hopeless. Then came the
visit to Brook Street, and Ayala returned quite an altered young
woman. It seemed as though she neither could nor would struggle
any longer. " I hate mutton-bones," she said to her aunt one morning
soon after her return.

" No doubt we would all like meat joints the best," said her aunt,
frowning.

" I hate joints too."

" You have, I dare say, been cockered up at the Marchesa's with
made dishes."

" I hate dishes," said Ayala, petulantly.

" You don't hate eating?"

" Yes, I do. It is ignoble. Nature should have managed it differ-
ently. We ought to have sucked it in from the atmosphere through
our fingers and hairs, as the trees do by their leaves. There should
have been no butchers, and no grease, and no nasty smells from the
kitchen,—and no gin."

This was worse than all,—this allusion to the mild but unfashionable
stimulant to which Mr. Dosett had been reduced by his good nature.
" You are flying in the face of the Creator, miss," said Aunt Margaret,
in her most angry voice,—" in the face of the Creator who made everything, and ordained what his creatures· should eat and drink by His
infinite wisdom."

" Nevertheless," said Ayala, " I think we might have done without
boiled mutton." Then she turned to some articles of domestic needle-
work which were in her lap as so to show that in spite of the wickedness
of her opinions she did not mean to be idle. But Mrs. Dosett, in her
wrath, snatched the work from her niece's hands and carried it out of
the room, thus declaring that not even a pillow-case in her house should
owe a stitch to the hands of a girl so ungrateful and so blasphemous.

The wrath wore off soon. Ayala, though not contrite was meek, and
walked home with her aunt on the following morning, patiently carrying a pound of butter, six eggs, and a small lump of bacon in a basket.

After that the pillow-case was recommitted to her. But there still was left evidence enough that the girl's mind had been upset by the luxuries of Brook Street,—evidence to which Aunt Margaret paid very much attention, insisting upon it in her colloquies with her husband. " I think that a little amusement is good for young people," said Uncle Reginald weakly.

" And for old people too. No doubt about it, if they can get it so as not to do them any harm at the same time. Nothing can be good for a young woman which unfits her for that state of life to which it has pleased God to call her. Ayala has to live with us. No doubt there was a struggle when she first came from your sister, Lady Tringle, but she made it gallantly, and I gave her great credit. She was just falling into a quiet mode of life when there came this invitation from the Marchesa Baldoni. Now she has come back quite an altered person, and the struggle has to be made all over again." Uncle Reginald again expressed his opinion that young people ought to have a little amusement, but he was not strong enough to insist very much upon his theory. It certainly, however, was true that Ayala, though she still struggled, had been very much disturbed by the visit.

Then came the invitation to Stalham. There was a very pretty note from Lady Albury to Ayala herself, saying how much pleasure she would have in seeing Miss Dormer at her house, where Ayala's old friends the Marchesa and Nina were then staying. This was accompanied by a long letter from Nina herself, in which all the charms of Stalham, including Mr. Ponsonby and lawn tennis, were set forth at full length. *Ayala had already heard much about Stalham and the Alburys* from her friend Nina, who had hinted in a whisper that such an invitation as this might perhaps be forthcoming. She was ready enough for the visit, having looked through her wardrobe, and resolved that things which had been good enough for Brook Street would still be good enough for Stalham. But the same post had brought a letter for Mrs. Dosett, and Ayala could see, that, as the letter was read, a frown came upon her aunt's brow, and that the look on her aunt's face was decidedly averse to Stalham. This took place soon after breakfast, when Uncle Reginald had just started for his office, and neither of them for awhile said a word to the other of the letter that had been received. It was not till after lunch that Ayala spoke. " Aunt," she said, " you have had a letter from Lady Albury?"

" Yes," said Mrs. Dosett, grimly, " I have had a letter from Lady Albury."

Then there was another silence, till Ayala, whose mind was full of promised delights, could not refrain herself longer. " Aunt Margaret," she said, " I hope you mean to let me go." For a minute or two there was no reply, and Ayala again pressed her question. "Lady Albury wants me to go to Stalham."

"She has written to me to say that she would receive you."

"And I may go?"

"I am strongly of opinion that you had better not," said Mrs. Dosett, confirming her decree by a nod which might have suited Jupiter.

"Oh, Aunt Margaret, why not?"

"I think it would be most prudent to decline."

"But why,—why,—why, Aunt Margaret?"

"There must be expense."

"I have money enough for the journey left of my own from what Uncle Tom gave me," said Ayala, pleading her cause with all her eloquence.

"It is not only the money. There are other reasons,—very strong reasons."

"What reasons, Aunt Margaret?"

"My dear, it is your lot to have to live with us, and not with such people as the Marchesa Baldoni and Lady Albury."

"I am sure I do not complain."

"But you would complain after having for a time been used to the luxuries of Albury Park. I do not say that as finding fault, Ayala. It is human nature that it should be so."

"But I won't complain. Have I ever complained?"

"Yes, my dear. You told me the other day that you did not like bones of mutton, and you were disgusted because things were greasy. I do not say this by way of scolding you, Ayala, but only that you may understand what must be the effect of your going from such a house as this to such a house as Stalham, and then returning back from Stalham to such a house as this. You had better be contented with your position——"

"I am contented with my position," sobbed Ayala.

"And allow me to write to Lady Albury refusing the invitation."

But Ayala could not be brought to look at the matter with her aunt's eyes. When her aunt pressed her for an answer which should convey her consent she would give none, and at last left the room bitterly sobbing. Turning the matter over in her own bosom upstairs she determined to be mutinous. No doubt she owed a certain amount of obedience to her aunt; but had she not been obedient, had she not worked hard and lugged about that basket of provisions, and endeavoured to take an interest in all her aunt's concerns? Was she so absolutely the property of her aunt that she was bound to do everything her aunt desired to the utter annihilation of all her hopes, to the extermination of her promised joys? She felt that she had succeeded in Brook Street. She had met no Angel of Light, but she was associated with people whom she had liked, and had been talked to by those to whom it had been a pleasure to listen. That colonel with the quaint name and the ugly face was still present to her memory as he had leaned over her shoulder at the theatre, making her now laugh by his drollery, and now filling her mind with interest by his description of the scenes which she was seeing. She was sure that all this, or something of the same nature, would be renewed for her delight at Stalham. And was she to be robbed of this,—the only pleasure which seemed to remain to her in this world,—merely because her aunt chose to entertain severe notions as to duty and pleasure? Other girls went out when they were asked. At Rome, when that question of the dance at the Marchesa's had been discussed, she had had her own way in opposition to her Aunt Emmeline and her cousin Augusta. No doubt she had, in consequence partly of her conduct on that occasion, been turned out of her Uncle Tom's house; but of that she did not think at the present moment. She would be mutinous, and would appeal to her Uncle Reginald for assistance.

But the letter which contained the real invitation had been addressed to her aunt, and her aunt could in truth answer it as she pleased. The answer might at this moment be in the act of being written, and should it be averse Ayala knew very well that she could not go in opposition to it. And yet her aunt came to her in the afternoon consulting her again, quite unconquered as to her own opinion, but still evidently unwilling to write the fatal letter without Ayala's permission. Then Ayala assured herself that she had rights of her own, which her aunt did not care to contravene. " I think I ought to be allowed to go,' she said, when her aunt came to her during the afternoon.

" When I think it will be bad for you!"

" It won't be bad. They are very good people. I think that I ought to be allowed to go."

" Have you no reliance on those who are your natural guardians?"

" Uncle Reginald is my natural guardian," said Ayala, through her tears.

" Very well! If you refuse to be guided by me as though I were not your aunt, and as you will pay no attention to what I tell you is proper for you and best, the question must be left till your uncle comes home. I cannot but be very much hurt that you should think so little of me. I have always endeavoured to do the best I could for you, just as though I were your mother."

" I think that I ought to be allowed to go," repeated Ayala.

As the first consequence of this, the replies to all the three letters

were delayed for the next day's post. Ayala had considered much with
what pretty words she might best answer Lady Albury's kind note,
and she had settled upon a form of words which she had felt to be very
pretty. Unless her uncle would support her, that would be of no
avail, and another form must be chosen. To Nina she would tell the
whole truth, either how full of joy she was,—or else how cruelly used
and how thoroughly broken-hearted. But she could not think that her
uncle would be unkind to her. Her uncle had been uniformly gentle.
Her uncle, when he should know how much her heart was set upon it,
would surely let her go.

The poor girl, when she tacitly agreed that her uncle should be the
arbiter in the matter, thus pledging herself to abide by her uncle's decision, let it be what it might, did not think what great advantage her
aunt would have over her in that discussion which would be held
upstairs while the master of the house was washing his hands before
dinner. Nor did she know of how much stronger will was her Aunt
Margaret than her Uncle Reginald. While he was washing his hands
and putting on his slippers, the matter was settled in a manner quite
destructive of poor Ayala's hopes. "I won't have it," said Mrs. Dosett,
in reply to the old argument that young people ought to have some
amusement. "If I am to be responsible for the girl I must be allowed
my own way with her. It is trouble enough, and very little thanks I get
for it. Of course she hates me. Nevertheless, I can endeavour to do
my duty, and I will. It is not thanks, nor love, nor even gratitude,
that I look for. I am bound to do the best I can by her because she
is your niece, and because she has no other real friends. I knew what
would come of it when she went to that house in Brook Street. I was
soft then and gave way. The girl has moped about like a miserable
creature ever since. If I am not to have my way now I will have done
with her altogether." Having heard this very powerful speech, Uncle
Reginald was obliged to give way, and it was settled that after dinner
he should convey to Ayala the decision to which they had come.

Ayala, as she sat at the dinner-table, was all expectation, but she
asked no question. She asked no question after dinner, while her
uncle slowly, solemnly, and sadly sipped his one beaker of cold gin-
and-water. He sipped it very slowly, no doubt because he was
anxious to postpone the evil moment in which he must communicate
her fate to his niece. But at last the melancholy glass was drained,
and then, according to the custom of the family, Mrs. Dosett led the
way up into the drawing-room, followed by Ayala and her husband.
He, when he was on the stairs, and when the eyes of his wife were not
upon him, tremulously put out his hand and laid it on Ayala's
shoulder, as though to embrace her. The poor girl knew well that

mark of affection. There would have been no need for such embracing had the offered joys of Stalham been in store for her. The tears were already in her eyes when she seated herself in the drawing-room, as far removed as possible from the arm-chair which was occupied by her aunt.

Then her uncle pronounced his judgment in a vacillating voice,—with a vacillation which was ineffectual of any good to Ayala. "Ayala," he said, "your aunt and I have been talking over this invitation to Stalham, and we are of opinion, my dear, that you had better not accept it."

"Why not, Uncle Reginald?"

"There would be expense."

"I can pay for my own ticket."

"There would be many expenses, which I need not explain to you more fully. The truth is, my dear, that poor people cannot afford to live with rich people, and had better not attempt it."

"I don't want to live with them."

"Visiting them is living with them for a time. I am sorry, Ayala, that we are not able to put you in a position in which you might enjoy more of the pleasures incidental to your age ; but you must take the things as they are. Looking at the matter all round, I am sure that your aunt is right in advising that you should stay at home."

"It isn't advice at all," said Ayala.

"Ayala !" exclaimed her aunt, in a tone of indignation.

"It isn't advice," repeated Ayala. "Of course, if you won't let me go, I can't."

"You are a very wicked girl," said Mrs. Dosett, "to speak to your uncle like that, after all that he has done for you."

"Not wicked," said the uncle.

"I say, wicked. But it doesn't matter. I shall at once write to Lady Albury, as you desire, and of course there will be no further question as to her going." Soon after that Mrs. Dosett sat down to her desk, and wrote that letter to which the Marchesa had alluded in hers to her nephew. No doubt it was stern and hard, and of a nature to make such a woman as the Marchesa feel that Mrs. Dosett would not be a pleasant companion for a girl like Ayala. But it was written with a full conviction that duty required it ; and the words, though hard and stiff, had been chosen with the purpose of showing that the doing of this disagreeable duty had been felt to be imperative.

When the matter had been thus decided, Ayala soon retreated to her own room. Her very soul was burning with indignation at the tyranny to which she thought herself subjected. The use of that weak word, advice, had angered her more than anything. It had not been advice. It had not been given as advice. A command had been laid upon her, a most cruel and unjust command, which she was forced to obey, because she lacked the power of escaping from her condition of slavery. Advice, indeed ? Advice is a thing with which the advised one may or may not comply, as that advised one may choose. A slave must obey an order! Her own papa and her own mamma had always advised her, and the advice had always been followed, even when read only in the glance of an eye, in a smile, or a nod. Then she had known what it was to be advised. Now she was ordered,—as slaves are ordered ; and there was no escape from her slavery !

She, too, must write her letter, but there was no need now of that pretty studied phrase, in which she had hoped to thank Lady Albury fitly for her great kindness. She found, after a vain attempt or two, that it was hopeless to endeavour to write to Lady Albury. The words would not come to her pen. But she did write to Nina ;—

" DEAR, DEAREST NINA,

" They won't let me go! Oh, my darling, I am so miserable! Why should they not let me go, when people are so kind, so very kind, as Lady Albury and your dear mamma! I feel as though I should like to run from the house, and never come back, even though I had to die in the streets. I was so happy when I got your letter and Lady Albury's, and now I am so wretched! I cannot write to Lady Albury. You must just tell her, with many thanks from me, that they will not let me go !

" Your unhappy but affectionate friend,

" AYALA."

CHAPTER XXII.

AYALA'S GRATITUDE.

THERE was much pity felt for Ayala among the folk at Stalham. The sympathies of them all should have been with Mrs. Dosett. They ought to have felt that the poor aunt was simply performing an unpleasant duty, and that the girl was impracticable if not disobedient. But Ayala was known to be very pretty, and Mrs. Dosett was supposed to be plain. Ayala was interesting, while Mrs. Dosett, from the nature of her circumstances, was most uninteresting. It was agreed on all sides, at Stalham, that so pretty a bird as Ayala should not be imprisoned for ever in so ugly a cage. Such a bird ought, at least, to be allowed its chance of captivating some fitting mate by its song and its plumage. That was Lady Albury's argument,—a woman very good-natured, a little given to match-making, a great friend to pretty girls, —and whose eldest son was as yet only nine, so that there could be no danger to herself or her own flock. There was much ridicule thrown on Mrs. Dosett at Stalham, and many pretty things said of the bird who was so unworthily imprisoned in Kingsbury Crescent. At last there was something like a conspiracy, the purport of which was to get the bird out of its cage in November.

In this conspiracy it can hardly be said that the Marchesa took an active part. Much as she liked Ayala, she was less prone than Lady Albury to think that the girl was ill-used. She was more keenly alive than her cousin,—or rather her cousin's wife,—to the hard necessities of the world. Ayala must be said to have made her own bed. At any rate there was the bed and she must lie on it. It was not the Dosetts' fault that they were poor. According to their means they were doing the best they could for their niece, and were entitled to praise rather than abuse. And then the Marchesa was afraid for her nephew. Colonel Stubbs, in his letter to her, had declared that he quite agreed with her views as to matrimony; but she was quite alive to her nephew's sarcasm. Her nephew, though he might in truth agree with her, nevertheless was sarcastic. Though he was sarcastic, still he might be made to accede to her views, because he did, in truth, agree with her. She was eminently an intelligent woman, seeing far into character, and she knew pretty well the real condition of her nephew's mind, and could foresee his conduct. He would marry before long, and might not improbably marry a girl with some money if one could be made to come in his way, who would, at the same time, suit his somewhat fastidious taste. But Ayala suited his taste, Ayala who had not a shilling, and the Marchesa thought it only too likely that if Ayala were released from her cage, and brought to Albury, Ayala might become Mrs. Jonathan Stubbs. That Ayala should refuse to become Mrs. Jonathan Stubbs did not present itself as a possibility to the Marchesa.

So the matters were when the Marchesa and Nina returned from Stalham to London, a promise having been given that Nina should go back to Stalham in November, and be allowed to see the glories of a hunt. She was not to ride to hounds. That was a matter of course, but she was to be permitted to see what a pack of hounds was like, and of what like were the men in their scarlet coats, and how the huntsman's horn would sound when it should be heard among the woods and fields. It was already decided that the Colonel should be there to meet her, and the conspiracy was formed with the object of getting Ayala out of her cage at the same time. Stalham was a hand-

some country seat, in the county of Rufford, and Sir Harry Albury
had lately taken upon himself the duties of Master of the Rufford and
Ufford United Pack.   Colonel Stubbs was to be there with his horses
in November, but had, in the meantime, been seen by Lady Albury,
and had been instigated to do something for the release of Ayala.   But
what could he do?   It was at first suggested that he should call at
Kinsbury Crescent, and endeavour to mollify the stony heart of Aunt
Dosett.   But, as he had said himself, he would be the worst person in
the world to perform such an embassy.   "I am not an Adonis, I
now," he said, "nor do I look like a Lothario, but still I am in some
prt a young man, and therefore certain to be regarded as pernicious,
as dangerous and damnable, by such a dragon of virtue as Aunt
Dosett.   I don't see how I could expect to have a chance."   This
interview took place in London during the latter end of October, and
it was at last decided that the mission should be made by Lady Albury
herself, and made, not to Mrs. Dosett, at Kingsbury Crescent, but to
Mr. Dosett at his office in Somerset House.   "I don't think I could
stand Mrs. D.," said Lady Albury.

Lady Albury was a handsome fashionable woman, rather tall, always
excellently dressed, and possessed of a personal assurance which
nothing could daunt.   She had the reputation of an affectionate wife
and a good mother, but was nevertheless declared by some of her
friends to be "a little fast."   She certainly was fond of comedy,—
those who did not like her were apt to say that her comedy was only
fun,—and was much disposed to have her own way when she could
get it.   She was now bent upon liberating Ayala from her cage, and
for this purpose had herself driven into the huge court belonging to
Somerset House.

Mr. Dosett was dignified at his office with the use of a room to
himself, a small room looking out upon the river, in which he spent
six hours on six days of the week in arranging the indexes of a volu-
minous library of manuscript letter-books.   It was rarely indeed that
he was disturbed by the presence of any visitor.   When, therefore, his
door was opened by one of the messengers, and he was informed that
Lady Albury desired to see him, he was for the moment a good deal
disturbed.   No option, however, was given to him as to refusing ad-
mission to Lady Albury.   She was in the room before the messenger
had completed his announcement, and had seated herself in one of the
two spare chairs which the room afforded as soon as the door was
closed   "Mr. Dosett," she said, "I have taken the great liberty of
talling to say a few words about your niece, Miss Ayala Dormer."

When the lady was first announced, Mr. Dosett, in his confusion,
aad failed to connect the name which he had heard with that of the

lady who had invited Ayala to her house. But now he recognised it, and knew who it was that had come to him. "You were kind enough," he said, "to invite my little girl to your house some weeks ago."

"And now I have come to invite her again."

Mr. Dosett was now more disturbed than ever. With what words was he to refuse the request which this kind but very grand lady was about to make? How could he explain to her all those details as to his own poverty, and as to Ayala's fate in having to share that poverty with him? How could he explain the unfitness of Ayala's temporary sojourn with people so wealthy and luxurious? And yet were he to yield in the least how could he face his wife on his return home to the Crescent? "You are very kind, Lady Albury," he said.

"We particularly wish to have her about the end of the first week in November," said the lady. "Her friend Nina Baldone will be there, and one or two others whom she knows. We shall try to be a little gay for a week or two."

"I have no doubt it would be gay, and we at home are very dull."

"Do you not think a little gaiety good for young people?" said her ladyship, using the very argument which poor Mr. Dosett had so often attempted to employ on Ayala's behalf.

"Yes; a little gaiety," he said, as though deprecating the excessive amount of hilarity which he imagined to prevail at Stalham.

"Of course you do," said Lady Albury. "Poor little girl! I have heard so much about her and of all your goodness to her. Mrs. Dosett I know is another mother to her; but still a little country air could not but be beneficial. Do say that she shall come to us, Mr. Dosett."

Then Mr. Dosett felt that, disagreeable as it was, he must preach the sermon which his wife had preached to him, and he did preach it. He spoke timidly of his own poverty, and the need which there was that Ayala should share it. He spoke a word of the danger which might come from luxury, and of the discontent which would be felt when the girl returned to her own home. Something he added of the propriety of like living with like, and ended by praying that Ayala might be excused. The words came from him with none of that energy which his wife would have used,—were uttered in a low melancholy drone; but still they were words hard to answer, and called upon Lady Albury for all her ingenuity in finding an argument against them.

But Lady Albury was strong-minded, and did find an argument. "You musn't be angry with me," she said, "if I don't quite agree with you. Of course you wish to do the best you can for this dear child."

"Indeed I do, Lady Albury."

"How is anything then to be done for her if she remains shut up in your house? You do not, if I understand, see much company yourselves."

"None at all."

"You won't be angry with me for my impertinence in alluding to it."

"Not in the least. It is the fact that we live altogether to ourselves."

"And the happiest kind of life too for married people," said Lady Albury, who was accustomed to fill her house in the country with a constant succession of visitors, and to have engagements for every night of the week in town. "But for young people it is not quite so good. How is a young lady to get herself settled in life?"

"Settled?" asked Mr. Dosett, vaguely.

"Married," suggested Lady Albury, more plainly. Mr. Dosett shook his head. No idea on the subject had ever flashed across his mind. To provide bread and meat, a bed and clothes, for his sister's child he had felt to be a duty,—but not a husband. Husbands came, or did not,—as the heavens might be propitious. That Ayala should go to Stalham for the sake of finding a husband was certainly beyond the extent of his providing care. "In fact how is a girl to have a chance at all unless she is allowed to see some one? Of course I don't say this with reference to our house. There will be no young men there, or anything of that kind. But, taking a broad view, unless you let a girl like that have what chances come in her way how is she to get on? I think you have hardly a right to do it."

"We have done it for the best."

"I am sure of that, Mr. Dosett. And I hope you will tell Mrs. Dosett, with my compliments, how thoroughly I appreciate her goodness. I should have called upon her instead of coming here, only that I cannot very well get into that part of the town."

"I will tell her what you are good enough to say."

"Poor Ayala! I am afraid that her other aunt, Aunt Tringle, was not as good to her as your wife. I have heard about how all that occurred in Rome. She was very much admired there. I am told that she is perfectly lovely."

"Pretty well."

"A sort of beauty that we hardly ever see now,--and very, very clever."

"Ayala is clever, I think."

"She ought to have her chance. She ought indeed. I don't think you quite do your duty by such a girl as that unless you let her have a chance. She is sure to get to know people, and that she is asked from one house to another. I speak plainly, for I really think you ought to let her come."

All this sank deeply into the heart of Uncle Reginald. Whether it was for good or evil it seemed to him at the moment to be unanswerable. If there was a chance of any good thing for Ayala, surely it could not be his duty to bar her from that chance. A whole vista of new views in reference to the treatment of young ladies was opened to him by the words of his visitor. Ayala certainly was pretty. Certainly she was clever. A husband with an income would certainly be a good thing. Embryo husbands with incomes do occasionally fall in love with pretty girls. But how can any pretty girl be fallen in love with unless some one be permitted to see her? At Kingsbury Crescent there was not a man to be seen from one end of the year to another. It occurred to him now, for the first time, that Ayala by her present life was shut out from any chance of marriage. It was manifestly true that he had no right to seclude her in that fashion. At last he made a promise, rashly, as he felt at the very moment of making it, that he would ask his wife to allow Ayala to go to Stalham. Lady Albury of course accepted this as an undertaking that Ayala should come, and went away triumphant.

Mr. Dosett walked home across the parks with a troubled mind, thinking much of all that had passed between him and the lady of fashion. It was with great difficulty that he could quite make up his mind which was right,—the lady of fashion or his wife. If Ayala was to live always as they lived at Kingsbury Crescent, if it should in process of time be her fate to marry some man in the same class as themselves, if continued care as to small pecuniary needs was to be her future lot, then certainly her comfort would only be disturbed by such a visit as that now proposed. And was it not probable that such would be the destiny in store for her? Mr. Dosett knew the world well enough to be aware that all pretty girls such as Ayala cannot find rich husbands merely by exhibiting their prettiness. Kingsbury Crescent, unalloyed by the dangers of Stalham, would certainly be the most secure. But then he had been told that Ayala now had special chances offered to her, and that he had no right to rob her of those chances. He felt this the more strongly, because she was not his daughter,—only his niece. With a daughter he and his wife might have used their own judgment without check. But now he had been told that he had no right to rob Ayala of her chances, and he felt that he had not the right. By the time that he reached Kingsbury Crescent he had, with many misgivings, decided in favour of Stalham.

It was now some weeks since the first invitation had been refused, and during those weeks life had not been pleasant at the Crescent.

Ayala moped and pined as though some great misfortune had fallen
upon her. When she had first come to the Crescent she had borne
herself bravely, as a man bears a trouble when he is conscious that he
has brought it on himself by his own act, and is proud of the act which
has done it. But when that excitement has gone, and the trouble still
remains, the pride wears off, and the man is simply alive to his suffering. So it had been with Ayala. Then had come the visit to Brook
Street. When, soon after that, she was invited to Stalham, it seemed
as though a new world was being opened to her. There came a moment
when she could again rejoice that she had quarrelled with her Aunt
Emmeline. This new world would be a much better world than the
Tringle world. Then had come the great blow, and it had seemed to
her as though there were nothing but Kingsbury Crescent before her
for the rest of her wretched life.

There was not a detail of all this hidden from the eyes of Aunt Margaret. Stalham had decided that Aunt Margaret was ugly and uninteresting. Stalham, according to its own views, was right. Nevertheless the lady in Kingsbury Crescent had both eyes to see and a heart
to feel. She was hot of temper, but she was forgiving. She liked her
own way, but she was affectionate. She considered it right to teach
her niece the unsavoury mysteries of economy, but she was aware that
such mysteries must be distasteful to one brought up as Ayala. Even
when she had been loudest in denouncing Ayala's mutiny, her heart
had melted in ruth because Ayala had been so unhappy. She, too,
had questioned herself again and again as to the justness of her decision. Was she entitled to rob Ayala of her chances? In her frequent
discussions with her husband she still persisted in declaring that Kingsbury Crescent was safe, and that Stalham would be dangerous. But,
nevertheless, in her own bosom she had misgivings. As she saw the
poor girl mope and weary through one day after another, she could not
but have misgivings.

" I have had that Lady Albury with me at the office to-day, and
have almost promised that Ayala shall go to her on the 8th of November." It was thus that Mr. Dosett rushed at once into his difficulty as
soon as he found himself up-stairs with his wife.

" You have ?"

" Well, my dear, I almost did. She said a great deal, and I could
not but agree with much of it. Ayala ought to have her chances."

" What chances ?" demanded Mrs. Dosett, who did not at all like
the expression.

" Well ; seeing people. She never sees anybody here."

" Nobody is better than some people," said Mrs. Dosett, meaning to
be severe on Lady Albury's probable guests.

"But if a girl sees nobody," said Mr. Dosett, "she can have no,—no,—no chances."

"She has the chance of wholesome victuals," said Mrs. Dosett, "and I don't know what other chances you or I can give her."

"She might see—a young man." This Mr. Dosett said very timidly.

"A young fiddlestick! A young man! Young men should be waited for till they come naturally, and never thought about if they don't come at all. I hate this looking after young men. If there wasn't a young man for the next dozen years we should do better,—so as just to get out of the way of thinking about them for a time." This was Mrs. Dosett's philosophy; but in spite of her philosophy she did yield, and on that night it was decided that Ayala after all was to be allowed to go to Stalham.

* * * * * *

To Mr. Dosett was deputed the agreeable task of telling Ayala on the next evening what was to befal her. If anything agreeable was to be done in that sombre house it was always deputed to the master.

"What!" said Ayala, jumping from her chair.

"On the eighth of November," said Mr. Dosett.

"To Stalham?"

"Lady Albury was with me yesterday at the office, and your aunt has consented."

"Oh, Uncle Reginald!" said Ayala, falling on her knees, and hiding her face on his lap. Heaven had been once more opened to her.

"I'll never forget it," said Ayala, when she went to thank her aunt,—"never."

"I only hope it may not do you a mischief."

"And I beg your pardon, Aunt Margaret, because I was,—I was,—because I was——" She could not find the word which would express her own delinquency, without admitting more than she intended to admit,—"too self-asserting, considering that I am only a young girl." That would have been her meaning, could she have found appropriate words.

"We need not go back to that now," said Aunt Margaret.

CHAPTER XXIII.

STALHAM PARK.

On the day fixed Ayala went down to Stalham. A few days before she started there came to her a letter, or rather an envelope, from her uncle Sir Thomas, inclosing a cheque for £20. The Tringle women had heard that Ayala had been asked to Stalham, and had mentioned the visit disparagingly before Sir Thomas. "I think it very wrong of my poor brother," said Lady Tringle. "She can't have a shilling even to get herself gloves." This had an effect which had not been intended, and Sir Thomas sent the cheque for £20. Then Ayala felt not only that the heavens were opened to her but that the sweetest zephyrs were blowing her on upon her course. Thoughts as to gloves had disturbed her, and as to some shoes which were wanting,—and especially as to a pretty hat for winter wear. Now she could get hat and shoes and gloves, and pay her fare, and go down to Stalham with money in her pocket. Before going she wrote a very pretty note to her Uncle Tom.

On her arrival she was made much of by everyone. Lady Albury called her the caged bird, and congratulated her on her escape from the bars. Sir Harry asked her whether she could ride to hounds. Nina gave her a thousand kisses. But perhaps her greatest delight was in finding that Jonathan Stubbs was at Albury. She had become so intimate with the Colonel that she regarded him quite like an old friend ;—and when a girl has a male friend, though he may be much less loved, or not loved at all, he is always more pleasant, or at any rate more piquant, than a female friend. As for love with Colonel Stubbs that was quite out of the question. She was sure that he would never fall in love with herself. His manner to her was altogether un-like that of a lover. A lover would be smooth, soft, poetic, and flattering. He was always a little rough to her,—sometimes almost scolding her. But then he scolded her as she liked to be scolded,—with a dash of fun and a greatly predominating admixture of good-nature. He was like a bear,—but a bear who would always behave himself pleasantly. She was delighted when Colonel Stubbs congratulated her on her escape from Kingsbury Crescent, and felt that he was justified by his intimacy when he called Mrs. Dosett a mollified she-Cerberus.

"Are you going to make one of my team ?" said the Colonel to her on the morning after her arrival. It was a non-hunting morning, and the gentlemen were vacant about the house till they went out for a little shooting later on in the day.

"What team ?" said Ayala, feeling that she had suddenly received a check to her happiness. She knew that the Colonel was alluding to those hunting joys which were to be prepared for Nina, and which were far beyond her own reach. That question of riding gear is terrible to young ladies who are not properly supplied. Even had time admitted she would not have dared to use her uncle's money for such a purpose, in the hope that a horse might be lent to her. She had told herself that it was out of the question, and had declared to herself that she was too thankful for her visit to allow any regret on such a matter to cross her mind. But when the Colonel spoke of his team there was something of a pang. How she would have liked to be one of such a team !

"My pony team. I mean to drive too. You mustn't think that I am taking a liberty when I say that they are to be called Nina and Ayala."

There was no liberty at all. Had he called her simply Ayala she would have felt it to be no more than pleasant friendship, coming from him. He was so big, and so red, and so ugly, and so friendly ! Why should he not call her Ayala? But as to that team,—it could not be. "If it's riding," she said, demurely, "I can't be one of the ponies."

"It is riding,—of course. Now the Marchesa is not here, we mean to call it hunting in a mild way."

"I can't," she said.

"But you've got to do it, Miss Dormer."

"I haven't got anything to do it with. Of course, I don't mind telling you."

"You are to ride the sweetest little horse that ever was foaled,— just bigger than a pony. It belongs to Sir Harry's sister who is away, and we've settled it all. There never was a safer little beast, and he can climb through a fence without letting you know that it's there."

"But I mean—clothes," said Ayala. Then she whispered, "I haven't got a habit, or anything else anybody ought to have."

"Ah," said the Colonel; "I don't know anything about that. I should say that Nina must have managed that. The horse department was left to me, and I have done my part. You will find that you will have to go out next Tuesday and Friday. The hounds will be here on Tuesday, and they will be at Rufford on Friday. Rufford is only nine miles from here, and it's all settled."

Before the day was over the difficulty had vanished. Miss Albury's horse was not only called into requisition but Miss Albury's habit also. Ayala had a little black hat of her own, which Lady Albury assured her would do excellently well for the hunting field. There was some fitting and some trying on, and perhaps a few moments of preliminary despair ; but on the Tuesday morning she rode away from the hall door at eleven o'clock mounted on Sprite, as the little horse was called, and felt herself from head to foot to be one of Colonel Stubbs's team. When at Glenbogie she had ridden a little, and again in Italy, and, being fearless by nature, had no trepidation to impair the fulness of her delight.

Hunting from home coverts rarely exacts much jumping from ladies. The woods are big, and the gates are numerous. It is when the far-

away homes of wild foxes are drawn,—those secluded brakes and
gorses where the nobler animal is wont to live at a distance from car-
riage-roads and other weak refuges of civilization,—that the riding
capacities of ladies must be equal to those of their husbands and
brothers. This present moment was an occasion for great delight,—
at least, so it was found by both Nina and Ayala. But it was not an
opportunity for great glory. Till it was time for lunch one fox after
another ran about the big woods of Albury in a fashion that seemed
perfect to the two girls, but which nearly broke the heart of old Tony,
who was still huntsman to the Ufford and Rufford United Hunt.
"Darm their nasty ways," said Tony to Mr. Larry Twentyman, who
was one of the popular habitués of the hunt; "they runs one a top of
another brushes, till there ain't a 'ound living knows t'other from
which. There's always a many on 'em at Albury, but I never knew an
Albury fox worth his grub yet." But there was galloping along roads
and through gates, and long strings of horsemen following each other up
and down the rides, and an easy coming back to the places from which
they started, which made the girls think that the whole thing was
divine. Once or twice there was a little bank, and once or twice a
little ditch,—just sufficient to make Ayala feel that no possible fence
would be a difficulty to Sprite. She soon learnt that mode of governing her body which leaping requires, and when she was brought into
lunch at about two she was sure that she could do anything which the
art of hunting required. But at lunch an edict went forth as to the two
girls, against further hunting for that day. Nina strove to rebel, and
Ayala attempted to be eloquent by a supplicating glance at the Colonel.
But they were told that as the horses would be wanted again on Friday
they had done enough. In truth, Tony had already trotted off with
the hounds to Pringle's Gorse, a distance of five miles, and the gentlemen who had lingered over their lunch had to follow him at their best
pace. "Pringle's Gorse is not just the place for young ladies," Sir
Harry said, and so the matter had been decided against Nina and
Ayala.

At about six Sir Harry, Colonel Stubbs, and the other gentlemen
returned, declaring that nothing quicker than their run from Pringle's
Gorse had ever been known in that country. "About six miles
straight on end in forty minutes," said the Colonel, "and then a kill
in the open."

"He was laid up under a bank," said young Gosling.

"He was so beat, he couldn't carry on a field farther," said Captain
Batsby, who was staying in the house.

"I call that the open," said Stubbs.

"I always think I kill a fox in the open," said Sir Harry, "when the hounds run into him, because he cannot run another yard with the country there before him." Then there was a long discussion, as they stood drinking tea before the fire, as to what "the open" meant, from which they went to other hunting matters. To all this Ayala listened with attentive ears, and was aware that she had spent a great day. Oh, what a difference was there between Stalham and Kingsbury Crescent!

The next two days were almost equally full of delight. She was taken into the stables to see her horse, and as she patted his glossy coat she felt that she loved Sprite with all her heart. Oh, what a world of joy was this;—how infinitely superior even to Queen's Gate and Glenbogie! The gaudy magnificence of the Tringles had been altogether unlike the luxurious comfort of Stalham, where everybody was at his ease, where everybody was good-natured, where everybody seemed to acknowledge that pleasure was the one object of life! On the evening before the Friday she was taken out to dinner by Captain Batsby. She was not sure that she liked Captain Batsby, who made little complimentary speeches to her. But her neighbour on the other side was Colonel Stubbs, and she was quite sure that she liked Colonel Stubbs.

"I know you'll go like a bird to-morrow," said Captain Batsby.

"I shouldn't like that, because there would be no jumping," said Ayala.

"But you'd be such a beautiful bird." The Captain, as he drawled out his words, made an eye at her, and she was sure that she did not like the Captain.

"At what time are we to start to-morrow?" she said, turning to the Colonel.

"Ten, sharp. Mind you're ready. Sir Harry takes us on the drag, and wouldn't wait for Venus, though she wanted five minutes more for her back hair."

"I don't suppose she ever wants any time for her back hair. I wouldn't if I were a goddess."

"Then you'd be a very untidy goddess, that's all. I wonder whether you are untidy."

"Well;—yes;—sometimes."

"I hate untidy girls."

"Thank you, Colonel Stubbs."

"What I like is a nice prim little woman, who never had a pin in the wrong place in her life. Her cuffs and collars are always as stiff as steel, and she never rubs the sleeves of her dresses by leaning about, like some young ladies.'

"That's what I do."

" My young woman never sits down lest she should crease her dress. My young woman never lets her ribbons get tangled. My young woman can dress upon £40 a-year, and always look as though she came out of a band-box."

" I don't believe you've got a young woman, Colonel Stubbs."

" Well ; no ; I haven't,—except in my imagination."

If so, he too must have his Angel of Light ! " Do you ever dream about her ?"

" Oh dear, yes. I dream that she does scold so awfully when I have her to myself. In my dreams, you know, I'm married to her, and she always wants me to eat hashed mutton. Now, if there is one thing that makes me more sick than another it is hashed mutton. Of course I shall marry her in some of my waking moments, and then I shall have to eat hashed mutton for ever."

Then Captain Batsby put in another word. " I should so like to be allowed to give you a lead to-morrow."

" Oh, thank you,—but I'd rather not have it," said Ayala, who was altogether in the dark, thinking that " a lead " might be some present which she would not wish to accept from Captain Batsby.

" I mean that I should like to show you a line if we get a run."

" What is a line ?" asked Ayala.

" A line ? Why a line is just a lead ;—keep your eye on me and I'll take the fences where you can follow without coming to grief."

" Oh," said Ayala, " that's a lead is it ? Colonel Stubbs is going to give my friend and me a lead, as long as we stay here."

" No man ever ought to coach more than one lady at once," said the Captain, showing his erudition. " You're sure to come on top of one another if there are two."

" But Colonel Stubbs is especially told by the Marchesa to look after both of us," said Ayala almost angrily. Then she turned her shoulder to him, and was soon intent upon further instructions from the Colonel.

The following morning was fine, and all the ladies in the house were packed on to the top of Sir Harry's drag. The Colonel sat behind Sir Harry on the plea that he was wanted to take care of the two girls. Captain Batsby and three other gentlemen were put inside, were they consoled themselves with unlimited tobacco. In this way they were driven to a spot called Rufford Cross Roads, where they found Tony Tappett sitting perfectly quiescent on his old mare, while the hounds were seated around him on the grassy sides of the roads. With him was talking a stout, almost middle-aged gentleman, in a scarlet coat, and natty pink-top boots, who was the owner of all the country around. This was Lord Rufford, who a few years since was known as one of the hardest riders in those parts ; but he had degenerated into matrimony, was now the happy father of half-a-dozen babies, and was hardly ever seen to jump over a fence. But he still came out when the meets were not too distant, and carefully performed that first duty of an English country gentleman,—the preservation of foxes. Though he did not ride much, no one liked a little hunting gossip better than Lord Rufford. It was, however, observed that even in regard to hunting he was apt to quote the authority of his wife.

" Oh, yes, my Lord," said Tony, " there'll sure to be a fox at Dills-borough. But we'll find one afore we get to Rufford, my Lord."

" Lady Rufford says there hasn't been a fox seen in the home woods this week."

" Her ladyship will be sure to know," said Tony.

" Do you remember that fence where poor Major Caneback got his fall six years ago ?" asked the Lord.

" Seven years next Christmas, my Lord," said Tony. " He never put a leg across a saddle again, poor fellow ? I remember him well, my Lord ; a man who could 'andle a 'orse wonderful, though he didn't know 'ow to ride to 'ounds ; not according to my idea. To get your animal to carry you through, never mind 'ow long the thing is ; that's my idea of riding to 'ounds, my Lord. The major was for always making a 'orse jump over everything. I never wants 'em to jump over nothing I can't 'elp ;—I don't, my Lord."

" That's just what her ladyship is always saying to me," said Lord Rufford, " and I do pretty much what her ladyship tells me."

On this occasion Lady Rufford had been quite right about the home covers. No doubt she generally was right in any assertion she made as to her husband's affairs. After drawing them Tony trotted on towards Dillsborough, running his hounds through a few little springs, which lay near his way. As they went Colonel Stubbs rode between the two girls. " Whenever 1 see Rufford," said the Colonel, " he does me a world of good."

" What good can a fat man like that do to you ?" said Nina.

" He is a continual sermon against marriage. If I could see Rufford once a week I know that I should be safe."

" He seems to me to be a very comfortable old gentleman," said Ayala.

" Old ! Seven years ago he was acknowledged to be the one undis-puted paragon of a young man in this county. No one else dreamed of looking at a young lady if he chose to turn his eyes in that direction. He was handsome as Apollo—— "

" He an Apollo !" said Nina.

" The best Apollo there then was in these parts, and every one knew that he had forty thousand a-year to spend. Now he is supposed to be the best hand in the house at rocking the cradle."

"Do you mean to say that he nurses the babies?" asked Ayala.

"He looks as if he did at any rate. He never goes ten miles away from his door without having Lady Rufford with him, and is always tucked up at night just at half-past ten by her ladyship's own maid. Ten years ago he would generally have been found at midnight with cards in his hand and a cigar in his mouth. Now he is allowed two cigarettes a-day. Well, Mr. Twentyman, how are you getting on?" This he said to a good-looking better sort of farmer, who came up, riding a remarkably strong horse, and dressed in pink and white cords.

"Thank ye, Colonel, pretty well, considering how hard the times are. A man who owns a few acres and tries to farm them must be on the road to ruin now-a-days. That's what I'm always telling my wife, so that she may know what she has got to expect." Mr. Twentyman had been married just twelve months.

"She isn't much frightened, I daresay," said the Colonel.

"She's young, you see," continued the farmer, "and hasn't settled herself down yet to the sorrows of life." This was that Mr. Lawrence Twentyman who married Kate Masters, the youngest daughter of old Masters, the attorney at Dillsborough, and sister of Mrs. Morton, wife of the squire of Bragton. "By the holy," said Twentyman, suddenly, "the hounds have put a fox out of that little spinney."

CHAPTER XXIV.

RUFFORD CROSS ROADS.

AYALA, who had been listening attentively to the conversation of Mr. Twentyman, and been feeling that she was being initiated every moment into a new phase of life,—who had been endeavouring to make some connection in her mind between the new charms of the world around her and that world of her dreams that was ever present to her, and had as yet simply determined that neither could Lord Rufford or Mr. Twentyman have ever been an Angel of Light,—at once straightened herself in her saddle, and prepared herself for the doing of something memorable. It was evident to her that Mr. Twentyman considered that the moment for action had come. He did not gallop off wildly, as did four or five others, but stood still for a moment looking intently at a few hounds who, with their tails feathering in the air and with their noses down, seemed at the same time to be irresolute and determined, knowing that the scent was there but not yet quite fixed as to its line. "Half a moment, Colonel," he said, standing up in his stirrups, with his left hand raised, while his right held his reins and his whip close down on his horse's neck. "Half a moment!" He only whispered, and then shook his head angrily, as he heard the ill-timed shouting of one or two men who had already reached the other side of the little skirting of trees. "I wish Fred Botsey's tongue were tied to his teeth," he said, still whispering. "Now, Colonel, they have it. There's a little lane to the right, and a gate. After that the country's open, and there's nothing which the ladies' nags can't do. I know the country so well, you'd perhaps better come with me for a bit."

"He knows all about it," said the Colonel to Ayala. "Do as he tells you."

Ayala and Nina both were quick enough to obey. Twentyman dashed along the lane, while the girls followed him with the Colonel after them. When they were at the hunting-gate already spoken of, old Tony Tappett was with them, trotting, impatient to get to the hounds, courteously giving place to the ladies,—whom, however, in his heart, he wished at home in bed,—and then thrusting himself through the gate in front of the Colonel. "D—— their pig-headed folly," he said, as he came up to his friend Twentyman—"they knows no more about it than if they'd just come from be'ind a counter,—'olloaing, 'olloaing, 'olloaing,—as if 'olloaing 'd make a fox break! 'Owsomever 'e's off now, and they've got Cranbury Brook between them and 'is line!" This he said in a squeaking little voice, intended to be jocose and satiric, shaking his head as he rode. This last idea seemed to give him great consolation.

It was the consideration, deep and well-founded, as to the Cranbury which had induced Larry Twentyman to pause on the road when he had paused, and then to make for the lane and the gate. The direction had hardly seemed to be that of the hounds, but Larry knew the spinney, knew the brook,—knew the fox, perhaps,—and was aware of the spot at which the brute would cross the water if he did cross it. The brute did cross the water, and therefore there was Cranbury Brook between many of the forward riders and his line.

Sir Harry was then with them, and two or three other farmers. But Larry had a lead, and the two girls were with him. Tony Tappett, though he had got up to his hounds, did not endeavour to ride straight to them as did Larry Twentyman. He was old and unambitious, very anxious to know where his hounds were, so that he might be with them should they want the assistance of his voice and counsel, anxious to be near enough to take their fox from them should they run into him, but taking no glory in jumping over a fence if he could avoid it, creeping about here and there, knowing from experience nearly every turn

in the animal's mind, aware of every impediment which would delay
him, riding fast only when the impediments were far between, taking
no amusement to himself out of the riding, but with his heart cruelly,
bloodily, ruthlessly set upon killing the animal before him. To kill
his fox he would imperil his neck, but for the glory of riding he would
not soil his boots if he could help it. After the girls came the Colonel,
somewhat shorn of his honour in that he was no longer giving them a
lead, but doing his best to maintain the pace, which Twentyman was
making, very good. "Now, young ladies," said Twentyman, "give
them their heads, and let them do it just as they please,—alongside of
each other, and not too near to me." It was a brook,—a confluent of
Cranbury Brook, and was wide enough to require a good deal of jumping. It may be supposed that the two young ladies did not understand
much of the instructions given to them. To hold their breath and be
brave was the only idea present to them. The rest must come from
instinct and chance. The other side of the brook was heaven ;—this
would be purgatory. Larry, fearing perhaps that the order as to their
not being too near might not be obeyed, added a little to his own pace
so as to be clear of them. Nevertheless they were only a few strides
behind, and had Larry's horse missed his footing there would have been
a mess. As it was they took the brook side by side close to each other,
and landed full of delight and glory on the opposite bank. "Bravo !
young ladies," shouted Twentyman.

"Oh, Nina, that is divine," said Ayala. Nina was a little too much
out of breath for answering but simply threw up her eyes to heaven
and made a flourish with her whip, intended to be expressive of her
perfect joy.

Away went Larry and away went the girls with him, quite unconscious that the Colonel's horse had balked the brook and then jumped
into it,—quite unconscious that Sir Harry seeing the Colonel's catastrophe had followed Tony a quarter of a mile up the brook to a
ford. Even in the soft bosoms of young ladies "the devil take the
hindmost" will be the motto most appropriate for hunting. Larry
Twentyman, of whom they had never heard before, was now the god
of their idolatry. Where Larry Twentyman might go it was manifestly their duty to follow, even though they should never see the poor
Colonel again. They recked nothing of the fox or of the hounds or of
the master or even of the huntsman. They had a man before them to
show them the way, and as long as they could keep him in sight
each was determined to be at any rate as good as the other. To
give Larry his due it must be acknowledged that he was thoroughly
thoughtful of them. At every fence encountered he studied the
spot at which they would be least likely to fall. He had to re-

member, also, that there were two of them together, and that he had made himself in a way responsible for the safety of both. All this he did, and did well, because he knew his business. With the exception of the water-jump, the country over which they passed was not difficult. For a time there was a run of gates, each of which their guide was able to open for them, and as they came near to Dillsborough Wood there were gaps in most of the fences; but it seemed to the girls that they had galloped over monstrous hedges and leapt over walls which it would almost take a strong man to climb. The brook, however,—the river as it seemed to them,—had been the crowning glory. Ayala was sure that that brook would never be forgotten by her. Even the Angel of Light was hardly more heavenly than the brook.

That the fox was running for Dillsborough Wood was a fact well known both to Tony Tappett and Mr. Larry Twentyman. A fox crossing the brook from the Rufford side would be sure to run to Dillsborough Wood. When Larry, with the two girls, were just about to enter the ride, there was old Tony standing up on his horse at the corner, looking into the covert. And now also a crowd of horsemen came rushing up, who had made their way along the road, and had passed up to the wood through Mr. Twentyman's farm-yard; —for, as it happened, here it was that Mr. Twentyman lived and farmed his own land. Then came Sir Harry, Colonel Stubbs, and some others who had followed the line throughout,—the Colonel with his boots full of water, as he had been forced to get off his horse in the bed of the brook. Sir Harry, himself, was not in the best of humours, —as will sometimes be the case with masters when they fail to see the cream of a run. "I never saw such riding in my life," said Sir Harry, as though some great sin had been committed by those to whom he was addressing himself. Larry turned round, and winked at the two girls, knowing that, if sin had been committed, they three were the sinners. The girls understood nothing about it, but still thought that Larry Twentyman was divine.

While they were standing about on the rides, Tony was still at his work. The riding was over, but the fox had to be killed, and Dillsborough Wood was a covert in which a fox will often require a large amount of killing. No happier home for the vulpine deity exists among the shires of England! There are earths there deep, capacious, full of nurseries; but these, on the present occasion, were debarred from the poor stranger by the wicked ingenuity of man. But there were deep dells, in which the brambles and bracken were so thick that no hound, careful of his snout, would penetrate them. The undergrowth of the wood was so interwoven that no huntsman could see through its depths.   There were dark nooks so impervious that any fox, ignorant of the theory of his own scent, must have wondered why a hound should have been induced to creep into spaces so narrow. From one side to another of the wood the hunted brute would traverse, and always seem to have at last succeeded in putting his persecutors at fault. So it was on this occasion. The run, while it lasted, had occupied, perhaps, three-quarters of an hour, and during a time equally long poor old Tony was to be seen scurrying from one side of the wood to another, and was to be heard loudly swearing at his attendant whips because the hounds did not follow his footsteps as quickly as his soul desired.

" I never mean to put on a pair of top-boots again, as long as I live," said the Colonel.   At this time a little knot of horsemen was stationed in a knoll in the centre of the wood, waiting till they should hear the fatal whoop.   Among them were Nina, Ayala, the Colonel, Larry Twentyman, and Captain Batsby.

" Give up top-boots?" said Larry.   " You don't mean to say you'll ride in black !"

" Top-boots, black boots, spurs, breeches, and red coat, I renounce them all from this moment.   If ever I'm seen in a hunting-field again it will be in a pair of trowsers with overalls."

" Now, you're joking, Colonel," said Larry.

" Why won't you wear a red coat any more ?" said Ayala.

" Because I'm disgraced for ever.   I came out to coach two young women, and give them a lead, and all I've done was to tumble into a brook, while a better man has taken my charge away from me."

" Oh, Jonathan, I am so sorry," said Nina, " particularly about your getting into the water."

" Oh, Colonel Stubbs, we ought to have stopped," said Ayala.

" It was my only comfort to see how very little I was wanted," said the Colonel.   " If I had broke my neck instead of wetting my feet it would have been just the same to some people."

" Oh, Jonathan !" said Nina, really shocked.

" We ought to have stopped.   I know we ought to have stopped," said Ayala, almost crying.

" Nobody ever stops for anyone out hunting," said Twentyman, laying down a great law.

" I should think not," said Captain Batsby, who had hardly been off the road all the time.

" I am sure the Colonel will not be angry with me because I took the young ladies on," said Larry.

" The Colonel is such a muff," said the Colonel himself, " that he will never presume to be angry with anybody again.   But if my cousin and Miss Dormer are not very much obliged to you for what you have done for them there will be nothing of gratitude left in the female British bosom. You have probably given to them the most triumphant moment of their existence."

"It was their own riding, Colonel; I had nothing to do with it."

"I am so much obliged to you, Sir," said Nina.

"And so am I," said Ayala, "though it was such a pity that Colonel Stubbs got into the water."

At that moment came the long-expected call. Tony Tappett had killed his fox, after crossing and re-crossing through the wood half a score of times. "Is it all over?" asked Ayala, as they hurried down the knoll and scurried down the line to get to the spot outside the wood to which Tony was dragging the carcase of his defeated enemy.

"It's all over for him," said Larry. "A good fox he was, but he'll never run again. He is one of them bred at Littlecotes. The foxes bred at Littlecotes always run."

"And is he dead?" asked Nina. "Poor fellow!--I wish it wasn't necessary to kill them." Then they stood by till they saw the body of the victim thrown up into the air, and fall amongst the blood-smirched upturned noses of the expectant pack.

"I call that a pretty little run, Sir Harry," said Larry Twentyman.

"Pretty well," said Sir Harry; "the pace wasn't very great, or that pony of mine which Miss Dormer is riding could not have lived with it."

"Horses, Sir Harry, don't want so much pace, if they are allowed to go straight. It's when a man doesn't get well away, or has made a mess with his fences, that he needs an extra allowance of pace to catch the hounds. If you're once with them and can go straight you may keep your place without such a deal of legs." To this Sir Harry replied only by a grunt, as on the present occasion he had "made a mess with his fences," as Larry Twentyman had called it.

"And now, young ladies," said Larry, "I hope you'll come in and see my missus and her baby, and have a little bit of lunch, such as it is."

Nina asked anxiously whether there would not be another fox. Ayala also was anxious lest in accepting the proffered hospitality she should lose any of the delights of the day. But it was at length arranged that a quarter of an hour should be allowed before Tony took his hounds over to the Bragton coverts. Immediately Larry was off his horse, rushing into the house and ordering everyone about it to come forth with bread and cheese and sherry and beer. In spite of what he had said of his ruin it was known that Larry Twentyman was

a warm man, and that no man in Rufford gave what he had to give with
a fuller heart. His house was in the middle of the Rufford and Ufford
hunting country, and the consumption there during the hunting
months of bread and cheese, sherry and beer, must have been
immense. Everyone seemed to be intimate with him, and all called
for what they wanted as if they were on their own premises. On such
occasions as these Larry was a proud man ; for no one in those parts
carried a lighter heart or was more fond of popularity.

The parlour inside was by no means big enough to hold the crowding
guests, who therefore munched their bread and cheese and drank their
beer round the front door, without dismounting from their horses ; but
Nina and Ayala with their friend the Colonel were taken inside to see
Mrs. Twentyman and her baby. "Now, Larry, what sort of a run
was it ?" said the young mother. "Where did you find him, and what
line did he take ?"

"I'll tell you all about it when I come back ; there are two young
ladies for you now to look after." Then he introduced his wife, and
the baby which was in her arms. "The little fellow is only six weeks
old, and yet she wanted to come to the meet. She'd have been riding
to hounds if I'd let her."

"Why not ?" said Mrs. Twentyman. "At any rate, I might have
gone in the pony carriage and had baby with me."

"Only six weeks old !" said Nina, stooping down and kissing the
child.

"He is a darling !" said Ayala. "I hope he'll go out hunting some
day."

"He'll want to go six times a week if he's anything like his father,"
said Mrs. Twentyman.

"And seven times if he's like his mother," said Larry. Then
again they mounted their nags, and trotted off across the high roads
to the Bragton coverts. Mrs. Twentyman with her baby in her arms
walked down to the gate at the high road and watched them with longing eyes, till Tony and the hounds were out of sight.

Nothing further in the way of hunting was done that day which
requires to be recorded. They drew various coverts and found a fox
or two, but the scent which had been so strong in the morning seemed
to have gone, and the glory of the day was over. The two girls and
the Colonel remained companions during the afternoon, and succeeded
in making themselves merry over the incident of the brook. The
Colonel was in truth well pleased that Larry Twentyman should have
taken his place, though he probably would not have been gratified had
he seen Captain Batsby assume his duties. It had been his delight to
see the two girls ride, and he had been near enough to see them. He

was one of those men who, though fond of hunting, take no special glory in it, and are devoid of the jealousy of riding. Not to have a good place in a run was no worse to him than to lose a game of billiards or a rubber of whist. Let the reader understand that this trait in his character is not mentioned with approbation. "Always to excel and to go ahead of everybody" should, the present writer thinks, be in the heart of every man who rides to hounds. There was in our Colonel a philosophical way of looking into the thing which perhaps became him as a man, but was deleterious to his character as a sportsman.

"I do so hope you've enjoyed yourself, Ayala!" he said, as he lifted her from her horse.

"Indeed,—indeed, I have!" said Ayala, not noticing the use of her Christian name. "I have been so happy, and I am so much obliged to you!"

CHAPTER XXV.

"YOU ARE NOT HE."

AYALA had been a week at Stalham, and according to the understanding which had existed she should now have returned to Kingsbury Crescent. She had come for a week, and she had had her week. Oh, what a week it had been, so thoroughly happy, without a cloud, filled full with ecstatic pleasures! Jonathan Stubbs had become to her the pleasantest of friends. Lady Albury had covered her with caresses and little presents. Nina was the most perfect of friends. Sir Harry had never been cross, except for that one moment in the wood. And as for Sprite,—Sprite had nearly realised her idea of an Angel of Light. Oh, how happy she had been! She was to return on the Monday, having thus comprised two Sundays within her elongated week. She knew that her heaven was to be at an end; but she was grateful, and was determined in her gratitude to be happy and cheerful to the close. But early on this Sunday morning Colonel Stubbs spoke a word to Lady Albury. "That little girl is so thoroughly happy here. Cannot you prolong it for her just for another three days?"

"Is it to be for her,—or for Colonel Stubbs, who is enamoured of the little girl?" asked Lady Albury.

"For both," said the Colonel, rather gravely.

"Are you in earnest?"

"What do you call earnest? I do love to see a pretty creature enjoy herself thoroughly as she does. If you will make her stay till Thursday Albury will let her ride the little horse again at Star Cross on Wednesday."

" Of course she shall stay,—all the season if you wish it. She is indeed a happy girl if you are in earnest."

Then it was settled, and Lady Albury in her happiest manner informed Ayala that she was not to be allowed to take her departure till after she had ridden Sprite once again. " Sir Harry says that you have given the little horse quite a name, and that you must finish off his character for him at Star Cross." As was the heart of the Peri when the gate of Paradise was opened for her so was the heart of Ayala. There were to be four days, with the fourth as a hunting-day, before she need think of going ! There was an eternity of bliss before her.

" But Aunt Margaret !" she said, not, however, doubting for a moment that she would stay. Who cares for a frowning aunt at the distance of an eternity. I fear that in the ecstasy of her joy she had forgotten the promise made, that she would always remember her aunt's goodness to her. " I will write a note to Mrs. Dosett, and make it all straight," said Lady Albury. The note was written, and, whether matters were straight or crooked at Kingsbury Crescent, Ayala remained at Albury.

Colonel Stubbs had thought about the matter, and determined that he was quite in earnest. He had, he told himself, enough for modest living,—for modest living without poverty. More would come to him when old General Stubbs, his uncle, should die. The general was already past seventy. What was the use of independence if he could not allow himself to have the girl whom he really loved ? Had any human being so perfectly lovely as Ayala ever flashed before his eyes before ? Was there ever a sweeter voice heard from a woman's mouth ? And then all her little ways and motions,—her very tricks,—how full of charm they were ! When she would open her eyes and nod her head, and pout with her lips, he would declare to himself that he could no longer live without her. And then every word that fell from her lips seemed to have something in it of pretty humour. In fact the Colonel was in love, and had now resolved that he would give way to his love in spite of his aunt, the Marchesa, and in spite of his own philosophy.

He felt by no means sure of success, but yet he thought that he might succeed. From the moment in which, as the reader may remember, he had accosted her at the ball, and desired her to dance with him in obedience to his aunt's behests, it had been understood by every one around him that Ayala had liked him. They had become fast friends. Ayala allowed him to do many little things which, by some feminine instinct of her own, would have been put altogether beyond the reach of Captain Batsby. The Colonel knew all this, and knew at the same time that he should not trust to it only. But still he

could not but trust to it in some degree. Lady Albury had told him
that Ayala would be a happy girl if he were in earnest, and he himself
was well aware of Ayala's dependent position, and of the discomforts of
Kingsbury Crescent. Ayala had spoken quite openly to him of Kingsbury Crescent as to a confidential friend. But on all that he did not
lean much as being in his favour. He could understand that such
a girl as Ayala would not accept a husband merely with the object of
avoiding domestic poverty. Little qualms of doubt came upon him as he
remembered the nature of the girl, so that he confessed to himself that
Lady Albury knew nothing about it. But, nevertheless, he hoped.
His red hair and his ugly face had never yet stood against him among
the women with whom he had lived. He had been taught by popularity to think himself a popular man ;— and then Ayala had shown so
many signs of her friendship!

There was shooting on Saturday, and he went out with the shooters,
saying nothing to any one of an intended early return ; but at three
o'clock he was back at the house. Then he found that Ayala was out
in the carriage, and he waited. He sat in the library pretending to
read, till he heard the sounds of the carriage-wheels, and then he met
the ladies in the hall. "Are they all home from shooting?" asked
Lady Albury. The Colonel explained that no one was home but himself. He had missed three cock-pheasants running, and had then
come away in disgust. "I am the most ignominious creature in existence," he said, laughing ; "one day I tumble into a ditch three feet
wide——"

"It was ten yards at least," said Nina, jealous as to the glory of her
jump.

"And to-day I cannot hit a bird. I shall take to writing a book
and leave the severer pursuit of sport to more enterprising persons."
Then suddenly turning round he said to Ayala, "Are you good-
natured enough to come and take a walk with me in the shrubbery?"

Ayala, taken somewhat by surprise at the request, looked up into
Lady Albury's face. "Go with him, my dear, if you are not tired,"
said Lady Albury. "He deserves consolation after all his good deeds
to you." Ayala still doubted. Though she was on terms of pleasant
friendship with the man, yet she felt almost awestruck at this sudden
request that she should walk alone with him. But not to do so, especially after Lady Albury's injunction, would have been peculiar. She
certainly was not tired, and had such a walk come naturally it would
have been an additional pleasure to her ; but now, though she went she
hesitated, and showed her hesitation.

"Are you afraid to come with me?" he said, as soon as they were
out on the gravel together.

" Afraid ! Oh, dear no, I should not be afraid to go anywhere with you, I think ; only it seemed odd that you did not ask Nina too."

" Shall I tell you why ?"

" Why was it ?"

" Because I have something to say to you which I do not want Nina to hear just at this moment. And then I thought that we were such friends that you would not mind coming with me."

" Of course we are," said Ayala.

" I don't know why it should be so, but I seem to have known you years instead of days."

" Perhaps that is because you knew papa."

" More likely because I have learnt to know your papa's daughter."

" Do you mean Lucy ?"

" I mean Ayala."

" That is saying the same thing twice over. You know me because you know me."

" Just that. How long do you suppose I have known that Mrs. Gregory, who sat opposite to us yesterday ?"

" How can I tell ?"

" Just fifteen years. I was going to Harrow when she came as a young girl to stay with my mother. Her people and my people had known each other for the last fifty years. Since that I have seen her constantly, and of course we are very intimate."

" I suppose so."

" I know as much about her after all that as if we had lived in two different hemispheres and couldn't speak a word of each other's language. There isn't a thought or a feeling in common between us. I ask after her husband and her children, and then tell her it's going to rain. She says something about the old General's health, and then there is an end of everything between us. When next we meet we do it all over again."

" How very uninteresting !" said Ayala.

" Very uninteresting. It is because there are so many Mrs. Gregorys about that I like to go down to Drumcaller and live by myself. Perhaps you're a Mrs. Gregory to somebody."

" Why should I be a Mrs. Gregory ? I don't think I am at all like Mrs. Gregory."

" Not to me, Ayala." Now she heard the " Ayala," and felt something of what it meant. There had been moments at which she had almost disliked to hear him call her Miss Dormer ; but now,—now she wished that he had not called her Ayala. She strove to assume a serious expression of face, but having done so she could not dare to turn it up towards him. The glance of her little anger, if there was any, fell only upon the ground. "It is because you are to me a creature so essentially different from Mrs. Gregory that I seem to know you so well. I never want to go to Drumcaller if you are near me ;—or, if I think of Drumcaller, it is that I might be there with you."

"I am sure the place is very pretty, but I don't suppose I shall ever see it."

"Do you know about your sister and Mr. Hamel?"

"Yes," said Ayala, surprised. "She has told me all about it. How do you know?"

"He was staying at Drumcaller,—he and I together with no one else,—when he went over to ask her. I never saw a man so happy as when he came back from Glenbogie. He had got all that he wanted in the world."

"I do so love him because he loves her."

"And I love her,—because she loves you."

"It is not the same, you know," said Ayala, trying to think it all out.

"May I not love her?"

"He is to be my brother. That's why I love him. She can't be your sister." The poor girl, though she had tried to think it all out, had not thought very far.

"Can she not?" he said.

"Of course not. Lucy is to marry Mr. Hamel."

"And whom am I to marry?" Then she saw it all. "Ayala,—Ayala,—who is to be my wife?"

"I do not know," she said,—speaking with a gruff voice, but still in a whisper, with a manner altogether different,—thinking how well it would be that she should be taken at once back into the house.

"Do you not know whom I would fain have as my wife?" Then he felt that it behoved him to speak out plainly. He was already sure that she would not at once tell him that it should be as he would have it,—that she would not instantly throw herself into his arms. But he must speak plainly to her, and then fight his cause as best he might. "Ayala, I have asked you to come out with me that I might ask you to be my wife. It is that that I did not wish Nina to hear at once. If you will put out your hand and say that it shall be so, Nina and all the world shall know it. I shall be as proud then as Hamel, and as happy, —happier, I think. It seems to me that no one can love as I do now, Ayala ; it has grown upon me from hour to hour as I have seen you. When I first took you away to that dance it was so already. Do you remember that night at the theatre,—when I had come away from everything and striven so hard that I might be near to you before you went back to your home? Ayala, I loved you then so dearly ;—but

not as I love you now.   When I saw you riding away from me yesterday, when I could not get over the brook, I told myself that unless I
might catch you at last, and have you all to myself, I could never
again be happy.   Do you remember when you stooped down and
kissed that man's baby at the farm-house?   Oh, Ayala, I thought then
that if you would not be my wife,—if you would not be my wife,—I
should never have wife, never should have baby, never should have
home of my own."   She walked on by his side, listening, but she had
not a word to say to him.   It had been easy enough to her to reject
and to rebuke and to scorn Tom Tringle, when he had persisted in his
suit; but she knew not with what words to reject this man who stood
so high in her estimation, who was in many respects so perfect, whom
she so thoroughly liked,—but whom, nevertheless, she must reject.
He was not the Angel of Light,—could never be the Angel of Light.
There was nothing there of the azure wings upon which should soar
the all but celestial being to whom she could condescend to give herself and her love.   He was pleasant, good, friendly, kind-hearted,—
all that a friend or a brother should be; but he was not the Angel of
Light.   She was sure of that.   She told herself that she was quite
sure of it, as she walked beside him in silence along the path.   "You
know what I mean, Ayala, when I tell you that I love you," he continued.   But still she made no answer.   "I have seen at last the one
human being with whom I feel that I can be happy to spend my life,
and, having seen her, I ask her to be my wife.   The hope has been
dwelling with me and growing since I first met you.   Shall it be a
vain hope?   Ayala, may I still hope?"

   "No," she said, abruptly.

   "Is that all?"

   "It is all that I can say."

   "Is that one 'no' to be the end of everything between us?"

   "I don't know what else I ought to say to you, Colonel Stubbs."

   "Do you mean that you can never love me?"

   "Never," she said.

   "That is a hard word,—and hardly friendly.   Is there to be no
more than one hard word between you and me?   Though I did not
venture to think that you could tell me that you loved me, I looked
for something kinder, something gentler than that."

> "From such a sharp and waspish word as 'no,'
> "To pluck the sting!"

Ayala did not know the lines I have quoted, but the idea conveyed
in them was present clearly to her mind.   She would fain have told

him, had she known how to do so, that her heart was very gentle towards him, was very kind, gentle and kind as a sister's;—but that she could not love him, so as to become his wife. "You are not he,—not he, not that Angel of Light, which must come to me, radiant with poetry, beautiful to the eye, full of all excellences of art, lifted above the earth by the qualities of his mind,—such a one as must come to me if it be that I am ever to confess that I love. You are not he, and I cannot love you. But you shall be the next to him in my estimation, and you are already so dear to me that I would be tender to you, would be gentle,—if only I knew how." It was all there, clear enough in her mind, but she had not the words. "I don't know what it is that I ought to say," she exclaimed through her sobs.

"The truth, at any rate," he answered, sternly, "but not the truth, half and half, after the fashion of some young ladies. Do not think that you should palter with the truth either because it may not be palatable to me, or seem decorous to yourself. To my happiness this matter is all important, and you are something to my happiness, if only because I have risked it on your love. Tell me;—why cannot you love me?"

The altered tone of his voice, which now had in it something of severity, seemed to give her more power.

"It is because——" Then she paused.

"Because why? Out with it, whatever it is. If it be something that a man may remedy I will remedy it. Do not fear to hurt me. Is it because I am ugly? That I cannot remedy." She did not dare to tell him that it was so, but she looked up at him, not dissenting by any motion of her head. "Then God help me, for ugly I must remain."

"It is not that only."

"Is it because my name is Stubbs,—Jonathan Stubbs?" Now she did assent, nodding her head at him. He had bade her tell him the truth, and she was so anxious to do as he bade her! "If it be so, Ayala, I must tell you that you are wrong,—wrong and foolish; that you are carried away by a feeling of romance, which is a false romance. Far be it from me to say that I could make you happy, but I am sure that your happiness cannot be made and cannot be marred by such accidents as that. Do you think that my means are not sufficient?"

"No;—no," she cried; "I know nothing of your means. If I could love you I would not condescend to ask,—even to hear."

"There is no other man, I think?"

"There is no other man."

"But your imagination has depicted to you something grander than

I am,"—then she assented quickly, turning round and nodding her head to him,—"some one who shall better respond to that spirit of poetry which is within you?" Again she nodded her head approvingly, as though to assure him that now he knew the whole truth. " Then, Ayala, I must strive to soar till I can approach your dreams. But, if you dare to desire things which are really grand, do not allow yourself to be mean at the same time. Do not let the sound of a name move you, or I shall not believe in your aspirations. Now shall I take you back to the house?"

Back to the house they went, and there was not another word spoken between them. By those last words of his she had felt herself to be rebuked. If it were possible that he could ask her again whether that sound, Jonathan Stubbs, had anything to do with it, she would let him know now, by some signal, that she no longer found a barrier in the name. But there were other barriers,—barriers which he himself had not pretended to call vain. As to his ugliness, that he had confessed he could not remedy ; calling on God to pity him because he was so. And as for that something grander which he had described, and for which her soul sighed, he had simply said that he would seek for it. She was sure that he would not find it. It was not to such as he that the something grander,—which was to be the peculiar attribute of the Angel of Light,—could be accorded. But he had owned that the something grander might exist.

CHAPTER XXVI.

" THE FINEST HERO THAT I EVER KNEW."

THE Colonel and Ayala returned to the house without a word. When they were passing through the hall she turned to go at once up the stairs to her own room. As she did so he put out his hand to her, and she took it. But she passed on without speaking, and when she was alone she considered it over all in her own mind. There could be no doubt that she was right. Of that she was quite sure. It was certainly a fixed law that a girl should not marry a man unless she loved him. She did not love this man, and therefore she ought not to marry him. But there were some qualms at her heart as to the possible reality of the image which she had created for her own idolatry. And she had been wounded when he told her that she should not allow herself to be mean amidst her soarings. She had been wounded, and yet she knew that he had been right. He had intended to teach her the same lesson when he told her the absurd story of the woman who had been flung out of the window. She could not love him ; but that name of his should never again be a reason for not doing so. Let the Angel of Light come to her with his necessary angelic qualities, and no want of euphony in a sound should be a barrier to him. Nor in truth could any outside appearance be an attribute of angelic light. The Angel of Light might be there even with red hair. Something as to the truth of this also came across her, though the Colonel had not rebuked her on that head.

But how should she carry herself now during the four days which remained to her at Stalham Park? All the loveliness seemed to depart from her prospect. She would hardly know how to open her mouth before her late friend. She suspected that Lady Albury knew with what purpose the Colonel had taken her out into the shrubbery, and she would not dare to look Lady Albury in the face. How should she answer Nina if Nina were to ask her questions about the walk. The hunt for next Wednesday was no longer a delight to which she could look forward. How would it be possible that Colonel Stubbs should direct her now as to her riding, and instruct her as to her conduct in the hunting-field? It would be better for her that she should return at once to Kingsbury Crescent.

As she thought of this there did come upon her a reflection that had she been able to accept Colonel Stubbs's offer there would have been an end for ever to the miseries of her aunt's house. She would have been lifted at once into the mode of life in which the man lived. Instead of being a stranger admitted by special grace into such an Elysium as that of Stalham Park, she would become one of those to whom such an Elysium belonged almost of right. By her own gifts she would have won her way into that upper and brighter life which seemed to her to be all smiles and all joy. As to his income she thought nothing and cared nothing. He lived with men who had horses and carriages, and who spent their time in pleasurable pursuits. And she would live amidst ladies who were always arrayed in bright garments, who, too, had horses and carriages at their command, and were never troubled by those sordid cares which made life at Kingsbury Crescent so sad and tedious. One little word would have done it all for her, would have enabled her to take the step by which she would be placed among the bright ones of the earth.

But the remembrance of all this only made her firmer in her resolution. If there was any law of right and wrong fixed absolutely in her bosom, it was this,—that no question of happiness or unhappiness, of suffering or joy, would affect her duty to the Angel of Light. She owed herself to him should he come to seek her. She owed herself to him no less, even should he fail to come. And she owed herself equally

whether he should be rich or poor. As she was fortifying herself with
these assurances, Nina came to ask her whether she would not come
down to tea. Ayala pleaded headache, and said that she would rest
till dinner. "Has anything happened?" asked Nina. Ayala simply
begged that she might be asked no questions then, because her head
was aching. "If you do not tell me everything, I shall think you are
no true friend," said Nina, as she left the room.

As evening drew on she dressed for dinner, and went down into the
drawing-room. In doing so it was necessary to pass through the billiard-room, and there she found Colonel Stubbs, knocking about the
balls. "Are you dressed for dinner?" he exclaimed; "I haven't begun
to think of it yet, and Sir Harry hates a man when he comes in late.
That wretch Batsby has beaten me four games." With that he rushed
off, putting down the cue with a rattle, and seeming to Ayala to have
recovered altogether from the late prostration of his spirits.

In the drawing-room Ayala was for a few minutes alone, and then,
as she was glad to see, three or four ladies all came in at once, so that
no question could be asked her by Lady Albury. They went into
dinner without the Colonel, who was in truth late, and she was taken
in by Mr. Gosling, whose pretty little wife was just opposite to her.
On the other side of her sat Lord Rufford, who had come to Stalham
with his wife for a day or two, and who immediately began to congratulate her on the performance of the day before. "I am told you
jumped the Cranbury Brook," he said. "I should as soon think of
jumping the Serpentine."

"I did it because somebody told me."

"Ah," said Lord Rufford, with a sigh, "there is nothing like
ignorance, innocence, and youth combined. But why didn't Colonel
Stubbs get over after you?"

"Because Colonel Stubbs couldn't," said that gentleman, as he took
his seat in the vacant chair.

"It may be possible," said Sir Harry, "that a gentleman should
not be able to jump over Cranbury Brook; but any gentleman, if he
will take a little trouble, may come down in time for dinner."

"Now that I have been duly snubbed right and left," said the
Colonel, "perhaps I may eat my soup."

Ayala, who had expected she hardly knew what further troubles,
and who had almost feared that nobody would speak to her because
she had misbehaved herself, endeavoured to take heart of grace when
she found that all around her, including the Colonel himself, were as
pleasant as ever. She had fancied that Lady Albury had looked at her
specially when Colonel Stubbs took his seat, and she had specially
noticed the fact that his chair had not been next her own. These

little matters she was aware Lady Albury managed herself, and was aware also that in accordance with the due rotation of things she and the Colonel should have been placed together. She was glad that it was not so, but at the same time she was confident that Lady Albury knew something of what had passed between herself and her suitor. The evening, however, went off easily, and nothing occurred to disturb her except that the Colonel had called her by her christian name, when as usual he brought to her a cup of tea in the drawing-room. Oh, that he would continue to do so, and yet not demand from her more than their old friendship !

The next morning was Sunday, and they all went to church. It was a law at Stalham that everyone should go to church on Sunday morning. Sir Harry himself, who was not supposed to be a peculiarly religious man, was always angry when any male guest did not show himself in the enormous family pew. " I call it d—— indecent," he has been heard to say. But nobody was expected to go twice,—and consequently nobody ever did go twice. Lunch was protracted later than usual. The men would roam about the grounds with cigars in their mouths, and ladies would take to reading in their own rooms, in following which occupation they would spend a considerable part of the afternoon asleep. On this afternoon Lady Albury did not go to sleep, but contrived to get Ayala alone upstairs into her little sitting-room. " Ayala," she said, with something between a smile and a frown, " I am afraid I am going to be angry with you."

" Please don't be angry, Lady Albury."

" If I am right in what I surmise, you had an offer made to you yesterday which ought to satisfy the heart of almost any girl in England." Here she paused, but Ayala had not a word to say for herself. " If it was so, the best man I know asked you to share his fortune with him."

" Has he told you ?"

" But he did ?"

" I shall not tell," said Ayala, proudly.

" I know he did. I knew that it was his intention before. Are you aware what kind of man is my cousin, Jonathan Stubbs ? Has it occurred to you that in truth and gallantry, in honour, honesty, courage, and real tenderness, he is so perfect as to be quite unlike to the crowd of men you see ?"

" I do know that he is good," said Ayala.

" Good ! Where will you find any one good like him ? Compare him to the other men around him, and then say whether he is good ! Can it be possible that you should refuse the love of such a man as that ?"

"I don't think I ought to be made to talk about it," said Ayala, hesitating.

"My dear, it is for your own sake and for his. When you go away from here it may be so difficult for him to see you again."

"I don't suppose he will ever want," said Ayala.

"It is sufficient that he wants it now. What better can you expect for yourself?"

"I expect nothing," said Ayala, proudly. "I have got nothing, and I expect nothing."

"He will give you everything, simply because he loves you. My dear, I should not take the trouble to tell you all this, did I not know that he is a man who ought to be accepted when he asks such a request as that. Your happiness would be safe in his hands." She paused but Ayala had not a word to say. "And he is not a man likely to renew such a request. He is too proud for that. I can conceive no possible reason for such a refusal unless it be that you are engaged. If there be some one else, then of course there must be an end of it."

"There is no one else."

"Then, my dear, with your prospects it is sheer folly. When the General dies he will have over two thousand a year."

"As if that had anything to do with it!" said Ayala, holding herself aloft in her wrath, and throwing angry glances at the lady.

"It is what I call romance," said Lady Albury. "Romance can never make you happy."

"At any rate it is not riches. What you call romance may be what I like best. At any rate if I do not love Colonel Stubbs I am sure I ought not to marry him;—and I won't."

After this there was nothing further to be said. Ayala thought that she would be turned out of the room,—almost out of the house, in disgrace. But Lady Albury, who was simply playing her part, was not in the least angry. "Well, my dear," she said, "pray,—pray, think better of it. I am in earnest, of course, because of my cousin,—because he seems to have put his heart upon it. He is just the man to be absolutely in love when he is in love. But I would not speak as I do unless I were sure that he would make you happy. My cousin Jonathan is to me the finest hero that I know. When a man is a hero he shouldn't be broken-hearted for want of a woman's smiles,—should he?"

"She ought not to smile unless she loves him," said Ayala, as she left the room.

The Monday and Tuesday went very quietly. Lady Albury said nothing more on the great subject, and the Colonel behaved himself exactly as though there had been no word of love at all. There was nothing special said about the Wednesday's hunt through the two days, till Ayala almost thought that there would be no hunt for her. Nor, indeed, did she much wish for it. It had been the Colonel who had instigated her to deeds of daring, and under his sanction that she had ventured to ride. She would hardly know how to go through the Wednesday,—whether still to trust him, or whether to hold herself aloof from him. When nothing was said on the subject till late on the evening of the Tuesday, she had almost resolved that she would not put on her habit when the morning came. But just as she was about to leave the drawing-room with her bed-candle Colonel Stubbs came to her. "Most of us ride to the meet to-morrow," he said; "but you and Nina shall be taken in the waggonette so as to save you a little. It is all arranged." She bowed and thanked him, going to bed almost sorry that it should have been so settled. When the morning came Nina could not ride. She had hurt her foot, and, coming early into Ayala's room, declared with tears that she could not go. "Then neither shall I," said Ayala, who was at that moment preparing to put on her habit.

"But you must. It is all settled, and Sir Harry would be offended if you did not go. What has Jonathan done that you should refuse to ride with him because I am lame?"

"Nothing," said Ayala.

"Oh, Ayala, do tell me. I should tell you everything. Of course you must hunt whatever it is. Even though he should have offered and you refused him, of course you must go."

"Must I?" said Ayala.

"Then you have refused him?"

"I have. Oh, Nina, pray do not speak of it. Do not think of it if you can help it. Why should everything be disturbed because I have been a fool?"

"Then you think you have been a fool?"

"Other people think so; but if so I shall at any rate be constant to my folly. What I mean is, that it has been done, and should be passed over as done with. I am quite sure that I ought not to be scolded; but Lady Albury did scold me." Then they went down together to breakfast, Ayala having prepared herself properly for the hunting-field.

In the waggonette there were with her Lady Albury, Mrs. Gosling, and Nina, who was not prevented by her lameness from going to the meet. The gentlemen all rode, so that there was no immediate difficulty as to Colonel Stubbs. But when she had been put on her horse by his assistance and found herself compelled to ride away from the carriage, apparently under his especial guidance, her heart misgave her, and she thoroughly wished that she was at home in the Crescent. Though she was specially under his guidance there were at first others close around her, and, while they were on the road going to the covert which they were to draw, conversation was kept up so that it was not necessary for her to speak ;—but what should she do when she should find herself alone with him as would certainly soon be the case? It soon was the case. The hounds were at work in a large wood in which she was told they might possibly pass the best part of the day, and it was not long before the men had dispersed themselves, some on this side some on that, and she found herself with no one near her but the Colonel. "Ayala," he said, "of course you know that it is my duty to look after you, and to do it better if I can than I did on Friday."

"I understand," she said.

"Do not let any remembrance of that walk on Saturday interfere with your happiness to-day. Who knows when you may be out hunting again?"

"Never!" she said; "I don't suppose I shall ever hunt again."

"Carpe diem," he said, laughing. "Do you know what 'carpe diem' means?"

"It is Latin perhaps."

"Yes ; and therefore you are not supposed to understand it. This is what it means. As an hour for joy has come, do not let any trouble interfere with it. Let it all be for this day at least as though there had been no walk in the Stalham Woods. There is Larry Twentyman. If I break down as I did on Friday you may always trust to him. Larry and you are old friends now."

"Carpe diem," she said to herself. "Oh, yes ; if it were only possible. How is one to 'carpe diem' with one's heart full of troubles?" And it was the less possible because this man whom she had rejected was so anxious to do everything for her happiness. Lady Albury had told her that he was a hero,—that he was perfect in honour, honesty, and gallantry ; and she felt inclined to own that Lady Albury was almost right. Yet,—yet how far was he from that image of manly perfection which her daily thoughts had created for her! Could she have found an appropriate word with which to thank him she would have done so ; but there was no such word, and Larry Twentyman was now with them, taking off his hat and overflowing with compliments. "Oh, Miss Dormer, I am so delighted to see you out again."

"How is the baby, Mr. Twentyman?"

"Brisk as a bee, and hungry as a hunter."

"And how is Mrs. Twentyman?"

"Brisker and hungrier than the baby. What do you think of the day, Colonel?"

"A very good sort of day, Twentyman, if we were anywhere out of these big woods." Larry shook his head solemnly. The Mudcombe Woods in which they were now at work had been known to occupy Tony Tappett and his whole pack from eleven o'clock till the dusk of evening. "We've got to draw them of course," continued the Colonel. Then Mr. Twentyman discoursed at some length on the excellence of Mudcombe Woods. What would any county be without a nursery for young foxes? Gorse coverts, hedge-rows, and little spinneys would be of no avail unless there were some grandly wild domain in which maternal and paternal foxes could roam in comparative security. All this was just as Ayala would have it, because it enabled her to ask questions, and saved her from subjects which might be painful to her.

The day, in truth, was not propitious to hunting even. Foxes were found in plenty, and two of them were killed within the recesses of the wood ; but on no occasion did they run a mile into the open. For Ayala it was very well, because she was galloping hither and thither, and because before the day was over she found herself able to talk to the Colonel in her wonted manner ; but there was no great glory for her as had been the glory of Little Cranbury Brook.

On the next morning she was taken back to London and handed over to her aunt in Kingsbury Crescent without another word having been spoken by Colonel Stubbs in reference to his love.

CHAPTER XXVII.

LADY ALBURY'S LETTER.

"I HAVE had a letter from Lady Albury," said Aunt Margaret, almost as soon as Ayala had taken off her hat and cloak.

"Yes, I know, Aunt Margaret. She wrote to ask that I might stay for four more days. I hope it was not wrong."

"I have had another letter since that, on Monday, about it ; I have determined to show it you. There it is. You had better read it by yourself, and I will come to you again in half an hour." Then, very solemnly, but with no trace of ill-humour, Mrs. Dosett left the room. There was something in her tone and gait so exceedingly solemn, that Ayala was almost frightened. Of course the letter must be about Colonel Stubbs, and of course the writer of it would find fault with her. She was conscious that she was adding one to her terribly long list of sins in not consenting to marry Colonel Stubbs. It was her misfortune that all her friends found fault with everything that she did. Among them there was not one, not even Nina, who fully sym-pathised with her. Not even to Lucy could she expatiate with a certainty of sympathy in regard to the Angel of Light. And now, though her aunt was apparently not angry,—only solemn,—she felt already sure that she was to be told that it was her duty to marry Colonel Stubbs. It was only the other day that her aunt was preaching to her as to the propriety of marrying her cousin Tom. It seemed, she said to herself, that people thought that a girl was bound to marry any man who could provide a house for her, and bread to eat, and clothes to wear. All this passed through her mind as she slowly drew Lady Albury's letter from the envelope, and prepared to read it. The letter was as follows ;—

"Albury, Monday, 18th November, 18—.

"DEAR MADAM,

"Your niece will return to you, as you request, on Thursday, but before she reaches you I think it my duty to inform you of a little circumstance which has occurred here. My cousin, Colonel Jonathan Stubbs, who is also the nephew of the Marchesa Baldoni, has made Miss Dormer an offer. I am bound to add that I did not think it improbable that it would be so, when I called on your husband, and begged him to allow your niece to come to us. I did not then know my cousin's intention as a fact. I doubt whether he knew it himself. But from what I had heard I thought it probable, and, as I conceive that any young lady would be fortunate in becoming my cousin's wife, I had no scruple.

"He has proposed to her, and she has rejected him. He has set his heart upon the matter, and I am most anxious that he should succeed, because I know him to be a man who will not easily brook disappointment where he has set his heart. Of all men I know he is the most stedfast in his purpose.

"I took the liberty of speaking to your niece on the subject, and am disposed to think that she is deterred by some feeling of foolish romance, partly because she does not like the name, partly because my cousin is not a handsome man in a girl's eyes ;—more probably, however, she has built up to herself some poetic fiction, and dreams of she knows not what. If it be so, it is a pity that she should lose an opportunity of settling herself well and happily in life. She gave as a reason that she did not love him. My experience is not so long as yours, perhaps, but such as I have has taught me to think that a wife will love her husband when she finds herself used well at all points. Mercenary marriages are, of course, bad ; but it is a pity, I think, that a girl, such as your niece, should lose the chance of so much happiness by a freak of romance.

"Colonel Stubbs, who is only twenty-eight years of age, has a staff appointment at Aldershot. He has private means of his own, on which alone he would be justified in marrying. On the death of his uncle, General Stubbs, he will inherit a considerable accession of fortune. He is not, of course, a rich man ; but he has ample for the wants of a family. In all other good gifts, temper, manliness, truth, and tenderness, I know no one to excel him. I should trust any young friend of my own into his hands with perfect safety.

"I have thought it right to tell you this. You will use your own judgment in saying what you think fit to your niece. Should she be made to understand that her own immediate friends approve of the offer, she would probably be induced to accept it. I have not heard my cousin say what may be his future plans. I think it possible that, as he is quite in earnest, he will not take one repulse. Should he ask again, I hope that your niece may receive him with altered views.

"Pray believe me to be, my dear Madam,

"Yours sincerely, ROSALINE ALBURY."

Ayala read the letter twice over before her aunt returned to her, and, as she read it, felt something of a feeling of renewed kindness come upon her in reference to the writer of it ;—not that she was in the least changed in her own resolution, but that she liked Lady Albury for wishing to change her. The reasons given, however, were altogether impotent with her. Colonel Stubbs had the means of keeping a wife ! If that were a reason then also ought she to marry her cousin, Tom Tringle. Colonel Stubbs was good and true ; but so also very probably was Tom Tringle. She would not compare the two men. She knew that her cousin Tom was altogether distasteful to her, while she took delight in the companionship of the Colonel. But the reasons for marrying one were to her thinking as strong as for marrying the other. There could be only one valid excuse for marriage,—that of adoring the man ;—and she was quite sure that she did not adore Colonel Jonathan Stubbs. Lady Albury had said, in her letter, that a girl would be sure to love a man who treated her well after marriage ; but that would not suffice for her. Were she to marry at all, it would be necessary that she should love the man before her marriage.

"Have you read the letter, my dear?" said Mrs. Dosett, as she entered the room and closed the door carefully behind her. She spoke almost in a whisper, and seemed to be altogether changed by the magnitude of the occasion.

"Yes, Aunt Margaret, I have read it?"

"I suppose it is true?"

"True ! It is true in part."

"You did meet this Colonel Stubbs?"

" Oh, yes ; I met him."

" And you had met him before ?"

" Yes, Aunt Margaret. He used to come to Brook Street. He is the Marchesa's nephew."

" Did he——." This question Aunt Margaret asked in a very low whisper, and her most solemn voice,—" Did he make love to you in Brook Street ?"

" No," said Ayala, sharply.

" Not at all ?"

" Not at all. I never thought of such a thing. I never dreamed of such a thing when he began talking to me out in the woods at Stalham on Saturday."

" Had you been—been on friendly terms with him ?"

" Very friendly terms. We were quite friends, and used to talk about all manner of things. I was very fond of him, and never afraid of anything that he said to me. He was Nina's cousin and seemed almost to be my cousin too."

" Then you do like him ?"

" Of course I do. Everybody must like him. But that is no reason why I should want to marry him."

Upon this Mrs. Dosett sat silent for awhile turning the great matter over in her thoughts. It was quite clear to her that every word which Ayala had spoken was true ; and probable also that Lady Albury's words were true. In her inmost thoughts she regarded Ayala as a fool. Here was a girl who had not a shilling of her own, who was simply a burden on relatives whom she did not especially love, who was doomed to a life which was essentially distasteful to her,—for all this in respect to herself and her house Mrs. Dosett had sense enough to acknowledge,—who seemed devoted to the society of rich and gay people, and yet would not take the opportunies that were offered her of escaping what she disliked and going to that which she loved ! Two offers had now been made to her, both of them thoroughly eligible, to neither of which would objection have been made by any of the persons concerned. Sir Thomas had shown himself to be absolutely anxious for the success of his son. And now it seemed that the grand relations of this Colonel Stubbs were in favour of the match. What it was in Ayala that entitled her to such promotion Mrs. Dosett did not quite perceive. To her eyes her niece was a fantastic girl, pretty indeed, but not endowed with that regular tranquil beauty which she thought to be of all feminine graces the most attractive. Why Tom Tringle should have been so deeply smitten with Ayala had been a marvel to her ; and now this story of Colonel Stubbs was a greater marvel. " Ayala," she said, " you ought to think better of it."

" Think better of what, Aunt Margaret ?"

" You have seen what this Lady Albury says about her cousin, Colonel Stubbs."

" What has that to do with it ?"

" You believe what she says ? If so why should you not accept him ?"

" Because I can't," said Ayala.

" Have you any idea what is to become of your future life ?" said Mrs. Dosett, very gravely.

" Not in the least," said Ayala. But that was a fib, because she had an idea that in the fullness of time it would be her heavenly fate to put her hand into that of the Angel of Light.

" Gentlemen won't come running after you always, my dear."

This was almost as bad as being told by her Aunt Emmeline that she had encouraged her cousin Tom. " It's a great shame to say that. I don't want anybody to run after me. I never did."

" No, my dear; no. I don't think that you ever did." Mrs. Dosett, who was justice itself, did acknowledge to herself that of any such fault as that suggested, Ayala was innocent. Her fault was quite in the other direction, and consisted of an unwillingness to settle herself and to free her relations of the burden of maintaining her when proper opportunities arose for doing so. " I only want to explain to you that people must,—must,—must make their hay while the sun shines. You are young now."

" I am not one-and-twenty yet," said Ayala, proudly.

" One-and-twenty is a very good time for a girl to marry,—that is to say if a proper sort of gentleman asks her."

" I don't think I ought to be scolded because they don't seem to me to be the proper sort. I don't want anybody to come. Nobody ought to be talked to about it at all. If I cared about anyone that you or Uncle Reginald did not approve, then you might talk to me. But I don't think that anything ought to be said about anybody unless I like him myself." So the conversation was over, and Mrs. Dosett felt that she had been entirely vanquished.

Lady Albury's letter was shown to Mr. Dosett, but he refused to say a word to his niece on the subject. In the argument which followed between him and his wife he took his niece's part, opposing altogether that idea that hay should be made while the sun shines. " It simply means selling herself," said Mr. Dosett.

" That is nonsense, Reginald. Of course such a girl as Ayala has to do the best she can with her good looks. What else has she to depend upon ?"

" My brother-in-law will do something for her."

" I hope he will,—though I do not think that a very safe reed to depend upon as she has twice offended him. But of course a girl thinks of marrying. Ayala would be very much disgusted if she were told that she was to be an old maid, and live upon £100 a year supplied by Sir Thomas's bounty. It might have been that she would have to do it ;—but now that chances are open she ought to take them. She should choose between her cousin Tom and this Colonel Stubbs ; and you should tell her that, if she will not, you will no longer be responsible for her."

To this Mr. Dosett turned altogether a deaf ear. He was quite sure that his responsibility must be continued till Ayala should marry, or till he should die, and he would not make a threat which he would certainly be unable to carry out. He would be very glad if Ayala could bring herself to marry either of the young men. It was a pity that she should feel herself compelled to refuse offers so excellent. But it was a matter for her own judgment, and one in which he would not interfere. For two days this almost led to a coldness between the man and his wife, during which the sufferings of poor Mrs. Dosett were heartrending.

Not many days after Ayala's return her sister Lucy came to see her. Certain reasons had caused Lady Tringle to stay at Glenbogie longer than usual, and the family was now passing through London on their way to Merle Park. Perhaps it was the fact that the Trafficks had been effectually extruded from Glenbogie, but would doubtless turn up at Merle Park, should Lady Tringle take up her residence there before the autumn was over. That they should spend their Christmas at Merle Park was an acknowledged thing ;—to mamma Tringle an acknowledged benefit, because she liked to have her daughter with her ; to papa Tringle an acknowledged evil, because he could not endure to be made to give more than he intended to give. That they should remain there afterwards through January, and till the meeting of Parliament, was to be expected. But it was hoped that they might be driven to find some home for themselves if they were left homeless by Sir Thomas for awhile. The little plan was hardly successful, as Mr. Traffick had put his wife into lodgings at Hastings, ready to pounce down on Merle Park as soon as Lady Tringle should have occupied the house a few days. Lady Tringle was now going there with the rest of the family, Sir Thomas having been in town for the last six weeks.

Lucy took advantage of the day which they passed in London, and succeeded in getting across to the Crescent. At this time she had heard nothing of Colonel Stubbs, and was full indeed of her own troubles. " You haven't seen him ?" she said to her sister.

" Seen who ?" asked Ayala, who had two " hims " to her bow,—and thought at the moment rather of her own two "hims" than of Lucy's one.

"Isadore. He said that he would call here." Ayala explained that she had not seen him, having been absent from town during the last ten days,—during which Mr. Hamel had in fact called at the house. "Ayala," continued Lucy, "what am I to do?"

"Stick to him," said Ayala, firmly.

"Of course I shall. But Aunt Emmeline thinks that I ought to give him up or——"

"Or what?"

"Or go away," said Lucy, very gravely.

"Where would you go to?"

"Oh, where indeed? Of course he would have me, but it would be ruin to him to marry a wife without a penny when he earns only enough for his own wants. His father has quarrelled with him altogether. He says that nobody can prevent our being married if we please, and that he is quite ready to make a home for me instantly; but I know that last year he hardly earned more than two hundred pounds after paying all his expenses, and were I to take him at his word I should ruin him."

"Would Uncle Tom turn you out?"

"He has been away almost ever since Mr. Hamel came to Glenbogie, and I do not know what he will say. Aunt Emmeline declares that I can only stay with them just as though I were her daughter, and that a daughter would be bound to obey her."

"Does Gertrude obey her about Mr. Houston?"

"Gertrude has her own way with her mother altogether. And of course a daughter cannot really be turned out. If she tells me to go, I suppose I must go."

"I should ask Uncle Tom," said Ayala. "She could not make you go out into the street. When she had to get rid of me, she could send me here in exchange; but she can't say now that you don't suit, and have me back again."

"Oh, Ayala, it is so miserable. I feel that I do not know what to do with myself."

"Nor do I," said Ayala, jumping up from the bed on which she was sitting. "It does seem to be so cross-grained. Nobody will let you marry, and everybody will make me."

"Do they still trouble you about Tom?"

"It is not Tom now, Lucy. Another man has come up."

"As a lover?"

"Oh, yes; quite so. His name is,—such a name Lucy,—his name is Colonel Jonathan Stubbs."

"That is Isadore's friend,—the man who lives at Drumcaller."

"Exactly. He told me that Mr. Hamel was at Drumcaller with him. And now he wants me to be his wife."

"Do you not like him?"

"That is the worst part of it all, Lucy. If I did not like him I should not mind it half so much. It is just because I like him so very much that I am so very unhappy. His hair is just the colour of Aunt Emmeline's big shawl."

"What does that signify?"

"And his mouth stretches almost from ear to ear."

"I shouldn't care a bit for his mouth."

"I don't think I do much, because he does look so good-natured when he laughs. Indeed he is always the most good-natured man that ever lived."

"Has he got an income enough for marriage?" asked Lucy, whose sorrows were already springing from that most fertile source of sorrowing.

"Plenty they tell me,—though I do not in the least know what plenty means."

"Then Ayala why should you not have him?"

"Because I can't," said Ayala. "How is a girl to love a man if she does not love him. Liking has nothing to do with it. You don't think liking ought to have anything to do with it?"

This question had not yet been answered when Aunt Margaret came into the room, declaring that the Tringle man-servant, who had walked across the park with Miss Dormer, was waxing impatient. The sisters, therefore, were separated, and Lucy returned to Queen's Gate.

CHAPTER XXVIII.

MISS DOCIMER.

"I TELL you fairly that I think you are altogether wrong;—that it is cowardly, unmanly, and disgraceful. I don't mean, you see, to put what you call a fine point upon it."

"No, you don't."

"It is one of those matters on which a person must speak the truth or not speak at all. I should not have spoken unless you forced it upon me. You don't care for her in the least."

"That's true. I do not know that I am especially quick at what you call caring for young ladies. If I care for anybody it is for you."

"I suppose so; but that may as well be dropped for the present.

You mean to marry this girl simply because she has got a lot of money ?"

" Exactly that ;—as you before long will marry some gentleman only because he has got money."

" You have no right to say so because I am engaged to no man. But, if I were so, it is quite different. Unless I marry I can be nobody. I can have no existence that I can call my own. I have no other way of pushing myself into the world's notice. You are a man."

" You mean to say that I could become a merchant or a lawyer,—be a Lord Chancellor in time, or perhaps an Archbishop of Canterbury."

" You can live and eat and drink and go where you wish without being dependent on anyone. If I had your freedom and your means do you think that I would marry for money ?"

In this dialogue the main part was taken by Mr. Frank Houston, whose ambition it was to marry Miss Gertrude Tringle, and the lady's part by his cousin and intimate friend, Miss Imogene Docimer. The scene was a walk through a pine-forest on the southern slopes of the Tyrolean Alps, and the occasion had been made a little more exhilarating than usual by the fact that Imogene had been strongly advised both by her brother, Mr. Mudbury Docimer, and by her sister-in-law, Mrs. Mudbury Docimer, not to take any more distant rambles with her far-away cousin Frank Houston. In the teeth of that advice this walk was taken, and the conversation in the pine-wood had at the present moment arrived at the point above given.

" I do not know that any two persons were ever further asunder in an argument than you and I in this," said Frank, not in the least disconcerted by the severe epithets which had been applied to him. " I conceive that you are led away by a desire to deceive yourself, whereas hypocrisy should only be used with the object of deceiving others."

" How do I deceive myself ?"

" In making believe that men are generally different from what they are ;—in trying to suppose that I ought to be, if I am not, a hero. You shall not find a man whose main object is not that of securing an income. The clergyman who preaches against gold licks the ground beneath the minister's feet in order that he may become a bishop. The barrister cares not with what case he may foul his hands so long as he may become rich. The man in trade is so aware of his own daily dishonesty that he makes two separate existences for himself, and endeavours to atone for his rascality in the City by his performance of all duties at the West End. I regard myself to be so infinitely cleaner in my conscience than other men that I could not bring myself to be a bishop, an Attorney-General, or a great merchant. Of all the ways open to me this seems to me to be the least sordid. I give her the only two things which she desires,—myself and a position. She will give me the only thing I desire, which is some money. When you marry you'll make an equally fine bargain,—only your wares will be your beauty."

" You will not give her yourself ;—not your heart."

" Yes, I shall. I shall make the most of her, and shall do so by becoming as fond of her as I can. Of course I like breeding. Of course I like beauty. Of course I like that aroma of feminine charm which can only be produced by a mixture of intellect, loveliness, taste, and early association. I don't pretend to say that my future would not be much sweeter before me with you as my wife,—if only either of us had a sufficiency of income. I acknowledge that. But then I acknowledge also that I prefer Miss Tringle, with £100,000, to you with nothing ; and I do not think that I ought to be called unmanly, disgraceful, and a coward, because I have courage enough to speak the truth openly to a friend whom I trust. My theory of life shocks you, not because it is uncommon, but because it is not commonly declared."

They were silent for a while as they went on through the path, and then Miss Docimer spoke to him in an altered voice. " I must ask you not to speak to me again as one who by any possibility could have been your wife."

·" Very well. You will not wish me to abandon the privilege of thinking of past possibilities ?"

" I would,—if it were possible."

" Quite impossible ! One's thoughts, I imagine, are always sup-posed to be one's own."

" You know what I mean. A gentleman will always spare a woman if he can do so ; and there are cases, such as have been ours, in which it is a most imperative duty to do so. You should not have followed us when you had made up your mind about this young lady."

" I took care to let you know, beforehand, that I intended it."

" You should not have thrown the weight upon me. You should not even have written to me."

" I wonder what you would have said then,—how loudly you would have abused me,—had I not written ! Would you not have told me then that I had not the courage to be open with you?" He paused for an answer, but she made none. " But I do recognise the necessity of my becoming subject to abuse in this state of affairs. I have been in no respect false, nor in any way wanting in affection. When I suggested to you that £600 a year between us, with an increasing family, and lodgings in Marylebone, would be uncomfortable, you shuddered at the prospect. When I explained to you that ˹ ˺ would have the worst of it, because my club would be open to me, you were almost angry with me because I seemed to imply that there would be any other than one decision."

"There could only be one decision,—unless you were man enough to earn your bread."

"But I wasn't. But I ain't. You might as well let that accident pass, sans dire. Was there ever a moment in which you thought that I should earn my bread ?"

"Never for a moment did I endow you with the power of doing anything so manly."

"Then why throw it in my teeth now ? That is not fair. However, I do own that I have to be abused. I don't see any way in which you and I are to part without it. But you need not descend to Billingsgate."

"I have not descended to Billingsgate, Mr. Houston."

"Upper-world Billingsgate ! Cowardice, as an accusation from a woman to a man, is upper-world Billingsgate. But it doesn't matter. Of course I know what it means. Do you think your brother wants me to go away at once ?"

"At once," she said.

"That would be disagreeable and absurd. You mean to sit to me for that head ?"

"Certainly not."

"I cannot in the least understand why not. What has a question of art to do with marriage or giving in marriage ? And why should Mrs. Docimer be so angry with me, when she has known the truth all along ?"

"There are questions which it is of no avail to answer. I have come out with you now because I thought it well that we should have a final opportunity of understanding each other. You understand me at any rate."

"Perfectly," he said. "You have taken especial care on this occasion to make yourself intelligible."

"So I intended. And as you do understand me, and know how far I am from approving your philosophy, you can hardly wish to remain with us longer." Then they walked on together in absolute silence for above a mile. They had come out of the wood, and were descending, by a steep and narrow path, to the village in which stood the hotel at which the party was staying. Another ten minutes would take them down to the high road. The path here ran by the side of a rivulet, the course of which was so steep that the waters made their way down in a succession of little cataracts. From the other side of the path was a fence so close to it, that on this particular spot there was room only for one to walk. Here Frank Houston stepped in front of his companion, so as to stop her. "Imogene," he said, "if it is intended that I am to start by the diligence for Innpruck this evening, you had better bid me farewell at once."

"I have bidden you farewell," she said.

"Then you have done it in so bitter a mood that you had better try your hand at it again. Heaven only knows in what manner you or I may meet again."

"What does it matter?" she asked.

"I have always felt that the hearts of men are softer than the hearts of women. A woman's hand is soft, but she can steel her heart when she thinks it necessary, as no man can do. Does it occur to you at this moment that there has been some true affection between you and me in former days."

"I wish it did not."

"It may be so that I wish it also; but there is the fact. No wishing will enable me to get rid of it. No wishing will save me from the memory of early dreams and sweet longings and vain triumphs. There is the remembrance of bright glory made very sad to me by the meanness of the existing truth. I do not say but that I would obliterate it if I could; but it is not to be obliterated; the past will not be made more pleasant to me by any pretence of present indignation. I should have thought that it would have been the same with you."

"There has been no glory," she said, "though I quite acknowledge the meanness."

"There has been at any rate some love."

"Misplaced. You had better let me pass on. I have, as you say, steeled myself. I will not condescend to any tenderness. In my brother's presence and my sister's I will wish you good-bye and express a hope that you may be successful in your enterprises. Here, by the brook-side, out upon the mountain-path, where there is no one to hear us but our two selves, I will bid you no farewell softer than that already spoken. Go and do as you propose. You have my leave. When it shall have been done there shall never be a word spoken by me against it. But, while you ask me whether you are right, I will only say that I think you to be wrong. It may be that you owe nothing to me;— but you owe something to her, and something also to yourself. Now, Mr. Houston, I shall be glad to pass on."

He shrugged his shoulders and then stepped out of the path, thinking as he did so how ignorant he had been, after all that had passed, of much of the character of Imogene Docimer. It could not be, he had thought, but that she would melt into softness at last. "I will not condescend to any tenderness." she had said. and it seemed that she would be as good as her word. He then walked down before her in silence, and in silence they reached the inn.

"Mr. Houston," said Mrs. Docimer, before they sat down to dinner together, "I thought it was understood that you and Imogene should not go out alone together again."

"I have taken my place to Innspruck by the diligence this evening," he answered.

"Perhaps it will be better so, though both Mudbury and I will be sorry to lose your company."

"Yes, Mrs. Docimer, I have taken my place. Your sister seemed to think that there would be great danger if I waited till to-morrow morning when I could have got a pleasant lift in a return carriage. I hate travelling at night and I hate diligences. I was quite prepared to post all the way, though it would have ruined me,—only for this accursed diligence."

"I am sorry you should be inconvenienced."

"It does not signify. What a man without a wife may suffer in that way never does signify. It's just fourteen hours. You wouldn't like Docimer to come with me."

"That's nonsense. You needn't go the whole way unless you like. You could sleep at Brunecken."

"Brunecken is only twelve miles, and it might be dangerous."

"Of course you choose to turn everything into ridicule."

"Better that than tears, Mrs. Docimer. What's the good of crying? I can't make myself an elder son. I can't endow Imogene with a hundred thousand pounds. She told me just now that I might earn my bread, but she knows that I can't. It's very sad. But what can be got by being melancholy?"

"At any rate you had better be away from her."

"I am going,—this evening. Shall I walk on, half a stage, at once, without any dinner? I wish you had heard the kind of things she said to me. You would not have thought that I had gone to walk with her for my own pleasure."

"Have you not deserved them?"

"I think not; but nevertheless I bore them. A woman, of course, can say what she pleases. There's Docimer,—I hope he won't call me a coward."

Mr. Docimer came out on the terrace, on which the two were standing, looking as sour as death. "He is going by the diligence to Innspruck this afternoon," said Mrs. Docimer.

"Why did he come? A man with a grain of feeling would have remained away."

"Now, Docimer," said Frank, "pray do not make yourself un-

pleasant. Your sister has been abusing me all the morning like a
pickpocket, and your wife looks at me as though she would say just as
much if she dared. After all, what is it I have done that you think
so wicked ?"

"What will everybody think at home," said Mrs. Docimer, "when
they know that you're with us again ? What chance is she to have if
you follow her about in this way ?"

"I shall not follow her very long," said Frank. "My wings will
soon be cut, and then I shall never fly again." They were at this
time walking up and down the terrace together, and it seemed for
awhile that neither of them had another word to say in the matter
of the dispute between them. Then Houston went on again in his
own defence. "Of course it is all bad," he said. "Of course we
have all been fools. You knew it, and allowed it ; and have no right
to say a word to me."

"We thought that when your uncle died there would have been
money," said Docimer, with a subdued growl.

"Exactly ; and so did I. You do not mean to say that I deceived
either you or her ?"

"There should have been an end of it when that hope was over."

"Of course there should. There should never have been a dream
that she or I could marry on six hundred a year. Had not all of us
been fools, we should have taken our hats off and bade each other farewell for ever when the state of the old man's affairs was known. We
were fools ; but we were fools together ; and none of us have a right
to abuse the others. When I became acquainted with this young lady
at Rome, it had been settled among us that Imogene and I must seek
our fortunes apart."

"Then why did you come after her ?" again asked Mr. Docimer.

At this moment Imogene herself joined them on the terrace.
"Mary," she said to her sister-in-law, "I hope you are not carrying
on this battle with Mr. Houston. I have said what there was to be
said."

"You should have held your tongue and said nothing," growled her
brother.

"Be that as it may I have said it, and he quite understands what I
think about it. Let us eat our dinner in peace and quietness, and
then let him go on his travels. He has the world free before him,
which he no doubt will open like an oyster, though he does not carry a
sword." Soon after this they did dine, and contented themselves with
abusing the meat and the wine, and finding fault with Tyrolese
cookery, just as though they had no deeper cares near their hearts.
Precisely at six the heavy diligence stopped before the hotel door, and

Houston, who was then smoking with Docimer on the Terrace, got up to bid them adieu. Mrs. Docimer was kind and almost affectionate, with a tear in her eye. "Well, old fellow," said Docimer, "take care of yourself. Perhaps everything will turn up right some of these days." "Good-bye, Mr. Houston," said Imogene, just giving him her hand to touch in the lightest manner possible. "God bless you, Imogene," said he. And there was a tear also in his eye. But there was none in hers, as she stood looking at him while he prepared himself for his departure; nor did she say another word to him as he went. "And now," said she, when the three of them were left upon the terrace, "I will ask a great favour of you both. I will beg you not to let there be another word about Mr. Houston among us." After that she rambled out by herself, and was not seen again by either of them that evening.

When she was alone she too shed her tears, though she felt impatient and vexed with herself as they came into her eyes. It was not perhaps only for her lost love that she wept. Had no one known that her love had been given and then lost she might have borne it without weeping. But now, in carrying on this vain affair of hers, in devoting herself to a lover who had, with her own consent, passed away from her, she had spent the sweet fresh years of her youth, and all those who knew her would know that it had been so. He had told her that it would be her fate to purchase for herself a husband with her beauty. It might be so. At any rate she did not doubt her own beauty. But, if it were to be so, then the romance and the charm of her life were gone. She had quite agreed that six hundred a year, and lodgings in Marylebone, would be quite unendurable; but what was there left for her that would be endurable? He could be happy with the prospect of Gertrude Tringle's money. She could not be happy, looking forward to that unloved husband who was to be purchased by her beauty.

CHAPTER XXIX.

AT MERLE PARK. NO. 1.

Sir Thomas took the real holiday of the year at Glenbogie,—where he was too far removed from Lombard Street to be drawn daily into the vortex of his millions. He would stay usually six weeks at Glenbogie,—which were by no means the happiest weeks of the year. Of all the grand things of the world which his energy and industry had produced for him, he loved his millions the best. It was not because they were his,—as indeed they were not. A considerable filing off them,—what he regarded as his percentage,—annually became his own; but it was not this that he loved. In describing a man's character it is the author's duty to give the man his due. Sir Thomas liked his own wealth well enough. Where is the rich man who does not?—or where is the poor man who does not wish that he had it to like? But what he loved were the millions with which Travers and Treason dealt. He was Travers and Treason, though his name did not even appear in the firm, and he dealt with the millions. He could affect the rate of money throughout Europe, and emissaries from national treasuries would listen to his words. He had been Governor and Deputy-Governor of the Bank of England. All the City respected him, not so much because he was rich, as that he was one who thoroughly understood millions. If Russia required to borrow some infinite number of roubles, he knew how to arrange it, and could tell to a rouble at what rate money could be made by it, and at what rate money would certainly be lost. He liked his millions, and was therefore never quite comfortable at Glenbogie. But at Merle Park he was within easy reach of London. At Merle Park he was not obliged to live, from week's end to week's end, without a sight of Lombard Street. The family might be at Merle Park, while he might come down on a Friday and remain till Tuesday morning. That was the plan proposed for Merle Park. As a fact he would spend four days in town, and only two down in the country. Therefore, though he spent his so-named holiday at Glenbogie, Merle Park was the residence which he loved.

In this autumn he went up to London long before his family, and then found them at Merle Park on the Saturday after their arrival there. They had gone down on the previous Wednesday. On the Saturday, when he entered the house, the first thing he saw was Mr. Traffick's hat in the hall. This was Saturday, 23rd November, and there would be three months before Parliament would meet! A curse was not muttered, but just formed between his teeth, as he saw the hat. Sir Thomas, in his angriest mood, never went so far as quite to mutter his curses. Will one have to expiate the anathemas which are well kept within the barrier of the teeth, or only those which have achieved some amount of utterance? Sir Thomas went on with a servant at his heels, chucking about the doors rather violently, till he found Mr. Traffick alone in the drawing-room. Mr. Traffick had had a glass of sherry and bitters brought in for his refreshment and Sir Thomas saw the glass on the mantelpiece. He never took sherry and bitters himself. One glass of wine, with his two o'clock mutton chop, sufficed him till dinner. It was all very well to be a Member of

Parliament, but, after all, Members of Parliament never do anything. Men who work don't take sherry and bitters! Men who work don't put their hats in other people's halls without leave from the master of the house! "Where's your mistress?" said Sir Thomas, to the man, without taking any notice of his son-in-law. The ladies had only just come in from driving, were very cold, and had gone up to dress. Sir Thomas went out of the room, again banging the door, and again taking no notice of Mr. Traffick. Mr. Traffick put his hand up to the mantelpiece, and finished his sherry and bitters.

"My dear," said Mr. Traffick to his wife, up in her bed-room, "your father has come down in one of his tantrums."

"I knew he would," said Augusta.

"But it does not signify the least. Give him a kiss when you see him, and don't seem to notice it. There is not a man in the world has a higher regard for me than your father, but if anyone were to see him in one of his tantrums they would suppose he meant to be uncivil."

"I hope he won't be downright unkind, Septimus," said his wife.

"Never fear! The kindest-hearted man in the world is your father."

"So he's here!" That was the first word of greeting which Sir Thomas addressed to his wife in her bed-room.

"Yes, Tom ;—they're here."

"When did they come?"

"Well ;—to tell the truth, we found them here."

"The —— !" But Sir Thomas restrained the word on the right, or inside, of the teeth.

"They thought we were to be here a day sooner, and so they came on the Wednesday morning. They were to come, you know."

"I wish I knew when they were to go."

"You don't want to turn your own daughter out of your own house?"

"Why doesn't he get a house of his own for her? For her sake why doesn't he do it? He has the spending of £6,000 a year of my money, and yet I am to keep him! No ;—I don't want to turn my daughter out of my house ; but it'll end in my turning him out."

When a week had passed by Mr. Traffick had not been as yet turned out. Sir Thomas, when he came back to Merle Park on the following Friday, condescended to speak to his son-in-law, and to say something to him as to the news of the day ; but this he did in an evident spirit of preconceived hostility. "Everything is down again," he said.

"Fluctuations are always common at this time of the year," said Traffick ; "but I observe that trade always becomes brisk a little before Christmas."

"To a man with a fixed income, like you, it doesn't much matter,' said Sir Thomas.

"I was looking at it in a public light."

"Exactly. A man who has an income, and never spends it, need not trouble himself with private views as to the money market." Mr. Traffick rubbed his hands, and asked whether the new buildings at the back of the Lombard Street premises were nearly finished.

Mr. Traffick's economy had a deleterious effect upon Gertrude, which she, poor girl, did not deserve. Sir Thomas, deeply resolving in his mind thåt he would, at some not very distant date, find means by which he would rid himself of Mr. Traffick, declared to himself that he would not, at any rate, burden himself with another son-in-law of the same kind. Frank Houston was, to his thinking, of the same kind, and therefore he hardened his heart against Frank Houston. Now Frank Houston, could he have got his wife with £6,000 a year,— as Mr. Traffick had done,—would certainly not have troubled the Tringle mansions with too much of his presence. It would have been his object to remove himself as far as possible from the Tringles, and to have enjoyed his life luxuriously with the proceeds of his wife's fortune. But his hopes in this respect were unjustly impeded by Mr. Traffick's parsimony. Soon after leaving the hotel in the Tyrol at which we lately saw him, Frank Houston wrote to his lady-love, declaring the impatience of his ardour, and suggesting that it would be convenient if everything could be settled before Christmas. In his letter he declared to Gertrude how very uncomfortable it was to him to have to discuss money matters with her father. It was so disagreeable that he did not think that he could bring himself to do it again. But, if she would only be urgent with her father, she would of course prevail. Acting upon this Gertrude determined to be urgent with her father on his second coming to Merle Park, when, as has been explained, Sir Thomas was in a frame of mind very much opposed to impecunious sons-in-law. Previous to attacking her father Gertrude had tried her hand again upon her mother, but Lady Tringle had declined. "If anything is to be done you must do it yourself," Lady Tringle had said.

"Papa," said Gertrude, having followed him into a little sitting-room where he digested and arranged his telegrams when at Merle Park, "I wish something could be settled about Mr. Houston."

Sir Thomas at this moment was very angry. Mr. Traffick had not only asked for the loan of a carriage to take him into Hastings, but had expressed a wish that there might be a peculiar kind of claret served at dinner with which he was conversant and to which he was much attached. "Then," said he, "you may as well have it all settled at once."

"How, papa?"

"You may understand for good and all that I will have nothing to do with Mr. Houston."

"Papa, that would be very cruel."

"My dear, if you call me cruel I will not allow you to come and talk to me at all. Cruel indeed! What is your idea of cruelty?"

"Everybody knows that we are attached to each other."

"Everybody knows nothing of the kind. I know nothing of the kind. And you are only making a fool of yourself. Mr. Houston is a penniless adventurer and is only attached to my money. He shall never see a penny of it."

"He is not an adventurer, papa. He is much less like an adventurer than Mr. Traffick. He has an income of his own, only it is not much."

"About as much as would pay his bill at the club for cigars and champagne. You may make your mind at rest, for I will not give Mr. Houston a shilling. Why should a man expect to live out of my earnings who never did a day's work in his life?"

Gertrude left the room despondently, as there was nothing more to be done on the occasion. But it seemed to her as though she were being used with the utmost cruelty. Augusta had been allowed to marry her man without a shilling, and had been enriched with £120,000. Why should she be treated worse than Augusta? She was very strongly of opinion that Frank Houston was very much better than Septimus Traffick. Mr. Traffick's aptitude for saving his money was already known to the whole household. Frank would never wish to save. Frank would spend her income for her like a gentleman. Frank would not hang about Glenbogie or Merle Park till he should be turned out. Everybody was fond of Frank. But she, Gertrude, had already learnt to despise Mr. Traffick, Member of Parliament though he was. She had already begun to think that having been chosen by Frank Houston, who was decidedly a man of fashion, she had proved herself to be of higher calibre than her sister Augusta. But her father's refusal to her had been not only very rough but very decided. She would not abandon her Frank. Such an idea never for a moment crossed her mind. But what step should she next take? Thinking over it during the whole of the day she did at last form a plan. But she greatly feared that the plan would not recommend itself to Mr. Frank Houston. She was not timid, but he might be so.

In spite of her father's anger and roughness she would not doubt his ultimate generosity; but Frank might doubt it. If Frank could be induced to come and carry her off from Merle Park and marry her in some manner approved for such occasions, she would stand the risk of getting the money afterwards. But she was greatly afraid that the risk would be too much for Frank. She did not, however, see any other scheme before her. As to waiting patiently till her father's obdurate heart should be softened by the greater obduracy of her own love, there was a tedium and a prolonged dullness in such a prospect which were anything but attractive to her. Had it been possible she would have made a bargain with her father. "If you won't give us £120,000 let us begin with £60,000." But even this she feared would not altogether be agreeable to Frank. Let her think of it how she would, that plan of being run away with seemed alone to be feasible, —and not altogether disagreeable.

It was necessary that she should answer her lover's letter. No embargo had as yet been put upon her correspondence, and therefore she could send her reply without external difficulty.

" Dear Frank," she said, " I quite agree with you about Christmas. It ought to be settled. But I have very bad news to send to you. I have been to papa as you told me, but he was very unkind. Nothing could be worse. He said that you ought to earn your bread, which is, of course, all humbug. He didn't understand that there ought to be some gentlemen who never earn their bread. I am sure, if you had been earning your bread by going to Lombard Street every day, I shouldn't have ever cared for you.

" He says that he will not give a single shilling. I think he is angry because Augusta's husband will come and live here always. That is disgusting, of course. But it isn't my fault. It is either that, or else some money has gone wrong;—or perhaps he had a very bad fit of indigestion. He was, however, so savage, that I really do not know how to go to him again. Mamma is quite afraid of him, and does not dare say a word, because it was she who managed about Mr. Traffick.

" What ought to be done? Of course, I don't like to think that you should be kept waiting. I am not sure that I quite like it myself. I will do anything you propose, and am not afraid of running a little risk. If we could get married without his knowing anything about it. I am sure he would give the money afterwards,—because he is always so good-natured in the long run, and so generous. He can be very savage, but he would be sure to forgive.

" How would it be if I were to go away? I am of age, and I believe that no one could stop me. If you could manage that we should get married in that way, I would do my best. I know people can get themselves married at Ostend. I do not see what else is to be done. You can write to me at present here, and nothing wrong will come of it. But Augusta says that if papa were to begin to suspect anything about my going away he would stop my letters.—Dear Frank, I am yours always, and always most lovingly, "GERTRUDE."

"You needn't be a bit afraid but that I should be quite up to going off if you could arrange it."

"I believe, papa," said Mrs. Traffick, on the afternoon of the day on which this was written, "that Gertrude is thinking of doing something wrong, and therefore I feel it to be my duty to bring you this letter." Augusta had not been enabled to read the letter, but had discussed with her sister the propriety of eloping. "I won't advise it," she had said, "but, if you do, Mr. Houston should arrange to be married at Ostend. I know that can be done." Some second thought had perhaps told her that any such arrangement would be injurious to the noble blood of the Traffick family, and she had therefore "felt it to be her duty" to extract the letter from the family letter-box, and to give it to her father. A daughter who could so excellently do her duty would surely not be turned out before Parliament met.

Sir Thomas took the letter and said not a word to his elder child. When he was alone he doubted. He was half-minded to send the letter on. What harm could the two fools do by writing to each other? While he held the strings of the purse there could be no marriage. Then he bethought himself of his paternal authority, of the right he had to know all that his daughter did,—and he opened the letter. "There ought to be gentlemen who don't earn their bread!" "Ought there?" said he to himself. If so these gentlemen ought not to come to him for bread. He was already supporting one such, and that was quite enough. "Mamma is quite afraid of him, and doesn't dare say a word." That he rather liked. "I am sure he would give the money afterwards." "I am sure he would do no such thing," he said to himself, and he reflected that in such a condition he should rather be delighted than otherwise in watching the impecunious importunities of his baffled son-in-law. The next sentence reconciled his girl to him almost entirely. "He is always so good-natured in the long run, and so generous!" For "good-natured" he did not care much, but he liked to be thought generous. Then he calmly took the letter, and restoring it to its envelope, put it back among his papers.

He sat for ten minutes thinking what he had better do, finding the task thus imposed upon him to be much more difficult than the distri-

bution of a loan.   At last he determined that, if he did nothing, things
would probably settle themselves.   Mr. Houston, when he received no
reply from his lady-love, would certainly be quiescent, and Gertrude,
without any assent from her lover, could hardly arrange her journey to
Ostend.   Perhaps it might be well that he should say a word of caution
to his wife ; but as to that he did not at present quite make up his
mind, as he was grievously disturbed while he was considering the
subject.

"If you please, Sir Thomas," said the coachman, hurrying into the
room almost without the ceremony of knocking,—"if you please,
Phœbe mare has been brought home with both her knees cut down to
the bone."

"What !" exclaimed Sir Thomas, who indulged himself in a taste
for horseflesh, and pretended to know one animal from another.

"Yes, indeed, Sir Thomas, down to the bone," said the coachman,
who entertained all that animosity against Mr. Traffick which domestics
feel for habitual guests who omit the ceremony of tipping.   "Mr.
Traffick brought her down on Windoverhill, Sir Thomas, and she'll
never be worth a feed of oats again.   I didn't think a man was born
who could throw that mare off her feet, Sir Thomas."   Now Mr.
Traffick, when he had borrowed the phaeton and pair of horses that
morning to go into Hastings, had dispensed with the services of a
coachman, and had insisted on driving himself.

CHAPTER XXX.

AT MERLE PARK.   NO. 2.

HAS any irascible reader,—any reader who thoroughly enjoys the
pleasure of being in a rage,—encountered suddenly some grievance
which, heavy as it may be, has been more than compensated by the
privilege it has afforded of blowing-up the offender?   Such was the
feeling of Sir Thomas as he quickly followered his coachman out of the
room.   He had been very proud of his Phœbe mare, who could trot with
him from the station to the house at the rate of twelve miles an hour.
But in his present frame of mind he had liked the mare less than he
disliked his son-in-law.   Mr. Traffick had done him this injury, and
he now had Mr. Traffick on the hip.   There are some injuries for
which a host cannot abuse his guest.   If your best Venetian decanter
be broken at table you are bound to look as though you liked it.   But
if a horse be damaged a similar amount of courtesy is hardly required.
The well-nurtured gentleman, even in that case, will only look unhappy

and say not a word. Sir Thomas was hardly to be called a well-nurtured gentleman; and then it must be remembered that the offender was his son-in-law. "Good heavens!" he exclaimed, hurrying into the yard. "What is this?"

The mare was standing out on the pavement with three men around her, of whom one was holding her head, another was down on his knees washing her wounds, and the third was describing the fatal nature of the wounds which she had received. Traffick was standing at a little distance, listening in silence to the implied rebukes of the groom. "Good heavens, what is this?" repeated Sir Thomas, as he joined the conclave.

"There are a lot of loose stones on that hill," said Traffick, "and she tripped on one and came down, all in a lump, before you could look at her. I'm awfully sorry, but it might have happened to anyone."

Sir Thomas knew how to fix his darts better than by throwing them direct at his enemy. "She has utterly destroyed herself," said he, addressing himself to the head-groom, who was busily employed with the sponge in his hand.

"I'm afraid she has, Sir Thomas. The joint-oil will be sure to run on both knees; the gashes is so mortal deep."

"I've driven that mare hundreds of times down that hill," said Sir Thomas, "and I never knew her to trip before."

"Never, Sir Thomas," said the groom.

"She'd have come down with you to-day," said Mr. Traffick, defending himself.

"It was my own fault, Bunsum. That's all that can be said about it." Bunsum the groom, kneeling as he was, expressed, by his grimaces, his complete agreement with this last opinion of his master. "Of course I ought to have known that he couldn't drive," said Sir Thomas.

"A horse may fall down with anybody," said Mr. Traffick.

"You'd better take her and shoot her," said Sir Thomas, still addressing the groom. "She was the best thing we had in the stable, but now she is done for." With that he turned away from the yard without having as yet addressed a word to his son-in-law.

This was so intolerable that even Mr. Traffick could not bear it in in silence. "I have told you that I am very sorry," said he, following Sir Thomas closely, "and I don't know what a man can do more."

"Nothing,—unless it be not to borrow a horse again."

"You may be sure I will never do that."

"I'm not sure of it at all. If you wanted another to-morrow you'd ask for him if you thought you could get him."

"I call that very uncivil, Sir Thomas,—and very unkind."

"Bother!" said Sir Thomas. "It is no good in being kind to a fellow like you. Did you ever hear what the cabman did who had a sovereign given to him for driving a mile. He asked the fool who gave it him to make it a guinea. I am the fool, and, by George, you are the cabman!" With this Sir Thomas turned into the house by a small door, leaving his son-in-law to wander round to the front by himself.

"Your father has insulted me horribly," he said to his wife, whom he found up in her bed-room.

"What is the matter now, Septimus?"

"That little mare of his, which I have no doubt has come down half a score of times before, fell with me and cut her knees."

"That's Phœbe," said Augusta. "She was his favourite."

"It's a kind of thing that might happen to anyone, and no gentleman thinks of mentioning it. He said such things to me that upon my word I don't think I can stop in the house any longer."

"Oh, yes, you will," said the wife.

"Of course, it is a difference coming from one's father-in-law. It's almost the same as from one's father."

"He didn't mean it, Septimus."

"I suppose not. If he had, I really couldn't have borne it. He does become very rough sometimes, but I know that at bottom he has a thorough respect for me. It is only that induces me to bear it." Then it was settled between husband and wife that they should remain in their present quarters, and that not a word further should be said at any rate by them about the Phœbe mare. Nor did Sir Thomas say another word about the mare, but he added a note to those already written in the tablets of his memory as to his son-in-law, and the note declared that no hint, let it be ever so broad, would be effectual with Mr. Traffick.

The next day was a Sunday, and then another trouble awaited Sir Thomas. At this time it was not customary with Tom to come often to Merle Park. He had his own lodgings in London and his own club, and did not care much for the rural charms of Merle Park. But on this occasion he had condescended to appear, and on the Sunday afternoon informed his father that there was a matter which he desired to discuss with him. "Father," said he, "I am getting confoundedly sick of all this."

"Confounded," said Sir Thomas, "is a stupid foolish word, and it means nothing."

"There is a sort of comfort in it, Sir," said Tom; "but if it's objectionable I'll drop it."

" It is objectionable."

" I'll drop it, Sir. But nevertheless I am very sick of it."

" What are you sick of, Tom ?"

" All this affair with my cousin."

" Then, if you take my advice, you'll drop that too."

" I couldn't do that, father. A word is all very well. A man can drop a word ; but a girl is a different sort of thing. One can't drop a girl, even if one tries."

" Have you tried, Tom ?"

" Yes, I have. I've done my best to try. I put it out of my mind for a fortnight and wouldn't think of her. I had a bottle of champagne every day at dinner and then went to the theatre. But it was all of no use. I have set my heart on it and I can't give her up. I'll tell you what I'd like to do. I'd like to give her a diamond necklace."

" It wouldn't be the slightest use," said Sir Thomas, shaking his head.

" Why not ? It's what other men do. I mean it to be something handsome ;—about three hundred pounds."

" That's a large sum of money for a necklace."

" Some of them cost a deal more than that."

" And you'd only throw away your money."

" If she took it, she'd take me too. If she didn't,—why I should still have the diamonds. I mean to try any way."

" Then it's of no use your coming to me."

" I thought you'd let me have the money. It's no good running into debt for them. And then if you'd add something of your own,— a locket, or something of that kind,—I think it would have an effect. I have seen a necklace at Ricolay's, and if I could pay ready money for it I could have 20 per cent. off it. The price named is three hundred guineas. That would make it £254 5s. £250 would buy it if the cheque was offered."

There was a spirit about the son which was not displeasing to the father. That idea that the gift if accepted would be efficacious, or if not that it would be rejected,—so that Tom would not lose his hopes and his diamonds together,—seemed to be sound. Sir Thomas, therefore, promised the money, with the distinct understanding that if the gift were not accepted by Ayala it should be consigned to his own hands. But as for any present from himself, he felt that this would not be the time for it. He had called upon his niece and solicited her himself, and she had been deaf to his words. After that he could not condescend to send her gifts. " Should she become my promised daughter-in-law then I would send her presents," said Sir Thomas.

The poor man certainly received less pleasure from his wealth than was credited to him by those who knew his circumstances. Yet he endeavoured to be good to those around him and especially good to his children. There had been present to him ever since the beginning of his successes,—ever since his marriage,—a fixed resolution that he would not be a curmudgeon with his money, that he would endeavour to make those happy who depended on him, and that he would be liberal in such settlements for his children as might be conducive to their happiness and fortunes in life. In this way he had been very generous to Mr. Traffick. The man was a Member of Parliament, the son of a peer, and laborious. Why should he expect more? Money was wanting, but he could supply the money. So he had supplied it, and had been content to think that a good man should be propped up in the world by his means. What that had come to the reader knows. He thoroughly detested his son-in-law, and would have given much to have had his money back again,—so that Mr. Traffick should have had no share in it.

Then there was his second daughter! What should be done with Gertrude? The money should be forthcoming for her too if the fitting man could be found. But he would have nothing further to do with a penniless lover, let his position in the world of fashion, or even in the world of politics, be what it might. The man should either have wealth of his own, or should be satisfied to work for it. Houston had been unfortunate in the moment of his approaches. Sir Thomas had been driven by his angry feelings to use hard, sharp words, and now was forced to act up to his words. He declared roughly that Mr. Houston should not have a shilling of his money,—as he had certainly been justified for doing;—and his daughter, who had always been indulged in every kind of luxury, had at once concocted a plot for running away from her home! As he thought of the plot it seemed to be wonderful to him that she should be willing to incur such a danger, —to be ready without a penny to marry a penniless man,—till he confessed to himself, that, were she to do so, she would certainly have the money sooner or later. He was capable of passion, capable of flying out and saying a very severe thing to Septimus Traffick or another when his temper was hot; but he was incapable of sustained wrath. He was already aware that if Mr. Traffick chose to stay he would stay; —that if Mr. Houston were brave enough to be persistent he might have both the money and the girl. As he thought of it all he was angry with himself, wishing that he were less generous, less soft, less forgiving.

And now here was Tom,—whom at the present moment he liked the best of all his children, who of the three was the least inclined to run counter to him,—ready to break his heart because he could not get a little chit of a girl of whom he would probably be tired in twelve months after he possessed her ! Remembering what Tom had been, he was at a loss to understand how such a lad should be so thoroughly in love. At the present moment, had Ayala been purchasable, he would have been willing to buy her at a great price, because he would fain have pleased Tom had it been possible. But Ayala, who had not a penny in the world,—who never would have a penny unless he should give it her,—would not be purchased, and would have nothing to do with Tom ! The world was running counter to him, so that he had no pleasure in his home, no pleasure in his money, no pleasure in his children. The little back-parlour in Lombard Street was sweeter to him than Merle Park, with all its charms. His daughter Gertrude wanted to run away from him, while by no inducement could he get Mr. Traffick to leave the house.

While he was in this humour he met his niece Lucy roaming about the garden. He knew the whole story of Lucy's love, and had been induced by his wife to acknowledge that her marriage with the sculptor was not to be sanctioned. He had merely expressed his scorn when the unfortunate circumstances of Hamel's birth had been explained to him again and again. He had ridiculed the horror felt by his wife at the equally ill-born brothers and sisters in Rome. He had merely shaken his head when he was told that Hamel's father never went inside of any place of worship. But when it was explained to him that the young man had, so to say, no income at all, then he was forced to acknowledge that the young man ought not to be allowed to marry his niece.

To Lucy herself he had as yet said nothing on the subject since he had asked the lover in to lunch at Glenbogie. He heard bad accounts of her. He had been told by his wife, on different occasions,—not in the mere way of conversation, but with a premeditated energy of fault-finding,—that Lucy was a disobedient girl. She was worse than Ayala. She persisted in saying that she would marry the penniless artist as soon as he should profess himself to be ready. It had been different, she had tried to explain to her aunt, before she had been engaged to him. Now she considered herself to be altogether at his disposal. This had been her plea, but her plea had been altogether unacceptable to Aunt Emmeline. " She can do as she pleases, of course," Sir Thomas had said. That might be all very well ; but Aunt Emmeline was strongly of opinion that an adopted daughter of Queen's Gate, of Glenbogie, and Merle Park, ought not to be allowed to do as she pleased with herself. A girl ought not to be allowed to have the luxuries of palatial residences, and the luxuries of

free liberty of choice at the same time. More than once it had
occurred to Sir Thomas that he would put an end to all these
miseries by a mere scratch of his pen. It need not be £120,000,
or £100,000 as with a daughter. A few modest thousands would
do it. And then this man Hamel, though the circumstances of
his birth had been unfortunate, was not an idler like Frank Houston.
As far as Sir Thomas could learn, the man did work, and was
willing to work. The present small income earned would gradually
become more. He had a kindly feeling towards Lucy, although he
had been inclined to own that her marriage with Hamel was out of the
question. "My dear," he said to her, "why are you walking about
alone?" She did not like to say that she was walking alone because
she had no one to walk with her,—no such companion as Isadore would
be if Isadore were allowed to come to Merle Park ; so she simply smiled,
and went on by her uncle's side. "Do you like this place as well as
Glenbogie?" he asked.

"Oh ; yes."

"Perhaps you will be glad to get back to London again ?"

"Oh ; no."

"Which do you like best, then ?"

"They are all so nice, if——"

"If what, Lucy ?"

"Cælum non animum mutant qui trans mare currunt," Lucy might
have said, had she known the passage. As it was, she put the same
feeling into simpler words, "I should like one as well as the other,
Uncle Tom, if things went comfortably."

"There's a great deal in that," he said. "I suppose the meaning
is, that you do not get on well with your aunt ?"

"I am afraid she is angry with me, Uncle Tom."

"Why do you make her angry, Lucy ? When she tells you what
is your duty, why do you not endeavour to do it ?"

"I cannot do what she tells me," said Lucy ; "and, as I cannot, I
think I ought not to be here."

"Have you anywhere else to go to ?" To this she made no reply,
but walked on in silence. "When you say you ought not to be here,
what idea have you formed in your own mind as to the future ?"

"That I shall marry Mr. Hamel, some day."

"Do you think it would be well to marry any man without an
income to live upon ? Would it be a comfort to him seeing that he
had just enough to maintain himself, and no more ?" These were
terrible questions to her,—questions which she could not answer, but
yet as to which her mind entertained an easy answer. A little help
from him, who was willing to indulge her with so many luxuries while

she was under his roof, would enable her to be an assistance rather than a burden to her lover. But of this she could not utter a word. " Love is all very well," continued Sir Thomas, in his gruffest voice ; " but love should be regulated by good sense. It is a crime when two beggars think of marrying each other,—two beggars who are not prepared to live as beggars do."

" He is not a beggar," said Lucy, indignantly. " He has begged nothing ; nor have I."

" Pshaw !" said Sir Thomas ; " I was laying down a general rule. I did not mean to call anybody a beggar. You shouldn't take me up like that."

" I beg your pardon, Uncle Tom," she said piteously.

" Very well ; very well ; that will do." But still he went on walking with her, and she felt she could not leave him till he gave her some signal that she was to go. They continued in this way till they had come nearly round the large garden ; when he stopped, as he was walking, and addressed her again. " I suppose you write to him sometimes."

" Yes," said Lucy, boldly.

" Write to him at once, and tell him to come and see me in Lombard Street on Tuesday, at two o'clock. Give me the letter, and I will take care it is sent to him directly I get to town. Now you had better go in, for it is getting very cold."

CHAPTER XXXI.

THE DIAMOND NECKLACE.

TOM went up to London intent upon his diamonds. To tell the truth he had already made the purchase subject to some question of ready money. He now paid for it after considerable chaffering as to the odd pounds, which he succeeded in bringing to a successful termination. Then he carried the necklace away with him, revolving in his mind the different means of presentation. He thought that a letter might be best if only he was master of the language in which such a letter should properly be written. But he entirely doubted his own powers of composition. He was so modest in this respect that he would not even make an attempt. He knew himself well enough to be aware that he was in many respects ignorant. He would have endeavoured to take the bracelet personally to Ayala had he not been conscious that he could not recommend his present with such romantic phrases and touches of poetry as would be gratifying to her fine sense. Were he to find himself in her presence with the necklace he must depend on himself for his words ; but a letter might be sent in his own hand-writing, the poetry and romance of which might be supplied by another.

Now it had happened that Tom had formed a marvellous friendship in Rome with Colonel Stubbs. They had been hunting together in the Campagna, and Tom had been enabled to accommodate the Colonel with the loan of a horse when his own had been injured. They had since met in London, and Stubbs had declared to more than one of his friends that Tom, in spite of his rings and his jewelry, was a very good fellow at bottom. Tom had been greatly flattered by the intimacy, and had lately been gratified by an invitation to Aldershot in order that the military glories of the camp might be shown to him. He had accepted the invitation, and a day in the present week had been fixed. Then it occurred to him suddenly that he knew no one so fitted to write such a letter as that demanded as his friend Colonel Jonathan Stubbs. He had an idea that the Colonel, in spite of his red hair and in spite of a certain aptitude for drollery which pervaded him, had a romantic side to his character ; and he felt confident that, as to the use of language, the Colonel was very great indeed. He therefore, when he went to Aldershot, carefully put the bracelet in his breast-pocket and determined to reveal his secret and to ask for aid.

The day of his arrival was devoted to the ordinary pursuits of Aldershot and the evening to festivities, which were prolonged too late into the night to enable him to carry out his purpose before he went to bed. He arranged to leave on the next morning by a train between ten and eleven, and was told that three or four men would come in to breakfast at half-past nine. His project then seemed to be all but hopeless. But at last with great courage he made an effort. " Colonel," said he, just as they were going to bed, " I wonder if you could give me half-an-hour before breakfast. It is a matter of great importance." Tom, as he said this, assumed a most solemn face.

" An hour if you like, my dear boy. I am generally up soon after six, and am always out on horseback before breakfast as soon as the light serves."

" Then if you'll have me called at half-past seven I shall be ever so much obliged to you."

The next morning at eight the two were closeted together, and Tom immediately extracted the parcel from his pocket and opened the diamonds to view. " Upon my word that is a pretty little trinket," said the Colonel, taking the necklace in his hand.

" Three hundred guineas !" said Tom, opening his eyes very wide.

" I daresay."

" That is, it would have been three hundred guineas unless I had come down with the ready. I made the fellow give me twenty per cent. off. You should always remember this when you are buying jewelry."

" And what is to be done with this pretty thing? I suppose it is intended for some fair lady's neck."

" Oh, of course."

" And why has it been brought down to Aldershot? There are plenty of fellows about this place who will get their hands into your pocket if they know that you have such a trinket as that about you."

" I will tell you why I brought it," said Tom, very gravely. " It is, as you say, for a young lady. I intend to make that young lady my wife. Of course this is a secret, you know."

" It shall be sacred as the Pope's toe," said Stubbs.

" Don't joke about it, Colonel, if you please. It's life and death to me."

" I'll keep your secret and will not joke. Now what can I do for you?"

" I must send this as a present with a letter. I must first tell you that she has,—well, refused me."

" That never means much the first time, old boy."

" She has refused me half-a-dozen times, but I mean to go on with it. If she refuses me two dozen times I'll try her a third dozen."

" Then you are quite in earnest?"

" I am. It's a kind of thing I know that men laugh about, but I don't mind telling you that I am downright in love with her. The governor approves of it."

" She has got money probably?"

" Not a shilling ;—not as much as would buy a pair of gloves. But I don't love her a bit the less for that. As to income, the governor will stump up like a brick. Now I want you to write the letter."

" It's a kind of thing a third person can't do," said the Colonel, when he had considered the request for a moment.

" Why not? Yes, you can."

" Do it yourself, and say just the simplest words as they come up. They are sure to go further with any girl than what another man may write. It is impossible that another man should be natural on such a task as that."

" Natural! I don't know about natural," said Tom, who was anxious now to explain the character of the lady in question. " I don't know that a letter that was particularly natural would please her. A touch of poetry and romance would go further than anything natural."

" Who is the lady?" asked the Colonel, who certainly was by this time entitled to be so far inquisitive.

"She is my cousin,—Ayala Dormer."

"Who ?"

"Ayala Dormer ;—my cousin. She was at Rome, but I do not think you ever saw her there."

"I have seen her since," said the Colonel.

"Have you ? I didn't know."

"She was with my aunt, the Marchesa Baldoni."

"Dear me ! So she was. I never put the two things together. Don't you admire her ?"

"Certainly I do. My dear fellow, I can't write this letter for you." Then he put down the pen which he had taken up as though he had intended to comply with his friend's request. "You may take it as settled that I cannot write it."

"No ?"

"Impossible. One man should never write such a letter for another man. You had better give the thing in person,—that is, if you mean to go on with the matter."

"I shall certainly go on with it," said Tom, stoutly.

"After a certain time, you know, reiterated offers do, you know,—do, —do,—partake of the nature of persecution."

"Reiterated refusals are the sort of persecution I don't like."

"It seems to me that Ayala,—Miss Dormer, I mean,—should be protected by a sort of feeling,—feeling of—of what I may perhaps call her dependent position. She is peculiarly,—peculiarly situated."

"If she married me she would be much better situated. I could give her everything she wants."

"It isn't an affair of money, Mr. Tringle."

Tom felt, from the use of the word Mister, that he was in some way giving offence ; but felt also that there was no true cause for offence. "When a man offers everything," he said, "and asks for nothing, I don't think he should be said to persecute."

"After a time it becomes persecution. I am sure Ayala would feel it so."

"My cousin can't suppose that I am ill-using her," said Tom, who disliked the "Ayala" quite as much as he did the "Mister."

"Miss Dormer, I meant. I can have nothing further to say about it. I can't write the letter, and I should not imagine that Ayala,— Miss Dormer,—would be moved in the least by any present that could possibly be made to her. I must go out now, if you don't mind, for half-an-hour ; but I shall be back in time for breakfast."

Then Tom was left alone with the necklace lying on the table before him. He knew that something was wrong with the Colonel, but could not in the least guess what it might be. He was quite aware that early in the interview the Colonel had encouraged him to persevere with the lady, and had then, suddenly, not only advised him to desist, but had told him in so many words that he was bound to desist out of consideration for the lady. And the Colonel had spoken of his cousin in a manner that was distasteful to him. He could not analyse his feelings. He did not exactly know why he was displeased, but he was displeased. The Colonel, when asked for his assistance, was, of course, bound to talk about the lady,—would be compelled, by the nature of the confidence, to mention the lady's name ;—would even have been called on to write her Christian name. But this he should have done with a delicacy ;—almost with a blush. Instead of that Ayala's name had been common on his tongue. Tom felt himself to be offended, but hardly knew why. And then, why had he been called Mister Tringle ? The breakfast, which was eaten shortly afterwards in the company of three or four other men, was not eaten in comfort ;—and then Tom hurried back to London and to Lombard Street.

After this failure Tom felt it to be impossible to go to another friend for assistance. There had been annoyance in describing his love to Colonel Stubbs, and pain in the treatment he had received. Even had there been another friend to whom he could have confided the task, he could not have brought himself to encounter the repetition of such treatment. He was as firmly fixed as ever in his conviction that he could not write the letter himself. And, as he thought of the words with which he should accompany a personal presentation of the necklace, he reflected that in all probability he might not be able to force his way into Ayala's presence. Then a happy thought struck him. Mrs. Dosett was altogether on his side. Everybody was on his side except Ayala herself, and that pigheaded Colonel. Would it not be an excellent thing to entrust the necklace to the hands of his Aunt Dosett, in order that she might give it over to Ayala with all the eloquence in her power. Satisfied with this project he at once wrote a note to Mrs. Dosett.

" MY DEAR AUNT,

" I want to see you on *most important business*. If I shall not be troubling you, I will call upon you to-morrow at ten o'clock, before I go to my place of business.

" Yours affectionately,   T. TRINGLE, Junior."

On the following morning he apparelled himself with all his rings. He was a good-hearted, well-intentioned young man, with excellent qualities ; but he must have been slow of intellect when he had not as yet learnt the deleterious effect of all those rings. On this occasion he put on his rings, his chains, and his bright waistcoat, and made himself a thing disgusting to be looked at by any well-trained female. As far as his aunt was concerned he would have been altogether indifferent as to his appearance, but there was present to his mind some small hope that he might be allowed to see Ayala, as the immediate result of the necklace. Should he see Ayala, then how unfortunate it would be that he should present himself before the eyes of his mistress without those adornments which he did not doubt would be grateful to her. He had heard from Ayala's own lips that all things ought to be pretty. Therefore he endeavoured to make himself pretty. Of course he failed,—as do all men who endeavour to make themselves pretty,— but it was out of the question that he should understand the cause of his failure.

"Aunt Dosett, I want you to do me a very great favour," he began, with a solemn voice.

"Are you going to a party, Tom," she said.

"A party! No,—who gives a party in London at this time of the day? Oh, you mean because I have just got a few things on. When I call anywhere I always do. I have got another lady to see, a lady of rank, and so I just made a change." But this was a fib.

"What can I do for you, Tom?"

"I want you to look at that." Then he brought out the necklace, and, taking it out of the case, displayed the gems tastefully upon the table.

"I do believe they are diamonds," said Mrs. Dosett.

"Yes; they are diamonds. I am not the sort of fellow to get anything sham. What do you think that little thing cost, Aunt Dosett?"

"I haven't an idea. Sixty pounds, perhaps!"

"Sixty pounds! Do you go into a jeweller's shop and see what you could do among diamonds with sixty pounds!"

"I never do go into jewellers' shops, Tom."

"Nor I, very often. It's a sort of place where a fellow can drop a lot of money. But I did go into one after this. It don't look much, does it?"

"It is very pretty."

"I think it is pretty. Well, Aunt Dosett, the price for that little trifle was three—hundred—guineas!" As he said this he looked into his aunt's face for increased admiration.

"You gave three hundred guineas for it!"

"I went with ready money in my hand, when I tempted the man with a cheque to let me have it for two hundred and fifty pounds. In buying jewelry you should always do that."

"I never buy jewelry," said Mrs. Dosett, crossly.

"If you should, I mean. Now, I'll tell you what I want you to do This is for Ayala."

"For Ayala !"

"Yes, indeed. I am not the fellow to stick at a trifle when I want to carry my purpose. I bought this the other day and gave ready money for it,—two hundred and fifty pounds,—on purpose to give it to Ayala. In naming the value,—of course you'll do that when you give it her,—you might as well say three hundred guineas. That was the price on the ticket. I saw it myself,—so there won't be any untruth, you know."

"Am I to give it her ?"

"That's just what I want. When I talk to her she flares up, and, as likely as not, she'd fling the necklace at my head."

"She wouldn't do that, I hope."

"It would depend upon how the thing went. When I do talk to her it always seems that nothing I say can be right. Now, if you will give it her you can put in all manner of pretty things."

"This itself will be the prettiest thing," said Mrs. Dosett.

"That's just what I was thinking. Everybody agrees that diamonds will go further with a girl than anything else. When I told the governor he quite jumped at the idea."

"Sir Thomas knows you are giving it ?"

"Oh, dear, yes. I had to get the rhino from him. I don't go about with two hundred and fifty pounds always in my own pocket."

"If he had sent the money to Ayala how much better it would have been," said poor Mrs. Dosett.

"I don't think that at all. Who ever heard of making a present to a young lady in money. Ayala is romantic, and that would have been the most unromantic thing out. That would not have done me the least good in the world. It would simply have gone to buy boots and petticoats and such like. A girl would never be brought to think of her lover merely by putting on a pair of boots. When she fastens such a necklace as this round her throat he ought to have a chance. Don't you think so, Aunt Dosett ?"

"Tom, shall I tell you something ?" said the aunt.

"What is it, Aunt Dosett ?"

"I don't believe that you have a chance."

"Do you mean that ?" he asked, sorrowfully.

"I do."

"You think that the necklace will do no good ?"

"Not the least. Of course I will offer it to her if you wish it, because her uncle and I quite approve of you as a husband for Ayala. But I am bound to tell you the truth. I do not think the necklace will do you any good." Then he sat silent for a time, meditating upon his condition. It might be imprudent;—it might be a wrong done to his father to jeopardise the necklace. How could it be if Ayala were to take the necklace and not to take him? "Am I to give it?" she asked.

"Yes," said he, bravely, but with a sigh; "give it her all the same."

"From you or from Sir Thomas?"

"Oh, from me;—from me. If she were told it came from the governor she'd keep it whether or no. I am sure I hope she will keep it," he said, trying to remove the bad impression which his former words might perhaps have left.

"You may be sure she will not keep it," said Mrs. Dosett, "unless she should intend to accept your hand. Of that I can hold out no hope to you. There is a matter, Tom, which I think I should tell you as you are so straightforward in your offer. Another gentleman has asked her to marry him."

"She has accepted him!" exclaimed Tom.

"No, she has not accepted him. She has refused him."

"Then I'm just where I was," said Tom.

"She has refused him, but I think that she is in a sort of way attached to him; and though he too has been refused I imagine that his chance is better than yours."

"And who the d—— is he?" said Tom, jumping up from his seat in great excitement.

"Tom!" exclaimed Mrs. Dosett.

"I beg your pardon; but you see this is very important. Who is the fellow?"

"He is one Colonel Jonathan Stubbs."

"Who?"

"Colonel Jonathan Stubbs."

"Impossible! It can't be Colonel Stubbs. I know Colonel Stubb ."

"I can assure you it is true, Tom. I have had a letter from a lady, —a relative of Colonel Stubbs,—telling me the whole story."

"Colonel Stubbs!" he said. "That passes anything I ever heard. She has refused him?"

"Yes, she has refused him."

"And has not accepted him since?"

"She certainly has not accepted him yet."

"You may give her the bracelet all the same," said Tom, hurrying out of the room. That Colonel Stubbs should have made an offer to Ayala, and yet have accepted his, Tom Tringle's, confidence!

CHAPTER XXXII.

TOM'S DESPAIR.

THE reader will understand that the fate of the necklace was very soon decided. Ayala declared that it was very beautiful. She had, indeed, a pretty taste for diamonds, and would have been proud enough to call this necklace her own ; but, as she declared to her aunt, she would not accept Tom though he were made of diamonds from head to foot. Accept Tom, when she could not even bring herself to think of becoming the wife of Jonathan Stubbs ! If Colonel Stubbs could not be received by her imagination as an Angel of Light, how immeasurably distant from anything angelic must be Tom Tringle ! " Of course it must go back," she said, when the question had to be decided as to the future fate of the necklace. As a consequence poor Mr. Dosett was compelled to make a special journey into the City and to deposit a well-sealed parcel in the hands of Tom Tringle himself. " Your cousin sends her kind regards," he said, " but cannot bring herself to accept your magnificent present."

Tom had been very much put about since his visit to the Crescent. Had his aunt merely told him that his present would be inefficacious, he would have taken that assurance as being simply her opinion, and would have still entertained some hopes in the diamonds. But these tidings as to another lover crushed him altogether. And such a lover ! The very man whom he had asked to write his letter for him ? Why had not Colonel Stubbs told him the truth when thus his own secret had become revealed by an accident ? He understood it all now,—the " Ayala," and the " Mister," and the reason why the Colonel could not write the letter. Then he became very angry with the Colonel, whom he bitterly accused of falsehood and treason. What right had the Colonel to meddle with his cousin at all ? And how false he had been to say nothing of what he himself had done when his rival had told him everything ! In this way he made up his mind that it was his duty to hate Colonel Stubbs, and if possible to inflict some personal punishment upon him. He was reckless of himself now, and, if he could only get one good blow at the Colonel's head with a thick stick, would be indifferent as to what the law might do with him afterwards. Or perhaps he might be able to provoke Colonel Stubbs to fight with him. He had an idea that duels at present were not in fashion. But nevertheless, in such a case as this, a man ought to fight. He could at any rate have the gratification of calling the Colonel a coward if he should refuse to fight.

He was the more wretched because his spirit within him was cowed by the idea of the Colonel. He did acknowledge to himself that his chance could be but bad while such a rival as Colonel Stubbs stood in his way. He tried to argue with himself that it was not so. As far as he knew, Colonel Stubbs was and would remain a very much less rich man than himself. He doubted very much whether Colonel Stubbs could keep a carriage in London for his wife, while it had been already arranged that he was to be allowed to do so should he succeed in marrying Ayala. To be a partner in the house of Travers and Treason was a much greater thing than to be a Colonel. But, though he assured himself of all this again and again, still he was cowed. There was something about the Colonel which did more than redeem his red hair and ugly mouth. And of this something poor Tom was sensible. Nevertheless, if occasion should arise he thought that he could "punch the Colonel's head;"—not without evil consequence to himself;—but still that he could "punch the Colonel's head," not minding the consequences.

Such had been his condition of mind when he left the Crescent, and it was not improved by the receipt of the parcel. He hardly said a word when his uncle put it into his hands, merely muttering something and consigning the diamonds to his desk. He did not tell himself that Ayala must now be abandoned. It would have been better for him if he could have done so. But all real, springing, hopeful hope departed from his bosom. This came from the Colonel, rather than from the rejected necklace.

" Did you send that jewelry ?" his father asked him some days afterwards.

" Yes ; I sent it."

" And what has now become of it ?"

" It is in my desk there."

" Did she send it back again ?"

" It came back. My Uncle Dosett brought it. I do not want to say anything more about it, if you please."

" I am sorry for that, Tom ;—very sorry. As you had set your heart upon it I wish it could have been as you would have it. But the necklace should not be left there." Tom shook his head in despair.

" You had better let me have the necklace. It is not that I should grudge it to you, Tom, if it could do you any good."

" You shall have it, Sir."

" It will be better so. That was the understanding." Then the necklace was transferred to some receptacle belonging to Sir Thomas himself, the lock of which might probably be more secure than that of Tom's desk, and there it remained in its case, still folded in the various papers in which Mrs. Dosett had encased it.

Then Tom found it necessary to adopt some other mode of life for his own consolation and support. He had told his father on one occasion that he had devoted himself for a fortnight to champagne and the theatres. But this had been taken has a joke. He had been fairly punctual at his place of business and had shown no symptoms of fast living. But now it occurred to him that fast living would be the only thing for him. He had been quite willing to apply himself to marriage and a steady life ; but fortune had not favoured him. If he drank too much now, and lay in bed, and became idle, it was not his fault. There came into his head an idea that Ayala and Colonel Stubbs between them must look to that. Could he meet Ayala he would explain to her how his character as a moral man had been altogether destroyed by her conduct ;—and should he meet Colonel Stubbs he would explain something to him also.

A new club had been established in London lately, called the Mountaineers, which had secured for itself handsome lodgings in Piccadilly, and considered itself to be, among clubs, rather a comfortable institution than otherwise. It did not as yet affect much fashion, having hitherto secured among its members only two lords,—and they were lords by courtesy. But it was a pleasant, jovial place, in which the delights of young men were not impeded by the austerity of their elders. Its name would be excused only on the plea that all other names available for a club had already been appropriated in the metropolis. There was certainly nothing in the club peculiarly applicable to mountains. But then there are other clubs in London with names which might be open to similar criticism. It was the case that many young men engaged in the City had been enrolled among its members, and it was from this cause, no doubt, that Tom Tringle was regarded as being a leading light among the Mountaineers. It was here that the champagne had been drunk to which Tom had alluded when talking of his love to his father. Now, in his despair, it seemed good to him to pass a considerable portion of his time among the Mountaineers.

" You'll dine here, Faddle ?" he said one evening to a special friend of his, a gentleman also from the City, with whom he had been dining a good deal during the last week.

" I suppose I shall," said Faddle, "but ain't we coming it a little strong ? They want to know at the Gardens what the deuce it is I'm about." The Gardens was a new row of houses, latterly christened Badminton Gardens, in which resided the father and mother of Faddle.

" I've given up all that kind of thing," said Tom.

" Your people are not in London."

" It will make no difference when they do come up. I call an evening in the bosom of one's family about the slowest thing there is. The bosom must do without me for the future."

" Won't your governor cut up rough ?"

" He must cut up as he pleases. But I rather fancy he knows all
about it. I shan't spend half as much money this way as if I had a
house and wife and family,—and what we may call a bosom of one's
own." Then they had dinner and went to the theatre, and played
billiards, and had supper, and spent the night in a manner very delightful, no doubt, to themselves, but of which their elder friends could
hardly have approved.

There was a good deal of this following upon the episode of the
necklace, and it must be told with regret that our young hero fell into
certain exploits which were by no means creditable to him. More than
one good-humoured policeman had helped him home to his lodgings ;
but alas, on Christmas Eve, he fell into the hands of some guardian of
the peace who was not quite sufficiently good-natured, and Tom passed
the night and the greater part of the following morning, recumbent,
he in one cell, and his friend Faddle in the next, with an intimation
that they would certainly be taken before a magistrate on the day after
Christmas Day.

Oh, Ayala ! Ayala ! It must be acknowledged that you were in a
measure responsible ;—and not only for the lamentable condition of
your lover, but also of that of his friend. For, in his softer moments,
Tom had told everything to Faddle, and Faddle had declared that he
would be true to the death to a friend suffering such unmerited misfortune. Perhaps the fidelity of Faddle may have owed something to the
fact that Tom's pecuniary allowances were more generous than those
accorded to himself. To Ayala must be attributed the occurrence of
these misfortunes. But Tom in his more fiery moments,—those
moments which would come between the subsidence of actual sobriety
and the commencement of intoxication,—attributed all his misfortunes
to the Colonel. " Faddle," he would say in these moments, " of course
I know that I'm a ruined man. Of course I'm aware that all this is
only a prelude to some ignominious end. I have not sunk to this kind
of thing without feeling it." " You'll be right enough some day, old
fellow," Faddle would reply. " I shall live to be godfather to the first
boy." " Never, Faddle !" Tom replied. " All those hopes have
vanished. You'll never live to see any child of mine. And I know
well where to look for my enemy. Stubbs indeed ! I'll Stubbs him.
If I can only live to be revenged on that traitor then I shall die contented. Though he shot me through the heart, I should die contented."

This had happened a little before that unfortunate Christmas Eve.
Up to this time Sir Thomas, though he had known well that his son
had not been living as he should do, had been mild in his remonstrances,
and had said nothing at Merle Park to frighten Lady Tringle. But the

affair of Christmas Eve came to his ears with all its horrors. A police-man whom Tom had struck with his fist in the pit of the stomach had not been civil enough to accept this mark of familiarity with good-humour. He had been much inconvenienced by the blow, and had insisted upon giving testimony to this effect before the magistrate. There had been half-an-hour, he said, in which he had hung dubious between this world and the next, so great had been the violence of the blow, and so deadly its direction! The magistrate was one of those just men who find a pleasure and a duty in protecting the police of the metropolis. It was no case, he declared, for a fine. What would be a fine to such a one as Thomas Tringle, junior! And Tom,—Tom Tringle, the only son of Sir Thomas Tringle, the senior partner in the great house of Travers and Treason,—was ignominiously locked up for a week. Faddle, who had not struck the blow, was allowed to depart with a fine and a warning. Oh, Ayala, Ayala, this was thy doing!

When the sentence was known Sir Thomas used all his influence to extricate his unfortunate son, but in vain. Tom went through his penalty, and, having no help from champagne, doubtless had a bad time of it. Ayala, Stubbs, the policeman, and the magistrate, seemed to have conspired to destroy him. But the week at last dragged itself out, and then Tom found himself confronted with his father in the back-parlour of the house in Queen's Gate. "Tom," he said, "this is very bad!"

"It is bad, Sir," said Tom.

"You have disgraced me, and your mother, and yourself. You have disgraced Travers and Treason!" Poor Tom shook his head. "It will be necessary, I fear, that you should leave the house altogether." Tom stood silent without a word. "A young man who has been locked up in prison for a week for maltreating a policeman can hardly expect to be entrusted with such concerns as those of Travers and Treason. I and your poor mother cannot get rid of you and the dis-grace which you have entailed upon us. Travers and Treason can easily get rid of you." Tom knew very well that his father was, in fact, Travers and Treason, but he did not yet feel that an opportunity had come in which he could wisely speak a word. "What have you got to say for yourself, Sir?" demanded Sir Thomas.

"Of course, I'm very sorry," muttered Tom.

"Sorry, Tom! A young man holding your position in Travers and Treason ought not to have to be sorry for having been locked up in prison for a week for maltreating a policeman! What do you think must be done, yourself?"

"The man had been hauling me about in the street."

" You were drunk, no doubt."

" I had been drinking. I am not going to tell a lie about it. But he needn't have done as he did. Faddle knows that, and can tell you."

" What can have driven you to associate with such a young man as Faddle? That is the worst part of it. Do you know what Faddle and Company are,—stock-jobbers, who ten years ago hadn't a thousand pounds in the way of capital among them! They've been connected with a dozen companies, none of which are floating now, and have made money out of them all! Do you think that Travers and Treason will accept a young man as a partner who associates with such people as that?"

" I have seen old Faddle's name and yours on the same prospectus together, Sir."

" What has that to do with it? You never saw him inside our counter. What a name to appear along with yours in such an affair as this! If it hadn't been for that, you might have got over it. Young men will be young men. Faddle! I think you will have to go abroad for a time, till it has been forgotten."

" I should like to stay, just at present, Sir," said Tom.

" What good can you do?"

" All the same, I should like to stay, Sir."

" I was thinking that, if you were to take a tour through the United States, go across to San Francisco, then up to Japan, and from thence through some of the Chinese cities down to Calcutta and Bombay, you might come back by the Euphrates Valley to Constantinople, see something of Bulgaria and those countries, and so home by Vienna and Paris. The Euphrates Valley Railway will be finished by that time, perhaps, and Bulgaria will be as settled as Hertfordshire. You'd see something of the world, and I could let it be understood that you were travelling on behalf of Travers and Treason. By the time that you were back, people in the City would have forgotten the policeman, and if you could manage to write home three or four letters about our trade with Japan and China, they would be willing to forget Faddle."

" But, Sir——"

" Shouldn't you like a tour of that kind?"

" Very much indeed, Sir ;—only——"

" Only what, Tom?"

" Ayala !" said Tom, hardly able to suppress a sob as he uttered the fatal name.

" Tom, don't be a fool. You can't make a young woman have you if she doesn't choose. I have done all that I could for you, because I saw that you'd set your heart upon it. I went to her myself, and then

I gave two hundred and fifty pounds for that bauble. I am told I shall have to lose a third of the sum in getting rid of it."

"Ricolay told me that he'd take it back at two hundred and twenty," said Tom, whose mind, prostrate as it was, was still alive to consideration of profit and loss.

"Never mind that for the present," said Sir Thomas. "Don't you remember the old song?—'If she will, she will, you may depend on't. And if she won't she won't; and there's an end on't.' You ought to be a man, and pluck up your spirits. Are you going to allow a little girl to knock you about in that way?" Tom only shook his head, and looked as if he was very ill. In truth, the champagne, and the imprisonment, and Ayala together, had altogether altered his appearance. "We've done what we could about it, and now it is time to give it over. Let me hear you say that you will give it over." Tom stood speechless before his father. "Speak the word, and the thing will be done," continued Sir Thomas, endeavouring to encourage the young man.

"I can't," said Tom, sighing.

"Nonsense!"

"I have tried, and I can't."

"Tom, do you mean to say that you are going to lose everything because a chit of a girl like that turns up her nose at you?"

"It's no use my going while things are like this," said Tom. "If I were to get to New York, I should come back by the next ship. As for letters about business, I couldn't settle my mind to anything of the kind."

"Then you're not the man I took you to be," said the father.

"I could be man enough," said Tom, clenching his fist, "if I could get hold of Colonel Stubbs."

"Colonel who?"

"Stubbs! Jonathan Stubbs! I know what I'm talking about. I'm not going to America, nor China, nor anything else, till I've polished him off. It's all very well your abusing me, but you don't know what it is I have suffered. As for being called a man I don't care about it. What I should like best would be to get Ayala on one side and Stubbs on the other, and then all three to go off the Duke of York's Column together. It's no good talking about Travers and Treason. I don't care for Travers and Treason as I am now. If you'll get Ayala to say that she'll have me, I'll go to the shop every morning at eight and stay till nine; and as for the Mountaineers it may all go to the d—— for me." Then he rushed out of the room, banging the door after him.

Sir Thomas, when he was thus left, stood for awhile with his hands

in his trousers' pockets, contemplating the condition of his son. It
was wonderful to him that a boy of his should be afflicted in this
manner. When he had been struck by the juvenile beauties of
Emmeline Dosett he had at once asked the young lady to share his
fortunes with him, and the young lady had speedily acceded to his
request. Then he had been married, and that was all he had ever
known of the troubles of love. He could not but think, looking back
at it as he did now from a distance, that had Emmeline been hard-
hearted he would have endured the repulse and have passed on
speedily to some other charmer. But Tom had been wounded after a
fashion which seemed to him to have been very uncommon. It might
be possible that he should recover in time, but while undergoing
recovery he would be ruined ;—so great were the young man's sufferings ! Now Sir Thomas, though he had spoken to Tom with all the
severity which he had been able to assume, though he had abused
Faddle, and had vindicated the injured dignity of Travers and Treason
with all his eloquence ; though he had told Tom it was unmanly to
give way to his love, yet, of living creatures, Tom was at this moment
the dearest to his heart. He had never for an instant entertained the
idea of expelling Tom from Travers and Treason because of the policeman, or because of Faddle. What should he do for the poor boy
now ? Was there any argument, any means of persuasion, by which he
could induce that foolish little girl to accept all the good things which
he was ready to do for her ? Could he try yet once again himself,
with any chance of success ? Thinking of all this, he stood there for
an hour alone with his hands in his trousers pockets.

CHAPTER XXXIII.

ISADORE HAMEL IN LOMBARD STREET.

In following the results of Tom's presentation of the necklace we
have got beyond the period which our story is presumed to have reached.
Tom was in durance during the Christmas week, but we must go back
to the promise which had been made by her uncle, Sir Thomas, to
Lucy about six weeks before that time. The promise had extended
only to an undertaking on the part of Sir Thomas to see Isadore Hamel
if he would call at the house in Lombard Street at a certain hour on a
certain day. Lucy was overwhelmed with gratitude when the promise
was made. A few moments previously she had been indignant because
her uncle had appeared to speak of her and her lover as two beggars,—
but Sir Thomas had explained and in some sort apologised, and then
had come the promise which to Lucy seemed to contain an assurance

effectual aid. Sir Thomas would not have asked to see the lover had he intended to be hostile to the lover. Something would be done to solve the difficulty which had seemed to Lucy to be so grave. She would not any longer be made to think that she should give up either her lover or her home under her uncle's roof. This had been terribly distressing to her because she had been well aware that on leaving her uncle's house she could be taken in only by her lover, to whom an immediate marriage would be ruinous. And yet she could not undertake to give up her lover. Therefore her uncle's promise had made her very happy, and she forgave the ungenerous allusion to the two beggars.

The letter was written to Isadore in high spirits. "I do not know what Uncle Tom intends, but he means to be kind. Of course you must go to him, and if I were you I would tell him everything about everything. He is not strict and hard like Aunt Emmeline. She means to be good too, but she is sometimes so very hard. I am happier now because I think something will be done to relieve you from the terrible weight which I am to you. I sometimes wish that you had never come to me in Kensington Gardens, because I have become such a burden to you."

There was much more in which Lucy no doubt went on to declare that burden as she was she intended to be persistent. Hamel, when he received this letter, was resolved to keep the appointment made for him, but his hopes were not very high. He had been angry with Lady Tringle,—in the first place, because of her treatment of himself at Glenbogie, and then, much more strongly, because she had been cruel to Lucy. Nor did he conceive himself to be under any strong debt of gratitude to Sir Thomas, though he had been invited to lunch. He was aware that the Tringles had despised him, and he repaid the compliment with all his heart by despising the Tringles. They were to him samples of the sort of people which he thought to be of all the most despicable. They were not only vulgar and rich, but purse-proud and conceited as well. To his thinking there was nothing of which such people were entitled to be proud. Of course they make money,—money out of money, an employment which he regarded as vile,—creating nothing either useful or beautiful. To create something useful was, to his thinking, very good. To create something beautiful was almost divine. To manipulate millions till they should breed other millions was the meanest occupation for a life's energy. It was thus, I fear, that Mr. Hamel looked at the business carried on in Lombard Street, being as yet very young in the world and seeing many things with distorted eyes.

He was aware that some plan would be proposed to him which might

probably accelerate his marriage, but was aware also that he would be
very unwilling to take advice from Sir Thomas. Sir Thomas, no doubt,
would be coarse and rough, and might perhaps offer him pecuniary
assistance in a manner which would make it impossible for him to
accept it. He had told himself a score of times that, poor as he was,
he did not want any of the Tringle money. His father's arbitrary
conduct towards him had caused him great misery. He had been
brought up in luxury, and had felt it hard enough to be deprived of
his father's means because he would not abandon the mode of life
that was congenial to him. But having been thus, as it were, cast off
by his father, he had resolved that it behoved him to depend only on
himself. In the matter of his love he was specially prone to be indignant and independent. No one had a right to dictate to him, and he
would follow the dictation of none. To Lucy alone did he acknowledge any debt, and to her he owed everything. But even for her sake
he could not condescend to accept Sir Thomas's money, and with his
money his advice. Lucy had begged him in her letter to tell everything to her uncle. He would tell Sir Thomas everything as to his
income, his prospects, and his intentions, because Sir Thomas, as Lucy's
uncle, would be entitled to such information. But he thought it very
improbable that he should accept any counsel from Sir Thomas.

Such being the condition of Hamel's mind it was to be feared that
but little good would come from his visit to Lombard Street. Lucy
had simply thought that her uncle, out of his enormous stores, would
provide an adequate income. Hamel thought that Sir Thomas, out of
his enormous impudence, would desire to dictate everything. Sir
Thomas was, in truth, anxious to be good-natured, and to do a kindness to his niece; but was not willing to give his money without being
sure that he was putting it into good hands.

"Oh, you're Hamel," said a young man to him, speaking to him
across the counter in the Lombard Street office. This was Tom, who,
as the reader will remember, had not yet got into his trouble on
account of the policeman.

Tom and Hamel had never met but once before, for a few moments
in the Coliseum at Rome, and the artist, not remembering him, did
not know by whom he was accosted in this familiar manner. "That
is my name, Sir," said Hamel. "Here is my card. Perhaps you will
do me the kindness to take it to Sir Thomas Tringle."

"All right, old fellow; I know all about it. He has got Puxley
with him from the Bank of England just at this moment. Come
through into this room. He'll soon have polished off old Puxley."
Tom was no more to Hamel than any other clerk, and he felt himself
to be aggrieved; but he followed Tom into the room as he was told,

and then prepared to wait in patience for the convenience of the great man. "So you and Lucy are going to make a match of it," said Tom.

This was terrible to Hamel. Could it be possible that all the clerks in Lombard Street talked of his Lucy in this way, because she was the niece of their senior partner? Were all the clerks, as a matter of course, instructed in the most private affairs of the Tringle family? "I am here in obedience to directions from Sir Thomas," said Hamel, ignoring altogether the impudent allusion which the young man had made.

"Of course you are. Perhaps you don't know who I am?"

"Not in the least," said Hamel.

"I am Thomas Tringle, junior," said Tom, with a little accession of dignity.

"I beg your pardon; I did not know," said Hamel.

"You and I ought to be thick," rejoined Tom, "because I'm going in for Ayala. Perhaps you've heard that before?"

Hamel had heard it and was well aware that Tom was to Ayala an intolerable burden, like the old man of the sea. He had heard of Tom as poor Ayala's pet aversion,—as a lover not to be shaken off though he had been refused a score of times. Ayala was to the sculptor only second in sacredness to Lucy. And now he was told by Tom himself that he was—"going in for Ayala." The expression was so distressing to his feelings that he shuddered when he heard it. Was it possible that any one should say of him that he was "going in" for Lucy? At that moment Sir Thomas opened the door, and grasping Hamel by the hand led him away into his own sanctum.

"And now, Mr. Hamel," said Sir Thomas, in his cheeriest voice, "how are you?" Hamel declared that he was very well, and expressed a hope that Sir Thomas was the same. "I'm not so young as I was, Mr. Hamel. My years are heavier and so is my work. That's the worst of it. When one is young and strong one very often hasn't enough to do. I daresay you find it so sometimes."

"In our profession," said Hamel "we go on working, though very often we do not sell what we do."

"That's bad," said Sir Thomas.

"It is the case always with an artist before he has made a name for himself. It is the case with many up to the last day of a life of labour. An artist has to look for that, Sir Thomas."

"Dear me! That seems very sad. You are a sculptor, I believe?"

"Yes, Sir Thomas."

"And the things you make must take a deal of room and be very heavy." At this Mr. Hamel only smiled. "Don't you think if you were to call an auction you'd get something for them?" At this suggestion the sculptor frowned but condescended to make no reply. Sir Thomas went on with his suggestion. "If you and half-a-dozen other beginners made a sort of gallery among you, people would buy them as they do those things in the Marylebone Road and stick them up somewhere about their grounds. It would be better than keeping them and getting nothing." Hamel had in his studio at home an allegorical figure of Italia United, and another of a Prostrate Roman Catholic Church, which in his mind's eye he saw for a moment stuck here or there about the gardens of some such place as Glenbogie ! Into them had been infused all the poetry of his nature and all the conviction of his intelligence. He had never dreamed of selling them. He had never dared to think that any lover of Art would encourage him to put into marble those conceptions of his genius which now adorned his studio, standing there in plaster of Paris. But to him they were so valuable, they contained so much of his thoughts, so many of his aspirations, that even had the marble counterparts been ordered and paid for nothing would have induced him to part with the originals. Now he was advised to sell them by auction in order that he might rival those grotesque tradesmen whose business it is to populate the gardens of wealthy but tasteless Britons ! It was thus that the idea represented itself to him. He simply smiled; but Sir Thomas did not fail to appreciate the smile.

"And now about this young lady?" said Sir Thomas, not altogether in so good a humour as he had been when he began his suggestion. "It's a bad look out for her when, as you say, you cannot sell your work when you've done it."

"I think you do not quite understand the matter, Sir Thomas."

"Perhaps not. It certainly does seem unintelligible that a man should lumber himself up with a lot of things which he cannot sell. A tradesman would know that he must get into the bankruptcy court if he were to go on like that. And what is sauce for the goose will be sauce for the gander also." Mr. Hamel again smiled but held his tongue. "If you can't sell your wares how can you keep a wife?"

"My wares as you call them are of two kinds. One, though no doubt made for sale, is hardly saleable. The other is done to order. Such income as I make comes from the latter."

"Heads," suggested Sir Thomas.

"Busts they are generally called."

"Well, busts. I call them heads. They are heads. A bust, I take it, is —— well, never mind." Sir Thomas found a difficulty in defining his idea of a bust. "A man wants to have something more or less like some one to put up in a church and then he pays you."

" Or perhaps in his library. But he can put it where he likes when he has bought it."

" Just so. But there ain't many of those come in your way, if I understand right."

" Not as many as I would wish."

" What can you net at the end of the year? That's the question."

Lucy had recommended him to tell Sir Thomas everything; and he had come there determined to tell at any rate everything referring to money. He had not the slightest desire to keep the amount of his income from Sir Thomas. But the questions were put to him in so distasteful a way that he could not bring himself to be confidential. " It varies with various circumstances, but it is very small."

" Very small? Five hundred a year?" This was ill-natured, because Sir Thomas knew that Mr. Hamel did not earn five hundred a year. But he was becoming acerbated by the young man's manner.

" Oh dear, no," said Hamel.

" Four hundred?"

" Nor four hundred,—nor three. I have never netted three hundred in one year after paying the incidental expenses."

" That seems to me to be uncommonly little for a young man who is thinking of marrying. Don't you think you had better give it up?"

" I certainly think nothing of the kind."

" Does your father do anything for you?"

" Nothing at all."

" He also makes heads?"

" Heads,—and other things."

" And sells them when he has made them."

" Yes, Sir Thomas; he sells them. He had a hard time once, but now he is run after. He refuses more orders than he can accept."

" And he won't do anything for you."

" Nothing. He has quarrelled with me."

" That is very bad. Well now, Mr. Hamel, would you mind telling me what your ideas are?" Sir Thomas, when he asked the question, still intended to give assistance, was still minded that the young people should by his assistance be enabled to marry. But he was strongly of opinion that it was his duty, as a rich and protecting uncle, to say something about imprudence, and to magnify difficulties. It certainly would be wrong for an uncle, merely because he was rich, to give away his money to dependent relatives without any reference to those hard principles which a possessor of money always feels it to be his business to inculcate. And up to this point Hamel had done nothing to ingratiate himself. Sir Thomas was beginning to think that the sculptor was an impudent prig, and to declare to himself that, should the marriage ever take place, the young couple would not be made welcome at Glenbogie or Merle Park. But still he intended to go on with his purpose, for Lucy's sake. Therefore he asked the sculptor as to his ideas generally.

"My idea is that I shall marry Miss Dormer, and support her on the earnings of my profession. My idea is that I shall do so before long, in comfort. My idea also is, that she will be the last to complain of any discomfort which may arise from my straitened circumstances at present. My idea is that *I* am preparing for myself a happy and independent life. My idea also is,—and I assure you that of all my ideas this is the one to which I cling with the fondest assurance,—that I will do my very best to make her life happy when she comes to grace my home."

There was a manliness in this which would have touched Sir Thomas had he been in a better humour, but, as it was, he had been so much irritated by the young man's manner, that he could not bring himself to be just. "Am I to understand that you intend to marry on something under three hundred a year?"

Hamel paused a moment before he made his reply. "How am I to answer such a question," he said, at last, "seeing that Miss Dormer is in your hands, and that you are unlikely to be influenced by anything that I may say?"

"I shall be very much influenced," said Sir Thomas.

".Were her father still alive, I think we should have put our hearts together, and between us decided on what might have been best for Lucy's happiness."

"Do you think that I'm indifferent to her happiness?" demanded Sir Thomas.

"I should have suggested to him," continued Hamel, not noticing the last question, "that she should remain in her own home till I could make one for her worthy of her acceptance. And then we should have arranged among us what would have been best for her happiness. I cannot do this with you. If you tell her to-morrow that she must give up either your protection or her engagement with me, then she must come to me, and make the best of all the little that I can do for her."

"Who says that I'm going to turn her out?" said Sir Thomas, rising angrily from his chair.

"I do not think that any one has said this of you."

"Then why do you throw it in my teeth?"

"Because your wife has threatened it."

Then Sir Thomas boiled over in his anger. "No one has threatened it. It is untrue. You are guilty both of impertinence and untruth in saying so." Here Hamel rose from his chair, and took up his hat. "Stop, young man, and hear what I have to say to you. I have done nothing but good to my niece."

"Nevertheless, it is true, Sir Thomas, that she has been told by your wife that she must either abandon me or the protection of your roof. I find no fault with Lady Tringle for saying so. It may have been the natural expression of a judicious opinion. But when you ask after my intentions in reference to your niece I am bound to tell you that I propose to subject her to the undoubted inconveniences of my poor home, simply because I find her to be threatened with the loss of another."

"She has not been threatened, Sir."

"You had better ask your wife, Sir Thomas. And, if you find that what I have said is true, I think you will own that I have been obliged to explain myself as I have done. As you have told me to my face that I have been guilty of untruth, I shall now leave you." With this he walked out of the room, and the words which Sir Thomas threw after him had no effect in recalling him.

It must be acknowledged that Hamel had been very foolish in referring to Aunt Emmeline's threat. Who does not know that words are constantly used which are intended to have no real effect? Who does not know that an angry woman will often talk after this fashion? But it was certainly the fact that Aunt Emmeline had more than once declared to Lucy that she could not be allowed to remain one of that family unless she would give up her lover. Lucy, in her loyal endeavours to explain to her lover her own position, had told him of the threat, and he, from that moment, had held himself prepared to find a home for his future wife should that threat be carried into execution. Sir Thomas was well aware that such words had been spoken, but he knew his wife, and knew how little such words signified. His wife, without his consent, would not have the power to turn a dog from Merle Park. The threat had simply been an argument intended to dissuade Lucy from her choice; and now it had been thrown in his teeth just when he had intended to make provision for this girl, who was not, in truth, related to him, in order that he might ratify her choice! He was very angry with the young prig who had thus rushed out of his presence. He was angry, too, with his wife, who had brought him into his difficulty by her foolish threat. But he was angry, also, with himself, knowing that he had been wrong to accuse the man of a falsehood.

CHAPTER XXXIV.

" I NEVER THREATENED TO TURN YOU OUT."

THEN there were written the following letters, which were sent and received before Sir Thomas went to Merle Park, and therefore, also, before he again saw Lucy.

DEAREST, DEAREST LOVE,

" I have been, as desired, to Lombard Street, but I fear that my embassy has not led to any good. I know myself to be about as bad an ambassador as any one can send. An ambassador should be soft and gentle,—willing to make the best of everything, and never prone to take offence, nor should he be addicted specially to independence. I am ungentle, and apt to be suspicious,—especially if anything be said derogatory to my art. I am proud of being an artist, but I am often ashamed of myself because I exhibit my pride. I may say the same of my spirit of independence. I am determined to be independent if I live,—but I find my independence sometimes kicking up its heels, till I hate it myself.

" From this you will perceive that I have not had a success in Lombard Street. I was quite willing to answer your uncle any questions he could ask about money. Indeed, I had no secret from him on any subject. But when he subjected me to cross-examination, forcing me into a bathos of poverty, as he thought, I broke down. ' Not five hundred a-year !' ' Not four !!' ' Not three !!!' ' Oh, heavens ! and you propose to take a wife !' You will understand how I writhed and wriggled under the scorn.

" And then there came something worse than this,—or rather, if I remember rightly, the worst thing came first. You were over in my studio, and will remember, perhaps, some of my own abortive treasures, those melancholy but soul-inspiring creations of which I have thought so much, and others have thought so little ? That no one else should value them is natural, but to me it seems unnatural, almost cruel, that any one should tell me to my face that they were valueless. Your uncle, of course, had never seen them, but he knew that sculptors are generally burdened with these ' wares,' as he called them ; and he suggested that I should sell them by auction for what they might fetch,— in order that the corners which they occupy might be vacant. He thought that, perhaps, they might do for country gentlemen to stick about among their shrubs. You, knowing my foolish soreness on the subject, will understand how well I must have been prepared by this to endure your uncle's cross-examination.

" Then he asked me as to my ideas,—not art ideas, but ideas as to bread and cheese for the future. I told him as exactly as I could. I explained to him that if you were left in possession of a comfortable home, such as would have been that of your father, I should think it best for your sake to delay our marriage till I should be prepared to do something better for you than I can at present; but that I hold myself ready to give you all that I have to give at a moment's notice, should you be required to leave his house. And, Lucy, speaking in your name, I said something further, and declared my belief that you, for my sake, would bear the inconveniences of so poor a home without complaining.

" Then there arose anger both on his side and on mine ; and I must say, insult ón his. He told me that I had no business to suggest that you would be expelled from his house. I replied that the threat had come, if not from him, then from Lady Tringle. Upon this he accused me of positive falsehood, asserting that your aunt had said nothing of the kind. I then referred him to Lady Tringle herself, but refused to stay any longer in the room with him, because he had insulted me.

" So you will see that I did less than nothing by my embassy. I told myself that it would be so as I descended into the underground cavern at the Gloucester Road Station. You are not to suppose that I blame him more, or, indeed, so much as I do myself. It was not to be expected that he should behave as a gentleman of fine feeling. But, perhaps, it ought to have been expected that I should behave as a man of common sense. I ought to have taken his advice about the auction, apparently, in good part. I ought not to have writhed when he scorned my poor earnings. When he asked as to my ideas, I should not have alluded to your aunt's threat as to turning you out. I should have been placid and humble ; and then his want of generous feeling would have mattered nothing. But spilt milk and broken eggs are past saving. Whatever good things may have come from your uncle's generosity had I brushed his hair for him aright, are now clean gone, seeing that I scrubbed him altogether the wrong way.

" For myself, I do not know that I should regret it very much. I have an idea that no money should be sweet to a man except that which he earns. And I have enough belief in myself to be confident that sooner or later I shall earn a sufficiency. But, dearest, I own that I feel disgusted with myself when I think that I have diminished your present comfort, or perhaps lessened for the future resources which would have been yours rather than mine. But the milk has been spilt, and now we must only think what we can best do without it. It seems to me that only two homes are possible for you,—one with Sir Thomas as his niece, and the other with me as my wife. I am conceited enough to think that you will prefer the latter even with many inconveniences(

Neither can your uncle or your aunt prevent you from marrying at a
very early day, should you choose to do so. There would be some
preliminary ceremony, of the nature of which I am thoroughly ignorant,
but which could, I suppose, be achieved in a month. I would advise
you to ask your aunt boldly whether she wishes you to go or to stay
with her, explaining, of course, that you intend to hold to your engagement, and explaining at the same time that you are quite ready to be
married at once if she is anxious to be quit of you. That is my
advice.

"And now, dear, one word of something softer! For did any lover
ever write to the lady of his heart so long a letter so abominably stuffed
with matters of business? How shall I best tell you how dearly I love
you? Perhaps I may do it by showing you that as far as I myself am
concerned I long to hear that your Aunt Emmeline and your Uncle
Tom are more hard-hearted and obdurate than were ever uncle and aunt
before them. I long to hear that you have been turned out into the
cold, because I know that then you must come to me, though it be even
less than three hundred a-year. I wish you could have seen your
uncle's face as those terribly mean figures reached his ears. I do not
for a moment fear that we should want. Orders come slow enough, but
they come a little quicker than they did. I have never for a moment
doubted my own ultimate success, and if you were with me I should
be more confident than ever. Nevertheless, should your aunt bid you
to stay, and should you think it right to comply with her desire, I will
not complain.

"Adieu! This comes from one who is altogether happy in his confidence that at any rate before long you will have become his wife.

                                        "ISADORE HAMEL.

"I quite expect to be scolded for my awkwardness. Indeed I shall
be disappointed if I am not."

The same post which brought Hamel's long letter to Lucy brought
also a short but very angry scrawl from Sir Thomas to his wife. No
eyes but those of Lady Tringle saw this epistle, and no other eyes shall
see it. But the few words which it contained were full of marital
wrath. Why had she threatened to turn her own niece out of his
doors? Why had she subjected him to the necessity of defending her
by a false assertion? Those Dormer nieces of hers were giving him an
amount of trouble and annoyance which he certainly had not deserved.
Lucy, though not a word was said to her of this angry letter, was conscious that something had been added to her aunt's acerbity. Indeed,
for the last day or two her aunt's acerbity towards her had been much
diminished. Lady Tringle had known that her husband intended to do

something by which the Hamel marriage would be rendered possible; and she, though she altogether disapproved of the Hamel marriage, would be obliged to accede to it if Sir Thomas acceded to it and encouraged it by his money. Let them be married, and then, as far as the Tringles were concerned, let there be an end of these Dormer troubles for ever. To that idea Lady Tringle had reconciled herself as soon as Sir Thomas had declared his purpose, but now,—as she declared to herself,—"all the fat was again in the fire." She received Lucy's salutations on that morning with a very bad grace.

But she had been desired to give no message, and therefore she was silent on the subject to Lucy. To the Honourable Mrs. Traffick she said a few words. "After all Ayala was not half as bad as Lucy," said Lady Tringle.

"There, mamma, I think you are wrong," said the Honourable Mrs. Traffick. "Of all the upsetting things I ever knew Ayala was the worst. Think of her conduct with Septimus." Lady Tringle made a little grimace, which, however, her daughter did not see. "And then with that Marchesa!"

"That was the Marchesa's fault."

"And with Tom!"

"I don't think she was so much to blame with Tom. If she were, why doesn't she take him now she can have him? He is just as foolish about her as ever. Upon my word I think Tom will make himself ill about it."

"You haven't heard it all, mamma."

"What haven't I heard?"

"Ayala has been down with the Alburys at Stalham."

"I did hear that."

"And another man has turned up. What on earth they see in her is what I can't understand."

"Another man has offered to her! Who is he?"

"There was a Colonel Stubbs down there. Septimus heard it all from young Batsby at the club. She got this man to ride about the country with her everywhere, going to the meets with him and coming home. And in this way she got him to propose to her. I don't suppose he means anything; but that is why she won't have anything to do with Tom now. Do you mean to say she didn't do all she could to catch Tom down at Glenbogie, and then at Rome? Everybody saw it. I don't think Lucy has ever been so bad as that."

"It's quite different, my dear."

"She has come from a low father," said the Honourable Mrs. Traffick proudly, "and therefore she has naturally attached herself to a low young man. There is nothing to be wondered at in that. I suppose they are fond of each other, and the sooner they are married the better."

" But he can't marry her because he has got nothing."

" Papa will do something."

" That's just what your papa won't. The man has been to your father in the City and there has been ever such a row. He spoke ill of me because I endeavoured to do my duty by the ungrateful girl. I am sure I have got a lesson as to taking up other people's children. I endeavoured to do an act of charity, and see what has come of it. I don't believe in charity."

" That is wicked mamma. Faith, Hope, and Charity ! But you've got to be charitable before you begin the others."

" I don't think it is wicked. People would do best if they were made to go along on what they've got of their own." This seemed to Augusta to be a direct blow at Septimus and herself. " Of course I know what you mean, mamma."

" I didn't mean anything."

" But, if people can't stay for a few weeks in their own parents' houses, I don't know where they are to stay."

" It isn't weeks, Augusta ; it's months. And as to parents, Lord Boardotrade is Mr. Traffick's parent. Why doesn't he go and stay with Lord Boardotrade ?" Then Augusta got up and marched with stately step out of the room. After this it was not possible that Lucy would find much immediate grace in her aunt's eyes.

From the moment that Lucy had received her letter there came upon her the great burthen of answering it. She was very anxious to do exactly as Hamel had counselled her. She was quite alive to the fact that Hamel had been imprudent in Lombard Street ; but not the less was she desirous to do as he bade her,—thinking it right that a woman should obey some one, and that her obedience could be due only to him. But in order to obey him she must consult her aunt. " Aunt Emmeline," she said that afternoon, " I want to ask you something ?"

" What is it now ?" said Aunt Emmeline, crossly.

" About Mr. Hamel."

" I don't want to hear any more about Mr. Hamel. I have heard quite enough of Mr. Hamel."

" Of course I am engaged to him, Aunt Emmeline."

" So I hear you say. I do not think it very dutiful of you to come and talk to me about him, knowing as you do what I think about him."

" What I want to ask is this. Ought I to stay here or ought I to go away ?"

" I never heard such a girl ! Where are you to go to? What makes you ask the question ?"

" Because you said that I ought to go if I did not give him up."

" You ought to give him up."

" I cannot do that, aunt."

" Then you had better hold your tongue and say nothing further about it. I don't believe he earns enough to give you bread to eat and decent clothes to wear. What would you do if children were to come year after year? If you really love him I wonder how you can think of being such a millstone round a man's neck !"

This was very hard to bear. It was so different from the delicious comfort of his letter. " I do not for a moment believe that we should want." " I have never for one moment doubted my own ultimate success." But after all was there not more of truth in her aunt's words, hard and cruel as they were? And on these words such as they were she must found her answer to her lover ; for he had bade her ask her aunt what she was to do as to staying or preparing herself for an immediate marriage. Then, before the afternoon was over, she wrote to Hamel as follows ;—

" DEAR ISADORE,

" I have got ever so much to say, but I shall begin by doing as you told me in your postscript. I won't quite scold you, but I do think you might have been a little gentler with poor Uncle Tom. I do not say this because I at all regret anything which perhaps he might have done for us. If you do not want assistance from him certainly I do not. But I do think that he meant to be kind ; and, though he may not be quite what you call a gentleman of fine feeling, yet he has taken me into his house when I had no other to go to, and in many respects has been generous to me. When he said that you were to go to him in Lombard Street, I am sure that he meant to be generous. And, though it has not ended well, yet he meant to be kind to both of us.

" There is what you will call my scolding ; though indeed, dearest, I do not intend to scold at all. Nor am I in the least disappointed except in regard to you. This morning I have been to Aunt Emmeline, as you desired, and I must say that she was very cross. Of course I know that it is because she is my own aunt that Uncle Tom has me here at all ; and I feel that I ought to be very grateful to her. But in spite of all that you say, laughing at Uncle Tom because he wants you to sell your grand work by auction, he is much more good-natured than Aunt Emmeline. I am quite sure my aunt never liked me, and that she will not be comfortable till I am gone. But when I asked her whether I ought to stay, or to go, she told me to hold my tongue, and say nothing further about it. Of course, by this, she meant that I was to remain at any rate for the present.

" My own dearest, I do think this will be best, though I need not

tell you how I look forward to leaving this, and being always with you.
For myself I am not a bit afraid, though Aunt Emmeline said dreadful
things about food and clothes, and all the rest of it.   But I believe
much more in what you say, that success will be sure to come.   But
still will it not be wise to wait a little longer?   Whatever I may have
to bear here, I shall think that I am bearing it for your dear sake;
and then I shall be happy.

"Believe me to be always and always your own

"LUCY."

This was written and sent on a Wednesday, and nothing further
was said either by Lucy herself, or by her aunt, as to the lover, till
Sir Thomas came down to Merle Park on the Saturday evening.   On
his arrival he seemed inclined to be gracious to the whole household,
even including Mr. Traffick, who received any attention of that kind
exactly as though the most amicable arrangements were always existing
between him and his father-in-law.   Aunt Emmeline, when it seemed
that she was to encounter no further anger on account of the revela-
tion which Hamel had made in Lombard Street, also recovered her
temper, and the evening was spent as though there were no causes for
serious family discord.   In this spirit, on the following morning, they
all went to church, and it was delightful to hear the flattering words
with which Mr. Traffick praised Merle Park, and everything belonging
to it, during the hour of lunch.   He went so far as to make some
delicately laudatory hints in praise of hospitality in general, and especially as to that so nobly exercised by London merchant-princes.   Sir
Thomas smiled as he heard him, and, as he smiled, he resolved that,
as soon as the Christmas festivities should be over, the Honourable
Septimus Traffick should certainly be turned out of that house.

After lunch there came a message to Lucy by a page-boy, who was
supposed to attend generally to the personal wants of Aunt Emmeline,
saying that her uncle would be glad of her attendance for a walk.
"My dear," said he, "have you got your thick boots on?   Then go
and put 'em on.   We will go down to the Lodge, and then come home
round by Windover Hill."   She did as she was bade, and then they
started.   "I want to tell you," said he, "that this Mr. Hamel of
yours came to me in Lombard Street."

"I know that, Uncle Tom."

"He has written to you, then, and told you all about it?"

"He has written to me, certainly, and I have answered him."

"No doubt.   Well, Lucy, I had intended to be kind to your Mr.
Hamel, but, as you are probably aware, I was not enabled to carry out
my intentions.   He seems to be a very independent sort of young man."

" He is independent, I think."

" I have not a word to say against it. If a man can be independent it is so much the better. If a man can do everything for himself, so as to require neither to beg nor to borrow, it will be much better for him. But, my dear, you must understand that a man cannot be independent with one hand, and accept assistance with the other, at one and the same time."

" That is not his character, I am sure," said Lucy, striving to hide her indignation while she defended her lover's character.

" I do not think it is. Therefore he must remain independent, and I can do nothing for him."

" He knows that, Uncle Tom."

" Very well. Then there's an end of it. I only want to make you understand that I was willing to assist him, but that he was unwilling to be assisted. I like him all the better for it, but there must be an end of it."

" I quite understand, Uncle Tom."

" Then there's one other thing I've got to say. He accused me of having threatened to turn you out of my house. Now, my dear——" Hereupon Lucy struggled to say a word, hardly knowing what word she ought to say, but he interrupted her,—" Just hear me out till I've done, and then there need not be another word about it. I never threatened to turn you out."

" Not you, Uncle Tom," she said, endeavouring to press his arm with her hand.

" If your aunt said a word in her anger you should not have made enough of it to write and tell him."

" I thought she meant me to go, and then I didn't know whom else to ask."

" Neither I nor she, nor anybody else, ever intended to turn you out. I have meant to be kind to you both,—to you and Ayala ; and if things have gone wrong I cannot say that it has been my fault. Now, you had better stay here, and not say a word more about it till he is ready to take you. That can't be yet for a long time. He is making, at present, not more than two hundred a year. And I am sure it must be quite as much as he can do to keep a coat on his back with such an income as that. You must make up your mind to wait, —probably for some years. As I told you before, if a man chooses to have the glory of independence he must also bear the inconvenience. Now, my dear, let there be an end of this, and never say again that I want to turn you out of my house."

CHAPTER XXXV.

TOM TRINGLE SENDS A CHALLENGE.

THE next six weeks went on tranquilly at Merle Park without a word spoken about Hamel. Sir Thomas, who was in the country as little as possible, showed his scorn to his son-in-law simply by the paucity of his words, speaking to him, when he did speak to him, with a deliberate courtesy which Mr. Traffick perfectly understood. It was that dangerous serenity which so often presages a storm. "There is something going to be up with your father," he said to Augusta. Augusta replied that she had never seen her father so civil before. "It would be a great convenience," continued the Member of Parliament, "if he could be made to hold his tongue till Parliament meets; but I'm afraid that's too good to expect." In other respects things were comfortable at Merle Park, though they were not always comfortable up in London. Tom, as the reader knows, was misbehaving himself sadly at the Mountaineers. This was the period of unlimited champagne, and of almost total absence from Lombard Street. It was seldom that Sir Thomas could get hold of his son, and when he did that broken-hearted youth would reply to his expostulations simply by asserting that if his father would induce Ayala to marry him everything should go straight in Lombard Street. Then came the final blow. Tom was of course expected at Merle Park on Christmas Eve, but did not make his appearance either then or on Christmas Day. Christmas fell on a Wednesday, and it was intended that the family should remain in the country till the following Monday. On the Thursday Sir Thomas went up to town to make inquiries respecting his heir, as to whom Lady Tringle had then become absolutely unhappy. In London he heard the disastrous truth. Tom, in his sportive mood, had caused serious inconvenience to a most respectable policeman, and was destined to remain another week in the hands of the Philistines. Then, for a time, all the other Tringle troubles were buried and forgotten in this great trouble respecting Tom. Lady Tringle was unable to leave her room during the period of incarceration. Mr. Traffick promised to have the victim liberated by the direct interference of the Secretary of State, but failed to get anything of the kind accomplished. The girls were completely cowed by the enormity of the misfortune; so that Tom's name was hardly mentioned except in sad and confidential whispers. But of all the sufferers Sir Thomas suffered the most. To him it was a positive disgrace, weighing down every moment of his life. At Travers and Treason he could not hold up his head boldly and open his mouth loudly as had always been his wont. At Travers and Treason there was not a clerk who did not know that "the governor" was an altered man since this misfortune had happened to the hope of the firm. What passed between Sir Thomas and his son on the occasion has already been told in a previous chapter. That Sir Thomas, on the whole, behaved with indulgence must be acknowledged; but he felt that his son must in truth absent himself from Lombard Street for a time.

Tom had been advised by his father to go forth and see the world. A prolonged tour had been proposed to him which to most young men might seem to have great attraction. To him it would have had attraction enough, had it not been for Ayala. There would have been hardly any limit to the allowance made to him, and he would have gone forth armed with introductions, which would have made every port a happy home to him. But as soon as the tour was suggested he resolved at once that he could not move himself to a distance from Ayala. What he expected,—what he even hoped,—he could not tell himself. But while Ayala was in London, and Ayala was unmarried, he could not be made to take himself far away.

He was thoroughly ashamed of himself. He was not at all the man who could bear a week of imprisonment and not think himself disgraced. For a day or two he shut himself up altogether in his lodgings, and never once showed himself at the Mountaineers. Faddle came to him, but he snubbed Faddle at first, remembering all the severe things his father had said about the Faddles in general. But he soon allowed that feeling to die away when the choice seemed to be between Faddle and solitude. Then he crept out in the dark and ate his dinners with Faddle at some tavern generally, paying the bill for both of them. After dinner he would play half-a-dozen games of billiards with his friend at some unknown billiard-room, and then creep home to his lodgings,—a blighted human being!

At last, about the end of the first week in January, he was induced to go down to Merle Park. There Mr. and Mrs. Traffick were still sojourning, the real grief which had afflicted Sir Thomas having caused him to postpone his intention in regard to his son-in-law. At Merle Park Tom was cosseted and spoilt by the women very injudiciously. It was not perhaps the fact that they regarded him as a hero simply because he had punched a policeman in the stomach and then been locked up in vindication of the injured laws of his country; but that incident in combination with his unhappy love did seem to make him heroic. Even Lucy regarded him with favour because of his constancy to her sister; whereas the other ladies measured their admiration for his persistency by the warmth of their anger against the silly girl who was causing so much trouble. His mother told him over and over

R

again that his cousin was not worth his regard ; but then, when he would throw himself on the sofa in an agony of despair,—weakened perhaps as much by the course of champagne as by the course of his love,—then she, too, would bid him hope, and at last promised that she herself would endeavour to persuade Ayala to look at the matter in a more favourable light. " It would all be right if it were not for that accursed Stubbs," poor Tom would say to his mother. " The man whom I called my friend ! The man I lent a horse to when he couldn't get one anywhere else ! The man to whom I confided everything, even about the necklace ! If it hadn't been for Stubbs I never should have hurt that policeman ! When I was striking him I thought that it was Stubbs !" Then the mother would heap feminine maledictions on the poor Colonel's head, and so together they would weep and think of revenge.

From the moment Tom had heard Colonel Stubbs's name mentioned as that of his rival he had meditated revenge. It was quite true when he said that he had been thinking of Stubbs when he struck the policeman. He had consumed the period of his confinement in gnashing his teeth, all in regard to our poor friend Jonathan. He told his father that he could not go upon his long tour because of Ayala. But in truth his love was now so mixed up with ideas of vengeance that he did not himself know which prevailed. If he could first have slaughtered Stubbs then perhaps he might have started ! But how was he to slaughter Stubbs ? Various ideas occurred to his mind. At first he thought that he would go down to Aldershot with the biggest cutting-whip he could find in any shop in Piccadilly ; but then it occurred to him that at Aldershot he would have all the British army against him, and that the British army might do something to him worse even than the London magistrate. Then he would wait till the Colonel could be met elsewhere. He ascertained that the Colonel was still at Stalham, where he had passed the Christmas, and he thought how it might be if he were to ttack the Colonel in the presence of his friends, the Alburys. He assured himself that, as far as personal injury went, he feared nothir.g. He had no disinclination to be hit over the head himself, if he could be sure of hitting the Colonel over the head. If it could be managed that they two should fly at each other with their fists, and be allowed to do the worst they could to each other for an hour, without interference, he would be quite satisfied. But down at Stalham that would not be allowed. All the world would be against him, and nobody there to see that he got fair play. If he could encounter the man in the streets of London it would be better ; but were he to seek the man down at Stalham he would probably find himself in the County Lunatic Asylum. What

must he do for his revenge? He was surely entitled to it. By all the
laws of chivalry, as to which he had his own ideas, he had a right to
inflict an injury upon a successful—even upon an unsuccessful—rival.
Was it not a shame that so excellent an institution as duelling should
have been stamped out? Wandering about the lawns and shrubberies
at Merle Park he thought of all this, and at last he came to a resolution.

The institution had been stamped out, as far as Great Britain was
concerned. He was aware of that. But it seemed to him that it had
not been stamped out in other more generous countries. He had
happened to notice that a certain enthusiastic politician in France had
enjoyed many duels, and had never been severely repressed by the
laws of his country. Newspaper writers were always fighting in
France, and were never guillotined. The idea of being hanged was
horrible to him,—so distasteful that he saw at a glance that a duel in
England was out of the question. But to have his head cut off, even
if it should come to that, would be a much less affair. But in Belgium, in Italy, in Germany, they never did cut off the heads of the
very numerous gentlemen who fought duels. And there were the
Southern States of the American Union, where he fancied that men
might fight duels just as they pleased. He would be ready to go even
to New Orleans at a day's notice if only he could induce Colonel
Stubbs to meet him there. And he thought that, if Colonel Stubbs
really possessed half the spirit which seemed to be attributed to him by
the British army generally, he would come, if properly invoked, and
fight such a duel as this, whether at New Orleans or at some other
well-chosen blood-allowing spot on the world's surface. Tom was
prepared to go anywhere for blood.

But the invocation must be properly made. When he had wanted
another letter of another kind to be written for him, the Colonel
himself was the man to whom he had gone for assistance. And, had
his present enemy been any other than the Colonel himself, he would
have gone to the Colonel in preference to anyone else for aid in this
matter. There was no one, in truth, in whom he believed so
thoroughly as in the Colonel. But that was out of the question.
Then he reflected what friend might now stand him in stead. He
would have gone to Houston, who wanted to marry his sister; but
Houston seemed to have disappeared, and he did not know where he
might be found. There was his brother-in-law, Traffick,—but he
feared lest Traffick might give him over once more into the hands of
the police. He thought of Hamel, as being in a way connected with
the family; but he had seen so little of Hamel, and had so much
disliked what he had seen, that he was obliged to let that hope go by.

There was no one left but Faddle whom he could trust. Faddle would do anything he was told to do. Faddle would carry the letter, no doubt, or allow himself to be named as a proposed second. But Faddle could not write the letter. He felt that he could write the letter himself better than Faddle.

He went up to town, having sent a mysterious letter to Faddle, bidding his friend attend him in his lodgings. He did not yet dare to go to the Mountaineers, where Faddle would have been found. But Faddle came, true to the appointment. " What is it, now ?" said the faithful friend. " I hope you are going back to Travers and Treasons'. That is what I should do, and walk in just as though nothing had happened."

" Not if you were me, you wouldn't."

" That does make a difference, of course."

" There is something else to be done before I can again darken the doors of Travers and Treason,—if I should ever do so !"

" Something particular ?"

" Something very particular. Faddle, I do think you are a true friend."

" You may say that. I have stuck to you always,—though you don't know the kind of things my people say to me about it. They say I am going to ruin myself because of you. The governor threatened to put me out of the business altogether. But I'm a man who will be true to my friend, whatever happens. I think you have been a little cool to me lately ; but even that don't matter."

" Cool ! If you knew the state that I'm in you wouldn't talk of a fellow being cool ! I'm so knocked about it all that I don't know what I'm doing."

" I do take that into consideration."

" Now, I'll tell you what I am going to do." Then he stood still, and looked Faddle full in the face. Faddle, sitting awe-struck on his chair, returned the gaze. He knew that a moment of supreme importance was at hand. " Faddle, I'll shoot that fellow down like a dog."

" Will you, indeed ?"

" Like a dog ;—if I can get at him. I should have no more compunction in taking his life than a mere worm. Why should I, when I know that he has sapped the very juice of my existence ?"

" Do you mean,—do you mean,—that you would—murder him ?"

" It would not be murder. Of course it might be that he would shoot me instead. Upon the whole, I think I should like that best."

" Oh; a duel !" said Faddle.

" That's what I mean. Murder him ! Certainly not. Though I should

like nothing half so well as to thrash him within an inch of his life. I
would not murder him. My plan is this,—I shall write to him a letter
inviting him to meet me in any corner of the globe that he may select.
Torrid zone or Arctic circle will be all the same to me. You will have
to accompany me as my second." Faddle shivered with excitement and
dread of coming events. Among other ideas there came the thought
that it might be difficult to get back from the Arctic circle without
money if his friend Tom should happen to be shot dead in that locality.
" But first of all," continued Tom, " you will have to carry a letter."

" To the Colonel ?" suggested Faddle.

" Of course. The man is now staying with friends of his named
Albury at a place called Stalham. From what I hear they are howling
swells. Sir Harry Albury is Master of the Hounds, and Lady Albury
when she is up in London has all the Royal Family constantly at her
parties. Stubbs is a cousin of his ; but you must go right away up to
him among 'em all, and deliver the letter into his hands without minding 'em a bit."

" Couldn't it go by post ?"

" No ; this kind of letter mustn't go by post. You have to be able
to swear that you delivered it yourself into his own hands. And then
you must wait for an answer. Even though he should want a day to
think of it, you must wait."

" Where am I to stay, Tom ?"

" Well ; it may be they'll ask you to the house, because, though
you carry the letter for me, you are not supposed to be his enemy. If
so, put a jolly face on it, and enjoy yourself as well as you can. You
must seem, you know, to be just as big a swell as any body there.
But if they don't ask you, you must go to the nearest inn. I'll pay
the bill."

" Shall I go to-day ?" asked Faddle.

" I've got to write the letter first. It'll take a little time, so that
you'd better put it off till to-morrow. If you will leave me now I'll
write it, and if you will come back at six we'll go and have a bit of dinner
at Bolivia's." This was an eating-house in the neighbourhood of Leicester Square, to which the friends had become partial during this
troubled period of their existence.

" Why not come to the Mountaineers, old boy ?" Tom shook his
head, showing that he was not yet up to such festivity as that ; and
then Faddle took his departure.

Tom at once got out his pen and paper, and began to write his letter.
It may be imagined that it was not written off-hand, or without many
struggles. When it was written it ran as follows :—

' Sir,

"You will not, I think, be surprised to hear from me in anything but a friendly spirit. I went down to you at Aldershot as to a friend whom I could trust with my bosom's dearest secret, and you have betrayed me. I told you of my love, a love which has long burned in my heart, and you received my confidence with a smile, knowing all the time that you were my rival. I leave it to you to say what reply you can make as to conduct so damning, so unmanly, so dastardly,—and so very unlike a friend as this!

"However, there is no place here for words. You have offered me the greatest insult and the greatest injury which one man can inflict upon another! There is no possibility of an apology, unless you are inclined to say that you will renounce for ever your claim upon the hand of Miss Ayala Dormer. This I do not expect, and, therefore, I call upon you to give me that satisfaction which is all that one gentleman can offer to another. After the injury you have done me I think it quite impossible that you should refuse.

"Of course, I know that duels cannot be fought in England because of the law. I am sorry that the law should have been altered, because it allows so many cowards to escape the punishment they deserve." Tom, as he wrote this, was very proud of the keenness of the allusion. "I am quite sure, however, that a man who bears the colours of a colonel in the British army will not try to get off by such a pretext." He was proud, too, about the colours. "France, Belgium, Italy, the United States, and all the world, are open! I will meet you wherever you may choose to arrange a meeting. I presume that you will prefer pistols.

"I send this by the hands of my friend, Mr. Faddle, who will be prepared to make arrangements with you, or with any friend on your behalf. He will bring back your reply, which no doubt will be satisfactory.—I am, Sir, your most obedient servant,

"Thomas Tringle, junior."

When, after making various copies, Tom at last read the letter as finally prepared, he was much pleased with it, doubting whether the Colonel himself could have written it better, had the task been confided to his hands. When Faddle came, he read it to him with much pride, and then committed it to his custody. After that they went out and ate their dinner at Bolivia's with much satisfaction, but still with a bearing of deep melancholy, as was proper on such an occasion.

CHAPTER XXXVI.

TOM TRINGLE GETS AN ANSWER.

FADDLE as he went down into the country made up his mind that the law which required such letters to be delivered by hand was an absurd law. The post would have done just as well, and would have saved a great deal of trouble. These gloomy thoughts were occasioned by a conviction that he could not carry himself easily or make himself happy among such " howling swells " as these Alburys. If they should invite him to the house the matter would be worse that way than the other. He had no confidence in his dress coat, which he was aware had been damaged by nocturnal orgies. It is all very well to tell a fellow to be as " big a swell " as anybody else, as Tom had told him. But Faddle acknowledged to himself the difficulty of acting up to such advice. Even the eyes of Colonel Stubbs turned upon him after receipt of the letter would oppress him.

Nevertheless he must do his best, and he took a gig at the station nearest to Albury. He was careful to carry his bag with him, but still he lived in hope that he would be able to return to London the same day. When he found himself within the lodges of Stalham Park he could hardly keep himself from shivering, and, when he asked the foot-man at the door whether Colonel Stubbs were there, he longed to be told that Colonel Stubbs had gone away on the previous day to some —he did not care what—distant part of the globe. But Colonel Stubbs had not gone away. Colonel Stubbs was in the house.

Our friend the Colonel had not suffered as Tom had suffered since his rejection ;—but nevertheless he had been much concerned. He had set his heart upon Ayala before he had asked her, and could not bring himself to change his heart because she had refused him. He had gone down to Aldershot and had performed his duties, abstaining for the present from repeating his offer. The offer of course must be repeated, but as to the when, the where, and the how, he had not as yet made up his mind. Then Tom Tringle had come to him at Alder-shot communicating to him the fact that he had a rival ;—and also the other fact that the other rival like himself had hitherto been unsuc-cessful. It seemed improbable to him that such a girl as Ayala should attach herself to such a man as her cousin Tom. But nevertheless he was uneasy. He regarded Tom Tringle as a miracle of wealth, and felt certain that the united efforts of the whole family would be used to arrange the match. Ayala had refused him also, and therefore, up to the present moment, the chances of the other man were no better than his own. When Tom left him at Aldershot he hardly remembered that

Tom knew nothing of his secret, whereas Tom had communicated **to** him his own. It never for a moment occurred to him that Tom would quarrel with him ; although he had seen that the poor fellow had been disgusted because he had refused to write the letter.

On Christmas Eve he had gone down to Stalham, and there he had remained discussing the matter of his love with Lady Albury. To no one else in the house had the affair been mentioned, and by Sir Harry he was supposed to remain there only for the sake of the hunting. With Sir Harry he was of all guests the most popular, and thus it came to pass that his prolonged presence at Stalham was not matter of special remark. Much of his time he did devote to hunting, but there were half-hours devoted in company with Lady Albury to Ayala's perfection and Ayala's obstinacy.

Lady Albury was almost inclined to think that Ayala should be given up. Married ladies seldom estimate even the girls they like best at their full value. It seems to such a one as Lady Albury almost a pity that such a one as Colonel Stubbs should waste his energy upon anything so insignificant as Ayala Dormer. The speciality of the attraction is of course absent to the woman, and unless she has considered the matter so far as to be able to clothe her thoughts in male vestments, as some women do, she cannot understand the longing that is felt for so small a treasure. Lady Albury thought that young ladies were very well, and that Ayala was very well among young ladies ; but Ayala in getting Colonel Stubbs for a husband would, as Lady Albury thought, have received so much more than her desert that she was now almost inclined to be angry with the Colonel. " My dear friend," he said to her one day, " you might as well take it for granted. I shall go after my princess with all the energy which a princess merits."

" The question is whether she be a princess," said Lady Albury.

" Allow me to say that that is a point on which I cannot admit a doubt. She is a princess to me, and just at present I must be regarded as the only judge in the matter."

" She shall be a goddess if you please," said Lady Albury.

" Goddess, princess, pink, or pearl ;—any name you please supposed to convey perfection shall be the same to me. It may be that she is in truth no better, or more lovely, or divine, than many another young lady who is at the present moment exercising the heart of many another gentleman. You know enough of the world to be aware that every Jack has his Gill. She is my Gill, and that's an end of it."

" I hope then that she may be your Gill."

" And, in order that she may, you must have her here again. I should absolutely not know how to go to work were I to find myself in the presence of Aunt Dosett in Kingsbury Crescent." In answer to this Lady Albury assured him that she would be quite willing to have the girl again at Stalham if it could be managed. She was reminding him, however, how difficult it had been on a previous occasion to overcome the scruples of Mrs. Dosett, when a servant brought in word to Colonel Stubbs that there was a man in the hall desirous of seeing him immediately on particular business. Then the servant presented our friend Faddle's card.

MR. SAMUEL FADDLE,

1, Badminton Gardens.

" Yes, Sir ;" said the servant. "He says he has a letter which he must put into your own particular hands."

" That looks like a bailiff," said Lady Albury, laughing. Colonel Stubbs, declaring that he had no special reason to be afraid of any bailiff, left the room and went down into the hall.

At Stalham the real hall of the house was used as a billiard-room, and here, leaning against the billiard table, the Colonel found poor Faddle. When a man is compelled by some chance circumstance to address another man whom he does not know, and whom by inspection he feels he shall never wish to know, he always hardens his face, and sometimes also his voice. So it was with the Colonel when he looked at Faddle. A word he did say, not in words absolutely uncivil, as to the nature of the business in hand. Then Faddle, showing his emotion by a quaver in his voice, suggested that as the matter was one of extreme delicacy some more private apartment might be provided. Upon this Stubbs led the way into a little room which was for the most part filled with hunting-gear, and offered the stranger one of the three chairs which it contained. Faddle sat down, finding himself so compelled, though the Colonel still remained standing, and then extracted the fatal epistle from his pocket. "Colonel Stubbs," said he, handing up the missive, "I am directed by my friend, Mr. Thomas Tringle, junior, to put this letter into your own hand. When you have read it I shall be ready to consult with you as to its contents." These few words he had learnt by heart on his journey down, having practised them continually.

The Colonel took the letter, and turning to the window read it with his back to the visitor. He read it twice from beginning to end in order that he might have time to resolve whether he would laugh aloud at both Faddle and Tringle, or whether it might not be better to endeavour to soften the anger of poor Tom by a message which should be at any rate kindly worded. "This is from my friend, Tom Tringle," he said.

" From Mr. Thomas Tringle, junior," said Faddle, proudly,

"So I perceive. I am sorry to think that he should be in so much trouble. He is one of the best fellows I know, and I am really grieved that he should be unhappy. This, you know, is all nonsense."

"It is not nonsense at all, Colonel Stubbs."

"You must allow me to be the judge of that, Mr. Faddle. It is at any rate nonsense to me. He wants me to go somewhere and fight a duel,—which I should not do with any man under any circumstances. Here there is no possible ground for any quarrel whatsoever,—as I will endeavour to explain, myself, to my friend, Mr. Tringle. I shall be sure to write to him at once,—and so I will bid you good afternoon."

But this did not at all suit poor Faddle after so long a journey. "I thought it probable that you would write, Colonel Stubbs, and therefore I am prepared to wait. If I cannot be accommodated here I will wait,—will wait elsewhere."

"That will not be at all necessary. We have a post to London twice a day."

"You must be aware, Colonel Stubbs, that letters of this sort should not be sent by post."

"The kind of letter I shall write may be sent by post very well. It will not be bellicose, and therefore there can be no objection."

"I really think, Colonel Stubbs, that you are making very little of a very serious matter."

"Mr. Faddle, I really must manage my own affairs after my own way. Would you like a glass of sherry? If not, I need hardly ask you to stay here any longer." Upon that he went out into the billiard-room and rang the bell. Poor Faddle would have liked the glass of sherry, but he felt that it would be incompatible with the angry dignity which he assumed, and he left the house without another word or even a gesture of courtesy. Then he returned to London, having taken his bag and dress-coat all the way to Stalham for nothing.

Tom's letter was almost too good to be lost, but there was no one to whom the joke could be made known except Lady Albury. She, he was sure, would keep poor Tom's secret as well as his own, and to her he showed the letter. "I pity him from the bottom of my heart," he said. Lady Albury declared that the writer of such a letter was too absurd for pity. "Not at all. Unless he really loved her he wouldn't have been so enraged. I suppose he does think that I injured him. He did tell me his story, and I didn't tell him mine. I can understand it all, though I didn't imagine he was such a fool as to invite me to travel all round the world because of the harsh laws of Great Britain. Nevertheless, I shall write to him quite an affectionate letter, remembering that, should I succeed myself, he will be my first cousin by marriage."

Before he went to bed that night he wrote his letter, and the reader may as well see the whole correspondence ;—

"MY DEAR TRINGLE,

"If you will think of it all round you will see that you have got no cause of quarrel with me any more than I have with you. If it be the case that we are both attached to your cousin, we must abide her decision whether it be in favour of either of us, or, as may be too probably the case, equally averse to both of us. If I understand your letter rightly, you think that I behaved unfairly when I did not tell you of my own affairs upon hearing yours from your own lips. Why should I? Why should I have been held to be constrained to tell my secret because you, for your own sake, had told me yours? Had I been engaged to your cousin,—which I regret to say is very far from the case,—I should have told you, naturally. I should have regarded the matter as settled, and should have acquainted you with a fact which would have concerned you. But, as such was not a fact, I was by no means bound to tell you how my affairs stood. This ought to be clear to you, and I hope will be when you have read what I say.

"I may as well go on to declare that under no circumstances should I fight a duel with you. If I thought I had done wrong in the matter I would beg your pardon. I can't do that as it is,—though I am most anxious to appease you,—because I have done you no wrong.

"Pray forget your animosity,—which is in truth unfounded,—and let us be friends as we were before.

"Yours very sincerely,   JONATHAN STUBBS."

Faddle reached London the evening before the Colonel's letter, and again dined with his friend at Bolivia's. At first they were both extremely angry, acerbating each other's wrath. Now that he was safe back in London Faddle thought that he would have enjoyed an evening among the "swells" of Stalham, and felt himself to be injured by the inhospitable treatment he had received—"after going all the way down there, hardly to be asked to sit down!"

"Not asked to sit down!"

"Well, yes, I was ;—on a miserable cane-bottomed chair in a sort of cupboard. And he didn't sit down. You may call them swells, but I think your Colonel Stubbs is a very vulgar sort of fellow. When I told him the post isn't the proper thing for such a letter, he only laughed. I suppose he doesn't know what is the kind of thing among gentlemen."

"I should think he does know," said Tom.

"Then why doesn't he act accordingly? Would you believe it; he never so much as asked me whether I had a mouth on. It was just luncheon time, too."

" I suppose they lunch late."

" They might have asked me. I shouldn't have taken it. He did say something about a glass of sherry, but it was in that sort of tone which tells a fellow that he is expected not to take it. And then he pretended to laugh. I could see that he was shaking in his shoes at the idea of having to fight. He go to the torrid zone ! He would much rather go to a police office if he thought that there was any fighting on hand. I should dust his jacket with a stick if I were you."

Later on in the evening Tom declared that this was what he would do, but, before he came to that, a third bottle of Signor Bolivia's champagne had been made to appear. The evening passed between them not without much enjoyment. On the opening of that third cork the wine was declared to be less excellent than what had gone before, and Signor Bolivia was evoked in person. A gentleman named Walker, who looked after the establishment, made his appearance, and with many smiles, having been induced to swallow a bumper of the compound himself, declared, with a knowing shake of the head and an astute twinkle of the eye, that the wine was not equal to the last. He took a great deal of trouble, he assured them, to import an article which could not be surpassed, if it could be equalled, in London, always visiting Epernay himself once a-year for the purpose of going through the wine-vaults. Let him do what he would an inferior bottle,—or, rather, a bottle somewhat inferior,—would sometimes make its way into his cellar. Would Mr. Tringle let him have the honour of drawing another cork, so that the exact amount of difference might be ascertained ? Tom gave his sanction ; the fourth cork was drawn ; and Mr. Walker, sitting down and consuming the wine with his customers, was enabled to point out to a hair's breadth the nature and the extent of the variation. Tringle still thought that the difference was considerable. Faddle was, on the whole, inclined to agree with Signor Bolivia. It need hardly be said that the four bottles were paid for,—or rather scored against Tringle, who at the present time had a little account at the establishment.

" Show a fellar fellar's letters morrer." Such or something like it was Faddle's last request to his friend as they bade each other farewell for the night in Pall Mall. But Faddle was never destined to see the Colonel's epistle. On his attempting to let himself in at Badminton Gardens, he was kidnapped by his father in his night-shirt and dressing-gown ; and was sent out of London on the following morning by long sea down to Aberdeen, whither he was intrusted to the charge of a stern uncle. Our friend Tom saw nothing more of his faithful friend till years had rolled over both their heads.

By the morning post, while Tom was still lying sick with headache, —for even with Signor Bolivia's wine the pulling of many corks is apt to be dangerous,—there came the letter from the Colonel. Bad as Tom was, he felt himself constrained to read it at once, and learned that neither the torrid zone or arctic circle would require his immediate attendance. He was very sick, and perhaps, therefore, less high in courage than on the few previous days. Partly, perhaps, from that cause, but partly, also, from the Colonel's logic, he did find that his wrath was somewhat abated. Not but what it was still present to his mind that if two men loved the same girl as ardently, as desperately, as eternally as he loved Ayala, the best thing for them would be to be put together like the Kilkenny cats, till whatever remnant should be left of one might have its chance with the young lady. He still thought that it would be well that they should fight to the death, but a glimmering of light fell upon his mind as to the Colonel's abnegation of all treason in the matter. " I suppose it wasn't to be expected that he should tell," he said to himself. " Perhaps I shouldn't have told in the same place. But as to forgetting animosity that is out of the question ! How is a man to forget his animosity when two men want to marry the same girl ?"

About three o'clock on that day he dressed himself, and sat waiting for Faddle to come to him. He knew how anxious his friend would be to see the Colonel's letter. But Faddle by this time had passed the Nore, and had added sea-sickness to his other maladies. Faddle came to him no more, and the tedious hours of the afternoon wore themselves away in his lodgings till he found his solitude to be almost more unbearable than his previous misfortunes. At last came the time when he must go out for his dinner. He did not dare to attempt the Mountaineers. And as for Bolivia, Bolivia with his corks, and his eating-house, and his vintages, was abominable to him. About eight o'clock he slunk into a quiet little house on the north side of Oxford Street, and there had two mutton chops, some buttered toast, and some tea. As he drank his tea he told himself that on the morrow he would go back to his mother at Merle Park, and get from her such consolation as might be possible.

CHAPTER XXXVII.

GERTRUDE IS UNSUCCESSFUL.

It was now the middle of January, and Gertrude Tringle had received no reply from her lover to the overture which she had made

him. Nor, indeed, had she received any letter from him since that
to which this overture had been a reply. It was now two months
since her proposition had been made, and during that time her anger
had waxed very hot against Mr. Houston. After all, it might be a
question whether Mr. Houston was worth all the trouble which she,
with her hundred thousand pounds, was taking on his behalf. She
did not like the idea of abandoning him, because, by doing so, she
would seem to yield to her father. Having had a young man of her
own, it behoved her to stick to her young man in spite of her parents.
But what is a girl to do with a lover who, at the end of two months,
has made no reply to an offer from herself that he should run away
with her, and take her to Ostend? She was in this frame of mind
when, lo and behold, she found her own letter, still inclosed in her
own envelope,—but opened, thrust in amongst some of her father's
papers. It was evident enough that the letter had never passed from
out of the house. There had been treachery on the part of some
servant ;—or perhaps her father might have condescended to search
the little box ;—or, more probable still, Augusta had betrayed her !
Then she reflected that she had communicated her purpose to her
sister, that her sister had abstained from any questions since the letter
had been written, and that her sister, therefore, no doubt, was the
culprit. There, however, was the letter, which had never reached her
lover's hands, and, as a matter of course, her affections returned with
all their full ardour to the unfortunate ill-used man. That her conduct was now watched would, she thought, be a matter of course.
Her father knew her purpose, and, like stern parents in general,
would use all his energies to thwart it. Sir Thomas had, in truth,
thought but little about the matter since he had first thrust the letter
away. Tom's troubles, and the disgrace brought by them upon
Travers and Treason generally, had so occupied his mind that he
cared but little for Gertrude and her lover. But Gertrude had no
doubt that she was closely watched, and in these circumstances
was driven to think how she could best use her wits so as to counter-
mine her father. To run away from Queen' Gate would, she thought,
be more difficult, and more uncomfortable, than to perform the same
operation at Merle Park. It was intended that the family should
remain in the country, at any rate, till Easter, and Gertrude resolved
that there might yet be time for another effort before Easter should be
past, if only she could avoid those hundred Argus eyes, which were,
no doubt, fixed upon her from all sides.

She prepared another letter to her lover, which she addressed to
him at his club in London. In this she told him nothing of her former
project, except that a letter written by her in November had fallen

into the hands of enemies. Then she gave him to understand that there was need of the utmost caution ; but that, if adequate caution were used, she did not doubt they might succeed. She said nothing about her great project, but suggested to him that he should run down into Sussex, and meet her at a certain spot indicated, outside the Park-palings, half-an-hour after dusk. It might be, she said, impossible that the meeting should be effected, but she thought that she could so manage as to leave the house unwatched at the appointed hour. With the object of being especially safe she began and concluded her letter without any names, and then managed to deposit it herself in the box of the village post-office.

Houston, when he received this letter, at once made up his mind that he would not be found on the outer side of the Park-palings on the evening named. He told himself that he was too old for the romance of love-making, and that should he be received, when hanging about in the dark, by some custodian with a cudgel he would have nothing to thank but his own folly. He wrote back therefore to say that he regarded the outside of the Park palings as indiscreet, but that he would walk up through the lodge-gate to the house at three o'clock in the afternoon of the day named, and he would take it as an additional mark of her favour if she would meet him on the road. Gertrude had sent him a mysterious address ; he was to direct the letter to " O. P. Q., Post Office, Hastings," and she was prepared to hire a country boy to act as Love's messenger on the occasion. But of this instruction Frank took no notice, addressing the letter to Merle Park in the usual way.

Gertrude received her letter without notice from any one. On that occasion Argus, with all his eyes, was by chance asleep. She was very angry with her lover,—almost determined to reject him altogether, almost disposed to yield to her angry parents and look out for some other lover who might be accepted in better part ; but still, when the day came she put on her hat and walked down the road towards the lodge.

As Fortune had it,—Fortune altogether unfavourable to those perils for which her soul was longing,—no one watched her, no one dogged her steps, no one took any notice of her, till she met Frank Houston when he had passed about a hundred yards on through the gates. " And so you have come," she said.

" Oh, yes ; I have come. I was sure to come when I said so. No man is more punctual than I am in these matters. I should have come before,—only I did not get your letter."

" Oh, Frank !"

" Well, my darling. You are looking uncommonly well, and I am so glad to see you. How are they all ?"

" Frank !"

" What is it ?"

" Oh, Frank, what are we to do?"

" The governor will give way at last, I should say."

" Never ;—that is while we are as we are now. If we were married——"

" Ah,—I wish we were ! Wouldn't it be nice ?"

" Do you really think so ?"

" Of course I do. I'm ready to-morrow for the matter of that."

" But could you do something great ?"

" Something great ! As to earning my bread, you mean ? I do not think I could do that. I didn't turn my hand to it early enough."

" I wasn't thinking of—your bread."

" You said,—could I do something great ?"

" Frank, I wrote you a letter and described it all. How I got the courage to do it I do not know. I feel as though I could not bring myself to say it now. I wonder whether you would have the courage."

" I should say so. I don't know quite what sort of thing it is ; but I generally have pluck enough for anything in a common way."

" This is something in an uncommon way."

" I couldn't break open Travers and Treason, and get at the safe, or anything in that way."

" It is another sort of safe of which you must break the lock, Frank; another treasure you must steal. Do you not understand me ?"

" Not in the least."

" There is Tom," said Gertrude. " He is always wandering about the place now like a ghost. Let us go back to the gate." Then Frank turned. " You heard, I suppose, of that dreadful affair about the policeman."

" There was a row, I was told."

" Did you feel that the family were disgraced ?"

" Not in the least. He had to pay five shillings,—hadn't he,—for telling a policeman to go about his business ?"

" He was—locked up," said Gertrude, solemnly.

" It's just the same. Nobody thinks anything about that kind of thing. Now, what is it I have got to do ? We had better turn back again as soon as we can, because I must go up to the house before I go."

" You will ?"

" Certainly. I will not leave it to your father to say that I came skulking about the place, and was ashamed to show my face. That would not be the way to make him give you your money."

" I'm sure he'd give it,—if we were once married."

" If we were married without having it assured before hand we should look very blue if things went wrong afterwards."

" I asked you whether you had courage."

" Courage enough, I think, when my body is concerned ; but I am an awful coward in regard to money. I wouldn't mind hashed mutton and baked potatoes for myself, but I shouldn't like to see you eating them, dearest, after all the luxuries to which you have been accustomed."

" I should think nothing of it."

" Did you ever try ? I never came absolutely to hashed mutton, but I've known how very uncomfortable it is not to be able to pay for the hot joints. I'm willing to own honestly that married life without an income would not have attractions for me."

" But if it was sure to come ?"

" Ah, then indeed,—with you ! I have just said how nice it would be."

" Have you ever been at Ostend ?" she asked, suddenly.

" Ostend. Oh, yes. There was a man there who used to cheat horribly at écarté. He did me out of nearly a hundred pounds one night."

" But there's a clergyman there, I'm told."

" I don't think this man was in orders. But he might have been. Parsons come out in so many shapes ! This man called himself a count. It was seven years ago."

" I am speaking of to day."

" I've not been there since."

" Would you like to go there,—with me ?"

" It isn't a nice sort of place, I should say, for a honeymoon. But you shall choose. When we are married you shall go where you like."

" To be married !" she exclaimed.

" Married at Ostend ! Would your mother like that ?"

" Mother ! Oh, dear !"

" I'll be shot if I know what you're after Gertrude. If you've got anything to say you'd better speak out. I want to go up to the house now."

They had now taken one or two turns between the lodge and a point in the road from which the house could be observed, and at which Tom could still be seen wandering about, thinking no doubt of Ayala. Here Frank stopped as though determined not to turn to the lodge again. It was wonderful to Gertrude that he should not have understood what she had already said. When he talked of her mother going with them to the Ostend marriage she was almost beside herself. This lover of

s

hers was a man of the world and must have heard of elopements. But now had come a time in which she must be plain, unless she made up her mind to abandon her plan altogether. " Frank," she said, " if you were to run away with me, then we could be married at Ostend."

" Run away with you !"

" It wouldn't be the first time that such a thing has been done."

" The commonest thing in the world, my dear, when a girl has got her money in her own hands. Nothing I should like so much."

" Money ! It's always money. It's nothing but the money, I believe."

" That's unkind, Gertrude."

" Ain't you unkind ? You won't do anything I ask."

" My darling, that hashed mutton and those baked potatoes are too clear before my eyes."

" You think of nothing, I believe, but your dinner."

" I think, unfortunately, of a great many other things. Hashed mutton is simply symbolical. Under the head of hashed mutton I include poor lodgings, growlers when we get ourselves asked to eat a dinner at somebody's table, limited washing-bills, table-napkins rolled up in their dirt every day for a week, antimacassars to save the backs of the chairs, a picture of you darning my socks while I am reading a newspaper hired at a halfpenny from the public-house round the corner, a pint of beer in the pewter between us,—and perhaps two babies in one cradle because we can't afford to buy a second."

" Don't, Sir."

" In such an emergency I am bound to give you the advantage both of my experience and imagination."

" Experience !"

" Not about the cradles ! That is imagination. My darling, it won't do. You and I have not been brought up to make ourselves happy on a very limited income."

" Papa would be sure to give us the money," she said, eagerly.

" In such a matter as this, where your happiness is concerned, my dear, I will trust no one."

" My happiness !"

" Yes, my dear, your happiness ! I am quite willing to own the truth. I am not fitted to make you happy, if I were put upon the hashed mutton régime as I have described to you. I will not run the risk,—for your sake."

" For your own you mean," she said.

" Nor for my own, if you wish me to add that also."

Then they walked up towards the house for some little way in silence. " What is it you intend then ?" she asked.

" I will ask your father once again."

" He will simply turn you out of the house," she said. Upon this he shrugged his shoulders, and they walked on to the hall-door in silence.

Sir Thomas was not at Merle Park, nor was he expected home that evening. Frank Houston could only therefore ask for Lady Tringle, and her he saw together with Mr. and Mrs. Traffick. In presence of them all nothing could be said of love affairs ; and, after sitting for half-an-hour, during which he was not entertained with much cordiality, he took his leave, saying that he would do himself the honour of calling on Sir Thomas in the City. While he was in the drawing-room Gertrude did not appear. She had retired to her room, and was there resolving that Frank Houston was not such a lover as would justify a girl in breaking her heart for him.

And Frank as he went to town brought his mind to the same way of thinking. The girl wanted something romantic to be done, and he was not disposed to do anything romantic for her. He was not in the least angry with her, acknowledging to himself that she had quite as much a right to her way of looking at things as he had to his. But he felt almost sure that the Tringle alliance must be regarded as impossible. If so, should he look out for another heiress, or endeavour to enjoy life, stretching out his little income as far as might be possible ;—or should he assume altogether a new character, make a hero of himself, and ask Imogene Docimer to share with him a little cottage, in whatever might be the cheapest spot to be found in the civilised parts of Europe ? If it was to be hashed mutton and a united cradle, he would prefer Imogene Docimer to Gertrude Tringle for his companion.

But there was still open to him the one further chance with Sir Thomas ; and this chance he could try with the comfortable feeling that he might be almost indifferent as to what Sir Thomas might say To be prepared for either lot is very self-assuring when any matter of difficulty has to be taken in hand. On arriving at the house in Lombard Street he soon found himself ushered once more into Sir Thomas' presence. " Well, Mr. Houston, what can I do for you to-day ?" asked the man of business, with a pleasant smile.

" It is the old story, Sir Thomas."

" Don't you think, Mr. Houston, that there is something,—a little,— unmanly shall I call it, in coming so often about the same thing ?"

" No, Sir Thomas, I do not. I think my conduct has been manly throughout."

" Weak, perhaps, would have been a better word. I do not wish to be uncourteous, and I will therefore withdraw unmanly. Is it not weak to encounter so many refusals on the same subject ?"

"I should feel myself to have been very strong if after so many refusals I were to be successful at last."

"There is not the least chance of it."

"Why should there be no chance if your daughter's happiness depends upon it?"

"There is no chance, because I do not believe that my daughter's happiness does depend upon it. She is foolish, and has made a foolish proposition to you."

"What proposition?" asked Houston, in surprise, having heard nothing of that intercepted letter.

"That journey to Ostend, with the prospect of finding a good-natured clergyman in the town! I hardly think you would be fool enough for that."

"No, Sir Thomas, I should not do that. I should think it wrong." This he said quite gravely, asking no questions; but was very much at a loss to know where Sir Thomas had got his information.

"I am sure you would think it foolish; and it would be foolish. I pledge you my word, that were you to do such a thing I should not give you a shilling. I should not let my girl starve; but I should save her from suffering in such a manner as to let you have no share of the sustenance I provided for her."

"There is no question of that kind," said Frank, angrily.

"I hope not;—only as I know that the suggestion has been made I have thought it well to tell you what would be my conduct if it were carried out."

"It will not be carried out by me," said Frank.

"Very well; I am glad to hear it. To tell the truth, I never thought that you would run the risk. A gentleman of your sort, when he is looking for a wife with money, likes to have the money quite certain."

"No doubt," said Frank, determined not to be brow-beaten.

"And now, Mr. Houston, let me say one word more to you and then we may part, as I hope, good friends. I do not mean my daughter Gertrude to marry any man such as you are;—by that I mean an idle gentleman without means. Should she do so in my teeth she would have to bear the punishment of sharing that poor gentleman's idleness and poverty. While I lived she would not be allowed absolutely to want, and when I died there would be some trifle for her, sufficient to keep the wolf from the door. But I give you my solemn word and honour that she shall never be the means of supplying wealth and luxury to such a husband as you would be. I have better purposes for my hard-earned money. Now, good-day." With that he rose from his chair and put out his hand. Frank rose also from his chair, took the hand that was offered him, and stepped out of Travers and Treason into Lombard Street, with no special desire to shake the dust off his feet as he did so. He felt that Sir Thomas had been reasonable,—and he felt also that Gertrude Tringle would perhaps have been dear at the money.

Two or three days afterwards he despatched the following little note to poor Gertrude at Merle Park ;—

"DEAR GERTRUDE,

"I have seen your father again, and found him to be absolutely obdurate. I am sure he is quite in earnest when he tells me that he will not give his daughter to an impoverished idle fellow such as I am. Who shall say that he is wrong ? I did not dare to tell him so, anxious as I was that he should change his purpose.

"I feel myself bound in honour, believing, as I do, that he is quite resolved in his purpose, to release you from your promise. I should feel that I was only doing you an injury were I to ask you to be bound by an engagement which could not, at any rate for many years, be brought to a happy termination.

"As we may part as sincere friends I hope you will consent to keep the little token of my regard which I gave you.

"FRANK HOUSTON."

CHAPTER XXXVIII.

FRANK HOUSTON IS PENITENT.

"AND now the Adriatic's free to wed another," said Houston to himself, as he put himself into a cab, and had himself carried to his club. There he wrote that valedictory letter to Gertrude which is given at the end of the last chapter. Had he reason to complain of his fate, or to rejoice ? He had looked the question of an establishment full in the face,—an establishment to be created by Sir Thomas Tringle's money, to be shared with Sir Thomas Tringle's daughter, and had made up his mind to accept it, although the prospects were not, as he told himself, 'altogether rosy.' When he first made up his mind to marry Gertrude,—on condition that Gertrude should bring with her, at any rate, not less than three thousand a-year, —he was quite aware that he would have to give up all his old ways of life, and all his little pleasures. He would become son-in-law to Sir Thomas Tringle, with a comfortable house to live in ; with plenty to eat and drink, and, probably, a horse or two to ride. If he could manage things at their best, perhaps he might be able to settle himself at Pau, or some other place of the kind, so as to be as far away as possible from Tringle influences. But his little dinners at one club, his little rubbers of whist at the other club, his evenings at the opera, the pleasant smiles of the ladies, whom he loved in a general way,— these would be done with for ever! Earn his own bread! Why, he was going to earn his bread, and that in a most disagreeable manner. He would set up an establishment, not because such an establishment would have any charms for him, but because he was compelled by lack of money to make some change in his present manner of life. And yet the time had been when he had looked forward to a marriage as the happiest thing that could befall him. As far as his nature could love, he had loved Imogene Docimer. There had come a glimpse upon him of something better than the little dinners and the little rubbers. There had been a prospect of an income,—not ample, as would have been that forthcoming from Sir Thomas,—but sufficient for a sweet and modest home, in which he thought that it would have sufficed for his happiness to paint a few pictures, and read a few books, and to love his wife and children. Even as to that there had been a doubt. There was a regret as to the charms of London life. But, nevertheless, he had made up his mind,—and she, without any doubt, had made up hers. Then that wicked uncle had died, and was found to have expended on his own pursuits the money which was to have been left to his nephew. Upon that there was an explanation between Frank and Imogene; and it was agreed that their engagement should be over, while a doubtful and dangerous friendship was to be encouraged between them.

Such was the condition of things when Frank first met Gertrude Tringle at Rome, now considerably more than twelve months since. When Gertrude had first received his proposition favourably he had written to Imogene a letter in that drolling spirit common to him, in which he declared his purpose;—or rather, not his purpose, but his untoward fate, should the gods be unkind to him. She had answered him after the same fashion, saying, that in regard to his future welcome she hoped that the gods would prove unkind. But had he known how to read all that her letter expressed between the lines, he would have perceived that her heart was more strongly moved than his own. Since that time he had learned the lesson. There had been a letter or two; and then there had been that walk in the wood on the Italian side of the Tyrolese Alps. The reader may remember how he was hurried away in the diligence for Innspruck, because it was considered that his further sojourn in the same house with Imogene was dangerous. He had gone, and even as he went had attempted to make a joke of the whole affair. But it had not been quite a joke to him even then. There was Imogene's love and Imogene's anger,—and together with these an aversion towards the poor girl whom he intended to marry,—

which became the stronger the more strongly he was convinced both of Imogene's love and of her anger.

Nevertheless, he persevered,—not with the best success. as has already been told. Now, as he left the house in Lombard Street, and wrote what was intended to be his last epistle to Gertrude, he was driven again to think of Miss Docimer. Indeed, he had in his pocket, as he sat at his club, a little note which he had lately received from that lady, which, in truth, had disturbed him much when he made his last futile efforts at Merle Park and in Lombard Street. The little note was as follows ;—

" DEAR FRANK,

" One little friendly word in spite of our storm on the Tyrolese hillside ! If Miss Tringle is to be the arbiter of your fate ;—why, then, let there be an end of everything between us. I should not care to be called upon to receive such a Mrs. Frank Houston as a dear friend. But if Tringle père should at the last moment prove hard-hearted, then let me see you again.—Yours,   " I."

With this letter in his pocket he had gone down to Merle Park, determined to put an end to the Tringle affair in one way or the other. His duty, as he had planned it to himself, would not be altered by Imogene's letter ; but if that duty should become impracticable,—why then it would be open to him to consider whatever Imogene might have to say to him.

The Docimers were now in London, where it was their custom to live during six months of the year ; but Houston had not been at their house since he had parted from them in the Tyrol. He had spent but little of his time in London since the autumn, and, when there, had not been anxious to see people who had, at any rate, treated him somewhat roughly. But now it would be necessary that he should answer Imogene's letter. What should be the nature of such answer he certainly had not as yet decided ; nor could he have decided before those very convincing assurances of Sir Thomas Tringle. That matter was at any rate over, and now the " Adriatic might wed another,"—if the Adriatic thought well to do so. The matter, however, was one which required a good deal of consideration. He gave to it ten minutes of intense thought, during which he consumed a cup of coffee and a cigarette ; and then, throwing away the burnt end of the paper, he hurried into the morning-room, and wrote to the lady as follows ;—

" DEAR IMOGENE,

" You will not have to press to your bosom as my wife the second daughter of Sir Thomas Tringle, Bart.   The high honour of that alliance has at last been refused by him in very plain language.   Had she become Mrs. Frank Houston, I do not doubt but you would have done your duty to your own cousin.   That lot, however, has not been written for me in the Book of Fates.   The father is persistent in looking upon me as an idle profligate adventurer ; and though he has been kind enough to hint more than once that it might be possible for me to achieve the young lady, he has succeeded in convincing me that I never should achieve anything beyond the barren possession of her beauty.   A wife and family on my present very moderate income would be burdensome ; and, therefore, with infinite regrets, I have bade adieu to Miss Tringle.

"I have not hitherto been to see either you or your brother or Mrs. Docimer because I have been altogether unaware whether you or your brother or Mrs. Docimer would be glad to see me.   As you say yourself, there was a storm on the Tyrolese hill-side,—in which there was more than one wind blowing at the same time.   I do not find fault with anybody,—perhaps a storm was needed to clear the air.   But I hate storms.   I do not pretend to be a very grand fellow, but I do endeavour not to be disagreeable.   Your brother, if you remember, was a little hard.   But, in truth, I say this only to account for my apparent incivility.

"And, perhaps, with another object ;—to gain a little time before I plunge into the stern necessity of answering all that you say in your very comprehensive letter of five lines.   The first four lines I have answered.   There will be no such Mrs. Frank Houston as that suggested.   And then, as to the last line.   Of course, you will see me again, and that very speedily.   So it would seem that the whole letter is answered.

"But yet it is not answered.   There is so much in it that whole sheets would not answer it.   A quire of note-paper stuffed full would hardly contain all that I might find to say in answer to it,—on one side and the other.   Nay, I might fill as many reams of folio as are required for a three-volume novel.   And then I might call it by one of two names, 'The Doubts of Frank Houston,' or 'The Constancy of Imogene Docimer,'—as I should at last bring my story to one ending or the other.   But the novel would contain that fault which is so prevalent in the novels of the present day.   The hero would be a very namby-mamby sort of a fellow, whereas the heroine would be too perfect for human nature.

"The hero would be always repeating to himself a certain line out of a Latin poet, which, of all lines, is the most heart-breaking ;—

> The better course I see and know ;—
> The worser one is where I go.

But then in novels the most indifferent hero comes out right at last. Some god comes out of a theatrical cloud and leaves the poor devil ten thousand a-year and a title. He isn't much of a hero when he does go right under such inducements, but he suffices for the plot, and everything is rose-coloured. I would be virtuous at a much cheaper rate ;—if only a young man with his family might have enough to eat and drink. What is your idea of the lowest income at which a prudent, —say not idiotically-quixotic hero,—might safely venture to be heroic?

"Now I have written to you a long letter, and think that I have indicated to you the true state of my feelings. Whatever may turn up I do not think I shall go fortune-hunting again. If half-a-million in female hands were to throw itself at my head, there is no saying whether I might not yield. But I do not think that I shall again make inquiry as to the amount of booty supposed to be within the walls of a city, and then sit down to besiege the city with regular lines of approach. It is a disgusting piece of work. I do not say but what I can lie, and did lie foully on the last siege operation ; but I do not like it. And then to be told that one is unmanly by the father, and a coward by the young lady, as occurred to me in this affair, is disheartening. They were both right, though I repudiated their assertions. This might be borne as a prelude to success ; but, as part of a failure, it is disgusting. At the present moment I am considering what economy might effect as to a future bachelor life, and am meditating to begin with a couple of mutton chops and half-a-pint of sherry for my dinner to-day. I know I shall break down and have a woodcock and some champagne.

"I will come to you about three on Sunday. If you can manage that your brother should go out and make his calls, and your sister attend divine service in the afternoon, it would be a comfort.

"Your always,   F. HOUSTON."

It was a long rambling letter, without a word in it of solid clearly-expressed meaning ; but Imogene, as she read it, understood very well its real purport. She understood more than its purport, for she could see by it,—more clearly than the writer did himself,—how far her influence over the man had been restored, and how far she might be able to restore it. But was it well that she should regain her influence? Her influence regained would simply mean a renewed engagement. No doubt the storm on the hill-side had come from the violence of true love on her part ! No doubt her heart had been outraged by the idea that he should give himself up to another woman after all that passed between them. She had been devoted to him altogether; but yet she had been taught by him to regard her love as a passion which of its nature contained something of the ridiculous. He had never ceased gently to laugh at himself, even in her presence, because he had subjected himself to her attraction. She had caught up the same spirit,—or at any rate the expression of spirit, and, deceived by that, he had thought that to relieve herself from the burden of her love would be as easy to her as to him. In making this mistake he had been ignorant of the intrinsic difference in the nature of a man's and of a woman's heart, and had been unaware that that, which to a man at his best can only be a part of his interest in his life's concerns, will to a woman be everything. She had attempted to follow his lead when it did not seem that by doing so she would lose anything. But when the moment of trial came she had not in truth followed his lead at all. She made the attempt, and in making the attempt gave him her permission to go from her; but when she realised the fact that he was gone,—or going,—then she broke down utterly. Then there came these contentions between her and her brother, and that storm on the hill-side.

After that she passed some months of wretchedness. There was no possibility for her to droll away her love. She had taught herself to love the man whether he were good or whether he were bad,—whether he were strong-hearted or whether he were fickle,—and the thing was there present to her, either as a permanent blessing, or, much more probably, a permanent curse. As the months went on she learned, though she never saw Frank himself, that his purpose of marrying Gertrude Tringle was not likely to be carried out. Then at last she wrote that comprehensive letter of five lines,—as Houston had called it. It had been intended to be comprehensive, and did, in fact, contain much more than it seemed to say. " If you can bring yourself to return to me, and to endure whatever inconveniences may be incidental to your doing so, I hereby declare that I will do the same; and I declare also that I can find for myself no other content in the world except what may come to me from such an agreement between us." It was this that she said in that last line, in which she had begged him to come to her, if at the last moment " Tringle père " should prove to be hard-hearted. All troubles of poverty, all the lingering annoyance of waiting, all her possible doubts as to his future want of persistency, would be preferable to the great loss which she found herself unable to endure.

Yes; it would be very well that both her brother and her sister-in-law should be absent when he came to her. To neither of them had she said a word of her last correspondence;—to neither of them a word of her renewed hopes. For the objections which might be raised by either of them would she care little if she could succeed with Frank. But while that success was still doubtful it would be well to get at any rate the assistance of her sister-in-law. On the Sunday afternoon Mr. Docimer would certainly be away from the house. It was his custom to go off among his friends almost immediately after lunch, and his absence might be counted on as assured. But with his wife it was different. That project of sending her to church was quite out of the question. Mrs. Docimer generally went to church of a Sunday morning, and then always considered herself to have performed the duties of the day. Nor did Imogene like the idea of this appointment with her lover without a word spoken about it to her sister-in-law. "Mary," she said, " Frank Houston is coming here on Sunday."

"Frank !" exclaimed Mrs. Docimer. "I thought we were to consider ourselves as altogether separated from that fortunate youth."

" I don't see why."

" Well ; he left us not with the kindest possible feelings in the Tyrol ; and he has allowed ever so many months to pass by without coming to see us. I asked Mudbury whether we should have him to dinner one day last week, and he said it would be better to let him go his own way."

" Nevertheless he is coming here on Sunday."

" Has he written to you ?"

" Yes, he has written to me,—in answer to a line from me. I told him that I wished to see him."

" Was that wise ?"

" Wise or not, I did so."

" Why should you wish to see him ?"

" Am I to tell you the truth or a lie ?"

" Not a lie, certainly. I will not ask for the truth if the truth be unpalatable to you."

" It is unpalatable ;—but yet I might as well tell it you. I wrote to ask him to come and see me, because I love him so dearly."

" Oh, Imogene !"

" It is the truth."

" Did you tell him so ?"

" No ; I told him nothing. I merely said, that, if this match was over between him and that girl of Sir Thomas Tringle, then he might come and see me again. That was all that I said. His letter was very much longer, but yet it did not say much. However he is to come, and I am prepared to renew our engagement should he declare that he is willing to do so."

" What will Mudbury say ?"

" I do not care very much what he says. I do not know that I am bound to care. If I have resolved to entangle myself with a long engagement, and Mr. Houston is willing to do the same, I do not think that my brother should interfere. I am my own mistress, and am dealing altogether with my own happiness."

" Imogene, we have discussed this so often before."

" Not a doubt ; and with such effect that with my permission Frank was enabled to ask this young woman with a lot of money to marry him. Had it been arranged, I should have had no right to find fault with him, however sore of heart I might have been. All that has fallen through, and I consider myself quite entitled to renew my engagement again. I shall not ask him you may be sure of that."

" It comes to the same thing, Imogene."

" Very likely. It often happens that ladies mean that to be expressed which it does not become them to say out loud. So it may be with me on this occasion. Nevertheless the word if it have to be spoken, will have to be spoken by him. What I want you to do now is to let me have the drawing-room alone at three o'clock on Sunday. If anything has to be said it will have to be said without witnesses."

With some difficulty Mrs. Docimer was induced to accede to the request, and to promise that, at any rate for the present, nothing should be said to her husband on the subject.

CHAPTER XXXIX.

CAPTAIN BATSBY.

In the meantime poor Ayala, whose days were running on in a very melancholy manner under her aunt's wings in Kingsbury Crescent, was creating further havoc and disturbing the bosom of another lover. At Stalham she had met a certain Captain Batsby, and had there attracted his attention. Captain Batsby had begged her to ride with him on one of those hunting-days, and had offered to give her a lead, —having been at the moment particularly jealous of Colonel Stubbs. On that day both Ayala and Nina had achieved great honour ;—but this, to the great satisfaction of Captain Batsby, had not been achieved under the leadership of Colonel Stubbs. Larry Twentyman, long famous among the riding-men of the Ufford and Rufford United Hunt, had been the hero of the hour. Thus Captain Batsby's feelings had been spared, and after that he had imagined that any kindly feelings which Ayala might have had for the Colonel had sunk into abeyance. Then he had sought some opportunity to push himself into Ayala's favour, but hitherto his success in that direction had not been great.

Captain Batsby was regarded by the inhabitants of Stalham as a nuisance,—but as a nuisance which could not be avoided. He was half-brother to Sir Harry, whose mother had married, as her second husband, a certain opulent Mr. Batsby out of Lancashire. They were both dead now, and nothing of them remained but this Captain. He was good-natured, simple, and rich, and in the arrangement of the Albury-cum-Batsby affairs, which took place after the death of Mrs. Batsby, made himself pleasant to everybody concerned. Sir Harry, who certainly had no particular affection for his half-brother, always bore with him on this account ; and Lady Albury was equally gracious, mindful of the wisdom of keeping on good terms with a rich relation. It was as yet quite on the cards that the Batsby money might come to some of the Albury scions.

But the Captain was anxious to provide himself with a wife who might be the mother of scions of his own. In fact he had fallen fearfully in love with Ayala, and was quite resolved to ask her to be his wife when he found that she was just on the point of flying from Stalham. He had intended to be quicker in his operations, but had lacked opportunity. On that last hunting-day the Colonel had always been still in his way, and circumstances had never seemed to favour him when he endeavoured to have a few words in private with the young lady. Then she was gone, and he could only learn respecting her that she lived with her aunt, Mrs. Dosett, in Kingsbury Crescent.

"I'm blessed if Benjamin isn't smitten with that girl!" Benjamin was Captain Batsby, and that girl was of course Ayala Dormer. The man who blessed himself was Sir Harry Albury, and the observation was addressed to his wife. This took place within an hour of Ayala's departure from Stalham.

"Benjamin in love with Ayala Dormer! I don't believe a word of it," said Lady Albury. It was not surprising that she should not believe it. There was her special favourite, Colonel Stubbs, infatuated by the same girl : and, as she was aware, Tom Tringle, the heir of Travers and Treason. was in the same melancholy condition. And, after all, according to her thinking, there was nothing in the girl to justify all this fury. In her eyes Ayala was pretty, but no more. She would have declared that Ayala had neither bearing, nor beauty, nor figure. A bright eye, a changing colour, and something of vivacity about her mouth, was all of which Ayala had to boast. Yet here were certainly the heir of the man of millions, and that Crichton of a Colonel, both knocked off their legs. And now she was told that Captain Batsby, who always professed himself hard to please in the matter of young ladies, was in the same condition. "Do you mean to say he told you?" she asked.

"No," said Sir Harry; "he is not at all the man to do that. In such a matter he is sure to have a great secret, and be sure also to let his secret escape in every word that he speaks. You will find that what I say is true."

Before the day was out Lady Albury did find her husband to be correct. Captain Batsby, though he was very jealous of his secret, acknowledged to himself the necessity of having one confidant. He could hardly, he thought, follow Ayala without some assistance. He knew nothing of Mrs. Dosett, nothing of Kingsbury Crescent, and very little as to Ayala herself. He regarded Lady Albury as his chosen friend, and generally communicated to her whatever troubles he might have. These had consisted chiefly of the persecutions to which he had been subjected by the mothers of portionless young ladies. How not to get married off against his will had been the difficulty of his life. His half sister-in-law had hitherto preserved him, and therefore to her he now went for assistance in this opposite affair. "Rosalind," he said in his gravest voice, "what do you think I have to tell you?"

Lady Albury knew what was coming, but of course she hid her knowledge. "I hope Mrs. Motherly has not written to you again," she said. Mrs. Motherly was a lady who had been anxious that her daughter should grace Captain Batsby's table, and had written to him letters, asking him his intentions.

"Oh, dear; nothing of that kind. I do not care a straw for Mrs. Motherly or the girl either. I never said a word to her that any one could make a handle of. But I want to say a word to somebody now."

"What sort of word is it to be, Ben?"

"Ah," he groaned. "Rosalind, you must understand that I never was so much in earnest in my life!"

"You are always in earnest."

Then he sighed very deeply. "I shall expect you to help me through this matter, Rosalind."

"Do I not always help you?"

"Yes; you do. But you must stick to me now like wax. What do you think of that young lady, Miss Dormer?"

"I think she is a pretty girl; and the gentlemen tell me that she rides bravely."

"Don't you consider her divine?" he asked.

"My dear Ben, one lady never considers another to be divine. Among ourselves we are terribly human, if not worse. Do you mean to tell me that you are in love with Ayala Dormer?"

"You have guessed it," said he. "You always do guess everything."

"I generally do guess as much as that, when young gentlemen find young ladies divine. Do you know anything about Miss Dormer?"

" Nothing but her beauty,—nothing but her wit ;—nothing but her grace ! I know all that, and I don't seem to want to know any more."

" Then you must be in love ! In the first place she hasn't got a sixpence in the world."

" I don't want sixpences," said the Captain, proudly.

" And in the next place I am not at all sure that you would like her people. Father and mother she has none."

" Then I cannot dislike them."

" But she has uncles and aunts, who are, I am afraid, objectionable. She lives with a Mr. Dosett, who is a clerk in Somerset House,—a respectable man, no doubt, but one whom you would not perhaps want at your house very often."

" I don't care about uncles and aunts," said Captain Batsby. " Uncles and aunts can always be dropped much easier than fathers and mothers. At any rate I am determined to go on, and I want you to put me in the way. How must I find her ?"

" Go to No. 10, Kingsbury Crescent, Bayswater. Ask for Mrs. Dosett and tell her what you've come about. When she knows that you are well off she will not turn a deaf ear to you. What the girl may do it is beyond me to say. She is very peculiar."

" Peculiar !" said the Captain with another sigh.

Lady Albury did, in truth, think Ayala was very peculiar, seeing that she had refused two such men as Tom Tringle in spite of his wealth, and Colonel Stubbs in spite of his position. This she had done though she had no prospects of her own before her, and no comfortable home at the present ! Might it not be more than probable that she would also refuse Captain Batsby, who was less rich than the one and certainly less known to the world than the other ? But as to this it was not necessary that she should say anything. To assist Colonel Stubbs she was bound by true affection for the man. In regard to her husband's half-brother she was only bound to seem to assist him. " I can write a line to Mrs. Dosett, if you wish it," she said, " or to Miss Dormer."

" I wish you would. It would be best to the aunt, and just tell her that I am fairly well off. She'll tell Ayala I could make quite a proper settlement on her. That kind of thing does go a long way with young ladies."

" It ought to do at any rate," said Lady Albury. " It certainly does with the old ladies." Then the matter was settled. She was to write to Mrs. Dosett and inform that lady that Captain Batsby intended to call in Kingsbury Crescent in the form of a suitor for Miss Ayala Dormer's hand. She would go on to explain that Captain Batsby was quite in a position to marry and maintain a wife.

" And if she should accept me you'll have her down here, Rosalind ?" Here was a difficulty, as it was already understood that Ayala was to be again brought down to Stalham on the Colonel's account ; but Lady Albury could make the promise, as, should the Captain be accepted, no harm would in that case be done to the Colonel. She was, however, tolerably sure that the Captain would not be accepted. " And if she shouldn't take me all at once, still you might have her," suggested the lover. As to this, which was so probable, there would be a great difficulty. Ayala was to be seduced into coming again to Stalham if possible,—but specially on the Colonel's behoof. In such a case it must be done behind the Captain's back. Lady Albury saw the troubles which were coming, but nevertheless she promised that she would see what could be done. All this having been settled, Captain Batsby took his leave and went off to London.

Mrs. Dosett, when she received Lady Albury's letter, was very much surprised. She too failed to understand what there was in Ayala to produce such a multiplicity of suitors, one after another. When Lucy came to her and had begun to be objectionable, she had thought that she might some day be relieved from her troubles by the girl's marriage. Lucy, to her eyes, was beautiful, and mistress of a manner likely to be winning in a man's eyes, though ungracious to herself. But in regard to Ayala she had expressed nothing of the kind. Ayala was little, and flighty, and like an elf,—as she had remarked to her husband. But now, within twelve months three lovers had appeared, and each of them suitable for matrimonial purposes. She could only tell her husband, and then tell Ayala.

" Captain Batsby ! I don't believe it !" said Ayala, almost crying. If Colonel Stubbs could not be made to assume the garb of an Angel of Light what was she to think of Captain Batsby ?

" You can read Lady Albury's letter."

" I don't want to read Lady Albury's letter. I won't see him. I don't care what my uncle says. I don't care what anybody says. Yes, I do know him. I remember him very well. I spoke to him once or twice, and I did not like him at all."

" You said the same of Colonel Stubbs."

" I didn't say the same of Colonel Stubbs. He is a great deal worse than Colonel Stubbs."

" And you said just the same of Tom."

" He is the same as Tom ;—just as bad. It is no good going on about him, Aunt Margaret. I won't see him. If I were locked up in a room with him I wouldn't speak a word to him. He has no right to come."

" A gentleman, my dear, has always a right to ask a lady to be his wife if he has got means."

" You always say so, Aunt Margaret, but I don't believe it. There should be,—there should have been,—I don't know what ; but I am quite sure the man has no right to come to me, and I won't see him." To this resolution Ayala clung, and, as she was very firm about it, Mrs. Dosett, after consultation with her husband, at last gave way, and consented to see Captain Batsby herself.

In due time Captain Batsby came. At any knock heard at the door during this period Ayala flew out of the drawing-room into her own chamber ; and at the Captain's knock she flew with double haste, feeling sure that this was the special knock. The man was shown up, and in a set speech declared his purpose to Mrs. Dosett, and expressed a hope that Lady Albury might have written on the subject. Might he be allowed to see the young lady ?

" I fear that it would be of no service, Captain Batsby."

" Of no service ?"

" On receiving Lady Albury's letter I was of course obliged to tell my niece the honour you proposed to do her."

" I am quite in earnest, you know," said the Captain.

" So I suppose, as Lady Albury would not have written, nor would you have come on such a mission. But so is my niece in earnest."

" She will at any rate hear what I have got to say."

" She would rather not," said Mrs. Dosett. " She thinks that it would only be painful to both of you. As she has quite made up her mind that she cannot accept the honour you propose to do her, what good would it serve ?"

" Is Miss Dormer at home ?" asked the Captain, suddenly. Mrs. Dosett hesitated for a while, anxious to tell a lie on the matter, but fearing to do so. "I suppose she is at home," continued the urgent lover.

" Miss Dormer is at present in her own chamber."

" Then I think I ought to see her," continued the Captain. " She can't know at present what is my income."

" Lady Albury has told us that it is sufficient."

" But that means nothing. Your niece cannot be aware that I have a very pretty little place of my own down in Berkshire."

" I don't think it would make a difference," said Mrs. Dosett.

" Or that I shall be willing to settle upon her a third of my income. It is not many gentlemen who will do as much as that for a young lady, when the young lady has nothing of her own."

" I am sure you are very generous."

" Yes, I am. I always was generous. And I have no impediments to get rid of; not a trouble of that kind in all the world. And I don't owe a shilling. Very few young men, who have lived as much in the world as I have, can say that."

T

" I am sure your position is all that is desirable."

" That's just it. No position could be more desirable. I should give up the service immediately as soon as I was married." At that Mrs. Dosett bowed, not knowing what words to find for further conversation. "After that," continued the Captain, "do you mean to say that I am not to be allowed to see the young lady ?"

" I cannot force her to come down, Captain Batsby."

" I would if I were you."

" Force a young lady ?"

" Something ought to be done," said he, beginning almost to whine. " I have come here on purpose to see her, and I am quite prepared to do what is handsome. My half-sister, Lady Albury, had her down at Stalham, and is quite anxious to have her there again. I suppose you have no objection to make to me, Mrs. Dosett !"

" Oh, dear no."

" Or Mr. Dosett ?"

" I do not say that he has, Captain Batsby ; but this is a matter in which a young lady's word must be paramount. We cannot force her to marry you, or even to speak to you." The Captain still went on with entreaties, till Mrs. Dosett found herself so far compelled to accede to him as to go up to Ayala's room and beg her to come down and answer this third suitor with her own voice. But Ayala was immovable. When her aunt came near her she took hold of the bed as though fearing an attempt would be made to drag her out of the room. She again declared that if she were forced into the room below nothing could oblige her to speak even a word.

" As for thanking him," she said, " you can do that yourself, Aunt Margaret, if you like. I am not a bit obliged to him ; but, if you choose to say so, you may ; only pray do tell him to go away,—and tell him never, never to come back any more." Then Mrs. Dosett returned to the drawing-room, and declared that her embassy had been quite in vain.

" In all my life," said Captain Batsby, as he took his leave, " I never heard of such conduct before." Nevertheless, as he went away he made up his mind that Lady Albury should get Ayala again down to Stalham. He was very angry, but his love remained as hot as ever.

" As I did not succeed in seeing her," he said, in a letter to his half-sister, " of course I do not know what she might have said to me herself. I might probably have induced her to give me another hearing. I put it all down to that abominable aunt, who probably has some scheme of her own, and would not let Miss Dormer come down to me. If you will have her again at Stalham, everything may be made to go right."

      ●   ●   ●   ●   ●

At home, in Kingsbury Crescent, when Ayala had gone to bed, both Mr. and Mrs. Dosett expressed themselves as much troubled by the peculiarity of Ayala's nature. Mrs. Dosett declared her conviction that that promised legacy from Uncle Tom would never be forthcoming, because he had been so much offended by the rejection of his own son. And, even should the legacy remain written in Sir Thomas's will, where would Ayala find a home if Mr. Dosett were to die before the baronet? This rejection of suitors,—of fit, well-to-do, unobjectionable suitors,— was held by Mrs. Dosett to be very wicked, and a direct flying in the face of Providence. "Does she think," said Mrs. Dosett, urging the matter with all her eloquence to her husband, "that young men with incomes are to be coming after her always like this?" Mr. Dosett shook his head and scratched it at the same time, which was always a sign with him that he was not at all convinced by the arguments used, but that he did not wish to incur further hostility by answering them. "Why shouldn't she see an eligible man when he comes recommended like this?"

"I suppose, my dear, she didn't think him nice enough."

"Nice! pshaw! I call it a direct flying in the face of Providence. If he were ever so nasty and twice so old she ought to think twice about it in her position. There is poor Tom, they say, absolutely ill. The housekeeper was over here from Queen's Gate the other day, and she declares that that affair about the policeman all came from his being in love. And now he has left the business and has gone to Merle Park, because he is so knocked in a heap that he cannot hold up his head."

"I don't see why love should make a man punch a policeman's breath out of him," said Mr. Dosett.

"Of course Tom was foolish; but he would do very well if she would have him. Of course your sister, and Sir Thomas, and all of them, will be very furious. What right will she have to expect money after that?"

"Tom is an ass," said Mr. Dosett.

"I suppose Colonel Stubbs is an ass too. What I want to know is what it is she looks for. Like any other girl, she expects to get married some day, I suppose; but she has been reading poetry, and novels, and trash, till she has got her head so full of nonsense that she doesn't know what it is she does want. I should like to shake her till I shook all the romance out of her. If there is anything I do hate it is romance while bread and meat, and coals, and washing, are so dear." With this Mrs. Dosett took herself and her troubles up to her bed-room.

Mr. Dosett sat for a while gazing with speculative eyes at the embers of the fire. He was conscious in his heart that some part of that attack upon romance in general was intended for himself. Though he did not look to be romantic, especially when seated at his desk in Somerset House, with his big index-book before him, still there was left about him some touch of poetry, and an appreciation of the finer feelings of our nature. Though he could have wished that Ayala should have been able to take one of these three well-to-do suitors, who were so anxious to obtain her hand, still he could not bring himself not to respect her, still he was unable not to love her, because she was stead-fastly averse to accept as a husband a man for whom she had no affec-tion. As he looked at the embers he asked himself how it ought to be? Here was a girl whose only gift in life was her own personal charm. That that charm must be powerful was evident from the fact that she could so attract such men as these. Of the good things of the world, of a pleasant home, of ample means, and of all that absence of care which comes from money, poor Mr. Dosett had by no means a poor appreciation. That men are justified in seeking these good things by their energy, industry, and talents, he was quite confident. How was it with a girl who had nothing else but her beauty,—or, perhaps, her wit,—in lieu of energy and industry? Was she justified in carrying her wares also into the market, and making the most of them? The embers had burned so low, and he had become so cold before he had settled the question in his own mind, that he was obliged to go up to bed, leaving it unsettled.

CHAPTER XL.

AUNT EMMELINE'S NEW PROPOSITION.

A FEW days after this, just as the bread and cheese had been put on the table for the modest mid-day meal at Kingsbury Crescent, there came a most unwonted honour on Mrs. Dosett. It was a call from no less a person than Lady Tringle herself, who had come all the way up from Merle Park on purpose. It was a Saturday. She had travelled by herself and intended to go back on the same day with her husband. This was an amount of trouble which she very seldom gave herself, not often making a journey to London during the periods of her rural sojourn; and, when she began by assuring her sister-in-law that she made the journey with no object but that of coming to Kingsbury Crescent, Mrs. Dosett was aware that something very important was to be communicated. Mrs. Dosett and Ayala were together in the dining-room when Lady Tringle appeared, and the embracings were very affec-tionate. They were particularly affectionate towards Ayala, who was kissed as though nothing had ever happened to interfere with the perfect love existing between the aunt and the niece. They were more than friendly, almost sisterly, towards Mrs. Dosett, whom in truth Lady Tringle met hardly more than once in a year. It was very manifest that Aunt Emmeline wanted to have something done. "Now, my darling," she said, turning to Ayala, "if you would not mind going away for ten minutes, I could say a few words on very particular business to your aunt." Then she gave her niece a tender little squeeze and assumed her sweetest smile.

It will be as well to go back a little and tell the cause which had produced this unexpected visit. There had been very much of real trouble at Merle Park. Everything was troublesome. Gertrude had received her final letter from her lover, had declared herself to be broken-hearted, and was evincing her sorrow by lying in bed half the day, abstaining from her meals, and relieving herself from famine by sly visits to the larder. It was supposed that her object was to bend the stony heart of her father, but the process added an additional trouble to her mother. Then the Trafficks were a sore vexation. It was now nearly the end of January and they were still at Merle Park. There had been a scene in which Sir Thomas had been very harsh. "My dear," he had said to his wife, "I find that something must be done to the chimney of the north room. The workmen must be in it by the first of February. See and have all the furniture taken out before they come." Now the north room was the chamber in which the Trafficks slept, and the Trafficks were present when the order was given. No one believed the story of the chimney. This was the mode of expulsion which Sir Thomas had chosen on the spur of the moment. Mr. Traffick said not a word, but in the course of the morning Augusta expostulated with her mother. This was also disagreeable. Then the condition of Tom was truly pitiable. All his trust in champagne, all his bellicose humour, had deserted him. He moped about the place the most miserable of human beings, spending hour after hour in imploring his mother's assistance. But Lucy with her quiet determination, and mute persistency in waiting, was a source of almost greater annoyance to her aunt than even her own children. That Lucy should in any degree have had her way with Mr. Hamel had gone against the grain with her. Mr. Hamel, to her thinking, was a person to be connected with whom would be a disgrace. She was always speaking of his birth, of his father's life, and of those Roman iniquities. She had given way for a time when she had understood that her husband intended to give the young people money enough to enable them to marry. In that case Lucy would at once be taken away from the house. But now all that had come to an end. Sir

Thomas had given no money, and had even refused to give any money. Nevertheless he was peacefully indulgent to Lucy, and was always scolding his wife because she was hostile to Lucy's lover.

In this emergency she induced him to accede to a proposition, by which one of her miseries would be brought to an end and another might perhaps be remedied. A second exchange should be made. Lucy should be sent back to Kingsbury Crescent, and Ayala should once more be brought into favour at Merle Park, Queen's Gate, and Glenbogie. "Your brother will never put up with it," said Sir Thomas. Lady Tringle was not afraid of her brother, and thought that by soft words she might even talk over her sister-in-law. Ayala, she knew, had been troublesome in Kingsbury Crescent. She was sure, she said, Ayala's whims would of their nature be more troublesome to such a woman as Mrs. Dosett, than Lucy's obstinacy. Ayala had no doubt been pert and disobedient at Glenbogie and at Rome, but there had been an unbending obduracy about Lucy which had been more distasteful to Aunt Emmeline than even Ayala's pert disobedience. "It will be the only way," she had said to Sir Thomas, "to put Tom on his legs again. If the girl comes back here she will be sure to have him at last." There was much in this which to Sir Thomas was weak and absurd. That prolonged journey round by San Francisco, Japan, and Pekin, was the remedy which recommended itself to him. But he was less able to despatch Tom at once to Japan than the elder Faddle had been to send off the younger Faddle to the stern realities of life in Aberdeen. He was quite willing that Tom should marry Ayala if it could be arranged, and therefore he gave his consent.

So armed, Lady Tringle had come up to Kingsbury Crescent, and was now about to undertake a task, which she acknowledged to herself to be difficult. She, in the first place, had had her choice and had selected a niece. Then she had quarrelled with her own selection, and had changed nieces. This had been done to accommodate her own fancy ; and now she wanted to change the nieces back again ! She felt aware that her request was unreasonable, and came, therefore, determined to wrap it up in her blandest smiles.

When Ayala had left the room Mrs. Dosett sat mute in attention. She was quite aware that something very much out of the ordinary way was to be asked of her. In her ordinary way Lady Tringle never did smile when she came to Kingsbury Crescent. She would be profuse in finery, and would seem to throw off sparks of wealth at every word she spoke. Now even her dress had been toned down to her humbler manner, and there was no touch of her husband's purse in her gait. "Margaret," she said, "I have a proposition of great importance to make to you." Mrs. Dosett opened her eyes wider and sat still mute. "That poor girl is not,—is not,—is not doing perhaps the very best for herself here at Kingsbury Crescent."

"Why is she not doing the best for herself?" asked Mrs. Dosett, angrily.

"Do not for a moment suppose that I am finding fault either with you or my brother."

"You'd be very wrong if you did."

"No doubt;—but I am not finding fault. I know how very generous you have both been. Of course Sir Thomas is a rich man, and what he gives to one of the girls comes to nothing. Of course it is different with you. It is hard upon my brother to have any such burden put upon him; and it is very good both in him and you to bear it!"

"What is it you want us to do now, Emmeline?"

"Well;—I was going to explain. I do think it a great pity that Tom and Ayala should not become man and wife. If ever any young man ever did love a girl I believe that he loves her."

"I think he does."

"It is dreadful. I never saw anything like it. He is just for all the world like those young men we read of who do all manner of horrible things for love,—smothering themselves and their young women with charcoal, or throwing them into the Regent's Canal. I am constantly afraid of something happening. It was all because of Ayala that he got into that terrible row at the police court,—and then we were afraid he was going to take to drink. He has given all that up now."

"1 am very glad he has given drink up. That wouldn't do him any good."

"He is quite different now. The poor fellow hardly takes anything. He will sit all the afternoon smoking cigarettes and sipping tea. It is quite sad to see him. Then he comes and talks to me, and is always asking me to make Ayala have him."

"I don't think that anybody can ever make Ayala do anything."

"Not quite by talking to her. I dare say not. I did not mean to say a word to her about it just now."

"We can do nothing, I fear," said Mrs. Dosett.

"I was going to suggest something. But I wanted first to say a word or two about poor Lucy." They were just at present all "poor" to Lady Tringle,—Ayala, Lucy, Tom, and Gertrude. Even Augusta was poor because she was to be turned out of her bedroom.

"Is she in trouble?"

"Oh, dear, yes. But," she added, thinking well to correct herself, so that Mrs. Dosett might not imagine that she would have to look forward to troubles with Lucy, "she could arrange her affairs, no doubt, if she were not with us. She is engaged to that Mr. Isadore Hamel, the sculptor."

"So I have heard."

"He does not earn very much just at present, I fear. Sir Thomas did offer to help him, but he was perhaps a little hoity-toity, giving himself airs. That, however, did not come off, and there they are, waiting. I don't mean to say a word against poor Lucy. I think it a pity, you know ; but perhaps it was natural enough. He isn't what I should have liked for a niece who was living with me just as though she was my daughter ; but I couldn't help that."

"But what are we to do, Emmeline ?"

"Let them just change places again."

"Change again ! Ayala go to you and Lucy come back here !"

"Just that. If Ayala were with us she would be sure to get used to Tom at last. And then Lucy could manage her affairs with Mr. Hamel so much better if she were with you."

"Why should she manage her affairs better if she were with us ?"

Lady Tringle was aware that this was the weak part of her case. On the poor Ayala and poor Tom side of the question there was a good deal which might be said. Then, though she might not convince, she might be eloquent. But, touching Lucy, she could say nothing which did not simply signify that she wanted to get rid of the girl. Now, Mrs. Dosett had also wanted to get rid of Lucy when the former exchange had been made. "What I mean is, that, if she were away, Sir Thomas would be more likely to do something for her." This was an invention at the spur of the moment.

"Do you not feel that the girls should not be chucked about like balls from a battledore ?" asked Mrs. Dosett.

"For their own good, Margaret. I only propose it for their own good. You can't but think it would be a good thing for Ayala to be married to our Tom."

"If she liked him."

"Why shouldn't she like him ? You know what that means. Poor Ayala is young, and a little romantic. She would be a great deal happier if all that could be knocked out of her. She has to marry somebody, and the sooner she settles down the better. Sir Thomas will do anything for them ;—a horse and carriage, and anything she could set her heart upon ! There is nothing Sir Thomas would not do for Tom so as to get him put upon his legs again."

"I don't think Ayala would go."

"She must, you know," whispered Lady Tringle, "if we both tell her."

"And Lucy ?"

"She must too," again whispered Lady Tringle.   "If they are told they are to go, what else can they do ? Why shouldn't Ayala wish to come ? "

" There were quarrels before."

" Yes ;—because of Augusta.   Augusta is married now."   Lady Tringle could not quite say that Augusta was gone.

" Will you speak to Ayala ? "

" Perhaps it would come better from you, Margaret, if you agree with me."

" I am not sure that I do.   I am quite sure that your brother would not force her to go whether she wished it or not.   No doubt we should be glad if the marriage could be arranged.   But we cannot force a girl to marry, and her aversion in this case is so strong——— "

" Aversion ! "

" Aversion to being married, I mean.   It is so strong that I do not think she will go of her own accord to any house where she is likely to meet her cousin.   I dare say she may be a fool.   I say nothing about that.   Of course, she shall be asked ; and, if she wishes to go, then Lucy can be asked too.   But of course it must all depend upon what your brother says."

Then Lady Tringle took her leave without again seeing Ayala herself, and as she went declared her intention of calling at Somerset House.   She would not think it right, she said, in a matter of such importance, to leave London without consulting her brother.   It might be possible, she thought, that she would be able to talk her brother over ; whereas his wife, if she had the first word, might turn him the other way.

" Is Aunt Emmeline gone ? " asked Ayala, when she came down. " I am glad she has gone, because I never know how to look when she calls me dear.   I know she hates me."

" I hope not, Ayala."

" I am sure she does, because I hated Augusta.   I do hate Augusta and my aunt hates me.   The only one of the lot I like is Uncle Tom."

Then the proposition was made, Ayala sitting with her mouth wide open as the details, one after another, were opened out to her.   Her aunt did it with exquisite fairness, abstaining from opening out some of the details which might be clear enough to Ayala without any explanation.   Her Aunt Emmeline was very anxious to have her back again,—the only reason for her former expulsion having been the enmity of Augusta.   Her Uncle Tom and her aunt, and, no doubt, Gertrude, would be very glad to receive her.   Not a word was said about Tom.   Then something was urged as to the material comforts of the Tringle establishments, and of the necessary poverty of Kingsbury Crescent.

"And Lucy is to have the poverty?" said Ayala, indignantly.

"I think it probable, my dear, that before long Lucy will become the wife of Mr. Hamel."

"And you want to get rid of me?" demanded Ayala.

"No, my dear; not so. You must not think that for a moment. The proposition has not originated with me at all. I am endeavouring to do my duty by explaining to you the advantages which you would enjoy by going to your Aunt Emmeline, and which you certainly cannot have if you remain here. And I must tell you, that, if you return to Sir Thomas, he will probably provide for you. You know what I mean by providing for you?"

"No, I don't," said Ayala, who had in her mind some dim idea that her cousin Tom was supposed to be a provision. She was quite aware that her Aunt Margaret, in her explanation as hitherto given, had not mentioned Tom's name, and was sure that it had not been omitted without reason.

"By providing, I mean that if you are living in his house he will leave you something in his will;—as would be natural that he should do for a child belonging to him. Your Uncle Reginald "——this she said in a low and very serious tone——"will, I fear, have nothing to leave to you." Then there was silence for some minutes, after which Mrs. Dosett asked the important question, "Well, Ayala, what do you think about it?"

"Must I go?" said Ayala. "May I stay?"

"Yes, my dear; you may certainly stay if you wish it."

"Then I will stay," said Ayala, jumping up on to her feet. "You do not want to turn me out, Aunt Margaret?" Then she went down on her knees, and, leaning on her aunt's lap, looked up into her face. "If you will keep me I will try to be good."

"My dear, you are good. I have nothing to complain of. Of course, we will keep you. Nobody has thought for a moment of bidding you go. But you should understand that when your aunt made the proposition I was bound to tell it you." Then there was great embracing and kissing, and Ayala felt that she was relieved from a terrible danger. She had often declared that no one could make her marry her cousin Tom; but it had seemed to her for a moment that if she were given up bodily to the Tringles no mode of escape would be open to her short of suicide. There had been a moment almost of regret that she had never brought herself to regard Jonathan Stubbs as an Angel of Light.

At Somerset House Lady Tringle made her suggestion to her brother with even more flowery assurance of general happiness than she had used in endeavouring to persuade his wife. Ayala would, of course, be married to Tom in the course of the next six months, and during the same period Lucy, no doubt, would be married to that very enterprising but somewhat obstinate young man, Mr. Hamel. Thus there would be an end to all the Dormer troubles ; "and you, Reginald," she said, "will be relieved from a burden which never ought to have been laid upon your shoulder."

"We will think of it," he said very gravely, over and over again. Beyond that " we will think of it " he could not be induced to utter a word.

CHAPTER XLI.

"A COLD PROSPECT !"

THREE days were allowed to Frank Houston to consider within his own mind what he would say for himself and what he would propose finally to do when he should see Miss Docimer on the appointed Sunday. He was called upon to decide whether, after so many resolutions made to the contrary, he would now at last bring himself to encounter poverty and a family,—genteel poverty with about seven hundred and fifty pounds a-year between himself and his wife. He had hitherto been very staunch on the subject, and had unfortunately thought that Imogene Docimer had been as firmly fixed in her determination. His theory had in itself been good. If two people marry they are likely, according to the laws of nature, to have very soon more than two. In the process of a dozen years they may not improbably become ever so many more than two. Funds which were barely enough, if enough, for two, would certainly fail to be enough for half-a-dozen. His means were certainly not enough for himself, as he had hitherto found them. Imogene's means were less even than his own. Therefore, it was clear that he and Imogene ought not to marry and encounter the danger of all those embryo mouths. There was a logic about it which had seemed to him to be unanswerable. It was a logic which applied to his case above all others. The man who had a hope of earning money need not be absolutely bound by it. To him the money might come as quickly as the mouths. With the cradles would arrive the means of buying the cradles. And to the man who had much more than enough for himself,—to such a man as he had expected to be while he was looking forward to the coffin of that iniquitous uncle,—the logic did not apply at all. In defending himself, both to himself and to Imogene, he was very strong upon that point. A man who had plenty and would not divide his plenty with another might with truth be called selfish. Rich old bachelors might with propriety

be called curmudgeons. But was it right that a man should be abused,
—even by a young lady to whom, under more propitious circumstances,
he had offered his heart,—when he declared himself unwilling to multi-
ply suffering by assisting to bring into the world human beings whom
he would be unable to support? He had felt himself to be very strong
in his logic, and had unfortunately made the mistake of supposing that
it was as clear to Imogene as to himself.

Then he had determined to rectify the inconvenience of his position.
It had become manifest to him whilst he was waiting for his uncle's
money that not only were his own means insufficient for married life
but even for single comfort. It would always come to pass that when
he had resolved on two mutton-chops and half-a-pint of sherry the
humble little meal would spread itself into woodcock and champagne.
He regarded it as an unkindness in Providence that he should not have
been gifted with economy. Therefore, he had to look about him for a
remedy; and, as Imogene was out of the question, he found a remedy
in Gertrude Tringle. He had then believed that everything was
settled for him,—not, indeed, in a manner very pleasant, but after a
fashion that would make life possible to him. Sir Thomas had given
one of his daughters, with a large sum of money, to such a man as
Septimus Traffick,—a man more impecunious than himself, one whom
Frank did not hesitate to pronounce to be much less of a gentleman.
That seat in the House of Commons was to him nothing. There were
many men in the House of Commons to whom he would hardly condescend to speak. To be the younger son of a latter-day peer was to
him nothing. He considered himself in all respects to be a more
eligible husband than Septimus Traffick. Therefore he had entertained
but little doubt when he found himself accepted by Gertrude herself
and her mother. Then by degrees he had learnt to know something
of the young lady to whom he intended to devote himself; and it had
come to pass that the better he had known the less he had liked her.
Nevertheless he had persevered, groaning in spirit as he thought of the
burden with which he was about to inflict himself. Then had come
the release. Sir Thomas had explained to him that no money would
be forthcoming; and the young lady had made to him a foolish proposition which, as he thought, fully justified him in regarding the match
as at an end.

And then he had three days in which to make up his mind. It may
be a question whether three days are ever much better than three
minutes for such a purpose. A man's mind will very generally refuse
to make itself up until it be driven and compelled by emergency. The
three days are passed not in forming but in postponing judgment. In
nothing is procrastination so tempting as in thought. So it came to

pass, that through the Thursday, the Friday, and the Saturday, Frank Houston came to no conclusion, though he believed that every hour of the time was devoted to forming one. Then, as he ate his dinner on Saturday night at his club, a letter was brought to him, the hand-writing of which was familiar to him. This letter assisted him little thinking.

The letter was from Gertrude Tringle, and need not be given in its entirety. There was a good deal of reproach, in that he had been so fickle as to propose to abandon her at the first touch of adversity. Then she had gone on to say, that knowing her father a great deal better than he could do, she was quite satisfied that the money would be all right. But the last paragraph of the letter shall be given. "Papa has almost yielded already. I have been very ill ;"—here the extent of her malady was shown by the strength of the underscoring with which the words were made significant.;—"very ill indeed," she went on to say, "as you will understand if you have ever really loved me. I have kept my bed almost ever since I got your cruel letter." Bed and cruel were again strenuously underscored. "It has made papa very unhappy, and, though he has said nothing to myself, he has told mamma that if I am really in earnest he will do something for us." The letter was long, but this is all the reader need see of it. But it must be explained that the young lady had greatly exaggerated her mother's words, and that her mother had exaggerated those which Sir Thomas had spoken. "She is a stupid idiot," Sir Thomas had said to his wife. "If she is obedient, and does her duty, of course I shall do something for her some day." This had been stretched to that promise of concession which Gertrude communicated to her lover.

This was the assistance which Frank Houston received in making up his mind on Saturday night. If what the girl said was true, there was still open to him the manner of life which he had prepared for himself ; and he did believe the announcement to be true. Though Sir Thomas had been so persistent in his refusals, his experience in life had taught him to believe that a parent's sternness is never a match for a daughter's obstinacy. Had there been a touch of tenderness in his heart to the young lady herself he would not have abandoned her so easily. But he had found his consolation when giving up his hope of Sir Thomas's money. Now, should he again take to the girl, and find his consolation in accepting the money ? Should he resolve upon doing so, this would materially affect any communication which he might make to Imogene on the following day.

While thus in doubt he went into the smoking-room and there he found any thinking to be out of the question. A great question was being debated as to club law. One man has made an assertion. He had declared that another man had been seen playing cards in a third man's company. A fourth man had, thereupon, put his hat on his head, and had declared contumaciously that the "assertion was not true." Having so declared he had contumaciously stalked out of the room, and had banged the door after him,—very contumaciously indeed. The question was whether the contumacious gentleman had misbehaved himself in accordance with the rules of the club, and, if so, what should be done to him. Not true is as bad as "false." "False," applied to a gentleman in a club, must be matter either of an apology or expulsion. The objectionable word had, no doubt, been said in defence of an absent man, and need not, perhaps, have been taken up had the speaker not at once put on his hat and stalked out of the room, and banged the door. It was asserted that a lie may be given by the way in which a door is banged. And yet no club punishes the putting on of hats, or stalking off, or the banging of doors. It was a difficult question, and occupied Frank Houston till two o'clock in the morning, to the exclusion of Gertrude Tringle and Imogene Docimer.

On the Sunday morning he was not up early, nor did he go to church. The contumacious gentleman was a friend of his, whom he knew that no arguments would induce to apologise. He believed also that gentleman No. 3 might have been seen playing cards with gentleman No. 2,—so that there was no valid excuse for the banging of the door. He was much exercised by the points to be decided, so that when he got into a cab to be taken to Mrs. Docimer's house he had hardly come to any other conclusion than that one which had arisen to him from a comparison between the two young ladies. Imogene was nearly perfect, and Gertrude was as nearly the reverse as a young lady could be with the proper number of eyes in her head and a nose between them. The style of her letter was abominable to him. "Very ill indeed ;—as you will understand, if you ever really loved me !" There was a mawkish clap-trap about it which thoroughly disgusted him. Everything from Imogene was straightforward and downright, whether it were love or whether it were anger. But then to be settled with an income of £3,000 a year would relieve him from such a load of care !

" And so Tringle père does not see the advantage of such a son-in-law," said Imogene, after the first greetings were over between them. The greetings had been very simple,—just a touch of the hand, just a civil word,—civil, but not in the least tender, just an inclination of the head, and then two seats occupied with all the rug between them.

" Yes, indeed !" said Frank. " The man is a fool, because he will probably get somebody who will behave less well to his daughter, and make a worse use of his money."

" Just so. One can only be astonished at his folly. Is there no hope left ?"

" A glimmer there is."

" Oh, indeed !"

" I got a letter last night from my lady-love, in which she tells me that she is very ill, and that her sickness is working upon her father's bowels."

" Frank !"

" It is the proper language ;—working upon her father's bowels of compassion. Fathers always have bowels of compassion at last."

" You will return them, of course ?"

" What do you say ?"

" As for myself,—or as for you ?"

" As a discreet and trusty counsellor. To me you have always been a trusty counsellor."

" Then I should put a few things into a bag, go down to Merle Park, and declare that, in spite of all the edicts that ever came from a father's mouth, you cannot absent yourself while you know that your Gertrude is ill."

" And so prepare a new cousin for you to press to your bosom."

" If you can endure her for always, why should not I for an hour or two, now and again ?"

" Why not, indeed ? In fact, Imogene, this enduring, and not enduring,—even this living and not living,—is, after all, but an affair of the imagination. Who can tell but, that as years roll on, she may be better-looking even than you ?"

" Certainly."

" And have as much to say for herself ?"

" A great deal more that is worth hearing."

" And behave herself as a mother of a family with quite as much propriety ?"

" In all that I do not doubt that she would be my superior."

" More obedient I am sure she would be."

" Or she would be very disobedient."

" And then she can provide me and my children with ample comforts."

" Which 1 take it is the real purpose for which a wife should be married."

" Therefore," said he,——and then he stopped.

" And therefore there should be no doubt."

" Though I hate her," he said, clenching his fist with violence as he spoke, " with every fibre of my heart,—still you think there should be no doubt ?"

"That, Frank, is violent language,—and foolish."

"And though I love you so intensely that whenever I see her the memory of you becomes an agony to me."

"Such language is only more violent and more foolish."

"Surely not, if I have made up my mind at last, that I never will willingly see Miss Tringle again." Here he got up, and walking across the rug, stood over her, and waited as though expecting some word from her. But she, putting her two hands up to her head, and brushing her hair away from her forehead, looked up to him for what further words might come to him. "Surely not," he continued, "if I have made up my mind at last, that nothing shall ever again serve to rob me of your love,—if I may still hope to possess it."

"Oh, Frank!" she said, "how mean I am to be a creature obedient to the whistle of such a master as you!"

"But are you obedient?"

"You know that well enough. I have had no Gertrude with whom I have vacillated, whether for the sake of love or lucre. Whatever you may be,—whether mean or noble,—you are the only man with whom I can endure to live, for whom I would endure to die. Of course I had not expected that your love should be like mine. How should it be so, seeing that you are a man and that I am but a woman." Here he attempted to seat himself by her on the sofa, which she occupied, but she gently repulsed him, motioning him towards the chair which he had occupied. "Sit there, Frank" she said, "so that we may look into each other's faces and talk seriously. Is it to come to this then, that I am to ruin you at last?"

"There will be no ruin."

"But there will, if we are married now. Shall I tell you the kind of life which would satisfy me?"

"Some little place abroad?" he asked.

"Oh, dear, no! No place to which you would be confined at all. If I may remain as I am, knowing that you intend to marry no one else, feeling confident that there is a bond binding us together even though we should never become man and wife, I should be, if not happy, at least contented."

"That is a cold prospect."

"Cold;—but not ice-cold, as would have been the other. Cold, but not wretchedly cold, as would be the idea always present to me that I had reduced you to poverty. Frank, I am so far selfish that I cannot bear to abandon the idea of your love. But I am not so far selfish as to wish to possess it at the expense of your comfort. Shall it be so?"

"Be how?" said he, speaking almost in anger.

"Let us remain just as we are. Only you will promise me, that as I cannot be your wife there shall be no other. I need hardly promise you that there will be no other husband." Now he sat frowning at her, while she, still pressing back her hair with her hands, looked eagerly into his face. "If this will be enough for you," she said, "it shall be enough for me."

"No, by G—d!"

"Frank!"

"It will certainly not be enough for me. I will have nothing to do with so damnable a compact."

"Damnable!"

"Yes; that is what I call it. That is what any man would call it, —and any woman, too, who would speak her mind."

"Then, Sir, perhaps you will be kind enough to make your proposition. I have made mine, such as it is, and am sorry that it should not have been received at any rate with courtesy." But as she said this there was a gleam of a bright spirit in her eyes, such as he had not seen since first the name of Gertrude had been mentioned to her.

"Yes," said he. "You have made your proposition, and now it is only fair that I should make mine. Indeed, I made it already when I suggested that little place abroad. Let it be abroad or at home, or of what nature it may,—so that you shall be there, and I with you, it shall be enough for me. That is my proposition; and, if it be not accepted, then I shall return to Miss Tringle and all the glories of Lombard Street."

"Frank——" she said. Then, before she could speak another word, he had risen from his seat, and she was in his arms. "Frank," she continued, pushing back his kisses, "how impossible it is that I should not be obedient to you in all things! I know,—I know that I am agreeing to that which will cause you some day to repent."

"By heavens, no!" said he. "I am changed in all that."

"A man cannot change at once. Your heart is soft, but your nature remains the same. Frank, I could be so happy at this moment if I could forget the picture which my imagination points to me of your future life. Your love and your generous words, and the look out of your dear eyes, are sweet to me now, as when I was a child, whom you first made so proud by telling her that she owned your heart. If I could only revel in the return of your affections——"

"It is no return," said he. "There has never been a moment in which my affections have not been the same."

"Well, then,—in these permitted signs of your affection,—if were not that I cannot shut out the future! Do not press me to name

U

any early day, because no period of my future life will be so happy to me as this."

    *   *   *   *   *

    "Is there any reason why I should not intrude?" said Mrs. Docimer, opening the door when the above conversation had been extended for perhaps another hour.

    "Not in the least, as far as I'm concerned," said Frank. "A few words have been spoken between us, all of which may be repeated to you if Imogene can remember them."

    "Every one of them," said Imogene; "but I hardly think that I shall repeat them."

    "I suppose they have been very much a matter of course," said Mrs. Docimer;—"the old story repeated between you two for the fourth or fifth time. Considering all things, do you think that I should congratulate you?"

    "I ask for no congratulation," said Imogene.

    "You may certainly congratulate me," said Frank. After that the conversation became tame, and the happy lover soon escaped from the house into the street. When there he found very much to occupy his mind. He had certainly made his resolution at last, and had done so in a manner which would now leave him no power of retrogression. The whole theory of his life had,—with a vengeance,—been thrown to the winds. "The little place abroad,"—or elsewhere,—was now a settled certainty. He had nearly got the better of her. He had all but succeeded in putting down his own love and hers by a little gentle ridicule, and by a few half-wise phrases which she at the moment had been unable to answer; but she now had in truth vanquished him by the absolute sincerity of her love.

CHAPTER XLII.

ANOTHER DUEL.

FRANK HOUSTON on that Sunday afternoon became an altered man. The reader is not to suppose by this that he is declared to have suddenly thrown off all his weaknesses, and to have succeeded in clothing himself in an armour of bright steel, proof for the rest of his life against all temptations. Such suits of armour are not to be had at a moment's notice; nor, as I fear, can a man ever acquire one quite perfect at all points who has not begun to make it for himself before Houston's age. But he did on that day dine off the two mutton-chops, and comforted himself with no more than the half-pint of sherry. It was a great beginning. Throughout the whole evening he could not be got for a moment to join any of the club juntas which were discussing the great difficulty of the contumacious gentleman. "I think he must really be going to be married at last!" one club pundit said when a question was asked as to Houston's singular behaviour on the occasion.

He was indeed very sober,—so sober that he left the smoking-room as soon as his one silent cigar was finished, and went out alone in order that he might roam the streets in thoughtful solitude. It was a clear frosty night, and as he buttoned his great coat around him he felt that the dry cold air would do him good, and assist his meditations. At last then everything was arranged for him, and he was to encounter exactly that mode of life which he had so often told himself to be most unfit for him. There were to be the cradles always full, and his little coffer so nearly empty! And he had done it all for himself. She, Imogene, had proposed a mode of life to him which would at any rate have saved him from this; but it had been impossible that he should accept a plan so cruel to her when the proposition came from herself. It must all soon be done now. She had asked that a distant day might be fixed for their marriage. Even that request, coming from her, made it almost imperative upon him to insist upon an early day. It would be well for him to look upon to-morrow, or a few morrows whose short distance would be immaterial, as the time fixed.

No;—there should be no going back now! So he declared to himself, endeavouring to prepare the suit of armour for his own wearing. Pau might be the best place,—or perhaps one of those little towns in Brittany. Dresden would not do, because there would be society at Dresden, and he must of course give up all ideas of society. He would have liked Rome; but Rome would be far too expensive, and then residents in Rome require to be absent three or four months every year. He and his wife and large family,—he had no doubt in life as to the large family,—would not be able to allow themselves any recreation such as that. He thought he had heard that the ordinary comforts of life were cheap in the west of Ireland,—or, if not cheap, unobtainable, which would be the same thing. Perhaps Castlebar might be a good locality for his nursery. There would be nothing to do at Castlebar,—no amusement whatever for such a one as himself, no fitting companion for Imogene. But then amusement for himself and companions for Imogene must of course be out of the question. He thought that perhaps he might turn his hand to a little useful gardening,—parsnips instead of roses,—while Imogene would be at work in the nursery. He would begin at once and buy two or three dozen pipes, because tobacco would be so much cheaper than cigars. He knew a shop at which were to be had some very pretty new-fashioned meerschaums, which, he had been told, smokers of pipes found to be excellent.   But, whether it should be Pau or whether it should be Castlebar, whether it should be pipes or whether, in regard to economy, no tobacco at all, the question now was at any rate settled for him.   He felt rather proud of his gallantry, as he took himself home to bed, declaring to himself that he would answer that last letter from Gertrude in a very few words and in a very decided tone.

There would be many little troubles.   On the Monday morning he got up early thinking that as a family man such a practice would be necessary for him.   When he had disturbed the house and nearly driven his own servant mad by demanding breakfast at an altogether unaccustomed hour, he found that he had nothing to do.   There was that head of Imogene for which she had only once sat, and at which he had occasionally worked from memory because of her refusal to sit again ; and he thought for a moment that this might be good employment for him now.   But his art was only an expense to him.   He could not now afford for himself paint and brushes and canvas, so he turned the half-finished head round upon his easel.   Then he took out his banker's book, a bundle of bills and some blotted scraps of ruled paper, with which he set himself to work to arrange his accounts. When he did this he must certainly have been in earnest.   But he had not as yet succeeded in seeing light through his figures when he was interrupted by the arrival of a letter which altogether arrested his attention.   It was from Mudbury Docimer, and this was the letter ;—

" DEAR HOUSTON,

" Of course I think that you and Imogene are two fools.   She has told me what took place here yesterday, and I have told her the same as I tell you.   I have no power to prevent it ; but you know as well as I do that you and she cannot live together on the interest of sixteen thousand pounds.   When you've paid everything that you owe I don't suppose there will be so much as that.   It had been arranged between you that everything should be over ; and if I had thought that anything of the kind would have occurred again I would have told them not to let you into the house.   What is the good of two such people as you making yourselves wretched for ever, just to satisfy the romance of a moment ?   I call it wicked.   So I told Imogene, and so I tell you.

" You have changed your mind so often that of course you may change it again.   I am sure that Imogene expects that you will.   Indeed I can hardly believe that you intend to be such a Quixote.   But at any rate I have done my duty.   She is old enough to look after herself, but as long as she lives with me as my sister I shall tell her what I think ; and until she becomes your wife,—which I hope she never will be,—I shall tell you the same.   " Yours truly,

"MUDBURY DOCIMER."

" He always was a hard, unfeeling fellow," said Frank to himself. Then he put the letter by with a crowd of others, assuring himself that it was one which required no answer.

On the afternoon he called at the house, as he did again on the Tuesday; but on neither day did he succeed in seeing Imogene. This he thought to be hard, as the pleasure of her society was as sweet to him as ever, though he was doubtful as to his wisdom in marrying her. On the Wednesday morning he received a note from her asking him not to come at once, because Mudbury had chosen to put himself into a bad humour. Then a few words of honey were added, " Of course you know that nothing that he can say will make a change. I am too well satisfied to allow of any change that shall not come from you yourself." He was quite alive to the sweetness of the honey, and declared to himself that Mudbury Docimer's ill-humour was a matter to him of no concern whatever.

But on the Wednesday there came also another letter,—in regard to which it will be well that we should travel down again to Merle Park. An answer altogether averse to the proposed changes as to the nieces had been received from Mrs. Dosett. " As Ayala does not wish it, of course nothing can be done." Such was the decision as conveyed by Mrs. Dosett. It seemed to Lady Tringle that this was absurd. It was all very well extending charity to the children of her deceased sister, Mrs. Dormer; but all the world was agreed that beggars should not be choosers. " As Ayala does not wish it." Why should not Ayala wish it? What a fool must Ayala be not to wish it! Why should not Ayala be made to do as she was told, whether she wished it or not? Such were the indignant questions which Lady Tringle asked of her husband. He was becoming sick of the young ladies altogether,—of her own girls as well as the Dormer girls. " They are a pack of idiots together," he said, " and Tom is the worst of the lot." With this he rushed off to London, and consoled himself with his millions.

Mrs. Dosett's letter had reached Merle Park on the Tuesday morning, Sir Thomas having remained down in the country over the Monday. Gertrude, having calculated the course of the post with exactness, had hoped to get a reply from Frank to that last letter of hers,—dated from her sick bed, but written in truth after a little surreptitious visit to the larder after the servants' dinner,—on the Sunday morning. This had been possible, and would have evinced a charming alacrity on the part of her lover. But this she had hardly ventured to expect. Then she had looked with anxiety to the arrival of letters on the Monday afternoon, but had looked in vain. On the Tuesday morning she had felt so certain that she had contrived to open the post-bag herself in spite of illness;—but there had been nothing for her. Then she sent the dispatch which reached Frank on the Wednesday morning, and immediately afterwards took to her bed again with such a complication of disorders that the mare with the broken knees was sent at once into Hastings for the doctor.

"A little rice will be the best thing for her," said the doctor.

"But the poor child takes nothing,—literally nothing," said Lady Tringle, who was frightened for her child. Then the doctor went on to say that arrowroot would be good, and sago, but offered no other prescription. Lady Tringle was disgusted by his ignorance, and thought that it might be well to send up to London for some great man. The doctor bowed, and made up his mind that Lady Tringle was an ass. But, being an honest man, and also tender-hearted, he contrived to get hold of Tom before he left the house.

"Your sister's health is generally good?" he said. Tom assented. As far as he knew, Gertrude had always been as strong as a horse. "Eats well?" asked the doctor. Tom, who occasionally saw the family at lunch, gave a description of his sister's general performance.

"She is a fine healthy young lady," said the doctor. Tom gave a brother's ready adhesion to the word healthy, but passed over the other epithet as being superfluous. "Now, I'll tell you what it is," said the doctor. "Of course I don't want to inquire into any family secrets."

"My father, you know," said Tom, "won't agree about the man she's engaged to."

"That is it? I knew there was some little trouble, but I did not want to ask any questions. Your mother is unnecessarily frightened, and I have not wished to disturb her. Your sister is taking plenty of nourishment?"

"She does not come to table, nor yet have it in her own room."

"She gets it somehow. I can say that it is so. Her veins are full, and her arms are strong. Perhaps she goes into the kitchen. Have a little tray made ready for her, with something nice. She will be sure to find it, and when she has found it two or three times she will know that she has been discovered. If Lady Tringle does send for a physician from London you could perhaps find an opportunity of telling him what I have suggested. Her mamma need know nothing about it." This took place on the Tuesday, and on the Wednesday morning Gertrude knew that she had been discovered,—at any rate by Tom and the doctor. "I took care to keep a wing for you," said Tom; "I carved them myself at dinner." As he so addressed her he came out from his hiding-place in the kitchen about midnight, and surprised her in the larder. She gave a fearful scream, which, however, luckily was not heard through the house. "You won't tell mamma, Tom, will you?" Tom promised that he would not, on condition that she would come down to breakfast on the following morning. This she did, and the London physician was saved the journey.

But, in the meantime, Gertrude's second letter had gone up to Frank, and also a very heartrending epistle from Lady Tringle to her husband. "Poor Gertrude is in a very bad state. If ever there was a girl really broken-hearted on account of love, she is one. I did not think she would ever set her heart upon a man with such violent affection. I do think you might give way when it becomes a question of life and death. There isn't anything really against Mr. Houston." Sir Thomas, as he read this, was a little shaken. He had hitherto been inclined to agree with Rosalind, "That men have died from time to time, and worms have eaten them, but not for love." But now he did not know what to think about it. There was Tom undoubtedly in a bad way, and here was Gertrude brought to such a condition, simply by her love, that she refused to take her meals regularly! Was the world come to such a pass that a father was compelled to give his daughter with a large fortune to an idle adventurer, or else to be responsible for his daughter's life? Would Augusta have pined away and died had she not been allowed to marry her Traffick? Would Lucy pine and die unless money were given to her sculptor? Upon the whole, Sir Thomas thought that the cares of his family were harder to bear than those of his millions. In regard to Gertrude, he almost thought that he would give way, if only that he might be rid of that trouble.

It must be acknowledged that Frank Houston, when he received the young lady's letter, was less soft-hearted than her father. The letter was, or should have been, heart-rending ;—

" You cruel Man,

" You must have received my former letter, and though I told you that I was ill and almost dying you have not heeded it! Three posts have come, and I have not had a line from you. In your last you were weak enough to say that you were going to give it all up because you could not make papa do just what you wanted all at once. Do you know what it is to have taken possession of a young lady's heart ; or is it true, as Augusta says of you, that you care for nothing but the money? If it is so, say it at once and let me die. As it is I am so very ill that I cannot eat a mouthful of anything, and have hardly strength left to me to write this letter.

" But I cannot really believe what Augusta says, though I daresay it may have been so with Mr. Traffick. Perhaps you have not been to your club, and so you have not got my former letter. Or it may be that you are ill yourself. If so, I do wish that I could come and nurse you, though indeed I am so ill that I am quite unable to leave my bed.

" At any rate, pray write immediately ;—and do come ! Mamma
seems to think that papa will give way because I am so ill. .If so, I
shall think my illness the luckiest thing in the world.—You must
believe, dearest Frank, that I am now, as ever, yours most affectionately,   " GERTRUDE."

Frank Houston was less credulous than Sir Thomas, and did not
believe much in the young lady's sickness. It was evident that the
young lady was quite up to the work of deceiving her father and
mother, and would no doubt be willing to deceive himself if anything
could be got by it. But, whether she were ill or whether she were
well, he could offer her no comfort. Nevertheless, he was bound to
send her some answer, and with a troubled spirit he wrote as follows ;—

" MY DEAR MISS TRINGLE,
   " It is to me a matter of inexpressible grief that I should have to
explain again that I am unable to persist in seeking the honour of your
hand in opposition to the absolute and repeated refusals which I have
received from your father. It is so evident that we could not marry
without his consent that I need not now go into that matter. But I
think myself bound to say that, considering the matter in all its bearing, I must regard our engagement as finally at an end. Were I to
hesitate in saying this very plainly I think I should be doing you an
injury.
   " I am sorry to hear that you are unwell, and trust that you may
soon recover your health.   Your sincere friend,
                                                        " FRANK HOUSTON."

On the next morning Gertrude was still in her bed, having there
received her letter, when she sent a message to her brother. Would
Tom come and see her ? Tom attended to her behest, and then sat
down by her bedside on being told in a mysterious voice that she had
to demand from him a great service. " Tom," she said, " that man
has treated me most shamefully and most falsely."
   " What man ?"
   " What man ? Why, Frank Houston. There has never been any
other man. After all that has been said and done he is going to throw
me over."
   " The governor threw him over," said Tom.
   " That amounts to nothing. The governor would have given way,
of course, and if he hadn't that was no matter of his. After he had
had my promise he was bound to go on with it. Don't you think so !"
   " Perhaps he was," said Tom, dubiously.
   " Of course he was. What else is the meaning of a promise ? Now

I'll tell you what you must do. You must go up to London and find him out. You had better take a stick with you, and then ask him what he means to do."

" And if he says he'll do nothing ?"

" Then, Tom, you should call him out. It is just the position in which a brother is bound to do that kind of thing for his sister. When he has been called out, then probably he'll come round, and all will be well."

The prospect was one which Tom did not at all like. He had had one duel on his hands on his own account, and had not as yet come through it with flying colours. There were still moments in which he felt that he would be compelled at last to take to violence in reference to Colonel Stubbs. He was all but convinced that were he to do so he would fall into some great trouble, but still it was more than probable that his outraged feelings would not allow him to resist. But this second quarrel was certainly unnecessary. " That's all nonsense, Gertrude," he said, " I can do nothing of the kind."

" You will not ?"

" Certainly not. It would be absurd. You ask Septimus and he will tell you that it is so."

" Septimus, indeed !"

" At any rate, I won't. Men don't call each other out now-a-days. I know what ought to be done in these kind of things, and such interference as that would be altogether improper."

" Then, Tom," said she, raising herself in bed, and looking round upon him, " I will never call you my brother again !"

CHAPTER XLIII.

ONCE MORE !

" PROBABLY you are not aware, Sir, that I am not at present the young lady's guardian." This was said at the office in Lombard Street by Sir Thomas, in answer to an offer made to him by Captain Batsby for Ayala's hand. Captain Batsby had made his way boldly into the great man's inner room, and had there declared his purpose in a short and business-like manner. He had an ample income of his own, he said, and was prepared to make a proper settlement on the young lady. If necessary, he would take her without any fortune ;—but it would, of course, be for the lady's comfort and for his own if something in the way of money were forthcoming. So much he added, having heard of this uncle's enormous wealth, and having also learned the fact that if Sir Thomas were not at this moment Ayala's guardian he had been not long ago. Sir Thomas listened to him with patience, and then replied to him as above.

"Just so, Sir Thomas. I did hear that. But I think you were once ; and you are still her uncle."

"Yes ; I am her uncle."

"And when I was so ill-treated in Kingsbury Crescent I thought I would come to you. It could not be right that a gentleman making an honourable proposition,—and very liberal, as you must acknowledge, —should not be allowed to see the young lady. It was not as though I did not know her. I had been ten days in the same house with her. Don't you think, Sir Thomas, I ought to have been allowed to see her ?"

"I have nothing to do with her," said Sir Thomas ;—"that is, in the way of authority." Nevertheless, before Captain Batsby left him, he became courteous to that gentleman, and though he could not offer any direct assurance he acknowledged that the application was reasonable. He was, in truth, becoming tired of Ayala, and would have been glad to find a husband whom she would accept, so that she might be out of Tom's way. He had been quite willing that Tom should marry the girl if it were possible, but he began to be convinced that it was impossible. He had offered again to open his house to her with all its wealth, but she had refused to come into it. His wife had told him that, if Ayala could be brought back in place of Lucy, she would surely yield. But Ayala would not allow herself to be brought back. And there was Tom as bad as ever. If Ayala were once married then Tom could go upon upon his travels and come back, no doubt, a sane man. Sir Thomas thought it might be well to make inquiry about this Captain, and then see if a marriage might be arranged. Mrs. Dosett, he told himself, was a hard, stiff woman, and would never get the girl married unless she allowed such a suitor as this Captain Batsby to have access to the house. He did make inquiry, and before the week was over had determined that if Ayala would become Mrs. Batsby there might probably be an end to one of his troubles.

As he went down to Merle Park he arranged his plan. He would, in the first place, tell Tom that Ayala had as many suitors as Penelope, and that one had come up now who would probably succeed. But when he reached home he found that his son was gone. Tom had taken a sudden freak, and had run up to London. "He seemed quite to have got a change," said Lady Tringle.

"I hope it was a change for the better as to that stupid girl." Lady Tringle could not say that there had been any change for the better, but she thought that there had been a change about the girl. Tom had, as she said, quite "brisked up," had declared that he was not going to stand this thing any longer, had packed up three or four port-manteaus, and had had himself carried off to the nearest railway station in time for an afternoon train up to London. " What is he going to do when he gets there ?" asked Sir Thomas. Lady Tringle had no idea what her son intended to do, but thought that something special was intended in regard to Ayala.

" He is an ass," said the father.

" You always say he is an ass," said the mother, complaining.

" No doubt I do. What else am I to call him ?" Then he went on and developed his scheme. " Let Ayala be asked to Merle Park for a week,—just for a week,—and assured that during that time Tom would not be there. Then let Captain Batsby also be invited." Upon this there followed an explanation as to Captain Batsby and his aspirations. Tom must be relieved after some fashion, and Sir Thomas declared that no better fashion seemed to present itself. Lady Tringle received her orders with sundry murmurings, still grieving for her son's grief ; —but she assented, as she always did assent, to her husband's propo-sitions.

Now we will accompany Tom up to London. The patient reader will perhaps have understood the condition of his mind when in those days of his sharpest agony he had given himself up to Faddle and champagne. By these means he had brought himself into trouble and disgrace, of which he was fully conscious. He had fallen into the hands of the police and had been harassed during the whole period by headache and nausea. Then had come the absurdity of his challenge to Colonel Stubbs, the folly of which had been made plain to him by the very letter which his rival had written to him. There was good sense enough about the poor fellow to enable him to understand that the police court, and the prison, that Faddle and the orgies at Bolivia's, that his challenge and the reply to it, were alike dishonourable to him. Then had come a reaction, and he spent a miserable fortnight down at Merle Park doing nothing, resolving on nothing, merely moping about and pouring the oft-repeated tale of his woes into his mother's bosom. These days at Merle Park gave him back at any rate his health, and rescued him from the intense wretchedness of his condition on the day after the comparison of Bolivia's wines. In this improved state he told himself that it behoved him even yet to do something as a man, and he came suddenly to the bold resolution of having,—as he called it to himself,—another " dash at Ayala."

How the " dash " was to be made he had not determined when he left home. But to this he devoted the whole of the following Sunday. He had received a lachrymose letter from his friend Faddle, at Aber-deen, in which the unfortunate youth had told him that he was destined to remain in that wretched northern city for the rest of his natural life. He had not as yet been to the Mountaineers since his mishap with the police, and did not care to show himself there at present. He was therefore altogether alone, and, walking all alone the entire round of the parks, he at last formed his resolution.

On the following morning when Mr. Dosett entered his room at Somerset House, a little after half-past ten o'clock, he found his nephew Tom there before him, and waiting for him. Mr. Dosett was somewhat astonished, for he too had heard of Tom's misfortunes. Some ill-natured chronicle of Tom's latter doings had spread itself among the Tringle and Dosett sets, and Uncle Reginald was aware that his nephew had been forced to relinquish his stool in Lombard Street. The vices of the young are perhaps too often exaggerated, so that Mr. Dosett had heard of an amount of champagne consumed and a number of policemen wounded, of which his nephew had not been altogether guilty. There was an idea at Kingsbury Crescent that Tom had gone nearly mad, and was now kept under paternal care at Merle Park. When, therefore, he saw Tom blooming in health, and brighter than usual in general appearance, he was no doubt rejoiced, but also surprised at the change. "What, Tom!" he said; "I'm glad to see you looking so well. Are you up in London again?"

"I'm in town for a day or two," said Tom.

"And what can I do for you?"

"Well, Uncle Reginald, you can do a great deal for me if you will. Of course you've heard of all those rows of mine?"

"I have heard something."

"Everybody has heard," said Tom, mournfully. "I don't suppose anybody was ever knocked so much about as I've been for the last six months."

"I'm sorry for that, Tom."

"I'm sure you are, because you're always good-natured. Now I wonder if you will do a great thing to oblige me."

"Let us hear what it is," said Uncle Reginald.

"I suppose you know that there is only one thing in the world that I want." Mr. Dosett thought that it would be discreet to make no reply to this, but, turning his chair partly round, he prepared to listen very attentively to what his nephew might have to say to him. "All this about the policeman and the rest of it has simply come from my being so unhappy about Ayala."

"It wouldn't be taken as a promise of your being a good husband, Tom, when you get into such a mess as that."

"That's because people don't understand," said Tom. "It is because I am so earnest about it, and because I can't bear the disappointment!

There isn't one at Travers and Treason who doesn't know that if I'd married Ayala I should have settled down as quiet a young man as there is in all London. You ask the governor else himself. As long as I thought there was any hope I used to be there steady as a rock at half-past nine. Everybody knew it. So I should again, if she'd only come round."

" You can't make a lady come round, as you call it."

" Not make her ; no. Of course you can't make a girl. But persuading goes a long way. Why shouldn't she have me ? As to all these rows she ought to feel at any rate that they're her doing. And what she's done it stands to reason she could undo if she would. It only wants a word from her to put me all right with the governor,—and to put me all right with Travers and Treason too. Nobody can love her as I do."

" I do believe that nobody could love her better," said Mr. Dosett, who was beginning to be melted by his nephew's earnestness.

" Oughtn't that to go for something ? And then she would have everything that she wishes. She might live anywhere she pleased,—so that I might go to the office every day. She would have her own carriage, you know."

" I don't think that would matter much with Ayala."

" It shows that I'm in a position to ask her," said Tom. " If she could only bring herself not to hate me——"

" There is a difference, Tom, between hating and not loving."

" If she would only begin to make a little way, then I could hope again. Uncle Reginald, could you not tell her that at any rate I would be good to her."

" I think you would be good to her," he said.

" Indeed, I would. There is nothing I would not do for her. Now will you let me see her just once again, and have one other chance ?"

This was the great thing which Tom desired from his uncle, and Mr. Dosett was so much softened by his nephew's earnestness that he did promise to do as much as this ;—to do as much as this, at least, if it were in his power. Of course, Ayala must be told. No good could be done by surprising her by a visit. But he would endeavour so to arrange it that, if Tom were to come to him on the following afternoon, they two should go to the Crescent together, and then Tom should remain and dine there,—or go away before dinner, as he might please, after the interview. This was settled, and Tom left Somerset House, rejoicing greatly at his success. It seemed to him that now at last a way was open to him.

Uncle Reginald, on his return home, took his niece aside and talked to her very gently and very kindly. " Whether you like him or whether you do not, my dear, he is so true to you that you are bound to see him again when he asks it." At first she was very stout, declaring that she would not see him. Of what good could it be, seeing that she would rather throw herself into the Thames than marry him? Had she not told him so over and over again, as often as he had spoken to her? Why would he not just leave her alone? But against all this her uncle pleaded gently but persistently. He had considered himself bound to promise so much on her behalf, and for his sake she must do as he asked. To this, of course, she yielded. And then he said many good things of poor Tom. His constancy was a great virtue. A man so thoroughly in love would no doubt make a good husband. And then there would be the assent of all the family, and an end, as far as Ayala was concerned, of all pecuniary trouble. In answer to this she only shook her head, promising, however, that she would be ready to give Tom an audience when he should be brought to the Crescent on the following day.

Punctually at four Tom made his appearance at Somerset House, and started with his uncle as soon as the index-books had been put in their places. Tom was very anxious to take his uncle home in a cab, but Mr. Dosett would not consent to lose his walk. Along the Embankmont they went, and across Charing Cross into St. James's Park, and then by Green Park, Hyde Park, and Kensington Gardens, all the way to Notting Hill. Mr. Dosett did not walk very fast, and Tom thought they would never reach Kingsbury Crescent. His uncle would fain have talked about the weather, or politics, or the hardships of the Civil Service generally; but Tom would not be diverted from his one subject. Would Ayala be gracious to him? Mr. Dosett had made up his mind to say nothing on the subject. Tom must plead his own cause. Uncle Reginald thought that he knew such pleading would be useless, but still would not say a word to daunt the lover. Neither could he say a word expressive of hope. As they were fully an hour-and-a-half on their walk, this reticence was difficult.

Immediately on his arrival, Tom was taken up into the drawing-room. This was empty, for it had been arranged that Mrs. Dosett should be absent till the meeting was over. " Now I'll look for this child," said Uncle Reginald, in his cheeriest voice as he left Tom alone in the room. Tom, as he looked round at the chairs and tables, remembered that he had never received as much as a kind word or look in the room, and then great drops of perspiration broke out all over his brow. All that he had to hope for in the world must depend upon the next five minutes,—might depend perhaps upon the very selection of the words which he might use.

Then Ayala entered the room and stood before him.

"Ayala," he said, giving her his hand.

"Uncle Reg. says that you would like to see me once again."

"Of course I want to see you once, and twice,—and always. Ayala, if you could know it! If you could only know it!" Then he clasped his two hands high upon his breast, not as though appealing to her heart, but striking his bosom in very agony. "Ayala, I feel that, if I do not have you as my own, I can only die for the want of you. Ayala, do you believe me?"

"I suppose I believe you, but how can I help it?"

"Try to help it! Try to try and help it! Say a word that you will perhaps help it by-and-bye." Then there came a dark frown upon her brow,—not, indeed, from anger, but from a feeling that so terrible a task should be thrown upon her. "I know you think that I am common."

"I have never said a word, Tom, but that I could not love you."

"But I am true,—true as the sun. Would I come again after all if it were not that I cannot help coming? You have heard that I have been,—been misbehaving myself?"

"I have not thought about that.'

"It has been so because I have been so wretched. Ayala, you have made me so unhappy. Ayala, you can make me the happiest man there is in London this day. I seem to want nothing else. As for drink, or clubs, or billiards, and all that, they are nothing to me,—unless when I try to forget that you are so—so unkind to me!"

"It is not unkind, not to do as you ask me."

"To do as I ask you,—that would be kind. Oh, Ayala, cannot you be kind to me." She shook her head, still standing in the place which she had occupied from the beginning. "May I come again? Will you give me three months, and then think of it? If you would only say that, I would go back to my work and never leave it." But she still shook her head. "Must I never hope?"

"Not for that, Tom. How can I help it?"

"Not help it!"

"No. How can I help it? One does not fall in love by trying,—nor by trying prevent it."

"By degrees you might love me,—a little." She had said all that she knew how to say, and again shook her head. "It is that accursed Colonel," he exclaimed, forgetting himself as he thought of his rival.

"He is not accursed," said Ayala, angrily.

"Then you love him?"

"No! But you should not ask. You have no right to ask. It is not proper."

"You are not engaged to him?"

"No ; I am not engaged to him. I do not love him. As you will ask, I tell you. But you should not ask; and he is not accursed. He is better than you,—though I do not love him. You should not have driven me to say this. I do not ask you questions."

"There is none that I would not answer. Stay, Ayala," for now she was going to leave the room. "Stay yet a moment. Do you know that you are tearing my heart in pieces? Why is it that you should make me so wretched? Dear Ayala;—dearest Ayala;—stay yet a moment."

"Tom, there is nothing more that I can say. I am very, very sorry if you are unhappy. I do think that you are good and true ; and, if you will shake hands with me, there is my hand. But I cannot say what you want me to say." Tom took her by the hand and tried to hold her, without, however, speaking to her again. But she slid away from him and left the room, not having for a moment sat down in his presence.

When the door was closed he stood a while looking round him, trying to resolve what he might do or what he might say next. He was now at any rate in the house with her, and did not know whether such an opportunity as that might ever occur to him again. He felt that there were words within his bosom which, if he could only bring them up to his mouth, would melt the heart of a stone. There was his ineffable love, his whole happiness at stake, his purpose,—his holy purpose, —to devote himself, and all that he had, to her well-being. Of all this he had a full conception within his own heart, if only he could express it so that others should believe him ! But of what use was it now? He had had this further liberty of speech accorded to him, and in it he had done nothing, made no inch of progress. She had hardly spoken a dozen words to him, but of those she had spoken two remained clear upon his memory. He must never hope, she had said ; and she had said also that that other man was better than he. Had she said that he was dearer, the word would hardly have been more bitter. All the old feeling came upon him of rage against his rival, and of a desire that something desperate should be done by which he might wreak his vengeance.

But there he was standing alone in Mrs. Dosett's drawing-room, and it was necessary that he should carry himself off. As for dining in that house, sitting down to eat and drink in Ayala's presence after such a conversation as that which was past, that he felt to be quite out of the question. He crammed his hat upon his head, left the room, and hurried down the stairs towards the door. In the passage he was met by his uncle, coming out of the dining-room. "Tom," he said, "you'll stay and eat your dinner?"

" No, indeed," said Tom, angrily.

" You shouldn't let yourself be disturbed by little trifles such as these," said his uncle, trying to put a good face upon the matter.

" Trifles !" said Tom Tringle. " Trifles !" And he banged the door after him as he left the house.

CHAPTER XLIV.

IN THE HAYMARKET.

It was now the beginning of February. As Tom and his uncle had walked from Somerset House the streets were dry and the weather fine ; but, as Mr. Dosett had remarked, the wind was changing a little out of the east and threatened rain. When Tom left the house it was already falling. It was then past six, and the night was very dark. He had walked there with a top coat and umbrella, but he had forgotten both as he banged the door after him in his passion ; and, though he remembered them as he hurried down the steps, he would not turn and knock at the door and ask for them. He was in that humour which converts outward bodily sufferings almost into a relief. When a man has been thoroughly illused in greater matters it is almost a consolation to him to feel that he has been turned out into the street to get wet through without his dinner,—even though he may have turned himself out.

He walked on foot, and as he walked became damp and dirty, till he was soon wet through. As soon as he reached Lancaster Gate he went into the park, and under the doubtful glimmer of the lamps trudged on through the mud and slush, not regarding his path, hardly thinking of the present moment in the full appreciation of his real misery. What should he do with himself ? What else was there now left to him ? He had tried everything and had failed. As he endeavoured to count himself up, as it were, and tell himself whether he were worthy of a happier fate than had been awarded to him, he was very humble,—humble, though so indignant ! He knew himself to be a poor creature in comparison with Jonathan Stubbs. Though he could not have been Stubbs had he given his heart for it, though it was absolutely beyond him to assume one of those tricks of bearing, one of those manly, winning ways, which in his eyes was so excellent in the other man, still he saw them and acknowledged them, and told himself that they would be all powerful with such a girl as Ayala. Though he trusted to his charms and his rings, he knew that his charms and his rings were abominable, as compared with that outside look an natural garniture which belonged to Stubbs, as though of right,—as though it had been born with him. Not exactly in those words, but with a full inward sense of the words, he told himself that Colonel Stubbs was a gentleman,—whereas he acknowledged himself to be a cad. How could he have hoped that Ayala should accept such a one, merely because he would have a good house of his own and a carriage? As he thought of all this, he hardly knew which he hated most,—himself or Jonathan Stubbs.

He went down to the family house in Queen's Gate, which was closed and dark,—having come there with no special purpose, but having found himself there, as though by accident, in the neighbourhood. Then he knocked at the door, which, after a great undoing of chains, was opened by an old woman, who with her son had the custody of the house when the family were out of town. Sir Thomas in these days had rooms of his own in Lombard Street in which he loved to dwell, and would dine at a city club, never leaving the precincts of the city throughout the week. The old woman was an old servant, and her son was a porter at the office. "Mr. Tom! Be that you? Why you are as wet as a mop!" He was wet as any mop, and much dirtier than a mop should be. There was no fire except in the kitchen, and there he was taken. He asked for a great coat, but there was no such thing in the house, as the young man had not yet come home. Nor was there any food that could be offered him, or anything to drink; as the cellar was locked up, and the old woman was on board wages. But he sat crouching over the fire, watching the steam as it came up from his damp boots and trousers. "And ain't you had no dinner, Mr. Tom?" said the old woman. Tom only shook his head. "And ain't you going to have none?" The poor wretch again shook his head. "That's bad, Mr. Tom." Then she looked up into his face. "There is something wrong I know, Mr. Tom. I hears that from Jem. Of course he hears what they do be saying in Lombard Street."

"What is it they say, Mrs. Tapp?"

"Well;—that you ain't there as you used to be. Things is awk'ard, and Sir Thomas, they say, isn't best pleased. But of course it isn't no affair of mine, Mr. Tom."

"Do they know why?" he asked.

"They do say it's some'at about a young lady."

"Yes; by heavens!" said Tom, jumping up out of his chair. "Oh, Mrs. Tapp, you can't tell the condition I'm in. A young lady indeed! D—— the fellow!"

"Don't 'ee now, Mr. Tom."

"D—— the fellow! But there's no good in my standing here cursing. I'll go off again. You needn't say that I've been here, Mrs. Tapp?"

"But you won't go out into the rain, Mr. Tom ?"

"Rain,—what matters the rain ?" Then he started again, disregard-ing all her prayers, and went off eastward on foot, disdaining the use of a cab because he had settled in his mind on no place to which he would go.

Yes ; they knew all about it, down to the very porters at the office. Everyone had heard of his love for Ayala ; and everyone had heard also that Ayala had scorned him. Not a man or woman connected by ever so slight a tie to the establishment was unaware that he had been sent away from his seat because of Ayala ! All this might have been borne easily had there been any hope ; but now he was forced to tell himself that there was none. He saw no end to his misery,—no possi-bility of escape. Where was he to go in this moment of his misery for any shred of comfort ? The solitude of his lodgings was dreadful to him ; nor had he heart enough left to him to seek companionship at his club.

At about ten o'clock he found himself, as it were, by accident, close to Mr. Bolivia's establishment. He was thoroughly wet through, jaded, wretched, and in want of sustenance. He turned in, and found the place deserted. The diners had gone away, and the hour had not come at which men in quest of later refreshment were wont to make their appearance. But there were still one or two gas-lights burning ; and he threw himself wearily into a little box or partition nearest to the fire. Here Signor Bolivia himself came to him, asking in com-miserating accents what had brought him thither in so wretched a plight. "I have left my coat and umbrella behind," said Tom, trying to pluck up a little spirit,—"and my dinner too."

"No dinner, Mr. Tringle ;—and you wet through like that ! What shall I get you, Mr. Tringle ?" But Tom declared that he would have no dinner. He was off his appetite altogether, he said. He would have a bottle of champagne and a devilled biscuit. Mr. Walker, who, as we are aware, put himself forward to the world generally as Signor Bolivia, felt for the moment a throb of pity, which overcame in his heart the innkeeper's natural desire to make the most he could of his customer. "Better have a mutton chop and a little drop of brandy and-water hot."

"I ain't up to it, Bolivia," said the young man. "I couldn't swallow it if I had it. Give us the bottle of champagne and the devilled biscuit." Then Mr. Walker,—for Bolivia was in truth Walker,—fetched the wine and ordered the biscuit ; and poor Tom was again brought back to the miserable remedy to which he had before applied himself in his misfortune. There he remained for about an hour, during a part of which he slept ; but before he left the house he

finished the wine. As he got up to take his departure Mr. Walker
scanned his gait and bearing, having a friendly feeling for the young
man, and not wishing him to fall again into the hands of the police.
But Tom walked forth apparently as sober as a judge, and as melancholy as a hangman. As far as Mr. Walker could see the liquor had
made no impression on him. "If I were you, Mr. Tringle," said the
keeper of the eating-house, "I'd go home at once, because you are so
mortal wet."

"All right," said Tom, going out into the pouring rain.

It was then something after eleven, and Tom instead of taking the
friendly advice which had been offered to him, walked, as fast as he
could, round Leicester Square ; and as he walked the fumes of the wine
mounted into his head. But he was not drunk,—not as yet so drunk
as to misbehave himself openly. He did not make his way round the
square without being addressed, but he simply shook off from him
those who spoke to him. His mind was still intent upon Ayala. But
now he was revengeful rather than despondent. The liquor had filled
him once again with a desire to do something. If he could destroy
himself and the Colonel by one and the same blow, how fitting a
punishment would that be for Ayala ! But how was he to do it? He
would throw himself down from the top of the Duke of York's column,
but that would be nothing unless he could force the Colonel to take
the jump with him ! He had called the man out and he wouldn't
come ! Now, with the alcohol in his brain, he again thought that the
man was a coward for not coming. Had not such a meeting been from
time immemorial the resource of gentlemen injured as he now was
injured ? The Colonel would not come when called,—but could he not
get at him so as to strike him ? If he could do the man a real injury
he would not care what amount of punishment he might be called upon
to bear.

He hurried at last out of the square into Coventry Street and down
the Haymarket. His lodgings were in Duke Street, turning out of
Piccadilly,—but he could not bring himself to go home to his bed.
He was unutterably wretched, but yet he kept himself going with some
idea of doing something, or of fixing some purpose. He certainly was
tipsy now, but not so drunk as to be unable to keep himself on his
legs. He gloried in the wet, shouting inwardly to himself that he in
his misery was superior to all accidents of the weather. Then he stood
for awhile watching the people as they came out of the Haymarket
Theatre. He was at this time a sorry sight to be seen. His hat was
jammed on to his head and had been almost smashed in the jamming.
His coat reeking wet through was fastened by one button across his
chest. His two hands were thrust into his pockets, and the bottle of

champagne was visible in his face. He was such a one,—to look at,—that no woman would have liked to touch or any man to address. In this guise he stood there amidst the crowd, foremost among those who were watching the ladies as they got into their vehicles. "And she might be as good as the best of them, and I might be here to hand her into her own carriage,"—said he to himself,—"if it were not for that intruder!"

At that moment the intruder was there before him, and on his arm was a lady whom he was taking across to a carriage, at the door of which a servant in livery was standing. They were followed closely by a pretty young girl who was picking her steps after them alone. These were Lady Albury and Nina, whom Colonel Stubbs had escorted to the play.

"You will be down by the twentieth?" said the elder lady.

"Punctual as the day comes," said the Colonel.

"And mind you have Ayala with you," said the younger.

"If Lady Albury can manage it with her aunt of course I will wait upon her," said the Colonel. Then the door of the carriage was shut, and the Colonel was left to look for a cab. He had on an overcoat and an opera hat, but otherwise was dressed as for dinner. On one side a link-boy was offering him assistance, and on another a policeman tendering him some service. He was one of those who by their outward appearance always extort respect from those around them.

As long as the ladies had been there,—during the two minutes which had been occupied while they got into the carriage,—Tom had been restrained by their presence. He had been restrained by their presence even though he had heard Ayala's name and had understood the commission given to the man whom he hated. Had Colonel Stubbs luckily followed the ladies into the carriage Tom, in his fury, would have taken himself off to his bed. But now,—there was his enemy within a yard of him! Here was the opportunity the lack of which seemed, a few moments since, to be so grievous to him! He took two steps out from the row in which he stood and struck his rival high on his breast with his fist. He had aimed at the Colonel's face but in his eagerness had missed his mark. "There," said he, "there! You would not fight me, and now you have got it." Stubbs staggered, and would have fallen but for the policeman. Tom, though no hero, was a strong young man and had contrived to give his blow with all his force. The Colonel did not at first see from whom the outrage had come, but at once claimed the policeman's help.

"We've got him, Sir;—we've got him," said the policeman.

"You've got me," said Tom, "but I've had my revenge." Then, though two policemen and one waterman were now holding him, he stretched himself up to his full height and glared at his enemy in the face.

"It's the chap who gave that hawful blow to Thompson in the bow'ls!" said one of the policemen, who by this time had both Tom's arms locked behind his own.

Then the Colonel knew who had struck him. "I know him," said the Colonel to the policeman. "It is a matter of no consequence."

"So do we, Sir. He's Thomas Tringle, junior."

"He's a friend of mine;" said the Colonel. "You must let him come with me."

"A friend, is he?" said an amateur attendant. The policeman, who had remembered the cruel onslaught made on his comrade, looked very grave, and still held Tom tight by the arms. "A very hugly sort of friend," said the amateur. Tom only stretched himself still higher, but remained speechless.

"Tringle," said the Colonel, "this was very foolish, you know,—a most absurd thing to do! Come with me, and we will talk it all over."

"He must come along with us to the watch-house just at present," said the policeman. "And you, Sir, if you can, had better please to come with us. It ain't far across to Vine Street, but of course you can have a cab if you like it." This was ended by two policemen walking off with Tom between them, and by the Colonel following in a cab, after having administered divers shillings to the amateur attendants. Though the journey in the cab did not occupy above five minutes, it sufficed to enable him to determine what step he should take when he found himself before the night officers of the watch.

When he found himself in the presence of the night officer he had considerable difficulty in carrying out his purpose. That Tom should be locked up for the night, and be brought before the police magistrate next morning to answer for the outrage he had committed, seemed to the officers to be a matter of course. It was long before the Colonel could persuade the officer that this little matter between him and Mr. Tringle was a private affair, of which he at least wished to take no further notice. "No doubt," he said, "he had received a blow on his chest, but it had not hurt him in the least."

"'E 'it the gen'leman with all his might and main," said the policeman."

"It is quite a private affair," said the Colonel. "My name is Colonel Stubbs; here is my card. Sir ———— ———— is a particular friend of mine." Here he named a pundit of the peace, very high in the estimation of all policemen. "If you will let the gentleman come away with me I will be responsible for him to-morrow, if it should be necessary to take any further step in the matter." This he said very eagerly, and with all the authority which he knew how to use. Tom, in the meantime, stood perfectly motionless, with his arms folded akimbo on his breast, wet through, muddy, still tipsy, a sight miserable to behold.

The card and the Colonel's own name, and the name of the pundit of the peace together, had their effect, and after a while Tom was dismissed in the Colonel's care. The conclusion of the evening's affair was, for the moment, one which Tom found very hard to bear. It would have been better for him to have been dragged off to a cell, and there to have been left to his miserable solitude. But as he went down through the narrow ways leading from the police-office out into the main street he felt that he was altogether debarred from making any further attack upon his protector. He could not strike him again, as he might have done had he escaped from the police by his own resources. His own enemy had saved him from durance, and he could not, therefore, turn again upon his enemy.

" In heaven's name, my dear fellow," said the Colonel, " what good do you expect to get by that ? You have hit me a blow when you knew that I was unprepared, and, therefore, unarmed. Was that manly ?" To this Tom made no reply. " I suppose you have been drinking ?" And Stubbs, as he asked this question, looked into his companion's face. " I see you have been drinking. What a fool you are making of yourself !"

" It is that girl," said Tom.

" Does that seem to you to be right ? Can you do yourself any good by that ? Will she be more likely to listen to you when she hears that you have got drunk, and have assaulted me in the street ? Have I done you any harm ?"

" She says that you are better than me," replied Tom.

" If she does, is that my doing ? Come, old fellow, try to be a man. Try to think of this thing rightly. If you can win the girl you love, win her ; but, if you cannot, do not be such an ass as to suppose that she is to love no one because she will not love you. It is a thing which a man must bear if it comes in his way. As far as Miss Dormer is concerned, I am in the same condition as you. But do you think that I should attack you in the street if she began to favour you to-morrow?"

" I wish she would ;—and then I shouldn't care what you did."

" I should think you a happy fellow, certainly ; and for a time I might avoid you, because your happiness would remind me of my own disappointment ; but I should not come behind your back and strike you ! Now, tell me where you live, and I will see you home." Then Tom told him where he lived, and in a few minutes the Colonel had left him within his own hall door.

CHAPTER XLV.

THERE IS SOMETHING OF THE ANGEL ABOUT HIM.

THE little accident which was recorded at the close of the last chapter occurred on a Tuesday night. On the following afternoon Tom Tringle, again very much out of spirits, returned to Merle Park. There was now nothing further for him to do in London. He had had his last chance with Ayala, and the last chance had certainly done him no good. Fortune, whether kindly or unkindly, had given him an opportunity of revenging himself upon the Colonel; he had taken advantage of the opportunity, but did not find himself much relieved by what he had done. His rival's conduct had caused him to be thoroughly ashamed of himself. It had at any rate taken from him all further hope of revenge. So that now there was nothing for him but to take himself back to Merle Park. On the Wednesday he heard nothing further of the matter; but on the Thursday Sir Thomas came down from London, and, showing to poor Tom a paragraph in one of the morning papers, asked whether he knew anything of the circumstance to which reference was made. The paragraph was as follows:—

"That very bellicose young City knight who at Christmas time got into trouble by thrashing a policeman within an inch of his life in the streets, and who was then incarcerated on account of his performance, again exhibited his prowess on Tuesday night by attacking Colonel ————, an officer than whom none in the army is more popular,—under the portico of the Haymarket theatre. We abstain from mentioning the officer's name,—which is, however, known to us. The City knight again fell into the hands of the police and was taken to the watch-house. But Colonel ————, who knew something of his family, accompanied him, and begged his assailant off. The officer on duty was most unwilling to let the culprit go; but the Colonel used all his influence and was successful. This may be all very well between the generous Colonel and the valiant knight. But if the young man has any friends they had better look to him. A gentleman with such a desire for the glories of battle must be restrained if he cannot control his propensities when wandering about the streets of the metropolis."

"Yes," said Tom,—who scorned to tell a lie in any matter concerning Ayala. "It was me. I struck Colonel Stubbs, and he got me off at the police office."

"And you're proud of what you've done?"

"No, Sir, I'm not. I'm not proud of anything. Whatever I do or whatever I say seems to go against me."

" He didn't go against you as you call it."

" I wish he had with all my heart.   I didn't ask him to get me off. I struck him because I hated him ; and whatever might have happened I would sooner have borne it than be like this."

" You would sooner have been locked up again in prison ?"

" I would sooner anything than be as I am."

" I tell you what it is, Tom," said the father.   " If you remain here any longer with this bee in your bonnet you will be locked up in a lunatic asylum, and I shall not be able to get you out again.   You must go abroad."   To this Tom made no immediate answer.   Lamentable as was his position, he still was unwilling to leave London while Ayala was living there.   Were he to consent to go away for any lengthened period, by doing so he would seem to abandon his own claim.   Hope he knew there was none ; but yet, even yet, he regarded himself as one of Ayala's suitors.   " Do you think it well," continued the father, " that you should remain in London while such paragraphs as these are being written about you ?"

" I am not in London now," said Tom.

" No, you are not in London while you are at Merle Park,—of course.   And you will not go up to London without my leave.   Do you understand that ?"   Here Tom again was silent.   " If you do," continued his father, " you shall not be received down here again, nor at Queen's Gate, nor will the cheques for your allowance be honoured any longer at the bank.   In fact if you do not obey me I will throw you off altogether.   This absurdity about your love has been carried on long enough."   And so it came to be understood in the family that Tom was to be kept in mild durance at Merle Park till everything should have been arranged for his extended tour about the world.   To this Tom himself gave no positive assent, but it was understood that when the time came he would yield to his father's commands.

It had thus come to pass that the affray at the door of the Haymarket became known to so much of the world at large as interested itself in the affairs either of Colonel Stubbs or of the Tringles.   Other paragraphs were written in which the two heroes of the evening were designated as Colonel J———— S——— and as T——— T———, junior, of the firm of T——— and T———, in the City.   All who pleased could read these initials, and thus the world was aware that our Colonel had received a blow, and had resented the affront only by rescuing his assailant from the hands of the police.   A word was said at first which seemed to imply that the Colonel had not exhibited all the spirit which might have been expected from him.   Having been struck should he not have thrashed the man who struck him ;—or at any rate have left the ruffian in the hands of the policemen for proper punishment ? But many days had not passed over before the Colonel's conduct had been viewed in a different light, and men and women were declaring that he had done a manly and a gallant thing. The affair had in this way become sufficiently well known to justify the allusion made to it in the following letter from Lady Albury to Ayala ;—

"Stalham, Tuesday, 11th February, 18—.

"MY DEAR AYALA,

"It is quite indispensable for the happiness of everybody, particularly that of myself and Sir Harry, that you should come down here on the twentieth. Nina will be here on her farewell visit before her return to her mother. Of course you have heard that it is all arranged between her and Lord George Bideford, and this will be the last opportunity which any of us will have of seeing her once again before her martyrdom. The world is to be told that he is to follow her to Rome, where they are to be married,—no doubt by the Pope himself under the dome of St. Peter's. But my belief is that Lord George is going to travel with her all the way. If he is the man I take him to be he will do so, but of course it would be very improper.

"You, however, must of course come and say pretty things to your friend ; and, as you cannot go to Rome to see her married, you must throw your old shoe after her when she takes her departure from Stalham. I have written a line to your aunt to press my request for this visit. This she will no doubt show to you, and you, if you please, can show her mine in return.

"And now, my dear, I must explain to you one or two other arrangements. A certain gentleman will *certainly* not be here. It was not my fault that a certain gentleman went to Kingsbury Crescent. The certain gentleman is, as you are aware, a great friend of ours, and was entitled to explain himself if it so seemed good to him ; but the certain gentleman was not favoured in that enterprise by the Stalham interest. At any rate, the certain gentleman will not be at Stalham on this occasion. So much for the certain gentleman.

"Colonel Stubbs will be here, and, as he will be coming down on the twentieth, would be glad to travel by the same train, so that he may look after your ticket and your luggage, and be your slave for the occasion. He will leave the Paddington Station by the 4 P.M. train if that will suit you.

"We all think that he behaved beautifully in that little affair at the Haymarket theatre. I should not mention it only that everybody has heard of it. Almost any other man would have struck the poor fellow again ; but he is one of the very few who always know what to do at the moment without taking time to think of it.

"Mind you come like a good girl.—Your affectionate friend,

"ROSALINE ALBURY."

It was in this way that Ayala heard what had taken place between her cousin Tom and Colonel Stubbs. Some hint of a fracas between the two men had reached her ears ; but now she asked various questions of her aunt, and at last elicited the truth. Tom had attacked her other lover in the street,—had attacked Colonel Stubbs because of his injured love, and had grossly misbehaved himself. As a consequence he would have been locked up by the police had not the Colonel himself interfered on his behalf. This to Ayala seemed to be conduct worthy almost of an Angel of Light.

Then the question of the proposed visit was discussed,—first with her aunt, and then with herself. Mrs. Dosett was quite willing that her niece should go to Stalham. To Mrs. Dosett's thinking, a further journey to Stalham would mean an engagement with Colonel Stubbs. When she had read Lady Albury's letter she was quite sure that that had been Lady Albury's meaning. Captain Batsby was not to receive the Stalham interest ;—but that interest was to be used on the part of Colonel Stubbs. She had not the slightest objection. It was clear to her that Ayala would have to be married before long. It was out of the question that one man after another should fall in love with her violently, and that nothing should come of it. Mrs. Dosett had become quite despondent about Tom. There was an amount of dislike which it would be impossible to overcome. And as for Captain Batsby there could be no chance for a man whom the young lady could not be induced even to see. But the other lover, whom the lady would not admit that she loved,—as to whom she had declared that she could never love him,—was held in very high favour. "I do think it was so noble not to hit Tom again," she had said. Therefore, as Colonel Stubbs had a sufficient income, there could be no reason why Ayala should not go again to Stalham. So it was that Mrs. Dosett argued with herself, and such was the judgment which she expressed to Ayala.

But there were difficulties. Ayala's little stock of cash was all gone. She could not go to Stalham without money, and that money must come out of her Uncle Reginald's pocket. She could not go to Stalham without some expenditure, which, as she well knew, it would be hard for him to bear. And then there was that terrible question of her clothes ! When that suggestion had been made of a further transfer of the nieces a cheque had come from Sir Thomas. "If Ayala comes to us she will want a few things," Sir Thomas had said in a note to Mrs. Dosett. But Mr. Dosett had chosen that the cheque should be sent back when it was decided that the further transfer should not take place. The cheque had been sent back, and there had been an end of it. There must be a morning dress, and there must be another hat, and there must be boots. So much Mrs. Dosett acknowledged.

Let them do what they might with the old things, Mrs. Dosett acknowledged that so much as that would at least be necessary. "We will both go to work," Mrs. Dosett said, "and we will ask your uncle what he can do for us." I think she felt that she had received some recompense when Ayala kissed her.

It was after this that Ayala discussed the matter with herself. She had longed to go once again to Stalham,—"dear Stalham," as she called it to herself. And as she thought of the place she told herself that she loved it because Lady Albury had been so kind to her, and because of Nina, and because of the hunting, and because of the general pleasantness and luxury of the big comfortable house. And yes ;—there was something to be said, too, of the pleasantness of Colonel Stubbs. Till he had made love to her he had been, perhaps, of all these fine new friends the pleasantest. How joyous his voice had sounded to her ! How fraught with gratification to her had been his bright ugly face ! How well he had known how to talk to her, and to make her talk, so that everything had been easy with her ! How thoroughly she remembered all his drollery on that first night at the party in London,—and all his keen sayings at the theatre ;—and the way he had insisted that she should hunt ! She thought of little confidences she had had with him, almost as though he had been her brother ! And then he had destroyed it all by becoming her lover !

Was he to be her lover still ;—and if so would it be right that she should go again to Stalham, knowing that she would meet him there ? Would it be right that she should consent to travel with him,—under his special escort ? Were she to do so would she not be forced to do more,—if he should again ask her ? It was so probable that he would not ask her again ! It was so strange that such a one should have asked her !

But if he did ask her ? Certainly he was not like that Angel of Light whom she had never seen, but of whom the picture in her imagination was as clearly drawn as though she were in his presence daily. No ;— there was a wave of hair and a shape of brow, and a peculiarity of the eye, with a nose and mouth cut as sharp as chisel could cut them out of marble, all of which graced the Angel but none of which belonged to the Colonel. Nor were these the chief of the graces which made the Angel so glorious to her. There was a depth of poetry about him, deep and clear, pellucid as a lake among grassy banks, which make all things of the world mean when compared to it. The Angel of Light lived on the essence of all that was beautiful, altogether unalloyed by the grossness of the earth. That such a one should come in her way ! Oh, no ; she did not look for it ! But, having formed

such an image of an angel for herself, would it be possible that she
should have anything less divine, less beautiful, less angelic?

Yes;—there was something of the Angel about him;—even about
him, Colonel Jonathan Stubbs.   But he was so clearly an Angel of the
earth, whereas the other one, though living upon the earth, would be
of the air, and of the sky, of the clouds, and of the heaven, celestial.
Such a one she knew she had never seen.   She partly dreamed that she
was dreaming.   But if so had not her dream spoilt her for all else?
Oh, yes; indeed he was good, this red-haired ugly Stubbs.   How well
had he behaved to Tom!   How kind he had been to herself!   How
thoughtful of her he was!   If it were not a question of downright love,
—of giving herself up to him, body and soul, as it were,—how pleasant
would it be to dwell with him!   For herself she would confess that she
loved earthly things,—such as jumping over the brook with Larry
Twentyman before her to show her the way.   But for her love, it was
necessary that there should be an Angel of Light.   Had she not read
that angels had come from heaven and taken in marriage the daughters
of men?

But was it right that she should go to Stalham, seeing that there
were two such strong reasons against it?   She could not go without
costing her uncle money, which he could ill afford; and if she did go
would she—would she not confess that she had abandoned her objection to the Colonel's suit.   She, too, understood something of that
which had made itself so plain to her aunt.   "Your uncle thinks it
is right that you should go," her aunt said to her in the drawing-
room that evening; "and we will set to work to-morrow and do the
best that we can to make you smart."

Her uncle was sitting in the room at the time, and Ayala felt herself compelled to go to him and kiss him, and thank him for all his
kindness.   "I am so sorry to cost you so much money, Uncle Reginald,"
she said.

"It will not be very much, my dear," he answered.   "It is hard
that young people should not have some amusement.   I only hope they
will make you happy at Stalham."

"They always make people happy at Stalham," said Ayala, energetically.

"And now, Ayala," said her aunt, "you can write your letter to
Lady Albury before we go out to-morrow.   Give her my compliments,
and tell her that as you are writing I need not trouble her."

Ayala, when she was alone in her bedroom, felt almost horrified as
she reflected that in this manner the question had been settled for her.
It had been impossible for her to reject her uncle's liberal offer when
it had been made.   She could not find the courage at that moment to

say that she had thought better of it all, and would decline the visit. Before she was well aware of what she was doing she had assented, and had thus, as it were, thrown over all the creations of her dream. And yet, as she declared herself, not even Lady Albury could make her marry this man, merely because she was at her house. She thought that, if she could only avoid that first journey with Colonel Stubbs in the railway, still she might hold her own. But, were she to travel with him of her own accord, would it not be felt that she would be wilfully throwing herself in his way? Then she made a little plan for herself, which she attempted to carry out when writing her letter to Lady Albury on the following morning. What was the nature of her plan, and how she effected it, will be seen in the letter which she wrote;—

"Kingsbury Crescent, Thursday.

"DEAR LADY ALBURY,

"It is so very good of you to ask me again, and I shall be so happy to visit Stalham once more! I should have been very sorry not to see dear Nina before her return to Italy. I have written to congratulate her of course, and have told her what a happy girl I think she is. Though I have not seen Lord George I take all that from her description. As she is going to be his wife immediately, I don't at all see why he should not go back with her to Rome. As for being married by the Pope, I don't think he ever does anything so useful as that. I believe he sits all day and has his toe kissed. That is what they told me at Rome.

"I am very glad of what you tell me about the certain gentleman, because I don't think I could have been happy at Stalham if he had been there. It surprised me so much that I could not think that he meant it in earnest. We never hardly spoke to each other when we were in the house together.

"Perhaps, if you don't mind, and I shan't be in the way,"—here she began to display the little plan which she had made for her own protection,—"I will come down by an earlier train than you mention. There is one at 2·15, and then I need not be in the dark all the way. You need not say anything about this to Colonel Stubbs, because I do not at all mind travelling by myself.—Yours affectionately,

"AYALA."

This was her little plan. But she was very innocent when she thought that Lady Albury would be blind to such a scheme as that. She got three words from Lady Albury, saying that the 2·15 train would do very well. and that the carriage would be at the station to meet her. Lady Albury did not also say in her note that she had communicated with Colonel Stubbs on the subject, and informed him that he must come up from Aldershot earlier than he intended in order that he might adapt himself to Ayala's whims. "Foolish little child," said Lady Albury to herself ! "As if that would make any difference !" It was clear to Lady Albury that Ayala must surrender now that she was coming to Stalham a second time, knowing that the Colonel would be there.

CHAPTER XLVI.

AYALA GOES AGAIN TO STALHAM.

THE correspondence between Lady Albury and Colonel Stubbs was close and frequent, the friendship between them being very close. Ayala had sometimes asked herself why Lady Albury should have been so kind and affectionate to her, and had failed to find any sufficient answer. She had been asked to Stalham at first,—so far as she knew,—because she had been intimate at Rome with the Marchesa Baldoni. Hence had apparently risen Lady Albury's great friendship, which had seemed even to herself to be strange. But in truth the Marchesa had had very little to do with it,—nor had Lady Albury become attached to Ayala for Ayala's own sake. To Lady Albury Colonel Stubbs was,—as she declared to herself very often,—"her own real brother." She had married a man very rich, well known in the world, whom she loved very well ; and she was not a woman who in such a position would allow herself to love another man. That there might certainly be no danger of this kind she was continually impressing on her friend the expediency of marriage,—if only he could find some one good enough to marry. Then the Colonel had found Ayala. Lady Albury at the beginning of all this was not inclined to think that Ayala was good enough. Judging at first from what she heard and then from what she saw, she had not been very favourable to Ayala. But when her friend had insisted,—had declared that his happiness depended on it,—had shown by various signs that he certainly would carry out his intentions, if not at Stalham then elsewhere, Lady Albury had yielded herself to him, and had become Ayala's great friend. If it was written in the book that Ayala was to become Mrs. Stubbs then it would certainly be necessary that she and Ayala should be friends. And she herself had such confidence in Jonathan Stubbs as a man of power, that she did not doubt of his success in any matter to which he might choose to devote himself. The wonder had been that Ayala should have rejected the chance when it had come in her way. The girl had been foolish, allowing herself to be influenced by the man's red hair and ill-sounding name,—not knowing a real pearl when she saw it. So Lady Albury had thought,—having only been partially right in so thinking,—not having gone to the depth of Ayala's power of dreaming. She was very confident, however, that the girl, when once again at Stalham, would yield herself easily ; and therefore she went to work, doing all that she could to smoothen love's road for her friend Jonathan. Her woman's mind had seen all those difficulties about clothes, and would have sent what was needful herself had she not feared to offend both the Dosetts and Ayala. Therefore she prepared a present which she could give to the girl at Stalham without offence. If it was to be the girl's high fate to become Mrs. Jonathan Stubbs, it would be proper that she should be adorned and decked, and made beautiful among others of her class,—as would become the wife of such a hero.

Of all that passed between her and Ayala word was sent down to Aldershot. " The stupid little wretch will throw you out, I know," wrote Lady Albury, " by making you start two hours before you have done your work. But you must let your work do itself for this occasion. There is nothing like a little journey together to make people understand each other."

The Colonel was clearly determined to have the little journey together. Whatever might be the present military duties at Aldershot, the duties of love were for the nonce in the Colonel's mind more imperative. Though His Royal Highness had been coming that afternoon to inspect all the troops, still he would have resolved so to have arranged matters as to travel down with Ayala to Stalham. But not only was he determined to do this, but he found it necessary also to arrange a previous meeting with Lady Albury before that important twentieth of the month. This he did by making his friend believe that her presence in London for a few hours would be necessary for various reasons. She came up as he desired, and there he met her at her hotel in Jermyn Street. On his arrival here he felt that he was almost making a fool of himself by the extent of his anxiety. In his nervousness about this little girl he was almost as insane as poor Tom Tringle, who, when she despised his love, was. altogether unable to control himself. " If I cannot persuade her at last, I shall be knocking somebody over the head, as he did." It was thus he was talking to himself as he got out of the cab at the door of the hotel.

" And now, Jonathan," said Lady Albury, " what can there possibly be to justify you in giving me all this trouble ?"

" You know you had to come up about that cook's character."

" I know that I have given that as a reason to Sir Harry; but I know also that I should have gone without a cook for a twelvemonth had you not summoned me."

" The truth is I could not get down to Stalham and back without losing an additional day, which I cannot possibly spare.   With you it does not very much matter how many days you spare."

" Nor how much money I spend, nor how much labour I take, so that I obey all the commands of Colonel Jonathan Stubbs !   What on earth is there that I can say or do for you more ?"

" There are one or two things," said he, " that I want you to understand.   In the first place, I am quite in earnest about this."

" Don't I know that you're in earnest ?"

" But perhaps you do not understand the full extent of my earnestness.   If she were to refuse me ultimately I should go away."

" Go away !   Go where ?

" Oh ; that I have not at all thought of ;—probably to India, as I might manage to get a regiment there.   But in truth it would matter very little."

" You are talking like a goose."

" That is very likely, because in this matter I think and feel like a goose.   It is not a great thing in a man to be turned out of his course by some undefined feeling which he has as to a young woman.   But the thing has occurred before now, and will occur again, in my case, if I am thrown over."

" What on earth is there about the girl ?" asked Lady Albury " There is that precious brother-in-law of ours going to hang himself incontinently because she will not look at him.   And that unfortunate friend of yours, Tom Tringle, is, if possible, worse than Ben Batsby or yourself."

" If two other gentlemen are in the same condition it only makes it the less singular that I should be the third.   At any rate, I am the third."

" You do not mean to liken yourself to them ?"

" Indeed I do.   As to our connection with Miss Dormer, I can see no difference.   We are all in love with her, and she has refused us all. It matters little whether a man's ugliness or his rings or his natural stupidity may have brought about this result."

" You are very modest, Jonathan."

" I always was, only you never could see it.   I am modest in this matter ; but not for that reason the less persistent in doing the best I can for myself.   My object now in seeing you is to let you understand that it is—well, not life and death, because she will not suffice either to kill me or to keep me alive,—but one of those matters which, in a man's career, are almost as important to him as life and death.   She was very decided in her refusal."

" So is every girl when a first offer is made to her.   How is any girl

Y

so to arrange her thoughts at a moment's notice as to accept a man off-hand ?"

" Girls do do so."

" Very rarely, I think ; and when they do they are hardly worth having," said Lady Albury, laying down the law on the matter with great precision. "If a girl accept a man all at once when she has had, as it were, no preparation for such a proposal, she must always surely be in a state of great readiness for matrimonial projects. When there has been a prolonged period of spooning then of course it is quite a different thing. The whole thing has in fact been arranged before the important word has been spoken."

" What a professor in the art you are !" said he.

" The odd thing is, that such a one as you should be so ignorant. Can't you understand that she would not come to Stalham if her mind were made up against you ? I said nothing of you as a lover, but I took care to let her know that you were coming. You are very ready to put yourself in the same boat with poor Ben Batsby or that other unfortunate wretch. Would she, do you think, have consented to come had she known that Ben would have been there, or your friend Tom Tringle ?"

There was much more of it, but the upshot was,—as the Colonel had intended that it should be,—that Lady Albury was made to understand that Ayala's good-will was essential to his happiness. "Of course I will do my best," she said, as he parted from her. "Though I am not quite as much in love with her myself as you are, yet I will do my best." Then when she was left alone, and was prosecuting her inquiries about the new cook, and travelling back in the afternoon to Stalham, she again considered how wonderful a thing it was such a girl as Ayala, so small, apparently so unimportant, so childish in her manner, with so little to say for herself, should become a person of such terrible importance.

The twentieth came, and at ten minutes before two Ayala was at the Paddington Railway Station. The train, which was to start at 2·15, had been chosen by herself so that she might avoid the Colonel, and there she was, with her aunt, waiting for it. Mrs. Dosett had thought it to be her duty to see her off, and had come with her in the cab. There were the two boxes laden with her wardrobe, such as it was. Both she and her aunt had worked hard ; for though,—as she had declared to herself,—there was no special reason for it, still she had wished to look her best. As she saw the boxes put into the van, and had told herself how much shabbier they were than the boxes of other young ladies who went visiting to such houses as Stalham, she rejoiced that Colonel Stubbs was not there to see them. And she considered whether it was possible that Colonel Stubbs should recognise a

dress which she had worn at Stalham before, which was now to appear
in a quite altered shape. She wondered also whether it would be possible that Colonel Stubbs should know how poor she was. As she was
thinking of all this there was Colonel Stubbs on the platform.

She had never doubted but that little plan would be efficacious.
Nor had her aunt doubted,—who had seen through the plan, though
not a word had been spoken between them on the subject. Mrs.
Dosett had considered it to be impossible that a Colonel engaged on
duties of importance at Aldershot should run away from them to wait
upon a child like Ayala,—even though he had professed himself to be
in love with the child. She had never seen the Colonel, and on this
occasion did not expect to see him. But there he was, all suddenly,
shaking hands with Ayala.

" My aunt, Mrs. Dosett," whispered Ayala. Then the Colonel
began to talk to the elder lady as though the younger lady were a
person of very much less importance. Yes ; he had run up from
Aldershot a little earlier than he had intended. There had been
nothing particular to keep him down at Aldershot. It had always
been his intention to go to Stalham on this day, and was glad of the
accident which was bringing Miss Dormer there just at the same time.
He spent a good deal of his time at Stalham because Sir Harry and
he, who were in truth cousins, were as intimate as brothers. He
always lived at Stalham when he could get away from duty and was
not in London. Stalham was a very nice place certainly ;—one of the
most comfortable houses he knew in England. So he went on till he
almost made Mrs. Dosett believe, and did make Ayala believe, that
his visit to Stalham had nothing to do with herself. And yet Mrs.
Dosett knew that the offer had been made. Ayala bethought herself
that she did not care so much for the re-manufactured frock after all,
nor yet for the shabby appearance of the boxes. The real Angel of
Light would not care for her frock nor for her boxes ;—and certainly
would not be indifferent after the fashion of,—of,— ! Then she began
to reflect that she was making a fool of herself.

She was put into the carriage, Mr. Dosett having luckily decided
against the use of the second-class. Going to such a house as Stalham
Ayala ought, said Mr. Dosett, to go as any other lady would. Had it
been himself or his wife it would have been very different ; but for
Ayala, on such an occasion as this, he would be extravagant. Ayala
was therefore put into her seat while the Colonel stood at the door
outside, still talking to Mrs. Dosett. " I don't think she will be let
to come away at the end of a week," said the Colonel. " Sir Harry
doesn't like people to come away very soon." Ayala heard this, and
thought that she remembered that Sir Harry himself was very indif-

ferent as to the coming and going of the visitors. "They go up to London about the end of March," said the Colonel, "and if Miss Dormer were to return about a week before it would do very well."

"Oh, no," said Ayala, putting her head out of the window; "I couldn't think of staying so long as that." Then the last final bustle was made by the guard; the Colonel got in, the door was shut, and Mrs. Dosett, standing on the platform, nodded her head for the last time.

There were only four persons in the carriage. In the opposite corner there were two old persons, probably a husband and wife, who had been very careful as to a foot-warming apparatus, and were muffled up very closely in woollen and furs. "If you don't mind shutting the door, Sir," said the old gentleman, rather testily, "because my wife has a pain in her face." The door absolutely was shut when the words were spoken, but the Colonel made some sign of closing all the apertures. But there was a ventilator above, which the old lady spied. "If you don't mind shutting that hole up there, Sir, because my husband is very bad with neuralgia." The Colonel at once got up and found that the ventilator was fast closed, so as not to admit a breath of air. "There are draughts come in everywhere," said the old gentleman. "The Company ought to be prosecuted." "I believe the more people they kill the better they like it," said the old lady. Then the Colonel looked at Ayala with a very grave face, with no hint at a smile, with a face which must have gratified even the old lady and gentleman. But Ayala understood the face, and could not refrain from a little laugh. She laughed only with her eyes,—but the Colonel saw it.

"The weather has been very severe all day," said the Colonel, in a severe voice.

Ayala protested that she had not found it cold at all. "Then, Miss, I think you must be made of granite," said the old lady. "I hope you'll remember that other people are not so fortunate." Ayala again smiled, and the Colonel made another effort as though to prevent any possible breath of air from making its way into the interior of the vehicle.

There was silence among them for some minutes, and then Ayala was quite surprised by the tone in which her friend addressed her. "What an ill-natured girl you must be," said he, "to have put me to such a terrible amount of trouble all on purpose."

"I didn't," said Ayala.

"Yes, you did. Why wouldn't you come down by the four o'clock train as I told you? Now I've left everything undone, and I shouldn't wonder if I get into such a row at the Horse Guards that I shall never hear the end of it. And now you are not a bit grateful."

" Yes, I am grateful ; but I didn't want you to come at all," she said.

" Of course I should come. I didn't think you were so perverse."

" I'm not perverse, Colonel Stubbs."

" When young persons are perverse, it is my opinion they oughtn't to be encouraged," said the old lady from her corner.

" My dear, you know nothing about it," said the old gentleman.

" Yes, I do," said the old lady. " I know all about it. Whatever she does a young lady ought not to be perverse. I do hate perversity. I am sure that hole up there must be open, Sir, for the wind does come in so powerful." Colonel Stubbs again jumped up and poked at the ventilator.

In the meantime Ayala was laughing so violently that she could with difficulty prevent herself from making a noise, which, she feared, would bring down increased wrath upon her from the old lady. That feigned scolding from the Colonel at once brought back upon her the feeling of sudden and pleasant intimacy which she had felt when he had first come and ordered her to dance with him at the ball in London. It was once again with her as though she knew this man almost more intimately, and certainly more pleasantly, than any of her other acquaintances. Whatever he said she could answer him now, and pretend to scold him, and have her joke with him as though no offer had ever been made. She could have told him now all the story of that turned dress, if that subject had come naturally to her, or have laughed with him at her own old boxes, and confided to him any other of the troubles of her poverty, as if they were jokes which she could share at any rate with him. Then he spoke again. " I do abominate a perverse young woman," he said. Upon this Ayala could no longer constrain herself, but burst into loud laughter.

After a while the two old people became quite familiar, and there arose a contest, in which the lady took part with the Colonel, and the old man protected Ayala. The Colonel spoke as though he were quite in earnest, and went on to declare that the young ladies of the present time were allowed far too much licence. " They never have their own bread to earn," he said, " and they ought to make themselves agreeable to other people who have more to do."

" I quite agree with you, Sir," said the old lady. " They should run about and be handy. I like to see a girl that can jump about the house and make herself useful."

" Young ladies ought to be young ladies," said the old man, putting his mouth for a moment up out of his comforter.

" And can't a young lady be useful and yet be a young lady ?" said the Colonel.

" It is her special province to be ornamental," said the old gentleman. " I like to see young ladies ornamental. I don't think young
ladies ought to be scolded, even if they are a little fractious."

" I quite agree with you, Sir," said Ayala. And so the fight went
on with sundry breaks and changes in the matter under discussion till
the station for Stalham had been reached. The old gentleman, indeed,
seemed to lose his voice before the journey was half over, but the lady
persevered, so that she and the Colonel became such fast friends that
she insisted on shaking hands with him when he left the carriage.

" How could you be so wicked as to go on hoaxing her like that ?"
said Ayala, as soon as they were on the platform.

" There was no hoax at all. I was quite in earnest. Was not every
word true that I said ? Now come and get into the carriage quickly,
or you will be as bad as the old gentleman himself."

Ayala did get into the carriage quickly, where she found Nina.

The two girls were full of conversation as they went to Stalham ;
but through it all Ayala could not refrain from thinking how the Jonathan Stubbs of to-day had been exactly like that Jonathan Stubbs she
had first known ;—and how very unlike a lover.

CHAPTER XLVII.

CAPTAIN BATSBY AT MERLE PARK.

WHEN Ayala went to Stalham Captain Batsby went to Merle Park.
They had both been invited by Lady Tringle, and when the letter was
written to Ayala she was assured that Tom should not be there. At
that time Tom's last encounter with the police had not as yet become
known to the Tringles, and the necessity of keeping Tom at the house
in the country was not manifest. The idea had been that Captain
Batsby should have an opportunity of explaining himself to Ayala.
The Captain came ; but, as to Ayala, Mrs. Dosett sent word to say that
she had been invited to stay some days just at that time with her
friend Lady Albury at Stalham.

What to do with Captain Batsby had been felt to be a difficulty by
Lady Albury. It was his habit to come to Stalham some time in
March and there finish the hunting season. It might be hoped that
Ayala's little affair might be arranged early in March, and then,
whether he came or whether he did not, it would be the same to
Ayala. But the Captain himself would be grievously irate when he
should hear the trick which would have been played upon him. Lady
Albury had already desired him not to come till after the first week in
March, having fabricated an excuse. She had been bound to keep the

coast clear both for Ayala's sake and the Colonel's ; but she knew that when her trick should be discovered there would be unmeasured wrath. " Why the deuce don't you let the two men come, and then the best man may win?" said Sir Harry, who did not doubt but that, in such a case, the Colonel would prove to be the best man. Here too there was another difficulty. When Lady Albury attempted to explain that Ayala would not come unless she were told that she would not meet the Captain, Sir Harry declared that there should be no such favour. " Who the deuce is this little girl," he asked, " that everybody should be knocked about in this way for her ?" Lady Albury was able to pacify the husband, but she feared that any pacifying of the Captain would be impossible. There would be a family quarrel ;—but even that must be endured for the Colonel's sake.

In the meantime the Captain was kept in absolute ignorance of Ayala's movements, and went down to Merle Park hoping to meet her there. He must have been very much in love, for Merle Park was by no means a spot well adapted for hunting. Hounds there were in the neighbourhood, but he turned up his nose at the offer when Sir Thomas suggested that he might bring down a hunter. Captain Batsby, when he went on hunting expeditions, never stirred without five horses, and always confined his operations to six or seven favoured counties. But Ayala just at present was more to him than hunting, and therefore, though it was now the end of February, he went to Merle Park.

" It was all Sir Thomas's doing." It was thus that Lady Tringle endeavoured to console herself when discussing the matter with her daughters. The Honourable Septimus Traffick had now gone up to London, and was inhabiting a single room in the neighbourhood of the House. Augusta was still at Merle Park, much to the disgust of her father. He did not like to tell her to be gone ; and would indeed have been glad enough of her presence had it not been embittered by the feeling that he was being " done." But there she remained, and in discussing the affairs of the Captain with her mother and Gertrude was altogether averse to the suggested marriage for Ayala. To her thinking Ayala was not entitled to a husband at all. Augusta had never given way in the affair of Tom ;—had declared her conviction that Stubbs had never been in earnest ; and was of opinion that Captain Batsby would be much better off at Merle Park without Ayala than he would have been in that young lady's presence. When he arrived nothing was said to him at once about Ayala. Gertrude, who recovered from the great sickness occasioned by Mr. Houston's misconduct though the recovery was intended only to be temporary, made herself as pleasant as possible. Captain Batsby was made welcome, and remained three days before he sought an opportunity of asking a question about Ayala.

During this time he found Gertrude to be a very agreeable companion, but he made Mrs. Traffick his first confidant. "Well, you know, Captain Batsby, to tell you the truth, we are not very fond of our cousin."

"Sir Thomas told me she was to be here."

"So we know. My father is perhaps a little mistaken about Ayala."

"Was she not asked?" demanded Captain Batsby, beginning to think that he had been betrayed.

"Oh, yes; she was asked. She has been asked very often, because she is mamma's niece, and did live with us once for a short time. But she did not come. In fact she won't go anywhere, unless——"

"Unless what?"

"You know Colonel Stubbs?"

"Jonathan Stubbs. Oh dear, yes; very intimately. He is a sort of connection of mine. He is my half-brother's second cousin by the father's side."

"Oh indeed! Does that make him very near?"

"Not at all. I don't like him, if you mean that. He always takes everything upon himself down at Stalham."

"What we hear is that Ayala is always running after him."

"Ayala running after Jonathan?"

"Haven't you heard of that?" asked Mrs. Traffick. "Why;—she is at Stalham with the Alburys this moment, and I do not doubt that Colonel Stubbs is there also. She would not have gone had she not been sure of meeting him."

This disturbed the Captain so violently that for two or three hours he kept himself apart, not knowing what to do with himself or where to betake himself. Could this be true about Jonathan Stubbs? There had been moments of deep jealousy down at Stalham; but then he had recovered from that, having assured himself that he was wrong. It had been Larry Twentyman and not Jonathan Stubbs who had led the two girls over the brook,—into which Stubbs had simply fallen, making himself an object of pity. But now again the Captain believed it all. It was on this account, then, that his half-sister-in-law, Rosaline, had desired him to stay away from Stalham for the present! He knew well how high in favour with Lady Albury was that traitor Stubbs;—how it was by her favour that Stubbs, who was no more than a second cousin, was allowed to do just what he pleased in the stables, while Sir Harry himself, the master of the hounds, confined himself to the kennel! He was determined at first to leave Merle Park and start instantly for Stalham, and had sent for his servant to begin the packing of his things ; but as he thought of it more maturely he considered that his arrival at Stalham would be very painful to himself as well as to others. For the others he did not much care, but he saw clearly that the pain to himself would be very disagreeable. No one at Stalham would be glad to see him. Sir Harry would be disturbed, and the other three persons with whom he was concerned,—Lady Albury, Stubbs, and Ayala,—would be banded together in hostility against him. What chance would he have under such circumstances? Therefore he determined that he would stay at Merle Park yet a little longer.

And, after all, was Ayala worth the trouble which he had proposed to take for her? How much had he offered her, how scornfully had his offer been received, and how little had she to give him in return! And now he had been told that she was always running after Jonathan Stubbs! Could it be worth his while to run after a girl who was always running after Jonathan Stubbs? Was he not much higher in the world than Jonathan Stubbs, seeing that he had, at any rate, double Stubbs's income? Stubbs was a red-haired, ugly, impudent fellow, who made his way wherever he went simply by "cheek"! Upon reflection, he found that it would be quite beneath him to run after any girl who could so demean herself as to run after Jonathan Stubbs. Therefore he came down to dinner on that evening with all his smiles, and said not a word about Ayala to Sir Thomas, who had just returned from London.

"Is he very much provoked?" Sir Thomas asked his wife that evening.

"Provoked about what?"

"He was expressly told that he would meet Ayala here."

"He seems to be making himself very comfortable, and hasn't said a word to me about Ayala. I am sick of Ayala. Poor Tom is going to be really ill." Then Sir Thomas frowned, and said nothing more on that occasion.

Tom was certainly in an uncomfortable position, and never left his bed till after noon. Then he would mope about the place, moping even worse than he did before, and would spend the evening all alone in the housekeeper's room, with a pipe in his mouth, which he seemed hardly able to take the trouble to keep alight. There were three or four other guests in the house, including two Honourable Miss Trafficks, and a couple of young men out of the City, whom Lady Tringle hoped might act as antidotes to Houston and Hamel. But with none of them would Tom associate. With Captain Batsby he did form some little intimacy ; driven to it, no doubt, by a community of interest. "I believe you were acquainted with my cousin, Miss Dormer, at Stalham?" asked Tom. At the moment the two were sitting over the fire in the housekeeper's room, and Captain Batsby was smoking a cigar, while Tom was sucking an empty pipe.

"Oh, yes," said Captain Batsby, pricking up his ears, "I saw a good deal of her."

"A wonderful creature!" ejaculated Tom.

"Yes, indeed!"

"For a real romantic style of beauty, I don't suppose that the world ever saw her like before. Did you?"

"Are you one among your cousin's admirers?" demanded the Captain.

"Am I?" asked Tom, surprised that there should be anybody who had not as yet heard his tragic story. "Am I one of her admirers? Why,—rather! Haven't you heard about me and Stubbs?"

"No, indeed."

"I thought that everybody had heard that. I challenged him, you know."

"To fight a duel?"

"Yes; to fight a duel. I sent my friend Faddle down with a letter to Stalham, but it was of no use. Why should a man fight a duel when he has got such a girl as Ayala to love him?"

"That is quite true, then?"

"I fear so! I fear so! Oh, yes; it is too true. Then you know;"—and as he came to this portion of his story he jumped up from his chair and frowned fiercely;—"then, you know, I met him under the portico of the Haymarket, and struck him."

"Oh,— was that you?"

"Indeed it was."

"And he did not do anything to you?"

"He behaved like a hero," said Tom. "I do think that he behaved like a hero,—though of course I hate him." The bitterness of expression was here very great. "He would'nt let them lock me up. Though, in the matter of that, I should have been best pleased if they would have me locked me up for ever, and kept me from the sight of the world. Admire that girl, Captain Batsby! I don't think that I ever heard of a man who loved a girl as I love her. I do not hesitate to say that I continue to walk the world,—in the way of not committing suicide, I mean,—simply because there is still a possibility while she has not as yet stood at the hymeneal altar with another man. I would have shot Stubbs willingly, though I knew I was to be tried for it at the Old Bailey,—and hung! I would have done it willingly,—willingly; or any other man." After that Captain Batsby thought it might be prudent not to say anything especial as to his own love.

And how foolish would it be for a man like himself, with a good fortune of his own, to marry any girl who had not a sixpence! The Captain was led into this vain thought by the great civility displayed to him by the ladies of the house. With Lucy, whom he knew to be Ayala's sister, he had not prospered very well. It came to his ears that she was out of favour with her aunt, and he therefore meddled with her but little. The Tringle ladies, however, were very kind to him,—so kind that he was tempted to think less than ever of one who had been so little courteous to him as Ayala. Mrs. Traffick was of course a married woman, and it amounted to nothing. But Gertrude ——! All the world knew that Septimus Traffick without a shilling of his own had become the happy possessor of a very large sum of money. He, Batsby, had more to recommend him than Traffick! Why should not he also become a happy possessor? He went away for a week's hunting into Northamptonshire, and then, at Lady Tringle's request, came back to Merle Park.

At this time Miss Tringle had quite recovered her health. She had dropped all immediate speech as to Mr. Houston. Had she not been provoked, she would have allowed all that to drop into oblivion. But a married sister may take liberties. "You are well rid of him, I think," said Augusta. Gertrude heaved a deep sigh. She did not wish to acknowledge herself to be rid of him until another string were well fitted to her bow. "After all, a man with nothing to do in the world, with no profession, no occupation, with no money——"

"Mr. Traffick had not got very much money of his own."

"He has a seat in Parliament, which is very much more than fortune, and will undoubtedly be in power when his party comes in. And he is a man of birth. But Frank Houston had nothing to recommend him."

"Birth!" said Gertrude, turning up her nose.

"The Queen, who is the fountain of honour, made his father a nobleman, and that constitutes birth." This the married sister said with stern severity of manner, and perfect reliance on the constitutional privileges of her Sovereign.

"I don't know that we need talk about it," said Gertrude.

"Not at all. Mr. Houston has behaved very badly, and I suppose there is an end of him as far as this house is concerned. Captain Batsby seems to me to be a very nice young man, and I suppose he has got money. A man should certainly have got money,—or an occupation."

"He has got both," said Gertrude,—which, however, was not true as Captain Batsby had left the service.

* * * * *

"Have you forgotten my cousin so soon?" Gertrude asked one day.

as she was walking with the happy Captain in the park. The Captain, no doubt, had been saying soft things to her.

" Do you throw that in my teeth as an offence ?"

" Inconstancy in men is generally considered as an offence," said Gertrude. What it might be in women she did not just then declare.

" After all I have heard oi your cousin since I have been here, I should hardly have thought that it would be reckoned so in this case."

" You have heard nothing against her from me."

" I am told that she has treated your brother very badly."

" Poor Tom !"

" And that she is flirting with a man I particularly dislike."

" I suppose she does make herself rather peculiar with that Colonel Stubbs."

" And, after all, only think how little I saw of her ! She is pretty."

" So some people think. I never saw it myself," said Gertrude. " We always thought her a mass of affectation. We had to turn her out of the house once you know. She was living here, and then it was that her sister had to come in her place. It is not their fault that they have got nothing ;—poor girls ! They are mamma's nieces, and so papa always has one of them." After that forgiveness was accorded to the Captain on account of his fickle conduct, and Gertrude consented to accept of his services in the guise of a lover. That this was so Mrs. Traffick was well aware. Nor was Lady Tringle very much in the dark. Frank Houston was to be considered as good as gone, and if so it would be well that her daughter should have another string. She was tired of the troubles of the girls around her, and thought that as Captain Batsby was supposed to have an income he would do as a son-in-law. But she had not hitherto been consulted by the young people, who felt among themselves that there still might be a difficulty. The difficulty lay with Sir Thomas. Sir Thomas had brought Captain Batsby there to Merle Park as Ayala's lover, and as he had been very little at home was unaware of the changes which had taken place. And then Gertrude was still supposed to be engaged to Mr. Houston, although this lover had been so violently rejected by himself. The ladies felt that, as he was made of sterner stuff than they, so would it be more difficult to reconcile him to the alterations which were now proposed in the family arrangements. Who was to bell the cat ? " Let him go to papa in the usual way, and ask his leave," said Mrs. Traffick.

" I did suggest that," said Gertrude, " but he seems not to like to do it quite yet."

" Is he such a coward as that ?"

" I do not know that he is more a coward than anybody else. I remember when Septimus was quite afraid to go near papa. But then Benjamin has got money of his own, which does make a difference."

"It's quite untrue saying that Septimus was ever afraid of papa. Of course he knows his position as a Member of Parliament too well for that. I suppose the truth is, it's about Ayala."

"It is a little odd about Ayala," said Gertrude, resuming her confidential tone. "It is so hard to make papa understand about these kind of things. I declare I believe he thinks that I never ought to speak to another man because of that scoundrel Frank Houston."

All this was in truth so strange to Sir Thomas that he could not understand any of the existing perplexities. Why did Captain Batsby remain as a guest at Merle Park? He had no special dislike to the man, and when Lady Tringle had told him that she had asked the Captain to prolong his visit he had made no objection. But why should the man remain there, knowing as he did now that there was no chance of Ayala's coming to Merle Park? At last, on a certain Saturday evening, he did make inquiry on the subject. "What on earth is that man staying here for?" he said to his wife.

"I think he likes the place."

"Perhaps he likes the place as well as Septimus Traffick, and means to live here always!" Such allusions as these were constant with Sir Thomas, and were always received by Lady Tringle with dismay and grief. "When does he mean to go away?" asked Sir Thomas, gruffly.

Lady Tringle had felt that the time had come in which some word should be said as to the Captain's intentions; but she feared to say it. She dreaded to make the clear explanation to her husband. "Perhaps," said she, "he is becoming fond of some of the young ladies."

"Young ladies! What young ladies? Do you mean Lucy?"

"Oh dear no!" said Lady Tringle.

"Then what the deuce do you mean? He came here after Ayala, because I wanted to have all that nonsense settled about Tom. Ayala is not here, nor likely to be here; and I don't know why he should stay here philandering away his time. I hate men in a country-house who are thorough idlers. You had better take an opportunity of letting him know that he has been here long enough."

All this was repeated by Lady Tringle to Mrs. Traffick, and by Mrs. Traffick to Gertrude. Then they felt that this was no time for Captain Batsby to produce himself to Sir Thomas as a suitor for his youngest daughter.

CHAPTER XLVIII.

THE JOURNEY TO OSTEND.

"No doubt it will be very hard to make papa understand." This
was said by Gertrude to her new lover a few days after that order had
been given that the lover should be sent away from Merle Park. The
purport of the order in all its severity had not been conveyed to
Captain Batsby. The ladies had felt,—Gertrude had felt very
strongly,—that were he informed that the master of the house
demanded his absence he would take himself off at once. But still
something had to be said,—and something done. Captain Batsby was,
just at present, in a matrimonial frame of mind. He had come to
Merle Park to look for a wife, and, as he had missed one, was, in his
present mood, inclined to take another. But there was no knowing
how long this might last. Augusta had hinted that "something must
be done, either with papa's consent or without it." Then there had
come the conversation in which Gertrude acknowledged the existing
difficulty. "Papa, too, probably, would not consent quite at once."

"He must think it very odd that I am staying here," said the
Captain.

"Of course it is odd. If you could go to him and tell him everything!" But the Captain, looking at the matter all round, thought that
he could not go to Sir Thomas and tell him anything. Then she
began gently to introduce the respectable clergyman at Ostend. It
was not necessary that she should refer at length to the circumstances
under which she had studied the subject, but she gave Captain Batsby
to understand that it was one as to which she had picked up a good
deal of information.

But the money! "If Sir Thomas were made really angry, the consequences would be disastrous," said the Captain. But Gertrude was
of a different way of thinking. Her father was, no doubt, a man who
could be very imperious, and would insist upon having his own way as
long as his own way was profitable to him. But he was a man who
always forgave.

"If you mean about the money," said Gertrude, "I am quite sure
that it would all come right." He did mean about the money, and
was evidently uneasy in his mind when the suggested step was made
manifest to him. Gertrude was astonished to see how long and melancholy his face could become. "Papa was never unkind about money
in his life," said Gertrude. "He could not endure to have any of us

On the next Saturday Sir Thomas again came down, and still found his guest at Merle Park. We are now a little in advance of our special story, which is, or ought to be, devoted to Ayala. But, with the affairs of so many lovers and their loves, it is almost impossible to make the chronicle run at equal periods throughout. It was now more than three weeks since Ayala went to Stalham, and Lady Albury had written to the Captain confessing something of her sin, and begging to be forgiven. This she had done in her anxiety to keep the Captain away. He had not answered his sister-in-law's letter, but, in his present frame of mind, was not at all anxious to finish up the hunting season at Stalham. Sir Thomas, on his arrival, was very full of Tom's projected tour. He had arranged everything,—except in regard to Tom's own assent. He had written to New York, and had received back a reply from his corresdondent assuring him that Tom should be made most heartily welcome. It might be that Tom's fighting propensities had not been made known to the people of New York. Sir Thomas had taken a berth on board of one of the Cunard boats, and had even gone so far as to ask the Captain to come down for a day or two to Merle Park. He was so much employed with Tom that he could hardly afford time and consideration to Captain Batsby and his affairs. Nevertheless he did ask a question, and received an answer with which he seemed to be satisfied. "What on earth is that man staying here for?" he said to his wife.

"He is going on Friday," replied Lady Tringle, doubtingly;—almost as though she thought that she would be subjected to further anger because of this delay. But Sir Thomas dropped the subject, and passed on to some matter affecting Tom's outfit. Lady Tringle was very glad to change the subject, and promised that everything should be supplied befitting the hottest and coldest climates on the earth's surface.

"She sails on the nineteenth of April," said Sir Thomas to his son.

"I don't think I could go as soon as that, Sir," replied Tom, whining.

"Why not? There are more than three weeks yet, and your mother will have everything ready for you. What on earth is there to hinder you?"

"I don't think I could go—not on the nineteenth of April."

"Well then, you must. I have taken your place, and Firkin expects you at New York. They'll do everything for you there, and you'll find quite a new life. I should have thought you'd have been delighted to get away from your wretched condition here."

"It is wretched," said Tom; "but I'd rather not go quite so soon."

"Why not?"

"Well. then——"

"What is it, Tom? It makes me unhappy when I see you such a fool."

"I am a fool! I know I am a fool!"

"Then make a new start of it. Cut and run, and begin the world again. You're young enough to forget all this."

"So I would, only——"

"Only what?"

"I suppose she is engaged to that man, Stubbs! If I knew it for certain then I would go. If I went before, I should only come back as soon as I got to New York. If they were once married and it were all done with I think I could make a new start."

In answer to this his father told him that he must go on the nineteenth of April, whether Ayala were engaged or disengaged, married or unmarried;—that his outfit would be bought, his cabin would be ready, circular notes for his use would be prepared, and everything would be arranged to make his prolonged tour as comfortable as possible; but that if he did not start on that day all the Tringle houses would be closed against him, and he would be turned penniless out into the world. "You'll have to learn that I'm in earnest," said Sir Thomas, as he turned his back and walked away. Tom took himself off to reflect whether it would not be a grand thing to be turned penniless out into the world,—and all for love!

By the early train on Monday Sir Thomas returned to London, having taken little or no heed of Captain Batsby during his late visit to the country. Even at Merle Park Captain Batsby's presence was less important than it would otherwise have been to Lady Tringle and Mrs. Traffick, because of the serious nature of Sir Thomas's decision as to his son. Lady Tringle perhaps suspected something. Mrs. Traffick, no doubt, had her own ideas as to her sister's position; but nothing was said and nothing was done. Both on the Wednesday and on the Thursday Lady Tringle went up to town to give the required orders on Tom's behalf. On the Thursday her elder daughter accompanied her, and returned with her in the evening. On their arrival they learnt that neither Captain Batsby nor Miss Gertrude had been seen since ten o'clock; that almost immediately after Lady Tringle's departure in the morning Captain Batsby had caused all his luggage to be sent into Hastings; and that it had since appeared that a considerable number of Miss Gertrude's things were missing. There could be no doubt that she had caused them to be packed up with the Captain's luggage. "They have gone to Ostend, mamma," said Augusta. "I was sure of it, because I've heard Gertrude say that people can always get themselves married at Ostend. There is a clergyman there on purpose to do it."

It was at this time past seven o'clock, and Lady Tringle when she heard the news was so astounded that she did not at first know how to act. It was not possible for her to reach Dover that night before the night-boat for Ostend should have started,—even could she have done any good by going there. Tom was in such a condition that she hardly dared to trust him; but it was settled at last that she should telegraph at once to Sir Thomas, in Lombard Street, and that Tom should travel up to London by the night train.

On the following morning Lady Tringle received a letter from Gertrude, posted by that young lady at Dover as she passed through on her road to Ostend. It was as follows;—

" DEAR MAMMA,

" You will be surprised on your return from London to find that we have gone. After much thinking about it we determined it would be best, because we had quite made up our mind *not to be kept separated.* Ben was so eager about it that I was obliged to yield. We were afraid that if we asked papa at once he would not have given his consent. Pray give him my most dutiful love, and tell him that I am sure he will never have occasion to be ashamed of his son-in-law. I don't suppose he knows, but it is the fact that Captain Batsby has about three thousand a year of his own. It is very different from having nothing, like that wretch Frank Houston, or, for that matter, Mr. Traffick. Ben was quite in a position to ask papa, but things had happened which made us both feel that papa would not like it just at present. We mean to be married at Ostend, and then will come back as soon as you and papa say that you will receive us. In the meantime I wish you would send some of my clothes after me. Of course I had to come away with very little luggage, because I was obliged to have my things mixed up with Ben's. I did not dare to have my boxes brought down by the servants. Could you send me the green silk in which I went to church the last two Sundays, and my pink gauze, and the grey poplin? Please send two or three flannel petticoats, as I could not put them among his things, and as many cuffs and collars as you can cram in. I suppose I can get boots at Ostend, but I should like to have the hat with the little brown feather. There is my silk jacket with the fur trimming; I should like to have that. I suppose I shall have to be married without any regular dress, but I am sure papa will make up my trousseau to me afterwards. I lent a little lace fichu to Augusta; tell her that I shall so like to have it.

" Give papa my best love, and Augusta, and poor Tom, and accept the same from your affectionate daughter,   " GERTRUDE."

" I suppose I must not add the other name yet."

z

Sir Thomas did not receive the telegram till eleven o'clock, when he returned from dinner, and could do nothing that night. On the next morning he was disturbed soon after five o'clock by Tom, who had come on the same errand. "Idiots!" exclaimed Sir Thomas, "What on earth can they have gone to Ostend for? And what can you do by coming up?"

"My mother thought that I might follow them to Ostend."

"They wouldn't care for you. No one will care for you until you have got rid of all this folly. I must go. Idiots! Who is to marry them at Ostend? If they are fools enough to want to be married why shouldn't they get married in England?"

"I suppose they thought you wouldn't consent."

"Of course I shan't consent. But why should I consent a bit more because they have gone to Ostend? I don't suppose anybody ever had such a set of fools about him as I have." This would have been hard upon Tom had it not been that he had got beyond the feeling of any hardness from contempt or contumely. As he once said of himself, all sense of other injury had been washed out of him by Ayala's unkindness.

On that very day Sir Thomas started for Ostend, and reached the place about two o'clock. Captain Batsby and Gertrude had arrived only during the previous night, and Gertrude, as she had been very sick, was still in bed. Captain Batsby was not in bed. Captain Batsby had been engaged since an early hour in the morning looking for that respectable clergyman of the Church of England of whose immediate services he stood in need. By the time that Sir Thomas had reached Ostend he had found that no such clergyman was known in the place. There was a regular English clergyman who would be very happy to marry him,—and to accept the usual fees,—after the due performance of certain preliminaries as ordained by the law, and as usual at Ostend. The lady, no doubt, could be married at Ostend, after such preliminaries,—as she might have been married also in England. All this was communicated by the Captain to Gertrude,—who was still very unwell,—at her bedroom door. Her conduct during this trying time was quite beyond reproach,—and also his,—as Captain Batsby afterwards took an opportunity of assuring her father.

"What on earth, Sir, is the meaning of all this?" said Sir Thomas, encountering the man who was not his son-in-law in the sitting-room of the hotel.

"I have just run away with your daughter, Sir Thomas. That is the simple truth."

"And I have got the trouble of taking her back again."

"I have behaved like a gentleman through it all, Sir Thomas," said the Captain, thus defending his own character and the lady's.

"You have behaved like a fool. What on earth am I to think of it, Sir? You were asked down to my house because you gave me to understand that you proposed to ask my niece, Miss Dormer, to be your wife; and now you have run away with my daughter. Is that behaving like a gentleman?"

"I must explain myself."

"Well, Sir!" Captain Batsby found the explanation very difficult; and hummed and hawed a great deal. "Do you mean to say that it was a lie from beginning to end about Miss Dormer?" Great liberties of speech are allowed to gentlemen whose daughters have been run away with, and whose hospitality has been outraged.

"Oh dear no. What I said then was quite true. It was my intention. But—but—." The perspiration broke out upon the unhappy man's brow as the great immediate trouble of his situation became clear to him. "There was no lie,—no lie at all. I beg to assure you, Sir Thomas, that I am not a man to tell a lie."

"How has it all been, then?"

"When I found how very superior a person your daughter was!"

"It isn't a month since she was engaged to somebody else," said the angry father, forgetting all propriety in his indignation.

"Gertrude?" demanded Captain Batsby.

"You are two fools. So you gave up my niece?"

"Oh dear yes, altogether. She didn't come to Merle Park, you know. How was I to say anything to her when you didn't have her there?"

"Why didn't you go away then, instead of remaining under a false pretence? Or why, at any rate, didn't you tell me the truth?"

"And what would you have me to do now?" asked Captain Batsby.

"Go to the d——," said Sir Thomas, as he left the room, and went to his daughter's chamber.

Gertrude had heard that her father was in the house, and endeavoured to hurry herself into her clothes while the interview was going on between him and her father. But she was not yet perfectly arrayed when her father burst into her room. "Oh, papa," she said, going down on her knees, "you do mean to forgive us?"

"I mean to do nothing of the kind. I mean to carry you home and have you locked up."

"But we may be married!"

"Not with my leave. Why didn't you come and ask if you wanted to get yourselves married? Why didn't you tell me?"

"We were ashamed."

"What has become of Mr. Houston, whom you loved so dearly?"

"Oh, papa!"

z 2

" And the Captain was so much attached to Ayala？"

" Oh, papa！"

" Get up, you stupid girl. Why is it that my children are so much more foolish than other people's？ I don't suppose you care for the man in the least."

" I do, I do. I love him with all my heart."

" And as for him,—how can he care for you when it is but the other day he was in love with your cousin."

" Oh, papa！"

" What he wants is my money, of course."

" He has got plenty of money, papa."

" I can understand him, fool as he is. There is something for him to get. He won't get it, but he might think it possible. As for you, I cannot understand you at all. What do you expect？ It can't be for love of a hatchet-faced fellow like that, whom you had never seen a fortnight ago."

" It is more than a month ago, papa."

" Frank Houston was, at any rate, a manly-looking fellow."

" He was a scoundrel," said Gertrude, now standing up for the first time.

" A good-looking fellow was Frank Houston ; that at least may be said for him," continued the father, determined to exasperate his daughter to the utmost. " I had half a mind to give way about him, because he was a manly, outspoken fellow, though he was such an idle dog. If you'd gone off with him I could have understood it ;—and perhaps forgiven it," he added.

" He was a scoundrel！" screamed Gertrude, remembering her ineffectual attempts to make her former lover perform this same journey.

" But this fellow？ I cannot bring myself to believe that you really care for him."

" He has a good income of his own, while Houston was little better than a beggar."

" I'm glad of that," said Sir Thomas, " because there will be something for you to live upon. I can assure you that Captain Batsby will never get a shilling of my money. Now, you had better finish dressing yourself, and come down and eat your dinner with me if you've got any appetite. You will have to go back to Dover by the boat to-night."

" May Ben dine with us？" asked Gertrude, timidly.

" Ben may go to the d——. At any rate he had better not show himself to me again," said Sir Thomas.

The lovers, however, did get an opportunity of exchanging a few words, during which it was settled between them that as the young lady must undoubtedly obey her father's behests, and return to Dover that night, it would be well for Captain Batsby to remain behind at Ostend. Indeed, he spoke of making a little tour as far as Brussels, in order that he might throw off the melancholy feelings which had been engendered. "You will come to me again, Ben," she said. Upon this he looked very grave. "You do not mean to say that after all this you will desert me?"

"He has insulted me so horribly!"

"What does that signify? Of course he is angry. If you could only hear how he has insulted me."

"He says that you were in love with somebody else not a month since."

"So were you, Ben, for the matter of that." He did, however, before they parted, make her a solemn promise that their engagement should remain an established fact, in spite both of father and mother.

Gertrude, who had now recovered the effects of her sea-sickness,—which, however, she would have to encounter again so very quickly,—contrived to eat a hearty dinner with her father. There, however, arose a little trouble. How should she contrive to pack up the clothes which she had brought with her, and which had till lately been mixed with the Captain's garments. She did, however, at last succeed in persuading the chamber-maid to furnish her with a carpet-bag, with which in her custody she arrived safely on the following day at Merle Park.

CHAPTER XLIX.

THE NEW FROCK.

AYALA'S arrival at Stalham was full of delight to her. There was Nina with all her new-fledged hopes and her perfect assurance in the absolute superiority of Lord George Bideford to any other man either alive or dead. Ayala was quite willing to allow this assurance to pass current, as her Angel of Light was as yet neither alive nor dead. But she was quite certain,—wholly certain,—that when the Angel should come forth he would be superior to Lord George. The first outpouring of all this took place in the carriage as Nina and Ayala were driven from the station to the house, while the Colonel went home alone in a dog-cart. It had been arranged that nothing should be said to Ayala about the Colonel, and in the carriage the Colonel's name was not mentioned. But when they were all in the hall at Stalham, taking off their cloaks and depositing their wraps, standing in front of the large fire, Colonel Stubbs was there. Lady Albury was present also, welcoming her guests, and Sir Harry, who had already come home from hunting, with one or two other men in red coats and top breeches, and a small bevy of ladies who were staying in the house. Lady Albury was anxious to know how her friend had sped with Ayala, but at such a moment no question could be asked. But Ayala's spirits were so high that Lady Albury was at a loss to understand whether the whole thing had been settled by Jonathan with success,—or whether, on the other hand, Ayala was so happy because she had not been troubled by a word of love.

" He has behaved so badly, Lady Albury," said Ayala.

" What ;—Stubbs ?" asked Sir Harry, not quite understanding all the ins and outs of the matter.

" Yes, Sir Harry. There was an old lady and an old gentleman. They were very funny, and he would laugh at them."

" I deny it," said the Colonel.

" Why shouldn't he laugh at them if they were funny ?" asked Lady Albury.

" He knew it would make me laugh out loud. I couldn't help my-self, but he could be as grave as a judge all the time. So he went till the old woman scolded me dreadfully."

" But the old man took your part," said the Colonel.

" Yes ;—he did. He said that I was ornamental."

" A decent and truth-speaking old gentleman," said one of the sportsmen in top-boots.

" Quite so ;—but then the old lady said that I was perverse, and Colonel Stubbs took her part. If you had been there, Lady Albury, you would have thought that he had been in earnest."

" So I was," said the Colonel.

All this was very pleasant to Ayala. It was a return to the old joyousness when she had first discovered the delight of having such a friend as Colonel Stubbs. Had he flattered her, paid her compli-ments, been soft and delicate to her,—as a lover might have been,— she would have been troubled in spirit and heavy at heart. But now it seemed as though all that love-making had been an episode which had passed away, and that the old pleasant friendship still remained. As yet, while they were standing there in the hall, there had come no moment for her to feel whether there was anything to regret in this. But certainly there had been comfort in it. She had been able to appear before all her Stalham friends, in the presence even of the man himself, without any of that consciousness which would have oppressed her had he come there simply as her acknowledged lover, and had she come there conscious before all the guests that it was so.

Then they sat for a while drinking tea and eating buttered toast in the drawing-room. A supply of buttered toast fully to gratify the wants of three or four men just home from hunting has never yet been created by the resources of any establishment. But the greater marvel is that the buttered toast has never any slightest effect on the dinner which is to follow in an hour or two. During this period the conversation turned chiefly upon hunting,—which is of all subjects the most imperious. It never occurs to a hunting-man to suppose that either a lady, or a bishop, or a political economist, can be indifferent to hunting. There is something beyond millinery,—beyond the interests of the church,—beyond the price of wheat,—in that great question whether the hounds did or did not change their fox in Gobblegoose Wood. On the present occasion Sir Harry was quite sure that the hounds did carry their fox through Gobblegoose Wood, whereas Captain Glomax, who had formerly been master of the pack which now obeyed Sir Harry, was perfectly certain that they had got upon another animal who went away from Gobblegoose as fresh as paint. He pretended even to ridicule Sir Harry for supposing that any fox could have run at that pace up Buddlecombe Hill who had travelled all the way from Stickborough Gorse. To this Sir Harry replied resentfully that the Captain did not know what were the running powers of a dog-fox in March. Then he told various stories of what had been done in this way at this special period of the year. Glomax, however, declared that he knew as much of a fox as any man in England, and that he would eat both the foxes, and the wood, and Sir Harry, and, finally, himself, if the animal which had run up Buddlecombe Hill was the same which they brought with them from Stickborough Gorse into Gobblegoose Wood. So the battle raged, and the ladies no doubt were much interested ;—as would have been the bishop had he been there, or the political economist.

After this Ayala was taken up into her room, and left to sit there by herself for a while till Lady Albury should send her maid. "My dear," said Lady Albury, "there is something on the bed which expect you to wear to-night. I shall be broken-hearted if it doesn fit you. The frock is a present from Sir Harry ; the scarf comes from me. Don't say a word about it. Sir Harry always likes to make presents to young ladies." Then she hurried out of the room while Ayala was still thanking her. Lady Albury had at first intended say something about the Colonel as they were sitting together ove Ayala's fire, but she had made up her mind against this as soon as she saw their manner towards each other on entering the house. I Ayala had accepted him at a word as they were travelling together then there would be need of no further interference in the matter

But if not, it would be better that she should hold her peace for the present.

Ayala's first instinct was to look at the finery which had been provided for her. It was a light grey silk, almost pearl colour, as to which she thought she had never seen anything so lovely before. She measured the waist with her eye, and knew at once that it would fit her. She threw the gauzy scarf over her shoulders and turned herself round before the large mirror which stood near the fire-place. " Dear Lady Albury !" she exclaimed ;—" dear Lady Albury !" It was impossible that she should have understood that Lady Albury's affection had been shown to Jonathan Stubbs much rather than to her when those presents were prepared.

She got rid of her travelling dress and her boots, and let down her hair, and seated herself before the fire, that she might think of it all in her solitude. Was she or was she not glad,—glad in sober earnest, glad now the moment of her mirth had passed by, the mirth which had made her return to Stalham so easy for her,—was she or was she not glad that this change had come upon the Colonel, this return to his old ways ? She had got her friend again, but she had lost her lover. She did not want the lover. She was sure of that. She was still sure that if a lover would come to her who would be in truth acceptable,—such a lover as would enable her to give herself up to him altogether, and submit herself to him as her lord and master,—he must be something different from Jonathan Stubbs. That had been the theory of her life for many months past, a theory on which she had resolved to rely with all her might from the moment in which this man had spoken to her of his love. Would she give way and render up herself and all her dreams simply because the man was one to be liked ? She had declared to herself again and again that it should not be so. There should come the Angel of Light or there should come no lover for her. On that very morning as she was packing up her boxes at Kingsbury Crescent she had arranged the words in which, should he speak to her on the subject in the railway train, she would make him understand that it could never be. Surely he would understand if she told him so simply, with a little prayer that his suit might not be repeated. His suit had not been repeated. Nothing apparently had been further from his intention. He had been droll, pleasant, friendly,—just like his old dear self. For in truth the pleasantness and the novelty of his friendship had made him dear to her. He had gone back of his own accord to the old ways, without any little prayer from her. Now was she contented ? As the question would thrust itself upon her in opposition to her own will, driving out the thoughts which she would fain have welcomed, she gazed listlessly at the fire. If it were so, then for what purpose, then for what reason, had Lady Albury procured for her the pale grey pearl-coloured dress ?

And why were all these grand people at Stalham so good to her,—to her, a poor little girl, whose ordinary life was devoted to the mending of linen and to the furtherance of economy in the use of pounds of butter and legs of mutton ? Why was she taken out of her own sphere and petted in this new luxurious world ? She had a knowledge belonging to her,—if not quite what we may call common sense,—which told her that there must be some cause. Of some intellectual capacity, some appreciation of things and words which were divine in their beauty, she was half conscious. It could not be, she felt, that without some such capacity she should have imaged to herself that Angel of Light. But not for such capacity as that had she been made welcome at Stalham. As for her prettiness, her beauty of face and form, she thought about them not at all,—almost not at all. In appearing in that pale-pearl silk, with that gauzy scarf upon her shoulders, she would take pride. Not to be shamed among other girls by the poorness of her apparel was a pride to her. Perhaps to excel some others by the prettiness of her apparel might be a pride to her. But of feminine beauty, as a great gift bestowed upon her, she thought not at all. She would look in the mirror for the effect of the scarf, but not for the effect of the neck and shoulders beneath it. Could she have looked in any mirror for the effect of the dreams she had thus dreamed,—ah ! that would have been the mirror in which she would have loved yet feared to look !

Why was Lady Albury so kind to her ? Perhaps Lady Albury did not know that Colonel Stubbs had changed his mind. She would know it very soon, and then, maybe, everything would be changed. As she thought of this she longed to put the pearl silk dress aside, and not to wear it as yet,—to put it aside so that it might never be worn by her if circumstances should so require. It was to be hoped that the man had changed his mind,—and to be hoped that Lady Albury would know that he had done so. Then she would soon see whether there was a change. Could she not give a reason why she should not wear the dress this night ? As she sat gazing at the fire a tear ran down her cheek. Was it for the dress she would not wear, or for the lover whom she would not love ?

The question as to the dress was settled for her very soon. Lady Albury's maid came into the room,—not a chit of a girl without a thought of her own except as to her own grandness in being two steps higher than the kitchen-maid,—but a well-grown, buxom powerful woman, who had no idea of letting such a young lady as Ayala do anything in the matter of dress but what she told her. When Ayala sug-

gested something as to the next evening in reference to the pale-pearl silk
the buxom powerful woman pooh-poohed her down in a moment. What;
—after Sir Harry had taken so much trouble about having it made;
having actually inquired about it with his own mouth. "To-night,
Miss; you must wear it to-night! My lady would be quite angry!"
"My lady not know what you wear! My lady knows what all the
ladies wear,—morning, noon, and night." That little plan of letting the
dress lie by till she should know how she should be received after
Colonel Stubbs's change of mind had been declared, fell to the ground
altogether under the hands of the buxom powerful woman.

When she went into the drawing-room some of the guests were
assembled. Sir Harry and Lady Albury were there, and so was
Colonel Stubbs. As she walked in Sir Harry was standing well in
front of the fire, in advance of the rug, so as to be almost in the middle
of the room. Captain Glomax was there also, and the discussion
about the foxes was going on. It had occurred to Ayala that as the
dress was a present from Sir Harry she must thank him. So she walked
up to him and made a little curtsey just before him. "Am I nice, Sir
Harry?" she said.

"Upon my word," said Sir Harry, "that is the best spent ten-
pound-note I ever laid out in my life." Then he took her by the
hand and gently turned her round, so as to look at her and her dress.

"I don't know whether I am nice, but you are," she said, curtsey-
ing again. Everybody felt that she had had quite a little triumph as
she subsided into a seat close by Lady Albury, who called her. As she
seated herself she caught the Colonel's eye, who was looking at her.
She fancied that there was a tear in it. Then he turned himself and
looked away into the fire.

"You have won his heart for ever," said Lady Albury.

"Whose heart?" asked Ayala, in her confusion.

"Sir Harry's heart. As for the other, cela va sans dire. You must
go on wearing it every night for a week or Sir Harry will want to know
why you have left it off. If the woman had made it on you it
couldn't have fitted better. Baker,—" Baker was the buxom female,
—"said that she knew it was right. You did that very prettily to
Sir Harry. Now go up and ask Colonel Stubbs what he thinks of
it."

"Indeed, I won't," said Ayala. Lady Albury, a few minutes afterwards, when she saw Ayala walking away towards the drawing-room
leaning on the Colonel's arm, acknowledged to herself that she did at
last understand it. The Colonel had been able to see it all, even without the dress, and she confessed in her mind that the Colonel had eyes
with which to see, and ears with which to hear, and a judgment with

which to appreciate. "Don't you think that girl very lovely?" she said to Lord Rufford, on whose arm she was leaning.

"Something almost more than lovely," said Lord Rufford, with unwonted enthusiasm.

It was acknowledged now by everybody. "Is it true about Colonel Stubbs and Miss Dormer?" whispered Lady Rufford to her hostess in the drawing-room.

"Upon my word, I never inquire into those things," said Lady Albury. "I suppose he does admire her. Everybody must admire her."

"Oh yes;" said Lady Rufford. "She is certainly very pretty. Who is she, Lady Albury?" Lady Rufford had been a Miss Penge, and the Penges were supposed to be direct descendants from Boadicea.

"She is Miss Ayala Dormer. Her father was an artist, and her mother was a very handsome woman. When a girl is as beautiful as Miss Dormer, and as clever, it doesn't much signify who she is.' Then the direct descendant from Boadicea withdrew, holding an opinion much at variance with that expressed by her hostess.

"Who is that young lady who sat next to you?" asked Captain Glomax of Colonel Stubbs, after the ladies had gone.

"She is a Miss Ayala Dormer."

"Did I not see her out hunting with you once or twice early in the season?"

"You saw her out hunting, no doubt, and I was there. I did not specially bring her. She was staying here, and rode one of Albury's horses."

"Take her top and bottom, and all round," said Captain Glomax, "she is the prettiest little thing I've seen for many a day. When she curtsyed to Sir Harry in the drawing-room I almost thought that I should like to be a marrying man myself." Stubbs did not carry on the conversation, having felt displeased rather than otherwise by the admiration expressed.

"I didn't quite understand before," said Sir Harry to his wife that night, "what it was that made Jonathan so furious about that girl; but I think I see it now."

"Fine feathers make fine birds," said his wife, laughing.

"Feathers ever so fine," said Sir Harry, "don't make well-bred birds."

"To tell the truth," said Lady Albury, "I think we shall all have to own that Jonathan has been right."

This took place upstairs, but before they left the drawing-room Lady Albury whispered a few words to her young friend. "We have had a terrible trouble about you, Ayala."

" A trouble about me, Lady Albury ?   I should be so sorry."

" It is not exactly your fault ;—but we haven't at all known what to do with that unfortunate man."

" What man ?" asked Ayala, forgetful at the moment of all men except Colonel Stubbs.

" You naughty girl ! Don't you know that my brother-in-law is broken-hearted about you ?"

" Captain Batsby !" whispered Ayala, in her faintest voice.

" Yes ; Captain Batsby. A Captain has as much right to be considered as a Colonel in such a matter as this." Here Ayala frowned, but said nothing. " Of course, I can't help it, who may break his heart, but poor Ben is always supposed to be at Stalham just at this time of the year, and now I have been obliged to tell him one fib upon another to keep him away. When he comes to know it all, what on earth will he say to me ?"

" I am sure it has not been my fault," said Ayala.

" That's what young ladies always say when gentlemen break their hearts."

When Ayala was again in her room, and had got rid of the buxom female who came to assist her in taking off her new finery, she was aware of having passed the evening triumphantly. She was conscious of admiration. She knew that Sir Harry had been pleased by her appearance. She was sure that Lady Albury was satisfied with her, and she had seen something in the Colonel's glance that made her feel that he had not been indifferent.   But in their conversation at the dinner table he had said nothing which any other man might not have said, if any other man could have made himself as agreeable. Those hunting days were all again described with their various incidents, with the great triumph over the brook, and Twentyman's wife and baby, and fat Lord Rufford, who was at the moment sitting there opposite to them ; and the ball in London, with the lady who was thrown out of the window ; and the old gentleman and the old lady of to-day who had been so peculiar in their remarks. There had been nothing else in their conversation, and it surely was not possible that a man who intended to put himself forward as a lover should have talked in such fashion as that ! But then there were other things which occurred to her. Why had there been that tear in his eye ? And that " cela va sans dire " which had come from Lady Albury in her railing mood ;—what had that meant ? Lady Albury, when she said that, could not have known that the Colonel had changed his purpose.

But, after all, what is a dress, let it be ever so pretty ? The Angel of Light would not care for her dress, let her wear what she might. Were he to seek her because of her dress, he would not be the Angel of Light of whom she had dreamed. It was not by any dress that she could prevail over him. She did rejoice because of her little triumph;—but she knew that she rejoiced because she was not an Angel of Light herself. Her only chance lay in this, that the angels of yore did come down from heaven to ask for love and worship from the daughters of men.

As she went to bed, she determined that she would still be true to her dream. Not because folk admired a new frock would she be ready to give herself to a man who was only a man,—a man of the earth really; who had about him no more than a few of the real attributes of an Angel of Light.

CHAPTER L.

GOBBLEGOOSE WOOD ON SUNDAY.

THE next two days were not quite so triumphant to Ayala as had been the evening of her arrival. There was hunting on both of those days, the gentlemen having gone on the Friday away out of Sir Harry's country to the Brake hounds. Ayala and the Colonel had arrived on the Thursday. Ayala had not expected to be asked to hunt again,—had not even thought about it. It had been arranged before on Nina's account, and Nina now was not to hunt any more. Lord George did not altogether approve of it, and Nina was quite in accord with Lord George,—though she had held up her whip and shaken it in triumph when she jumped over the Cranbury Brook. And the horse which Ayala had ridden was no longer in the stables. "My dear, I am so sorry; but I'm afraid we can't mount you," Lady Albury said. In answer to this Ayala declared that she had not thought of it for a moment. But yet the days seemed to be dull with her. Lady Rufford was,—well,—perhaps a little patronising to her, and patronage such as that was not at all to Ayala's taste. "Lady Albury seems to be quite a kind friend to you," Lady Rufford said. Nothing could be more true. The idea implied was true also,—the idea that such a one as Ayala was much in luck's way to find such a friend as Lady Albury. It was true no doubt; but, nevertheless, it was ungracious, and had to be resented. 'A very kind friend indeed. Some people only make friends of those who are as grand as themselves."

"I am sure we should be very glad to see you at Rufford if you remain long in the country," said Lady Rufford, a little time afterwards. But even in this there was not a touch of that cordiality which might have won Ayala's heart. "I am not at all likely to stay," said Ayala. 'I live with my uncle and aunt at Notting Hill, and I very rarely go away from home." Lady Rufford, however, did not quite understand it. It had been whispered to her that morning that Ayala was certainly going to marry Colonel Stubbs ; and, if so, why should she not come to Rufford ?

On that day, the Friday, she was taken out to dinner by Captain Glomax. "I remember quite as if it were yesterday," said the Captain. "It was the day we rode the Cranbury Brook."

Ayala looked up into his face, also remembering everything as well as it were yesterday. "Mr. Twentyman rode over it," she said, "and Colonel Stubbs rode into it."

"Oh, yes ; Stubbs got a ducking ; so he did." The Captain had not got a ducking, but then he had gone round by the road. "It was a good run that."

"I thought so."

"We haven't been lucky since Sir Harry has had the hounds somehow. There doesn't seem to be the dash about 'em there used to be when I was here. I had them before Sir Harry, you know." All this was nearly in a whisper.

"Were you Master?" asked Ayala, with a tone of surprise which was not altogether pleasing to the Captain.

"Indeed, I was. But the fag of it was too great, and the thanks too small, so I gave it up. They used to get four days a week out of me." During the two years that the Captain had had the hounds there had been, no doubt, two or three weeks in which he had hunted four days.

Ayala liked hunting, but she did not care much for Captain Glomax, who, having seen her once or twice on horseback, would talk to her about nothing else. A little away on the other side of the table Nina was sitting next to Colonel Stubbs, and she could hear their voices and almost their words. Nina and Jonathan were first cousins, and, of course, could be happy together without giving her any cause for jealousy ;—but she almost envied Nina. Yet she had hoped that it might not fall to her lot to be taken out again that evening by the Colonel. Hitherto she had not even spoken to him during the day. They had started to the meet very early, and the gentlemen had almost finished their breakfast before she had come down. If there had been any fault it was her fault, but yet she almost felt that there was something of a disruption between them. It was so evident to her that he was perfectly happy whilst he was talking to Nina.

After dinner it seemed to be very late before the men came into the drawing-room, and then they were still engaged upon that weary talk about hunting, till Lady Rufford, in order to put a stop to it, offered to sing. "I always do" she said, "if Rufford ventures to

name a fox in the drawing-room after dinner." She did sing, and
Ayala thought that the singing was more weary than the talk about
hunting.

While this was going on, the Colonel had got himself shut up in a
corner of the room. Lady Albury had first taken him there, and
afterwards he had been hemmed in when Lady Rufford sat down to the
piano. Ayala had hardly ventured even to glance at him, but yet she
knew all that he did, and heard almost every word that he spoke.
The words were not many, but still when he did speak his voice was
cheerful. Nina now and again had run up to him, and Lady Rufford
had asked him some questions about the music. But why didn't he
come out and speak to her? thought Ayala. Though all that nonsense
about love was over, still he ought not to have allowed a day to pass at
Stalham without speaking to her. He was the oldest friend there in that
house except Nina. It was indeed no more than nine months since she
had first seen him, but still it seemed to her that he was an old friend.
She did feel, as she endeavoured to answer the questions that Lord Rufford was asking her, that Jonathan Stubbs was treating her unkindly.

Then came the moment in which Lady Albury marshalled her guests
out of the room towards their chambers. " Have you found yourself
dull without the hunting?" the Colonel said to Ayala.

" Oh dear no ; I must have a dull time if I do, seeing that I have
only hunted three days in my life." There was something in the tone
of her voice which, as she herself was aware, almost expressed dis-
satisfaction. And yet not for worlds would she have shown herself to
be dissatisfied with him, could she have helped it.

" I thought that perhaps you might have regretted the little pony,"
he said.

" Because a thing has been very pleasant, it should not be regretted
because it cannot be had always."

" To me, a thing may become so pleasant, that unless I can have it
always my life must be one long regret."

" The pony is not quite like that," said Ayala, smiling, as she followed the other ladies out of the room.

On the next morning the meet was nearer, and some of the ladies
were taken there in an open carriage. Lady Rufford went, and Mrs.
Gosling, and Nina and Ayala. " Of course there is a place for you,"
Lady Albury had said to her. " Had I wanted to go I would have
made Sir Harry send the drag ; but I've got to stop at home and see
that the buttered toast is ready by the time the gentlemen all come
back." The morning was almost warm, so that the sportsmen were
saying evil things of violets and primroses, as is the wont of sportsmen on such occasions, and at the meet the ladies got out of the car-

riage and walked about among the hounds, making civil speeches to old Tony. "No, my lady," said Tony, "I don't like these sunshiny mornings at all ; there ain't no kind of scent, and I goes riding about these big woods, up and down, till my shirt is as wet on my back with the sweat as though I'd been pulled through the river," Then Lady Rufford walked away and did not ask Tony any more questions.

Ayala was patting one of the hounds when the Colonel, who had given his horse to a groom, came and joined her. "If you don't regret that pony," said he, "somebody else does."

" I do regret him in one way, of course. I did like it very much ; but I don't think it nice, when much has been done for me, to say that I want to have more done."

" Of course I knew what you meant."

" Perhaps you would go and tell Sir Harry, and then he would think me very ungrateful."

" Ayala," he said, "I will never say anything of you that will make anybody think evil of you. But, between ourselves, as Sir Harry is not here, I suppose I may confess that I regret the pony."

" I should like it, of course," whispered Ayala.

" And so should I,—so much ! I suppose all these men here would think me an ass if they knew how little I care about the day's work,— whether we find, or whether we run; or whether we kill,—just because the pony is not here. If the pony were here I should have that feeling of expectation of joy, which is so common to girls when some much-thought-of ball or promised pleasure is just before them." Then Tony went off with his hounds, and Jonathan, mounting his horse, followed with the ruck.

Ayala knew very well what the pony meant, as spoken of by the Colonel. When he declared that he regretted the pony, it was because the pony might have carried herself. He had meant her to understand that the much-thought-of ball or promised pleasure would have been the delight of again riding with herself. And then he had again called her Ayala. She could remember well every occasion on which he had addressed her by her Christian name. It had been but seldom. Once, however, it had occurred in the full flow of their early intimacy, before that love-making had been begun. It had struck her as being almost wrong, but still as very pleasant. If it might be made right by some feeling of brotherly friendship, how pleasant would it be ! And now she would like it again, if only it might be taken as a sign of friendship rather than of love. It never occurred to her to be angry as she would have been angry with any other man. How she would have looked at Captain Batsby had he dared to call her Ayala ! Colonel

Stubbs should call her Ayala as long as he pleased,—if it were done only in friendship.

After that they were driven about for a while, seeing what Tony did with the hounds, as tidings came to them now and again that one fox had broken this way and another had gone the other. But Ayala, through it all, could not interest herself about the foxes. She was thinking only of Jonathan Stubbs. She knew that she was pleased because he had spoken to her, and had said kind, pleasant words to her. She knew that she had been displeased while he had sat apart from her, talking to others. But yet she could not explain to herself why she had been either pleased or displeased. She feared that there was more than friendship,—than mere friendship in that declaration of his that he did in truth regret the pony. His voice had been, oh, so sweet as he had said it! Something told her that men do not speak in mere friendship after that fashion. Not even in the softness of friendship between a man and a woman will the man's voice become as musical as that! Young as she was, child as she was, there was an instinct in her breast which declared to her that it was so. But then, if it were so, was not everything again wrong with her? If it were so, then must that condition of things be coming back which it had been, and still was, her firm resolve to avoid. And yet, as the carriage was being driven about, and as the frequent exclamations came that the fox had traversed this way or that, her pride was gratified and she was happy.

"What was Colonel Stubbs saying to you?" asked Nina, when they were at home at the house after lunch.

"He was talking about the dear pony which I used to ride."

"About nothing else?"

"No;—about nothing else." This Ayala said with a short, dry manner of utterance which she would assume when she was determined not to have a subject carried on.

"Ayala, why do you not tell me everything? I told you everything as soon as it happened."

"Nothing has happened."

"I know he asked you," said Nina.

"And I answered him."

"Is that to be everything?"

"Yes;—that is to be everything," said Ayala, with the short, dry manner of utterance. It was so plain, that even Nina could not pursue the subject.

There was nothing done on that day in the way of sport. Glomax thought that Tony had been idle, and had made a holiday of the day from the first. But Sir Harry declared that there had not been a rd of scent. The buttered toast, however, was eaten, and the regular sporting conversation was carried on. Ayala, however, was not there to hear it. Ayala was in her own room dreaming.

She was taken in to dinner by a curate in the neighbourhood,—to whom she endeavoured to make herself very pleasant, while the Colonel sat at her other side. The curate had a good deal to say as to lawn tennis. If the weather remained as it was, it was thought that they could all play lawn tennis on the Tuesday,—when there would be no hunting. The curate was a pleasant young fellow, and Ayala devoted herself to him and to their joint hopes for next Tuesday. Colonel Stubbs never once attempted to interfere with the curate's opportunity. There was Lady Rufford on the other side of him, and to Lady Rufford he said all that he did say during dinner. At one period of the repast she was more than generally lively, because she felt herself called upon to warn her husband that an attack of the gout was imminent, and would be certainly produced instantaneously if he could not deny himself the delight of a certain diet which was going the round of the table. His lordship smiled and denied himself,—thinking, as he did so, whether another wife, plus the gout, would or would not have been better for him. All this either amused Colonel Stubbs so sufficiently, or else made him so thoughtful, that he made no attempt to interfere with the curate. In the evening there was again music,—which resulted in a declaration made upstairs by Sir Harry to his wife that that wife of Rufford's was a confounded bore. "We all knew that, my dear, as soon he married her?" said Lady Albury.

"Why did he marry a bore?"

"Because he wanted a wife to look after himself, and not to amuse his friends. The wonder used to be that he had done so well."

Not a word had there been,—not a word, since that sound of "Ayala" had fallen upon her ears. No ;—he was not handsome, and his name was Jonathan Stubbs ;—but surely no voice so sweet had ever fallen from a man's lips ! So she sat and dreamed far into the night. He, the Angel of Light, would certainly have a sweeter voice ! That was an attribute without which no angel could be angelic ! As to the face and the name, that would not, perhaps, signify. But he must have an intellect high soaring, a mind tuned to music, and a mind versed in nothing but great matters. He might be an artist, or more probably a poet ;—or perhaps a musician. Yet she had read of poets, artists, and musicians, who had misused their wives, been fond of money, and had perhaps been drunkards. The Angel of Light must have the gifts, and must certainly be without the vices.

The next day was Sunday and they all went to church. In the afternoon they, as many of them as pleased, were to walk as far as Gobblegoose Wood, which was only three miles from the house. They could not hunt and therefore they must go to the very scene of the late contest and again discuss it there. Sir Harry and the Captain would walk and so would Ayala and Nina and some others. Lord Rufford did not like walking and Lady Rufford would stay at home to console him. Ayala used her little wiles to keep herself in close company with Nina; but the Colonel's wiles were more effective;—and then, perhaps, Nina assisted the Colonel rather than Ayala. It came to pass that before they had left Gobblegoose Wood Ayala and the Colonel were together. When it was so he did not beat about the bush for a moment longer. He had fixed his opportunity for himself and he put it to use at once. "Ayala," he said, "am I to have any other answer?"

"What answer?"

"Nay, my dearest,—my own, own dearest as I fain would have you,—who shall say what answer but you? Ayala, you know that I love you!"

"I thought you had given it up."

"Given it up. Never,—never! Does a man give up his joy,—the pride of his life,—the one only delight on which his heart has set itself? No, my darling, I have not given it up. Because you would not have it as I wished when I first spoke to you, I have not gone on troubling you. I thought I would wait till you were used again to the look of me, and to my voice. I shall never give it up, Ayala. When you came into the room that night with your new frock on——" Then he paused, and she glanced round upon him, and saw that a tear again was in his eye. "When you came in and curtseyed to Sir Harry I could hardly keep within myself because I thought you were so beautiful."

"It was the new gown which he had given me."

"No, my pet;—no! You may add a grace to a dress, but it can do but little for you. It was the little motion, the little word, the light in your eye! It twinkles at me sometimes when you glance about, so that I do not know whether it is meant for me or not. I fear that it is never meant for me."

"It is meant for nothing," said Ayala.

"And yet it goes into my very bosom. When you were talking to that clergyman at dinner I could see every sparkle that came from it. Then I wonder to myself whether you can ever be thinking of me as I am always thinking of you." She knew that she had been thinking of him every waking moment since she had been at Albury and through many of her sleeping moments also. "Ayala, one little word, one other glance from your eyes, one slightest touch from your hand upon my arm, shall tell me,—shall tell me,—shall tell me that I am the happiest, the proudest man in all the world." She walked on stead-fastly, closing her very teeth against a word, with her eyes fixed before her so that no slightest glance should wander. Her two hands were in her little muff, and she kept them with her fingers clasped together, as though afraid lest one might rebel, and fly away, and touch the sleeve of his coat. " Ayala, how is it to be with me ?"

" I cannot," she said, sternly. And her eyes were still fixed before her, and her fingers were still bound in one with another. And yet she loved him. Yet she knew that she loved him. She could have hung upon his arm and smiled up into his face, and frowned her refusal only with mock anger as he pressed her to his bosom,—only that those dreams were so palpable to her and so dear, had been to her so vast a portio of her young life ! " I cannot," she said again. " I cannot."

" Is that to be your answer for ever ?" To this she made no immediate reply. " Must it be so, Ayala ?"

" I cannot " she said. But the last little word was so impeded by the sobs which she could not restrain as almost to be inaudible.

" I will not make you unhappy, Ayala ?" Yes, she was unhappy. She was unhappy because she knew that she could not rule herself to her own happiness ; because, even at this moment, she was aware that she was wrong. If she could only release part of herself from the other, then could she fly into his arms and tell him that that spirit which had troubled her had flown. But the spirit was too strong for her, and would not fly. " Shall we go and join them ?" he asked her in a voice altered, but still so sweet to her ears.

" If you think so," she replied.

" Perhaps it will be best, Ayala. Do not be angry with me now. I will not call you so again.' Angry ! Oh, no ! She was not angry with him ! But it was very bitter to her to be told that she should never hear the word again from his lips.

" The hunted fox never went up Buddlecombe Hill ;—never. If he did I'll eat every fox in the Rufford and Offord country." This was heard, spoken in most angry tones by Captain Glomax, as the Colonel and Ayala joined the rest of the party.

CHAPTER LI.

" NO !"

AYALA, on her return from the walk to the wood, spent the remainder of the afternoon in tears. During the walk she kept close to Sir

Harry, pretending to listen to the arguments about the fox, but she
said nothing. Her ears were really intent on endeavouring to catch
the tones of her lover's voice as he went on in front of them talking to
Nina. Nothing could be more pleasant than the sound as he said a
word or two now and again, encouraging Nina in her rhapsodies as to
Lord George and all Lord George's family. But Ayala learned nothing
from that. She had come to know the man well enough to be aware
that he could tune his voice to the occasion, and could hide his feelings let them be ever so strong. She did not doubt his love now. She
did not doubt but that at this moment his heart was heavy with
rejected love. She quite believed in him. But nevertheless his words
were pleasant and kind as he encouraged Nina.

Nor did she doubt her own love. She was alone in her room that
afternoon till she told herself at last the truth. Oh, yes; she loved
him. She was sure of that. But now he was gone! Why had she
been so foolish? Then it seemed as though at that moment the
separation took place between herself and the spirit which had haunted
her. She seemed to know now,—now at this very moment,—that the
man was too good for her. The knowledge had been coming to her.
It had almost come when he had spoken to her in the wood. If it
could only have been that he should have delayed his appeal to her
yet for another day or two! She thought now that if he could have
delayed it but for a few hours the cure would have been complete. If
he had talked to her as he so well knew how to talk while they were
in the wood together, while they were walking home,—so as to have
exorcised the spirit from her by the sweetness of his words,—and then
have told her that there was his love to have if she chose to have it,
then she thought she would have taken it. But he had come to her
while those words which she had prepared under the guidance of the
spirit were yet upon her tongue. "I cannot," she had said. "I cannot." But she had not told him that she did not love him.

"I did love him," she said to herself, almost acknowledging that
the spirit had been wholly exorcised. The fashion of her mind was
altogether different from that which had so strongly prevailed with her.
He was an honest, noble man, high in the world's repute, clever,
a gentleman, a man of taste, and possessed of that gentle ever-
present humour which was so inexpressibly delightful to her. She
never again spoke to herself even in her thoughts of that Angel of
Light,—never comforted herself again with the vision of that which
was to come! There had appeared to her a man better than all other
men, and when he had asked her for her hand she had simply said,—
"I cannot." And yet she had loved him all the time. How foolish,
how false, how wicked she had been! It was thus that she thought of

it all as she sat there alone in her bedroom through the long hours of the afternoon. When they sent up for her asking her to come down, she begged that she might be allowed to remain there till dinner-time, because she was tired with her walk.

He would not come again now. Oh, no,—he was too proud, too firm, too manly for that. It was not for such a one as he to come whining after a girl,—like her cousin Tom. Would it be possible that she should even yet tell him? Could she say to him one little word, contradicting that which she had so often uttered in the wood? "Now I can," once whispered in his ear, would do it all. But as to this she was aware that there was no room for hope. To speak such a word, low as it might be spoken, simple and little as it might be, was altogether impossible. She had had her chance and had lost it,—because of those idle dreams. That the dreams had been all idle she declared to herself,—not aware that the Ayala whom her lover had loved would not have been an Ayala to be loved by him, but for the dreams. Now she must go back to her uncle and aunt and to Kingsbury Crescent, with the added sorrow that the world of dreams was closed to her for ever. When the maid came to her she consented to have the frock put on, the frock which Sir Harry had given her, boldly resolving to struggle through her sorrow till Lady Albury should have dismissed her to her home. Nobody would want her now at Stalham, and the dismissal would soon come.

While she had been alone in her room the Colonel had been closeted with Lady Albury. They had at least been thus shut up together for some half-hour during which he had told his tale. "I have to own," said he, half-laughing as he began his tale, "that I thoroughly respect Miss Dormer."

"Why is she to be called Miss Dormer?"

"Because she has shown herself worthy of my respect."

"What is it that you mean, Jonathan?"

"She knew her own mind when she told me at first that she could not accept the offer which I did myself the honour of making her, and now she sticks to her purpose. I think that a young lady who will do that should be respected."

"She has refused you again?"

"Altogether."

"As how?"

"Well, I hardly know that I am prepared to explain the 'as how,' even to you. I am about as thick-skinned a man in such matters as you may find anywhere, but I do not know that even I can bring myself to tell the 'as how.' The 'as how' was very clear in one respect. It was manifest that she knew her own mind, which is a knowledge not in the possession of all young ladies. She told me that she could not marry me."

" I do not believe it."

" Not that she told me so ?"

" Not that she knew her own mind. She is a little simple fool, who with some vagary in her brain is throwing away utterly her own happiness, while she is vexing you."

" As to the vexation you are right."

" Cross-grained little idiot !"

" An idiot she certainly is not ; and as to being cross-grained I have never found it. A human being with the grains running more directly all in the same way I have never come across."

" Do not talk to me, Jonathan, like that," she said. " When I call her cross-grained I mean that she is running counter to her own happiness."

" I cannot tell anything about that. I should have endeavoured, I think, to make her happy. She has certainly run counter to my happiness."

" And now ?"

" What ;—as to this very moment ! I shall leave Stalham to-morrow."

" Why should you do that ! Let her go if one must go."

" That is just what I want to prevent. Why should she lose her little pleasure ?"

" You don't suppose that we can make the house happy to her now ! Why should we care to do so when she will have driven you away?" He sat silent for a minute or two looking at the fire, with his hands on his two knees. " You must acknowledge, Jonathan," continued she, " that I have taken kindly to this Ayala of yours."

" I do acknowledge it."

" But it cannot be that she should be the same to us simply as a young lady, staying here as it were on her own behalf, as she was when we regarded her as your possible wife. Then every little trick and grace belonging to her endeared itself to us because we regarded her as one who was about to become one of ourselves. But what are her tricks and graces to us now ?"

" They are all the world to me," said the Colonel.

" But you must wipe them out of your memory,—unless, indeed, you mean to ask her again."

" Ah !—that is it."

" You will ask her again ?"

" I do not say so ; but I do not wish to rob myself of the chance. It may be that I shall. Of course I should to-morrow if I thought there was a hope. To-morrow there would be none,—but I should like to know, that I could find her again in hands so friendly as yours, if at the end of a month I should think myself strong enough to encounter the risk of another refusal. Would Sir Harry allow her to remain here for another month?"

"He would say, probably, nothing about it."

"My plan is this," he continued; "let her remain here, say, for three weeks or a month. Do you continue all your kindness to her,— if not for her sake then for mine. Let her feel that she is made one of yourselves, as you say."

"That will be hard," said Lady Albury.

"It would not be hard if you thought that she was going to become so at last. Try it, for my sake. Say not a word to her about me,— though not shunning my name. Be to her as though I had told you nothing of this. Then when the period is over I will come again,—if I find that I can do so. If my love is still stronger than my sense of self-respect, I shall do so." All this Lady Albury promised to do, and then the interview between them was over.

"Colonel Stubbs is going to Aldershot to-morrow," said she to Ayala in the drawing-room after dinner. "He finds now that he cannot very well remain away." There was no hesitation in her voice as she said this, and no look in her eye which taught Ayala to suppose that she had heard anything of what had occurred in the wood.

"Is he indeed?" said Ayala, trying, but in vain, to be equally undemonstrative.

"It is a great trouble to us, but we are quite unable to prevent it,— unless you indeed can control him."

"I cannot control him," said Ayala, with that fixed look of resolution with which Lady Albury had already become familiar.

That evening before they went to bed the Colonel bade them all good-bye, as he intended to start early in the morning. "I never saw such a fellow as you are for sudden changes," said Sir Harry.

"What is the good of staying here for hunting when the ground and Tony's temper are both as hard as brick-bats. If I go now I can get another week further on in March if the rain should come." With this Sir Harry seemed to be satisfied; but Ayala felt sure that Tony's temper and the rain had had nothing to do with it.

"Good-bye, Miss Dormer," he said, with his pleasantest smile, and his pleasantest voice.

"Good-bye," she repeated. What would she not have given that her voice should be as pleasant as his, and her smile! But she failed so utterly that the little word was inaudible,—almost obliterated by the choking of a sob. How bitterly severe had that word, Miss Dormer, sounded from his mouth! Could he not have called her Ayala for the last time,——even though all the world should have heard it? She was wide awake in the morning and heard the wheels of his cart as he was driven off. As the sound died away upon her ear she felt that he was gone from her for ever. How had it been that she had said, "I cannot," so often, when all her heart was set upon "I can?"

And now it remained to her to take herself away from Stalham as fast as she might. She understood perfectly all those ideas which Lady Albury had expressed to her well-loved friend. She was nothing to anybody at Stalham, simply a young lady staying in the house;— as might be some young lady connected with them by blood, or some young lady whose father and mother had been their friends. She had been brought there to Stalham, now this second time, in order that Jonathan Stubbs might take her as his wife. Driven by some madness she had refused her destiny, and now nobody would want her at Stalham any longer. She had better begin to pack up at once,—and go. The coldness of the people, now that she had refused to do as she had been asked, would be unbearable to her. And yet she must not let it appear that Stalham was no longer dear to her merely because Colonel Stubbs had left it. She would let a day go by, and then say with all the ease she could muster that she would take her departure on the next. After that her life before her would be a blank. She had known up to this,—so at least she told herself,—that Jonathan Stubbs would afford her at any rate another chance. Now there could be no other chance.

The first blank day passed away, and it seemed to her almost as though she had no right to speak to any one. She was sure that Lady Rufford knew what had occurred, because nothing more was said as to the proposed visit. Mrs. Colonel Stubbs would have been welcome anywhere, but who was Ayala Dormer? Even though Lady Albury bade her come out in the carriage, it seemed to her to be done as a final effort of kindness. Of course they would be anxious to be rid of her. That evening the buxom woman did not come to help her dress herself. It was an accident. The buxom woman was wanted here and there till it was too late, and Ayala had left her room. Ayala, in truth, required no assistance in dressing. When the first agonizing moment of the new frock had been passed over, she would sooner have arrayed herself without assistance. But now it seemed as though the buxom woman was running away, because she, Ayala, was thought to be no longer worthy of her services.

On the next morning she began her little speech to Lady Albury. " Going away to-morrow?" said Lady Albury.

" Or perhaps the next day," suggested Ayala.

" My dear, it has been arranged that you should stay here for another three weeks."

" No."

" I say it was arranged. Everybody understood it. I am sure your aunt understood it. Because one person goes, everybody else isn't to follow so as to break up a party. Honour among thieves !"

" Thieves !"

" Well ;—anything else you like to call us all. The party has been made up. And to tell the truth I don't think that young ladies have the same right of changing their minds and rushing about as men assume. Young ladies ought to be more steady. Where am I to get another young lady at a moment's notice to play lawn tennis with Mr. Greene ? Compose yourself and stay where you are, like a good girl."

" What will Sir Harry say ?"

" Sir Harry will probably go on talking about the Stillborough fox and quarreling with that odious Captain Glomax. That is, if you remain here. If you go all of a sudden, he will perhaps hint——"

" Hint what, Lady Albury ?"

" Never mind. He shall make no hints if you are a good girl." Nothing was said at the moment about the Colonel,—nothing further than the little allusion made above. Then there came the lawn tennis, and Ayala regained something of her spirits as she contrived with the assistance of Sir Harry to beat Nina and the curate. But on the following day Lady Albury spoke out more plainly. " It was because of Colonel Stubbs that you said that you would go away."

Ayala paused a moment, and then answered stoutly, " Yes, it was because of Colonel Stubbs."

" And why ? "

Ayala paused again and the stoutness almost deserted her. " Because——"

" Well, my dear ?"

" I don't think I ought to be asked," said Ayala.

" Well, you shall not be asked. I will not be cruel to you. But do you not know that if I ask anything it is with a view to your own good ?"

" Oh, yes," said Ayala.

" But though I may not ask I suppose I may speak." To this Ayala made no reply, either assenting or dissenting. " You know, do you not, that I and Colonel Stubbs love each other like brother and sister,—more dearly than many brothers and sisters ?"

" I suppose so."

"And that therefore he tells me everything. He told me what took place in the wood,—and because of that he has gone away."

"Of course you are angry with me ;—because he has gone away."

"I am sorry that he has gone,—because of the cause of it. I always wish that he should have everything that he desires ; and now I wish that he should have this thing because he desires it above all other things." Does he desire it above all other things ?—thought Ayala to herself. And, if it be really so, cannot I now tell her that he shall have it ? Cannot I say that I too long to get it quite as eagerly as he longs to have it ? The suggestion rushed quickly to her mind ; but the answer to it came as quickly. No ;—she would not do so. No offer of the kind would come from her. By what she had said must she abide,—unless, indeed, he should come to her again. "But why should you go, Ayala, because he has gone ? Why should you say aloud that you had come here to listen to his offer, and that you had gone away as soon as you had resolved that, for this reason or that, it was not satisfactory to you ?"

"Oh, Lady Albury."

"That would be the conclusion drawn. Remain here with us, and see if you can like us well enough to be one of us."

"Dear Lady Albury, I do love you dearly."

"What he may do I cannot say. Whether he may bring himself to try once again I do not know,—nor will I ask you whether there might possibly be any other answer were he to do."

"No !" said Ayala, driven by a sudden fit of obstinacy which she could not control.

"I ask no questions about it, but I am sure it will be better for you to remain here for a few weeks. We will make you happy if we can, and you can learn to think over what has passed without emotion." Thus it was decided that Ayala should prolong her visit into the middle of March. She could not understand her own conduct when she again found herself alone. Why had she ejaculated that sudden "No," when Lady Albury had suggested to her the possibility of changing her purpose ? She knew that she would fain change it if it were possible ; and yet when the idea was presented to her she replied with a sudden denial of its possibility. But still there was hope, even though the hope was faint. "Whether he may bring himself to try again I do not know." So it was that Lady Albury had spoken of him, and of what Lady Albury said to her she now believed every word. "Whether he could bring himself !" Surely such a one as he would not condescend so far as that. But if he did one word should be sufficient. By no one else would she allow it to be thought, for an instant, that she would wish to reverse her decision. It must still be No to any other person from whom such suggestion might come. But should he give her the chance she would tell him instantly the truth of everything. "Can I love you! Oh, my love, it is impossible that I should not love you!" It would be thus that the answer should be given to him, should he allow her the chance of making it.

CHAPTER LII.

"I CALL IT FOLLY."

THREE weeks passed by, and Ayala was still at Stalham. Colonel Stubbs had not as yet appeared, and very little had been said about him. Sir Henry would sometimes suggest that if he meant to see any more hunting he had better come at once, but this was not addressed to Ayala. She made up her mind that he would not come, and was sure that she was keeping him away by her presence. He could not— "bring himself to try over again," as Lady Albury had put it! Why should he—"bring himself"—to do anything on behalf of one who had treated him so badly? It had been settled that she should remain to the 25th of March, when the month should be up from the time in which Lady Albury had decided upon that as the period of her visit. Of her secret she had given no slightest hint. If he ever did come again it should not be because she had asked for his coming? As far as she knew how to carry out such a purpose, she concealed from Lady Albury anything like a feeling of regret. And she was so far successful that Lady Albury thought it expedient to bring in other assistance to help her cause,—as will be seen by a letter which Ayala received when the three weeks had passed by.

In the meantime there had been at first dismay, then wonder, and lastly, some amusement, at the condition of Captain Batsby. When Captain Batsby had first learned at Merle Park that Ayala and Jonathan Stubbs were both at Stalham, he wrote very angrily to Lady Albury. In answer to this his sister-in-law had pleaded guilty,—but still defending herself. How could she make herself responsible for the young lady,—who did not indeed seem ready to bestow her affections on any of her suitors? But still she acknowledged that a little favour was being shown to Colonel Stubbs,—wishing to train the man to the idea that, in this special matter, Colonel Stubbs must be recognised as the Stalham favourite. Then no further letters were received from the Captain, but there came tidings that he was staying at Merle Park. Ayala heard continually from her sister, and Lucy sent some revelations as to the Captain. He seemed to be very much at home at Merle Park, said Lucy; and then, at last, she expressed her own opinion that Captain Batsby and Gertrude were becoming very fond of each other. And yet the whole story of Gertrude and Mr. Houston was known, of course, to Lucy, and through Lucy to Ayala. To Ayala these sudden changes were very amusing, as she certainly did not wish to retain her own hold on the Captain and was not specially attached to her cousin Gertrude. From Ayala the tidings went to Lady Albury, and in this way the fears which had been entertained as to the Captain's displeasure were turned to wonder and amusement. But up to this period nothing had been heard of the projected trip to Ostend.

Then came the letter to Ayala, to which allusion has been made,—a letter from her old friend the Marchesa, who was now at Rome. It was ostensibly in answer to a letter from Ayala herself, but was written in great part in compliance with instructions received from Lady Albury. It was as follows ;—

" DEAR AYALA,—

" I was glad to get your letter about Nina. She is very happy, and Lord George is here. Indeed, to tell the truth, they arrived together,— which was not at all proper ; but everything will be made proper on Tuesday, 8th April, which is the day at last fixed for the wedding. I wish you could have been here to be one of the bridesmaids. Nina says that you will have it that the Pope is to marry her. Instead of that, it is going to be done by Lord George's uncle, the Dean of Dorchester, who is coming for this purpose. Then they are going up to a villa they have taken on Como, where we shall join them some time before the spring is over. After that they seem to have no plans,— except plans of connubial bliss which is never to know any interruption.

" Now that I have come to connubial bliss, and feel so satisfied as to Nina's prospects, I have a word or two to say about the bliss of somebody else. Nina is my own child, and of course comes first. But one Jonathan Stubbs is my nephew, and is also very near to my heart. From all that I hear, I fancy that he has set his mind also on connubial bliss. Have you not heard that it is so ?

" A bird has whispered to me that you have not been kind to him. Why should it be so ? Nobody knows better than I do that a young lady is entitled to the custody of her own heart, and that she should not be compelled, or even persuaded, to give her hand in opposition to her own feelings. If your feelings and your heart are altogether opposed to the poor fellow, of course there must be an end of it. But I had thought that from the time you first met him he had been a favourite of yours ;—so much so that there was a moment in which I feared that you might think too much of the attentions of a man who has ever been a favourite with all who have known him. But I have found that in this I was altogether mistaken. When he came that evening to see the last of you at the theatre, taking, as I knew he did, considerable trouble to release himself from other engagements, I was pretty sure how it was going to be. He is not a man to be in love with a girl for a month and then to be in love with another the next month. When once he has allowed himself to think that he was in love, the thing was done and fixed either for his great delight,—or else to his great trouble.

"I knew how it was to be, and so it has been. Am I not right in saying that on two occasions, at considerable intervals, he has come to you and made distinct offers of his hand? I fear, though I do not actually know it, that you have just as distinctly rejected those offers. I do not know it, because none but you and he can know the exact words with which you received from him the tender of all that he had to give you. I can easily believe that he, with all his intelligence, might be deceived by the feminine reserve and coyness of such a girl as you. If it be so, I do pray that no folly may be allowed to interfere with his happiness and with yours.

"I call it folly, not because I am adverse to feminine reserves, not because I am prone to quarrel even with what I call coyness; but because I know his nature so well, and feel that he would not bear rebuffs of which many another man would think nothing;—that he would not bring himself to ask again, perhaps even for a seventh time, as they might do. And, if it be that by some frequent asking his happiness and yours could be insured, would it not be folly that such happiness should be marred by childish disinclination on your part to tell the truth?

"As I said before, if your heart be set against him, there must be an end of it. I can understand that a girl so young as you should fail to see the great merit of such a man. I therefore write as I do, think-ing it possible that in this respect you may be willing to accept from my mouth something as to the man which shall be regarded as truth. It is on the inner man, on his nature and disposition, that the happi-ness of a wife must depend. A more noble nature, a more truthful spirit than his, I have never met. He is one on whom in every phase of life you may depend,—or I may depend,—as on a rock. He is one without vacillation, always steady to his purpose, requiring from him-self in the way of duty and conduct infinitely more than he demands from those around him. If ever there was a man altogether manly, he is one. And yet no woman, no angel, ever held a heart more tender within his bosom. See him with children! Think of his words when he has spoken to yourself! Remember the estimation in which those friends hold him who know him best,—such as I and your friend, Lady Albury, and Sir Harry, and his cousin Nina. I could name many others, but these are those with whom you have seen him most frequently. If you can love such a man, do you not think that he would make you happy? And if you cannot must there not be something wrong in your heart,—unless indeed it be already predisposed to some one else? Think of all this, dear Ayala, and remember that I am always " Your affectionate friend,

" JULIA BALDONI."

Ayala's first feeling as she read the letter was a conviction that her friend had altogether wasted her labour in writing it. Of what use was it to tell her of the man's virtues,—to tell her that the man's heart was as tender as an angel's, his truth as assured as a god's, his courage that of a hero,—that he was possessed of all those attributes which should by right belong to an Angel of Light? She knew all that without requiring the evidence of a lady from Rome,—having no need of any evidence on that matter from any other human being. Of what use could any evidence be on such a subject from the most truthful lips that ever spoke! Had she not found it all out herself would any words from others have prevailed with her? But she had found it out herself. It was already her gospel. That he was tender and true, manly, heroic,—as brightly angelic as could be any Angel of Light,—was already an absolute fact to her. No!—her heart had never been predisposed to anyone else. It was of him she had always dreamed even long before she had seen him. He was the man, perfect in all good things, who was to come and take her with him ;—if ever man should come and take her. She wanted no Marchesa Baldoni now to tell her that the angel had in truth come and realised himself before her in all his glory.

But she had shown herself to be utterly unfit for the angel. Though she recognised him now, she had not recognised him in time ;—and even when she had recognised him she had been driven by her madness to reject him. Feminine reserve and coyness! Folly! Yes, indeed; she knew all that, too, without need of telling from her elders. The kind of coyness which she had displayed had been the very infatuation of feminine imbecility. It was because nature had made her utterly unfit for such a destiny that she had been driven by coyness and feminine reserve to destroy herself! It was thus that Ayala conversed with herself.

" I know his nature so well, and feel that he would not bear rebuffs of which many another man would think nothing." Thus, she did not doubt, the Marchesa had spoken very truly. But of what value was all that now? She could not recall the rebuff. She could not now eradicate the cowardice which had made her repeat those wicked fatal words,—"I cannot." "I cannot." "I cannot." The letter had come too late, for there was nothing she could do to amend her doom. She must send some answer to her friend in Italy, but there could be nothing in her answer to her to assist her. The feminine reserve and coyness had become odious to her,—as it had been displayed by herself to him. But it still remained in full force as to any assistance from others. She could not tell another to send him back to her. She could not implore help in her trouble. If he would come himself,—himself of his own accord,—himself impelled once more by his great tenderness of heart,—himself once more from his real, real love ; then there should be no more coyness. " If you will still have me,—oh, yes !"

But there was the letter to be written. She so wrote it that by far the greater part of it,—the larger part at least,—had reference to Nina and her wedding. " I will think of her on the 8th of April," she said. " I shall then be at home in Kingsbury Crescent, and I shall have nothing else to think of." In that was her first allusion to her own condition with her lover. But on the last side of the sheet it was necessary that she should say more than that. Something must be said thoughtfully, carefully, and gratefully in reply to so much thought and care, and friendship, as had been shown to her. But it must be so written that nothing of her secret should be read in it. The task was so troublesome that she was compelled to recopy the whole of her long letter, because the sentences as first written did not please her. " I am so much obliged to you," she said, " by your kindness about Colonel Stubbs. He did do me the honour of asking me to be his wife. And I felt it so. You are not to suppose that I did not understand that. It is all over now, and I cannot explain to you why I felt that it would not do. It is all over, and therefore writing about it is no good. Only I want you to be sure of two things,—that there is no one else, and that I do love you so much for all your kindness. And you may be sure of a third thing, too,—that it is all over. I do hope that he will still let me be his friend. As a friend I have always liked him so much." It was brave and bold, she thought, in answer to such words as the Marchesa's ; but she did not know how to do it any better.

On Tuesday, the 25th of March, she was to return to Kingsbury Crescent. Various little words were said at Stalham indicating an intended break in the arrangement. "The Captain certainly won't come now," said Lady Albury, alluding to the arrangement as though

It had been made solely with the view of saving Ayala from an encounter with her objectionable lover. "Croppy has come back," said Sir Harry one day ;—Croppy being the pony which Ayala had ridden. "Miss Dormer can have him now for what little there is left of the hunting." This was said on the Saturday before she was to go. How could she ride Croppy for the rest of the hunting when she would be at Kingsbury Crescent? On neither of these occasions did she say a word, but she assumed that little look of contradiction which her friends at Stalham already knew how to read. Then, on the Sunday morning, there came a letter for Lady Albury. "What does he say?" asked Sir Harry, at breakfast. "I'll show it you before you go to church," answered his wife. Then Ayala knew that the letter was from Colonel Stubbs.

But she did not expect that the letter should be shown to her,— which, however, came to be the case. When she was in the library, waiting to start to church, Lady Albury came in and chucked the letter to her across the table. "That concerns you," she said,—"you had better read it." There was another lady in the room, also waiting to start on their walk across the park, and therefore it was natural that nothing else should be said at the moment. Ayala read the letter, returned it to the envelope, and then handed it back to Lady Albury, —so that there was no word spoken about it before church. The letter, which was very short, was as follows ;—

" I shall be at Stalham by the afternoon train on Sunday, 30th,—in time for dinner, if you will send the dog-cart. I could not leave this most exigeant of all places this week. I suppose Albury will go on in the woodlands for a week or ten days in April, and I must put up with that. I hear that Batsby is altogether fixed by the fascinations of Merle Park. I hope that you and Albury will receive consolation in the money." Then there was a postscript. "If Croppy can be got back again, Miss Dormer might see me tumble into another river."

It was evident that Lady Albury did not expect anything to be said at present. She put the letter into her pocket, and there, for the moment, was the end of it. It may be feared that Ayala's attention was not fixed that morning so closely as it should have been on the services of the Church. There was so much in that little letter which insisted upon having all her attention! Had there been no postscript, the letter would have been very different. In that case the body of the letter itself would have intended to have no reference to her,—or rather it would have had a reference altogether opposite to that which the postscript gave it. In that case it would have been manifest to her that he had intentionally postponed his coming till she had left Stalham. Then his suggestion about the hunting would

2 B

have had no interest for her. Everything would have been over. She would have been at Kingsbury Crescent, and he would have been at Stalham. But the postscript declared his intention of finding her still in the old quarters. She would not be there,—as she declared to herself. After this there would be but one other day, and then she would be gone. But even this allusion to her and to the pony made the letter something to her of intense interest. Had it not been so Lady Albury would not have shown it to her. As it was, why had Lady Albury shown it to her in that quiet, placid, friendly way,—as though it were natural that any letter from Colonel Stubbs to Stalham should be shown to her?

At lunch Sir Harry began about the pony at once. "Miss Dormer," he said, "the pony will hardly be fit to-morrow, and the distances during the rest of the week are all too great for you; you had better wait till Monday week, when Stubbs will be here to look after you."

"But I am going home on Tuesday," said Ayala.

"I've had the pony brought on purpose for you," said Sir Harry.

"You are not going at all," said Lady Albury. "All that has to be altered. I'll write to Mrs. Dosett."

"I don't think——" began Ayala.

"I shall take it very much amiss," said Sir Harry, "if you go now. Stubbs is coming on purpose."

"I don't think——" began Ayala again.

"My dear Ayala, it isn't a case for thinking," said Lady Albury. "You most positively will not leave this house till some day in April, which will have to be settled hereafter. Do not let us have a word more about it." Then, on that immediate occasion, no further word about it was spoken. Ayala was quite unable to speak as she sat attempting to eat her lunch.

CHAPTER LIII.

HOW LUCY'S AFFAIRS ARRANGED THEMSELVES.

WE must go again to Merle Park, where the Tringle family was still living,—and from which Gertrude had not as yet been violently abducted at the period to which the reader has been brought in the relation which has been given of the affairs at Stalham. Jonathan Stubbs's little note to Lady Albury was received on Sunday, 23rd March, and Gertrude was not abducted till the 29th. On Sunday, the 30th, she was brought back,—not in great triumph. At that time the house was considerably perturbed. Sir Thomas was very angry with his daughter Augusta, having been led to believe that she had been privy to Gertrude's escapade,—so angry that very violent words had been spoken as to her expulsion from the house. Tom also was ill, absolutely ill in bed, with a doctor to see him,—and all from love, declaring that he would throw himself over the ship's side and drown himself while there was yet a chance left to him for Ayala. And in the midst of this Lady Tringle herself was by no means exempt from the paternal wrath. She was told that she must have known what was going on between her daughter and that idiot Captain,—that she encouraged the Trafficks to remain,—that she coddled up her son till he was sick from sheer lackadaisical idleness. The only one in the house who seemed to be exempt from the wrath of Sir Thomas was Lucy,—and therefore it was upon Lucy's head that fell the concentrated energy of Aunt Emmeline's revenge. When Captain Batsby was spoken of with contumely in the light of a husband,—this being always done by Sir Thomas,—Lady Tringle would make her rejoinder to this, when Sir Thomas had turned his back, by saying that a captain in Her Majesty's army, with good blood in his veins and a competent fortune, was at any rate better than a poor artist, who had, so to say, no blood, and was unable to earn his bread; and when Tom was ridiculed for his love for Ayala she would go on to explain,—always after Sir Thomas's back had been turned,—that poor Tom had been encouraged by his father, whereas Lucy had taken upon herself to engage herself in opposition to her pastors and masters. And then came the climax. It was all very well to say that Augusta was intruding,—but there were people who intruded much worse than Augusta, without half so much right. When this was said the poor sore-hearted woman felt her own cruelty, and endeavoured to withdraw the harsh words; but the wound had been given, and the venom rankled so bitterly that Lucy could no longer bear her existence among the Tringles. "I ought not to remain after that," she wrote to her lover. "Though I went into the poor-house I ought not to remain."

"I wrote to Mr. Hamel," she said to her aunt, "and told him that as you did not like my being here I had better,—better go away."

"But where are you to go? And I didn't say that I didn't like you being here. You oughtn't to take me up in that way."

"I do feel that I am in the way, aunt, and I think that I had better go."

"But where are you to go? I declare that everybody says everything to break my heart. Of course you are to remain here till he has got a house to keep you in." But the letter had gone and a reply had come telling Lucy that whatever might be the poor-house to which she would be destined he would be there to share it with her.

Hamel wrote this with high heart. He had already resolved, previous to this, that he would at once prepare a home for his coming bride, though he was sore distressed by the emergency of his position. His father had become more and more bitter with him as he learned that his son would in no respect be guided by him. There was a sum of money which he now declared to be due to him, and which Isadore acknowledged to have been lent to him. Of this the father demanded repayment. "If," said he, "you acknowledge anything of the obedience of a son, that money is at your disposal,—and any other that you may want. But, if you determine to be as free from my control and as deaf to my advice as might be any other young man, then you must be to me as might be any other young man." He had written to his father saying that the money should be repaid as soon as possible. The misfortune had come to him at a trying time. It was, however, before he had received Lucy's last account of her own misery at Merle Park, so that when that was received he was in part prepared.

Our Colonel, in writing to Lady Albury, had declared Aldershot to be a most exigeant place,—by which he had intended to imply that his professional cares were too heavy to allow his frequent absence; but nevertheless he would contrive occasionally to fly up to London for a little relief. Once when doing so he had found himself sitting in the sculptor's studio, and there listening to Hamel's account of Lucy's troubles at Merle Park. Hamel said nothing as to his own difficulties, but was very eager in explaining the necessity of removing Lucy from the tyranny to which she was subjected. It will perhaps be remembered that Hamel down in Scotland had declared to his friend his purpose of asking Lucy Dormer to be his wife, and also the success of his enterprise after he had gone across the lake to Glenbogie. It will be borne in mind also that should the Colonel succeed in winning Ayala to his way of thinking the two men would become the husbands of the two sisters. Each fully sympathised with the other, and in this way they had become sincere and intimate friends.

"Is she like her sister?" asked the Colonel, who was not as yet acquainted with Lucy.

"Hardly like her; although in truth there is a family likeness. Lucy is taller, with perhaps more regular features, and certainly more quiet in her manner."

"Ayala can be very quiet, too," said the lover.

"Oh, yes,—because she varies in her moods. I remember her almost as a child, when she would remain perfectly still for a quarter of an hour, and then would be up and about the house everywhere, glancing about like a ray of the sun reflected from a mirror as you move it in your hand."

" She has grown steadier since that," said the Colonel.

" I cannot imagine her to be steady,—not as Lucy is steady. Lucy, if it be necessary, can sit and fill herself with her own thoughts for the hour together."

" Which of them was most like their father ?"

" They were both of them like him in their thorough love for things beautiful ;—but they are both of them unlike him in this, that he was self-indulgent, while they, like women in general, are always devoting themselves to others." She will not devote herself to me, thought Jonathan Stubbs to himself, but that may be because, like her father, she loves things beautiful. "My poor Lucy," continued Hamel, " would fain devote herself to those around her if they would only permit it."

" She would probably prefer devoting herself to you," said the Colonel.

" No doubt she would,—if it were expedient. If I may presume that she loves me, I may presume also that she would wish to live with me."

" Is it not expedient ?" asked the other.

" It will be so, I trust, before long."

" But it seems to be so necessary just at present." To this the sculptor at the moment made no reply. "If," continued Stubbs, " they treat her among them as you say, she ought at any rate to be relieved from her misery."

" She ought to be relieved certainly. She shall be relieved."

" But you say that it is not expedient."

" I only meant that there were difficulties ;—difficulties which will have to be got over. I think that all difficulties are got over when a man looks at them steadily."

" This, I suppose, is an affair of money."

" Well, yes. All difficulties seem to me to be an affair of money. A man, of course, would wish to earn enough before he marries to make his wife comfortable. I would struggle on as I am, and not be impatient, were it not that I fear she is more uncomfortable as she is now than she would be here in the midst of my poverty."

" After all, Hamel, what is the extent of the poverty ? What are the real circumstances ? As you have gone so far you might as well tell me everything." Then after considerable pressure the sculptor did tell him everything. There was an income of less than three hundred a-year,—which would probably become about four within the nex twelvemonth. There were no funds prepared with which to buy the necessary furniture for the incoming of a wife, and there was that debt demanded by his father.

" Must that be paid ?" asked the Colonel.

" I would starve rather than not pay it," said Hamel, " if I alone were to be considered. It would certainly be paid within the next six months if I were alone, even though I should starve."

Then his friend told him that the debt should be paid at once. It amounted to but little more than a hundred pounds. And then, of course, the conversation was carried further. When a friend inquires as to the pecuniary distresses of a friend he feels himself as a matter of course bound to relieve him. He would supply also the means necessary for the incoming of the young wife. With much energy, and for a long time, Hamel refused to accept the assistance offered to him; but the Colonel insisted in the first place on what he considered to be due from himself to Ayala's sister, and then on the fact that he doubted not in the least the ultimate success which would attend the professional industry of his friend. And so before the day was over it was settled among them. The money was to be forthcoming at once, so that the debt might be paid and the preparations made, and Hamel was to write to Lucy and declare that he should be ready to receive her as soon as arrangements should be made for their immediate marriage. Then came the further outrage,—that cruel speech as to intruders, and Lucy wrote to her lover, owning that it would be well for her that she should be relieved.

The news was, of course, declared to the family at Merle Park. " I never knew anything so hard," said Aunt Emmeline. " Of course you have told him that it was all my fault." When Lucy made no answer to this, she went on with her complaint. " I know that you have told him that I have turned you out,—which is not true."

" I told him it was better I should go, as you did not like my being here."

" I suppose Lucy was in a little hurry to have the marriage come off," said Augusta,—who would surely have spared her cousin if at the moment she had remembered the haste which had been displayed by her sister.

" I thought it best," said Lucy.

" I am sure I don't know how it is to be done," said Aunt Emmeline. " You must tell your uncle yourself. I don't know how you are to be married from here, seeing the trouble we are in."

" We shall be up in London before that," said Gertrude.

" Or from Queen's Gate either," continued Aunt Emmeline.

" I don't suppose that will much signify. I shall just go to the church."

" Like a servant-maid ?" asked Gertrude.

' Yes ;—like a servant-maid," said Lucy. " That is to say, a servant-maid would, I suppose, simply walk in and be married ; and shall do the same."

"I think you had better tell your uncle," said Aunt Emmeline "But I am sure I did not mean that you were to go away like this. It will be your own doing, and I cannot help it if you will do it.

Then Lucy did tell her uncle. "And you mean to live upon three hundred a year !" exclaimed Sir Thomas. "You don't know what you are talking about."

"I think Mr. Hamel knows."

"He is as ignorant as a babe unborn ;—I mean about that kind of thing. I don't doubt he can make things in stone as well as anybody."

"In marble, Uncle Tom."

"Marble is stone, I suppose ;—or in iron."

"Bronze, Uncle Tom."

"Very well. There is iron in bronze, I suppose. But he doesn't know what a wife will cost. Has he bought any furniture?"

"He is going to buy it,—just a little ;—what will do?"

"Why should you want to bring him into this?" Lucy looked wistfully up into his face. He himself had been personally kind to her, and she found it to be impossible to complain to him of her aunt. "You are not happy here?"

"My aunt and cousins think that I am wrong ;—but I must be married to him now, Uncle Tom."

"Why did he kick up his heels when I wanted to help him?" Nevertheless, he gave his orders on the subject very much in Lucy's favour. She was to be married from Queen's Gate, and Gertrude must be her bridesmaid. Ayala no doubt would be the other. When his wife expostulated, he consented that the marriage should be very quiet, but still he would have it as he had said. Then he bestowed a cheque upon Lucy,—larger in amount than Stubbs's loan,—saying that after what had passed in Lombard Street he would not venture to send money to so independent a person as Mr. Isadore Hamel ; but adding that Lucy, perhaps, would condescend to accept it. There was a smile in his eye as he said the otherwise ill-natured word, so that Lucy, without any wound to her feelings, could kiss him and accept his bounty.

"I suppose I am to have nothing to do in settling the day," said Aunt Emmeline. It was, however, settled between them that the marriage should take place on a certain day in May. Upon this Lucy was of course overjoyed, and wrote to her lover in a full flow of spirits. And she sent him the cheque, having written her name with great pride on the back of it. There was a little trouble about this as a part of it had to come back as her trousseau, but still the arrangement was pleasantly made. Then Sir Thomas again became more kind to her, in his rough manner,—even when his troubles were at the worst after the return of Gertrude. "If it will not be altogether oppressive to his pride you may tell him that I shall make you an allowance of a hundred a year as my niece,—just for your personal expenses."

"I don't know that he is so proud, Uncle Tom."

"He seemed so to me. But if you say nothing to him about it, and just buy a few gowns now and again, he will perhaps be so wrapt up in the higher affairs of his art as not to take any notice."

"I am sure he will notice what I wear," said Lucy. However she communicated her uncle's intentions to her lover, and he sent back his grateful thanks to Sir Thomas. As one effect of all this the Colonel's money was sent back to him, with an assurance that as things were now settling themselves such pecuniary assistance was not needed. But this was not done till Ayala had heard what the Angel of Light had done on her sister's behalf. But as to Ayala's feelings in that respect we must be silent here, as otherwise we should make premature allusion to the condition in which Ayala found herself before she had at last managed to escape from Stalham Park.

"Papa," said Gertrude, to her father one evening, "don't you think you could do something for me too now?" Just at this time Sir Thomas, greatly to his own annoyance, was coming down to Merle Park every evening. According to their plans as at present arranged, they were to stay in the country till after Easter, and then they were to go up to town in time to despatch poor Tom upon his long journey round the world. But poor Tom was now in bed, apparently ill, and there seemed to be great doubt whether he could be made to go on the appointed day in spite of the taking of his berth and the preparation of his outfit. Tom, if well enough, was to sail on the nineteenth of April, and there now wanted not above ten days to that time. "Don't you think you could do something for me now?" asked Gertrude. Hitherto Sir Thomas had extended no sign of pardon to his youngest daughter, and never failed to allude to her and to Captain Batsby as "those two idiots," whenever their names were mentioned before him.

"Yes, my dear; I will endeavour to do a good deal for you if you will behave yourself."

"What do you call behaving myself, papa?"

"In the first place telling me that you are very sorry for your misbehaviour with that idiot."

"Of course I am sorry if I have offended you."

"Well, that shall go for something. But how about the idiot?"

"Papa!" she exclaimed.

" Was he not an idiot ?   Would any one but an idiot have gone on such an errand as that ?"

" Gentlemen and ladies have done it before, papa."

" I doubt it," he said.   " Gentlemen have run away with young ladies before and generally have behaved very badly when they have done so.   He behaved very badly indeed, because he had come to my house, with my sanction, with the express purpose of expressing his affection for another young lady.   But I think that his folly in this special running away was worse even than his conduct.   How did he come to think that he could get himself married merely by crossing over the sea to Ostend ?   I should be utterly ashamed of him as a son-in-law,—chiefly because he has shown himself to be an idiot."

" But, papa, you will accept him ;—won't you."

" No, my dear, I will not."

" Not though I love him ?"

" If I were to give you a choice which would you take,—him or Mr. Houston ?"

" Houston is a scoundrel."

" Very likely ; but then he is not an idiot.   My choice would be altogether in favour of Mr. Houston.   Shall I tell you what I will do, my dear ?   I will consent to accept Captain Batsby as my son-in-law if he will consent to become your husband without having a shilling with you."

" Would that be kind, papa ?"

" I do not think that I can show you any greater kindness than to protect you from a man who I am quite sure does not care a farthing about you.   He has, you tell me, an ample income of his own."

" Oh yes, papa."

" Then he can afford to marry you without a fortune.   Poor Mr. Houston could not have done so, because he had nothing of his own. I declare, as I think of it all, I am becoming very tender-hearted towards Mr. Houston.   Don't you think we had better have Mr. Houston back again ?   I suppose he would come if you were to send for him."   Then she burst into tears and went away and hid herself.

CHAPTER LIV.

TOM'S LAST ATTEMPT.

WHILE Gertrude was still away on her ill-omened voyage in quest of a parson, Lady Tringle was stirred up to a great enterprise on behalf of her unhappy son.   There wanted now little more than a fortnight before the starting of the ship which his father still declared should carry him out across the world, and he had progressed so far in contemplating the matter as to own to himself that it would be best for him to obey his father if there was no hope. But his mind was still swayed by a theory of love and constancy. He had heard of men who had succeeded after a dozen times of asking. If Stubbs, the hated but generous Stubbs, were in truth a successful rival, then indeed the thing would be over ;—then he would go, the sooner the better ; and, as he told his mother half-a-dozen times a-day, it would matter nothing to him whether he were sent to Japan, or the Rocky Mountains, or the North Pole. In such case he would be quite content to go, if only for the sake of going. But how was he to be sure? He was, indeed, nearly sure in the other direction. If Ayala were in truth engaged to Colonel Stubbs it would certainly be known through Lucy. Then he had heard, through Lucy, that, though Ayala was staying at Stalham, the Colonel was not there. He had gone, and Ayala had remained week after week without him. Then, towards the end of March, he wrote a letter to his Uncle Reginald, which was very piteous in its tone ;—

" DEAR UNCLE REGINALD," the letter said,

" I don't know whether you have heard of it, but I have been very ill,—and unhappy. I am now in bed, and nobody here knows that I am sending this letter to you. It is all about Ayala, and I am not such a fool as to suppose that you can do anything for me. If you could I think you would,—but of course you can't. She must choose for herself,—only I do so wish that she should choose me. Nobody would ever be more kind to her. But you can tell me really how it is. Is she engaged to marry Colonel Stubbs? I know that she refused him, because he told me so himself. If she is not engaged to him I think that I would have another shy at it. You know what the poet says,— 'Faint heart never won fair lady.' Do tell me if she is or is not engaged. I know that she is with those Alburys, and that Colonel Stubbs is their friend. But they can't make her marry Colonel Stubbs any more than my friends can make her marry me. I wish they could. I mean my friends, not his.

" If she were really engaged I would go away and hide myself in the furthermost corner of the world. Siberia or Central Africa would be the same to me. They would have little trouble in getting rid of me if I knew that it was all over with me. BUT I WILL NEVER STIR FROM THESE REALMS TILL I KNOW MY FATE !—Therefore, waiting your reply, I am your affectionate nephew,

" THOMAS TRINGLE, junior,"

Mr. Dosett, when he received this letter, consulted his wife before he replied to it, and then did so very shortly;—

" MY DEAR TOM,

" As far as I know, or her aunt, your cousin Ayala is not engaged to marry any one. But I should deceive you if I did not add my belief that she is resolved not to accept the offer you have done her the honour to make her.—Your affectionate uncle,

" REGINALD DOSETT."

The latter portion of this paragraph had no influence whatsoever on Tom. Did he not know all that before ? Had he ever attempted to conceal from his relations the fact that Ayala had refused him again and again ? Was not that as notorious to the world at large as a minister's promise that the income-tax should be abolished ? But the income-tax was not abolished,—and, as yet, Ayala was not married to any one else. Ayala was not even engaged to any other suitor. Why should she not change her mind as well as the minister ? Certainly he would not go either to the North Pole or to New York as long as there should be a hope of bliss for him in England. Then he called his mother to his bedside.

" Go to Stalham, my dear !" said his mother.

" Why not ? They can't eat you. Lady Albury is no more than a baronet's wife,—just the same as you."

" It isn't about eating me, Tom. I shouldn't know what to say to them."

" You need not tell them anything. Say that you had come to call upon your niece."

" But it would be such an odd thing to do. I never do call on Ayala,—even when I am in London."

" What does it matter being odd ? You could learn the truth at any rate. If she does not care for any one else why shouldn't she have me ? I could make her a baronet's wife,—that is, some day when the governor——"

" Don't, Tom ;—don't talk in that way."

" I only mean in the course of nature. Sons do come after their fathers, you know. And as for money, I suppose the governor is quite as rich as those Alburys."

" I don't think that would matter."

" It does count, mother. I suppose Ayala is the same as other girls, in that respect. I am sure I don't know why it is that she should have taken such an aversion to me. I suppose it is that she doesn't think me so much,—quite such a swell as some other men."

" One can't account for such things, Tom."

" No ;—that is just it. And therefore she might come round without accounting for it. At any rate, you might try. You might tell her that it is ruining me ;—that I shall have to go about wandering over all the world because she is so hard-hearted."

" I don't think I could, my dear," said Lady Tringle, after considering the matter for awhile.

" Why not ? Is it because of the trouble ?"

" No, my dear ; a mother does not think what trouble she may take for her child, if any good may be done. It is not the trouble. I would walk all round England to get her for you if that would do it."

" Why not, then ? At any rate you might get an answer from her. She would tell you something of her intention. Mother, I shall never go away till I know more about it than I do now. The governor says that he will turn me out. Let him turn me out. That won't make me go away."

" Oh, Tom, he doesn't mean it."

" But he says it. If I knew that it was all over,—that every chance was gone, then I would go away."

" It is not the Alburys that I am afraid of," said Lady Tringle.

" What then ?"

" It is your father. I cannot go if he will not let me." Nevertheless she promised before she left his bedside that she would ask Sir Thomas when he came home whether he would permit her to make the journey. All this occurred while Sir Thomas was away in quest of his daughter. And it may be imagined that immediately after his return he was hardly in a humour to yield to any such request as that which had been suggested. He was for the moment almost sick of his children, sick of Merle Park, sick of his wife, and inclined to think that the only comfort to be found in the world was to be had among his millions, in that little back parlour in Lombard Street.

It was on a Sunday that he returned, and on that day he did not see his son. On the Monday morning he went into the room, and Tom was about to press upon him the prayer which he had addressed to his mother when his lips were closed by his father's harshness. " Tom," he said, " you will be pleased to remember that you start on the nineteenth."

" But, father ——"

" You start on the nineteenth," said Sir Thomas. Then he left the room, closing the room behind him with none of the tenderness generally accorded to an invalid.

" You have not asked him ?" Tom said to his mother shortly afterwards.

" Not yet, my dear. His mind is so disturbed by this unfortunate affair."

" And is not my mind disturbed ? You may tell him that I will not go, though he should turn me out a dozen times, unless I know more about it than I do now."

Sir Thomas came home again that evening, very sour in temper, and nothing could be said to him. He was angry with everybody, and Lady Tringle hardly dared to go near him, either then or on the following morning. On the Tuesday evening, however, he returned somewhat softened in his demeanour. The millions had perhaps gone right, though his children would go so wrong. When he spoke either to his younger daughter or of her he did so in that jeering tone which he afterwards always assumed when allusion was made to Captain Batsby, and which, disagreeable as it was, seemed to imply something of forgiveness. And he ate his dinner, and drank his glass of wine, without making any allusion to the parsimonious habits of his son-in-law, Mr. Traffick. Lady Tringle, therefore, considered that she might approach him with Tom's request.

" You go to Stalham !" he exclaimed.

" Well, my dear, I suppose I could see her ?"

" And what could you learn from her ?"

" I don't suppose I could learn much. She was always a pig-headed, stiff-necked creature. I am sure it wouldn't be any pleasure to me to see her."

" What good would it do ?" demanded Sir Thomas.

" Well, my dear ; he says that he won't go unless he can get a message from her. I am sure I don't want to go to Stalham. Nothing on earth could be so disagreeable. But perhaps I could bring back a word or two which would make him go upon his journey."

" What sort of word ?"

" Why ;—if I were to say that she were engaged to this Colonel Stubbs, then he would go. He says that he would start at once if he knew that his cousin were really engaged to somebody else."

" But if she be not ?"

" Perhaps I could just colour it a little. It would be such a grand thing to get him away, and he in this miserable condition ! If he were once on his travels, I do think he would soon begin to forget it all."

" Of course he would," said Sir Thomas.

" Then I might as well try. He has set his heart upon it, and if he thinks that I have done his bidding then he will obey you. As for turning him out, Tom, of course you do not really mean that !"

In answer to this Sir Thomas said nothing. He knew well enough that Tom couldn't be turned out. That turning out of a son is a difficult task to accomplish, and one altogether beyond the power of Sir Thomas. The chief cause of his sorrow lay in the fact that he, as the head of Travers and Treason, was debarred from the assistance and companionship of his son. All Travers and Treason was nothing to him, because his son would run so far away from the right path. There was nothing he would not do to bring him back. If Ayala could have been bought by any reasonable, or even unreasonable, amount of thousands, he would have bought her willingly for his boy's delight. It was a thing wonderful to him that Tom should have been upset so absolutely by his love. He did appreciate the feeling so far that he was willing to condone all those follies already committed if Tom would only put himself in the way of recovery. That massacreing of the policeman, those ill-spent nights at the Mountaineers and at Bolivia's, that foolish challenge, and the almost more foolish blow under the portico at the Haymarket, should all be forgiven if Tom would only consent to go through some slight purgation which would again fit him for Travers and Treason. And the purgation should be made as pleasant as possible. He should travel about the world with his pocket full of money and with every arrangement for luxurious comfort. Only he must go. There was no other way in which he could be so purged as to be again fit for Travers and Treason. He did not at all believe that Ayala could now be purchased. Whether pig-headed or not, Ayala was certainly self-willed. No good such as Tom expected would come from this projected visit to Stalham. But if he would allow it to be made in obedience to Tom's request,—then perhaps some tidings might be brought back which, whether strictly true or not, might induce Tom to allow himself to be put on board the ship. Arguing thus with himself, Sir Thomas at last gave his consent.

It was a most disagreeable task which the mother thus undertook. She could not go from Merle Park to Stalham and back in one day. It was necessary that she should sleep two nights in London. It was arranged, therefore, that she should go up to London on the Thursday; then make her journey down to Stalham and back on the Friday, and get home on the Saturday. There would then still remain nearly a fortnight before Tom would have to leave Merle Park. After much consideration it was decided that a note should be written to Ayala apprising her of her aunt's coming. " I hope Lady Albury will not be surprised at my visit," said the note, " but I am so anxious to see you, just for half-an-hour, upon a matter of great importance, that I shall run my chance." She would prefer to have seen the girl without any notice; but then, had no notice been given, the girl would perhaps have been out of the way. As it was a telegram was received back in reply. "I shall be at home. Lady Albury will be very glad to see you at lunch. She says there shall be a room all ready if you will sleep."

"I certainly shall not stay there," Lady Tringle said to Mrs. Traffick, "but it is as well to know that they will be civil to me."

"They are stuck-up sort of people I believe," said Augusta; "just like that Marchesa Baldoni, who is one of them. But, as to their being civil, that is a matter of course. They would hardly be uncivil to any one connected with Lord Boardotrade!"

Then came the Thursday on which the journey was to be commenced. As the moment came near Lady Tringle was very much afraid of the task before her. She was afraid even of her niece Ayala, who had assumed increased proportions in her eyes since she had persistently refused not only Tom but also Colonel Stubbs and Captain Batsby, and then in spite of her own connexion with Lord Boardotrade,—of whom since her daughter's marriage she had learned to think less than she had done before,—she did feel that the Alburys were fashionable people, and that Ayala as their guest had achieved something for herself. Stalham was, no doubt, superior in general estimation to Merle Park, and with her there had been always a certain awe of Ayala which she had not felt in reference to Lucy. Ayala's demand that Augusta should go upstairs and fetch the scrap-book had had its effect,—as had also her success in going up St. Peter's and to the Marchesa's dance; and then there would be Lady Albury herself,—and all the Alburys! Only that Tom was very anxious she would even now have abandoned the undertaking.

"Mother," said Tom, on the last morning, "you will do the best you can for me."

"Oh yes, my dear."

"I do think that, if you would make her understand the real truth, she might have me yet. She wouldn't like that a fellow should die."

"I am afraid that she is hard-hearted, Tom."

"I do not believe it, mother. I have seen her when she wouldn't kill even a fly. If she could only be made to see all the good she could do."

"I am afraid she won't care for that unless she can bring herself really to love you."

"Why shouldn't she love me?"

"Ah, my boy; how am I to tell you? Perhaps if you hadn't loved her so well it might have been different. If you had scorned her——"

"Scorn her! I couldn't scorn her. I have heard of that kind of thing before, but how is one to help oneself? You can't scorn a friend just because you choose to say so to yourself. When I see her she is something so precious to me that I could not be rough to her to save my life. When she first came it wasn't so. I could laugh at her then. But now——! They talk about goddesses, but I am sure she is a goddess to me."

"If you had made no more than a woman of her it might have been better, Tom." All that was too late now. The doctrine which Lady Tringle was enunciating to her son, and which he repudiated, is one that has been often preached and never practised. A man when he is conscious of the presence of a mere woman, to whom he feels that no worship is due, may for his own purpose be able to tell a lie to her, and make her believe that he acknowledges a divinity in her presence. But, when he feels the goddess, he cannot carry himself before her as though she were a mere woman, and, as such, inferior to himself in her attributes. Poor Tom had felt the touch of something divine, and had fallen immediately prostrate before the shrine with his face to the ground. His chance with Ayala could in no circumstances have been great; but she was certainly not one to have yielded to a prostrate worshipper.

"Mother!" said Tom, recalling Lady Tringle as she was leaving the room.

"What is it, my dear? I must really go now or I shall be too late for the train."

"Mother, tell her,—tell her,—tell her that I love her." His mother ran back, kissed his brow, and then left the room.

Lady Tringle spent that evening in Queen's Gate, where Sir Thomas remained with her. The hours passed heavily, as they had not much present to their mind with which to console each other. Sir Thomas had no belief whatever in the journey except in so far as it might help to induce his son to proceed upon his travels;—but his wife had been so far softened by poor Tom's sorrows as to hope a little, in spite of her judgment, that Ayala might yet relent. Her heart was soft towards her son, so that she felt that the girl would deserve all manner of punishment unless she would at last yield to Tom's wishes. She was all but sure that it could not be so, and yet, in spite of her convictions, she hoped.

On the next morning the train took her safely to the Stalham Road Station, and as she approached the end of her journey her heart became heavier within her. She felt that she could not but fail to give any excuse to the Alburys for such a journey,—unless, indeed, Ayala should do as she would have her. At the station she found the Albury carriage, with the Albury coachman, and the Albury footman, and the Albury liveries, waiting for her. It was a closed carriage, and for a moment she thought that Ayala might be there. In that case she could have performed her commission in the carriage, and then have returned to London without going to the house at all. But Ayala was not there. Lady Tringle was driven up to the house, and then taken through the hall into a small sitting-room, where for a moment she was alone. Then the door opened, and Ayala, radiant with beauty, in all the prettiness of her best morning costume, was in a moment in her arms. She seemed in her brightness to be different from that Ayala who had been known before at Glenbogie and in Rome. "Dear aunt," said Ayala, "I am so delighted to see you at Stalham!"

CHAPTER LV.

IN THE CASTLE THERE LIVED A KNIGHT.

AYALA was compelled to consent to remain at Stalham. The "I don't think" which she repeated so often was, of course, of no avail to her. Sir Harry would be angry, and Lady Albury would be disgusted, were she to go,—and so she remained. There was to be a week before Colonel Stubbs would come, and she was to remain not only for the week but also for some short time afterwards,—so that there might be yet a few days left of hunting under the Colonel. It could not, surely, have been doubtful to her after she had read that letter,—with the postscript,—that if she remained her happiness would be insured! He would not have come again and insisted on her being there to receive him if nothing were to come of it. And yet she had fought for permission to return to Kingsbury Crescent after her little fashion, and had at last yielded,—as she told Lady Albury,— because Sir Harry seemed to wish it. "Of course he wishes it," said Lady Albury. "He has got the pony on purpose, and nobody likes being disappointed when he has done a thing so much as Sir Harry." Ayala, delighted as she was, did not make her secret known. She was fluttered, and apparently uneasy,—so that her friend did not know what to make of it, or which way to take it. Ayala's secret was to herself a secret still to be maintained with holy reticence. It might still be possible that Jonathan Stubbs should never say another word to her of his love. If he did,—why then all the world might know. Then there would be no secret. Then she could sit and discuss her love, and his love, all night long with Lady Albury, if Lady Albury would listen to her. In the meantime the secret must be a secret,

2 C

To confess her love, and then to have her love disappointed,—that would be death to her!

And thus it went on through the whole week, Lady Albury not quite knowing what to make of it. Once she did say a word, thinking that she would thus extract the truth, not as yet understanding how potent Ayala could be to keep her secret. "That man has, at any rate, been very true to you," she said. Ayala frowned, and shook her head, and would not say a word upon the subject. "If she did not mean to take him now, surely she would have gone," Lady Albury said to her husband.

"She is a pretty little girl enough," said Sir Harry, "but I doubt whether she is worth all the trouble."

"Of course she is not. What pretty little girl ever was? But as long as he thinks her worth it the trouble has to be taken."

"Of course she'll accept him?"

"I am not at all so sure of it. She has been made to believe that you wanted her to stay, and therefore she has stayed. She is quite master enough of herself to ride out hunting with him again and then to refuse him." And so Lady Albury doubted up to the Sunday, and all through the Sunday,—up to the very moment when the last preparations were to be made for the man's arrival.

The train reached the Stalham Road Station at 7 P.M., and the distance was five miles. On Sundays they usually dined at Stalham at 7·30. The hour fixed was to be 8 on this occasion,—and even with this there would be some bustling. The house was now nearly empty, there being no visitors there except Mr. and Mrs. Gosling and Ayala. Lady Albury gave many thoughts to the manner of the man's reception, and determined at last that Jonathan should have an opportunity of saying a word to Ayala immediately on his arrival if he so pleased. "Mind you are down at half-past seven," she said to Ayala, coming to her in her bedroom.

"I thought we should not dine till eight."

"There is no knowing. Sir Harry is so fussy. I shall be down, and I should like you to be with me." Then Ayala promised. "And mind you have his frock on."

"You'll make me wear it out before any one else sees it," she said, laughing. But again she promised. She got a glimmer of light from it all, nearly understanding what Lady Albury intended. But against such intentions as these she had no reason to fight. Why should she not be ready to see him? Why should she not have on her prettiest dress when he came? If he meant to say the word,—then her prettiest dress would all be too poor, and her readiest ears not quick enough to meet so great a joy. If he were not to say the other word,

—then should she shun him by staying behind, or be afraid of the encounter? Should she be less gaily attired because it would be unnecessary to please his eye?

Oh, no! "I'll be there at half-past seven," she said. "But I know the train will be late, and Sir Harry won't get his dinner till nine."

"Then, my dear, great as the Colonel is, he may come in and get what is left for him in the middle. Sir Harry will not wait a minute after eight."

The buxom woman came and dressed her. The buxom woman probably knew what was going to happen;—was perhaps more keenly alive to the truth than Lady Albury herself. "We have taken great care of it, haven't we, miss?" she said, as she fastened the dress behind. "It's just as new still."

"New!" said Ayala. "It has got to be new with me for the next two years."

"I don't know much about that, Miss. Somebody will have to pay for a good many more new dresses before two years are over, I take it." To this Ayala made no answer, but she was quite sure that the buxom woman intended to imply that Colonel Stubbs would have to pay for the new dresses.

Punctually at half-past seven she was in the drawing-room, and there she remained alone for a few minutes. She endeavoured to sit down and be quiet, but she found it impossible to compose herself. Almost immediately he would be there, and then,—as she was quite sure,—her fate would be known to her instantly. She knew that the first moment of his presence in the room with her would tell her everything. If that were told to her which she desired to hear, everything should be re-told to him as quickly. But, if it were otherwise, then she thought that when the moment came she would still have strength enough to hide her sorrow. If he had come simply for the hunting,—simply that they two might ride-a-hunting together so that he might show to her that all traces of his disappointment were gone,—then she would know how to teach him to think that her heart towards him was as it had ever been. The thing to be done would be so sad as to call from her tears almost of blood in her solitude; but it should be so done that no one should know that any sorrow such as this had touched her bosom. Not even to Lucy should this secret be told.

There was a clock on the mantelpiece to which her eye was continually turned. It now wanted twenty minutes to eight, and she was aware that if the train was punctual he might now be at the hall-door. At this moment Lady Albury entered the room. "Your knight has come at last," she said. "I hear his wheels on the gravel."

" He is no knight of mine," said Ayala, with that peculiar frown of hers.

" Whose ever knight he is, there he is. Knight or not, I must go and welcome him." Then Lady Albury hurried out of the room and Ayala was again alone. The door had been left partly open, so that she could hear the sound of voices and steps across the inner hall or billiard-room. There were the servants waiting upon him, and Sir Harry bidding him to go up and dress at once so as not to keep the whole house waiting, and Lady Albury declaring that there was yet ample time as the dinner certainly would not be on the table for half-an-hour. She heard it all, and heard him to whom all her thoughts were now given laughing as he declared that he had never been so cold in his life, and that he certainly would not dress himself till he had warmed his fingers. She was far away from the door, not having stirred from the spot on which she was standing when Lady Albury left her ; but she fancied that she heard the murmur of some slight whisper, and she told herself that Lady Albury was telling him where to seek her. Then she heard the sound of the man's step across the billiard-room, she heard his hand upon the door, and there he was in her presence !

When she thought of it all afterwards, as she did so many scores of times, she never could tell how it had occurred. When she accused him in her playfulness, telling him that he had taken for granted that of which he had had no sign, she never knew whether there had been aught of truth in her accusation. But she did know that he had hardly closed the door behind him when she was in his arms, and felt the burning love of his kisses upon her cheeks. There had been no more asking whether he was to have any other answer. Of that she was quite sure. Had there been such further question she would have answered him, and some remembrance of her own words would have remained with her. She was quite sure that she had answered no question. Some memory of mingled granting and denying, of repulses and assents all quickly huddled one upon another, of attempts to escape while she was so happy to remain, and then of a deluge of love terms which fell upon her ears,—" his own one, his wife, his darling, his Ayala, at last his own sweet Ayala,"—this was what remained to her of that little interview. She had not spoken a word. She thought she was sure of that. Her breath had left her,—so that she could not speak. And yet it had been taken for granted,—though on former occasions he had pleaded with slow piteous words ! How had it been that he had come to know the truth so suddenly ? Then she became aware that Lady Albury was speaking to Mrs. Gosling in the billiard-room outside, detaining her other guest till the scene within should be ever. At that moment she did speak a word which she remembered afterwards. " Go ;—go ; you must go now." Then there had been one other soft repulse, one other sweet assent, and the man had gone. There was just a moment for her, in which to tell herself that the Angel of Light had come for her, and had taken her to himself.

Mrs. Gosling, who was a pretty little woman, crept softly into the room, hiding her suspicion if she had any. Lady Albury put out her hand to Ayala behind the other woman's back, not raising it high, but just so that her young friend might touch it if she pleased. Ayala did touch it, sliding her little fingers into the offered grasp. " I thought it would be so," whispered Lady Albury. " I thought it would be so."

" What the deuce are you all up to," said Sir Harry, bursting into the room. " It's eight now, and that man has only just gone up to his room."

" He hasn't been in the house above five minutes yet," said Lady Albury, " and I think he has been very quick." Ayala thought so too.

During dinner and afterwards they were very full of hunting for the next day. It was wonderful to Ayala that there should be thought for such a trifle when there was such a thing as love in the world. While there was so much to fill her heart, how could there be thoughts of anything else ? But Jonathan,—he was Jonathan to her now, her Jonathan, her Angel of Light,—was very keen upon the subject. There was but one week left. He thought that Croppy might manage three days as there was to be but one week. Croppy would have leisure and rest enough afterwards. " It's a little sharp," said Sir Harry.

" Oh, pray don't," said Ayala.

But Lady Albury and Jonathan together silenced Sir Harry, and Mrs. Gosling proved the absurdity of the objection by telling the story of a pony who had carried a lady three days running. " I should not have liked to be either the pony, or the owner, or the lady," said Sir Harry. But he was silenced. What did it matter though the heavens fell, so that Ayala was pleased ? What is too much to be done for a girl who proves herself to be an angel by accepting the right man at the right time ?

She had but one moment alone with her lover that night. " I always loved you," she whispered to him as she fled away. The Colonel did not quite understand the assertion, but he was contented with it as he sat smoking his cigar with Sir Harry and Mr. Gosling.

But, though she could have but one word that night with her lover there were many words between her and Lady Albury before they

went to bed. "And so, like wise people, you have settled it al
between you at last," said Lady Albury.

"I don't know whether he is wise."

"We will take that for granted. At any rate he has been very
true."

"Oh, yes!"

"And you,—you knew all about it."

"No ;—I knew nothing. I did not think he would ever ask again
I only hoped."

"But why on earth did you give him so much trouble?"

"I can't tell you," said Ayala, shaking her head.

"Do you mean that there is still a secret?"

"No ; not that. I would tell you anything that I could tell, because
you have been so very, very good to me. But I cannot tell. I cannot
explain it even to myself. Oh, Lady Albury, why have you been so
good to me?"

"Shall I say because I have loved you?"

"Yes ;—if it be true?"

"But it is not true."

"Oh, Lady Albury!"

"I do love you dearly. I shall always love you now. I do hope I
shall love you now, because you will be his wife. But I have not been
kind to you as you call it because I loved you."

"Then why?"

"Because I loved him. Cannot you understand that? Because I
was anxious that he should have all that he wanted. Was it not necessary that there should be some house in which he might meet you?
Could there have been much of a pleasant time for wooing between you
in your aunt's drawing-room in Kingsbury Crescent?"

"Oh, no," said Ayala.

"Could he have taken you out hunting unless you had been here?
How could he and you have known each other at all unless I had been
kind to you? Now you will understand."

"Yes," said Ayala, "I understand now. Did he ask you?"

"Well ;—he consulted me. We talked you all over, and made up
our minds, between us, that if we petted you down here that would be
the best way to win you. Were we not right?"

"It was a very nice way. I do so like to be petted."

"Sir Harry was in the secret, and he did his petting by buying the
frock. That was a success too, I think."

"Did he care about that, Lady Albury?"

"What he?"

"Jonathan," said Ayala, almost stumbling over the word, as she
pronounced it aloud for the first time.

" I think he liked it.   But whether he would have persevered without it you must ask yourself.   If he tells you that he would never have said another word to you only for this frock, then I think you ought to thank Sir Harry, and give him a kiss."

" I am sure he will not tell me that," said Ayala, with mock indignation.

" And now, my dear, as I have told you all my secret, and have explained to you how we laid our heads together, and plotted against you, I think you ought to tell me your secret.   Why was it that you refused him so pertinaciously on that Sunday when you were out walking, and yet you knew your mind about it so clearly as soon as he arrived to-day ?"

" I can't explain it," said Ayala.

" You must know that you liked him."

" I always liked him."

" You must have more than liked on that Sunday."

" I adored him."

" Then I don't understand you."

" Lady Albury, I think I fell in love with him the first moment I saw him.   The Marchesa took me to a party in London, and there he was."

" Did he say anything to you then ?"

" No.   He was very funny,—as he often is.   Don't you know his way ?   I remember every word he said to me.   He came up without any introduction and ordered me to dance with him."

" And you did ?"

" Oh yes.   Whatever he told me I should have done.   Then he scolded me because I did not stand up quick enough.   And he invented some story about a woman who was engaged to him and would not marry him because he had red hair and his name was Jonathan.   I knew it was all a joke, and yet I hated the woman."

" That must have been love at first sight."

" I think it was.   From that day to this I have always been thinking about him."

" And yet you refused him twice over ?"

" Yes."

" At ever so long an interval ?"   Ayala bobbed her head at her companion.   " And why ?"

" Ah ;—that I can't tell.   I shall try to tell him some day, but know that I never shall.   It was because ——.   But, Lady Albury, cannot tell it.   Did you ever picture anything to yourself in a waking dream ?"

" Build castles in the air ?" suggested Lady Albury.

" That's just it.

" Very often. But they never come true."

" Never have come true,—exactly. I had a castle in the air, and in the castle lived a knight." She was still ashamed to say that the inhabitant of the castle was an Angel of Light. "I wanted to find out whether he was the knight who lived there. He was."

" And you were not quite sure till to-day?"

" I have been sure a long time. But when we walked out on that Sunday I was such an idiot that I did not know how to tell him. Oh, Lady Albury, I was such a fool! What should I have done if he hadn't come back?"

" Sent for him."

" Never;—never! I should have been miserable always! But now I am so happy."

" He is the real knight?"

" Oh, yes; indeed. He is the real,—real knight, that has always been living in my castle."

Ayala's promotion was now so firmly fixed that the buxom female came to assist her off with her clothes when Lady Albury had left her. From this time forth it was supposed that such assistance would be necessary. "I take it, Miss," said the buxom female, "there will be a many new dresses before the end of this time two years." From which Ayala was quite sure that everybody in the house knew all about it.

* * * * *

But it was now, now when she was quite alone, that the great sense of her happiness came to her. In the fulness of her dreams there had never been more than the conviction that such a being, and none other, could be worthy of her love. There had never been faith in the hope that such a one would come to her,—never even though she would tell herself that angels had come down from heaven and had sought in marriage the hands of the daughters of men. Her dreams had been to her a barrier against love rather than an encouragement. But now he that she had in truth dreamed of had come for her. Then she brought out the Marchesa's letter and read that description of her lover. Yes; he was all that; true, brave, tender,—a very hero. But then he was more than all that,—for he was in truth the very " Angel of Light."

CHAPTER LVI.

GOBBLEGOOSE WOOD AGAIN.

THE Monday was devoted to hunting. I am not at all sure that riding about the country with a pack of hounds is an amusement specially compatible with that assured love entertainment which was now within the reach of Ayala and her Angel. For the rudiments of love-making, for little endearing attentions, for a few sweet words to be whispered with shortened breath as one horse gallops beside another, perhaps for a lengthened half-hour together, amidst the mazes of a large wood when opportunities are no doubt given for private conversation, hunting may be very well. But for two persons who are engaged, with the mutual consent of all their friends, a comfortable sofa is perhaps preferable. Ayala had heard as yet but very little of her lover's intentions ;—was acquainted only with that one single intention which he had declared in asking her to be his wife. There were a thousand things to be told,—the how, the where, and the when. She knew hitherto the why, and that was all. Nothing could be told her while she was galloping about a big wood on Croppy's back. "I am delighted to see you again in these parts, Miss," said Larry Twentyman, suddenly.

"Oh, Mr. Twentyman ; how is the baby ?"

"The baby is quite well, Miss. His mamma has been out ever so many times."

"I ought to have asked for her first. Does baby come out too ?"

"Not quite. But when the hounds are near mamma comes for an hour or so. We have had a wonderful season,—quite wonderful. You have heard, perhaps, of our great run from Dillsborough Wood. We found him there, close to my place, you know, and run him down in the Brake country after an hour and forty minutes. There were only five or six of them. You'd have been one, Miss, to a moral, if you'd have been here on the pony. I say we never changed our fox."

Ayala was well disposed towards Larry Twentyman, and was quite aware that, according to the records and established usages of that hunt, he was a man with whom she might talk safely. But she did not care about the foxes so much as she had done before. There was nothing now for which she cared much, except Jonathan Stubbs. He was always riding near her throughout the day, so that he might be with her should there arise anything special to be done ; but he was not always close to her,—as she would have had him. He had gained his purpose, and he was satisfied. She had entered in upon the fruition of positive bliss, but enjoyed it in perfection only when she heard the sound of his voice, or could look into his eyes as she spoke to him.

She did not care much about the great run from Dillsborough, or even
for the compliment with which Mr. Twentyman finished his narrative. They were riding about the big woods all day, not without killing
a fox, but with none of the excitement of a real run. "After that
Croppy will be quite fit to come again on Wednesday," suggested the
Colonel, on their way home. To which Sir Harry assented.

"What do you folks mean to do to-day," asked Lady Albury at
breakfast on the following morning. Ayala had her own little plan in
her head, but did not dare to propose it publicly. "Will you choose to
be driven, or will you choose to walk?" said Lady Albury, addressing
herself to Ayala. Ayala, in her present position, was considered to be
entitled to special consideration. Ayala thought she would prefer to
walk. At last there came a moment in which she could make her
request to the person chiefly concerned. "Walk with me to the wood
with that absurd name," suggested Ayala.

"Gobblegoose Wood," suggested the Colonel. Then that was arranged according to Ayala's wishes.

A walk in a wood is perhaps almost as good as a comfortable seat
in a drawing-room, and is, perhaps, less liable to intrusion. They
started and walked the way which Ayala remembered so well when she
had trudged along, pretending to listen to Sir Harry and Captain
Glomax as they carried on their discussion about the hunted fox, but
giving all her ears to the Colonel, and wondering whether he would
say anything to her before the day was over. Then her mind had
been in a perturbed state which she herself had failed to understand.
She was sure that she would say "No" to him, should he speak, and
yet she desired that it should be "Yes." What a fool she had been,
she told herself as she walked along now, and how little she had deserved all the good that had come to her!

The conversation was chiefly with him as they went. He told her
much now of the how, and the when, and the where. He hoped there
might be no long delay. He would live, he said, for the next year or two
at Aldershot, and would be able to get a house fit for her on condition
that they should be married at once. He did not explain why the
house could not be taken even though their marriage were delayed
two or three months,—but as to this she asked no questions. Of course
they must be married in London if Mrs. Dosett wished it; but if not
it might be arranged that the wedding should take place at Stalham.
Upon all this and many other things he had much to propose, and all
that he said Ayala accepted as gospel. As the Angel of Light had
appeared,—as the knight who was lord of the castle had come forth,—
of course he must be obeyed in everything. He could hardly have
made a suggestion to which she would not have acceded. When they

had entered the wood Ayala in her own quiet way led him to the very spot in which on that former day he had asked her his question. "Do you remember this path?" she asked.

"I remember that you and I were walking here together," he said.

"Ay, but this very turn? Do you remember this branch?"

"Well, no ; not the branch."

"You put your hand on it when you said that 'never,—never,' to me."

"Did I say 'never,—never'?"

"Yes, you did ;—when I was so untrue to you."

"Were you untrue?" he asked.

"Jonathan, you remember nothing about it. It has all passed away from you just as though you were talking to Captain Glomax about the fox."

"Has it, dear?"

"I remember every word of it. I remember how you stood and how you looked, even to the hat you wore and the little switch you held in your hand,—when you asked for one little word, one glance, one slightest touch. There, now ;—you shall have all my weight to bear." Then she leant upon him with both her hands, turned round her arm, glanced up into his face, and opened her lips as though speaking that little word. "Do you remember that I said I thought you had given it all up?"

"I remember that, certainly."

"And was not that untrue? Oh, Jonathan, that was such a story. Had I thought so I should have been miserable."

"Then why did you swear to me so often that you could not love me?"

"I never said so," replied Ayala ; "never."

"Did you not?" he asked.

"I never said so. I never told you such a story as that. I did love you then, almost as well as I do now. Oh, I had loved you for so long a time !"

"Then why did you refuse me?"

"Ah ; that is what I would explain to you now,—here on this very spot,—if I could. Does it not seem odd that a girl should have all that she wants offered to her, and yet not be able to take it?"

"Was it all that you wanted?"

"Indeed it was. When I was in church that morning I told myself that I never, never, could be happy unless you came to me again."

"But when I did come you would not have me."

"I knew how to love you," she said, "but I did not know how to tell you that I loved you. I can tell you now; cannot I?" and then she looked up at him and smiled. "Yes, I think I shall never be tired of telling you now. It is sweet to hear you say that you love me, but it is sweeter still to be always telling you. And yet I could not tell you then. Suppose you had taken me at my word!"

"I told you that I should never give you up."

"It was only that that kept me from being altogether wretched. I think that I was ashamed to tell you the truth when I had once refused to do as you would have me. I had given you so much trouble all for nothing. I think that if you had asked me on that first day at the ball in London I should have said yes, if I had told the truth."

"That would have been very sudden. I had never seen you before that."

"Nevertheless it was so. I don't mind owning it to you now, though I never, never, would own it to any one else. When you came to us at the theatre I was sure that no one else could ever have been so good. I certainly did love you then."

"Hardly that, Ayala."

"I did," she said. "Now I have told you everything, and if you choose to think I have been bad,—why you must think so, and I must put up with it."

"Bad, my darling!"

"I suppose it was bad to fall in love with a man like that; and very bad to give him the trouble of coming so often. But now I have made a clean breast of it, and if you want to scold me you must scold me now. You may do it now, but you must never scold me afterwards,—because of that." It may be left to the reader to imagine the nature of the scolding which she received.

Then on their way home she thanked him for all the good that he had done to all those belonging to her. "I have heard it all from Lucy;—how generous you have been to Isadore."

"That has all come to nothing," he said.

"How come to nothing? I know that you sent him the money."

"I did offer to lend him something, and, indeed, I sent him a cheque; but two days afterwards he returned it. That tremendous uncle of yours——"

"Uncle Tom?"

"Yes, your Uncle Tom; the man of millions! He came forward and cut me out altogether. I don't know what went on down there in Sussex, but when he heard that they intended to be married shortly he put his hand into his pocket as a magnificent uncle, overflowing with millions, ought to do."

"I did not hear that."

" Hamel sent my money back at once."

" And poor Tom ! You were so good to poor Tom."

" I like Tom."

" But he did behave badly."

" Well ; yes. One gentleman shouldn't strike another even though he be ever so much in love. It's an uncomfortable proceeding, and never has good results. But then, poor fellow, he has been so much in earnest."

" Why couldn't he take a No when he got it ?"

" Why didn't I take a No when I got it ?"

" That was very different. He ought to have taken it. If you had taken it you would have been very wrong and have broken a poor girl's heart. I am sure you knew that all through."

" Did I ?"

" And then you were too good-natured. That was it. I don't think you really love me ;—not as I love you. Oh, Jonathan, if you were to change your mind now ! Suppose you were to tell me that it was a mistake ! Suppose I were to awake and find myself in bed at Kingsbury Crescent !"

" I hope there may be no such waking as that !"

" I should go mad,—stark mad. Shake me till I find out whether it is real waking, downright, earnest. But, Jonathan, why did you call me Miss Dormer when you went away ? That was the worst of all. I remember when you called me Ayala first. It went through and through me like an electric shock. But you never saw it ;—did you ?"

On that afternoon when she returned home she wrote to her sister Lucy, giving a sister's account to her sister of all her happiness. " I am sure Isadore is second best, but Jonathan is best. I don't want you to say so; but if you contradict me I shall stick to it. You remember my telling you that the old woman in the railway said that I was perverse. She was a clever old woman and knew all about it, for I was perverse. However, it has come all right now, and Jonathan is best of all. Oh, my man,—my man ! Is it not sweet to have a man of one's own to love ?" If this letter had been written on the day before,—as would have been the case had not Ayala been taken out hunting,—it would have reached Merle Park on the Wednesday, the news would have been made known to Aunt Emmeline, and so conveyed to poor Tom, and that disagreeable journey from Merle Park to Stalham would have been saved. But there was no time for writing on the Monday. The letter was sent away in the Stalham post-bag on the Tuesday evening, and did not reach Merle Park till the Thursday, after Lady Tringle had left the house. Had it been known on that morning that Ayala was engaged to Colonel Stubbs that would have

sufficed to send Tom away upon his travels without any more direct
messenger from Stalham.

On the Wednesday there was more hunting, and on this day Ayala,
having liberated her mind to her lover in Gobblegoose Wood, was
able to devote herself more satisfactorily to the amusement in hand.
Her engagement was now an old affair. It had already become matter
for joking to Sir Harry, and had been discussed even with Mrs. Gosling. It was, of course, " a joy for ever,"—but still she was beginning
to descend from the clouds and to walk the earth,—no more than a
simple queen. When, therefore, the hounds went away and Larry
told her that he knew the best way out of the wood, she collected her
energies and rode " like a little brick," as Sir Harry said when they
got back to Stalham. On that afternoon she received the note from
her aunt and replied to it by telegram.

On the Thursday she stayed at home and wrote various letters. The
first was to the Marchesa, and then one to Nina,—in both of which
much had to be said about "Jonathan." To Nina also she could
repeat her idea of the delight of having a man to love. Then there
was a letter to Aunt Margaret,—which certainly was due, and another
to Aunt Emmeline,—which was not however received until after Lady
Tringle's visit to Stalham. There was much conversation between her
and Lady Albury as to the possible purpose of the visit which was to
be made on the morrow. Lady Albury was of opinion that Lady
Tringle had heard of the engagement, and was coming with the intention of setting it on one side on Tom's behalf. " But she can't do
that, you know," said Ayala, with some manifest alarm. " She is
nothing to me now, Lady Albury. She got rid of me, you know. I
was changed away for Lucy."

" If there had been no changing away, she could no nothing," said
Lady Albury.

About a quarter of an hour before the time for lunch on the following day Lady Tringle was shown into the small sitting-room which
has been mentioned in a previous chapter, and Ayala radiant with
happiness and beauty appeared before her. There was a look about
her of being at home at Stalham, as though she were almost a daughter
of the house, that struck her aunt with surprise. There was nothing
left of that submissiveness which, though Ayala herself had not been
submissive, belonged, as of right, to girls so dependent as she and her
sister Lucy. " I am so delighted to see you at Stalham," said Ayala,
as she embraced her aunt.

" I am come to you," said Lady Tringle, " on a matter of very particular business." Then she paused, and assumed a look of peculiar
solemnity.

" Have you got my letter ?" demanded Ayala.

" I got your telegram, and I thought it very civil of Lady Albury. But I cannot stay. Your poor cousin Tom is in such a condition that I cannot leave him longer than I can help."

" But you have not got my letter ?"

" I have had no letter from you, Ayala."

" I have sent you such news,—oh, such news, Aunt Emmeline !"

" What news, my dear ?" Lady Tringle as she asked the question seemed to become more solemn than ever.

" Oh, Aunt Emmeline——; I am—— "

" You are what, Ayala ?"

" I am engaged to be married to Colonel Jonathan Stubbs."

" Engaged !"

" Yes, Aunt Emmeline ;—engaged. I wrote to you on Tuesday to tell you all about it. I hope you and Uncle Tom will approve. There cannot possibly be any reason against it,—except only that I have nothing to give him in return ; that is in the way of money. Colonel Stubbs, Aunt Emmeline, is not what Uncle Tom will call a rich man, but everybody here says that he has got quite enough to be comfort-able. If he had nothing in the world it could not make any difference to me. I don't understand how anybody is to love anyone or not to love him just because he is rich or poor."

" But you are absolutely engaged !" exclaimed Lady Tringle.

" Oh dear yes. Perhaps you would like to ask Lady Albury about it. He did want it before, you know."

" But now you are engaged to him ?" In answer to this Ayala thought it sufficient simply to nod her head. " It is all over then ?"

" All over !" exclaimed Ayala. " It is just going to begin."

" All over for poor Tom," said Lady Tringle.

" Oh yes. It was always over for him, Aunt Emmeline. I told him ever so many times that it never could be so. Don't you know, Aunt Emmeline, that I did ?"

" But you said that to this man just the same."

" Aunt Emmeline," said Ayala, putting on all the serious dignity which she knew how to assume, " I am engaged to Colonel Stubbs, and nothing on earth that anybody can say can change it. If you want to hear all about it, Lady Albury will tell you. She knows that you are my aunt, and therefore she will be quite willing to talk to you. Only nothing that anybody can say can change it."

" Poor Tom !" ejaculated the rejected lover's mother.

" I am very sorry if my cousin is displeased."

" He is ill,—terribly ill. He will have to go away and travel all about the world, and I don't know that ever he will come back again. I am sure this Stubbs will never love you as he has done."

' Oh, aunt, what is the use of that ?"

" And then Tom will have twice as much. But, however——" Ayala stood silent, not seeing that any good could be done by addition to her former assurances. " I will go and tell him, my dear, that's all. Will you not send him some message, Ayala ?"

" Oh, yes ; any message that I can that shall go along with my sincere attachment to Colonel Stubbs. You must tell him that I am engaged to Colonel Stubbs. You will tell him, Aunt Emmeline ?"

" Oh, yes ; if it must be so."

" It must," said Ayala. " Then you may give him my love, and tell him that I am very unhappy that I should have been a trouble to him, and that I hope he will soon be well, and come back from his travels." By this time Aunt Emmeline was dissolved in tears. " I could not help it, Aunt Emmeline, could I ?" Her aunt had once terribly outraged her feelings by telling her that she had encouraged Tom. Ayala remembered at this moment the cruel words and the wound which they had inflicted on her; but, nevertheless, she behaved tenderly, and endeavoured to be respectful and submissive. " I could not help it,—could I, Aunt Emmeline ?"

" I suppose not, my dear."

After that Lady Tringle declared that she would return to London at once. No ;—she would rather not go in to lunch. She would rather go back at once to the station if they would take her. She had been weeping, and did not wish to show her tears. Therefore, at Ayala's request, the carriage came round again,—to the great disgust, no doubt, of the coachman,—and Lady Tringle was taken back to the station without having seen any of the Albury family.

CHAPTER LVII.

CAPTAIN BATSBY IN LOMBARD STREET.

It was not till Colonel Stubbs had been three or four days at Stalham, basking in the sunshine of Ayala's love, that any of the Stalham family heard of the great event which had occurred in the life of Ayala's third lover. During that walk to and from Gobblegoose Wood something had been said between the lovers as to Captain Batsby,— something, no doubt, chiefly in joke. The idea of the poor Captain having fallen suddenly into so melancholy a condition was droll enough. " But he never spoke to me," said Ayala. " He doesn't speak very much to any one," said the Colonel, " but he thinks a great deal about

things. He has had ever so many affairs with ever so many ladies,
who generally, I fancy, want to marry him because of his money.
How he has escaped so long nobody knows." A man when he has
just engaged himself to be married is as prone as ever to talk of other
men " escaping," feeling that, though other young ladies were no better
than evils to be avoided, his young lady is to be regarded as almost a
solitary instance of a blessing.   Then, two days afterwards, arrived
the news of the trip to Ostend.   Sir Harry received a letter from a
friend in which an account was given of his half-brother's adventure.
" What do you think has happened ?" said Sir Harry, jumping up from
his chair at the breakfast table.

" What has happened ?" asked his wife.

" Benjamin has run off to Ostend with a young lady."

" Benjamin,—with a young lady !" exclaimed Lady Albury. Ayala
and Stubbs were equally astonished, each of them knowing that the
Captain had been excluded from Stalham because of the ardour of his
unfortunate love for Ayala.   " Ayala, that is your doing !"

" No !" said Ayala.   " But I'm very glad if he's happy."

" Who is the young lady ?" asked Stubbs.

" It is that which makes it so very peculiar," said Sir Harry, looking
at Ayala. He had learned something of the Tringle family, and was
aware of Ayala's connection with them.

" Who is it, Harry ?" demanded her ladyship.

" Sir Thomas Tringle's younger daughter."

" Gertrude !" exclaimed Ayala, who also knew of the engagement
with Mr. Houston.

" But the worst of it is," continued Sir Harry, " that he is not at
all happy.   The young lady has come back, while nobody knows what
has become of Benjamin."

" Benjamin never will get a wife," said Lady Albury.   Thus all the
details of the little event became known at Stalham,—except the
immediate condition and whereabouts of the lover.

Of the Captain's condition and whereabouts something must be told.
When the great disruption came, and he had been abused and
ridiculed by Sir Thomas at Ostend, he felt that he could neither remain
there where the very waiters knew what had happened, nor could he
return to Dover in the same vessel with Sir Thomas and his daughter.
He therefore took the first train and went to Brussels.

But Brussels did not offer him many allurements in his present frame
of mind. He found nobody there whom he particularly knew, and
nothing particular to do.   Solitude in a continental town with no
amusements beyond those offered by the table d'hôte and the theatre
is oppressing.   His time he endeavoured to occupy with thinking of

the last promise he had made to Gertrude. Should he break it or should he keep it? Sir Thomas Tringle was, no doubt, a very rich man,—and then there was the fact which would become known to all the world that he had run off with the young lady. Should he ultimately succeed in marrying the young lady the enterprise would bear less of an appearance of failure than it would do otherwise. But then, should the money not be forthcoming, the consolation coming from the possession of Gertrude herself would hardly suffice to make him a happy man. Sir Thomas, when he came to consider the matter, would certainly feel that his daughter had compromised herself by her journey, and that it would be good for her to be married to the man who had taken her. It might be that Sir Thomas would yield, and consent to make, at any rate, some compromise. A rumour had reached his ears that Traffick had received £200,000 with the elder daughter. He would consent to take half that sum. After a week spent amidst the charms of Brussels he returned to London, without any public declaration of his doing so,—"sneaked back," as a friend of his said of him at the club;—and then went to work to carry out his purpose as best he might. All that was known of it at Stalham was that he had returned to his lodgings in London.

On Friday, the 11th of April, when Ayala was a promised bride of nearly two weeks' standing, and all the uncles and aunts were aware that her lot in life had been fixed for her, Sir Thomas was alone in the back-room in Lombard Street with his mind sorely diverted from the only joy of his life. The whole family were now in town, and Septimus Traffick with his wife was actually occupying a room in Queen's Gate. How it had come to pass Sir Thomas hardly knew. Some word had been extracted from him signifying a compliance with a request that Augusta might come to the house for a night or two until a fitting residence should be prepared for her. Something had been said of Lord Boardotrade's house being vacated for her and her husband early in April. An occurrence to which married ladies are liable was about to take place with Augusta, and Sir Thomas certainly understood that the occurrence was to be expected under the roof of the coming infant's noble grandfather. Something as to ancestral halls had been thrown out in the chance way of conversation. Then he certainly had assented to some minimum of London hospitality for his daughter,— as certainly not including the presence of his son-in-law; and now both of them were domiciled in the big front spare bed-room at Queen's Gate! This perplexed him sorely. And then Tom had been brought up from the country still as an invalid, his mother moaning and groaning over him as though he were sick almost past hope of recovery. And yet the nineteenth of the month, now only eight days distant, was still fixed for his departure. Tom, on the return of his mother from Stalham, had to a certain extent accepted as irrevocable the fact of which she bore the tidings. Ayala was engaged to Stubbs, and would, doubtless, with very little delay, become Mrs. Jonathan Stubbs. "I knew it," he said; "I knew it. Nothing could have prevented it unless I had shot him through the heart. He told me that she had refused him; but no man could have looked like that after being refused by Ayala." Then he never expressed a hope again. It was all over for him as regarded Ayala. But still he refused to be well, or even, for a day or two, to leave his bed. He had allowed his mother to understand that if the fact of her engagement were indubitably brought home to him he would gird up his loins for his journey and proceed at once wherever it might be thought good to send him. His father had sternly reminded him of his promise; but, when so reminded, Tom had turned himself in his bed and uttered groans instead of replies. Now he had been brought up to London and was no longer actually in bed; but even yet he had not signified his intention of girding up his loins and proceeding upon his journey. Nevertheless the preparations were going on, and, under Sir Thomas's directions, the portmanteaus were already being packed. Gertrude also was a source of discomfort to her father. She considered herself to have been deprived of her two lovers, one after the other, in a spirit of cruel parsimony. And with this heavy weight upon her breast she refused to take any part in the family conversations. Everything had been done for Augusta, and everything was to be done for Tom. For her nothing had been done, and nothing had been promised;—and she was therefore very sulky. With these troubles all around him, Sir Thomas was sitting oppressed and disheartened in Lombard Street on Friday, the 11th of April.

Then there entered to him one of the junior clerks with a card announcing the name of Captain Batsby. He looked at it for some seconds before he gave any notification of his intention, and then desired the young man to tell the gentleman that he would not see him. The message had been delivered, and Captain Batsby with a frown of anger on his brow was about to shake the dust off from his feet on the uncourteous threshold when there came another message saying that Captain Batsby could go in and see Sir Thomas if he wished it. Upon this he turned round and was shown into the little sitting-room. "Well, Captain Batsby," said Sir Thomas; "what can I do for you now? I am glad to see that you have come back safely from foreign parts."

"I have called," said the Captain, "to say something about your daughter."

2 D 2

" What more can you have to say about her ?"

At this the Captain was considerably puzzled. Of course Sir Thomas must know what he had to say. "The way in which we were separated at Ostend was very distressing to my feelings."

" I daresay."

" And also I should think to Miss Tringle's."

" Not improbably. I have always observed that when people are interrupted in the performance of some egregious stupidity their feelings are hurt. As I said before what can I do for you now ?"

" I am very anxious to complete the alliance which I have done myself the honour to propose to you."

" I did not know that you had proposed anything. You came down to my house under a false pretence ; and then you persuaded my daughter,—or else she persuaded you,—to go off together to Ostend. Is that what you call an alliance ?"

" That, as far as it went was,—was an elopement."

" Am I to understand that you now want to arrange another elopement, and that you have come to ask my consent ?"

" Oh dear no."

" Then what do you mean by completing an alliance ?"

" I want to make," said the Captain, " an offer for the young lady's hand in a proper form. I consider myself to be in a position which justifies me in doing so. I am possessed of the young lady's affections, and have means of my own equal to those which I presume you will be disposed to give her."

" Very much better means I hope, Captain Batsby. Otherwise I do not see what you and your wife would have to live upon. I will tell you exactly what my feelings are in this matter. My daughter has gone off with you, forgetting all the duty that she owed to me and to her mother, and throwing aside all ideas of propriety. After that I will not say that you shall not marry her if both of you think fit. I do not doubt your means, and I have no reason for supposing that you would be cruel to her. You are two fools, but after all fools must live in the world. What I do say is, that I will not give a sixpence towards supporting you in your folly. Now, Captain Batsby, you can complete the alliance or not as you please."

Captain Batsby had been called a fool also at Ostend, and there, amidst the distressing circumstances of his position, had been constrained to bear the opprobrious name, little customary as it is for one gentleman to allow himself to be called a fool by another ; but now he had collected his thoughts, had reminded himself of his position in the world, and had told himself that it did not become him to be too humble before this City man of business. It might have been all very well at Ostend ; but he was not going to be called a fool in London without resenting it. " Sir Thomas," said he, " fool and folly are terms which I cannot allow you to use to me."

" If you do not present yourself to me here, Captain Batsby, or at my own house,—or, perhaps I may say, at Ostend,—I will use no such terms to you."

" I suppose you will acknowledge that I am entitled to ask for your daughter's hand."

" I suppose you will acknowledge that when a man runs away with my daughter I am entitled to express my opinion of his conduct."

" That is all over now, Sir Thomas. What I did I did for love. There is no good in crying over spilt milk. The question is as to the future happiness of the young lady."

" That is the only wise word I have heard you say, Captain Batsby. There is no good in crying after spilt milk. Our journey to Ostend is done and gone. It was not very agreeable, but we have lived through it. I quite think that you show a good judgment in not intending to go there again in quest of a clergyman. If you want to be married there are plenty of them in London. I will not oppose your marriage, but I will not give you a shilling. No man ever had a better opportunity of showing the disinterestedness of his affection. Now, good morning."

" But, Sir Thomas——"

" Captain Batsby, my time is precious. I have told you all that there is to tell." Then he stood up, and the Captain with a stern demeanour and angry brow left the room and took himself in silence away from Lombard Street.

" Do you want to marry Captain Batsby ?" Sir Thomas said to his daughter that evening, having invited her to come apart with him after dinner.

" Yes, I do."

" You think that you prefer him on the whole to Mr. Houston ?"

" Mr. Houston is a scoundrel. I wish that you would not talk about him, papa."

" I like him so much the best of the two," said Sir Thomas. " But of course it is for you to judge. I could have brought myself to give something to Houston. Luckily, however, Captain Batsby has got an income of his own."

" He has, papa."

" And you are sure that you would like to take him as your husband ?"

" Yes, papa."

" Very well. He has been with me to-day."

" Is he in London ?"

" I tell you that he has been with me to-day in Lombard Street."

" What did he say ? Did he say anything about me ?"

" Yes, my dear. He came to ask me for your hand."

" Well, papa !"

" I told him that I should make no objection,—that I should leave it altogether to you. I only interfered with one small detail as to my own wishes. I assured him that I should never give him or you a single shilling. I don't suppose it will matter much to him, as he has, you know, means of his own." It was thus that Sir Thomas punished his daughter for her misconduct.

Captain Batsby and the Trafficks were acquainted with each other. The Member of Parliament had, of course, heard of the journey to Ostend from his wife, and had been instigated by her to express an opinion that the young people ought to be married. " It is such a very serious thing," said Augusta to her husband, " to be four hours on the sea together ! And, then, you know——!" Mr. Traffick acknowledged that it was serious, and was reminded by his wife that he, in the capacity of brother, was bound to interfere on his sister's behalf. " Papa, you know, understands nothing about these kind of things. You, with your family interest, and your seat in Parliament, ought to be able to arrange it." Mr. Traffick probably knew how far his family interest and his seat in Parliament would avail. They had, at any rate, got him a wife with a large fortune. They were promising for him, still further, certain domiciliary advantages. He doubted whether he could do much for Batsby ; but still he promised to try. If he could arrange these matters it might be that he would curry fresh favour with Sir Thomas by doing so. He therefore made it his business to encounter Captain Batsby on the Sunday afternoon at a club to which they both belonged. " So you have come back from your little trip ?" said the Member of Parliament.

The Captain was not unwilling to discuss the question of their family relations with Mr. Traffick. If anybody would have influence with Sir Thomas it might probably be Mr. Traffick. " Yes ; I have come back."

" Without your bride."

" Without my bride,—as yet. That is a kind of undertaking in which a man is apt to run many dangers before he can carry it through."

" I dare say. I never did anything of the kind myself. Of course you know that I am the young lady's brother-in-law."

" Oh yes."

" And therefore you won't mind me speaking. Don't you think
you ought to do something further ?"

" Something further ! By George, I should think so," said the
Captain, exultingly. " I mean to do a great many things further.
You don't suppose I am going to give it up ?"

" You oughtn't, you know. When a man has taken a girl off with
him that way, he should go on with it. It's a deuced serious thing,
you know."

" It was his fault in coming after us."

" That was a matter of course. If he hadn't done it, I must. I
have made the family my own, and, of course, must look after its
honour." The noble scion of the house of Traffick, as he said this,
showed by his countenance that he perfectly understood the duty
which circumstances had imposed upon him.

" He made himself very rough, you know," said the Captain.

" I dare say he would."

" And said things,—well,—things which he ought not to have
said."

" In such a case as that a father may say pretty nearly what comes
uppermost."

" That was just it. He did say what came uppermost,—and very
rough it was."

" What does it matter ?"

" Not much if he'd do as he ought to do now. As you are her
brother-in-law, I'll tell you just how it stands. I have been to him
and made a regular proposal."

" Since you have been back ?"

" Yes ; the day before yesterday. And what do you think he
says ?"

" What does he say ?"

" He gives his consent ; only——"

" Only what ?"

" He won't give her a shilling ! Such an idea, you know ! As
though she were to be punished after marriage for running away with
the man she did marry."

" Take your chance, Batsby," said the Member of Parliament.

" What chance ?"

" Take your chance of the money. I'd have done it ; only, of course,
it was different with me. He was glad to catch me, and therefore the
money was settled."

" I've got a tidy income of my own, you know," said the Captain,
thinking that he was entitled to be made more welcome as a son-in-law
than the younger son of a peer who had no income.

" Take your chance," continued Traffick. " What on earth can a man like Tringle do with his money except give it to his children? He is rough, as you say, but he is not hard-hearted, nor yet stubborn. I can do pretty nearly what I like with him."

" Can you, though?"

" Yes ; by smoothing him down the right way. You run your chance, and we'll get it all put right for you." The Captain hesitated, rubbing his head carefully to encourage the thoughts which were springing up within his bosom. The Honourable Mr. Traffick might perhaps succeed in getting the affair put right, as he called it, in the interest rather of the elder than of the second daughter. " I don't see how you can hesitate now, as you have been off with the girl," said Mr. Traffick.

" I don't know about that. I should like to see the money settled."

" There would have been nothing settled if you had married her at Ostend."

" But I didn't," said the Captain. " I tell you what you might do. You might talk him over and make him a little more reasonable. I should be ready to-morrow if he'd come forward."

" What's the sum you want?"

" The same as yours, I suppose."

" That's out of the question," said Mr. Traffick, shaking his head. " Suppose we say sixty thousand pounds." Then after some chaffering on the subject it was decided between them that Mr. Traffick should use his powerful influence with his father-in-law to give his daughter on her marriage,—say a hundred thousand pounds if it were possible, or sixty thousand pounds at the least.

CHAPTER LVIII.

MR. TRAFFICK IN LOMBARD STREET.

MR. TRAFFICK entertained some grand ideas as to the house of Travers and Treason. Why should not he become a member, and ultimately the leading member, of that firm? Sir Thomas was not a young man, though he was strong and hearty. Tom had hitherto succeeded only in making an ass of himself. As far as transacting the affairs of the firm Tom,—so thought Mr. Traffick,—was altogether out of the question. He might perish in those extensive travels which he was about to take. Mr. Traffick did not desire any such catastrophe;— but the young man might perish. There was a great opening. Mr. Traffick, with his thorough knowledge of business, could not but see that there was a great opening. Besides Tom, there were but two daughters, one of whom was his own wife. Augusta, his wife, was, he thought, certainly the favourite at the present moment. Sir Thomas could, indeed, say rough things even to her; but then, Sir Thomas was of his nature rough. Now, at this time, the rough things said to Gertrude were very much the rougher. In all these circumstances the wisdom of interfering in Gertrude's little affairs was very clear to Mr. Traffick. Gertrude would, of course, get herself married sooner or later, and almost any other husband would obtain a larger portion than that which would satisfy Batsby. Sir Thomas was now constantly saying good things about Mr. Houston. Mr. Houston would be much more objectionable than Captain Batsby,—much more likely to interfere. He would require more money at once, and might possibly come forward himself in the guise of a partner. Mr. Traffick saw his way clearly. It was incumbent upon him to see that Gertrude should become Mrs. Batsby with as little delay as possible.

But one thing he did not see. One thing he had failed to see since his first introduction to the Tringle family. He had not seen the peculiar nature of his father-in-law's foibles. He did not understand either the weakness or the strength of Sir Thomas,—either the softness or the hardness. Mr. Traffick himself was blessed with a very hard skin. In the carrying out of a purpose there was nothing which his skin was not sufficiently serviceable to endure. But Sir Thomas, rough as he was, had but a thin skin ;—a thin skin and a soft heart. Had Houston and Gertrude persevered he would certainly have given way. For Tom, in his misfortune, he would have made any sacrifice. Though he had given the broadest hints which he had been able to devise, he had never as yet brought himself absolutely to turn Traffick out of his house. When Ayala was sent away he still kept her name in his will, and added also that of Lucy as soon as Lucy had been entrusted to him. Had things gone a little more smoothly between him and Hamel when they met,—had he not unluckily advised that all the sculptor's grand designs should be sold by auction for what they would fetch,—he would have put Hamel and Lucy upon their legs. He was a soft-hearted man ;—but there never was one less willing to endure interference in his own affairs.

At the present moment he was very sore as to the presence of Traffick in Queen's Gate. The Easter parliamentary holidays were just at hand, and there was no sign of any going. Augusta had whispered to her mother that the poky little house in Mayfair would be very uncomfortable for the coming event,—and Lady Tringle, though she had not dared to say even as much as that in plain terms to her husband, had endeavoured to introduce the subject by little

hints,—which Sir Thomas had clearly understood.   He was hardly the
man to turn a daughter and an expected grandchild into the streets ;
but he was, in his present mood, a father-in-law who would not unwillingly have learned that his son-in-law was without a shelter except
that afforded by the House of Commons.   Why on earth should he
have given up one hundred and twenty thousand pounds,—£6,000
a-year as it was under his fostering care,—to a man who could not even
keep a house over his wife's head ?   This was the humour of Sir
Thomas when Mr. Traffick undertook to prevail with him to give an
adequate fortune to his youngest daughter on her marriage with
Captain Batsby.

The conversation between Traffick and Batsby took place on a Sunday.
On the following day the Captain went down to the House and saw the
Member.   "No ; I have not spoken to him yet."

"I was with him on Friday, you know," said Batsby.   "I can't well
go and call on the ladies in Queen's Gate till I hear that he has changed
his mind."

"I should.   I don't see what difference it would make."

Then Captain Batsby was again very thoughtful.   "It would make
a difference, you know.   If I were to say a word to Gertrude now,—as
to being married or anything of that kind,—it would seem that I
meant to go on whether I got anything or not."

"And you should seem to want to go on," said Traffick, with all
that authority which the very surroundings of the House of Commons
always give to the words and gait of a Member.

"But then I might find myself dropped in a hole at last."

"My dear Batsby, you made that hole for yourself when you ran off
with the young lady."

"We settled all that before."

"Not quite.   What we did settle was that we'd do our best to fill
the hole up.   Of course you ought to go and see them.   You went off
with the young lady,—and since that have been accepted as her suitor
by her father.   You are bound to go and see her."

"Do you think so?"

"Certainly ! Certainly !   It never does to talk to Tringle about
business at his own house.   I'll make an hour to see him in the City
to-morrow.   I'm so pressed by business that I can hardly get away
from the House after twelve ;—but, I'll do it.   But, while I'm in Lombard Street, do you go to Queen's Gate."   The Captain after further
consideration said that he would go to Queen's Gate.

At three o'clock on the next day he did go to Queen's Gate.   He
had many misgivings, feeling that by such a step he would be committing himself to matrimony with or without the money.   No doubt

he could so offer himself, even to Lady Tringle, as a son-in-law, that it should be supposed that the offer would depend upon the father-in-law's goodwill. But then the father-in-law had told him that he would be welcome to the young lady,—without a farthing. Should he go on with his matrimonial purpose, towards which this visit would be an important step, he did not see the moment in which he could stop the proceedings by a demand for money. Nevertheless he went, not being strong enough to oppose Mr. Traffick.

Yes ;—the ladies were at home, and he found himself at once in Lady Tringle's presence. There was at the time no one with her, and the Captain acknowledged to himself that a trying moment had come to him. "Dear me! Captain Batsby!" said her ladyship, who had not seen him since he and Gertrude had gone off together.

"Yes, Lady Tringle. As I have come back from abroad I thought that I might as well come and call. I did see Sir Thomas in the City."

"Was not that a very foolish thing you did?"

"Perhaps it was, Lady Tringle. Perhaps it would have been better to ask permission to address your daughter in the regular course of things. There was, perhaps,—perhaps a little romance in going off in that way."

"It gave Sir Thomas a deal of trouble."

"Well, yes ; he was so quick upon us you know. May I be allowed to see Gertrude now?"

"Upon my word I hardly know," said Lady Tringle, hesitating.

"I did see Sir Thomas in the City."

"But did he say you were to come and call?"

"He gave his consent to the marriage."

"But I am afraid there was to be no money," whispered Lady Tringle. "If money is no matter I suppose you may see her." But before the Captain had resolved how he might best answer this difficult suggestion the door opened, and the young lady herself entered the room, together with her sister."

"Benjamin," said Gertrude, "is this really you?" And then she flew into his arms.

"My dear," said Augusta, "do control your emotions."

"Yes, indeed, Gertrude," said the mother. "As the things are at present you should control yourself. Nobody as yet knows what may come of it."

"Oh, Benjamin !" again exclaimed Gertrude, tearing herself from his arms, throwing herself on the sofa, and covering her face with both her hands. "Oh, Benjamin,—so you have come at last."

"I am afraid he has come too soon," said Augusta, who however had received her lesson from her husband, and had communicated some portion of her husband's tidings to her sister.

"Why too soon?" exclaimed Gertrude. "It can never be too soon. Oh, mamma, tell him that you make him welcome to your bosom as your second son-in-law."

"Upon my word, my dear, I do not know, without consulting your father."

"But papa has consented," said Gertrude.

"But only if——"

"Oh, mamma," said Mrs. Traffick, "do not talk about matters of business on such an occasion as this. All that must be managed between the gentlemen. If he is here as Gertrude's acknowledged lover, and if papa has told him that he shall be accepted as such, I don't think that we ought to say a word about money. I do hate money. It does make things so disagreeable."

"Nobody can be more noble in everything of that kind than Benjamin," said Gertrude "It is only because he loves me with all his heart that he is here. Why else was it that he took me off to Ostend?"

Captain Batsby as he listened to all this felt that he ought to say something. And yet how dangerous might a word be! It was apparent to him, even in his perturbation, that the ladies were in fact asking him to renew his offer, and to declare that he renewed it altogether independently of any money consideration. He could not bring himself quite to agree with that noble sentiment in expressing which Mrs. Traffick had declared her hatred of money. In becoming the son-in-law of a millionaire he would receive the honest congratulations of all his friends,—on condition that he received some comfortable fraction out of the millions, but he knew well that he would subject himself to their ridicule were he to take the girl and lose the plunder. If he were to answer them now as they would have him answer he would commit himself to the girl without any bargain as to the plunder. And yet what else was there for him to do? He must be a brave man who can stand up before a girl and declare that he will love her for ever,—on condition that she shall have so many thousand pounds; but he must be more than brave, he will be heroic, who can do so in the presence not only of the girl but of the girl's mother and married sister as well. Captain Batsby was no such hero. "Of course," he said at last.

"Of course what?" asked Augusta.

"It was because I loved her."

"I knew that he loved me," sobbed Gertrude.

"And you are here, because you intend to make her your wife in presence of all men?" asked Augusta.

" Oh certainly."

" Then I suppose that it will be all right," said Lady Tringle.

" It will be all right," said Augusta. " And now, mamma, I think that we may leave them alone together." But to this Lady Tringle would not give her assent. She had not had confided to her the depth of Mr. Traffick's wisdom, and declared herself opposed to any absolute overt love-making until Sir Thomas should have given his positive consent.

" It is all the same thing, Benjamin, is it not ?" said Augusta, assuming already the familiarity of a sister-in-law.

" Oh quite," said the Captain.

But Gertrude looked as though she did not think it to be exactly the same. Such deficiency as that, however, she had to endure ; and she received from her sister after the Captain's departure full congratulations as to her lover's return. " To tell you the truth," said Augusta, " I didn't think that you would ever see him again. After what papa said to him in the City he might have got off and nobody could have said a word to him. Now he's fixed."

Captain Batsby effected his escape as quickly as he could, and went home a melancholy man. He, too, was aware that he was fixed ; and. as he thought of this, a dreadful idea fell upon him that the Honourable Mr. Traffick had perhaps played him false.

In the meantime Mr. Traffick was true to his word and went into the City. In the early days of his married life his journeys to Lombard Street were frequent. The management and investing of his wife's money had been to him a matter of much interest, and he had felt a gratification in discussing any money matter with the man who handled millions. In this way he had become intimate with the ways of the house, though latterly his presence there had not been encouraged. " I suppose I can go in to Sir Thomas," he said, laying his hand upon a leaf in the counter, which he had been accustomed to raise for the purpose of his own entrance. But here he was stopped. His name should be taken in, and Sir Thomas duly apprised. In the meantime he was relegated to a dingy little waiting-room, which was odious to him, and there he was kept waiting for half-an-hour. This made him angry, and he called to one of the clerks. " Will you tell Sir Thomas that I must be down at the House almost immediately, and that I am particularly anxious to see him on business of importance ?" For another ten minutes he was still kept, and then he was shown into his father-in-law's presence. " I am very sorry, Traffick," said Sir Thomas, " but I really can't turn two Directors of the Bank of England out of my room, even for you."

" I only thought I would just let you know that I am in a hurry."

" So am I, for the matter of that. Have you gone to your father's house to-day, so that you would not be able to see me in Queen's Gate ?"

This was intended to be very severe, but Mr. Traffick bore it. It was one of those rough things which Sir Thomas was in the habit of saying, but which really meant nothing. " No. My father is still at his house as yet, though they are thinking of going every day. It is about another matter, and I did not want to trouble you with it at home."

" Let us hear what it is."

" Captain Batsby has been with me."

" Oh, he has, has he ?"

" I've known him ever so long. He's a foolish fellow."

" So he seems.'

" But a gentleman."

" Perhaps I am not so good a judge of that. His folly I did perceive."

" Oh yes ; he's a gentleman. You may take my word for that. And he has means."

" That's an advantage."

" While that fellow Houston is hardly more than a beggar. And Batsby is quite in earnest about Gertrude."

" If the two of them wish it he can have her to-morrow. She has made herself a conspicuous ass by running away with him, and perhaps it's the best thing she can do."

" That's just it. Augusta sees it quite in the same light."

" Augusta was never tempted. You wouldn't have run away."

" It wasn't necessary, Sir Thomas, was it ? There he is,—ready to marry her to-morrow. But, of course, he is a little anxious about the money."

" I dare say he is."

" I've been talking to him,—and the upshot is, that I have promised to speak to you. He isn't at all a bad fellow."

" He'd keep a house over his wife's head, you think ?" Sir Thomas had been particularly irate that morning, and before the arrival of his son-in-law had sworn to himself that Traffick should go. Augusta might remain, if she pleased, for the occurrence ; but the Honourable Septimus should no longer eat and drink as an inhabitant of his house.

" He'd do his duty by her as a man should do," said Traffick, determined to ignore the disagreeable subject.

" Very well. There she is."

" But of course he would like to hear something about money."

" Would he ?"

" That's only natural."

" You found it so,—did you not ? What's the good of giving a girl money when her husband won't spend it. Perhaps this Captain Batsby would expect to live at Queen's Gate or Merle Park."

It was impossible to go on enduring this without notice. Mr. Traffick, however, only frowned and shook his head. It was clear at last that Sir Thomas intended to be more than rough, and it was almost imperative upon Mr. Traffick to be rough in return. " I am endeavouring to do my duty by the family," he said.

" Oh indeed."

" Gertrude has eloped with this man, and the thing is talked about everywhere. Augusta feels it very much."

" She does, does she ?"

" And I have thought it right to ask his intentions."

" He didn't knock you down, or anything of that sort ?"

" Knock me down !"

" For interfering. But he hasn't pluck for that. Houston would have done it immediately. And I should have said he was right. But if you have got anything to say, you had better say it. When you have done, then I shall have something to say."

" I've told him that he couldn't expect as much as you would have given her but for this running away."

" You told him that ?"

" Yes ; I told him that. Then some sum had to be mentioned. He suggested a hundred thousand pounds."

" How very modest ! Why should he have put up with less than you, seeing that he has got something of his own ?"

" He hasn't my position, Sir. You know that well enough. Now to make a long and short of it, I suggested sixty."

" Out of your own pocket ?"

" Not exactly."

" But out of mine ?"

" You're her father, and I suppose you intend to provide for her."

" And you have come here to dictate to me the provision which I am to make for my own child ! That is an amount of impudence which I did not expect even from you. But suppose that I agree to the terms. Will he, do you think, consent to have a clause put into the settlement ?"

" What clause ?"

" Something that shall bind him to keep a house for his own wife's use, so that he should not take my money and then come and live upon me afterwards."

" Sir Thomas," said the Member of Parliament, " that is a mode of expression so uncourteous that I cannot bear it even from you."

" Is there any mode of expression that you cannot bear ?"

" If you want me to leave your house say it at once."

" Why I have been saying it for the last six months ! I have been saying it almost daily since you were married."

" If so you should have spoken more clearly, for I have not understood you."

" Heavens and earth !" ejaculated Sir Thomas.

" Am I to understand that you wish your child to leave your roof during this inclement weather in her present delicate condition ?"

" Are you in a delicate condition ?" asked Sir Thomas. To this Mr. Traffick could condescend to make no reply. " Because, if not, you, at any rate, had better go,—unless you find the weather too inclement."

" Of course I shall go," said Mr. Traffick. " No consideration on earth shall induce me to eat another meal under your roof until you shall have thought good to have expressed regret for what you have said."

" Then it is very long before I shall have to give you another meal."

" And now what shall I say to Captain Batsby."

" Tell him from me," said Sir Thomas, " that he cannot possibly set about his work more injudiciously than by making you his ambassador." Then Mr. Traffick took his departure.

It may be as well to state here that Mr. Traffick kept his threat religiously,—at any rate, to the end of the Session. He did not eat another meal during that period under his father-in-law's roof. But he slept there for the next two or three days until he had suited himself with lodgings in the neighbourhood of the House. In doing this, however, he contrived to get in and out without encountering Sir Thomas. His wife in her delicate condition,—and because of the inclemency of the weather,—awaited the occurrence at Queen's Gate.

CHAPTER LIX.

TREGOTHNAN.

THE writer, in giving a correct chronicle of the doings of the Tringle family at this time, has to acknowledge that Gertrude, during the prolonged absence of Captain Batsby at Brussels,—an absence that was cruelly prolonged for more than a week,—did make another little effort in another direction. Her father, in his rough way, had expressed an opinion that she had changed very much for the worse in transferring her affections from Mr. Houston to Captain Batsby, and had almost gone so far as to declare that had she been persistent with her Houston the money difficulty might have been overcome. This was imprudent,—unless, indeed, he was desirous of bringing back Mr. Houston into the bosom of the Tringles. It instigated Gertrude to another attempt,—which, however, she did not make till Captain Batsby had been away from her for at least four days without writing a letter. Then it occurred to her that if she had a preference it certainly was for Frank Houston. No doubt the general desirability of marriage was her chief actuating motive. Will the world of British young ladies be much scandalised if I say that such is often an actuating motive? They would be justly scandalised if I pretended that many of its members were capable of the speedy transitions which Miss Tringle was strong enough to endure; but transitions do take place, and I claim, on behalf of my young lady, that she should be regarded as more strong-minded and more determined than the general crowd of young ladies. She had thought herself to be off with the old love before she was on with the new. Then the "new" had gone away to Brussels,—or heaven only knows where,—and there seemed to be an opportunity of renewing matters with the "old." Having perceived the desirability of matrimony, she simply carried out her purpose with a determined will. It was with a determined will, but perhaps with deficient judgment, that she had written as follows:

"Papa has altered his mind altogether. He speaks of you in the highest terms, and says that had you persevered he would have yielded about the money. Do try him again. When hearts have been united it is terrible that they should be dragged asunder." Mr. Traffick had been quite right in telling his father-in-law that "the thing had been talked about everywhere." The thing talked about had been Gertrude's elopement. The daughter of a baronet and a millionnaire cannot go off with the half-brother of another baronet and escape that penalty. The journey to Ostend was in everybody's mouth, and had surprised Frank Houston the more because of the recent termination of his own little affair with the lady. That he should already have re-accommodated himself with Imogene was intelligible to him, and seemed to admit of valid excuse before any jury of matrons. It was an old affair, and the love,—real, true love,—was already existing. He, at any rate, was going back to the better course,—as the jury of matrons would have admitted. But Gertrude's new affair had had to be arranged from the beginning, and shocked him by its celerity. "Already!" he had said to himself,—"gone off with another man already!" He felt himself to have been wounded in a tender part, and was conscious of a feeling that he should like to injure the successful lover,—blackball him at a club, or do him some other mortal mischief. When, therefore, he received from the young lady the little billet above

given, he was much surprised. Could it be a hoax? It was certainly
the young lady's handwriting. Was he to be enticed once again
into Lombard Street, in order that the clerks might set upon him in a
body and maltreat him? Was he to be decoyed into Queen's Gate,
and made a sacrifice of by the united force of the housemaids? Not
understanding the celerity of the young lady, he could hardly believe
the billet.

When he received the note of which we have here spoken two
months had elapsed since he had seen Imogene and had declared to her
his intention of facing the difficulties of matrimony in conjunction
with herself as soon as she would be ready to undergo the ceremony
with him. The reader will remember that her brother, Mudbury
Docimer, had written to him with great severity, abusing both him
and Imogene for the folly of their intention. And Houston, as he
thought of their intention, thought to himself that perhaps they were
foolish. The poverty, and the cradles, and the cabbages, were in
themselves evils. But still he encouraged himself to think that there
might be an evil worse even than folly. After that scene with Imogene,
in which she had offered to sacrifice herself altogether, and to be bound
to him, even though they should never be married, on condition that
he should take to himself no other wife, he had quite resolved that it
behoved him not to be exceeded by her in generosity. He had stoutly
repudiated her offer, which he had called a damnable compact. And
then there had been a delightful scene between them, in which it had
been agreed that they should face the cradles and the cabbages with bold
faces. Since that he had never allowed himself to fluctuate in his purpose. Had Sir Thomas come to him with Gertrude in one hand and the
much-desired £120,000 in the other, he would have repudiated the lot of
them. He declared to himself with stern resolution that he had altogether washed his hands from dirt of that kind. Cabbages and cradles
for ever was the unpronounced cry of triumph with which he buoyed
up his courage. He set himself to work earnestly, if not altogether
steadfastly, to alter the whole tenor of his life. The champagne and
the woodcocks,—or whatever might be the special delicacies of the
season,—he did avoid. For some few days he absolutely dined upon a
cut of mutton at an eating-house, and as he came forth from the unsavoury doors of the establishment regarded himself as a hero. Cabbages and cradles for ever! he would say to himself, as he went away
to drink a cup of tea with an old maiden aunt, who was no less
surprised than gratified by his new virtue. Therefore, when it had at
last absolutely come home to him that the last little note had in truth
been written by Gertrude with no object of revenge, but with the
intention of once more alluring him into the wealth of Lombard Street,

he simply put it into his breastcoat-pocket, and left it there un-answered.

Mudbury Docimer did not satisfy himself with writing the very uncourteous letter which the reader has seen, but proceeded to do his utmost to prevent the threatened marriage. "She is old enough to look after herself," he had said, as though all her future actions must be governed by her own will. But within ten days of the writing of that letter he had found it expedient to go down into the country, and to take his sister with him. As the head of the Docimer family he possessed a small country-house almost in the extremity of Cornwall; and thither he went. It was a fraternal effort made alto-gether on his sister's behalf, and was so far successful that Imogene was obliged to accompany him. It was all very well for her to feel that as she was of age she could do as she pleased. But a young lady is con-strained by the exigencies of society to live with somebody. She can-not take a lodging by herself, as her brother may do. Therefore, when Mudbury Docimer went down to Cornwall, Imogene was obliged to accompany him.

"Is this intended for banishment?" she said to him, when they had been about a week in the country.

"What do you call banishment? You used to like the country in the spring." It was now the middle of April.

"So I do, and in summer also. But I like nothing under con-straint."

"I am sorry that circumstances should make it imperative upon me to remain here just at present."

"Why cannot you tell the truth, Mudbury?"

"Have I told you any falsehood?"

"Why do you not say outright that I have been brought down here to be out of Frank Houston's way."

"Because Frank Houston is a name which I do not wish to mention to you again,—at any rate for some time."

"What would you do if he were to show himself here?" she asked.

"Tell him at once that he was not welcome. In other words, I would not have him here. It is very improbable I should think that he would come without a direct invitation from me. That invitation he will never have until I feel satisfied that you and he have changed your mind again, and that you mean to stick to it."

"I do not think we shall do that."

"Then he shall not come down here; nor, as far as I am able to arrange it, shall you go up to London."

"Then I am a prisoner?"

"You may put it as you please," said her brother. "I have no

power of detaining you.   Whatever influence I have I think it right to
use.   I am altogether opposed to this marriage, believing it to be an
absurd infatuation.   I think that he is of the same opinion."

"No!" said she, indignantly."

"That I believe to be his feeling," he continued, taking no notice of
her assertion.   "He is as perfectly aware as I am that you two are not
adapted to live happily together on an income of a few hundreds a
year.   Some time ago it was agreed between you that it was so.
You both were quite of one mind, and I was given to understand that
the engagement was at an end.   It was so much at an end that he
made an arrangement for marrying another woman.   But your feelings are stronger than his, and you allowed them to get the better of
you.   Then you enticed him back from the purpose on which you had
both decided."

"Enticed!" said she.   "I did nothing of the kind!"

"Would he have changed his mind if you had not enticed him?"

"I did nothing of the kind.   I offered to remain just as we are."

"That is all very well.   Of course he could not accept such an offer.
Thinking as I do, it is my duty to keep you apart as long as I can.
If you contrive to marry him in opposition to my efforts, the misery of
both of you must be on your head.   I tell you fairly that I do not
believe he wishes anything of the kind."

"I am quite sure he does," said Imogene.

"Very well.   Do you leave him alone ; stay down here, and see
what will come of it.   I quite agree that such a banishment, as you call
it, is not a happy prospect for you ;—but it is happier than that of a
marriage with Frank Houston.   Give that up, and then you can go
back to London and begin the world again."

Begin the world again!   She knew what that meant.   She was to
throw herself into the market, and look for such other husband as
Providence might send her.   She had tried that before, and had convinced herself that Providence could never send her any that could be
acceptable.   The one man had taken possession of her, and there never
could be a second.   She had not known her own strength,—or her own
weakness as the case might be,—when she had agreed to surrender the
man she loved because there had been an alteration in their prospects
of an income.   She had struggled with herself, had attempted to amuse
herself with the world, had told herself that somebody would come
who would banish that image from her thoughts and heart.   She had
bade herself to submit to the separation for his welfare.   Then she had
endeavoured to quiet herself by declaring to herself that the man was
no hero,—was unworthy of so much thinking.   But it had all been of
no avail.   Gertrude Tringle had been a festering sore to her.   Frank

whether a hero or only a commonplace man, was,—as she owned to herself,—hero enough for her. Then came the opening for a renewal of the engagement. Frank had been candid with her, and had told her everything. The Tringle money would not be forthcoming on his behalf. Then,—not resolving to entice him back again,—she had done so. The word was odious to her, and was rejected with disdain when used against her by her brother;—but, when alone, she acknowledged to herself that it was true. She had enticed her lover back again,—to his great detriment. Yes; she certainly had enticed him back. She certainly was about to sacrifice him because of her love. "If I could only die, and there be an end of it!" she exclaimed to herself.

Though Tregothnan Hall, as the Docimers' house was called, was not open to Frank Houston, there was the post running always. He had written to her half-a-dozen times since she had been in Cornwall, and had always spoken of their engagement as an affair at last irrevocably fixed. She, too, had written little notes, tender and loving, but still tinged by that tone of despondency which had become common to her. "As for naming a day," she said once, "suppose we fix the first of January, ten years hence. Mudbury's opposition will be worn out by old age, and you will have become thoroughly sick of the pleasures of London." But joined to this there would be a few jokes, and then some little word of warmest, most enduring, most trusting love. "Don't believe me if I say that I am not happy in knowing that I am altogether your own." Then there would come a simple "I" as a signature, and after that some further badinage respecting her "Cerberus," as she called her brother.

But after that word, that odious word, "enticed," there went another letter up to London of altogether another nature.

"I have changed my mind again," she said, "and have become aware that though I should die in doing it,—though we should both die if it were possible,—there should be an end of everything between you and me. Yes, Frank; there! I send you back my troth, and demand my own in return. After all why should not one die;—hang oneself if it be necessary? To be self-denying is all that is necessary,—at any rate to a woman. Hanging or lying down and dying, or lingering on and saying one's prayers and knitting stockings, is altogether immaterial. I have sometimes thought Mudbury to be brutal to me, but I have never known him to be untrue,—or even, as I believe, mistaken. He sees clearly and knows what will happen. He tells me that I have enticed you back. I am not true as he is. So I threw him back the word in his teeth,—though its truth at the moment was going like a dagger through my heart. I know myself to have been selfish, unfeeling, unfeminine, when I induced you to surrender your-

self to a mode of life which will make you miserable. I have sometimes been proud of myself because I have loved you so truly ; but
now I hate myself and despise myself because I have been incapable of
the first effort which love should make. Love should at any rate be
unselfish.

" He tells me that you will be miserable and that the misery will be
on my head,—and I believe him. There shall be an end of it. I want
no promise from you. There may, perhaps, be a time in which
Imogene Docimer as a sturdy old maid shall be respected and serene
of mind. As a wife who had enticed her husband to his misery she
would be respected neither by him nor by herself,—and as for serenity
it would be quite out of the question. I have been unfortunate. That
is all ;—but not half so unfortunate as others that I see around me.

" *Pray, pray,* PRAY, take this as final, and thus save me from renewed trouble and renewed agony.

" Now I am yours truly,

—" never again will I be affectionate to any one with true
feminine love, " IMOGENE DOCIMER."

Houston when he received the above letter of course had no alternative but to declare that it could not possibly be regarded as having any
avail. And indeed he had heart enough in his bosom to be warmed to
something like true heat by such words as these. The cabbages and
cradles ran up in his estimation. The small house at Pau, which in
some of his more despondent moments had assumed an unqualified
appearance of domestic discomfort, was now ornamented and accoutred
till it seemed to be a little paradise. The very cabbages blossomed
into roses, and the little babies in the cradles produced a throb of
paternal triumph in his heart. If she were woman enough to propose
to herself such an agony of devotion, could he not be man enough to
demand from her a devotion of a different kind? As to Mudbury
Docimer's truth, he believed in it not at all, but was quite convinced
of the man's brutality. Yes ; she should hang herself—but it should be
round his neck. The serenity should be displayed by her not as an
aunt but as a wife and mother. As for enticing, did he not now,—just
in this moment of his manly triumph,—acknowledge to himself that she
had enticed him to his happiness, to his glory, to his welfare? In this
frame of mind he wrote his answer as follows ;—

" MY DEAREST,

" You have no power of changing your mind again. There must be
some limit to vacillations, and that has been reached. Something
must be fixed at last. Something has been fixed at last, and I most

certainly shall not consent to any further unfixing. What right has Mudbury to pretend to know my feelings ? or, for the matter of that, what right have you to accept his description of them ? I tell you now that I place my entire happiness in the hope of making you my wife. I call upon you to ignore all the selfish declarations as to my own ideas which I have made in times past. The only right which you could now possibly have to separate yourself from me would come from your having ceased to love me. You do not pretend to say that such is the case ; and therefore, with considerable indignation, but still very civilly, I desire that Mudbury with his hard-hearted counsels may go to the ——"

" Enticed ! Of course you have enticed me. I suppose that women do as a rule entice men, either to their advantage or disadvantage. I will leave it to you to say whether you believe that such enticement, if it be allowed its full scope, will lead to one or the other as far as I am concerned. I never was so happy as when I felt that you had enticed me back to the hopes of former days.

" Now I am yours, as always, and most affectionately,
" FRANK HOUSTON."

" I shall expect the same word back from you by return of post scored under as eagerly as those futile " prays."

Imogene when she received this was greatly disturbed,—not knowing how to carry herself in her great resolve,—or whether indeed that resolve must not be again abandoned. She had determined, should her lover's answer be as she had certainly intended it to be when she wrote her letter, to go at once to her brother and to declare to him that the danger was at an end, and that he might return to London without any fear of a relapse on her part. But she could not do so with such a reply as that she now held in her pocket. If that reply could, in very truth be true, then there must be another revulsion, another change of purpose, another yielding to absolute joy. If it could be the case that Frank Houston no longer feared the dangers that he had feared before, if he had in truth reconciled himself to a state of things which he had once described as simple poverty, if he really placed his happiness on the continuation of his love, then,—then, why should she make the sacrifice ? Why should she place such implicit confidence in her brother's infallibility against error, seeing that by doing so she would certainly shipwreck her own happiness,—and his too, if his words were to be trusted ?

He called upon her to write to him again by return of post. She was to write to him and unsay those prayers, and comfort him with a repetition of that dear word which she had declared that she would never use again with all its true meaning. That was his express order to her. Should she obey it, or should she not obey it? Should she vacillate again, or should she leave his last letter unanswered with stern obduracy? She acknowledged to herself that it was a dear letter, deserving the best treatment at her hands,—giving her lover credit, probably, for more true honesty than he deserved. What was the best reatment? Her brother had plainly shown his conviction that the best treatment would be to leave him without meddling with him any further. Her sister-in-law, though milder in her language, was, she feared, of the same opinion. Would it not be better for him not to be meddled with? Ought not that to be her judgment, looking at the matter all round?

She did not at any rate obey him at all points, for she left his letter in her pocket for three or four days while she considered the matter backwards and forwards.

CHAPTER LX.

AUNT ROSINA.

During this period of heroism it had been necessary to Houston to have some confidential friend to whom from time to time he could speak of his purpose. He could not go on eating slices of boiled mutton at eating-houses, and drinking dribblets of bad wine out of little decanters no bigger than the bottles in a cruet-stand, without having some one to encourage him in his efforts. It was a hard apprenticeship, and, coming as it did rather late in life for such a beginning and after much luxurious indulgence, required some sympathy and consolation. There were Tom Shuttlecock and Lord John Battledore at the club. Lord John was the man as to whose expulsion because of his contumacious language so much had been said, but who lived through that and various other dangers. These had been his special friends, and to them he had confided everything in regard to the Tringle marriage. Shuttlecock had ridiculed the very idea of love, and had told him that everything else was to be thrown to the dogs in pursuit of a good income. Battledore had reminded him that there was "a deuced deal of cut-and-come-again in a hundred and twenty thousand pounds." They had been friends, not always altogether after his own heart, but friends who had served his purpose when he was making his raid upon Lombard Street. But they were not men to whom he could descant on the wholesomeness of cabbages as an article of daily food, or who would sympathise with the struggling joys of an embryo father. To their thinking, women were occasionally very convenient as being the depositaries of some of the accruing wealth of the world. Frank had been quite worthy of their friendship as having "spotted" and nearly "run down" for himself a well-laden city heiress. But now Tom Shuttlecock and Lord John Battledore were distasteful to him,—as would he be to them. But he found the confidential friend in his maiden aunt.

Miss Houston was an old lady,—older than her time as are some people,—who lived alone in a small house in Green Street. She was particular in calling it Green Street, Hyde Park. She was very anxious to have it known that she never occupied it during the months of August, September, and October,—though it was often the case with her that she did not in truth expatriate herself for more than six weeks. She was careful to have a fashionable seat in a fashionable church. She dearly loved to see her name in the papers when she was happy enough to be invited to a house whose entertainments were chronicled. There were a thousand little tricks,—I will not be harsh enough to call them unworthy,—by which she served Mammon. But she did not limit her service to the evil spirit. When in her place in church she sincerely said her prayers. When in London, or out of it, she gave a modicum of her slender income to the poor. And, though she liked to see her name in the papers as one of the fashionable world, she was a great deal too proud of the blood of the Houstons to toady any one or to ask for any favour. She was a neat, clean, nice-looking old lady, who understood that if economies were to be made in eating and drinking they should be effected at her own table and not at that of the servants who waited upon her. This was the confidential friend whom Frank trusted in his new career.

It must be explained that Aunt Rosina, as Miss Houston was called, had been well acquainted with her nephew's earlier engagement, and had approved of Imogene as his future wife. Then had come the unexpected collapse in the uncle's affairs, by which Aunt Rosina as well as others in the family had suffered,—and Frank, much to his aunt's displeasure, had allowed himself to be separated from the lady of his love on account of his comparative poverty. She had heard of Gertrude Tringle and all her money,—but from a high standing of birth and social belongings had despised all the Tringles and all their money. To her, as a maiden lady, truth in love was everything. To her, as a well-born lady, good blood was everything. Therefore, though there had been no quarrel between her and Frank, there had been a cessation of sympathetic interest, and he had been thrown into the hands of the Battledores and Shuttlecocks. Now again the old

sympathies were revived, and Frank found it convenient to drink tea
with his aunt when other engagements allowed it.

"I call that an infernal interference," he said to his aunt, showing
her Imogene's letters.

"My dear Frank, you need not curse and swear," said the old lady.

"Infernal is not cursing nor yet swearing." Then Miss Houston,
having liberated her mind by her remonstrance, proceeded to read the
letter. "I call that abominable," said Frank, alluding of course to
the allusions made in the letter to Mudbury Docimer.

"It is a beautiful letter;—just what I should have expected from
Imogene. My dear, I will tell you what I propose. Remain as you
are both of you for five years."

"Five years. That's sheer nonsense."

"Five years, my dear, will run by like a dream. Five years to look
back upon is as nothing."

"But these five years are five years to be looked forward to. It is
out of the question."

"But you say that you could not live as a married man."

"Live! I suppose we could live." Then he thought of the cabbages
and the cottage at Pau. "There would be seven hundred a-year I
suppose."

"Couldn't you do something, Frank?"

"What, to earn money? No; I don't think I could. If I attempted to break stones I shouldn't break enough to pay for the ham-
mers."

"Couldn't you write a book?"

"That would be worse than the stones. I sometimes thought I
could paint a picture,—but, if I did, nobody would buy it. As to
making money that is hopeless. I could save some, by leaving off
gloves and allowing myself only three clean shirts a-week."

"That would be dreadful, Frank."

"It would be dreadful, but it is quite clear that I must do something.
An effort has to be made." This he said with a voice the tone of
which was almost heroic. Then they discussed the matter at great
length, in doing which Aunt Rosina thoroughly encouraged him in his
heroism. That idea of remaining unmarried for another short period
of five years was allowed to go by the board, and when they parted on
that night it was understood that steps were to be taken to bring about
a marriage as speedily as possible.

"Perhaps I can do a little to help," said Aunt Rosina, in a faint
whisper as Frank left the room.

Frank Houston, when he showed Imogene's letter to his aunt,
had already answered it. Then he waited a day or two, not very

patiently, for a further rejoinder from Imogene,—in which she of course was to unsay all that she had said before. But when, after four or five days, no rejoinder had come, and his fervour had been increased by his expectation, then he told his aunt that he should immediately take some serious step. The more ardent he was the better his aunt loved him. Could he have gone down and carried off his bride, and married her at once, in total disregard of the usual wedding-cake and St.-George's-Hanover-Square ceremonies to which the Houston family had always been accustomed, she could have found it in her heart to forgive him. "Do not be rash, Frank," she said. He merely shook his head, and as he again left her declared that he was not going to be driven this way or that by such a fellow as Mudbury Docimer.

"As I live, there's Frank coming through the gate." This was said by Imogene to her sister-in-law, as they were walking up and down the road which led from the lodge up to the Tregothnan house. The two ladies were at that moment discussing Imogene's affairs. No rejoinder had as yet been made to Frank's last letter, which, to Imogene's feeling, was the most charming epistle which had ever come from the hands of a true lover. There had been passion and sincerity in every word of it ;—even when he had been a little too strong in his language as he denounced the hard-hearted counsels of her brother. But yet she had not responded to all this sincerity, nor had she as yet withdrawn the resolution which she had herself declared. Mrs. Docimer was of opinion that that resolution should not be withdrawn, and had striven to explain that the circumstances were now the same as when, after full consideration, they had determined that the engagement should come to an end. At this very moment she was speaking words of wisdom to this effect, and as she did so Frank appeared, walking up from the gate.

"What will Mudbury say?" was Mrs. Docimer's first ejaculation. But Imogene, before she had considered how this danger might be encountered, rushed forward and gave herself up,—I fear we must confess,—into the arms of her lover. After that it was felt at once that she had withdrawn all her last resolution and had vacillated again. There was no ground left even for an argument now that she had submitted herself to be embraced. Frank's words of affection need not here be repeated, but they were of a nature to leave no doubt on the minds of either of the ladies.

Mudbury had declared that he would not receive Houston in his house as his sister's lover, and had expressed his opinion that even Houston would not have the face to show his face there. But Houston had come, and something must be done with him. It was soon ascertained that he had walked over from Penzance, which was but two miles off, and had left his portmanteau behind him. "I wouldn't bring anything," said he. "Mudbury would find it easier to maltreat my things than myself. It would look so foolish to tell the man with a fly to carry them back at once. Is he in the house?"

"He is about the place," said Mrs. Docimer, almost trembling.

"Is he very fierce against me?"

"He thinks it had better be all over."

"I am of a different way of thinking, you see. I cannot acknowledge that he has any right to dictate to Imogene."

"Nor can I," said Imogene.

"Of course, he can turn me out."

"If he does I shall go with you," said Imogene.

"We have made up our minds to it," said Frank, "and he had better let us do as we please. He can make himself disagreeable, of course ; but he has got no power to prevent us." Now they had reached the house, and Frank was of course allowed to enter. Had he not entered neither would Imogene, who was so much taken by this further instance of her lover's ardour that she was determined now to be led by him in everything. His explanation of that word "enticed" had been so thoroughly satisfactory to her that she was no longer in the least angry with herself because she had enticed him. She had quite come to see that it is the duty of a young woman to entice a young man.

Frank and Imogene were soon left alone, not from any kindness of feeling on the part of Mrs. Docimer, but because the wife felt it necessary to find her husband. "Oh, Mudbury, who do you think has come? He is here!"

"Houston!"

"Yes ; Frank Houston!"

"In the house?"

"He is in the house. But he hasn't brought anything. He doesn't mean to stay."

"What does that matter? He shall not be asked even to dine here."

"If he is turned out she will go with him ! If she says so, she will do it. You cannot prevent her. That's what would come of it if she were to insist on going up to London with him."

"He is a scoundrel !"

"No ; Mudbury ;—not a scoundrel. You cannot call him a scoundrel. There is something firm about him ; isn't there?"

"To come to my house when I told him not?"

"But he does really love her."

" Bother !"

" At any rate there they are in the breakfast-parlour, and something must be done. I couldn't tell him not to come in. And she wouldn't have come without him. There will be enough for them to live upon. Don't you think you'd better ?" Docimer, as he returned to the house, declared that he " did not think he'd better." But he had to confess to himself that, whether it were better or whether it were worse, he could do very little to prevent it.

The greeting of the two men was anything but pleasant. " What I have got to say I would rather say outside," said Docimer.

" Certainly," said Frank. " I suppose I'm to be allowed to return ?"

" If he does not,"—said Imogene, who at her brother's request had left the room, but still stood at the open door,—" if he does not I shall go to him in Penzance. You will hardly attempt to keep me a prisoner."

" Who says that he is not to return ? I think that you are two idiots, but I am quite aware that I cannot prevent you from being married if you are both determined." Then he led the way out through the hall, and Frank followed him. " I cannot understand that any man should be so fickle," he said, when they were both out on the walk together.

" Constant, I should suppose you mean."

" I said fickle, and I meant it. It was at your own suggestion that you and Imogene were to be separated."

" No doubt ;—it was at my suggestion, and with her consent. But you see that we have changed our minds."

" And will change them again."

" We are steady enough in our purpose, now, at any rate. You hear what she says. If I came down here to persuade her to alter her pur-pose,—to talk her into doing something of which you disapproved, and as to which she agreed with you,—then you might do something by quarreling with me. But what's the use of it, when she and I are of one mind ? You know that you cannot talk her over."

" Where do you mean to live ?"

" I'll tell you all about that if you'll allow me to send into Penzance for my things. I cannot discuss matters with you if you proclaim yourself to be my enemy. You say we are both idiots."

" I do."

" Very well. Then you had better put up with two idiots. You can't cure their idiocy. Nor have you any authority to prevent them from exhibiting it." The argument was efficacious though the idiocy was acknowledged. The portmanteau was sent for, and before the evening was over Frank had again been received at Tregothnan as Imogene's accepted lover.

Then Frank had his story to tell and his new proposition to make. Aunt Rosina had offered to join her means with his. The house in Green Street, no doubt, was small, but room it was thought could be made, at any rate till the necessity had come for various cribs and various cradles. "I cannot imagine that you will endure to live with Aunt Rosina," said the brother.

"Why on earth shall I object to Aunt Rosina?" said Imogene. "She and I have always been friends." In her present mood she would hardly have objected to live with any old woman, however objectionable. "And we shall be able to have a small cottage somewhere," said Frank. "She will keep the house in London, and we shall keep the cottage."

"And what on earth will you do with yourself?"

"I have thought of that too," said Frank. "I shall take to painting pictures in earnest;—portraits probably. I don't see why I shouldn't do as well as anybody else."

"That head of yours of old Mrs. Jones," said Imogene, "was a great deal better than dozens of things one sees every year in the Academy."

"Bother!" exclaimed Docimer.

"I don't see why he should not succeed, if he really will work hard," said Mrs. Docimer.

"Bother!"

"Why should it be bother?" said Frank, put upon his mettle. "Ever so many fellows have begun and have got on, older than I am. And, even if I don't earn anything, I've got an employment."

"And is the painting-room to be in Green Street also?" asked Docimer.

"Just at present I shall begin by copying things at the National Gallery," explained Houston, who was not as yet prepared with his answer to that difficulty as to a studio in the little house in Green Street.

When the matter had been carried as far as this it was manifest enough that anything like opposition to Imogene's marriage was to be withdrawn. Houston remained at Tregothnan for a couple of days and then returned to London. A week afterwards the Docimers followed him, and early in the following June the two lovers, after all their troubles and many vacillations, were made one at St. George's church, to the great delight of Aunt Rosina. It cannot be said that the affair gave equal satisfaction to all the bridegroom's friends, as may be learnt from the following narration of two conversations which took place in London very shortly after the wedding.

"Fancy after all that fellow Houston going and marrying such a

girl as Imogene Docimer, without a single blessed shilling to keep themselves alive." This was said in the smoking-room of Houston's club
by Lord John Battledore to Tom Shuttlecock ; but it was said quite
aloud, so that Houston's various acquaintances might be enabled to offer
their remarks on so interesting a subject ; and to express their pity for
the poor object of their commiseration.

"It's the most infernal piece of folly I ever heard in my life," said
Shuttlecock. "There was that Tringle girl with two hundred thousand pounds to be had just for the taking ;—Traffick's wife's sister, you
know."

"There was something wrong about that," said another. "Benjamin Batsby, that stupid fellow who used to be in the twentieth, ran
off with her just when everything had been settled between Houston
and old Tringle."

"Not a bit of it," said Battledore. "Tringle had quarrelled with
Houston before that. Batsby did go with her, but the governor
wouldn't come down with the money. Then the girl was brought back
and there was no marriage." Upon that the condition of poor Gertrude
in reference to her lovers and her fortune was discussed by those present with great warmth ; but they all agreed that Houston had proved
himself to be a bigger fool than any of them had expected.

"By George, he's going to set up for painting portraits," said Lord
John, with great disgust.

In Queen's Gate the matter was discussed by the ladies there very
much in the same spirit. At this time Gertrude was engaged to Captain Batsby, if not with the full approbation at any rate with the consent both of her father and mother, and therefore she could speak of
Frank Houston and his bride, if with disdain, still without wounded
feelings. "Here it is in the papers, Francis Houston and Imogene
Docimer," said Mrs. Traffick.

"So she has really caught him at last !" said Gertrude.

"There was not much to catch," rejoined Mrs. Traffick. "I doubt
whether they have got £500 a-year between them."

"It does seem so very sudden," said Lady Tringle.

"Sudden !" said Gertrude. "They have been about it for the last
five years. Of course he has tried to wriggle out of it all through.
I am glad that she has succeeded at last, if only because he deserves it."

"I wonder where they'll find a place to live in," said Augusta. This
took place in the bedroom which Mrs. Traffick still occupied in
Queen's Gate, when she had been just a month a mother.

Thus, with the kind assistance of Aunt Rosina, Frank Houston and
Imogene Docimer were married at last, and the chronicler hereby
expresses a hope that it may not be long before Frank may see a pic-

ture of his own hanging on the walls of the Academy, and that he may
live to be afraid of the coming of no baby.

CHAPTER LXI.

TOM TRINGLE GOES UPON HIS TRAVELS.

We must again go back and pick up our threads to April, having
rushed forward to be present at the wedding of Frank Houston and
Imogene Docimer, which did not take place till near Midsummer.
This we must do at once in regard to Tom Tringle, who, if the matter
be looked at aright, should be regarded as the hero of this little
history. Ayala indeed, who is no doubt the real heroine among so
many young ladies who have been more or less heroic, did not find in
him the angel of whom she had dreamed, and whose personal appearance on earth was necessary to her happiness. But he had been able
very clearly to pick out an angel for himself, and, though he had failed
in his attempts to take the angel home with him, had been constant in
his endeavours as long as there remained to him a chance of success.
He had shown himself to be foolish, vulgar, and ignorant. He had
given way to Bolivian champagne and Faddle intimacies. He had
been silly enough to think that he could bribe his Ayala with diamonds
for herself, and charm her with cheaper jewelry on his own person.
He had thought to soar high by challenging his rival to a duel, and
had then been tempted by pot courage to strike him in the streets. A
very vulgar and foolish young man! But a young man capable of a
persistent passion! Young men not foolish and not vulgar are, perhaps, common enough. But the young men of constant heart and
capable of such persistency as Tom's are not to be found every day
walking about the streets of the metropolis. Jonathan Stubbs was
constant, too; but it may be doubted whether the Colonel ever really
despaired. The merit is to despair and yet to be constant. When a
man has reason to be assured that a young lady is very fond of him,
he may always hope that love will follow,—unless indeed the love
which he seeks has been already given away elsewhere. Moreover,
Stubbs had many substantial supports at his back;—the relationship
of the Marchesa, the friendship of Lady Albury, the comforts of Stalham,—and not least, if last, the capabilities and prowess of Croppy.
Then, too, he was neither vulgar nor foolish nor ignorant. Tom
Tringle had everything against him,—everything that would weigh
with Ayala; and yet he fought his battle out to the last gasp. Therefore, I desire my hearers to regard Tom Tringle as the hero of the

transactions with which they have been concerned, and to throw their old shoes after him as he starts away upon his grand tour.

"Tom, my boy, you have to go, you know, in four days," said his father to him. At this time Tom had as yet given no positive consent as to his departure. He had sunk into a low state of moaning and groaning, in which he refused even to accede to the doctrine of the expediency of a manly bearing. "What's the good of telling a lie about it?" he would say to his mother. "What's the good of manliness when a fellow would rather be drowned?" He had left his bed indeed, and had once or twice sauntered out of the house. He had been instigated by his sister to go down to his club, under the idea that by such an effort he would shake off the despondency which overwhelmed him. But he had failed in the attempts, and had walked by the doors of the Mountaineers, finding himself unable to face the hall-porter. But still the preparations for his departure were going on. It was presumed that he was to leave London for Liverpool on the Friday, and his father had now visited him in his own room on the Tuesday evening with the intention of extorting from him his final consent. Sir Thomas had on that morning expressed himself very freely to his son-in-law Mr. Traffick, and on returning home had been glad to find tha this words had been of avail, at any rate as regarded the dinner-hour. He was tender-hearted towards his son, and disposed to tempt him rather than threaten him into obedience.

"I haven't ever said I would go," replied Tom.

"But you must, you know. Everything has been packed up, and I want to make arrangements with you about money. I have got a cabin for you to yourself, and Captain Merry says that you will have a very pleasant passage. The equinoxes are over."

"I don't care about the equinoxes," said Tom. "I should like bad weather if I am to go."

"Perhaps you may have a touch of that, too."

"If the ship could be dashed against a rock I should prefer it!" exclaimed Tom.

"That's nonsense. The Cunard ships never are dashed against rocks. By the time you've been three days at sea you'll be as hungry as a hunter. Now, Tom, how about money?"

"I don't care about money," said Tom.

"Don't you? Then you're very unlike anybody else that I meet. I think I had better give you power to draw at New York, San Francisco, Yokohama, Pekin, and Calcutta."

"Am I to go to Pekin?" asked Tom, with renewed melancholy.

"Well, yes;—I think so. You had better see what the various houses are doing in China. And then from Calcutta you can go up

2 F

the country. By that time I daresay we shall have possession of Cabul. With such a government as we have now, thank God ! the Russians will have been turned pretty nearly out of Asia by this time next year."*

" Am I to be away more than a year ?"

" If I were you," said the father, glad to catch the glimmer of assent which was hereby implied,—" if I were you I would do it thoroughly whilst I was about it. Had I seen so much when I was young I should have been a better man of business."

" It's all the same to me," said Tom. " Say ten years, if you like it ! Say twenty ! I shan't ever want to come back again. Where am I to go after Cabul ?"

" I didn't exactly fix it that you should go to Cabul. Of course you will write home and give me your own opinion as you travel on. You will stay two or three months probably in the States."

" Am I to go Niagara ?" he asked.

" Of course you will, if you wish it. The Falls of Niagara, I am told, are very wonderful."

" If a man is to drown himself," said Tom, " it's the sort of place to do it effectually."

" Oh, Tom !" exclaimed his father. " Do you speak to me in that way when I am doing everything in my power to help you in your trouble?"

" You cannot help me," said Tom.

" Circumstances will. Time will do it. Employment will do it. A sense of your dignity as a man will do it, when you find yourself amongst others who know nothing of what you have suffered. You revel in your grief now because those around you know that you have failed. All that will be changed when you are with strangers. You should not talk to your father of drowning yourself !"

" That was wrong. I know it was wrong," said Tom, humbly. " I won't do it if I can help it,—but perhaps I had better not go there. And how long ought I to stay at Yokohama ? Perhaps you had better put it all down on a bit of paper." Then Sir Thomas endeavoured to explain to him that all that he said now was in the way of advice. That it would be in truth left to himself to go almost where he liked, and to stay at each place almost as long as he liked ;—that he would be his own master, and that within some broad and undefined limits he would have as much money as he pleased to spend. Surely no preparations for a young man's tour were ever made with more alluring circumstances ! But Tom could not be tempted into any expression of satisfaction.

---

* It has to be stated that this story was written in 1878.

This, however, Sir Thomas did gain,—that before he left his son's room it was definitely settled,—that Tom should take his departure on the Friday, going down to Liverpool by an afternoon train on that day. "I tell you what," said Sir Thomas; "I'll go down with you, see you on board the ship, and introduce you to Captain Merry. I shall be glad of an opportunity of paying a visit to Liverpool." And so the question of Tom's departure was settled.

On the Wednesday and Thursday he seemed to take some interest in his bags and portmanteaus, and began himself to look after those assuagements of the toils of travel which are generally dear to young men. He interested himself in a fur coat, in a well-arranged despatch box, and in a very neat leathern case which was intended to hold two brandy flasks. He consented to be told of the number of his shirts, and absolutely expressed an opinion that he should want another pair of dress-boots. When this occurred every female bosom in the house, from Lady Tringle's down to the kitchenmaid's, rejoiced at the signs of recovery which evinced themselves. But neither Lady Tringle nor the kitchenmaid, nor did any of the intermediate female bosoms, know how he employed himself when he left the house on that Thursday afternoon. He walked across the Park, and, calling at Kingsbury Crescent, left a note addressed to his aunt. It was as follows:—"I start tomorrow afternoon,—I hardly know whither. It may be for years or it may be for ever. I should wish to say a word to Ayala before I go. Will she see me if I come at twelve o'clock exactly to-morrow morning? I will call for an answer in half-an-hour. T. T., junior. Of course I am aware that Ayala is to become the bride of Colonel Jonathan Stubbs." In half-an-hour he returned, and got his answer. "Ayala will be glad to have an opportunity of saying good-bye to you to-morrow morning."

From this it will be seen that Ayala had at that time returned from Stalham to Kingsbury Crescent. She had come back joyful in heart, thoroughly triumphant as to her angel, with everything in the world sweet and happy before her,—desirous if possible to work her fingers off in mending the family linen, if only she could do something for somebody in return for all the joy that the world was giving her. When she was told that Tom wished to see her for the last time,—for the last time at any rate before her marriage,—she assented at once. "I think you should see him as he asks it," said her aunt.

"Poor Tom! Of course I will see him." And so the note was written which Tom received when he called the second time at the door.

At half-past eleven he skulked out of the house in Queen's Gate, anxious to avoid his mother and sisters, who were on their side anxious to devote every remaining minute of the time to his comfort and wel-

2 F 2

fare. I am afraid it must be acknowledged that he went with all his jewelry. It could do no good. At last he was aware of that. But still he thought that she would like him better with his jewelry than without it. Stubbs wore no gems, not even a ring, and Ayala when she saw her cousin enter the room could only assure herself that the male angels certainly were never be-jewelled. She was alone in the drawing-room, Mrs. Dosett having arranged that at the expiration of ten minutes, which were to be allowed to Tom for his private adieux, she would come down to say good-bye to her nephew. "Ayala!" said Tom.

"So you are going away,—for a very long journey, Tom."

"Yes, Ayala ; for a very long journey ;—to Pekin and Cabul, if I live through, to get to those sort of places."

"I hope you will live through, Tom."

"Thank you, Ayala. Thank you. I daresay I shall. They tell me I shall get over it. I don't feel like getting over it now."

"You'll find some beautiful young lady at Pekin, perhaps."

"Beauty will never have any effect upon me again, Ayala. Beauty indeed ! Think what I have suffered from oeauty ! From the first moment in which you came down to Glenbogie I have been a victim to it. It has destroyed me,—destroyed me !"

"I am sure you will come back quite well," said Ayala, hardly knowing how to answer the last appeal.

"Perhaps I may. If I can only get my heart to turn to stone, then I shall. I don't know why I should have been made to care so much about it. Other people don't."

"And now we must say, Good-bye, I suppose."

"Oh, yes ;—good-bye ! I did want to say one or two words if you ain't in a hurry. Of course you'll be his bride now."

"I hope so," said Ayala.

"I take that for granted. Of course I hate him."

"Oh, Tom ; you shan't say that."

"It's human nature ! I can tell a lie if you want it. I'd do anything for you. But you may tell him this : I'm very sorry I struck him."

"He knows that, Tom. He has said so to me."

"He behaved well to me,—very well,—as he always does to everybody."

"Now, Tom, that is good of you. I do like you so much for saying that."

"But I hate him !"

"No !"

"The evil spirits always hate the good ones. I am conscious of an evil spirit within my bosom. It is because my spirit is evil that you would not love me. He is good, and you love him."

"Yes; I do," said Ayala.

"And now we will change the conversation. Ayala, I have got a little present which you must take from me."

"Oh, no!" said Ayala, thinking of the diamond necklace.

"It's only a little thing,—and I hope you will." Then he brought out from his pocket a small brooch which he had selected from his own stock of jewelry for the occasion. "We are cousins, you know."

"Yes, we are cousins," said Ayala, accepting the brooch, but still accepting it unwillingly.

"He must be very disdainful if he would object to such a little thing as this," said Tom, referring to the Colonel.

"He is not at all disdainful. He will not object in the least. I am sure of that, Tom. I will take it then, and I will wear it sometimes as a memento that we have parted like friends,—as cousins should do."

"Yes, as friends," said Tom, who thought that even that word was softer to his ears than cousins. Then he took her by the hand and looked into her face wistfully, thinking what might be the effect if for the last and for the first time he should snatch a kiss. Had he done so I think she would have let it pass without rebuke under the guise of cousinship. It would have been very disagreeable ;—but then he was going away for so long a time, for so many miles! But at the moment Mrs. Dosett came in, and Ayala was saved. "Good-bye," he said ; "good-bye," and without waiting to take the hand which his aunt offered him he hurried out of the room, out of the house, and back across the Gardens to Queen's Gate.

At Queen's Gate there was an early dinner, at three o'clock, at which Sir Thomas did not appear, as he had arranged to come out of the city and meet his son at the railway station. There were, therefore, sitting at the board for the last time the mother and the two sisters with the intending traveller. "Oh, Tom," said Lady Tringle, as soon as the servant had left them together, "I do so hope you will recover."

"Of course he will recover," said Augusta.

"Why shouldn't he recover?" asked Gertrude. "It's all in a person's mind. If he'd only make up his mind not to think about her the thing would be done, and there would be nothing the matter with him."

"There are twenty others, ever so much better than Ayala, would have him to-morrow," said his mother.

"And be glad to catch him," said Gertrude. "He's not like one of those who haven't got anything to make a wife comfortable with."

" As for Ayala," said Augusta, " she didn't deserve such good luck. I am told that that Colonel Stubbs can't afford to keep any kind of carriage for her. But then, to be sure, she has never been used to a carriage."

" Oh, Tom, do look up," said his mother, " and say that you will try to be happy."

" He'll be all right in New York," said Gertrude. " There's no place in the world, they say, where the girls put themselves forward so much, and make things so pleasant for the young men."

" He will soon find some one there," said Augusta, " with a deal more to say for herself than Ayala, and a great deal better-looking."

" I hope he will find some one who will really love him," said his mother.

Tom sat silent, while he listened to all this encouragement, turning his face from one speaker to the other. It was continued, with many other similar promises of coming happiness, and assurances that he had been a gainer in losing all that he lost, when he suddenly turned sharply upon them, and strongly expressed his feelings to his sisters. " I don't believe that either of you know anything about it," he said.

" Don't know anything about what?" said Augusta, who as a lady who had been married over twelve months, and was soon about to become a mother, felt that she certainly did know all about it.

" Why don't we know as well as you?" asked Gertrude, who had also had her experiences.

" I don't believe you do know anything about it ;—that's all," said Tom. " And now there's the cab. Good-bye, mother ! Good-bye, Augusta. I hope you'll be all right." This alluded to the baby. " Good-bye, Gertrude. I hope you'll get all right too some day." This alluded to Gertrude's two lovers. Then he left them, and as he got into his cab declared to himself that neither of them had ever, or would ever, know anything of that special trouble which had so nearly overwhelmed himself.

" Upon my word, Tom," said his father, walking about the vessel with him, " I wish I were going to New York myself with you ;—it all looks so comfortable."

" Yes," said Tom, " it's very nice."

" You'll enjoy yourself amazingly. There is that Mrs. Thompson has two as pretty daughters with her as ever a man wished to see." Tom shook his head. " And you're fond of smoking. Did you see the smoking-room ? They've got everything on board these ships now. Upon my word I envy you the voyage."

" It's as good as anything else, I daresay," said Tom. " Perhaps it's better than London."

Then his father, who had been speaking aloud to him, whispered a word in his ear. "Shake yourself, Tom;—shake yourself, and get over it."

"I am trying," said Tom.

"Love is a very good thing, Tom, when a man can enjoy it, and make himself warm with it, and protect himself by it from selfishness and hardness of heart. But when it knocks a man's courage out of him, and makes him unfit for work, and leaves him to bemoan himself, there's nothing good in it. It's as bad as drink. Don't you know that I am doing the best I can for you, to make a man of you?"

"I suppose so."

"Then shake yourself, as I call it. It is to be done, if you set about it in earnest. Now, God bless you, my boy." Then Sir Thomas got into his boat, and left his son to go upon his travels and get himself cured by a change of scene.

I have no doubt that Tom was cured, if not before he reached New York, at any rate before he left that interesting city;—so that when he reached Niagara, which he did do in company with Mrs. Thompson and her charming daughters, he entertained no idea of throwing himself down the Falls. We cannot follow him on that prolonged tour to Japan and China, and thence to Calcutta and Bombay. I fancy that he did not go on to Cabul, as before that time the Ministry in England was unfortunately changed, and the Russians had not as yet been expelled from Asia;—but I have little doubt that he obtained a great deal of very useful mercantile information, and that he will live to have a comfortable wife and a large family, and become in the course of years the senior partner in the great house of Travers and Treason. Let us, who have soft hearts, now throw our old shoes after him.

CHAPTER LXII.

HOW VERY MUCH HE LOVED HER.

WE have seen how Mr. Traffick was finally turned out of his father-in-law's house;—or, rather, not quite finally when we last saw him, as he continued to sleep at Queen's Gate for two or three nights after that, until he had found shelter for his head. This he did without encountering Sir Thomas,—Sir Thomas pretending the while to believe that he was gone; and then in very truth his last pair of boots was removed. But his wife remained, awaiting the great occurrence with all the paternal comforts around her,—Mr. Traffick having been quite right in surmising that the father would not expose his daughter in her delicate condition to the inclemencies of the weather.

But this no more than natural attention on the part of the father and grandfather to the needs of his own daughter and grandchild did not in the least mitigate in the bosom of the Member of Parliament the wrath which he felt at his own expulsion. It was not, as he said to himself, the fact that he was expelled, but the coarseness of the language used. "The truth is," he said to a friend in the House, "that, though it was arranged I should remain there till after my wife's confinement, I could not bear his language." It will probably be acknowledged that the language was of a nature not to be borne.

When, therefore, Captain Batsby went down to the House on the day of Tom's departure to see his counsellor he found Mr. Traffick full rather of anger than of counsel. "Oh, yes," said the Member, walking with the Captain up and down some of the lobbies, "I spoke to him, and told him my mind very freely. When I say I'll do a thing, I always do it. And, as for Tringle, nobody knows him better than I. It does not do to be afraid of him. There is a little bit of the cur about him."

"What did he say?"

"He didn't like it. The truth is——. You know I don't mind speaking to you openly."

"Oh, no," said Batsby.

"He thinks he ought to do as well with the second girl as he has done with the first." Captain Batsby at this opened his eyes, but he said nothing. Having a good income of his own, he thought much of it. Not being the younger son of a lord, and not being a Member of Parliament, he thought less of the advantages of those high privileges. It did not suit him, however, to argue the question at the present moment. "He is proud of his connection with our family, and looks perhaps even more than he ought to do to a seat in the House."

"I could get in myself if I cared for it," said Batsby.

"Very likely. It is more difficult than ever to find a seat just now. A family connection of course does help one. I had to trust to that a good deal before I was known myself."

"But what did Sir Thomas say?"

"He made himself uncommonly disagreeable;—I can tell you that. He couldn't very well abuse me, but he wasn't very particular in what he said about you. Of course he was cut up about the elopement. We all felt it. Augusta was very much hurt. In her precarious state it was so likely to do a mischief."

"It can't be undone now."

"No —it can't be undone. But it makes one feel that you can't make a demand for money as though you set about it in the other way. When I made up my mind to marry I stated what I thought I had a right to demand, and I got it. He knew very well that I shouldn't take a shilling less. It does make a difference when he knows very well that you've got to marry the girl whether with or without money."

" I haven't got to marry the girl at all."

" Haven't you? I rather think you have, old fellow. It is generally considered that when a gentleman has gone off with a girl he means to marry her."

" Not if the father comes after her and brings her back."

" And when he has gone afterwards to the family house and proposed himself again in the mother's presence." In all this Mr. Traffick received an unfair advantage from the communications which were made to him by his wife. " Of course you must marry her. Sir Thomas knows that, and, knowing it, why should he be flush with his money? I never allowed myself to say a single word they could use against me till the ready-money-down had been all settled."

" What was it he did say?" Batsby was thoroughly sick of hearing his counsellor tell so many things as to his own prudence and his own success, and asked the question in an angry tone.

" He said that he would not consider the question of money at all till the marriage had been solemnised. Of course he stands on his right. Why shouldn't he? But, rough as he is, he isn't stingy. Give him his due. He isn't stingy. The money's there all right; and the girl is his own child. You'll have to wait his time;— that's all."

" And have nothing to begin with?"

" That'll be about it, I think. But what does it matter, Batsby? You are always talking about your income."

" No, I ain't ; not half so much as you do of your seat in Parliament,—which everybody says you're likely to lose at the next election." Then, of course, there was a quarrel. Mr. Traffick took his offended dignity back to the House,—almost doubting whether it might not be his duty to bring Captain Batsby to the bar for contempt of privilege ; and the Captain took himself off in thorough disgust.

Nevertheless there was the fact that he had engaged himself to the young lady a second time. He had run away with her with the object of marrying her, and had then,—according to his own theory in such matters,—been relieved from his responsibility by the appearance of the father and the re-abduction of the young lady. As the young lady had been taken away from him it was to be supposed that the intended marriage was negatived by a proper authority. When starting for

Brussels he was a free man ; and had he been wise he would have
remained there, or at some equally safe distance from the lady's
charms. Then, from a distance, he might have made his demand for
money, and the elopement would have operated in his favour rather
than otherwise. But he had come back, and had foolishly allowed
himself to be persuaded to show himself at Queen's Gate. He had
obeyed Traffick's advice, and now Traffick had simply thrown him over
and quarrelled with him. He had too promised, in the presence both
of the mother and the married sister, that he would marry the young
lady without any regard to money. He felt it all and was very angry
with himself, consoling himself as best he might with the reflection
that Sir Thomas's money was certainly safe and that Sir Thomas himself was a liberal man. In his present condition it would be well for
him, he thought, to remain inactive and see what circumstances would
do for him.

But circumstances very quickly became active. On his return to
his lodgings, after leaving Mr. Traffick, he found a note from Queen's
Gate. "Dearest Ben,—Mamma wants you to come and lunch to-
morrow. Papa has taken poor Tom down to Liverpool, and won't be
back till dinner-time.—G." He did not do as he was bid, alleging
some engagement of business. But the persecution was continued in
such a manner as to show him that all opposition on his part would be
hopeless unless he were to proceed on some tour as prolonged as that
of his future brother-in-law. "Come and walk at three o'clock in
Kensington Gardens to-morrow." This was written on the Saturday
after his note had been received. What use would there be in con-
tinuing a vain fight? He was in their hands, and the more gracefully
he yielded the more probable it would be that the father would evince
his generosity at an early date. He therefore met his lady-love on
the steps of the Albert Memorial, whither she had managed to take
herself all alone from the door of the family mansion.

"Ben," she said, as she greeted him, "why did you not come for
me to the house?"

" I thought you would like it best."

" Why should I like it best? Of course mamma knows all about it.
Augusta would have come with me just to see me here, only that she
cannot walk out just at present." Then he said something to her
about the Monument, expressed his admiration of the Prince's back,
abused the east wind, remarked that the buds were coming on some of
the trees, and suggested that the broad road along by the Round Pond
would be drier than the little paths. It was not interesting, as Gertrude
felt ; but she had not expected him to be interesting. The interest
she knew must be contributed by herself. "Ben," she said, "I was
so happy to hear what you said to mamma the other day."

" What did I say ?"

" Why, of course, that, as papa has given his consent, our engagement is to go on just as if ——"

" Just as if what ?"

" As if we had found the clergyman at Ostend."

" If we had done that we should have been married now," suggested Batsby.

" Exactly. And it is almost as good as being married ;—isn't it ?"

" I suppose it comes to the same thing."

" Hadn't you better go to papa again and have it all finished ?"

" He makes himself so very unpleasant."

" That's only because he wants to punish us for running away. I suppose it was wrong. I shall never be sorry, because it made me know how very, very much you loved me. Didn't it make you feel how very, very dearly I loved you,—to trust myself all alone with you in that way ?"

" Oh, yes ; of course."

" And papa can't bite you, you know. You go to him, and tell him that you hope to be received in the house as my,—my future husband, you know."

" Shall I say nothing else ?"

" You mean about the day ?"

" I was meaning about money."

" I don't think I would. He is very generous, but he does not like to be asked. When Augusta was to be married he arranged all that himself after they were engaged."

" But Traffick demanded a certain sum ?" This question Captain Batsby asked with considerable surprise, remembering what Mr. Traffick had said to him in reference to Augusta's fortune.

" Not at all. Septimus knew nothing about it till after the engagement. He was only too glad to get papa's consent. You mustn't believe all that Septimus says, you know. You may be sure of this,—that you can trust papa's generosity." Then, before he landed her at the door in Queen's Gate, he had promised that he would make another journey to Lombard Street, with the express purpose of obtaining Sir Thomas's sanction to the marriage,—either with or without money.

" How are you again ?" said Sir Thomas, when the Captain was for the third time shown into the little back parlour. " Have you had another trip to the continent since I saw you ?" Sir Thomas was in a good humour. Tom had gone upon his travels ; Mr. Traffick had absolutely taken himself out of the house ; and the millions were accommodating themselves comfortably.

" No, Sir Thomas ; I haven't been abroad since then. I don't keep on going abroad constantly in that way."

" And what can I do for you now ?"

" Of course it's about your daughter. I want to have your permission to consider ourselves engaged."

" I explained to you before that if you and Gertrude choose to marry each other I shall not stand in your way."

" Thank you, Sir."

" I don't know that it is much to thank me for. Only that she made a fool of herself by running away with you I should have preferred to wait till some more sensible candidate had proposed himself for her hand. I don't suppose you'll ever set the Thames on fire."

" I did very well in the army."

" It's a pity you did not remain there, and then, perhaps, you would not have gone to Ostend with my daughter. As it is, there she is. I think she might have done better with herself ; but that is her fault. She has made her bed and she must lie upon it."

" If we are to be married, I hope you won't go on abusing me always, Sir Thomas."

" That's as you behave. You didn't suppose that I should allow such a piece of tomfoolery as that to be passed over without saying anything about it ! If you marry her and behave well to her I will——" Then he paused.

" What will you do, Sir Thomas ?"

" I'll say as little as possible about the Ostend journey."

" And as to money, Sir Thomas ?"

" I think I have promised quite enough for you. You are not in a position, Captain Batsby, to ask me as to money ;—nor is she. You shall marry her without a shilling,—or you shall not marry her at all. Which is it to be ? I must have an end put to all this. I won't have you hanging about my house unless I know the reason why. Are you two engaged to each other ?"

" I suppose we are," said Batsby, lugubriously.

" Suppose is not enough."

" We are," said Batsby, courageously.

" Very well. Then, from this moment, Ostend shall be as though there weren't such a seaport anywhere in Europe. I will never allude to the place again,—unless, perhaps, you should come and stay with me too long when I am particularly anxious to get rid of you. Now you had better go and settle about the time and all that with Lady Tringle, and tell her that you mean to come and dine to-morrow or next day, or whenever it suits. Come and dine as often as you please, only do not bring your wife to live with me pertinaciously when you're not asked,"

All this Captain Batsby did not understand, but, as he left Lombard Street, he made up his mind that of all the men he had ever met, Sir Thomas Tringle, his future father-in-law, was the most singular. "He's a better fellow than Traffick," said Sir Thomas to himself when he was alone, "and as he has trusted me so far I'll not throw him over."

The Captain now had no hesitation in taking himself to Queen's Gate. As he was to be married he might as well make the best of such delights as were to be found in the happy state of mutual affection. "My dear, dearest Benjamin, I am so happy," said Lady Tringle, dissolved in tears as she embraced her son-in-law that was to be. "You will always be so dear to me!" In this she was quite true. Traffick was not dear to her. She had at first thought much of Mr. Traffick's position and noble blood, but, of late, she too had become very tired of Mr. Traffick. Augusta took almost too much upon herself, and Mr. Traffick's prolonged presence had been an eyesore. Captain Batsby was softer, and would be much more pleasant as a son-in-law. Even the journey to Ostend had had a good effect in producing a certain humility.

"My dear Benjamin," said Augusta, "we shall always be so happy to entertain you as a brother. Mr. Traffick has a great regard for you, and said from the first that if you behaved as you ought to do after that little journey he would arrange that everything should go straight between you and papa. I was quite sure that you would come forward at once as a man."

But Gertrude's delight was, of course, the strongest, and Gertrude's welcoming the warmest,—as was proper. "When I think of it," she said to him, "I don't know how I should ever have looked anybody in the face again,—after our going away with our things mixed up in that way."

"I am glad rather now that we didn't find the clergyman."

"Oh, certainly," said Gertrude. "I don't suppose anybody would have given me anything. Now there'll be a regular wedding, and, of course, there will be the presents."

"And, though nothing is to be settled, I suppose he will do something."

"And it would have been very dreadful, not having a regular trousseau," said Gertrude. "Mamma will, of course, do now just as she did about Augusta. He allowed her £300! Only think;—if we had been married at Ostend you would have had to buy things for me before the first month was out. I hadn't more than half-a-dozen pair of stockings with me."

"He can't but say now that we have done as he would have us," added the Captain. "I do suppose that he will not be so unnatural as not to give something when Augusta had £200,000."

"Indeed, she had not. But you'll see that sooner or later papa will do for me quite as well as for Augusta." In this way they were happy together, consoling each other for any little trouble which seemed for a while to cloud their joys, and basking in the full sunshine of their permitted engagement.

The day was soon fixed, but fixed not entirely in reference to the wants of Gertrude and her wedding. Lucy had also to be married from the same house, and the day for her marriage had already been arranged. Sir Thomas had ordered that everything should be done for Lucy as though she were a daughter of the house, and her wedding had been arranged for the last week in May. When he heard that Ayala and Colonel Stubbs were also engaged he was anxious that the two sisters should be "buckled," as he called it, on the same occasion, —and he magnanimously offered to take upon himself the entire expense of the double arrangement, intimating that the people in Kingsbury Crescent had hardly room enough for a wedding. But Ayala, acting probably under Stalham influences, would not consent to this. Lady Albury, who was now in London, was determined that Ayala's marriage should take place from her own house ; and, as Aunt Margaret and Uncle Reginald had consented, that matter was considered as settled. But Sir Thomas, having fixed his mind upon a double wedding, resolved that Gertrude and Lucy should be the joint brides. Gertrude, who still suffered perhaps a little in public estimation from the Ostend journey, was glad enough to wipe out that stain as quickly as possible, and did not therefore object to the arrangement. But to the Captain there was something in it by which his more delicate feelings were revolted. It was a matter of course that Ayala should be present at her sister's wedding, and would naturally appear there in the guise of a bridesmaid. She would also, now, act as a bridesmaid to Gertrude,—her future position as Mrs. Colonel Stubbs giving her, as was supposed, sufficient dignity for that honourable employment. But Captain Batsby, not so very long ago, had appeared among the suitors for Ayala's hand ; and therefore, as he said to Gertrude, he felt a little shamefaced about it. "What does that signify ?" said Gertrude. "If you say nothing to her about it, I'll be bound she'll say nothing to you." And so it was on the day of the wedding. Ayala did not say a word to Captain Batsby, nor did Captain Batsby say very much to Ayala.

On the day before his marriage Captain Batsby paid a fourth visit to Lombard Street in obedience to directions from Sir Thomas. "There, my boy," said he, " though you and Gertrude did take a little journey on the sly to a place which we will not mention, you shan't take her altogether empty-handed." Then he explained certain arrangements which he had made for endowing Gertrude with an allowance, which under the circumstance the bridegroom could not but feel to be liberal. It must be added, that, considering the shortness of time allowed for getting them together, the amount of wedding presents bestowed was considered by Gertrude to be satisfactory. As Lucy's were exhibited at the same time the show was not altogether mean. " No doubt I had twice as much as the two put together," said Mrs. Traffick to Ayala up in her bedroom, " but then of course Lord Boardotrade's rank would make people give."

CHAPTER LXIII.

AYALA AGAIN IN LONDON.

AFTER that last walk in Gobblegoose Wood, after Lady Tringle's unnecessary journey to Stalham on the Friday, and the last day's hunting with Sir Harry's hounds,—which took place on the Saturday,—Ayala again became anxious to go home. Her anxiety was in its nature very different from that which had prompted her to leave Stalham on an appointed day lest she should seem to be waiting for the coming of Colonel Stubbs. " No ; I don't want to run away from him any more," she said to Lady Albury. " I want to be with him always, and I hope he won't run away from me. But I've got to be somewhere where I can think about it all for a little time."

" Can't you think about it here ?"

" No ;—one can never think about a thing where it has all taken place. I must be up in my own little room in Kingsbury Crescent, and must have Aunt Margaret's work around me,—so that I may realise what is going to come. Not but what I mean to do a great deal of work always."

" Mend his stockings ?"

" Yes,—if he wears stockings. I know he doesn't. He always wears socks. He told me so. Whatever he has, I'll mend,—or make if he wants me.

'I can bake and I can brew,
    And I can make an Irish stew ;—
    Wash a shirt, and iron it too.'"

Then, as she sang her little song, she clapped her hands together.

" Where did you get all your poetry ?"

" He taught me that. We are not going to be fine people,—except sometimes when we may be invited to Stalham. But I must go on Thursday, Lady Albury. I came for a week and I have been here ever since the middle of February. It seems years since the old woman told me I was perverse, and he said that she was right."

" Think how much you have done since that time."

" Yes, indeed. I very nearly destroyed myself ;—didn't I ?"

" Not very nearly."

" I thought I had. It was only when you showed me his letter on that Sunday morning that I began to have any hopes. I wonder what Mr. Greene preached about that morning. I didn't hear a word. I kept on repeating what he said in the postscript."

" Was there a postscript ?"

" Of course there was. Don't you remember ?"

" No, indeed ; not I."

" The letter would have been nothing without the postscript. He said that Croppy was to come back for me. I knew he wouldn't say that unless he meant to be good to me. And yet I wasn't quite sure of it. I know it now ; don't I ? But I must go, Lady Albury. I ought to let Aunt Margaret know all about it." Then it was settled that she should go on the Thursday,—and on the Thursday she went. As it was now considered quite wrong that she should travel by the railway alone,—in dread, probably, lest the old lady should tell her again how perverse she had been,—Colonel Stubbs accompanied her. It had then been decided that the wedding must take place at Stalham, and many messages were sent to Mr. and Mrs. Dosett assuring them that they would be made very welcome on the occasion. " My own darling Lucy will be away at that time with her own young man," said Ayala, in answer to further invitations from Lady Albury.

" And so you've taken Colonel Stubbs at last," said her Aunt Margaret.

" He has taken me, aunt. I didn't take him."

" But you refused him ever so often."

" Well ;—yes. I don't think I quite refused him."

" I thought you did."

" It was a dreadful muddle, Aunt Margaret ;—but it has come right at last, and we had better not talk about that part of it."

" I was so sure you didn't like him."

" Not like him ? I always liked him better than anybody else in the world that I ever saw."

" Dear me !"

" Of course I shouldn't say so if it hadn't come right at last. I may say whatever I please about it now, and I declare that I always loved him. A girl can be such a fool ! I was, I know. I hope you are glad, aunt."

" Of course I am. I am glad of anything that makes you happy. It seemed such a pity that when so many gentlemen were falling in love with you all round you couldn't like anybody."

"But I did like somebody, Aunt Margaret. And I did like the best,—didn't I?" In answer to this Mrs. Dosett made no reply, having always had an aunt's partiality for poor Tom, in spite of all his chains.

Her uncle's congratulations were warmer even than her aunt's. "My dear girl," he said, "I am rejoiced indeed that you should have before you such a prospect of happiness. I always felt how sad for you was your residence here, with two such homely persons as your aunt and myself."

"I have always been happy with you," said Ayala,—perhaps straining the truth a little in her anxiety to be courteous. "And I know," she added, "how much Lucy and I have always owed you since poor papa's death."

"Nevertheless, it has been dull for a young girl like you. Now you will have your own duties, and if you endeavour to do them properly the world will never be dull to you." And then there were some few words about the wedding. "We have no feeling, my dear," said her uncle, "except to do the best we can for you. We should have been glad to see you married from here if that had suited. But, as this lover of yours has grand friends of his own, I dare say their place may be the better." Ayala could hardly explain to her uncle that she had acceded to Lady Albury's proposal because, by doing so, she would spare him the necessary expense of the wedding.

But Ayala's great delight was in meeting her sister. The two girls had not seen each other since the engagement of either of them had been ratified by their friends. The winter and spring, as passed by Lucy at Merle Park, had been very unhappy for her. Things at Merle Park had not been pleasant to any of the residents there, and Lucy had certainly had her share of the unpleasantness. Her letters to Ayala had not been triumphant when Aunt Emmeline had more than once expressed her wish to be rid of her, and when the news reached her that Uncle Tom and Hamel had failed to be gracious to each other. Nor had Ayala written in a spirit of joy before she had been able to recognise the Angel of Light in Jonathan Stubbs. But now they were to meet after all their miseries, and each could be triumphant.

It was hard for them to know exactly how to begin. To Lucy, Isadore Hamel was, at the present moment, the one hero walking the face of this sublunary globe; and to Ayala, as we all know, Jonathan Stubbs was an Angel of Light, and, therefore, more even than a hero. As each spoke, the "He's" intended took a different personification; so that to any one less interested than the young ladies themselves there

2 G

might be some conrusion as to which "He" might at the moment be under discussion. "It was bad," said Lucy, "when Uncle Tom told him to sell those magnificent conceptions of his brain by auction!"

"I did feel for him certainly," said Ayala.

"And then when he was constrained to say that he would take me at once without any preparation because Aunt Emmeline wanted me to go, I don't suppose any man ever behaved more beautifully than he did."

"Yes, indeed," said Ayala. And then she felt herself constrained to change the subject by the introduction of an exaggerated superlative in her sister's narrative. Hamel, no doubt, had acted beautifully, but she was not disposed to agree that nothing could be more beautiful. "Oh, Lucy," she said, "I was so miserable when he went away after that walk in the road. I thought he never would come back again when I had behaved so badly. But he did. Was not that grand in him?"

"I suppose he was very fond of you."

"I hope he was. I hope he is. But what should I have done if he had not come back? No other man would have come back after that. You never behaved unkindly to Isadore?"

"I think he would have come back a thousand times," said Lucy; "only I cannot imagine that I should ever have given him the necessity of coming back even a second. But then I had known him so much longer."

"It wasn't that I hadn't known him long enough," said Ayala. "I seemed to know all about him almost all at once. I knew how good he was, and how grand he was, long before I had left the Marchesa up in London. But I think it astounded me that such a one as he should care for me." And so it went on through an entire morning, each of the sisters feeling that she was bound to listen with wrapt attention to the praises of the other's "him" if she wished to have an opportunity of singing those of her own.

But Lucy's marriage was to come first by more than two months, and therefore in that matter she was allowed precedence. And at her marriage Ayala would be present, whereas with Ayala's Lucy would have no personal concern. Though she did think that Uncle Tom had been worse than any Vandal in that matter of selling her lover's magnificent works, still she was ready to tell of his generosity. In a manner of his own he had sent the money which Hamel had so greatly needed, and had now come forward to provide, with a generous hand, for the immediate necessities, and more than the necessities, of the wedding. It was not only that she was to share the honours of the two wedding-cakes with Gertrude, and that she was to be taken as a bride from the gorgeous mansion in Queen's Gate, but that he had provided for her bridal needs almost as fully as for those of his own daughter. "Never mind what she'll be able to do afterwards," he said to his wife, who ventured on some slight remonstrance with him as to the unnecessary luxuries he was preparing for the wife of a poor man. "She won't be the worse for having a dozen new petticoats in her trunk, and, if she don't want to blow her nose with as many handkerchiefs this year as Gertrude does, she'll be able to keep them for next year." Then Aunt Emmeline obeyed without further hesitation the orders which were given her.

Nor was his generosity confined to the niece who for the last twelve-months had been his property. Lucy was still living in Queen's Gate, though at this time she spent much of each day in Kingsbury Crescent, and on one occasion she brought with her a little note from Uncle Tom. "Dear Ayala," said the little note,

"As you are going to be married too, you, I suppose, will want some new finery. I therefore send a cheque. Write your name on the back of it, and give it to your uncle. He will let you have the money as you want it.   "Yours affectionately,
                                            "T. TRINGLE."
"I hope your Colonel Stubbs will come and see me some day."

"You must go and see him," she said to her Colonel Stubbs, when he called one day in Kingsbury Crescent. "Only for him I shouldn't have any clothes to speak of at all, and I should have to be married in my old brown morning frock."

"It would be just as good as any other for my purpose," said the Colonel.

"But it wouldn't for mine, Sir. Fine feathers make fine birds, and I mean to be as fine as Lady Albury's big peacock. So if you please you'll go to Queen's Gate, and Lombard Street too, and show yourself. Oh, Jonathan, I shall be so proud that everybody who knows me should see what sort of a man has chosen to love me."

Then there was a joint visit paid by the two sisters to Mr. Hamel's studio,—an expedition which was made somewhat on the sly. Aunt Margaret in Kingsbury Crescent knew all about it, but Aunt Emmeline was kept in the dark. Even now, though the marriage was sanctioned and was so nearly at hand, Aunt Emmeline would not have approved of such a visit. She still regarded the sculptor as improper,—at any rate not sufficiently proper to be treated with full familiarity,—partly on account of his father's manifest improprieties, and partly because of his own relative poverty and unauthorised position in the world. But Aunt Margaret was more tolerant, and thought that the sister-in-law was entitled to visit the workshop in which her sister's future bread was to be earned. And then, starting from Kingsbury Crescent, they could go in a cab; whereas any such proceeding emanating from Queen's Gate would have required the carriage. There was a wickedness in this starting off in a Hansom cab to call on an unmarried young man, doing it in a manner successfully concealed from Aunt Emmeline, on which Ayala expatiated with delight when she next saw Colonel Stubbs.

"You don't come and call on me," said the Colonel.

"What!—all the way down to Aldershot? I should like, but I don't quite dare to do that."

The visit was very successful. Though it was expected, Hamel was found in his artist's costume, with a blouse or loose linen tunic fitted closely round his throat, and fastened with a belt round his waist. Lucy thought that in this apparel he was certainly as handsome as could ever have been any Apollo,—and, so thinking, had contrived her little plans in such a way that he should certainly be seen at his best. To her thinking Colonel Stubbs was not a handsome man. Hamel's hair was nearly black, and she preferred dark hair. Hamel's features were regular, whereas the Colonel's hair was red, and he was known for a large mouth and broad nose, which were not obliterated though they were enlightened by the brightness of his eyes. "Yes," said Ayala to herself, as she looked at Hamel; "he is very good looking, but nobody would take him for an Angel of Light."

"Ayala has come to see you at your work," said Lucy, as they entered the studio.

"I am delighted to see her. Do you remember where we last met, Miss Dormer?"

"Miss Dormer, indeed," said Ayala. "I am not going to call you Mr. Hamel. Yes; it was high up among the seats of the Coliseum. There has a great deal happened to us all since then."

"And I remember you at the Bijou."

"I should think so. I knew then so well what was going to happen," said Ayala.

"What did you know?"

"That you and Lucy were to fall in love with each other."

"I had done my part of it already," said he.

"Hardly that, Isadore," said Lucy, "or you would not have passed me in Kensington Gardens without speaking to me."

"But I did speak to you. It was then I learned where to find you."

"That was the second time. If I had remained away, as I ought to have done, I suppose you never would have found me."

Ayala was then taken round to see all those magnificent groups and figures which Sir Thomas would have disposed of at so many shillings apiece under the auctioneer's hammer. "It was cruel,—was it not?" said Lucy.

"He never saw them, you know," said Ayala, putting in a good-natured word for her uncle.

"If he had," said the sculptor, "he would have doubted the auctioneer's getting anything. I have turned it all in my mind very often since, and I think that Sir Thomas was right."

"I am sure he was wrong," said Lucy. "He is very good-natured, and nobody can be more grateful to another person than I am to him;—but I won't agree that he was right about that."

"He never would have said it if he had seen them," again pleaded Ayala.

"They will never fetch anything as they are," continued the sculptor, "and I don't suppose that when I made them I thought they would. They have served their purpose, and I sometimes feel inclined to break them up and have them carted away."

"Isadore!" exclaimed Lucy.

"For what purpose?" asked Ayala.

"They were the lessons which I had to teach myself, and the play which I gave to my imagination. Who wants a great figure of Beelzebub like that in his house?"

"I call it magnificent," said Ayala.

"His name is Lucifer,—not Beelzebub," said Lucy. "You call him Beelzebub merely to make little of him."

"It is difficult to do that, because he is nearly ten feet high. And who wants a figure of Bacchus? The thing is whether, having done a figure of Bacchus, I may not be better able to do a likeness of Mr. Jones, when he comes to sit for his bust at the request of his admiring friends. For any further purpose that it will answer, Bacchus might just as well be broken up and carted away in the dust-cart." To this, however, the two girls expressed their vehement opposition, and were of opinion that the time would come when Beelzebub and Bacchus, transferred to marble, would occupy places of honour in some well-proportioned hall built for the purpose of receiving them. "I shall be quite content," said Hamel, "if the whole family of the Jones's will have their busts done about the size of life, and stand them up over their bookshelves. My period for Beelzebubs has gone by." The visit, on the whole, was delightful. Lucy was contented with the almost more than divine beauty of her lover, and the two sisters, as they made their return journey to Kingsbury Crescent in another Hansom, discussed questions of art in a spirit that would have been delightful to any aspiring artist who might have heard them.

Then came the wedding, of which some details were given at the close of the last chapter, at which two brides who were very unlike to each other were joined in matrimony to two bridegrooms as dissimilar. But the Captain made himself gracious to the sculptor who was now to be connected with him, and declared that he would always look upon Lucy as a second sister to his dear Gertrude. And Gertrude was equally gracious, protesting, when she was marshalled to walk up to the altar first, that she did not like to go before her darling Lucy. But the dimensions of the church admitted but of one couple at a time, and Gertrude was compelled to go in advance. Colonel Stubbs was there acting as best man to Hamel, while Lord John Battledore performed the same service for Captain Batsby. Lord John was nearly broken-hearted by the apostacy of a second chum, having heard that the girl whom Frank Houston had not succeeded in marrying was now being taken by Batsby without a shilling. "Somebody had to bottle-hold for him," said Lord John, defending himself at the club afterwards, "and I didn't like to throw the fellow over, though he is such a fool! And there was Stubbs, too," continued his Lordship, "going to take the other girl without a shilling! There's Stubbs, and Houston, and Batsby, all gone and drowned themselves. It's just the same as though they'd drowned themselves!" Lord John was horrified, —nay, disgusted,—by the folly of the world. Nevertheless, before the end of the year, he was engaged to marry a very pretty girl as devoid of fortune as our Ayala.

CHAPTER LXIV.

AYALA'S MARRIAGE.

Now we have come to our last chapter, and it may be doubted whether any reader,—unless he be some one specially gifted with a genius for statistics,—will have perceived how very many people have been made happy by matrimony. If marriage be the proper ending for a novel,—the only ending, as this writer takes it to be, which is not discordant,—surely no tale was ever so properly ended, or with so full a concord, as this one. Infinite trouble has been taken not only in arranging these marriages but in joining like to like,—so that, if not happiness, at any rate sympathetic unhappiness, might be produced. Our two sisters will, it is trusted, be happy. They have chosen men from their hearts, and have been chosen after the same fashion. Those two other sisters have been so wedded that the one will follow the idiosyncrasies of her husband, and the other bring her husband to follow her idiosyncrasies, without much danger of mutiny or revolt.

As to Miss Docimer there must be room for fear. It may be questioned whether she was not worthy of a better lot than has been achieved for her by joining her fortunes to those of Frank Houston. But I, speaking for myself, have my hopes of Frank Houston. It is hard to rescue a man from the slough of luxury and idleness combined. If anything can do it, it is a cradle filled annually. It may be that he will yet learn that a broad back with a heavy weight upon it gives the best chance of happiness here below. Of Lord John's married prospects I could not say much as he came so very lately on the scene; but even he may perhaps do something in the world when he finds that his nursery is filling.

For our special friend, Tom Tringle, no wife has been found. In making his effort,—which he did manfully,—he certainly had not chosen the consort who would be fit for him. He had not seen clearly, as had done his sisters and cousins. He had fallen in love too young, —it being the nature of young men to be much younger than young ladies, and, not knowing himself, had been as might be a barn-door cock who had set his heart upon some azure-plumaged, high-soaring lady of the woods. The lady with the azure plumes had, too, her high-soaring tendencies, but she was enabled by true insight to find the male who would be fit for her. The barn-door cock, when we left him on board the steamer going to New York, had not yet learned the nature of his own requirements. The knowledge will come to him. There may be doubts as to Frank Houston, but we think that there need be none as to Tom Tringle. The proper wife will be forthcoming; and in future years, when he will probably have a Glenbogie and a Merle Park of his own, he will own that Fortune did well for him in making his cousin Ayala so stern to his prayers.

But Ayala herself,—Ayala our pet heroine,—had not been yet married when the last chapter was written, and now there remains a page or two in which the reader must bid adieu to her as she stands at the altar with her Angel of Light. She was at Stalham for a fortnight before her marriage, in order, as Lady Albury said, that the buxom ladysmaid might see that everything had been done rightly in reference to the trousseau. "My dear," said Lady Albury, "it is important, you know. I dare say you can bake and brew, because you say so; but you don't know anything about clothes." Ayala, who by this time was very intimate with her friend, pouted her lips, and said that if "Jonathan did not like her things as she chose to have them he might do the other thing." But Lady Albury had her way, inducing Sir Harry to add something even to Uncle Tom's liberality, and the buxom woman went about her task in such a fashion that if Colonel Stubbs were not satisfied he must have been a very unconscionable Colonel,

He probably would know nothing about it,—except that his bride in her bridal array had not looked so well as in any other garments, which, I take it, is invariably the case,—till at the end of the first year a glimmer of the truth as to a lady's wardrobe would come upon him. " I told you there would be a many new dresses before two years were over, Miss," said the buxom female, as she spread all the frocks and all the worked petticoats and all the collars and all the silk stockings and all the lace handkerchiefs about the bedroom to be inspected by Lady Albury, Mrs. Gosling, and one or two other friends, before they were finally packed up.

Then came the day on which the Colonel was to reach Stalham, that day being a Monday, whereas the wedding was to take place on Wednesday. It was considered to be within the bounds of propriety that the Colonel should sleep at Stalham on the Monday, under the same roof with his bride ; but on the Tuesday it was arranged that he should satisfy the decorous feeling of the neighbourhood by removing himself to the parsonage, which was distant about half-a-mile across the park, and was contiguous to the church. Here lived Mr. Greene, the bachelor curate, the rector of the parish being an invalid and absent in Italy.

" I don't see why he is to be sent away after dinner to walk across the park in the dark," said Ayala, when the matter was discussed before the Colonel's coming.

" It is a law, my dear," said Lady Albury, " and has to be obeyed whether you understand it or not, like other laws. Mr. Greene will be with him, so that no one shall run away with him in the dark. Then he will be able to go into church without dirtying his dress boots."

" But I thought there would be half-a-dozen carriages at least."

" But there won't be room in one of them for him. He is to be nobody until he comes forth from the church as your husband. Then he is to be everybody. That is the very theory of marriage."

$$* \quad * \quad * \quad * \quad *$$

" I think we managed it all very well between us," said Lady Albury afterwards, " but you really cannot guess the trouble we took."

" Why should there have been trouble ?"

" Because you were such a perverse creature, as the old lady said. I am not sure that you were not right, because a girl does so often raise herself in her lover's estimation by refusing him half-a-dozen times. But you were not up to that."

" Indeed I was not. I am sure I did not intend to give any trouble to anybody."

" But you did. Only think of my going up to London to meet him, and of him coming from Aldershot to meet me, simply that we might put our heads together how to overcome the perversity of such a young woman as you !" There then came a look almost of pain on Ayala's brow. "But I do believe it was for the best. In this way he came to understand how absolutely necessary you were to him."

" Am I necessary to him ?"

" He thinks so."

" Oh, if I can only be necessary to him always ! But there should have been no going up to London. I should have rushed into his arms at once."

" That would have been unusual."

" But so is he unusual," said Ayala.

It is probable that the Colonel did not enjoy his days at Stalham before his marriage,—except during the hour or two in which he was allowed to take Ayala out for a last walk. Such days can hardly be agreeable to the man of whom it is known by all around him that he is on the eve of committing matrimony. There is always, on such occasions, a feeling of weakness, as though the man had been subdued, brought at length into a cage and tamed, so as to be made fit for domestic purposes, and deprived of his ancient freedom amongst the woods ; —whereas the girl feels herself to be the triumphant conqueror, who has successfully performed this great act of taming. Such being the case, the man had perhaps better keep away till he is forced to appear at the church-door.

Nevertheless our Colonel did enjoy his last walk. " Oh, yes," she said, " of course we will go the old wood. Where else ? I am so glad that poor fox went through Gobblegoose ;—otherwise we should never have gone there, and then who knows whether you and I would ever have been friends again any more ?"

" If one wood hadn't been there, I think another would have been found."

" Ah, that's just it. You can know that you had a purpose, and perhaps were determined to carry it out."

" Well, rather."

" But I couldn't be sure of that. I couldn't carry out my purpose, even if I had one. I had to doubt, and to be unhappy, and to hate myself, because I had been perverse. I declare, I do think you men have so much the best of it. How glorious would it have been to be able to walk straight up and say, Jonathan Stubbs, I love you better than all the world. Will you be my husband ?"

" But suppose the Jonathan Stubbs of the occasion were to decline the honour. Where would you be then ?"

" That would be disagreeable," said Ayala.

" It is disagreeable,—as you made me feel twice over."

" Oh, Jonathan, I am so sorry."

"Therefore it is possible that you may have the best of it."

*   *   *   *   *

"And so you never will take another walk with Ayala Dormer!" she said, as they were returning home.

"Never another," he replied.

"You cannot think how I regret it. Of course I am glad to become your wife. I do not at all want to have it postponed. But there is something so sweet in having a lover;—and you know that though I shall have a husband I shall never have a lover again,—and I never had one before, Jonathan. There has been very little of it. When a thing has been so sweet it is sad to think that it must be gone for ever!" Then she leaned upon him with both her hands, and looked up at him and smiled, with her lips a little open,—as she knew that he liked her to lean upon him and to look,—for she had caught by her instinct the very nature of the man, and knew how to witch him with her little charms. "Ah, me! I wonder whether you'll like me to lean upon you when a dozen years have gone by."

"That depends on how heavy you may be."

"I shall be a fat old woman, perhaps. But I shall lean upon you,—always, always. What else shall I ever have to lean upon now?"

"What else should you want?"

"Nothing,—nothing,—nothing! I want nothing else. I wonder whether there is anybody in all the world who has got so completely everything that she ever dreamed of wanting as I have. But if you could have been only my lover for a little longer——!" Then he assured her that he would be her lover just the same, even though they were husband and wife. Alas, no! There he had promised more than it is given to a man to perform. Faith, honesty, steadiness of purpose, joined to the warmest love and the truest heart, will not enable a husband to maintain the sweetness of that aroma which has filled with delight the senses of the girl who has leaned upon his arm as her permitted lover.

"What a happy fellow you are!" said Mr. Greene, as, in the intimacy of the moment, they walked across the park together.

"Why don't you get a wife for yourself?"

"Yes; with £120 a-year!"

"With a little money you might."

"I don't want to have to look for the money; and if I did I shouldn't get it. I often think how very unfairly things are divided in this world."

"That will all be made up in the next."

"Not if one covets one's neighbour's wife,—or even his ass," said Mr. Greene.

On the return of the two lovers to the house from their walk there were Mr. and Mrs. Dosett, who would much rather have stayed away had they not been unwilling not to show their mark of affection to their niece. I doubt whether they were very happy, but they were at any rate received with every distinction. Sir Thomas and Aunt Emmeline were asked, but they made some excuse. Sir Thomas knew very well that he had nothing in common with Sir Harry Albury; and, as for Aunt Emmeline, her one journey to Stalham had been enough for her. But Sir Thomas was again very liberal, and sent down as his contribution to the wedding presents the very necklace which Ayala had refused from her cousin Tom. "Upon my word, your uncle is magnificent," said Lady Albury, upon which the whole story was told to her. Lucy and her husband were away on their tour, as were Gertrude and hers on theirs. This was rather a comfort, as Captain Batsby's presence at the house would have been a nuisance. But there was quite enough of guests to make the wedding, as being a country wedding, very brilliant. Among others, old Tony Tappett was there, mindful of the manner in which Cranbury Brook had been ridden, and of Croppy's presence when the hounds ran their fox into Dillsborough Wood. "I hope she be to ride with us, off and on, Colonel," said Tony, when the ceremony had been completed.

"Now and then, Tony, when we can get hold of Croppy."

"Because, when they come out like that, Colonel, it's a pity to lose 'em, just because they's got their husbands to attend to."

And Lord Rufford was there, with his wife, who on this occasion was very pressing with her invitations. She had heard that Colonel Stubbs was likely to rise high in his profession, and there were symptoms, of which she was an excellent judge, that Mrs. Colonel Stubbs would become known as a professional beauty. And Larry Twentyman was there, who, being in the neighbourhood, was, to his great delight, invited to the breakfast.

Thus, to her own intense satisfaction, Ayala was handed over to her

ANGEL OF LIGHT.

PRINTED AT THE BEDFORD PRESS, 20 AND 21, BEDFORDBURY, LONDON, W.C.
2

THE SELECT LIBRARY OF FICTION.

Price 2s. each; or cloth gilt, 2s. 6d.

By CHARLES LEVER.

39 Jack Hinton.
40 Harry Lorrequer.
41 The O'Donoghue.
42 The Fortunes of Glencore.
43 One of Them.
44 Sir Jasper Carew.
45 A Day's Ride: a Life's Romance
46 Maurice Tiernay.
47 Barrington.
48 Luttrell of Arran.
49 Rent in a Cloud.
50 Sir Brook Fossbrooke
51 The Bramleighs.
52 Tony Butler.
53 That Boy of Norcott's.
54 Lord Kilgobbin.
55 Cornelius O'Dowd.
56 Nuts and Nutcrackers.
57 Tales of the Trains.
58 Paul Goslett's Confessions.

2s. 6d. each; cloth, 3s.

59 Charles O'Malley.
60 The Daltons.
61 Knight of Gwynne.
62 Dodd Family Abroad.
63 Tom Burke.
64 Davenport Dunn.
65 Roland Cashel.
66 Martins of Cro' Martin.

By HARRISON AINSWORTH.

73 Cardinal Pole.
74 Constable of the Tower.
75 Leaguer of Lathom.
76 Spanish Match.
77 Constable de Bourbon.
78 Old Court.
79 Myddleton Pomfret.
80 Hilary St. Ives.

81 Lord Mayor of London.
82 John Law.

By HENRY KINGSLEY.

103 Geoffry Hamlyn.
104 Ravenshoe.
105 Hillyars and Burtons.
106 Silcote of Silcotes.
107 Leighton Court.
108 Austin Elliot.
109 Reginald Hetherege.

By WHYTE-MELVILLE.

115 Tilbury Nogo.
116 Uncle John.
117 The White Rose.
118 Cerise.
119 Brookes of Bridlemere.
120 "Bones and I."
121 "M. or N."
122 Contraband.
123 Market Harborough.
124 Sarchedon.
125 Satanella.
126 Katerfelto.
127 Sister Louise
128 Rosine.
129 Roy's Wife.
130 Black, but Comely.
131 Riding Recollections.
132 Songs and Verses.
133 The True Cross.

By Mrs. OLIPHANT.

146 May.
147 For Love and Life.
148 Last of the Mortimers.
149 Squire Arden.
150 Ombra.
151 Madonna Mary.
152 Days of my Life.

London: WARD, LOCK & CO., Salisbury Square, E.C.
New York: 10, Bond Street.

THE SELECT LIBRARY OF FICTION.

Price 2s. each; or cloth gilt, 2s. 6d.

153 Harry Muir.
154 Heart and Cross.
155 Magdalene Hepburn.
156 House on the Moor.
157 Lilliesleaf.
158 Lucy Crofton.

By HAWLEY SMART.
165 Broken Bonds.
166 Two Kisses.
167 False Cards.
168 Courtship.
169 Bound to Win.
170 Cecile.
171 Race for a Wife.
172 Play or Pay.
173 Sunshine and Snow.
174 Belles and Ringers.
175 Social Sinners.
176 The Great Tontine.

By JANE AUSTEN.
187 Sense and Sensibility:
188 Emma.
189 Mansfield Park.
190 Northanger Abbey.
191 Pride and Prejudice.

By VICTOR HUGO.
195 Jean Valjean (Les Miserables):
196 Cosette and Marius (Les Miserables).
197 Fantine (Les Miserables).
198 By the King's Command.

By CHARLES DICKENS.
203 Pickwick Papers.
204 Nicholas Nickleby.
229 Picnic Papers. (Edited by C. Dickens.)

By Sir WALTER SCOTT.
230 Waverley.
231 Kenilworth.
232 Ivanhoe.
233 The Antiquary.

By LYTTON BULWER.
264 Paul Clifford.
265 Last Days of Pompeii.
266 Eugene Aram.
267 Pelham.

By Captain MARRYAT.
298 Midshipman Easy.
299 Japhet in Search of a Father.
300 Jacob Faithful.
301 Peter Simple.

By MAX ADELER.
322 Out of the Hurly Burly.
323 Elbow Room.
324 Random Shots.
325 An Old Fogey.

By C. C. CLARKE.
332 Charlie Thornhill.
333 Flying Scud.
334 Crumbs from a Sportsman's Table.
335 Which is the Winner.
336 Lord Falconberg's Heir.
337 The Beaucleros.
338 Box for the Season.

By ANNIE THOMAS.
343 Theo Leigh.
344 Dennis Donne.
345 Called to Account
346 A Passion in Tatters.
347 He Cometh Not, She Said.
348 No Alternative.

London: WARD, LOCK & CO., Salisbury Square, E.C.
New York: 10, Bond Street.

THE SELECT LIBRARY OF FICTION.

Price 2s. each; or cloth gilt, 2s. 6d.

349 A Narrow Escape.
350 Blotted Out.
351 A Laggard in Love.
352 High Stakes.
353 Best for Her.

By E. P. ROE.

370 Opening a Chestnut Burr
371 A Face Illumined.
372 Barriers Burned Away.
373 What Can She Do?
374 A Day of Fate.
375 Without a Home.
376 A Knight of the 19th Century.
377 Near to Nature's Heart.
378 From Jest to Earnest.

By Miss E. MARLITT.

387 Old Maid's Secret.
388 Gold Elsie.
389 The Second Wife.
390 The Little Moorland Princess.

By AMELIA B. EDWARDS.

398 In the Days of My Youth.
399 Miss Carew.
400 Debenham's Vow.
401 Monsieur Maurice.

By ALEXANDRE DUMAS.

407 Count of Monte-Christo.

By JAMES GRANT.

428 Secret Dispatch.

By G. P. R. JAMES.

435 Bernard Marsh.

By OLIVER WENDELL HOLMES.

440 Elsie Venner.
441 Autocrat of the Breakfast Table.

By SAMUEL LOVER.

446 He Would be a Gentleman.
447 Irish Stories and Legends.

By Mrs. MARSH.

451 Father Darcy.
452 Time, the Avenger.
453 Emilia Wyndham.
454 Mount Sorrel.

By ELEANOR F. TROLLOPE.

459 Aunt Margaret.
460 A Charming Fellow.
461 Veronica.
462 Sacristan's Household.

By ALBERT SMITH.

465 Christopher Tadpole.

By BRET HARTE.

468 Complete Tales.
469 The Heathen Chinee.
470 Wan Lee, the Pagan, &c.
471 Deadwood Mystery, and MARK TWAIN's Nightmare.

By Capt. MAYNE REID.

474 The Mountain Marriage.

By Mrs. LYNN LINTON.

478 Lizzie Lorton.
479 The Mad Willoughbys.

By IVAN TURGENIEFF.

483 Virgin Soil.
484 Smoke.
485 Fathers and Sons.
486 Dimitri Roudine.
487 Liza; or, A Noble Nest.

By NATHANIEL HAWTHORNE.

491 Blithedale Romance.

By Mrs. CASHEL HOEY.

492 No Sign.
493 Blossoming of an Aloe.

London: WARD, LOCK & CO., Salisbury Square, E.C.
New York: 10, Bond Street.

Price 2s. each; or cloth gilt, 2s. 6d.

London: WARD, LOCK & CO., Salisbury Square, E.C.
New York: 10, Bond Street.

THE SELECT LIBRARY OF FICTION.

Price 2s. each; or cloth gilt, 2s. 6d.

By Mrs. W. M. L. JAY.
602 Shiloh.
603 Holden with the Cords.

By Miss R. M. KETTLE.
606 Smugglers and Foresters.
607 Mistress of Langdale Hall.
608 Hillsden on the Moors.
609 Under the Grand Old Hills.
610 Fabian's Tower.
611 The Wreckers.
612 My Home in the Shires.
613 The Sea and the Moor.

By MICHAEL SCOTT.
620 Tom Cringle's Log.
621 Cruise of the "Midge."

By JEAN MIDDLEMASS.
625 Wild Georgie.

By the Author of "OLIVE VARCOE."
629 Forgotten Lives.
630 The Kiddle-a-Wink.
631 Love's Bitterness.
632 In the House of a Friend.

By GEORGE MEREDITH.
635 Tragic Comedians.

By Capt. ARMSTRONG.
638 Queen of the Seas.
639 The Sailor Hero.
640 Cruise of the "Daring."
641 The Sunny South.

By Miss PARDOE.
644 The Jealous Wife.
645 Rival Beauties.

By W. STEPHENS HAYWARD.
650 Eulalie.
651 The Diamond Cross.

By ANNA H. DRURY.
654 Deep Waters.
655 Misrepresentations.
656 The Brothers.

By DOUGLAS JERROLD.
660 The Brownrigg Papers.

By Lady EDEN.
661 Dumbleton Common.
662 Semi-Attached Couple.
663 Semi-Detached House.

By Miss C. J. HAMILTON.
664 Marriage Bonds.
665 The Flynns of Flynnville.

By HOLME LEE.
673 Hawksview.
674 Gilbert Messenger.
675 Thorney Hall.

By HENRY COCKTON.
676 Valentine Vox.

By KATHARINE KING.
677 Lost for Gold.
678 Queen of the Regiment.
679 Off the Roll.
680 Our Detachment.

By S. W. FULLOM.
683 Man of the World.
684 King and Countess.

By the Author of "CASTE," &c.
687 Colonel Dacre.
688 My Son's Wife.
689 Entanglements.
690 Mr. Arle.
691 Bruna's Revenge.
692 Pearl.
693 Caste.

London: WARD, LOCK & CO., Salisbury Square, E.C.
New York: 10, Bond Street.

THE SELECT LIBRARY OF FICTION.

Price 2s. each; or cloth gilt, 2s. 6d.

By Rev. R. COBBOLD.
696 Margaret Catchpole.
697 The Suffolk Gipsy.

By Mrs. PARSONS.
698 Beautiful Edith.
699 Sun and Shade.
700 Ursula's Love Story.

By ARTEMUS WARD.
703 His Book; and Travels among the Mormons.
704 Letters to Punch; and MARK TWAIN's Practical Jokes.

By ANNA C. STEELE.
705 Condoned.
706 Gardenhurst.
707 Broken Toys.

By Mrs. WHITNEY.
710 Odd or Even?

By EMILIE CARLEN.
711 Twelve Months of Matrimony.
712 The Brilliant Marriage.

By WILLIAM CARLETON.
715 Squanders of Castle Squander.

By W. S. MAYO.
720 Never Again.
721 The Berber.

By Mrs. FORRESTER.
722 Olympus to Hades.
723 Fair Women.

By AUGUSTUS MAYHEW.
724 Faces for Fortunes.

By MARK LEMON.
725 Leyton Hall.

By Miss BURNEY.
726 Evelina.

By HONORE DE BALZAC.
728 Unrequited Affection.

By JANE PORTER.
732 The Scottish Chiefs.

By HANS C. ANDERSEN.
734 The Improvisatore.

By KATHARINE MACQUOID.
735 A Bad Beginning.
736 Wild as a Hawk.
737 Forgotten by the World (2s. 6d. and 3s.)

By A. LAMARTINE.
741 Genevieve, and The Stonemason.

By GUSTAV FREYTAG.
744 Debit and Credit.

By Author of "ST. AUBYN OF ST. AUBYN'S."
745 Charlie Nugent.
746 St. Aubyn of St. Aubyn's.

By "WATERS."
747 The Heir at Law.
748 Romance of the Seas.

By EDGAR ALLAN POE.
749 Tales of Mystery, &c.

By HENRY J. BYRON.
750 Paid in Full.

By THOMAS MILLER.
754 Royston Gower.

By Mrs. S. C. HALL.
756 The Whiteboy.

By Lady CHATTERTON.
757 The Lost Bride.

London: WARD, LOCK & CO., Salisbury Square, E.C.
New York: 10, Bond Street.

THE SELECT LIBRARY OF FICTION.

Price 2s. each; or cloth gilt, 2s. 6d.

By WILLIAM GILBERT.
758 Dr. Austin's Guests.

By VARIOUS AUTHORS.
759 Melincourt. T. PEACOCK.
761 Maretime. BAYLE ST. JOHN.
762 Jacob Bendixen. C. GOLD-SCHMIDT.
763 The Only Child. Lady SCOTT.
765 Image of his Father. Bros. MAYHEW.
767 Belial. A Popular Author.
768 Highland Lassies. E. MAC-KENZIE.
769 Rose Douglas. S. W. R.
770 O. V. H. WAT BRADWOOD.
771 Esther's Sacrifice. ALICE PERRY.
772 Ladies of Bever Hollow. A. MANNING.
773 Madeline. JULIA KAVANAGH.
774 Hazarene. Author of "Guy Livingstone."
776 First in the Field.
777 Lilian's Penance. Mrs. HOUSTON.
778 Off the Line. Lady THYNNE.
779 Queen of Herself. A. KING.
780 A Fatal Error. J. MASTER-MAN.
781 Mainstone's Housekeeper. E. METEYARD.
782 Wild Hyacinth. RANDOLPH.

783 All for Greed. Baroness DE BURY.
785 Kelverdale. Earl DESART.
786 Dark and Light Stories. M. HOPE.
788 Leah, the Jewish Maiden.
789 Zana, the Gipsy. STEVENS.
790 Margaret. SYLVESTER JUDD.
791 The Conspirators. A. DE VIGNY.
792 Chelsea Pensioners. GLEIG.
793 A Lease for Lives. A. DE FONBLANQUE.
794 The Backwoodsman. Sir E. WRAXALL.
795 Almost a Quixote. LEVIEN.
796 Janetta, and Blythe Hern-don.
797 Margaret's Ordeal. JUNCKER
798 Philiberta. THORPE TALBOT.
799 Our Helen. By SOPHIE MAY.
800 Little Ragamuffins of Out-cast London. J. GREENWOOD.

By CATHARINE SINCLAIR.
850 Beatrice.
851 Modern Accomplishments.
852 Holiday House,

By JULES VERNE.
856 Five Weeks in a Balloon.

By ERCKMANN-CHATRIAN.
876 The Great Invasion.
877 Campaign in Kabylia.

LIBRARY EDITION OF THE BEST AUTHORS.

Crown 8vo, neat cloth gilt, price 3s. 6d. each.

1 The Pickwick Papers. By CHARLES DICKENS. With Original Illustrations by A. B. FROST.
2 Nicholas Nickleby. By CHAS. DICKENS. With the Original Illus-trations by "PHIZ."
3 Virgin Soil. By IVAN TURGE-NIEFF
4 Smoke. By IVAN TURGENIEFF.

5 Fathers and Sons. By IVAN TURGENIEFF.
6 Dimitri Roudine. By Ditto.
7 Hector O'Halloran. By W. H. MAXWELL. Illustrated by LEECH.
8 Christopher Tadpole. By ALBERT SMITH. Illustrated.
9 Charles O'Malley. By C. LEVER. Plates by PHIZ. Half-bd.

London: WARD, LOCK & CO., Salisbury Square, E.C.
New York: 10, Bond Street.

The Codes Of Hammurabi And Moses
W. W. Davies

QTY

The discovery of the Hammurabi Code is one of the greatest achievements of archaeology, and is of paramount interest, not only to the student of the Bible, but also to all those interested in ancient history...

Religion　ISBN: *1-59462-338-4*　　Pages:132
MSRP *$12.95*

The Theory of Moral Sentiments
Adam Smith

QTY

This work from 1749. contains original theories of conscience amd moral judgment and it is the foundation for systemof morals.

Philosophy　ISBN: *1-59462-777-0*　　Pages:536
MSRP *$19.95*

Jessica's First Prayer
Hesba Stretton

QTY

In a screened and secluded corner of one of the many railway-bridges which span the streets of London there could be seen a few years ago, from five o'clock every morning until half past eight, a tidily set-out coffee-stall, consisting of a trestle and board, upon which stood two large tin cans, with a small fire of charcoal burning under each so as to keep the coffee boiling during the early hours of the morning when the work-people were thronging into the city on their way to their daily toil...

Childrens　ISBN: *1-59462-373-2*　　Pages:84
MSRP *$9.95*

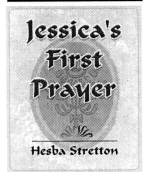

My Life and Work
Henry Ford

QTY

Henry Ford revolutionized the world with his implementation of mass production for the Model T automobile. Gain valuable business insight into his life and work with his own auto-biography... "We have only started on our development of our country we have not as yet, with all our talk of wonderful progress, done more than scratch the surface. The progress has been wonderful enough but..."

Biographies/　ISBN: *1-59462-198-5*　Pages:300
MSRP *$21.95*

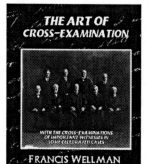

The Art of Cross-Examination
Francis Wellman

QTY

I presume it is the experience of every author, after his first book is published upon an important subject, to be almost overwhelmed with a wealth of ideas and illustrations which could readily have been included in his book, and which to his own mind, at least, seem to make a second edition inevitable. Such certainly was the case with me; and when the first edition had reached its sixth impression in five months, I rejoiced to learn that it seemed to my publishers that the book had met with a sufficiently favorable reception to justify a second and considerably enlarged edition. ..

Reference   **ISBN:** *1-59462-647-2*

Pages:412
MSRP $19.95

On the Duty of Civil Disobedience
Henry David Thoreau

QTY

Thoreau wrote his famous essay, On the Duty of Civil Disobedience, as a protest against an unjust but popular war and the immoral but popular institution of slave-owning. He did more than write—he declined to pay his taxes, and was hauled off to gaol in consequence. Who can say how much this refusal of his hastened the end of the war and of slavery ?

Law   **ISBN:** *1-59462-747-9*

Pages:48
MSRP $7.45

Dream Psychology Psychoanalysis for Beginners
Sigmund Freud

QTY

Sigmund Freud, born Sigismund Schlomo Freud (May 6, 1856 - September 23, 1939), was a Jewish-Austrian neurologist and psychiatrist who co-founded the psychoanalytic school of psychology. Freud is best known for his theories of the unconscious mind, especially involving the mechanism of repression; his redefinition of sexual desire as mobile and directed towards a wide variety of objects; and his therapeutic techniques, especially his understanding of transference in the therapeutic relationship and the presumed value of dreams as sources of insight into unconscious desires.

Psychology   **ISBN:** *1-59462-905-6*

Pages:196
MSRP $15.45

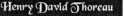

The Miracle of Right Thought
Orison Swett Marden

QTY

Believe with all of your heart that you will do what you were made to do. When the mind has once formed the habit of holding cheerful, happy, prosperous pictures, it will not be easy to form the opposite habit. It does not matter how improbable or how far away this realization may see, or how dark the prospects may be, if we visualize them as best we can, as vividly as possible, hold tenaciously to them and vigorously struggle to attain them, they will gradually become actualized, realized in the life. But a desire, a longing without endeavor, a yearning abandoned or held indifferently will vanish without realization.

Self Help   **ISBN:** *1-59462-644-8*

Pages:360
MSRP $25.45

QTY

The Rosicrucian Cosmo-Conception Mystic Christianity *by Max Heindel* ISBN: *1-59462-188-8* **$38.95**
The Rosicrucian Cosmo-conception is not dogmatic, neither does it appeal to any other authority than the reason of the student. It is: not controversial, but is: sent forth in the, hope that it may help to clear.. New Age/Religion Pages 646

Abandonment To Divine Providence *by Jean-Pierre de Caussade* ISBN: *1-59462-228-0* **$25.95**
"The Rev. Jean Pierre de Caussade was one of the most remarkable spiritual writers of the Society of Jesus in France in the 18th Century. His death took place at Toulouse in 1751. His works have gone through many editions and have been republished... Inspirational/Religion Pages 400

Mental Chemistry *by Charles Haanel* ISBN: *1-59462-192-6* **$23.95**
Mental Chemistry allows the change of material conditions by combining and appropriately utilizing the power of the mind. Much like applied chemistry creates something new and unique out of careful combinations of chemicals the mastery of mental chemistry... New Age Pages 354

The Letters of Robert Browning and Elizabeth Barret Barrett 1845-1846 vol II ISBN: *1-59462-193-4* **$35.95**
by Robert Browning and Elizabeth Barrett Biographies Pages 596

Gleanings In Genesis (volume I) *by Arthur W. Pink* ISBN: *1-59462-130-6* **$27.45**
Appropriately has Genesis been termed "the seed plot of the Bible" for in it we have, in germ form, almost all of the great doctrines which are afterwards fully developed in the books of Scripture which follow... Religion/Inspirational Pages 420

The Master Key *by L. W. de Laurence* ISBN: *1-59462-001-6* **$30.95**
In no branch of human knowledge has there been a more lively increase of the spirit of research during the past few years than in the study of Psychology, Concentration and Mental Discipline. The requests for authentic lessons in Thought Control, Mental Discipline and... New Age/Business Pages 422

The Lesser Key Of Solomon Goetia *by L. W. de Laurence* ISBN: *1-59462-092-X* **$9.95**
This translation of the first book of the "Lernegton" which is now for the first time made accessible to students of Talismanic Magic was done, after careful collation and edition, from numerous Ancient Manuscripts in Hebrew, Latin, and French... New Age/Occult Pages 92

Rubaiyat Of Omar Khayyam *by Edward Fitzgerald* ISBN:*1-59462-332-5* **$13.95**
Edward Fitzgerald, whom the world has already learned, in spite of his own efforts to remain within the shadow of anonymity, to look upon as one of the rarest poets of the century, was born at Bredfield, in Suffolk, on the 31st of March, 1809. He was the third son of John Purcell... Music Pages 172

Ancient Law *by Henry Maine* ISBN: *1-59462-128-4* **$29.95**
The chief object of the following pages is to indicate some of the earliest ideas of mankind, as they are reflected in Ancient Law, and to point out the relation of those ideas to modern thought. Religion/History Pages 452

Far-Away Stories *by William J. Locke* ISBN: *1-59462-129-2* **$19.45**
"Good wine needs no bush, but a collection of mixed vintages does. And this book is just such a collection. Some of the stories I do not want to remain buried for ever in the museum files of dead magazine-numbers an author's not unpardonable vanity..." Fiction Pages 272

Life of David Crockett *by David Crockett* ISBN: *1-59462-250-7* **$27.45**
"Colonel David Crockett was one of the most remarkable men of the times in which he lived. Born in humble life, but gifted with a strong will, an indomitable courage, and unremitting perseverance.. Biographies/New Age Pages 424

Lip-Reading *by Edward Nitchie* ISBN: *1-59462-206-X* **$25.95**
Edward B. Nitchie, founder of the New York School for the Hard of Hearing, now the Nitchie School of Lip-Reading, Inc, wrote "LIP-READING Principles and Practice". The development and perfecting of this meritorious work on lip-reading was an undertaking... How-to Pages 400

A Handbook of Suggestive Therapeutics, Applied Hypnotism, Psychic Science ISBN: *1-59462-214-0* **$24.95**
by Henry Munro Health/New Age/Health/Self-help Pages 376

A Doll's House: and Two Other Plays *by Henrik Ibsen* ISBN: *1-59462-112-8* **$19.95**
Henrik Ibsen created this classic when in revolutionary 1848 Rome. Introducing some striking concepts in playwriting for the realist genre, this play has been studied the world over. Fiction/Classics/Plays 308

The Light of Asia *by sir Edwin Arnold* ISBN: *1-59462-204-3* **$13.95**
In this poetic masterpiece, Edwin Arnold describes the life and teachings of Buddha. The man who was to become known as Buddha to the world was born as Prince Gautama of India but he rejected the worldly riches and abandoned the reigns of power when... Religion/History/Biographies Pages 170

The Complete Works of Guy de Maupassant *by Guy de Maupassant* ISBN: *1-59462-157-8* **$16.95**
"For days and days, nights and nights, I had dreamed of that first kiss which was to consecrate our engagement, and I knew not on what spot I should put my lips..." Fiction/Classics Pages 240

The Art of Cross-Examination *by Francis L. Wellman* ISBN: *1-59462-309-0* **$26.95**
Written by a renowned trial lawyer, Wellman imparts his experience and uses case studies to explain how to use psychology to extract desired information through questioning. How-to/Science/Reference Pages 408

Answered or Unanswered? *by Louisa Vaughan* ISBN: *1-59462-248-5* **$10.95**
Miracles of Faith in China Religion Pages 112

The Edinburgh Lectures on Mental Science (1909) *by Thomas* ISBN: *1-59462-008-3* **$11.95**
This book contains the substance of a course of lectures recently given by the writer in the Queen Street Hall, Edinburgh. Its purpose is to indicate the Natural Principles governing the relation between Mental Action and Material Conditions.. New Age/Psychology Pages 148

Ayesha *by H. Rider Haggard* ISBN: *1-59462-301-5* **$24.95**
Verily and indeed it is the unexpected that happens! Probably if there was one person upon the earth from whom the Editor of this, and of a certain previous history, did not expect to hear again... Classics Pages 380

Ayala's Angel *by Anthony Trollope* ISBN: *1-59462-352-X* **$29.95**
The two girls were both pretty, but Lucy who was twenty-one who supposed to be simple and comparatively unattractive, whereas Ayala was credited, as her Bombwhat romantic name might show, with poetic charm and a taste for romance. Ayala when her father died was nineteen... Fiction Pages 434

The American Commonwealth *by James Bryce* ISBN: *1-59462-286-8* **$34.45**
An interpretation of American democratic political theory. It examines political mechanics and society from the perspective of Scotsman James Bryce Politics Pages 572

Stories of the Pilgrims *by Margaret P. Pumphrey* ISBN: *1-59462-116-0* **$17.95**
This book explores pilgrims religious oppression in England as well as their escape to Holland and eventual crossing to America on the Mayflower, and their early days in New England... History Pages 268

QTY

The Fasting Cure *by Sinclair Upton*
ISBN: *1-59462-222-1* **$13.95**

In the Cosmopolitan Magazine for May, 1910, and in the Contemporary Review (London) for April, 1910, I published an article dealing with my experiences in fasting. I have written a great many magazine articles, but never one which attracted so much attention... New Age/Self Help/Health Pages 164

Hebrew Astrology *by Sepharial*
ISBN: *1-59462-308-2* **$13.45**

In these days of advanced thinking it is a matter of common observation that we have left many of the old landmarks behind and that we are now pressing forward to greater heights and to a wider horizon than that which represented the mind-content of our progenitors... Astrology Pages 144

Thought Vibration or The Law of Attraction in the Thought World
ISBN: *1-59462-127-6* **$12.95**

by William Walker Atkinson
Psychology/Religion Pages 144

Optimism *by Helen Keller*
ISBN: *1-59462-108-X* **$15.95**

Helen Keller was blind, deaf, and mute since 19 months old, yet famously learned how to overcome these handicaps, and spread her lectures promoting optimism. An inspiring read for everyone... Biographies/Inspirational Pages 84

Sara Crewe *by Frances Burnett*
ISBN: *1-59462-360-0* **$9.45**

In the first place, Miss Minchin lived in London. Her home was a large, dull, tall one, in a large, dull square, where all the houses were alike, and all the sparrows were alike, and where all the door-knockers made the same heavy sound... Childrens/Classic Pages 88

The Autobiography of Benjamin Franklin *by Benjamin Franklin*
ISBN: *1-59462-135-7* **$24.95**

The Autobiography of Benjamin Franklin has probably been more extensively read than any other American historical work, and no other book of its kind has had such ups and downs of fortune. Franklin lived for many years in England, where he was agent... Biographies/History Pages 332

Name	
Email	
Telephone	
Address	
City, State ZIP	

☐ **Credit Card**   ☐ **Check / Money Order**

Credit Card Number	
Expiration Date	
Signature	

Please Mail to: Book Jungle
PO Box 2226
Champaign, IL 61825
or Fax to: 630-214-0564

ORDERING INFORMATION

web: *www.bookjungle.com*
email: *sales@bookjungle.com*
fax: *630-214-0564*
mail: *Book Jungle PO Box 2226 Champaign, IL 61825*
or PayPal *to sales@bookjungle.com*

Please contact us for bulk discounts

DIRECT-ORDER TERMS

**20% Discount if You Order
Two or More Books**
Free Domestic Shipping!
Accepted: Master Card, Visa,
Discover, American Express

Printed in the United States
120512LV00006B/38/A